Acclaim for the authors of *Pocketful of Blessings*

CAROLYNE AARSEN

"A gentle story of spiritual healing."
—*Romantic Times* on *Homecoming*

"Another delightful romance by Carolyne Aarsen sure to bring a smile to your lips."
—*Romantic Times* on *Twin Blessings*

"Carolyne Aarsen just keeps getting better."
—*Romantic Times* on *A Hero for Kelsey*

CYNTHIA RUTLEDGE

"There is nothing typical about this wonderful story…another winner from start to finish!"
—*Romantic Times* on *Undercover Angel*

"A fresh detour from the conservative inspirational romance…this author will no doubt gain a faithful readership."
—*Romantic Times* on *Undercover Angel*

"…a poignant tale, filled with powerful emotions."
—*Romantic Times* on *Trish's Not-So-Little Secret*

VALERIE HANSEN

"…memorable scenes."
—*Romantic Times* on *The Perfect Couple*

"…a tender, well-written story of forgiveness, God's great sense of humor and how falling in love is never easy."
—*Romantic Times* on *The Troublesome Angel*

"…a delightful work of fiction… great sparring dialogue, well-defined characters and just a hint of suspense."
—*Romantic Times* on *The Wedding Arbor*

POCKETFUL OF BLESSINGS

CAROLYNE AARSEN

CYNTHIA RUTLEDGE

VALERIE HANSEN

Love Inspired®

Published by Steeple Hill Books™

STEEPLE HILL BOOKS

ISBN 0-373-78523-2

POCKETFUL OF BLESSINGS

This edition published by arrangement with Steeple Hill Books.

Visit us at www.steeplehill.com

Printed in U.S.A.

CONTENTS

Books by Carolyne Aarsen

Love Inspired

Homecoming #24
Ever Faithful #33
A Bride at Last #51
The Cowboy's Bride #67
**A Family-Style Christmas* #86
A Mother at Heart #94
A Family at Last #121
A Hero for Kelsey #133
Twin Blessings #149
Toward Home #215

*Stealing Home

CAROLYNE AARSEN

lives in Alberta on a small ranch with her husband and the youngest of their four children. Carolyne's writing skills have been honed between being a stay-at-home mom, wife, foster mother, columnist and business partner with her husband in their logging operation and cattle ranch. Writing for Love Inspired has given her the wonderful opportunity to combine her love of the Lord with her love of a romantic story.

HOMECOMING

Carolyne Aarsen

To Richard;
my husband, my critic,
my inspiration, my friend.

Chapter One

Mark tugged on the brim of his hat, and shoved open the dented metal door.

Noise poured out like a wave, pulsating, raucous, the air heavily laced with the smell of smoke. He stepped inside squinting in the dim light as the door shut behind him. Not for the first time that day he wished he could head back to Sweet Creek and tell Ed he simply couldn't find her.

Then he remembered the feel of Ed's fingers clutching his and the entreaty in his eyes. Mark was too close to quit. With a glance around the semidarkness, he worked his way through the crowded room to an empty table and dropped into the chair, scanning the crowd.

Half an hour ago, he had tracked Sheryl's address down to a dingy apartment block, three miles from here. No one was home but the policeman parked across the road had recognized the picture Mark had shown him and sent him here.

A slim-figured girl approached the bar, carrying an empty tray. A long swath of blond hair hung down her back almost to the waistband of a tight, short skirt. Mark peered through the haze trying to get a better look at her.

"What'll you have?" Another waitress stood in front of him, tray tucked under one arm, her hand shoving her frizzy red hair out of her face.

The question took him by surprise. He only wanted to ask

a few questions but he would probably be less conspicuous if he looked like a customer.

"I'll have a beer."

She quirked a bored eyebrow up. "Really?"

"That one," Mark amended, pointing to a name that flashed blue and white behind the bar. It *had* been a while since he'd been in a bar.

The red-haired waitress returned quickly and set a frosted bottle and glass on the table, then waited to be paid.

"Does Sheryl Kyle work here?" Mark asked pulling out his wallet.

The girl eyed him with distrust. "Why?" she asked handing him his change.

Mark pulled out a worn picture, seeking to allay her suspicions. "I'm from Sweet Creek, B.C. She used to live there with Ed Krickson, her stepfather."

The waitress glanced at the picture. "I'll see if I can find her," she said with a shrug.

Mark sat back. *Please, Lord, let this work,* he thought, the irony of praying in a bar making him smile.

But he needed all the prayers he could send out. He needed to get back to the ranch and he knew if he came without Sheryl, Ed would lose all will to live.

"Two pilsners and two ale."

Sheryl gave her order to the bartender and leaned on the bar. She eased her aching feet out of her two-inch-high heels. Dave, her boss, thought they made his waitresses look alluring.

Sheryl wiggled her toes, relishing the soothing coolness of the hard cement floor, hoping the guys she had shouldered past to put in her order wouldn't step on her feet with their heavy work boots.

She wished she could relieve the pounding in her head that was keeping time with the resonant bass of the jukebox, pouring out its unintelligible tales of heartache and woe. The habitual haze of cigarette smoke hung in a gray-blue pall over the rowdy patrons competing with the music.

Friday and payday for the municipal workers had customers lined two-deep at the bar, flirting, making noise and wasting time.

The bartender pushed the frosted bottles toward her, Sheryl slipped the beers onto the tray. With a tired sigh, she wriggled her swelling feet back into her shoes, and turned almost bumping into Tory.

"Sheryl, you're a brat," the other waitress said, her tray making a metallic clatter as she dropped it on the wet bar.

"You're the one that just about dumped my order," Sheryl groused, ignoring the complaints from the men beside her as she balanced her tray.

"You've been holding out on me," Tory continued, hanging well over the bar to take a quick drag off a cigarette that lay smoldering in an ashtray out of their boss's sight. She tossed Sheryl a sidelong glance.

"What do you mean?" Sheryl looked around, hoping Dave didn't notice either her lingering or Tory's smoking.

"There's this absolute hunk of a guy asking for you." Tory fluttered her eyelashes.

"By name?"

"He asked for a Sheryl Kyle." Tory took another quick puff and stubbed her cigarette out. "He knows everything..." Tory grinned at Sheryl's shocked look. "Just kidding. Said you used to live in Sweet Creek, British Columbia. Showed me a picture." Tory lifted one plucked eyebrow expectantly.

"What did he want?" Sheryl ignored Tory's obvious curiosity, stifling a rising clutch of panic. Sweet Creek hadn't been a part of her life for seven years. "Is anyone with him?"

"Drinking alone." Tory pouted at Sheryl's reticence, her lipstick faded away to a thin, red outline. "Actually sitting alone. He hasn't popped the top off the beer yet. Asked if you could talk to him."

"Where is he?"

Tory raised a hand to point, and Sheryl grabbed it.

''Don't do that,'' she said. ''I want a better look at him first. Just tell me where he's sitting.''

''By the west wall, toward the back exit. Can't miss the honey. He's the only one with a cowboy hat.'' Tory leveled a serious glance at her. ''You in trouble?''

''I'm just being careful.''

''So what are you going to do?''

''Nothing until I scope him out.''

Sheryl lifted the tray of drinks and, working her way through the jumble of tables, managed an occasional glance over her shoulder. A cowboy hat shouldn't be too hard to spot amongst all the baseball caps and bare heads.

By the time she delivered the drinks, her customers were growling. She flashed them her best smile and took a few moments to laugh with them. She managed to sidestep one customer's hand and pocket his cash in one fluid movement, smiling all the while. No easy feat considering the snug fit of her skirt.

As she looked up, she saw him.

All that showed beneath the brim of the battered cowboy hat were the narrow line of his lips, the clean sweep of his jaw. Dark brown hair hung well over the collar of a faded denim jacket that sat easily on broad shoulders.

Everything about him spoke of working cowboy. From the frayed cuffs of the denim jacket to the jeans that sculpted his long, lean legs stretched out in front of him and the scuffed, slant-heeled cowboy boots, crossed indolently over each other.

He was nursing a beer, not really drinking, just holding it and looking as out of place in this bar as a horse would in the parking lot outside.

Sheryl's mind raced, trying to place him. Definitely not one of Jason Kyle's buddies or a cop. He was too relaxed to be either.

He pushed his hat back and looked her way. Dark brows ran in a straight line across his forehead, not quite meeting over the bridge of a long, narrow nose. But it was his eyes that held her—steel gray and piercing.

She swallowed and took a step backward.

"Kyle!" Dave's all-too-familiar voice bellowed from behind her. "Get moving or you're history, babe."

Sheryl gritted her teeth at her boss's comments, pitched, as usual, three decibels higher than the jukebox.

He stood beside her now, heavyset and domineering, his cologne overpowering the smell of cigarette smoke and liquor. Sheryl could tell by the set of his bulldog jaw he felt edgy. "I've got thirsty customers and you're just standing there holding that tray like it was a rosary," he growled. "One more slipup and you're gone."

"Sorry, Dave." She eased away from him, knowing she was treading on thin ice. She knew it would take only one more infinitesimal misjudgment on her part and she would be out of a job. Much as she hated the work, it paid the rent and covered the costs of her classes.

"I asked to talk to Sheryl. That's why she wasn't serving anyone." Now holding his hat, the stranger stood in front of them, a hint of contempt in his deep voice.

"Who are you?" Dave turned on the cowboy. "I didn't know there was a rodeo in town."

"Neither did I." The man smiled, set his hat on a nearby table and pulled out his wallet. "I just need a few moments of Sheryl's time." He handed Dave a folded bill.

Dave glanced at it, then with a leer chucked Sheryl under the chin. "Five minutes, Kyle." He shoved the money in his pocket.

Unconsciously Sheryl wiped her face, then turned on the cowboy, feeling cheap and humiliated. "Who do you think you are, paying him for my time?"

"I wanted him out of the way for a while," the dark stranger interrupted. "I figured he would understand a nice crisp bill."

"I don't need to talk to you." She turned to go.

"It's about your stepfather, Ed."

Sheryl stopped, feeling like he had just doused her with ice water.

"Are you coming?" he continued, retrieving his hat. "Your boss is checking his watch."

"I don't even know who you are." Sheryl found her voice again, shock making her movements automatic. She followed him to his table. He didn't look like anyone she'd ever met in the eight years she'd lived in Sweet Creek, British Columbia.

"Sorry." He glanced around at the seedy bar, laying his hat on the table beside his beer. "I didn't think formal introductions would be necessary. I'm Mark Andrews, partner and brother-in-law of your stepbrother, Nate. Your stepfather sent me because he didn't think you'd talk to Nate." He pulled out a letter, unfolded it and handed it to her.

Sheryl took it, her hands trembling. Though the spidery handwriting wandered across the unlined page, it was unmistakably Ed's.

Swallowing, she slowly sat down, laying the creased paper on the table. What did he want, after all this time? And why send a personal messenger after so many silent years? "How did you manage to find me?" she asked finally.

Mark sat down across from her and laid a photograph on the table beside the letter. "Ed gave me this old picture of you. I knew you lived in Edmonton, and I had a few prayers on my side." Mark leaned forward, spinning the beer bottle between his fingers, his eyes on her. "I found your place by eliminating all the other Kyles. The policeman parked across from your apartment was very helpful. I guess he comes here once in a while."

"So what do you want?"

He toyed with the bottle some more. "Do you and your husband have any children?"

"Why?"

"I was wondering if you were able to travel."

"Why do I need to do that?"

''Do you answer all questions with another question?'' he asked, his voice tight.

''Depends who's asking.'' Sheryl glanced pointedly at her watch. ''Look, I really hate this place, and I really hate this job, but I don't want to lose it. I'd appreciate it if you would tell me what Ed wants.''

Mark looked up at her, his gaze level. A thin thread of fear spiraled through her when she met his steely eyes.

''Would your husband mind if you went away for a while?''

''Jason's dead.'' Sheryl twisted her watch around her wrist. The harshness of those two clipped words jolted her again. The sorrow she'd felt at Jason's death had been eclipsed by relief as she walked away from his grave.

''What about children?''

''No kids,'' she answered shortly. ''Now could you please tell me what you really came all this way for?''

Mark hesitated, pushed his beer around his hat and, just when Sheryl was about to get up, he spoke. ''Ed's been hospitalized for a stroke. He's been asking for you constantly.''

The mighty Ed Krickson felled by a stroke?

Sheryl blinked, staring past him, dredging up her last memory of Ed. He had stood on the porch as Jason had thrown her suitcase in the back of his battered old pickup. Ed's arms had been crossed tightly over his broad chest, eyes narrowed, saying nothing. What else could have been added to the yelling that had reverberated through the house every time Sheryl had stepped out of the door, every time she'd dressed up, every time she'd ignored him and his dire imprecations of spiritual ruin for the previous eight years?

Sheryl had only glanced once at him as she'd gotten in beside Jason, then turned her head resolutely ahead as they'd driven away. Nothing held her in Sweet Creek anymore. Her mother lay in a grave. The prospect of living with Ed and the constant judgment of a God so different from her natural father's teachings had sent her on a one-way trip with the only person brave enough to stand up to Ed—Jason Kyle, the valley's wild child.

And now his partner said Ed had been asking for her. She had thought she'd been cut out of the Krickson family, possibly even erased out of the family Bible.

"Kyle," Dave's nasal voice pierced her memories. "Time's up."

Sheryl pulled her thoughts to the present. "Look, I'm really touched he still remembers who I am." Sheryl stood, taking her tray with her. "But somehow between then and now, I don't really care what Ed Krickson needs or wants anymore."

"I said time's up, missy." Dave stood beside her, his narrow eyes almost impaling her.

"I'm coming already," she snapped.

"Ed is dying, Sheryl." Mark's deep voice didn't go up a single decibel, but as his words registered they fairly roared in Sheryl's ears.

She turned to face this long, tall, stranger, her tray hanging at her side, questions tumbling through her mind.

"Kyle, if you don't get a move on, you've had it."

She whirled on Dave, her voice tight with mixed emotions and confusion. "Just lay off for a bit."

"I wouldn't use that tone with me, missy." Dave leaned closer pressing a nicotine-stained finger against her forehead.

Sheryl slapped his hand away. Dave's face registered shock, his hand flew back, and instinctively Sheryl flinched, her tray clattering to the floor, her arm raised.

As soon as she did, she felt foolish. Dave wouldn't dare hit her in front of his customers.

She dropped her arm in time to see Mark put his hand on Dave's shoulder. "Leave her alone," he said quietly. Dave spun around, his face twisted with anger.

"Get out, jerk." Dave pushed Mark away.

Sheryl didn't know what happened next. She saw Dave stumble, take a step back, then fall heavily to the floor.

Fight she thought, seeing anger on Mark's face.

Sheryl straightened, self-preservation kicking in. At the rear of the building an exit sign's red glow caught her eye. Sheryl ran, reached the door, whacked her hands against the metal bar and slipped out into the cool night air. She fell against the brick wall, eyes closed, adrenaline still coursing through her. Her breath came in quick gasps as her anger grew.

It was a sure bet she would be hitting the unemployment office again, she thought, clenching her fists, banging them once against the hard edges of the brick wall. She wished she could use them on any guy that happened within five feet of her right.

The door opened again, the uproar of voices inside the bar pouring out, getting cut off as the metal door slammed shut.

She got her wish. It was Mark Andrews.

"You okay?" His voice registered concern.

"What do you care?" She glared at him. "Thanks to you I just lost the last job in Edmonton. You're such a guy." She shoved her hands in her pocket. She still had the crumpled bills and odd change from her last three orders. Her purse inside held slightly more.

Mark stood in front of her, his stance easy but wary. The light from the street lamp cast his angular features into shadow. "He was going to hit you."

"Are you kidding? Dave prefers more serious threats, like firing me." Sheryl shivered, her satin shirt offering scant warmth in the cool of the evening.

Sheryl pushed herself away from the wall. "Thanks to you I don't even dare go back inside to get my purse and coat."

"I'll get them for you."

"I wouldn't recommend it. The lion's den would be tame compared to what Dave will be like if he sees you again. You embarrassed him." Sheryl dragged a hand over her face. She didn't want to think about the implications of losing her job and her purse with her last few dollars still inside.

The door opened again and Sheryl jumped. Mark, she noticed lifted his hands slightly, as if ready.

Tory slipped through the narrow opening, carrying a coat.

"I heard Dave muttering as he walked over that this was

it, he was canning you. I thought I would cover for you and grabbed your things.'' Tory handed Sheryl her coat, purse and running shoes, glancing over her shoulder as the door closed behind her. ''He's pretty ticked. I wouldn't go back in there if I were you.'' She turned to Mark and winked at him. ''Why didn't you deck him?''

''I don't waste my time with guys like him,'' Mark said.

Sheryl frowned. He didn't fight with Dave? That was a first. ''Don't blame you. He'd probably sue.''

Tory snorted. She turned to Sheryl, her face suddenly melancholy. ''And you, hon, what are you going to do?''

Sheryl shrugged, not wanting to voice her own fears. Instead she bent over, yanked off the high heels and slipped her feet into her old, comfortable running shoes. ''Hit the employment office again.''

''It's payday today, I'll get your cheque and mail it to you.''

''If Dave lets you.'' Sheryl picked up the offending shoes and, with a crooked grin, wound up and threw them as far as she could. A moment of silence, then they clattered against a metal Dumpster. Sheryl turned back to Tory, ignoring Mark's surprised look.

Tory laid a hand on Sheryl's arm. Sheryl instinctively pulled back, and Tory gave her a sad smile. ''I would love to see a sparkle in those pretty green eyes someday.''

''I'll be okay.'' Sheryl felt a rush of thankfulness for her friend, feeling sorry at her reaction to Tory's touch, and then forced herself to lean over to give her friend a hug. ''Thanks for being around. There aren't many like you.''

Tory clasped her hands between hers and from the expression on her face, Sheryl could see that she had caught her off guard.

''You're full of surprises, Sheryl Kyle.'' She smiled and squeezed her hands. ''If you need a place…''

''I paid my rent for two months, so I'm okay for a while.'' Sheryl bit her lip, trying to quell the unexpected tears that threatened. Tory was rough, hard edged but generous to a fault. ''You better get back.''

Tory stretched up and pulled a card out of her pocket. ''My man Mike was talking to one of his customers in the garage, a lawyer. He was complaining that his secretary's quitting in two weeks.'' Tory handed the card to Sheryl with a shrug. ''You said you worked in an office before, so I thought it would be worth a try.''

Sheryl took the grease-stained business card. She didn't know if she could wait a couple of weeks, but tucked the card in her purse anyway.

''Well. I better get back. I can't afford to lose this job, either, at least not until we got our down payment for Mike's business together.'' Tory hesitated, then caught Sheryl in a hug. ''I have a good feeling about this hunk,'' she murmured in Sheryl's ear. ''Be nice to him.''

Tory pulled away, grinned at Mark, then slipped back inside.

Avoiding his eyes, Sheryl put on her coat and drew her purse over her shoulder.

''I've been pushing my luck already,'' she said to Mark, glancing behind her. ''I'd better get going.''

She turned and walked away.

Mark caught up easily, his hands shoved in the pockets of his jean jacket.

''I hate to state the obvious, but what are you going to do now?'' he asked.

''That isn't your concern,'' she replied curtly.

Ignoring him, Sheryl paused at the end of the alley, habit making her glance both ways down the sidewalk bordering the busy street that fronted the bar. A steady stream of semis, full and empty, lumbered past them interspersed with cars and light trucks.

The sun still hovered over what she could see of the horizon, and Sheryl steeled herself for the long walk home. She couldn't afford to waste her tip money on a bus ride tonight.

Mark still stood beside her, the slight evening breeze lifting his hair from the neck of his coat. She shot him a sideways glance, wishing he would leave.

"Sheryl," his deep voice was quiet. "What about Ed?"

All she wanted was her apartment, a hot bath and a nap. She didn't want to think about Ed, or her past.

He's dying.

The thought caught her up short. If Mark spoke the truth, then she needed to face Ed before that happened. She had too many questions that needed answers.

There's nothing for you here, her thoughts mocked her. She clutched her purse tighter, trying to think, to plan. But she was too tired. With a sigh that came from her aching heels, she slowly nodded her head.

"How long will I be gone?"

Mark lifted one broad shoulder. "That's up to you. Nate has a small cabin back of his place you can stay in if you want privacy."

Sheryl squinted at the traffic, not replying. Overhead a plane, engines screaming, dropped down, heading toward the airport across the road. Threaded through that sound was the screech of trains from the rail yard behind them. From the nether reaches of her mind came the picture of azure hills giving way to rugged mountains, the tantalizing image of deep woods, silent and waiting.

It hurt. She knew it would. That's why she kept those memories buried deep. At the mention of the cabin they had slowly spiraled to the surface.

It was to that cabin she used to retreat when she needed space and privacy. It was her private domain, and no one bothered her there. Ed had fixed it up for her, and Nate had helped. That was in the beginning, when things were still easy between them.

"I can pick you up first thing in the morning," Mark said, his voice a quiet sound that registered through the commotion of the city. "I've brought my truck."

Sheryl looked him over again. Tall, broad-shouldered, arrestingly attractive.

Unknown.

Would she be crazy to spend a day cooped up in a vehicle with him?

With a fatalistic shrug she nodded. What would be, would be. In her youth she believed in a God that watched over her, but experience had taught her differently. God had been conspicuously absent in her life in the past years. Dependence created instability. She had to make decisions for herself and live with the consequences.

"I'll be ready. Do you know where I live?"

He nodded. "Is six o'clock okay?"

"Sure." Sheryl kept her eyes averted, her long hair slipping loose from her ponytail, hiding her face. Then she turned with a fatalistic shrug.

"Sheryl, wait. I'll give you a ride," Mark called after her.

She didn't feel like spending any more time with him. Her stomach knotted up at the thought of seeing her stepfather, and she still shook after that business with Dave. But she faced an hour of walking before she was home, and if she was going to be spending the whole day with him tomorrow, a ten-minute drive could hardly be more dangerous. She stopped, shoved her hands in her pockets and followed him back to his truck.

He stood by a dusty, silver Ford, and when she came near he went ahead of her to the passenger door and opened it. Shooting him an oblique glance she shrugged and threw her purse in.

Mark sauntered around the front of the truck his fingers trailing on the hood.

One quick step onto the running board and a jump got her into the front seat before Mark opened his door. She tugged on her skirt trying to at least get it back over her thighs. As soon as she was home this particular piece of clothing was heading for the garbage bin.

She watched Mark as he got in the truck. As if aware of her scrutiny he returned her gaze. His gray eyes met hers, and a gentle smile hovered on his well-shaped mouth. He was entirely too handsome and too much of a puzzle.

She looked ahead as he turned the truck on and reversed, wondering again what she was getting tangled in. It had taken her three months after the accident to find another job, and it was only in the past few weeks that she felt as if her life was getting under her own control.

I shouldn't go, she thought, a shiver of apprehension skittering down her neck. It was as if life had caught her and dragged her back into its current. She felt propelled along a course, clinging to whatever happened to come by.

Drawing in a deep breath, she settled back. When she got back to the apartment, she'd run a bath, go over her assignment…and that was as far as her plans were going for now.

"Sufficient unto the day is the trouble thereof." The quote from the Bible would just have to hold her for now.

Mark pulled up in front of her apartment building, and for a moment she saw it through a stranger's eyes. Built after World War II, it squatted back from the street, square and ugly. Patches of stucco had fallen off, exposing the wires beneath. For two years Sheryl and Jason had called a basement suite in this dull, squat building home.

She should have moved right out after Jason died, but it was the cheapest apartment block she could find close enough to her work and school. The money she saved would pay for two more courses next year.

"Thanks for the ride," she said, turning to Mark.

"Hey, I'm really sorry about your job." He pushed his hat back on his head, sighing lightly. "And your husband."

Sheryl bit back a retort. "Don't lie awake about either. I won't." She glanced at him, surprised to see real remorse on his face. "Dave was just waiting for an excuse to fire me."

"Why is that?"

"It doesn't matter," she answered shortly. Mark didn't need to know any more than the bare details of her life. He was just a blip.

She stepped out of the truck and walked up to her apartment. As she unlocked the front door, she glanced over her shoulder.

He waited, watching her, and when she stepped into the dank lobby, she heard the truck start up, and he left.

She leaned against the locked door, drawing a deep breath. *Enough girl,* she reprimanded herself, *Tomorrow, think about it then.*

Mark hit the remote button, and the picture on the TV screen shrank and faded away. He dropped the remote and clasped his hands behind his head as he leaned back against the headboard, trying to meld his first impression of Sheryl with the stories he'd heard. The short skirt, the satin shirt and high heels all fit with what Nate and Ed said the few times they talked of her.

Mark picked up the photograph that lay beside him on the bed. Sheryl looked about fifteen, her hair swirling around her face, her mouth twisted in a wry smile. It resembled her enough for identification, but didn't adequately portray the delicate line of her features, the elusive color of her long hair. Sheryl was taller than he had imagined, slender, with an easy grace in her movements—a direct contrast to the hardened edge of her manner.

He remembered again the sight of her clutching her head, and another wave of anger coursed through him. She said Dave wouldn't have hit her, and in retrospect he knew she was right. Dave looked like he worked on intimidation and threats. So what had caused her quick response?

He dropped the picture on the bed.

With a frustrated sigh, he pulled the phone toward him and dialed.

"I found her," Mark said when Nate answered.

"So how was my sister?" Nate's voice held anger that Mark knew had as much to do with his worry over his father as his long history with Sheryl.

"Broke, out of a job, scared."

''Sheryl, scared? I can't imagine that. How's the husband?''

Mark sighed as he leaned back, pinching the bridge of his nose. ''He's dead.''

''What?'' Nate's voice exploded in his ear. ''Since when?''

''I don't know. We didn't really exchange much in the way of polite chitchat. I'm surprised you didn't know. Didn't Jason have family in Sweet Creek?''

''He only had his mother, and she moved to Toronto right after they left.'' Nate sounded flustered. ''Why didn't she tell us?''

''I get the feeling from her that she thought no one cared.''

Nate fell quiet and Mark, sensing guilt, waited. ''How did you manage to talk her into coming?'' Nate asked after a lengthy pause.

''She didn't have much choice. Thanks to me she lost her job.''

''How's that?''

''I tangled with her boss.''

A pause at the other end of the line told Mark that Nate was absorbing his second shock of the night.

''Whatever happened to turning the other cheek, Mark?''

''It wasn't *my* cheek I thought he was going to hit,'' Mark replied, his mouth set in grim lines. ''Anyhow,'' Mark continued, wanting to forget the debacle, ''she agreed to come with me. If we leave on time in the morning I'll probably head straight to the hospital.'' He didn't speak of his reason for haste, but it hung between them.

''If all goes well, Dad will be discharged in a couple of days,'' Nate said. ''The doctor says he can't live at his own place anymore, so he'll come and stay with us.''

''That's going to make things busy for you and Elise.'' Mark frowned. Elise had enough to do with three little kids. He wondered about the wisdom of bringing Ed there, as well.

''Speaking of busy,'' Nate said, ignoring his comment, ''I checked the hay today. It's ready to bale.''

''Did you manage to get hold of a baling crew?''

"Yah, Rob and Conrad. I rented an extra baler. So all that's left is to pray for good weather."

"That's all we can do anyway, Nate." Mark stifled a yawn. "You got any ideas of what I can talk to Sheryl about? Twelve hours is a lot of time to be cooped up in a vehicle with someone you've never met before."

"Ask her what she's been doing the past eight years. We sure don't have a clue." Nate's voice was abrupt, and Mark let that matter drop.

"Okay. Then, I'll see you tomorrow." Mark hung up, staring at the phone, feeling an unexpected pang of sympathy for Sheryl.

Her face came back to him: delicate features, soft green eyes framed with lightly arched brows, and hair that went on forever, tempting a man to run his fingers through it. He had seen many beautiful girls, but somehow she held a certain fascination for him, and when she smiled…

Mark laughed shortly. He was acting like a kid himself instead of an experienced man of thirty-four. He'd had girlfriends enough, just never the right one. The life he had lived didn't lend itself to finding a girl willing to share his life, his faith in God, the isolation of his ranch and the hard work that came with it. Living on the ranch kept him too busy to go looking. And after Tanya, he didn't have much inclination.

He got up, restlessness sending him to the window. Lately the old feeling seemed to come upon him more often.

Nate and Elise already had three children, and Elise, his baby sister, was five years younger than him. As for himself…no one.

He shrugged, attributing his restlessness to spending most of the day driving around busy streets trying to find the bar Sheryl worked. The city always gave him that claustrophobic feeling, and each time he went there for business or visits he couldn't wait until he was back in the open hills riding his horse into the wind.

Mark dropped his shoulder against the cool window of his

air-conditioned room, hands shoved in his jeans pockets, frowning at the cars below wishing he was back on the ranch.

He thought again of Sheryl, trying to imagine her on a horse. Nate said she used to ride every chance she got. He couldn't visualize it, not after seeing her this evening, serving drinks in a smoky, noisy bar wearing that narrow short skirt.

He pushed himself away from the window with a sigh and dropped on the bed, tugging his cowboy boots off. He pulled his Bible out of his suitcase, and lay back, paging through the Psalms, looking for inspiration, comfort…wisdom.

With a wry grin he flipped to Proverbs. Between Nate, Sheryl and Ed, he would need the wisdom of Solomon to understand them and all the undercurrents that swirled around their lives.

For now he was only the messenger. Once he brought Sheryl to Sweet Creek, his job would be over and he could get back to the business of keeping his beloved ranch afloat.

Chapter Two

Even though warm sunshine slanted into the cab of the truck, Mark shivered as he turned onto Sheryl's street. He wasn't looking forward to spending the long drive with this self-contained girl. Besides, the work he'd left behind at the ranch lay heavy on his mind. Knowing the hay was ready to bale made him fidgety.

He glanced down the street toward Sheryl's apartment, wondering if she had changed her mind. But as he drew closer to her building, he saw her waiting, a small suitcase on the sidewalk beside her, a backpack slung over one shoulder.

He pulled to a stop in front of her, and she tossed her suitcase in the truck's box and opened the door, flipping her backpack into the cab before he could get out to help.

"Good morning, Sheryl," he said instead, settling back into the seat.

She only nodded at him, climbing easily into the truck. This morning she wore blue jeans and a loose-fitting track coat over a soft pink T-shirt. Mark was disappointed to see that her hair hung in a neat braid down her back.

"Do you want breakfast?" he asked, hoping her lack of greeting wasn't an indication of what the next twelve hours would be like.

"I ate already. Thanks."

"Okay." Great conversation starter, Mark, he thought as

he spun the truck in a tight U-turn. No wonder he was always such a hit with the ladies.

He sped down the street and turned onto the Yellowhead, glad to put this district of Edmonton behind him, restless to see the city skyline in his rearview mirror.

The hum of the tires and the occasional muted swish of a vehicle passing them were the only sounds in the cab of the truck—a cab that seemed to grow smaller with each passing block.

It was going to be a long drive.

Finally they hit the last traffic lights on the freeway until the town of Edson, more than a two-hour drive away. Mark stepped down on the accelerator and Sheryl turned, looking over her shoulder at the city they left behind.

''Second thoughts?'' Mark asked.

She turned to him, her face expressionless. ''That's a waste of time,'' she replied her voice terse.

The tone of her voice didn't exactly encourage conversation, but Mark persisted. ''How long did you live in Edmonton?''

''Five years.''

''Where were you before that?''

''Prince George.''

Well things were going great guns, he thought ruefully. At this rate the trip would crawl by.

Mark took his cue from the resolute set of her jaw and turned on the radio. ''Do you have any preferences?''

''I don't listen to the radio much.''

Mark couldn't imagine that. Driving anywhere back in the valley took time and the only thing that broke the monotony was the radio. Market reports, weather, news, music. Didn't matter much. It was noise and company, and the way things were going he would need both.

Sheryl turned away again.

With a sigh Mark leaned forward, resting his forearms on the steering wheel as he watched the road flow past. One part of his mind on the work that waited back home.

He and Nate had cut the hay before he'd left. If it didn't rain today it would be ready to bale. He was glad Nate had managed to get hold of a haying crew. They were going to need all the hands they could get. Square bales were labor intensive, but the price had gone through the roof for good hay. The buyer from the lower mainland wanted only hay baled in manageable square bales. The money would help nudge the ranch out of the hole it had been languishing in since the drop in cattle prices.

The interchange for Westlock flew past, then Spruce Grove then Stony Plain. The speed limit increased and Mark leaned back.

''Do you have to drive so fast?''

Mark jumped at the sound of Sheryl's voice. He assumed she had fallen asleep. Instead she sat rigid, arms clasped across her stomach, face pale.

''This isn't fast.'' He glanced at the speedometer—110 kilometers per hour. ''I'm going close to the speed limit.''

''I'm not comfortable with speed.''

''Well we've got over 1,000 kilometers ahead of us and the only way we're going to get anywhere is to step on it.''

Mark waited for a response, but she only bit her lip and settled back, rubbing her palms over the legs of her jeans.

''You'll just have to trust my driving.''

''I can't.'' She pressed her hands between her knees.

She didn't look like she could, either, thought Mark. Her pale face and white lips showed him clearly how uncomfortable she was. Biting back an impatient sigh, Mark slowed down and set the cruise at 105. Dropping the speed would add an extra sixty minutes of scintillating silence to an already long trip.

They drove over the interchange for Peace River an hour later, and Mark switched the radio off.

''Are you warm enough?'' he asked Sheryl, taking another stab at conversation.

''I'm fine.''

He decided to press on. It felt unnatural to share a vehicle with someone without even commenting on the scenery.

"How long has it been since you were in the valley?"

"I left eight years ago."

"With Jason?"

Sheryl only nodded.

Five words. Three more than the last sentence. At this rate she might be up to a paragraph by Little Fort.

He hadn't perfected the outright nosiness of his mother and sister but he was persistent. One way or another he meant to find out something about this enigmatic girl even if all he got was yes and no answers.

"How long ago did Jason die?" He glanced her way, trying to gauge her reaction.

"Eight months." She blinked but continued staring out the window.

"I'm sorry to hear that."

Sheryl shot him a glance and then looked straight ahead again, not replying.

Mark tapped his fingers on the steering wheel. Nate always complained that Sheryl would talk his ear off with her constant chatter. He hoped he was taking the right person back.

"What happened?" he finally asked.

"Car accident."

Well that explained her dislike of speed.

"And you've been on your own since then?"

"If you mean living on my own, yes. If you mean boyfriends, you're right as well."

Two sentences. Disdainful sentences but at least things were picking up. "So what do you plan to do once you're back in Edmonton?"

"I don't plan that far ahead." Sheryl leaned over, unbuckled her backpack and pulled out a book.

Mark glanced at the cover. *Paradise Lost.*

"Don't tell me you're reading that for pleasure?" he asked, ignoring her signal. He kept his tone light, hoping she would warm up to his irresistible charm.

''Actually it's for a course I'm taking.''

''College or university?''

''I wish.'' She opened the book but didn't look at it. ''Correspondence course.''

''That's pretty impressive.''

She frowned at him as if she sensed ridicule.

''Seriously,'' he protested. ''I spent four years getting my MBA, and got away from classes as soon as possible. I couldn't imagine the discipline required to struggle through Milton on your own.''

''I like learning.''

''What's the course for?''

She shrugged, riffling the corners of the pages with her thumb. ''Bachelor of Education.'' Her voice held a note of deprecation.

''Any specialty?''

''High school English.''

''Then you have my prayers. Anyone wanting to try to instill in teenagers an appreciation for Shakespeare and poetry will need them,'' Mark said with a grin.

''You can save your breath. Prayers are a waste of time.'' Sheryl paused, a hint of pain crossing her face, then she bent her head to the book, eyes narrowed as if concentrating.

That brief look of vulnerability caught Mark by surprise. He glanced at her again, his eyes following the clean line of her features, the smooth curve of her neck. He had seen pictures of her as a young girl, but most of them were amateur and blurred. None of them had even begun to capture her good looks.

Mark jerked his head back to the road, staring out the window with determination.

They also didn't give a hint of how cold and self-possessed she could be.

Sheryl twisted her head around, trying to ease the crook in her neck. From Edson to Jasper, she had alternately dozed and read and from Little Fort to 100 Mile House she merely stared out the window, trying to keep her mind off what waited for her at the end of the journey. The basic fact of the here and now was that she was in a truck with a man who looked like he preferred to be anywhere else.

After his few attempts at conversation, the ride had been painfully quiet. Sheryl found it difficult to ignore him, however. He exuded a quiet strength that made his presence known with no effort on his part.

By the time they reached Valemount, halfway on the trip, she felt tense and saw how rude she'd been. It wasn't Mark's fault that Ed had felt sudden remorse or whatever emotion it was that had sent Mark across British Columbia and half of Alberta. So she swallowed her pride, her antagonism to men in general, and asked a few questions herself.

Mark told her about Ed and his stroke—how, during the course of the tests, they had found the fatal aneurysm. It was inoperable and now only a matter of time.

She also discovered that Nate had met Elise, Mark's sister, a few months after Sheryl and Jason had left. Mark's parents had bought the Simpson ranch five miles down the road from the Krickson place. Three years later Mark sold his real estate business in Vancouver and joined up with Nate and Ed.

The conversation had wound down after that, and they were back to the radio and strained silence.

Sheryl found it difficult to maintain a polite interest in her stepfather and stepbrother's life, and after discovering that Nate and Elise also had three children, she didn't want to talk anymore.

Sheryl had opened her book again, trying to follow the unfamiliar cadence of words and phrases from another time. But they dealt with the justice of a God she neither trusted nor wholly believed in. If it hadn't been required reading for the course, she would have thrown it out months ago.

The words on the page blurred, and she drifted back in time, remembering life in the valley, recalling working on the ranch, fighting with Ed and Nate. Whenever she pulled herself back to the present and the book on her lap, Milton's words echoed her life too closely, its laments of brokenness struck too near her pain.

Giving up, she straightened, glancing at Mark as she did so.

He lounged against the seat, steering one-handed, his fingers resting on the bottom of the wheel. He looked tired and bored, his finely shaped mouth pulled down at the corners, his thickly lashed eyes, heavy-lidded as he stared with disinterest at the road ahead of him. His hair was long, flowing well past his collar, hanging almost in his eyes. He had pulled off his jacket halfway through the trip and rolled up the sleeves of his denim shirt, revealing muscular forearms. He was a very attractive man, she gave him that. He carried himself with a quiet strength that she wouldn't want to have to face down.

She was glad he hadn't pushed her harder, inquired any further into her own life. She meant nothing to him, he nothing to her.

They were approaching Williams Lake now, and Sheryl sat up, struck by an unexpected jolt of familiarity at the smooth summer brown hills laced with dark green pine ridges.

They rounded a corner, and the lake came into view below them, its waters sparkling in the late-afternoon sun. The hills were staggered against each other, and tapered down toward the lake, surrounding it protectively. It looked like home.

Sheryl bit her lip as she shook that particular feeling off. There was no home waiting for her. God and home were a small part of other memories better left buried.

''We'll be there pretty soon now,'' Mark said. ''Do you want to go straight to the hospital, or did you want to head to your brother's place first?''

''May as well get this part of the trip over and done with,'' she said with a sigh. She felt a nervous clenching of her stomach at the thought of finally facing Ed after all the silent years.

Against her will she relived the weeks after she sent her letter five years ago. She had set aside her stubborn pride and written, pleading for sanctuary. She had no other place to go.

Each time she picked up the mail it was with shaking fingers and fear that Jason would find out. Then the one and only time Jason picked up the mail, the letter came.

Only it was her own—resealed and marked ''Return to Sender.'' She never wrote another one and heard nothing from Ed since.

They pulled into the parking lot of the Cariboo Memorial Hospital and Mark shut off the truck's engine. He leaned back, pulling his hands over his face, blowing out his breath. He looked tired, Sheryl thought, feeling a faint pull of attraction. Understandably. His even features and thickly lashed eyes had made women's heads turn each place they'd stopped.

Sheryl shook her head, angry with herself for even acknowledging his good looks. Men were nothing but trouble and heartache. She should know that by now.

''So, ready to go in?'' Mark asked, slowly opening his door.

Sheryl shrugged in reply, slipping her book into the knapsack and buckling it shut. She opened her door just as Mark came around the front of the truck.

He frowned at her as she stepped out, slamming the door behind her. ''I was going to open it for you,'' he said.

''Are you kidding?'' Sheryl almost laughed. ''That went out with feathered helmets and armor.''

''No it didn't,'' was his quiet response.

Sheryl raised her eyebrows at him as she stepped away from the truck, and without a backward glance, she walked down the sidewalk, effectively cutting off the conversation.

A few strides of his long legs put him ahead of her and, reaching around her, he opened the hospital door. ''You're going to make me hustle to prove my point, aren't you?''

''What point?'' Sheryl squinted up at him against the bright sun.

''That some mothers still raise their sons to be gentlemen.'' Mark smiled down at her, his one hand shoved in the pocket of his coat, the other still holding the door.

''Trust me, mister, the words *gentle* and *men* do not belong together,'' Sheryl replied, a mocking tone in her voice.

''My name is Mark.''

His voice was quiet, but Sheryl sensed the light note of rebuke in it.

He may be a man but he had done nothing to deserve being addressed so impersonally. She paused. ''I'm sorry…Mark.'' Their eyes met, and it was as if a tenuous connection had been created by her using his name.

He only nodded, his expression suddenly serious.

Sheryl looked away, took a breath and stepped into the hospital. All thoughts of gentlemen and chivalry were abruptly cut off as the nauseatingly familiar smells of the hospital wafted over her.

The hallways were hushed, the aroma of disinfectant stronger now. Sheryl fought the urge to turn and run, to forget about Ed. But Mark strode inexorably on, boot heels ringing out on the polished floor. Sheryl followed him.

Mark paused at the doorway to a darkened hospital room, knocked lightly on the open door and walked in. Sheryl wiped her damp palms on the legs of her denim jeans, took a steadying breath and followed him inside.

She didn't recognize the figure lying on the bed. The sheets outlined a body that had hollows instead of muscles. The once-black hair was peppered with gray and visibly thinning. His eyes were closed, the lids shot with broken blood vessels.

His skin had an unhealthy grayish pallor and one side of his face was pulled down in a perpetual frown. Tubes and lines snaked out from his body, connected to an IV and monitors that bleeped from a shelf above his head.

Mark bent over and shook Ed's shoulder lightly. One eye opened fully, the other drooped. Even with Mark's warnings, Sheryl still felt shocked at how his stroke had felled this proud man.

''I've brought Sheryl, Ed.'' Mark's voice broke the silence of the hushed darkness of the room.

Ed blinked and stared past Mark, squinting with his good

eye. Then he struggled to sit up, using only one arm, the other falling uselessly to one side, bandaged and connected to an intravenous machine.

"Sheryl? You brought her?" One corner of his mouth lifted in a parody of a smile, the other stayed resolutely where it was. "Come closer." His slurred speech made him sound drunk, a condition scrupulously foreign to Ed Krickson.

Sheryl unclenched her rigid jaw, struggled to still the erratic beating of her heart. Anger, guilt, frustration, sorrow all warred within her, each trying to make a claim.

Blindly she took a step past Mark, almost tripping over the base of the IV stand.

Mark caught her, his hands warm through the thin material of her jacket. Sheryl flinched and pulled away. She took a steadying breath, her iron control over her emotions slipping.

"Hello, Ed," was all she could manage to say as she faced her stepfather.

"Sheryl." Ed reached out to catch her hand, but she drew back. "You…came. Need to see you…to talk to you."

His halting expression of concern was in total opposition to the Ed she remembered. She had been prepared to face a strong adversary, but this man was not the Ed Krickson she had yelled at and fought with as a willful teenager.

"I've been…feeling…vulnerable," he continued, not noticing her silence. "How…are…you?" He took a breath, swallowed. "Are you…happy?"

What should she say? she thought, clasping her waist with her arms. Did he want to hear about the past eight years, would it vindicate everything he had ever told her? Could she tell this broken man about her pain? Did she want to give him that kind of ammunition?

She settled for the superficial, the inane.

"I'm fine."

"Are…you?" His one eye, as blue as the Chilcotin skies, seemed to pierce her, to bore into her very soul.

Unnerved, she took a step back almost bumping into Mark in the close quarters of the hospital room.

Ed lifted a hand to his head as if it pained him. "Sheryl...I've had...burden for you...needed to...see you." The words came out slowly, tortured, and for a moment Sheryl felt pity for him. Until he spoke again.

"I...do...love you...I need to tell..."

Sheryl swayed, his words echoing in her ears. He couldn't mean it. Did someone who loved you push you and force you to become someone you weren't? Did someone who loved you ignore a cry for help?

His words created a hunger for something that had been missing so long from her life—family and a family's love. A home.

His paltry offering was too little too late.

The ceiling pressed down to meet a floor tilting beneath her feet. The echoing became a roar, and she took a halting step away from the bed. Only a few minutes had elapsed since she stepped into this room, but she felt as if she had lived through a lifetime of emotions. She couldn't stay.

"I'm sorry," she mumbled, turning. "I've got to go." Surprisingly Mark stepped back, giving her room, and without looking back, she stumbled out.

Once out in the hallway, she turned, not sure of her direction but aware of a need to escape, to leave behind Ed's empty words spoken from some need to fix what could never be repaired.

The double doors loomed ahead, and she pushed them open, slipping between them. Forcing down a rising wave of panic, she slowed her steps and walked through the entrance and out into the blessed fresh air and warmth of the parking lot.

She found Mark's truck easily and leaned against it, soaking up the warmth it had absorbed from the sun, trying to dispel the chill deep within her.

Slowly the emptiness became smaller, more manageable. Sheryl inhaled. Vulnerability was weakness. She could depend on no one. Love was a word, only a word, she repeated to herself like a litany.

* * *

''I'm sorry Nate isn't here. He had to go up to Lac La Hache today to pick up a bull,'' Elise, Nate's wife, apologized as she led Sheryl down an overgrown path to the cabin tucked away behind the ranch-style home.

Sheryl was relieved. To face Nate so soon after her visit with Ed would have been too hard on emotions still raw from that afternoon.

When Mark had driven up the driveway to the house, Sheryl experienced a sense of déjà vu. She was again fifteen years old, coming home from another day at school in Nate's truck, looking forward to a quick ride on her horse before chores needed to be done.

The house standing so solidly amongst the fir trees, exuded a sense of permanence. Placed against the rootless years she had spent with Jason, it was another painful reminder of might-have-beens.

Even now, as she followed a pathway narrowed by shrubs and ferns and darkened by towering fir trees, she felt as if all the intervening years had slipped away, and once again she was retreating to her sanctuary.

''The girls and I cleaned out the cabin.'' Elise grinned at Sheryl over her shoulder as she opened the door. ''Now there's room to move around.''

Sheryl followed Elise into the cabin. The wave of nostalgia was unexpected, and for the second time in as many days she felt the unwelcome prick of tears. Eight years of hard-won self-control were brushed away as easily as the cobwebs Elise must have cleaned out of this cabin.

She quickly turned away from Elise, concentrating on the room instead. The old metal bed, bought at an auction sale, sat in the same place against the wall, the quilt her mother had made out of her old clothes still covered the mattress. Opposite the bed was a walled-in area that held the toilet and shower, and tucked in the corner between that wall and the cabin wall stood a chest of drawers, an old scarf of her mother's hiding the scarred and gouged top that no amount of sanding could erase.

Sunlight, muted and crosshatched by the limbs of the fir trees, fell through the window and across the old wooden desk that had been the command post of the dreams and adventures of a young girl who longed to be anywhere but here.

Sheryl was drawn to it, and as her fingers unconsciously traced the initials she had labored over, she glanced out the window to the swaying trees and the creek that tumbled over the rocks at their base. How many dreams hadn't she spun, staring out this speckled glass, chin on her hand, elbow on the desk?

Sheryl shook her head to dispel the insidious memories, turning back to Elise, who stood just inside the door.

"Sorry." Sheryl smiled, a sad twisting of her lips. "It feels like I never left."

"I'm glad it looks the same. Nate didn't have time to help, so the girls and I relied on instinct." Elise shoved her hands in the back pocket of her jeans, and in that movement Sheryl recognized one of the similarities between her and Mark. There were others. Both shared thickly lashed eyes, high cheekbones, strong jaws, but where Mark's dark hair flowed past his collar, Elise's was cut short. However, she looked as feminine with her short hair as he looked masculine in spite of the length of his.

"Nate tells me you used to stay in the cabin quite a bit," Elise continued.

"My stays here started out as a punishment, and soon the cabin became a retreat." She smiled at Elise to ease the bitter note that had crept into her voice. "I probably spent more time here than I should have."

"The girls went riffling through the desk once, looking for paper for airplanes. I'm afraid they took some away. I took the rest and put them in a box under the bed. I'm sorry about that." Elise rocked back on the heels of her runners, looking apologetic.

"Doesn't matter," Sheryl reassured her. "They were just old stories and poems. I'm surprised you kept them."

‘‘They were part of your past, and everyone should have something to remember their childhood by.’’

‘‘Probably,’’ she replied.

‘‘I’m even sorrier to hear about your husband....’’

Sheryl only nodded, letting an awkward silence drift between them.

‘‘Well,’’ Elise said as she brushed nonexistent dirt off her pants, that single hesitant word signaling the end of their conversation. ‘‘I’ve got to get the urchins cleaned up and in bed. You’re welcome to come by the house once you’ve rested.’’

Sheryl knew she wouldn’t. ‘‘I’d like to thank you for having me here,’’ she said finally. ‘‘I know it must be inconvenient for you, knowing how Nate feels about me...’’ Sheryl let the last part of the sentence drift away.

‘‘Nate is a good man, a caring husband, but he has his Krickson moments of righteous indignation. Between him and Ed I’ve learned that I’m better off to draw my own conclusions about people.’’ Elise tilted her head to one side, as if studying Sheryl, her gray eyes soft. ‘‘I’ll get to know you on my own terms.’’ She lifted a hand in farewell. ‘‘See you tomorrow.’’

Elise carefully closed the door, her footsteps fading quickly away, leaving Sheryl feeling both bemused and warmed by Elise’s words. Elise had a quiet strength about her, much like her brother Mark.

With a short laugh Sheryl picked her suitcase up from beside the door. Her impressions of these people didn’t matter much. She was only staying long enough to give Ed the peace of mind he seemed to crave, and then she was off, back to Edmonton, back to...

She clutched a shirt she had just unpacked to her stomach, looking over her shoulder at the window and the play of sunlight through the trees. The hushed sounds of the brook filtered through the walls, laying down a gentle counterpoint to the wind sifting through the trees.

Shaking her head, she turned resolutely back to her clothes, hanging them up with rigid determination.

Don't even think about it, she warned herself. There's nothing, not one thing here for you, no life, no friends, no welcome. You made your choice when you ran away from here with Jason.

She heard a soft knock on the door. Elise must have forgotten something, she thought, dropping her clothes on the bed to open the door.

Two girls stood on the shadowed deck, each clutching a handful of wildflowers—lupins, daisies and paintbrush. Each wore dirty T-shirts, and bare feet poked out from the frayed hems of blue jeans. Sheryl guessed their ages to be five and six. These must be the ''urchins'' Elise set out looking for. Nate's little girls, her nieces. Stepnieces, she corrected herself.

The oldest smiled, hesitantly, showing a mouth bereft of front teeth, and thrust her flowers forward.

''These are for you,'' she lisped, grinning.

''Thank you.'' Sheryl took the flowers, unable to keep from smiling.

''And I have some, too,'' the second girl, a dark copy of her blond sister, pushed her bouquet toward Sheryl, as well.

''My name is Crystal, this is Marla,'' the older girl said. ''And we helped my mom clean the cabin for you.'' She peered past Sheryl into the cabin. ''Pretty clean huh?''

''Very clean,'' Sheryl agreed, sniffing the flowers. ''And these flowers will be just the thing it needs to make it look like a home.'' Sheryl hesitated, watching the two girls, suddenly jealous of Nate.

Elise's distant voice drifted up to them.

''Oh, brother, there's my mom. She probably wants us to have a bath.'' Crystal turned to Sheryl. ''Will we see you tomorrow?''

Sheryl nodded uncertainly, still holding the flowers. With another grin, they both turned and skipped down the path toward the house, arms outstretched, giggles trailing behind them.

Nate's family. Nate's place. Nate's home.

Sheryl stopped herself. She was getting maudlin.

She glanced down at the bouquet of flowers in her hand, touching them with a forefinger. It was funny. In all the years she had lived here, this was the most welcome she had ever felt.

Chapter Three

As Mark approached Nate and Elise's driveway the next day, he hesitated, then touched the brake, slowing the truck down. Elise had told him she and Nate would visit Ed before church, so he'd left his own home earlier in the hopes of catching them.

He came to a complete halt just before the turnoff and tapped his thumbs on the steering wheel. Would it be obvious if he stopped in? Would he look too much like a nosy Andrews?

Ever since he'd found Sheryl in the hospital parking lot, huddled against his truck, she had been on his mind. Ed and Nate's part of the story he knew by rote. Now, suddenly it had another side.

On the way back from the hospital, she had sat across the seat from him, arms clasped tightly across her stomach, her face averted.

Thankfully Nate was gone when he dropped her off, but Mark knew she would have to meet him today. Would their meeting have the same emotional undercurrents that Sheryl's and Ed's had? Nate had never spoken kindly of Sheryl.

Mark hesitated, then spun the wheel and stepped on the gas before he changed his mind. Dust billowed behind him as the truck flew up the hill. Cresting it, he slowed, then coasted down the other side, stopping behind Nate and Elise's minivan.

Crystal and Marla sat on the verandah, chins on hands, elbows planted on knees, and ruffled skirts brushing the tops of black patent leather shoes.

They jumped up, tripping down the stairs. ''Uncle Mark, Uncle Mark,'' they both shouted, running toward him.

Mark slammed the door behind him and, bending over, scooped up little Marla in his arms and swung her around. He retained his hold on her and pulled Crystal against him. As always, their unabashed welcome warmed him, filling the empty spots of his life.

''We didn't see you for a long time, Uncle Mark,'' Marla admonished, leaning back as if to make sure he was still the same favorite uncle.

''I was only gone a few days, punky.'' Mark squeezed both girls. ''How do you like what I brought back for you all the way from Edmonton?''

''Mommy told me she used to sleep in my room,'' Marla hooked a slender arm around Mark's neck. ''And I think she's pretty.''

''Did you see her hair, Uncle Mark? I bet she can almost sit on it.'' Crystal tugged at the fine wisps of hair that Mark knew Elise had spent twenty minutes curling. ''I wish I had hair like that, then I'd be pretty.''

''Don't let Grandma hear you say that,'' Mark chuckled.

''I know what she would say,'' Marla interrupted. ''She'll say that 'grace is defeatful and beauty is a pain, but...''' She frowned, chewing on her lip. Then with a shrug, dismissed the mangled quote.

'''But a woman that fears the Lord, she shall be praised.''' Mark kissed his youngest niece, stifling his own laughter, and set her on the ground.

''Mom said she probably won't come to church with us. I want her to come because Mr. Hankinson said we should bring a visitor to church, but we never have any visitors,'' Crystal complained.

Mark stroked Crystal's crisp, sun-warmed hair. ''I don't think Sheryl is used to coming to church, Crissie.''

''Then she should come for sure, shouldn't she, Marla?''

Marla nodded seriously, twisting the hem of her ruffled skirt around her fingers.

''Can't you ask her, Uncle Mark?''

''I don't think it will help if I ask her.'' Besides he was unsure of his own reception after what had happened yesterday.

''Of course it will matter,'' Crystal said, interrupting his thoughts. ''Mommy says that all the girls think you're a hunk.'' Crystal's eyes sparkled.

''You don't need to use words like that, Crissie.''

''Like what? Hunk? It's not a swear is it?''

Mark shook his head as he felt a rush of love for these two precious lives. Nate leaned toward a stern upbringing, and it was difficult not to intervene. And as children would, they got very adept at knowing which adult they could cajole and which one would not be led.

''Could you ask her to come?'' Marla's voice was soft, her expression wistful. Crystal leaned against him, sighing.

Mark knew they were playing him along, yet he already felt himself softening.

''It would be good for her to go to church,'' Marla continued.

Marla grabbed his one hand, Crystal the other, and they tugged, pulling him down the path toward the cabin.

''C'mon girls, I don't think she's even awake.'' *Aren't you the firm uncle,* he thought wryly, unable to resist the encouraging smiles they were throwing his way.

Crystal ran up the steps, Marla behind her, each disregarding her long skirt. Mark hung back as Crystal knocked confidently on the door. The speed with which the door opened was as much of a surprise as the smile on Sheryl's face at the sight of the two girls.

''Well, hello again.'' She hunkered down, the hair that Crystal so admired falling to one side like a golden, shimmering curtain. ''Did you girls bring me that delicious breakfast?''

Her face was animated, her green eyes sparkling, and Mark felt an unexplained tug of attraction.

"We tried not to wake you up," Marla offered.

Crystal stepped forward. "Do you want to come to church with us?"

Mark almost groaned. Crystal's approach was pure Krickson. Full speed ahead, ignore all comers.

The smile on Sheryl's face faded, and slowly she straightened, catching sight of Mark. She paused, their eyes meeting and holding. Mark had to stop himself from taking a step toward her. She looked away, breaking the connection. "I'm not dressed for church."

"That doesn't matter, Auntie Sheryl, we can wait."

"Please come," Marla added her voice to Crystal's. "We never have a visitor, and Daddy said you're only staying a couple of days." Marla turned to Mark, ready to plead her cause, but he saw Sheryl's discomfort.

"We had a long drive yesterday, and Sheryl's probably tired." Mark kept his voice firm, wishing, not for the first time, that his nieces were sweet, shy and tractable.

"I think God wants you to come, Auntie Sheryl." Crystal caught Sheryl's hand and turned her own soft blue eyes up to Sheryl's green ones. A look of pain flitted across her face, so momentary that Mark thought he imagined it.

"Maybe He does, sweetheart." Sheryl smiled down at Crystal, a tight movement of her lips. "Do I have time to change?"

Crystal clenched one fist and jerked it down toward a lifted knee in a childish parody of a hockey player's victory dance. Mark made a note to tell Nate that Crystal was possibly watching a little too much television.

Sheryl grinned, and as she looked up she met Mark's eyes again.

"We'd like it if you came," he said.

"Okay." She lifted her hands up as if in surrender. "I'll be real quick."

Mark caught Crystal's hand and gave it a tug. "We'll wait for you by my truck."

Sheryl appeared around the corner of the house two minutes later, dressed in a loose, flowing skirt and brown T-shirt that set off to perfection the gold of her hair.

The girls ran up to meet her just as Nate and Elise came down the steps of the verandah.

Nate was the first to see her. He paused, his son balanced on one arm, his face suddenly cold, hard, and Mark knew they hadn't seen each other yet.

"Hello, Sheryl." Nate's voice had a tight edge to it.

Sheryl's step faltered, her smile faded.

"Hey, Mom and Dad, Auntie Sheryl is coming to church." Crystal skipped up to her dad, hands flapping in excitement.

The tension between Sheryl and Nate was palpable, but somehow she overcame her obvious reluctance and walked over to Nate, her hand outstretched.

Nate hesitated, and for a moment Mark thought he was going to ignore her. Instead he shifted the baby to his other arm and caught Sheryl's hand in his.

"Thanks for letting me stay in the cabin," she said quietly. "It's like old times again."

Nate nodded, releasing her hand, clasping his son closer.

"Is this the baby?" Sheryl asked, her voice and manner hesitant, totally at odds with the tight, controlled woman Mark had spent the past two days with.

"Yes. His name is Benjamin."

Mark could almost feel the yearning in her as she reached out and touched Benjamin's chubby hand.

Nate didn't even look at her, instead concentrated on his son. Sheryl stroked Benjamin's arm then her hand fell to her side.

Mark wondered how Nate could pretend indifference to Sheryl as she stood before him, her face betraying her inner struggle?

Mark could take no more.

"Why don't you ride with me, Sheryl," he offered. "And

Marla can ride on the way up, Crystal on the way home,'' he quickly added as both girls clamored to be the third passenger.

Sheryl bit her lip, her hands clutching her elbows. She looked like she was caught between two evils, and he remembered.

''I'll drive slowly,'' he added softly.

Her shoulders seemed to sag in relief, and without a backward glance she walked over to Mark's truck.

A few quick steps got him to the passenger door in time to open it for her. She shot him an oblique glance and got in behind Marla.

Mark closed the door, watching her as he rounded the hood of the truck, still trying to absorb who the real Sheryl was, the self-controlled, secretive woman he spent an entire day with yesterday, or the vulnerable girl she became around Nate and Ed?

Marla chattered to Sheryl as he got in on his side of the truck. ''I don't like buckling up.''

''It's safer if you do.'' Sheryl ignored Marla's protests and clicked the belt over her stomach, pulling it snug. She looked up at Mark as he clipped his own seat belt. ''Thanks for the ride, Mark.'' Her voice was soft, husky, and hearing her say his name gave his heart a nudge.

He only nodded in acknowledgment and started the truck, fully aware of her on the other side of the cab, wondering himself what created these unexpected feelings.

As he pulled away from the house, he glanced at her. The sun coming through the windshield caught her hair making it shine and glimmer. Her soft green eyes were downcast, shaded by a sweep of sable lashes. As she spoke to Marla, she smiled, a gentle movement of soft, full lips.

The girls were wrong. She was more than pretty. Now, with her barriers pulled down, she was stunning.

The rustle of papers and coughs of people subsided like a wave as the minister raised his hands for the blessing.

Sheryl clutched the pew in front of her. It had been years since she had attended a church service.

Her natural father had given her a youthful and carefree trust in God that had managed to withstand the rigors of Ed's interpretation of parents and duty. But it hadn't been able to withstand the reality of being Jason's wife. Broken promises and unanswered prayers had worn her faith down until it had become only a part of her past, like her father's name.

But Crystal and Marla showed such exuberance and so easily had overridden her objections. Had she known that it would include a visit with Ed, she would have been more firm. Thankfully Ed didn't pay much attention to her, and during the visit she stayed in the background, netting yet another disapproving look from Nate.

As the organ played the familiar introduction to the closing song, she remembered standing in the pew, singing the song with glad enthusiasm, Ed frowning at her, Nate rolling his eyes and Blythe trying to restrain her with a pleading glance.

Now the familiar words and tune created a desire for that comforting closeness with the God from her past.

She sighed and cut that thought off. God required something she could never afford to give Him, or anyone else—vulnerability and love.

Mark's deep baritone struck out beside her. He held the book loosely in one hand, his other tucked casually in the front pocket of black pants. He sang the words with enthusiasm, and Sheryl felt jealous of his faith and security.

As if he sensed her scrutiny, he glanced sidelong at her, and in between stanzas quirked a half grin at her. An answering flutter of her heart surprised Sheryl, and she turned ahead.

The song wound down to the "Amen," and Sheryl looked ahead, thankful that it was over.

The organist paused a moment then segued into the postlude, and Sheryl steeled herself to face the knowing looks of people who remembered her as a young and willful girl and Jason Kyle's girlfriend.

"Auntie Sheryl," Crystal called out, slipping through the people as they gave way. "Auntie Sheryl, wait for us."

That name again. Auntie. So easily they used it to claim a relationship Sheryl knew wouldn't last longer than the few days she stayed.

But being with them was preferable to facing curious glances and the usual valley nosiness. So Sheryl waited for them as they worked their way through the exiting worshippers.

"Did you see us looking at you," Crystal whispered, as she caught Sheryl's hand in hers.

"I waved, too," Marla put in, trying to wiggle past Crystal to get to Sheryl's other hand.

"Hey, girls," Mark's voice came from behind them, sounding wounded. "Doesn't anyone want to hold my hand?"

"You can carry me," Marla offered just as she got a solid grip on Sheryl's hand.

"Thank you, Your Majesty." Mark swung Marla up in his arms with a laugh.

Marla still clung to Sheryl's hand and because of that, Mark ended up walking close beside Sheryl, his proximity unnerving. Her shoulder bumped his arm, and her hip hit his, but Marla wouldn't release her grip.

They made their way out of church this way, looking for all the world like a little family. Sheryl wondered how the people of the valley would look upon this little scene.

They stepped out into the warm sunshine, people of all ages and sizes milling about below them on the grass surrounding the church.

"Sheryl…Sheryl Kyle?" A woman the same age as Sheryl came up to them, shoulder-length dark hair framing a pleasant face.

Sheryl stared at her blankly, feeling like her mind had shut down.

"Lainie Saunders," the woman prompted. "We used to skip out of Mr. Kuric's class and go swimming in the Horsefly River."

''I remember.'' Sheryl smiled as happier memories intruded, brushing aside the darker ones from the church service. ''I flunked biology because of it.''

''So did I.'' Lainie laughed, glancing curiously at Mark. ''My parents were so mad. I ended up taking summer school.''

''I spent the entire summer cleaning out calf pens by hand,'' Sheryl commented dryly, surprised at the quick stab of anger that accompanied the recollection. It had happened almost ten years ago.

''Remember that time we floated all the way down to the lake?'' Lainie went on. ''And that young Fish-and-Wildlife officer caught us...''

''Anthony Jesperson.''

''I think that meeting was meant to be. We've been married four years this spring.''

The conversation hit a pause. ''And you're expecting?'' Sheryl asked, glancing at Lainie's obviously protruding midriff.

''In two months,'' Lainie said, with pride tingeing her voice. ''I feel like a beached whale, and I'm only seven months along.'' Lainie smoothed a hand over her stomach self-consciously. ''What about you? Did you and Jason...''

''No. No kids.'' Sheryl withdrew her hand from Marla's and Crystal's, the warmth of their fingers suddenly burning.

''And where is Jason?''

''He passed away about eight months ago.'' Sheryl felt a tightening around her temples.

''Oh, no. I'm sorry to hear that.''

''It's okay.'' She swallowed, her throat suddenly thickening.

''Do you want to come over for coffee and catch up?'' Lainie asked, laying a gentle hand on Sheryl's shoulder, her face expressing concern.

She shook her head, glancing behind her at Mark who still held Marla. ''I...I...should get going. I got a ride with Mark, and I think he wants to leave.'' Sheryl shot Mark a pleading glance, and thankfully he picked up the cue without a pause.

''Sorry, Lainie. My brothers and sisters are coming for the day, and I think we're already late.''

''Let's make it another time. I'm sure we've lots to catch up on,'' Lainie replied, her expression one of concern.

''Sure. I'll give you a call.'' Sheryl took a step down the stairs, then another and, with a quick wave at her old friend, turned and almost ran to Mark's truck.

''Don't spill, now.'' Elise handed Marla and Crystal each a cup of juice and added a frown for good measure.

Mark leaned an elbow on the counter of his mother's kitchen, tracing a pattern in the spilled sugar on the gray arborite. ''So, Elise, how do you read Sheryl?'' he asked.

''Like a closed book.'' Elise opened one of the many containers on the counter and began arranging cookies and squares on a tray. ''You've spent more time with her than I have.''

''She seems like a different person in each different place.'' Mark pushed the sugar into a neat pile with his pinky, frowning at it. ''Lainie talked to her after church today, and I thought I caught a glimpse of what she used to be like. Then it's like someone hit a switch, and she's the girl I met in the bar.''

''She lost her husband only eight months ago. A person's emotions are very unstable for almost a year after a death.''

''Probably,'' Mark said, rearranging the sugar again. ''But I get the feeling that she's not too sorry her husband's gone.''

''Well I know Nate isn't. He's hated Jason for years.'' Elise set out some cups on the tray, her lips pursed. ''From what I've heard he was a pretty hardened character before Sheryl went out with him.''

Mark shrugged, pressing a finger on the pile of sugar he had created, still frowning. ''What have you heard?''

''He was wild, rough, drank, got into plenty of trouble…''

Elise shrugged. ''Even if half of the rumors I heard are true, he wasn't husband material.''

''So why did Sheryl take off with him and stay with him for eight years?''

''Why don't you ask her?''

Mark curled his lip. ''Good idea, 'Lise. She's so talkative.''

She flashed him a mischievous grin. ''Well, get Mom to ask.'' Elise closed a sugar container and pushed it aside. ''Do you know how long she's going to stay around?''

''I think she's going to make the visit as short as possible.''

''What does she have to go back for?''

''Nothing, unless you want to count a run-down apartment.'' Mark brushed the sugar into his hand and reached over the counter to dump it into the sink. ''I guess what she does shouldn't matter.''

''Probably not, but I get the sense it does.'' Elise winked at him. ''She's good-looking enough.''

''Well as Marla said this morning, 'Grace is defeatful and beauty is a pain'...''

Elise looked puzzled, and as comprehension dawned, she burst out laughing. ''That's cute.'' She pushed the tray of mugs across the counter to Mark. ''Anyhow, big brother, here's your chance to show Sheryl what a man of the nineties you are. Don't spill, now,'' she added with a wicked grin.

''Cute, 'Lise.'' He picked up the tray and headed from the relative peace of the kitchen to the din of the living room and another Andrews family gathering.

The two couches facing each other were full of bodies, others sat on the floor braced against them, chairs from the kitchen were pulled up, and in one corner of the spacious room a group of teenagers were sprawled on the floor playing an unusually noisy game of Monopoly.

Empty, the room had grace, elegance and style. The fireplace that dominated the center of one wall was built of soft, sand-colored brick and flanked by two floor-to-ceiling windows draped with lace curtains.

Mark almost groaned when he spied Sheryl seated at the

opposite end of the living room on a kitchen chair between his parents, Lenore and Nick. As soon as he was done his duties, he would head over and rescue her. Once Lenore got hold of her she wouldn't rest until she got Sheryl's birth weight and grades in school.

"Ah, coffee." Mark's brother, Allen, disentangled himself from his wife and his nephew Benjamin and reached up for the cup that Mark offered him. "You are almost an angel."

"If serving coffee is all that takes then I'm honorary member of the crowd before the throne in heaven," his wife, Diane, said with a laugh. She took a cup and flashed a thankful smile at Mark.

"Saying 'I do' to Allen was enough to bring you there, Diane," Brad, Mark's younger brother, said with a laugh. "Say Mark, we don't have to tip you do we?"

"Just leave donations in the cup when you're done. I'll put them towards the Nate and Mark Eternal Debt Fund." Mark returned.

"Hey, little brother, I'll have a cup of that stuff, too," said Rick, Mark's other brother.

"I don't know how you can still call him 'little,'" sang out Brad. "He's at least five inches taller than you."

"Two," Rick held up two fingers as if to emphasize the point. "Two lousy inches, brat."

"Must be all that hair that makes you think that," said Allen.

Mark shook his head and bent over so Rick could get a cup off the tray. His brother glanced past him toward Sheryl. "Is she the reason you're lowering yourself, brother?"

Mark turned the tray half a turn. "Cream or sugar?" was all he said.

"Right," Rick replied, settling back on the couch with a smirk.

Mark ignored him and worked his way past the younger nieces and nephews leaning against their parents legs, toward the chairs that flanked the fireplace. He felt sorry for Sheryl—she looked a little dazed. And for good reason. Mark had two sisters and three brothers, all married. Only Elaine and Drew had no children. An Andrews gathering was something you eased into, one family at a time, not dived into on a day when all the members were together.

"Noisy enough for you, Mother?" Mark set the tray down on the table, pushing a couple of books out of the way. He spooned some sugar into her cup, poured in some cream and handed it to her.

"It's like music, don't you think, dear?" Lenore asked of her husband as she took her cup from Mark.

"I prefer Bach, myself," Nick grumbled, and raised his eyebrows as a cry went up from the corner of the living room where the teenagers were.

"I've got two hotels on Park Place. You're toast, Jennifer," one of the nephews crowed.

Mark handed his father a cup, offered the tray to Sheryl who shook her head. He took the last cup and eased himself down at his mother's feet.

"How are you feeling, Dad?" he asked, leaning his head back against his mother's chair.

"I got to slow down, doctor said," Nick retorted dryly. "I'm retired. How slow am I supposed to go?"

"He's grumpy because he's not allowed to help you and Nate with the haying," Lenore said, stroking her son's head.

Mark quirked his mother a lazy grin. "I don't know if he's that much help anyhow...."

"Watch what you say, Mark," Lenore admonished, giving his long hair a tug. "You'll goad him into coming out anyway. And when are you going to get your hair cut?"

"I'm trying to save money," returned Mark, winking at Sheryl.

Her only response was to take another sip of coffee.

Elise and the girls set trays of sandwiches and squares on the already-full coffee table, and the noise level immediately decreased.

"How is the ranch doing, Mark?" Brad leaned past his wife

to address him. "Nate was saying that you landed a decent hay contract with a guy in Langley?"

"Yeah, Thomason up at the One-Oh-Eight put me on to him. He supplies a lot of hobby farmers and will take all we can give him. If the price is as good as he says, irrigating that hay land will more than pay for itself this year." Mark popped a cookie in his mouth, and the talk turned toward the weather, loan payments and cattle futures.

Nate wandered into the room and joined in the conversation. Mark glanced at Sheryl who ignored both Nate and him, concentrating on the sandwich she held. Someone asked him a question, but as he answered it, he listened with half an ear to the conversation going on behind him, wondering if the dry wit of his father or the nosiness of his mother could draw Sheryl out.

Her replies were quiet, her manner self-contained, and after half an hour the only new thing Mark discovered was that she'd had chicken pox when she was nine, that she usually didn't have time for lunch and that her visit with her father went fine.

If you could call standing against the wall, arms crossed across her stomach, "fine." Mark knew her answer was an evasion, but with Sheryl, what else did he expect?

The afternoon wore on, and the older men took the kids outside to play volleyball. Diane and Elise were cleaning up in the kitchen, and Brad's wife kept Crystal, Marla and her own youngest son entertained.

Mark felt relaxed, comfortable, the welcoming ambience of his mother's home working its familiar magic. Wherever they had lived, Lenore had made each house a home, each place a focal point for their family to gather, talk and share fellowship.

Sheryl had moved to one of the couches, and as the room emptied, he dropped himself down on the one across from her.

"Oh, honey," his mother said suddenly, spying a red-cheeked Benjamin in the doorway of the living room, blanket tucked under one arm, book under the other. ''Couldn't you sleep?''

He shook his head and toddled over toward his grandmother. But when he spied Sheryl, he veered off course and clambered up beside her, slapping his book on her lap.

''Read,'' he demanded, dragging his blanket up alongside, leaning against her.

Sheryl pulled away, then as she looked down on Benjamin's tousled head Mark could see her soften.

Her hand slowly lifted and touched a wayward lock of hair, straightening it, and a look of such yearning came over her it hit Mark deep and low.

The stern lines of her face smoothed, the hardness drifted away, and she was transformed into the same beautiful girl that had fussed over Marla's seat belt this morning.

Mark was inexplicably jealous of Benjamin. Jealous of the way Sheryl's delicate fingers drifted over his head, the soft smile she bestowed on him when he looked up at her. Why was it that this young child brought out this soft part of her, a part she never showed to any adult?

Mark wondered if he would ever know.

Chapter Four

The sun was up; however, the air wafting into the cabin was still cool and laced with the scent of fir and moldering underbrush.

The smell of the mountains. Sheryl stopped sweeping and closed her eyes. Effortlessly she drifted back over the years, remembering walks with her mother as they had discovered this new place. It had been so different from the prairies and the grain farm that Sheryl's first father had worked. These mountains, cradling wide-open valleys, held an elemental fascination for them.

Sheryl smiled as she relived those moments of discovery, happiness and a mother's love.

A quick shake of her head brought her back to the bleak present. Love was a scarce commodity, she reminded herself. God parceled it out in small portions, and it seemed she used up her share as a young child.

She bent over to sweep under the bed, and her broom hit something solid. Puzzled, she got down on her knees. A box.

Sheryl dropped the broom, pulled the box forward and opened the flaps. Loose papers, old scribblers and dog-eared paperback novels filled it. With a rueful grin Sheryl drew out a hard-cover journal that lay on the top. It had been a gift from her mother for her tenth birthday, the first one she'd celebrated here.

Sheryl sat back on her heels, running her fingers over the

figure of the old-fashioned lady embossed on the cover. How she'd hated to ruin the clean, white pages when she'd first gotten it. But a need to express herself had overcome her reluctance and soon she'd written in it every day.

Sheryl opened the cover and saw the first words on the page, remembering again what it was like to be ten years old, confused and missing her father:

> I dreamed me and Mom and Dad still lived in Alberta. I dreamed Daddy was still alive. But then I woke up. I had to cry. I miss him so much.

Sheryl smiled ruefully, touching the childish writing with her finger, remembering the pain of a loss she didn't dare express. Her tears made her mother sad which would bother Ed.

> Mr. Ed Krickson wants me to call him Dad. He's really my stepdad but it sounds funny to call him that.

And that had been the beginning of the conflict, thought Sheryl.

She flipped past long and rambling descriptions of the cows, horses, plants and mountains. She remembered a young girl impressed with her surroundings.

"I like living here now." She had written this a few months later.

> I don't miss Daddy as much. But there's so much to do. I have to feed the orphaned calves, and my hands get so cold. I lost a mitten and Mr. Ed Krickson says I can't have another one for at least a month. So I stole one from Nate. Just when I feed the calves, though. Then I put it back.

Sheryl closed the book. Now, looking at it from an adult's perspective, the incident seemed even more harsh and cruel than it had as a young child, when she'd been called irresponsible and careless. She put it away, determined to close the box and push it back under the bed, but another book caught her eye. A coiled scribbler. She'd started keeping her diary in leftover scribblers from school, because Ed had found her first diary and had punished her for the sins she had confessed to in it.

> Jason smiled at me today. He's so cute, and Lainie thinks so, too. Nate, the daddy's boy, says he's trouble. I hate the way Nate stares at me lately.

As Sheryl read, she remembered how deep their antagonism had run. At first it had been fun having an older brother. But as they got older, Sheryl's battles with Ed escalated, and as a consequence, so did Nate's anger with her.

Sheryl turned over another page.

> Jason wants me to go out with him on Friday. I shouldn't go, but I know Jason will talk me into it. Nate still won't talk much to me at the supper table. Just sits there and stares. I was supposed to pray tonight and told Ed I didn't want to. Mom started crying. I like to talk to God, but up in the mountains, away from them, not at the table in front of them where they can criticize what I say.

Sheryl frowned at the last sentences and closed the book. It seemed difficult to believe that she had once had such a simple faith in God.

She looked outside at the sunlight dancing between the branches of the fir trees. That God had made this part of the world was easy to see.

It was harder to see God in a city. It was even harder to talk to God when you were just trying to survive the bleakness.

And now?

Sheryl shrugged as she packed the books back in the box. She had drifted so far from God, it was improbable that she could find her way back to Him.

"Auntie Sheryl." Marla's voice shrilled through the silence. "Auntie Sheryl, you have to help." The voice came closer and as Sheryl got up she saw Marla coming at a dead run up the path.

She made it up the steps and sagged against the door frame.

"What's the matter, honey?" Sheryl ran to the door and fell on her knees before the panting little girl.

"My daddy...fell...down the stairs...in the house."

Sheryl jumped up and took off down the path.

"Wait for me...Auntie Sheryl?" Marla shouted, trying desperately to keep up.

Sheryl grabbed Marla's hand, almost dragging her around the front of the house and through the door.

Nate lay on the floor at the bottom of the stairs. His face was pale, his teeth clenched. Elise was crouched on her knees beside him, and Sheryl recognized her younger sister, Elaine, hovering behind her.

"Just lie still and tell me where it hurts," Elise cried, her hands fluttering over his chest.

"My leg." Nate sucked in a painful breath. "Maybe a broken rib or two."

Marla dropped down in a nearby chair and began to cry.

Elise glanced up at Sheryl, eyes wide, scared. "What do I do?"

Sheryl knelt beside Nate, across from Elise, and carefully felt down his leg. Nate winced when she reached his lower leg, and she stopped.

"Do you have anything long and flat that we can tie his leg to?" Sheryl asked. "We'll have to immobilize it for the trip to the hospital."

Elise covered her mouth with one hand, Marla's sobs increased.

"There's some one-inch boards in the garage," Nate ground out through clenched teeth.

"Elise, get some pieces of cloth we can rip up. Elaine, you help Marla." Sheryl snapped out her orders, turned and ran out to the shed.

When she returned with a suitable length of board, Elise was ripping material into strips, and Elaine was comforting Marla, who stared at her father, eyes wide, mouth still trembling.

With quick but careful movements, Sheryl tied his leg to the board, ordering Elaine to bring the van to the front door so they could load him inside.

"Sheryl," Nate caught her hand.

Sheryl paused, surprised at his acknowledgment of her.

"I'm supposed to drive my tractor to Mark. Can you do that for me?"

Sheryl turned her attention back to the knot she was tying and nodded.

Nate grimaced in pain. "Just go up the road to the old Simpson place. He'll be in the lower fields, along the creek."

"Sure" was all she could say. Nate hadn't spoken more than ten words to her since she had come, and now, even though he was in pain, all he could talk about was the ranch. It shouldn't hurt, but it did.

"I'll need you to help me take the seats out," Elaine called out after she parked the van.

Sheryl left to help, and after they had dragged the bench out, Elise showed up with a sleeping bag to lay down on the floor.

It took the three of them to move him, ignoring his shouts of pain and Marla's increasing tears.

"When are you going on that diet, Nate?" Elise groaned as they finally got him settled.

He smiled wanly at her, his face pale. She leaned over, kissed him lightly and climbed into the driver's seat. Elaine and Sheryl closed the door, and with a rumble of gravel, reminiscent of her brother's driving, Elise tore out of the yard.

The dust from her retreating van still hung in the valley when Sheryl felt reaction set in.

Too vividly she remembered a body at the foot of another set of stairs, a shadowy, menacing figure at the top. After that time Jason had given her a dozen roses. The next time, carnations.

She clutched her stomach as if to hold the memories in and turned to Elaine, pulling in a shaky breath. She was needed and had no time for histrionics.

"Can you stay here with Marla and Benjamin? I should take that tractor to Mark."

"Just give me a minute to check on Benjamin." Elaine ran up the stairs, pausing to pick up the toy truck Nate had slipped on.

Sheryl knelt down in front of Marla, stroking a lock of hair away from her damp cheeks.

"When your daddy comes back he'll have a hard white cast on his leg and a smile on his face." She had an inspiration. "You should make a card for him and when Crystal comes home from school, you could pick some flowers, like you did for me."

"My daddy won't die will he?" Marla sniffed, her eyes shiny with tears.

Sheryl frowned. "Of course not. It's just a broken leg."

"Daddy said Grandpa will probably die in the hospital."

Sheryl caught Marla in a quick hug. "Your daddy is big and strong," she reassured her. "I remember when he fell off the machine shed. He broke his arm, and it got fixed really good."

"Did you and Grandpa pray about it, is that why it got fixed?" Marla wiped her eyes with the heel of her hand, leaving brown smudges on her cheeks.

"I'm sure we did." It was all she could say. She remembered many prayers, but not one for mended arms.

"Well then, Auntie Elaine and I will pray that Daddy's leg gets better, too."

Sheryl smiled at her innocence and stood up. "I better go tell your uncle Mark your daddy won't be coming to help."

"He won't be happy. Uncle Mark said they had to finish this week."

Elaine came back down the stairs. "Benny's still sleeping.

Thanks so much for helping,'' she said to Sheryl. ''I don't know what Elise and I would have done without you.''

''Managed, I guess.'' Sheryl shrugged, stroked Marla's cheek once more, then left.

''Conrad, toss me that can of lubricant,'' Mark strained at a nut under the tractor. The wrench slipped, and his knuckles scraped painfully across a metal bar. He sucked in his breath, and the heavy tool fell out of his hands onto his forehead. Shards of pain shot through his skull.

Conrad hunkered down beside him, holding out the spray can. ''It's your p.t.o. clutch, man. That's why the baler don't work.''

Mark closed his eyes, rubbing his sore head, stifling the urge to scream. Could the day get any worse? It had taken him and Nate almost an hour to get the baler they'd rented from Jacksons' to work. Rob had taken his sweet time coming this morning, and now this tractor had broken down after they'd done one whole bale.

He grabbed the tractor tire with one hand, picked up the wrench with the other and dragged himself out from underneath, the hay stubble scratching his back as his shirt pulled up.

''At least we can still drive this piece of junk to the edge of the field. We'll need to pull out the clutch and take it in to get fixed, if Nate doesn't get here pretty quick with the other tractor.''

''So what do you figure, Mark?'' Conrad hovered beside him, his face expectant. ''Do you want me and Rob to head into town?''

''Don't get your hopes up, buster. You guys can start with my tractor. I'll wait for Nate to come.''

Conrad sighed and returned to Mark's tractor. He started it and, putting it into gear, roared off toward the other baler.

Mark bent over, snatched his hat off the ground and flipped it on his head. He yanked on his gloves and blew out his breath. A baler that wasn't working properly, one bum tractor and rain in the forecast. And where was Nate? How long did it take to run home and get a tractor, anyhow?

He vaulted up onto the crippled tractor, shoved it into gear and moved it slowly into the shade of the fir trees on the field's edge.

Mark turned around as a tractor roared into the field. That took him long enough, he thought, anxious to get going.

The tractor came closer and Mark leaned forward as if to see better. Since when did Nate have a pink T-shirt and long blond hair?

It was Sheryl.

She rolled noisily past Mark and stopped beside the baler. Shoving the gearshift into neutral she pushed the throttle down. She waited a moment to make sure the tractor had come to a complete halt and then climbed out.

"I brought the tractor over." Sheryl raised her voice above the roar of the engine, looking up at him as he came closer. She wore the same faded pink T-shirt and blue jeans she'd had on the day they'd driven here. Her hair hung in a braid over one shoulder, but a few wisps had worked loose to blow around her face. Her cheeks had a glow to them, her mouth a soft smile. Mark felt mesmerized, then shook his head, belatedly yanking his hat off his head.

"I'm glad to see you and the tractor, but what happened to Nate?" he asked.

Her smile disappeared. "He broke his leg."

Mark stared her and as her words registered he closed his eyes, wondering what he had done the past few days to deserve this.

"Elise is bringing him into town, and Elaine is staying with Benjamin and Marla," she continued. "I don't know when they'll be back, but I don't suppose he'll be in any condition to drive a tractor for a while."

"That's obvious," Mark said, unable to keep the frustration out of his voice. "Well, thanks for bringing it here in one piece."

Not that it did much good now. Making square bales required two people per tractor, one driving, the other stuking the bales. They didn't have an automatic bale stacker, at least not this year. If they could make enough money on the bales they could look at a more efficient system for next year.

But if they didn't get these fields baled by the end of the week, they might lose the contract entirely. What a time for Nate to break his leg!

Sheryl pointed her chin in the direction of an old, rusted truck parked in the shade beside the broken-down tractor. ''Mind if I take that back with me?''

''Go ahead,'' Mark answered, absently. ''Rob can drive the tractor back tonight.''

She nodded and turned to leave. Mark watched her go, a sudden inspiration hitting him.

''Hey, Sheryl,'' he called, running to catch up with her.

She stopped and glanced over at him, lifting one delicately arched eyebrow.

''Nate said you used to help on the farm....'' He hesitated in the face of her cool, ever-present self-control.

''Of course. Everyone pitched in when there was hay to be baled.'' She smiled to take the sting off her words. ''Why?''

Mark was hesitant to ask for her help, but the impending rain pushed aside his indecision.

''I don't imagine you would be willing to give me a hand?''

Sheryl tilted her head to one side, as if studying him, then she smiled a soft smile. ''I probably could,'' she said.

Mark pushed his hat back on his head with a surge of relief.

''That's great.'' he said with a grin. ''That's just great. If you just hitch Nate's tractor up to this baler we can get going.''

The sun hung directly above them, beating down relentlessly. Sheryl's T-shirt stuck to her back and her head ached in spite of wearing Mark's hat. He'd given it to her when he'd seen her constantly shading her eyes against the glare of the sun. It was too big, but it gave her tired eyes and hot head some measure of relief.

She still didn't know what had come over her when she'd accepted Mark's offer of work. Part of it was his hesitant request. He'd seemed unsure of her response, which seemed a surprisingly unmasculine position.

As well, driving the tractor down the road this morning brought back good memories. These were the kind she cherished and hung on to, to keep the bad ones at bay.

Her eyes swept the golden field ahead. Dust from the baler hung in a soft haze. In the distance Rob drove the tractor and Conrad stuked, making their own circles. She had lost track of how many times she and Mark had gone around.

They followed the cool shade of the trees edging the creek, turned and headed toward the farmyard and corrals. The next turn followed the fence line and Sheryl caught periodic glimpses of the old Simpson house, now Mark's, that she had always admired as a girl. Then they headed back toward the creek, finishing the circle. And hovering over them as they worked, always within view—the mountains.

They were directly ahead of her now. Sheryl followed with her eyes the contours of the land, along the field ahead and up the dark green of the timber that broke here and there, and finally up to the gray unyielding rock swept by white snow, crisp against an achingly blue sky.

She drank it in, a feeling of belonging surging through her as she remembered stolen horseback rides up into their beguiling beauty. As a young girl she often lasted only one day of haying before the mountains called and she stole a quick ride on her horse up them the next morning, promising herself she would be back before Ed and Nate got started the next day.

She never made it.

Sheryl turned away from the view and rubbed her neck. It was sore from turning back and forth, first watching the swath, then the baler and always, in spite of herself, Mark.

The baler spat out another bale, and Mark grabbed it with gloved hands. He flexed his well-muscled shoulders, swinging the bale onto the stuker behind him. His motions were easy, fluid and as often as Sheryl looked away, her eyes kept returning to him. His T-shirt clung to his chest and his back in wet triangles. A red sweat-stained bandana held his long dark hair down.

Mark glanced up at her then, flashed her a smile, a white slash against his dark skin, and Sheryl's heart skipped a beat.

Flustered she looked ahead. He disturbed her even as he attracted her. It was disconcerting.

''Hey, Sheryl. Stop,'' Mark yelled. Sheryl jumped and instinctively stepped on the brakes. She slapped the throttle down with one hand and the p.t.o. drive with the other, then turned around. Mark was already at the front of the baler, yanking the cover off.

''It's jammed. Grab the toolbox, will you?'' Mark didn't even look at her as he pulled hay out of the baler. ''Probably busted a shear pin, too,'' he said with disgust.

The baler must have hit a thick patch in the swath. Angry at her own inattentiveness, Sheryl grabbed the toolbox and got off the tractor. She set it beside Mark, annoyed at her pounding heart and yet unable to quell the coil of fear that began at the sound of his irate voice.

''Hand me the pliers, would you,'' Mark said looking up at her. He straightened, his outstretched hand falling to his side. ''What's the matter?''

He had seen her fear. Sheryl thought all the years of living with Jason had schooled her into keeping her emotions hidden, concealed. Weakness gave the other person power. Angry at her lack of self-control, she turned to the toolbox and found the pliers.

''It's no big deal, Sheryl,'' Mark said, his voice reassuring as he took the pliers. ''Balers jam up all the time.''

''I know that,'' she snapped, stepping back as he turned to the baler.

It was more than the baler, and she knew that, too. It was this place, so rife with memories that created this vulnerability. The mountains, the rivers, the trees. It tricked her into lowering her guard, into hoping that somewhere, somehow she could recapture the brief, happy moments she had once enjoyed.

Mark slammed the lid shut and turned to hand Sheryl the toolbox. "Are you okay, Sheryl?" he asked, his expression puzzled.

"I'm fine." She grabbed the toolbox and set it in the tractor cab, wishing her hands would stop trembling. Adrenaline, that's all it was.

"I wasn't going to hurt you." His voice was soft, his expression observant.

Sheryl took a deep breath. "I know," she said with a careless shrug. "We'd better get back to work." She climbed back onto the sun-warmed seat and glanced back at Mark.

He stood on the stuker, gloved hands on his hips, frowning. But when he caught her glance he quirked a grin at her. Sheryl blinked then started the tractor up, feeling oddly reassured.

Two hot, dusty hours later Mark signaled to her to stop. He jerked a thumb over his shoulder when she frowned, puzzled as to why they stopped.

A truck waited in the shade of the trees alongside the corrals, and Rob and Conrad were already walking toward it.

"Lunchtime, Sheryl," Mark called.

She turned off the tractor and paused a moment, letting her eyes drift over the field and all the triangular stacks of hay bales at regular intervals. It had been a satisfying morning.

She climbed off the tractor, Mark's hat falling over her face, and she pulled it off, lifting her heavy braid from the back of her neck. It had been a while since she had done any work outside, had sweated, had wiped hay dust from her eyes. It sure felt a lot better than aching feet from high heels and a burning throat from cigarette smoke.

Mark waited by the baler for her, and she couldn't help but comment.

"You still trying to prove your point?" she asked dryly as he fell into step with her.

"What point?"

"When we came to the hospital, you said that your mother

raised you to be a gentleman and you were going to prove it to me.''

''I'd forgotten about that.'' He flashed her a grin as he wiped off his face with his bandana. ''So you think this is part of my campaign?''

''Isn't it?''

Mark paused by an overhanging tree and hung his bandana in it to dry and smiled. ''So am I doing it?''

''What?''

''Proving my point to you?''

''Do you always answer questions with a question?'' she countered with a sly grin, remembering their first conversation.

Mark laughed.

Funny that the sound of his laughter could kindle this gentle warmth within her, she thought as they walked toward the truck. To make someone laugh was a gift, but she felt as if Mark had just given her something instead.

Elaine had set a picnic cooler on a blanket laid out in the shade of the trees. Marla and Benjamin were jumping all over Rob and Conrad by the time Mark and Sheryl arrived.

''I'm going to throw you in the creek if you don't stop it, Bunny,'' Rob laughed, throwing Benjamin up in the air.

''He's not Bunny, he's Benjamin,'' Marla said indignantly, giving Rob's shoulder a push.

''Marla, don't be rude,'' Mark warned, his voice firm but quiet.

''Yeah, Marla.'' Conrad stuck his tongue out at her but stopped when he caught Mark's admonishing look.

''You're going to get kids just like you, you know,'' Mark warned them.

''His poor wife.'' Elaine laughed, setting out plates and sandwiches.

''Have you heard from Elise?'' Mark asked as he took the plate Elaine had filled for him.

''Nate broke some bone in his lower leg, I can't remember

which, and bruised some ribs. Elise was waiting for the plaster to dry, and then they were going to head back."

"Poor guy." Mark sighed. "I imagine he'll be out of commission for a few days.

"The cast has to stay on for about six weeks." Elaine smiled up at Sheryl. "I didn't even realize you didn't come back until I picked Benjamin up from his nap. Were you here all morning?"

"I stayed to help when I brought the tractor."

"Good for you. I sure couldn't do this work. Too hot and dusty." Elaine gave her a plate with a sandwich and some vegetables on it. "I think it's bad enough bringing lunch out."

Sheryl just smiled as she took the food and turned around, hesitating.

"Sit by me Auntie Sheryl," Marla dropped down beside Mark and patted the empty spot beside her.

With a shrug, she complied, stepping over Mark's long legs.

As Sheryl lifted her sandwich to take a bite, she saw Mark and Elaine bow their heads. Sheryl paused, not knowing where to look, uncomfortable, feeling like she should do the same but knowing it would be hypocritical.

Mark finished, looked up at her and winked at her as he took a bite out of his sandwich. He turned his attention to Rob and Conrad who had also paused.

"How's the tractor running?" he asked them.

With those prosaic words the spell broke, and Sheryl felt as if something precious had slipped away from her.

"Okay," Conrad mumbled around a mouthful of food. "But I'm going to need some more twine and a couple of extra sheer pins. We busted three so far."

"That's three more than us." Mark said, turning his head to grin at Sheryl.

"What?" Rob sputtered. "How did you pull that off?"

"Skillful driving and close attention to details."

"I would say it had more to do with light swaths," Sheryl said easily.

"And some skill." Mark reached past Marla and gently wiped a trickle of sweat from Sheryl's temple. "How are you feeling now?"

Sheryl's hand halted midway, frozen at his touch. Her heart stopped, did a slow flip and raced on. "I'm sorry, what did you say?"

"You looked flushed before I gave you my hat. I thought you might have a headache."

"No, I'm fine." Sheryl swallowed, still flustered at the casual touch of his callused fingertip on her temple. "Do you want your hat back?"

"No. With your fair skin and hair, you'll burn to a crisp without that hat."

"Is Sheryl going to help you this afternoon, too?" Elaine asked Mark as she fed Benjamin.

Mark turned his head slightly, his gray eyes holding Sheryl's. "That's entirely up to her."

He did it again, she thought. Either he was bound and determined to make his point about chivalry with each thing he did and said or it came naturally to him.

"I'll stay. I like to finish what I start."

She was supposed to have visited Ed this afternoon. That would just have to be put off until tonight. She'd much rather be outside, working, regardless of how dusty, hot and tiring it may be.

Mark smiled, a lazy movement of his well-shaped mouth, and Sheryl's heart skipped again.

"So, Sheryl, how long has it been since you were in the valley?" Elaine asked conversationally.

"I left the Cariboo about eight years ago." Sheryl replied, glad of the diversion.

"And you worked in Edmonton?"

Sheryl turned Mark's hat over in her hands, her elbows resting on her knees. "Yes," she said finally. "I did a number of different jobs but my last one was in a bar."

"Really," Rob lifted his head from his supine position.

"Ed must have had asphyxiation when he found out. I just can't feature Ed Krickson's daughter working in a bar."

"Stepdaughter," Sheryl corrected, unable to keep the harsh tone out of her voice.

"How does that work?"

"Sheryl's mother was married before," Mark interjected.

"Oh, right. I remember my mom and dad talking about his stepdaughter. I didn't know that was you, Sheryl." Rob looked as if he wanted to say more.

"We'd better get back to work." Mark stood up, signaling the end of the conversation. Elaine looked disappointed, and Sheryl felt faintly relieved. It didn't seem to matter what the topic was, it always came back to things she didn't want to talk about.

Everyone got up at once. Mark explained to Rob and Conrad what he wanted them to do, and Sheryl helped Elaine clean up.

Benjamin leaned on the cooler, rooting around in the food. Sheryl laid the dirty plates inside and, giving in to an impulse, picked him up. He was so soft and rounded and appealing. She inhaled the sun-warmed smell of him and felt a melting inside of her.

"You're such a cutie, you know," she murmured in his ear. He pulled away, his soft blue eyes fixed intently on her face. One chubby hand reached out and grabbed a fistful of hair and he gurgled his pleasure.

Mark was finished with the boys and he sauntered over, Marla's hand in his. He stopped beside Sheryl and stroked Benjamin's cheek, his finger dark against the baby's fair skin.

"Hey, buddy, how're the teeth coming?" As if in answer, Ben grabbed Mark's finger with his free hand and tried to stick it in his mouth. "I don't think so," Mark warned pulling his hand away. "That's a yucky finger, full of grease and dust."

He wasn't touching her. In fact he stood almost a foot away, yet Sheryl was completely aware of him, the warmth that emanated from him, the faint smell of sweat overlaid with the dusty scent of hay. Unconsciously she took a step away, but Benjamin still held Mark's finger in one hand and her hair in another.

"Here," Mark pulled his finger away from Benjamin and, reaching around, disentangled her hair from the little boy's sticky hand.

Mark's fingers feathered her cheek, sending an unexpected shiver skittering down her back. She tried to keep her head down, but it was as if an unseen force drew her chin up, pulling her eyes toward his.

All the world seemed to drop away as she felt herself melting into soft gray eyes fringed with thick dark lashes. His eyelids drooped, and he came closer, closer.

"C'mon, Uncle Mark, you have to get back to work."

Marla's shrill voice broke the spell his nearness had woven around her, and Sheryl blinked, stepping away.

Benjamin leaned back in her arms, reaching out to Elaine, and Sheryl relinquished her hold on the baby, trying to still the pounding of her heart.

She swung around and walked back to the tractor, her steps brisk, her manner determined. She didn't know what was wrong with her, but somehow Mark was getting under her guard.

Too dangerous, she warned herself as she swung up the steps.

Chapter Five

Sheryl rolled her head to take the tightness out of her neck. A delicious weariness engulfed her. The day had been good, satisfying.

Her plans to visit Ed had, of necessity, been altered. Not that it mattered. It was a relief not to have to face any more of Ed's hesitant declarations of love.

It was only imminent death that had brought them forward, she thought, rubbing her neck. But even as she formulated the doubt, another part of her mind, the one that cried out for family and place, longed to have those words repeated for her to hold to herself.

She shook her head, as if to discard the confusion.

As she pulled her tired shoulders up to ease the persistent ache in them, she glanced across the truck at Mark.

His dusty face was shadowed along his lean jawline, and his hair was still held down by the red bandana he had rolled up and tied around his head that morning.

He looked almost like a pirate in the gathering dusk. Except pirates didn't have such long dark eyelashes, nor did pirates let their mothers stroke their hair, like Lenore had done yesterday. She envied him both his family and the absolute sense of rightness that surrounded his work. He was so obviously a part of this land that it was a stretch to imagine him making his living in the city.

Just then he looked over at her, his dark eyes gleaming in

the dusk. His face was expressionless, his eyes piercing, and she looked away, berating herself for entertaining too many thoughts of him.

One more visit with Ed, and she was out of here, she promised herself.

"Looks like Nate is home," Mark said as they pulled into the driveway. He came to a stop and slowly pushed the gearshift into reverse. He turned to Sheryl, "Are you going to come in for something to eat—"

His question was cut off by the piercing honk of a horn as headlights swept behind them and shut off.

Sheryl turned, opening her door. She could see Lenore and Nick getting out of a small car. Nick bent over to take a box out of the back seat, and Lenore walked up to Sheryl her hands outstretched in greeting. "Sheryl, hello," she said with a smile. She caught Sheryl's hands before she had a chance to pull away.

"Goodness gracious, girl, what have you been doing today?" Lenore turned Sheryl's hands over and held them up to the light spilling from the verandah onto the vehicles. "You've got blisters on your palms." She looked over at Mark, who leaned against his truck, chatting with his father. "Mark, how did Sheryl get these blisters on her hands?"

Mark glanced over his shoulder at his mother, one eyebrow quirked at her demanding tone. "She was driving Nate's old Massey. Nate, you will remember, broke his leg and couldn't drive."

"Don't be flippant. Were you baling today?"

"On the fields below my house."

Lenore turned back to Sheryl, her face indignant. "It got up to eighty-five degrees today," Lenore fumed. "Don't tell me you were working in this heat, driving a tractor without a cab on it?"

"I had a hat on," Sheryl replied, bemused at Lenore's anger. What did it matter to Lenore what she did?

Still holding on to Sheryl, Lenore dragged her around the

front of the truck, holding out the palms of her hands for Mark's inspection.

"Look at that, Mark. I can't believe you made her help you with such a horrible job. I know you were in a bind, but I'm sure you could have found someone in town."

Sheryl couldn't help but smile at the sight of this five-foot-nothing of a woman glaring up at her son who towered above her.

Mark shrugged helplessly, looking to his father.

"Why don't we do what we came here for, and that's see how Nate is doing and help Elise with supper?" Nick asked, pulling his wife toward him and winking at Mark.

"Are you two coming?" Lenore asked, looking back at them as her husband ushered her up the stairs to the verandah.

Sheryl opened her mouth to protest.

"I know what you're going to say," Mark said, touching her shoulder lightly. "But please don't start with that, Sheryl. Come on in, wash up and have something to eat, or my mother's going to think I'm a total boor."

Sheryl's stomach rumbled, and as she glanced at the brightly lit house a burst of laughter came from within. It was more appealing than her cabin with its meagre propane lantern light.

"As long as Elise doesn't mind dusty blue jeans on her chairs."

"She won't even notice."

The kitchen table was already set. Lenore was unpacking a pot of soup from the box Nick brought in, and Elaine was grilling cheese sandwiches. The smells made Sheryl's stomach clench with hunger.

"Did you want to give the children some of this soup, as well, Elaine?" Lenore asked as she put the pot on the stove.

"Just a bit. They should get to bed."

Lenore looked up as Sheryl and Mark came into the room. "Goodness, you two are even dirtier in the light. Mark you use the sink in the porch, Sheryl you can wash up in the one down the hall....'' Lenore waved a spoon in the direction of the bathroom.

''I think Sheryl remembers where it is, Mom,'' Mark reprimanded his mother his tone light.

Lenore frowned at him, then as comprehension dawned, she laughed. ''I forgot. You probably know this house better than I do, Sheryl.''

''I used to. It looks so different now.'' She took a moment to appreciate the changes that Elise had wrought in what was once a dark and run-down room.

The cupboards had been covered with a fresh coat of white paint and trimmed with blue porcelain handles. The dusty-blue countertop was new as were the flowered tiles against the wall. Gaily patterned paper and bunches of dried flower arrangements decorated the wall, and in one corner white chairs with blue cushions were pushed up against a table topped with a blue-and-white-checked cloth.

''I like this kitchen,'' she said, smiling at Elise, who stood watching her, almost anxiously. ''You've made it look fresh and inviting.''

''Thank you. It was a bit of a battle to convince Ed and Nate that it needed a woman's touch, but once I started, they came around.''

Sheryl smiled wryly, wondering why her mother had never dared to stand up to Ed. Maybe she had too much to lose, she thought as she walked down the hall to the bathroom, another room transformed from dull to bright.

As she washed her hands she caught her reflection in the mirror and grimaced. Rivulets of sweat had dried, leaving dark tracks on her dusty skin. Her eyes were rimmed with brown, her hair dull. Not much to look at now, not much to look at then, she thought, remembering the taunts of childhood.

She soaped down her hands and rinsed off her face.

As the brown water swirled down the drain she remembered a rebellious young girl who had refused to wear the skirts and dresses that Ed had insisted were proper for a young lady. The clothes that had made her classmates laugh at her.

As he had become more determined to bend and shape her and she had become even more determined to stay who she was, the battle had escalated. Push and shove, back and forth, neither yielding.

She looked in the mirror again and picked up a brush, wondering what would have happened if her mom had stood up for her? Or what would have happened if Sheryl had not resented Ed his place in her mother's life.

Sheryl sighed as she ran a brush through her long hair. It was all past, impossible to fix or relive. She rebraided her hair, noting with dismay the flecks of hay that dotted the immaculate floor.

She stepped out of the bathroom to get a broom, almost bumping into Nate.

"Hi," she stammered. "How are you feeling?"

"I ache all over," he mumbled, pulling one crutch closer to let her pass.

He closed his eyes, his face pale. "I didn't say it before, but thanks for what you did."

"You're welcome." She bit her lip, feeling the tension between them. "Do you need any help now?"

"No. I'll manage on my own."

Sheryl hesitated a moment. He still didn't move, so she stepped carefully past him and walked down the hallway to the kitchen.

Marla and Crystal were eating already. One sat on each side of Mark, as he fed Benjamin some soup. Mark's movements were awkward, the tiny spoon almost lost in his hands, and with each spoonful he gave Benjamin, he unconsciously opened his mouth as well.

Sheryl's steps slowed. He looked far too appealing now, his hair still dented from the bandana he'd worn all day, his lean jaw shadowed with whiskers. He looked darkly handsome, dangerous, the image so at odds with the domestic scene in which he seemed so comfortable.

"Oh, there's Sheryl...and Nate." Lenore rushed past

Sheryl to Nate, hovering as Nate clumped down into the kitchen and eased himself into a nearby chair.

"Daddy!" Marla and Crystal cried out in unison. They jumped from their seats, jostling Mark.

"Whoa, girls," he reprimanded, almost spilling the spoonful of soup he was transferring to Benjamin's waiting mouth.

Marla and Crystal eased themselves around him, then scampered over to their dad's side.

Sheryl couldn't help but watch as Nate's children hovered, his wife slipped her arms around his shoulders and his mother-in-law fussed over him. Why did it hurt? Why did it matter that Nate was the one everyone ran to. This was his house, his place.

Swallowing, she slipped into a chair on the opposite end of the table, one over from Mark.

"So your face didn't go permanently brown," he commented with a grin.

"I feel like I left a bale of hay in Elise's bathroom.... Oh, no, I was going to sweep it up." She rose, but was forestalled by Mark's hand on her forearm.

"Don't worry about it. Elaine or Elise can get to it after. The haying crew gets preferential treatment."

"So, can we eat this soup or are we going to live on love?" Nick complained.

In a flurry of people and chairs moving, the family sat around the table. An expectant pause hovered just before the meal when Nick looked around, smiling. He held out his hands to Elise on one side and Lenore on the other. Marla sat on one side of Sheryl, Crystal on the other, and they both clasped her hands in theirs, as well.

Nick bowed his head and began to pray.

Sheryl blinked a moment, bowed her head but kept her eyes fixed on the oil stain on her left leg.

But Nick's gentle voice and soft-spoken prayer drew Sheryl in. He thanked the Lord for the weather and for the work that was done. He thanked God that Sheryl could have helped Nate and that she was able to help Mark, as well. From thanks he moved on to requests for Ed's return to health and to spare his life. Nick's words, spoken with a quiet confidence, were simple and straightforward, more like a conversation than a listing of confessions.

Sheryl closed her eyes as a faint remembrance of her own prayers trickled upward. How long had it been since she'd felt her prayers were getting through to God? She had winged enough heavenward those first few years.

But here, now, with Nick's soft prayers drawing her up, she felt the faint touch of eternity. And as Nick said amen, Sheryl felt bereft. She kept her head down, drawing herself back into this room, composing herself. When she looked up it was to smiling faces drawing her into their meal and their communion.

The first few moments were quiet as Elaine, Elise and the children finished their interrupted meal. They then excused themselves.

''Kiss your dad good night girls and it's off to bed with you.'' Crystal and Marla protested, but Elise held firm.

Nate hugged his daughters, wincing as he did so, gave Benjamin a soft kiss on his red cheek and watched them as they left the room. Then he turned back to Mark.

''So how did baling go?''

''We got most of my field done,'' Mark replied, hunched over his soup. ''We'll be able to move the tractors to the river-bottom land tomorrow.''

''What?'' Nate looked up from his supper. ''How did you manage that with only one tractor and baler?''

''Sheryl brought your tractor over and stayed and helped until we were done.''

Nate's spoon hovered in midair, his mouth open. He blinked, looked at Sheryl, frowning. ''Why?''

''Why what?'' Mark laughed.

''I mean, why did you help, Sheryl?''

Sheryl stirred her soup, lifting one shoulder in a negligent shrug. ''I had nothing else to do, and I know how busy haying season can be.'' She toyed with a noodle, avoiding his eyes.

''And what about tomorrow?'' Nate's question hung between them. ''I seem to remember that you never seemed to be around the next day.''

Sheryl knew he alluded to the times she would steal a quick ride up into the mountains on those glorious mornings that were also perfect haying weather. She chose not to respond.

''You mean to say you helped with the haying when you were young?'' Lenore asked.

''I only had to drive the tractor when we were stuking and when we were picking up the bales,'' Sheryl replied, surprised at the incredulous tone of Lenore's voice.

''How old were you when you started?''

Sheryl pursed her lips, thinking back. ''Probably about eleven or twelve.''

''What?'' Lenore looked first at Sheryl, then at Nate, her eyes wide. ''Your feet barely reached the floor at that age. I can't believe Ed actually made her do that, Nate.''

''We had a ranch to run. Everyone had to pitch in.'' Nate's tone was defensive.

''If a ranch depends on twelve-year-old girls driving tractors then I don't think it has a right to keep going,'' Lenore returned.

''It was only during haying season,'' Sheryl put in, trying to ease the gathering tension.

Lenore opened her mouth to speak again.

''Can I bother you to get me some more soup, my dear and docile wife?'' Nick interrupted.

''Good idea, Dad.'' Mark held out his bowl, as well, grinning at his mother. ''Keep her feet moving and they might not end up in her mouth.''

Lenore glared at her husband, then her son, but got up. The rest of the meal passed quickly and soon Sheryl could feel the effect of working outside all day. The room was warm, and the edges of everything in her line of vision grew fuzzy.

She gave her head a shake. She had to get moving or she'd fall asleep. She got up and began stacking the empty bowls, Mark laid a restraining hand on her arm.

''Elaine and Elise can do it. You've had a busy day.''

The warmth of his fingers sent a quiver through her stomach. She knew she should pull away, keep moving, but somehow her body wouldn't respond to her mind.

''I...I should go, anyway. I'm tired, and if you need help tomorrow, then I need my sleep.''

''You're not going to do that dusty, dirty job tomorrow, too, are you?'' Lenore asked.

''I want to, Mrs. Andrews. It's okay.'' She smiled at Lenore. ''Say good night to Elise for me, please. And thanks for the delicious meal.''

''You're welcome.'' Lenore smiled warmly, and Sheryl couldn't help but return it.

Mark got up, as well, leaned over and kissed his mother on the cheek. ''I think I'll head back, too. Tomorrow's going to be a long day.''

''Are you going to give Sheryl a chance to come in and see Ed sometime in the next couple of days?'' Lenore asked.

''That's up to her,'' Mark replied quietly, straightening.

''I can come and get you tomorrow afternoon,'' Lenore said to Sheryl.

Sheryl threw a questioning look at Mark, who only shrugged.

''How about later on in the day,'' Mark suggested with a yawn. He rubbed his neck and blinked. ''Late afternoon should give us enough time.''

''I'll bring a late lunch at two-thirty. Nick could manage a few turns around the field. Couldn't you Nick?''

''As long as I can drive slow,'' he replied dryly. He grinned at his wife's puzzled look. ''Doctor's orders, remember.''

Sheryl watched the give-and-take between them, smiling at the total lack of conflict in Mark's family, so different from the atmosphere that had pervaded this kitchen when she and her mother had lived there. She shook her head, dispelling the mood and turned to leave.

The porch door squeaked open behind her. A quick glance

over her shoulder showed her that Mark was following her out.

''Wait a sec. I'll walk you home,'' he said, pausing to pull on his battered cowboy boots.

''It's not that far,'' Sheryl replied, but she waited anyway, a gentle warmth suffusing her cheeks. She put it down to being outside all day, but as they walked in silence down the darkened pathway to her cabin, a sense of waiting drifted around her.

Leaves rustled as they passed by, and far off a coyote threw its lonesome wail out into the soft night.

Sheryl stopped by the door of her cabin. ''This is a first for me, you know,'' she joked, trying to lighten a mood that felt sombre.

''What's that?'' Mark leaned one shoulder against the door frame, his eyes resting on her.

''Having a man walk me to my door.''

''Jason never did?''

Sheryl laughed. ''Jason would drop me off at the end of the driveway, and I would climb up the verandah and sneak into my room.''

''Ed didn't like him, did he?''

''Ed hated him.'' Sheryl looked away. ''Nate didn't like him, either. I guess that's one of the things they were right about.''

''What do you mean?'' Mark's voice was quiet, prompting, but Sheryl didn't get drawn in.

''It doesn't matter anymore.'' She took a breath, but to her own surprise it was a little shaky. Fatigue, she thought. ''It's all past and things have to move on.''

''I don't know if our past is ever past...''

''Please don't start analyzing my life,'' Sheryl interrupted, trying to soften her words with a light laugh.

''Hobby of mine,'' was all he said, leaning one shoulder against the door frame. It put him a little too close to her, but she refused to let his size, height and mere presence intimidate her. ''I think much of what happened to us in the past shapes the decisions we make for our future.''

''So what made you leave Vancouver to come here?'' Sheryl verbally sidestepped, changing the direction of the conversation.

Mark rubbed the side of his nose, as if thinking about the answer.

''Well,'' she prompted.

''When I was a young boy, I used to dream of being a cowboy. Used to sit on a fence, wearing my cowboy hat and boots, just sitting, staring off into the distance. But in my mind I was on the Goodnight-Loving trail, pushing horns, eating dust and fording rivers.'' He laughed softly. ''I'm sure for a while there my parents thought I was losing it.''

''So how did you end up in real estate?''

''It was a place to make money. I spent enough years in college and thought I could make a quick buck on the side.''

Sheryl frowned. ''You don't seem the avaricious type.''

''Thanks for that.'' Mark pushed his hair out of his eyes and grinned down at her. ''I was at that time though. Made a pile of money and thought I had the world by the tail.''

''So what made you sell out?''

Mark sighed, staring past her. ''I saw what was happening to my friends. Saw the emptiness in their lives and how few of them were really doing what they wanted. As a Christian I couldn't see myself wasting my life like that. So when my parents told me that there was a place for sale beside Nate and Elise's, I chucked it all and came out here.'' He reached out and touched her hair, his fingers warm on her forehead. In the pale light his eyes seemed to glow, and Sheryl felt a shiver of apprehension. ''And here is where I want to stay.'' He dropped his hand. ''And what about you?''

''I have plans.''

''College?''

Sheryl nodded.

''And after that?''

''A job as a teacher, I hope.''

''No marriage plans?''

''Been there. Done that.'' She flicked her hands deprecatingly, as if the past eight years were a mere blip in her life.

''Not all men are like Jason, you know.''

''I've met more that are than aren't.'' She replied, uncomfortable with the intensity she saw in his probing gaze. ''So we'll just change that subject.''

''Okay.'' Mark smiled lazily at her flippant reply. He shifted his stance so his back was against the wall of the cabin. ''I love this time of the evening,'' he said, falling in with her request. ''I love looking at the stars, even though it makes me feel small and unimportant.'' He hooked his thumbs in the belt loops of his pants as he stared at the stars strewn across the inky black darkness. ''Isn't it amazing how vast the universe is?''

Sheryl bit her lip, sensing where the conversation was going this time, and she didn't know if she liked it anymore. She said nothing.

Mark didn't seem to notice her silence.

''God sure made a beautiful world.''

''This part of it, yes,'' she replied.

He glanced at her as if encouraging her to say more.

''God hasn't been around my part of the world much these past few years,'' she added, trying to keep her voice matter-of-fact.

''If you seek Him, you will find Him,'' Mark replied softly.

''I don't want to talk about God, either.''

Mark straightened, then turned back to her, lifting her hand, and Sheryl wondered what he was up to. She wasn't used to the casual touches he bestowed so freely. ''My mom was right,'' was all he said. ''You do have blisters.'' He traced them lightly with the tip of his other finger.

''It doesn't matter.'' She could barely get the words past the constriction of her throat. She tried to pull back, but this time he held firm. Then he bent over and kissed her palm, closing her fingers over the warmth his mouth left behind as if to save it.

Sheryl's heart slammed into her chest, and she snatched her hand away from him, her cheeks burning.

"Thanks for helping," he whispered. "I'll pick you up around eight o'clock tomorrow." And with another wink, he turned and left her.

Unable to keep her eyes off his retreating figure, she watched him, his soft whistling marking his progress until he disappeared. A few moments later Sheryl heard his truck start and drive away.

She uncurled her hand, looking down at it, expecting to see a mark where his lips had touched her palm. All she saw were lines of grime she couldn't wash out and two red blisters. What was he trying to do to her? she thought as she leaned back against the door, suddenly chilled. She didn't need his solicitous concern, his questions that probed deeper than "Are you free tonight?"

She turned and retreated into her cabin.

But as she lay in bed, all she could think of was hair that almost hung in soft gray eyes, the feel of his mouth on her palm and his quiet faith in God. A faith she knew she could never share.

Chapter Six

Sheryl peeled her orange slowly, her ear attuned for the sound of Mark's truck. The early morning sun finally found its way through the thick foliage, touching the porch with a soft warmth.

Two hours ago she'd given up trying to sleep, and after getting dressed she'd stolen into Elise's kitchen to grab a bite to eat. Thankfully no one had been awake, so she'd helped herself to a couple of bran muffins and an orange and wrote Elise a note.

The moments of wakefulness had given her time to regret her offer to help Mark. She may as well face the fact, she thought, pulling another piece of peel off the orange. Mark scared her. His charm and interest in her life created a potent combination she was unused to dealing with.

Sheryl pulled a face and popped a section into her mouth. She remembered too well each one of Mark's casual touches, his intent looks.

Probably treated all girls the same, she thought, finishing her orange and wiping her hands on her pants. She clung to that notion, because dwelling on any other possibility was too distracting.

She knew she wanted to take this job from start to finish. Nate practically challenged her to last night. She was determined to show him that he was wrong.

Sheryl picked up her orange peels and tossed them deep in

the bush. Suddenly restless, she got up and began walking down the driveway. She would finish what she started, she promised herself. As for Mark, well she would treat him with the same lighthearted humor that she did any of the men who had shown interest in her over the years. Guys tended to leave you alone if you treated them like you were a brother, she'd found out.

The muted roar of a truck's engine bounced off the hills, drawing nearer, and suddenly, there he was, dust roiling in his wake as his truck bore down on her.

Mark stopped beside her with a rumble of gravel, and before he could roll down his window, Sheryl ran over to the passenger door and jumped in the cab.

''Aren't you the eager and willing worker?'' he said with a grin as he reversed and spun the truck around.

''I like that,'' she returned, forcing a light tone into her voice. ''Demoted from lifesaver to worker. You didn't even try to open my door for me.''

''I'd have had to stop twenty feet in front of you in order to beat you to it.'' He winked at her, stepped on the accelerator and bounced over the cattle guard that divided the yard from the road.

Sheryl sat back, pleased with herself. It was surprisingly easy to sit in his truck, to think of spending the whole day together. Perhaps she had only imagined the undercurrents that seemed to flow around them last night.

At the end of the driveway Mark turned right this time, toward the river.

''Rob and Conrad moved the tractors down to the river-bottom land last night. We'll be working there for a few days,'' he explained as the truck picked up speed. The scenery flew by, towering fir trees hovering along every curve as they dropped lower into the valley. Ahead of them Sheryl caught a glimpse of the river, flanked by fields ridged with thick swaths of hay.

''How do you get to the fields on the other side?''

''There's a wooden bridge around the next curve of the

river. We'll work on this side the next couple of days and if all goes well, we'll cross and spend the rest of the week on the other side."

"Are the cows still in the upper pastures?"

Mark nodded. "I have to check them as soon as haying is done. My family usually organizes a pack trip in conjunction with that and escorts me and whoever is coming along, half-way there."

"Sounds like fun."

"You can come if you want."

"Right."

"Serious." Mark looked at her, his eyes wide. "I bet Elise will ask you, anyway."

"I don't think I'll be around by then." Sheryl couldn't imagine accompanying such a close-knit family on what was obviously a family event. Sunday dinner at Mark's mother and father's place had been difficult enough.

"I see," he said, grinning at her. "You're one of these transient workers who just drifts in and out with the tide, looking for whatever work comes your way."

"That was Jason's line," she replied with a light laugh, trying to get caught up in his banter.

Mark seemed to hesitate a moment, his wrist resting on the steering wheel as he frowned at the road ahead. "What exactly did Jason do for a living?"

Sheryl tilted a wry look his way, puzzled at his interest. "You mean all the helpful gossips in the valley haven't filled you in on Jason Kyle and his famous escapades?"

"I haven't lived here long enough. The only people who I've heard talk about Jason are Ed and Nate."

"I'm sure they had a lot to say about him."

Mark shrugged, his eyes still on the road. "They didn't like him. I gathered that much."

Sheryl said nothing at that. *Hate* was a more apt description than *didn't like,* except good Christian men like Nate and Ed would never admit to feeling that way about another human being.

"So what kind of work did Jason do?"

"You really are persistent...."

"No, I'm an Andrews." Mark tossed her a quick grin. "And I've learned everything I know about asking questions from my mom and sister."

"Well then, I'm out of my league." Sheryl laughed, relaxing around his lighthearted manner. "Jason started out as a helper for a carpenter, and once he figured he knew enough, he started working for himself. And from there things went from worse to worser."

"How did that happen?"

Sheryl sighed, clasping her arms across her stomach, not really wanting to talk about this, but unable to formulate a reason she shouldn't.

"Jason didn't do really well at his business, and he started drinking." She gave a short laugh. "And with the prices of liquor it doesn't take much to drink away a week's wages, especially if your buddies are thirsty, too."

Mark was silent at that. "I'm sorry, Sheryl. I didn't know...."

"That's okay, Mark."

"Maybe." He glanced at her, his expression serious. "I can't explain it, but I have a need to know more about you, to know where you stand with God. It matters to me, but I don't want you to feel that I'm pushing you."

Sheryl held his gaze a moment, touched by his honesty. "You're some kind of guy, Mark Andrews," she said with a rueful shake of her head.

Mark pulled up beside the tractor and baler they used yesterday. The other tractor and baler was parked farther down the field, silent, waiting. Sheryl stepped out of the truck, inhaling the scent of mown hay that still lingered in the morning dew.

The air held a slight chill this far down the valley, and Sheryl hugged herself against it. She took a few steps into the field, dropped her head back and looked around, turning a slow circle. The clouds were hard white against the sharp blue of the sky, the contrast almost painful to see. Purple-tinged mountains, skiffed with a dusting of snow on their peaks surged down to green and brown hills. The shushing sounds of the river at their feet softened and lulled the vastness of the landscape.

She took a deep breath and released it, as if cleansing herself. The years of living in the city had buried these pictures, blurred them. She couldn't stop the smile that curved her lips as the familiar countryside became once more a part of her.

"Ready for some more blisters?" Mark's deep voice beside her made her jump, breaking the moment.

She glanced up at him. His tall figure blocked the sun, casting his features in shadows. Unconsciously Sheryl took a step back.

"Don't be so skittish," he said, holding out a hat. "I just wanted to give you this."

He took a step closer, and Sheryl steeled herself to stand still as he dropped the hat on her head. "Now you have your own." She felt the warmth of his hands through the hat's material as he set it at the correct angle on her head. "It should be straw, but this is all I could find." His gray eyes glinted at her, and as Sheryl held his gaze, something indefinable held them and she couldn't look away.

"Feels good, thanks." Her voice was shaky, and she swallowed, willing her legs to move. If she was smart, she would turn around right now, head down that road and keep going. She was crazy to think that she could keep him at arm's length. Mark was attractive, decent, honest and far too compelling.

"We better get going," she said, trying to keep her voice light and carefree. She scrambled up the steps to the seat of the tractor and concentrated on the job at hand.

Sheryl had picked up the rhythm of the tractor again, slowing down when the swaths were heavier, speeding up along the treeline. The hay didn't grow as thick there because of the nutrients the trees took up from the soil. But everywhere else the swaths were dense and rich, the fragrant dust swirling around the tractor in an ever-present haze.

In the distance Mark saw Rob and Conrad making their own tedious circles, the "chunk, chunk" of their baler and the chug of the tractor's engine, muted by the distance.

He stood easily on the drag, waiting for the baler to spit out another bale. He grabbed it, braced it on one thigh and using the weight of the bale and its momentum, turned and swung it around, dropping it neatly beside the other three so it sat like a square diamond between the pipes, the tops of the bales forming a zigzag pattern. He straightened, paused and grabbed the next one, dropping it neatly into the open triangle formed by two bales side by side, making the next layer. Ten bales to a triangular stuke, hit the release pedal, and the pipes lowered until the bottoms of the bales hit the ground and pulled away from the stuker.

Mark glanced up at Sheryl who sat half-turned on the tractor seat, her long hair tied up in a loose braid, hanging beneath the battered felt hat. She pulled her shoulder up to her chin, wiping a trickle of sweat that reached her chin, leaving a track in the dust on her face. Mentally he compared her to the carefully coiffed and expensively tailored girls he once had squired around Vancouver, trying to imagine any of them perched on a tractor with a brown cowboy hat, two sizes too big shading a dusty face.

The picture made him laugh. As he did so, Sheryl caught his eye, held it for a heartbeat, then blinked and looked away again, and Mark followed the direction of her gaze.

The mountains.

Whenever she had a chance, her gaze would fly to the mountains.

The words of Psalm 100 came to mind. "I lift up mine eyes to the hills, from whence cometh my help." His help came from God. Sheryl claimed she didn't need any help.

He caught another bale, and when he had straightened, she was looking at him again. He smiled back, trying to coax a smile from her, and when she responded, the quickening of his own heart caught him by surprise.

She was completely the wrong person for him, and she made that very clear with each word she spoke in anger against God.

Yet...

When her iron self-control slipped, her vulnerability showed. It was this girl that drew him.

They made a few more rounds when the sound of a horn's insistent honking penetrated the growling of the tractor's engine. He caught sight of his mother, standing in the shade of the trees, her hands on her hips. Even from this distance he could sense her displeasure. Well she could grumble all she wanted. Sheryl seemed determined to finish this job and Mark wasn't going to argue. He needed the help and, curiously, he enjoyed being with her.

The next time Sheryl looked back, Mark pointed to his watch. She waited until the next bale was forced out and stopped the tractor.

Mark dropped the bale into the stuke and pulled his already damp bandana from the release lever of the stuker, wiping his face with it.

Sheryl paused a moment, her eyes wandering over the field, a soft smile teasing the corner of her mouth. Mark watched her, bemused at her obvious love for the land, puzzled that she couldn't see the Creator behind the creation.

He waited until she climbed down off the tractor and fell into step with her.

"Tired?" His voice resonated with concern.

"Yeah." She took off the hat and handed it back to him. "I feel like falling into a tub of water and not coming up for air the rest of the day."

"I get the feeling you're not looking forward to seeing Ed again?"

"It's the reason I made the trip out here." She looked away, her feet dragging in the hay stubble as she rubbed her neck.

"Do you want me to come with you?"

She twisted her head around, her expression puzzled. "Why would you want to do that?"

He didn't know, himself, except that he felt she wasn't ready to face Ed and whatever buried memories might surface, and he felt a curious protectiveness toward her. "I guess I'm not sick of spending time with you yet." His tone was light, but the eyes that held hers were steady.

"I'll be okay." She pushed her hair back from her face, tucking the sweat-dampened tendrils behind her ears, turning away from him, shutting him out. But the trembling of her fingers belied the firm tone of her voice.

"Then why do you look scared?"

She clenched her hands into fists and stared ahead. "I'm not scared," she replied, her voice hard.

Mark only sighed. Why did he keep trying? The precious little she gave away was only what slipped past her control. Nothing was relinquished willingly.

Rob and Conrad were already sitting down eating, by the time Sheryl and Mark came.

"It took you long enough," Lenore scolded. "Come sit here, Sheryl, I've brought a lawn chair for you. Just pull up beside Nick." Lenore handed Sheryl a plate of food, an assortment of cold cuts, a bun and some fruit slices.

"And what about your own son?" Mark complained, an unexpected irritation flickering in his voice.

"My own son is perfectly capable of bringing his own lawn chair in his own truck." Lenore said briskly.

Lunch was quiet, the talk desultory in the energy-sapping heat.

Nick, Mark and Lenore exchanged idle chat, Rob and Conrad dozed and Sheryl said nothing.

Mark tried to catch her eye, but she kept them either on her food or tilted up and away from him, toward the hills that cradled the river. He tried to analyze what it was about her that kept drawing him back to her. She made him feel both frustrated and content, sad and yet peaceful. She seemed to belong here, yet she made it very clear that she would leave once her obligations were fulfilled.

When Lenore got up, Sheryl followed suit, picking up the empty plates, gathering up the remnants of food and repacking the picnic cooler.

''When do you expect to be back?'' Mark asked as he tugged on the blanket, waking Rob and Conrad. They stretched and got up, grumbling about slave-driving bosses. He shook the leaves and bits of hay off it and folded it up.

''I thought Sheryl could have supper with us. Then Nick can take her home.'' Lenore closed the cooler and brushed her hands off on her blue jeans.

''Okay. Just drive carefully.''

Lenore shot Mark an oblique glance. ''Actually I thought I might go flying through the valley as fast as you usually do.''

''Rob and Conrad almost hit a couple of deer close to the bend by the old Newkiwski homestead.'' Mark lifted up the cooler with a grunt. ''That's why I was telling you to be careful.'' He carried it back to the car, waiting for his father to open it.

''Point taken, son.'' Lenore smiled at him. ''Sheryl, you just sit in the car and take it easy. I'll be there in a minute.''

Sheryl hesitated, and Mark saw it again. That brief flash of fear. He took a step toward her, then stopped himself. Why did he always fall for those few scraps of emotion that she allowed to eke out? Why did it take so precious little on her part for him to try so hard to connect with her. He turned back to his parents' car, slamming the trunk closed just a little too hard.

''Easy on my car, son.'' Lenore frowned at him but he didn't reply. ''Are you going to bring your father home? Because if you are, then you can have supper with Sheryl and us.''

''Naw.'' Mark tossed a quick glance at Sheryl, who still hesitated by the door of the car, then turned resolutely away.

''Dad can take the old brown truck home. Rob can get it when we need it.''

He shouldn't try to spend any more time than he had to with Sheryl. She didn't need anyone. She certainly didn't need him.

''I thought I would give you a chance to visit with Ed for a while, by yourself.'' Lenore pulled into an empty spot in the parking lot and left the car running.

''Okay.'' Sheryl put her hand on the door's handle, hesitating.

''Ed has been very eager to see you.'' Lenore turned to Sheryl, touching her shoulder lightly. ''He isn't always the easiest person to be around, but I can assure you he has changed.''

Sheryl nodded as the words that whirled around her head all afternoon increased their tempo and finally slipped out. ''He told me he loved me,'' she said, her voice bitter. ''The whole time I lived with him and my mom, he never said that to me. Why now?'' Sheryl bit her lip, rubbing a trembling finger against her temple, her eyes closed.

Lenore's hand tightened on her shoulder as anger and sorrow contended with each other. She looked sidelong at Lenore. ''I wasn't the easiest daughter, I know that, but was I so unlovable?''

''I wish I knew, honey,'' Lenore said softly. ''You should ask Ed.''

Sheryl blinked, her finger still pressed against her head as if to draw out the questions that begged answers. ''I know I should.... But where do I start?''

''With the question you ask yourself the most.'' Lenore smiled softly at her. ''You won't be going there on your own strength, I'll be praying for you.''

''For what that's worth,'' Sheryl said as she opened the door.

Lenore leaned over, catching the door before Sheryl shut it. ''God has the power to change people, Sheryl.''

Sheryl held the open door, looking down on Lenore and the assurance she saw there. For a moment she believed her. Just for a moment.

"Thanks, I think." She gave Lenore a wan smile, turned and walked up the sidewalk to the hospital, a soft breeze cooling the heat of her cheeks, teasing her freshly washed hair, enveloping her with the soft fragrance of the shampoo she had used at Lenore's.

As she approached the glass doors, she stopped. What was she doing here? she thought, her hand resting on the sun-warmed handle. It wouldn't change anything, either in the past or present. She could just turn around and go back.

Just then brisk steps sounded behind her, and a work-roughened hand reached around her to open the door.

Sheryl spun around, the bright sun blinding her. All she saw was a tall figure wearing a cowboy hat.

Mark.

Her heart skipped, she began to smile in greeting, surprised to see him here.

"Do you need some help?" The figure spoke, and Sheryl felt the keen edge of disappointment.

She stepped back as the man opened the door and waited for her to go in. The singular smell of the hospital assailed her nostrils, and she hesitated.

"Well, if you won't go in, I will," the man growled, stepping past her. Sheryl caught the door on the backswing, berating herself for her foolish notions. Mark was in the field, baling, and she was on her own. Taking a fortifying breath of fresh air, she stepped into the darkened hallway.

Ed sat by the window when the nurse ushered her into his room. The loose hospital gown was covered with a brown bathrobe that hung loosely on his large frame, and he wore leather slippers.

He looked like an old tired man, and as he turned, Sheryl swallowed. For a fleeting moment she thought she saw pain in his eyes.

"How...are you?" he asked, his words slurred by his misshapen mouth.

"Fine." Sheryl sat down in the hard vinyl chair across from him, the daylight from the window further illuminating the ravages the stroke had wrought in this once-proud man. The droop of his eye was more noticeable in the unforgiving light of the sun, the gray in his hair more pronounced. His entire body listed to one side, propped up by pillows.

Sheryl leaned back, crossing her arms as she faced the man she had so many questions to ask. It was easy for Lenore to encourage her to start with the one she asked herself most. It was also the one that caused the most anguish.

"How are you feeling?" she asked, opting for safe ground even though the question sounded trite in the face of his obvious decline. Lenore also said that God had the power to change people. Well if that's what had happened to Ed Krickson, then she didn't know if she wanted to get too close to God.

"I...wanted so bad...to see...you." Ed shifted his weight, trying to lean forward, his one good eye piercing, probing. "How are you? Are you...right...with...God?"

"What does it matter to you, Dad?" She hadn't meant to call him that, but the situation hearkened so strongly back to her past the name slipped out. "God and I understand each other. He leaves me alone, and I leave him alone."

"No...no...Sheryl." He reached out to her looking distressed, his hand barely lifting off the arm of the chair. "You...can't leave...God alone. He'll find...you."

Sheryl closed her eyes, wishing she could as easily shut out the all-too-familiar words. "I've been in deep and dark places since I left, Dad, and God hasn't found me in them."

"What...places?"

Sheryl shook her head. *Tell him,* her thoughts urged. *Let him know what it's been like for you.*

"Sheryl...I wish...I could...help you. I was...so wrong."

She sat up at that, leaning forward now, his confession bringing questions to the fore.

''Why did you turn me away, Dad? Why did you let me down when I needed you?''

Ed shifted, trying to move, as Sheryl got up, her arms wrapped tightly around her middle, wrinkling her T-shirt. Slow down, she warned herself. You're all alone, no one will help you through this. She took a deep breath to still the voices and her beating heart.

''I'm sorry...''

Sheryl rubbed her upper arm again and again as if to erase the memory of the pain. ''Sorry.'' The word came out in a burst of disbelieving anger. ''You think you can get rid of it all with that feeble word.'' She bit her lip. This wasn't going at all as she had thought it should. She was supposed to be in control, calmly asking him about the letter he returned, asking for some kind of restitution. But what could she ask from this frail man who could barely talk? What could he give her now that would change anything?

''Mark said...Jason's dead.'' Ed's words came out in a tortured sound, and when Sheryl turned to him a lone tear sparkled on his wrinkled cheek.

She only nodded, unable to tear her gaze away from the path of the tear as it slowly drifted down to his chin, puzzled that the news of Jason's death should cause it.

''How?''

''Car accident.'' She clutched herself harder, concentrating on the color of his hair, the droop of his shoulders. She had to be strong, his tears were too late and didn't help her now.

''Do you...miss...him?''

Sheryl looked away, biting her lip. Her stepfather, the man who had hated Jason before they'd left, now looked as if he was grieving Jason's death, whereas she, his wife, had not shed a tear. She pressed her fingers to her eyes as if to force something from them. ''I don't miss him, Dad.''

''Did you...love him?'' Ed tried to lean forward.

Sheryl felt the beginnings of a headache building behind her eyes. This was even harder than she had envisioned. Ed challenging her, blustering at her—these she had ready answers for.

Not this unexpected concern, his probing questions—these she wasn't prepared for. They came around behind her and pushed away all the defenses she had built against him. Now he could be proved right, and while her prideful nature didn't want to admit it, she knew that if she was to have any kind of peace in her life, if she was to regain any kind of power over her future, she had to admit her part in what had happened in the past.

"Did...he love...you?" Ed asked this time.

Sheryl felt a catch in her throat. Had anyone cared in the past few years whether she had received love? "I think he wanted to," she replied carefully. Slowly she lowered herself into the chair across from Ed. "Jason wasn't a good husband, Dad. But I stayed with him because that's what wives do. That's what you taught me."

Ed said nothing, his eyes holding hers as another tear formed. "I'm sorry."

Sheryl only nodded, his tears touching her emotions in a place she didn't think Ed would ever have access to again. "I'm glad you're sorry, Dad. I'm sorry, too. Sorry that I ever married him. Hard as it is for me to say it, you were right about him." She smoothed the wrinkles out of the worn skirt, the confession draining her.

She had come for vindication, for this chance to find out whys and why nots and suddenly it became wearying, draining. But she pressed on. The threat of his death demanded that the events of her past find some kind of finish, closure. "I just wish I could know why you and Nate couldn't let me be part of your family."

"I never...had a girl."

But you had a son, Sheryl thought. You loved him.

"I don't think...I even...knew how to love Nate."

Sheryl's heart skipped at his response. It was as if he'd read her mind. "Why did you marry my mom?" Sheryl avoided his eyes, pleating her skirt, her voice soft as she moved on to other questions.

"She was pretty…and so sad." Ed sighed. "I wanted…to help her…help you."

Sheryl rubbed her finger over the crease she had made in her skirt, his confessions settling into her memories.

"I needed…her," Ed said softly.

"And what about me?" She looked up at him, questioning. "Did you need me, too?"

"Yes. I loved her…I love you. Please believe…I love… you."

Sheryl sighed, rubbing her forehead. She stood, looking down at this broken man. She couldn't dredge up enough anger to hate him. Tucking her hair behind her ear she tilted her head to one side. "Well you had a strange way of showing it," she said quietly.

Ed blinked slowly, concentrating on her, shaking his head with long tired movements. "I'm sorry…so sorry…"

Sheryl felt a strange thickening in her throat. She swallowed it down, willing the emotions back where she had consigned so many more.

And as she forced her emotions back to equilibrium, as she battled with old dull pain, Ed closed his eyes.

Sheryl felt her heart stop, and she rushed over to his side, almost praying that it wasn't so. Frantically she grabbed his hand, searching for his pulse.

He twitched and his head fell forward as Sheryl felt the faint, but regular heartbeat. She sat back on her heels, her own heart bursting in her chest. He had fallen asleep and there was nothing left for her to say, so she quietly left.

Chapter Seven

Mark reached back and pulled his shirt off in one easy motion, ignoring the buttons. Balling it up he tossed it in a corner of the kitchen, joining the rest of his laundry.

Scratching his chest, he wandered to the fridge, pulled it open and grimaced at the contents. He took an apple out of a broken cellophane bag and took a quick swig of milk right out of the carton.

Another nourishing meal, he thought as he kicked the door of the fridge closed behind him.

He walked into the living room. Should clean this up, too, he thought, munching on his apple.

A wood stove sat smugly on a brick pad, awaiting chilly fall nights and cold winter days when it would radiate welcome heat. For now it held an assortment of dust-laden pictures: wedding portraits, family pictures and school pictures from nieces and nephews.

A wave of melancholy washed over Mark as he walked through the empty room on his way upstairs to his bedroom. When he'd first seen the house, the Simpson family had lived here, and kids and furniture had filled it. It looked better then.

He finished his apple as he trudged up the stairs. It was still early in the evening. The dew came down too soon to hay longer into the night. Tomorrow, after two dry days, they would be able to go until dark.

The rest of the evening stretched before him, empty,

quiet...boring. His dad had repeated his mother's invitation to supper, but he'd declined. In spite of his better judgment he found himself inexplicably drawn to Sheryl, and he couldn't understand her. She made it fairly clear any time he tried to get past her guard that she didn't want his concern.

But he couldn't stop thinking about her. Better that he stay at home instead of subjecting himself to more of the same. Humiliation wasn't an emotion that sat well with him, so why seek it out. It had taken a while to get over Tanya's rejection, he shouldn't be in such a hurry to let another woman give him more of the same.

Mark walked over to the window, opened it and threw his apple core out, pausing to appreciate the view. Five years he had lived here, yet he never tired of the view.

The corrals lay below him, laid out in squares of graduating sizes. It had taken almost an entire summer to build up his corral system to make it easier for him to sort his cows. The work reaped its own rewards, he thought, remembering the past fall and how much quicker he and Nate had separated the heifers from the steers and the calves from the cows.

Beyond the corrals lay the hay fields, neat triangles of stuked hay dotting the clipped field. In two days they would have the lower fields done and then they could haul the bales to Nate's place where they would await the trucks from Langley. It had taken a few years and a lot of hard work. This hay contract and the increase in cattle prices should help the ranch turn a healthy profit, for a change. If things held, the partnership would be well able to support two families.

Mark laughed ruefully. Make that one family and one bachelor.

He glanced over his shoulder at the spacious bedroom behind him. A mattress pushed against one wall served as his bed, the rumpled sheets mocking his mother's constant nagging as he grew up. It looked lost in the room.

The condo he'd owned in Vancouver had come furnished, and a cleaning lady used to come in once a week. It had never felt like a home, but at least it had been neater than this place, he thought, running a finger through the dust that layered the windowsill.

This house needs a family.

In spite of his earlier resolve, his thoughts wandered to Sheryl. In his mind he saw her again on a tractor seat, working in heat and dust, never complaining, a faint smile curving her lips, softening the hard lines of her face. She looked more appealing all dusty and dirty, manhandling Nate's old Massey around the corners, than Tanya or any of the women before her ever could after spending an afternoon in their salons. In Sheryl he sensed a love for the land that so closely echoed his own, and it called to a deeper part of him.

Tanya had never wanted to share this life, had wanted no part of it. Whenever he'd brought her out here, she'd complained about the distance, politely declined offers to go riding and smiled deprecatingly at his family. Tanya fit in Vancouver, but not out here.

With a short laugh, he spun away from the window and off to a much-needed shower. Sheryl had her own plans, as well, and they didn't include a bachelor rancher.

But as the hot water poured down over him he couldn't help but remember those brief moments of vulnerability that seemed to call out to him.

Lenore's house exuded a quiet peace that enveloped Sheryl as soon as she stepped inside. It was as if the house, which had held so many people on Sunday, had shrunk down, pulled into itself. The living room was symmetrical again, the couches neatly facing each other across a delicate Queen Anne coffee table, whose legs seemed to barely touch the deep pile of the carpet, wing chairs flanking the fireplace presiding over the room.

In the kitchen the counters were visible again, an oak table had also shrunk down, four chairs neatly surrounding it, the crystal vase of flowers reflected in the gleaming surface of the table.

"Just sit down, Sheryl. I'll make some tea while we wait

for Nick to come back.'' Lenore dropped her bags of groceries on the countertop with a muted clunk. ''I'll phone Elise to tell her you're here for supper, so she and Nate don't worry.''

Sheryl almost laughed at that. ''That's not necessary. I'm sure it doesn't matter whether I show up or not.''

Lenore paused, her hand still holding on to a cupboard door. She let it slip shut and leaned back against the cupboard, her arms crossed over each other.

''Now I know you're not a whiner, so I don't think that's one of those 'feel sorry for me' kinds of statements. They do worry about you.''

Sheryl didn't want to get into a discussion over Nate's lack of fraternal devotion—he obviously had Lenore fooled—so she merely shrugged in answer.

''Nate and Elise often wondered how you were doing when you lived in Edmonton,'' Lenore continued, concern furrowing her forehead. ''He tried to get hold of you...''

''Please, Lenore,'' Sheryl interrupted, suddenly tired of seeing Nate as the blue-eyed boy. ''Nate knew Jason's last name, he knew where we lived. He never once tried to contact me.'' She caught Lenore's eyes and held them, the emotions of the day catching up on her. She felt a sob begin way down in her chest.

Then the all-too-familiar invisible hand closed off her throat, pushed closed the crack in her defenses, and the heartache subsided. For a fleeting moment Sheryl wished the tears would come, wished the pain could be lanced, but knew that her solitary life could not allow her to get swept up in the ensuing emotional storm.

''Are you okay?'' Lenore came around the counter to kneel beside her, gentle hands covering Sheryl's tightly clenched fingers. ''Is it Ed?''

Sheryl shook her head. ''I don't know what's wrong with me these days.'' She drew in a shaky breath, forcing herself to relax. ''Ed told me...'' But she stopped. What could she possibly gain from opening up to Lenore? She didn't need to hear confessions from someone who was such a small part of her life. ''Sorry,'' Sheryl said, drawing her hands away. ''It's been a tiring day.''

The back door opened just then, deep voices laughing, bursting into the house, bringing vitality and breaking the quiet.

''That sounds like Mark.'' Frowning, Lenore got up, leaving Sheryl to compose herself and at the same time try to stop the foolish trill of her heart at the sound of Mark's voice, the mention of his name.

''How fast did you have to drive to get here the same time as your father, Mark?'' Lenore asked as both men walked into the kitchen at the same time.

''Dad drives like an old lady,'' Mark said, quirking a tired smile at his mother.

''I thought I'd give you enough time to get supper on the table, but I see I should have driven even slower,'' Nick joked. He turned to Sheryl. ''So how's Ed?''

Sheryl got up, suddenly self-conscious of her faded denim skirt and too-large white T-shirt. Strange that a pair of gray eyes focused on her should bring that out. She never cared what she looked like before. ''He was sitting up today. They took him off the monitors.''

It bothered her that it mattered, and as she looked past Nick's smiling face to Mark's serious one, things other than her clothes took precedence: like the clean sweep of his freshly shaven jaw; how his brown hair, still damp from his shower, swept just above his dark eyebrows; how his eyes seemed to delve into hers, seeking, drawing her out. She faintly heard Lenore's laughter, Nick's dry answer. On the periphery of her vision she saw them move past her, but she couldn't take her eyes away from Mark's, couldn't break the connection that seemed to grow with each step he took closer to her until he stood in front of her.

''Hi,'' he said, his deep voice soft, the single word winging home to a heart that hungered for more.

''I thought you were going home?'' she replied, her voice unsteady.

"I did and then changed my mind."

Her heart lifted and thrummed as time slowed and all else seemed to fade. She caught herself, blinked, swallowed and forced her leaden feet to step away.

Mark was a complication she could ill afford. Solid, secure in his faith and surrounded by family and community.

She turned away, breaking the contact by force of her will. "Do you need any help with supper, Mrs. Andrews?" Sheryl offered, her voice rough edged. She cleared her throat and caught Lenore's scrutinizing glance.

"You can start browning the hamburger," she said, handing Sheryl a fork.

Sheryl had a hard time working, knowing that Mark's eyes followed her every move. It was disconcerting, puzzling and exciting, and she didn't know which emotion took precedence.

By the time they sat down to supper she felt wound up tighter than a spring.

Lenore was well organized and in less than twenty minutes managed to pull together a Stroganoff-based sauce over buttered noodles with a crisp salad on the side. They seated themselves around the table, Sheryl between Lenore and Mark, and as Nick paused, she knew what was coming. Too late she tried to drop her hands to her lap. Lenore had already captured one and Mark held out his hand for the other one. She hesitated, and he laid his hand, callused palm up, on the table, inviting yet not pushing. It would have looked ungracious to refuse, so, reluctantly she laid her hand in his large one, quenching the light trill that quivered up her arm at his touch.

Then his fingers wrapped around hers, firm, hard, secure, and as they bowed their heads Sheryl felt peace flow through her that was a combination of Mark holding her hand and the communion of four people united in prayer.

When Nick quietly said amen, Sheryl carefully slid her hand out of Mark's, thankful that he loosened his hold on her and, picking up her fork, tried to eat.

"How much more baling do you have to do?" Nick asked Mark.

"Three more days, tops. I'm thankful it's been going so well."

"I can't come tomorrow and help you, I'm afraid," Nick began.

"I'll help again." Sheryl interrupted, her voice quiet.

Mark almost dropped his fork. He had been hoping, praying, that she would offer. He didn't dare ask.

"You don't have to," Lenore said. "I'm sure Nick can..."

Sheryl smiled at Lenore. "I'm sure he can, too, but this time I want to finish what I start."

"Now what do you mean by that?" Lenore asked.

Sheryl looked down at her plate. "When I was younger I used to drive the tractor, but could only last a few days. Then I would take off..." She let the sentence hang, and Mark tried to decipher her expression, but a heavy swag of golden hair hid her face from him.

"I still think it's a bit much to expect a young girl like you to help with that dusty, dirty job." Lenore placed her knife and fork together on her plate and pushed it slightly away from her.

"Well I'm glad she doesn't mind," Mark replied. "It sure helps me out a lot."

"I don't imagine you worked on a farm in Edmonton?" Lenore asked, ignoring Mark's warning glance.

Sheryl pushed the noodles around her plate as if contemplating the easiest way to answer the question. "I worked in a bar."

"How did you like that?"

Mark stifled a groan. His mother, soft-spoken though she pretended to be, could never manage to get away from her tendency to be nosy.

Surprisingly, Sheryl smiled. "I disliked it thoroughly. I can't imagine a more futile occupation than serving drinks."

"How long did you do that?" Lenore asked, resting her elbows on the table, her chin propped on her hands.

"Too long." Sheryl looked up and smiled a wry smile. "When we first moved to Edmonton, I took some secretarial courses, then got a job working at a lawyer's office.'' For a moment she seemed far away, then with a shrug she looked down at her supper. ''But things slowed down, and I got laid off.''

''Mark tells me that you are studying again.''

Mark almost groaned. Sheryl must think that she was discussed at every possible moment. As if to confirm that, she glanced sidelong at him.

Mark paused as their eyes held. It was like a reaching out and touching, he was so aware of her. He swallowed and, trying to relieve the tension that sprang between them, winked. She blinked, smiled back.

Something inside of him turned slowly over then. So many things that should matter didn't. Against his better judgment, he was falling for her. The signs were clear to him. The urge to touch, the constant seeking out of her company, the feeling of completeness when they were together.

He looked away, breaking the connection, suddenly sorry he had.

She was wrong for him in so many different ways. She gave nothing of herself. She claimed no relationship with God, she had no intention of pursuing one. Her stay here was only temporary; that point she made very clear.

Mark listed all the reasons, trying to be rational about his feelings for her.

He looked at her again, watching her hands, the cuticles of her nails still lined with dirt that he knew would only come out after the season was over.

In his mind he saw again her hands clutching the steering wheel of the tractor as she manhandled it around the corner, leaning into the turn, a smile tugging the corners of her mouth.

In as many ways as she was wrong for him, she was right. She loved the land as he did; the work didn't bother her. She was independent and self-contained enough to be able to endure being isolated....

''Are you done, Mark?'' His mother was asking.

With a jolt he pulled himself back to the present. "Sorry," he mumbled, handing his mother his plate.

"And where were you?" she asked as she gathered up the remains of the supper.

Mark said nothing, realizing that the question needn't be answered.

Bible reading followed dessert, Mark studiously avoiding eye contact with Sheryl. When prayers were over, he got up, feeling suddenly self-conscious.

"What's your rush?" Nick asked as he leaned back in his chair, a cup of steaming coffee resting in front of him.

"With the warm weather we've been having, the dew will be off the swaths early tomorrow," Mark said, pushing his chair carefully under the table. "I want to get an early start."

"Well, then, maybe you should drive Sheryl home. I had planned on taking her myself, but it would be easier if you did," Nick said.

"She might not want to come right now...." The excuse sounded lame in his ears. The prospect of having her in the truck with him for another hour, coming so close on the heels of his own discovery, would be awkward.

A silence greeted his remark, and Mark realized the difficult position he'd put Sheryl in. To agree would inconvenience his parents, to disagree would sound ungracious. "I guess it does make more sense, if I take her home," he amended. Great, Mark, he thought, now she'll feel like it's too much trouble.

"Will Elise be bringing you lunch tomorrow?" Lenore asked as he bent over to kiss her goodbye.

"I hope so." He waved to his father and waited for Sheryl to get up and say her goodbyes, wondering why this reticent girl could make him feel like an inept teenager.

"You're welcome to come anytime, Sheryl," his mother said, taking her hand. "Just ask Mark to bring you, he'll use any excuse to get some of his mom's cooking."

"Thank you." She smiled, said her farewells to Mark's father and walked past Mark out to the truck.

The ride was made in silence, broken only by the ping of gravel on the truck's undercarriage.

Sheryl looked out the window, fully aware of Mark lounging behind the wheel beside her as he drove in his usual full-speed-ahead fashion. It still frightened her to see the scenery fly by in a green and blue blur, so she kept her eyes fastened on the mountains above them, which moved past at a more sedate pace.

"How did your visit with your father go?"

Sheryl jumped at the sound of Mark's voice breaking her concentration.

"It went," she replied, as a fresh pain clutched her heart at the thought of Ed and his declaration of love. Why now? Had God truly changed his heart? "I didn't stay long…he fell asleep."

Mark slowed and turned into the Kricksons' driveway, pulling up to the house and switching off the lights.

"Thanks again for helping me." He half turned, tapping his fingers on the steering wheel. "You seem to enjoy the work."

She shrugged, wanting to leave, yet loath to exchange the cozy intimacy of the cab and his company for her lonely cabin.

Mark studied her, his head tilted to one side as if trying to figure her out. "You know, I've heard Ed and Nate talk about you, and I have to confess that for a time I didn't think particularly well of you." He shrugged. "I'm sorry about that. Since I've met you I know there's another side to this story of rebellion and mistrust."

Sheryl sighed, her usual reticence wearing away under the concern and caring shown her by Mark's family and, yes, Mark himself. "I don't know if it's worth delving into. It's over…."

"Maybe. But whatever happened is affecting your relationships now." Mark leaned back and smiled encouragingly at her. "Tell me about your first father. Wasn't his name Bill?"

And in that moment, Sheryl felt she could unburden herself. No one had ever asked about Bill Reilly before.

"Bill Reilly," she replied, pleased that he knew her father's name. "He was a good father, a caring man." Sheryl sat back, not realizing until then how tense she was. "We had a ranch in Southern Alberta, the most beautiful part of the country."

"Prettier than this part?" he asked with a soft laugh.

Sheryl turned to Mark, smiling. "It's pretty in a different way. You should go there once, to see the sweep of the land as it moves toward the mountains. It's majestic, open and different…and the same."

"I might do that," Mark said, his voice quiet, his whole posture relaxed.

"My dad and I went everywhere together. We covered a lot of country." Sheryl sighed, drifting back to a happy, almost magical time. "He used to take me with him on the tractor, in front of him on the horse. I was an only child, and probably spoiled, though I never felt that way until I moved here. I just know, for that time in my life I was safe, secure and loved." She clasped her hands in her lap, circling her thumbs slowly. "When he died I felt as if I would never laugh again, never be happy again."

"That must have been a difficult time for you and your mother." Mark's soft voice was sympathetic.

Sheryl only nodded, remembering an old sorrow made less painful by the passage of time.

"So how did you end up in Williams Lake?"

"My mom's cousin had a rental house there, and she found my mom a job. So we moved."

"Why didn't you stay on the ranch?"

"My dad, though loving to a fault, was not much of a manager. The ranch had to be sold to pay the debts. My mother was ill prepared for making a living, and things got very tight. My mom's cousin introduced her to Ed, and that ended her brief but short career in the Laundromat." Sheryl pressed her thumbs together, watching her nails turn white under the pressure. "They got married, and Ed started his campaign to change what he saw as a willful and spoiled child.''

''Didn't he love you?''

Ed's words from this afternoon reverberated through her head. She glanced over at Mark. He lay back against his door, one arm resting along the back of the seat his other hand supporting his head.

''I suppose he wanted to,'' she continued, reassured by his casual pose. ''Though I don't think he quite knew what to do with me. He loved my mother, in his own way, though I saw early on that she was intimidated by him.'' Sheryl sighed, recalling frowns and puzzlement on his part, resentment on hers. ''I never wanted him to take the place of my father, and I have to confess that my part in the whole relationship was to defy him just for the sake of staying loyal to my father's memory and showing Ed that he would never replace Bill Reilly in my life.''

''How long after your father died did you mother remarry?''

Sheryl frowned, thinking. ''About six months.''

Mark lifted his eyebrows. ''So soon?''

''Like I said, money was tight, and my mother didn't seem able to cope without a man to support her.''

''And you moved right onto the ranch from Williams Lake?''

''I loved it at first. And at first I suppose Ed did try. He taught me how to saddle and care for a horse, something my father always did for me. I was allowed to ride whenever I wanted, as long as my chores were done for the day.''

''And that included baling hay…''

''Among other things. I fed orphaned calves, mucked out the calving pens, helped with the fencing, rode out with Nate to check on upper pastures…''

''And you were ten years old?'' Mark lifted his head, frowning at her.

''Yes.''

''And as you grew older…''

"Things went from difficult to worse. I didn't mind the work at first, but it seemed that the rides became fewer and farther between." Sheryl pulled her hands over her face as angry confrontations between her, Nate and Ed came to mind. "I would sneak off whenever I could, leaving them to do the work. This of course created more anger and punishment, which meant more chores, which made me more determined to fight them, and away we went. Soon we were fighting over what I wore, how I acted. God was drawn into every discussion on my hell-bent nature. I didn't like God very much. He seemed an angry dictator at best, a despot at worst."

"How did your mother deal with it all?"

"I think she was afraid to oppose Ed and stand up for me. She was a good mother, but not a strong woman."

"And where did Jason come into the equation?"

"Early on." Sheryl scratched her head with one finger, sighing. "Jason was exactly the opposite of what Ed saw as fine and upstanding in a young man."

"I've heard about Jason...."

"Everything you have heard is true." Mark hadn't moved but his stillness created an air of waiting, listening. He hadn't made any judgments on her behavior, hadn't offered any comments. He just asked those quiet questions that encouraged.

"At first I saw him as a misunderstood young man. But he wasn't. Those who knew him understood him completely. He was angry, rebellious and sadistic."

"What do you mean?"

"He used to hit me." She kept her voice even, glossing over the humiliation.

Mark said nothing, but Sheryl could see his hands tightening on the steering wheel.

"But that was only for the first few years."

"What do you mean?" Mark's voice was harsh, controlled.

Sheryl lifted her mouth in a cynical parody of a smile, turning to face Mark as if challenging him. "I started fighting back."

Mark's gaze was level, his eyes slightly narrowed. "Why didn't you leave him?"

"And go where?" Sheryl laughed shortly. "I had no place and no money."

"Why didn't you tell Ed? No matter what you may think of him, he would have helped you, let you come back...."

"I tried to tell him..." Sheryl turned away. She had said enough, had said too much. She was venturing too close to the true pain, buried deep where she didn't dare venture. "Look, I've got to go." She fumbled for the door, unable to find the latch in the darkened cab.

Mark reached across her and opened the door for her and she slipped out.

"Hey wait a minute." His voice was suddenly quiet.

Sheryl stopped, biting her lip, not wanting to break the moment they had shared, but knowing she had to.

"Aren't you even going to say thanks for the ride?"

She turned back, studying him. His hair framed his face, and in the glow of the dash, his features were all angles and shadows. He was handsome and appealing in a very frightening way. His questions had given her a first chance to tell someone her part of the story, and her ensuing confidences had made her feel vulnerable to him.

"You look scared again," Mark continued, his gray eyes holding her. "It makes me sad for you."

She said nothing, thinking of Jason, Ed, Nate—men who, as far as she could remember, had never felt sad for her—a painful breathlessness pulling on her chest as she faced one who did. Sighing, she leaned her head against the door, clutching the frame as she felt herself drift into his smoldering eyes.

"My mom was right, you know," he said, his voice hushed.

Sheryl frowned, not comprehending the direction of his words.

"I don't think twelve-year-old girls should be driving tractors, either." His level gaze and serious expression gave

Sheryl approbation while creating a newer anger for the pain she now lived with.

"Don't do this," she whispered, almost pleading.

"Don't do what?" Mark leaned forward. "Don't try to understand what you lived with? Don't try to figure out what made you who you are now?"

"I can't do this. I can't give you what you want...." She pushed down the pain and memories. "I'm not going to delve any deeper and open myself to anyone again." But she could only look as far as the open vee of his gleaming white shirt as she spoke.

"I still haven't heard the whole story, Sheryl. I know you aren't the selfish person Nate led me to believe you were." He ran a finger along the steering wheel, then looked up at her. "I'm sorry I prejudged you. It wasn't Christlike, and it wasn't right. I guess I've come to respect you and know there's more that you're not telling me."

"Please..."

"I won't dig anymore. I'll leave you alone." He quirked her a wry smile. "For now."

Sheryl felt again the unwelcome prick of tears behind her eyelids. Why did he do this to her? What did her life matter to him? How did he manage to make her feel vulnerable, when she promised herself it would never happen again?

She slammed the door shut, the sound ricocheting off the buildings in the yard. Without a second glance, she strode away, her hands shoved in the pockets of her skirt, head down. She would finish what she started and thereby prove to Nate and herself that she was dependable and worthy. Then she would return to Edmonton, back to her studies, back to...

Sheryl bit her lip, her step faltering. Clenching her teeth, she reminded herself of her plans, her first small steps to an independent life.

Chapter Eight

As the tractor slowed, Mark watched the last bale clunk its way out of the baler, a grin lifting his mouth. He caught the bale, winked at Sheryl, who watched him over her shoulder, and dropped it on the top of the last stuke.

Relief, fulfillment and just plain happiness surged through him, and with a whoop he jumped off the stuker and ran toward the tractor. He caught Sheryl around the waist just as she was getting down and set her on the ground.

''We're done,'' he shouted. He caught her hands in his, pressing them against his stubbled face. He looked heavenward and called out ''Thank you, Lord.'' As he looked back down, he grinned at Sheryl's incredulous face. She blinked and grinned back, her sea green eyes limned with dust, her hair sticking out, dust smears on her cheek.

She looked gorgeous.

''You are a wonder, my girl,'' he exulted, catching her by her slender waist and swinging her up and around, his own happiness overcoming his resolve to be careful with her. Her hat flew off in one direction and her feet in another.

By the time she touched ground again, she was laughing, her white teeth a sharp contrast to her tanned and dirty face. ''I don't suppose you do this to Nate, when the first cut is baled,'' she called out.

''Nate isn't nearly as good-looking as you are.'' He winked at her. Giving in to an impulse, he dropped a kiss on her forehead. He thought she would jerk away, but to his surprise she only blinked and then smiled back. "I don't know if I've said it enough, but thanks," he added, suddenly serious.

"I enjoyed it."

"I know." He couldn't seem to stop himself—the need to connect with her was too strong—and he reached up and palmed her hair away from her face, cupping it gently, his gloved hand looking incongruous against her delicate features. "I've never met anyone like you before."

"I believe that." She stepped away then, breaking the contact. "Here come Rob and Conrad."

Mark glanced over his shoulder at the approaching tractor, frustrated at the intrusion.

Rob drove, and Conrad hung from the cab, singing. They pulled up beside Mark with a hoot.

"All done, slave driver." Rob called down from his perch. "We'll bring this rig to your place and then me and Conrad are heading to town."

Mark pulled his gloves off and shoved them in his back pocket. "I'll have a cheque for both of you in the mail in the next couple of days."

He sighed as they jumped back on the tractor, wondering again at the exuberance and stupidity of youth. They were probably headed off to the bar where they would promptly drink away half of what they made in the past week.

"I guess baling's thirsty work," said Sheryl with a wry note in her voice. "I wish they could see what they are wasting."

Mark glanced over at her, and she caught his look. With a deprecating shrug she turned back to the still-running tractor. "We should get this unit back to the farm. I imagine you'll want to service the tractor, return the baler…"

Mark caught her arm, and she turned to face him, her eyebrows lifted in question.

"Thanks a lot for helping."

"You already said it."

"But I don't know if you realize what this means to me and to Nate...."

"I didn't do it for him, I did it to help you out. I like the work...I love being outside." She laughed shortly and turned her gaze back to him. "I guess I just spent too many years here, hating it when I had to help, hating where I lived, that I never really appreciated it like I should."

"You probably didn't have a chance to appreciate it."

Sheryl shrugged. "You don't need to defend my actions. In a way Nate was right. I wasn't always dependable." She smiled at Mark. "Now I've made up for that."

Back at the farm Sheryl helped him clean up the baler, grease the tractor and gas it up. She hadn't forgotten what needed to be done and was quick, efficient and capable. Nate and Ed had taught her well, Mark conceded.

She returned from parking the tractor, brushing loose bits of hay off her pants. "I guess I'm done."

Mark nodded, watching the play of sun and wind in her hair, wishing he had the nerve to reach over and take the braid out, to see it loose again.

"Do you need to return the baler right away?" she asked, quirking him a questioning look.

He pulled his thoughts together. "No," he answered shortly. "I'll return it when we come back."

"Come back...?"

"From the pack trip."

Sheryl nodded as comprehension dawned on her face. "I forgot about that."

"Aren't you coming?"

"No, I can't."

Mark felt disappointment cut through him. He had so hoped she was coming, had hoped that once she was on a horse in the mountains she so clearly loved, she would lower her defenses, would open up...

To what? he thought deprecatingly. Your suaveness and irresistible charm?

"So what were you going to do?"

She shoved her hands in her pockets, pursing her lips. ''I was going to head back to Edmonton.''

''For what?''

''My apartment...my studies.''

Mark nodded, dropping the rag into the empty pail beside him. ''Of course. I forgot.''

He sighed, cleaned up the tools, Sheryl helping him of course, and when they were done he drove her back to Nate's place. The drive was quiet.

He pulled up to Nate's house and stopped.

''So,'' he said, turning to Sheryl, the truck still running. ''Thanks again.''

She looked down at the old felt hat she still held and nodded. ''You're welcome again.'' Then she caught his eyes and smiled. ''I really enjoyed it, truly.''

''So when are you heading back?''

She shrugged, ''A bus leaves from Williams Lake at midnight for Prince George. I can visit Ed once more before I leave.''

''Tomorrow night?''

She frowned at him. ''No. Tonight.''

''What?'' He couldn't stop the exclamation of surprise. ''Why didn't you tell me?''

''I knew we'd be finished early today...''

''I don't care about the baling. I just thought you might let me know...'' His voice trailed off.

She glanced at him, her expression surprised, and as their eyes met Mark felt it again, that clutch in the pit of his stomach that hurt and made him angry at the same time. Couldn't she see what effect she had on him? Didn't it matter to her?

''Mark, what's the matter?''

He shook his head, wondering whether she was just blind or indifferent. ''I can't believe you didn't tell me when you were going.'' He shoved his hair out of his eyes with a quick movement, unable to keep the words down. ''I mean, we spent the entire week working together, and I didn't have a clue.''

"You knew I was only going to be here awhile..."

"Of course I knew that, I just thought you might want to stay and spend some time here without having to work like a dog."

"I told you already I enjoyed it." She handed him his hat and reached for the door handle. "Anyhow I have to leave sometime."

Mark couldn't stop himself and caught her arm. "I don't want you to go. Come on the pack trip, spend some time in the mountains.

She said nothing, only stared ahead, her face suddenly harsh.

"Nate won't be coming, if that's what you're afraid of."

She shook her head and then turned to him, her face drawn and tight. Mark felt a chill shiver through him as he faced again the same withdrawn Sheryl he had met in the bar over a week ago.

"It doesn't matter, Mark. I can't go."

And before he could challenge her comment, she stepped out of the truck without a backward glance.

But as Mark watched her, he felt as if she'd taken part of him with her.

Sheryl waited until she heard Mark's truck reverse and tear down the driveway. Only then did she dare turn around, watching him hungrily as he left, just as she did each night he brought her home, knowing this would be her last glimpse of him. The red bandana still held down his long hair, and from his posture, Sheryl knew he was angry.

She was fully aware of the undercurrents that flowed between them, she knew he was attracted to her, even though it seemed that to recognize it was a type of pride.

But it was there, and to ignore it would be to encourage him. He was not for her. The very things that made him so incredibly appealing also pushed her away. He had a place, security, but more importantly, a sincere faith. His spontaneous prayer that morning had shown her more clearly than anything he could say that he had a real and solid relationship with God.

She turned, her feet dragging, knowing if she had given him any encouragement at all, things might have been different. But then what? She knew that the most basic ingredient of any relationship was the ability to open up to each other. And she knew she couldn't give any man any kind of power over her.

She pushed open the door of her cabin, surprised to see Marla and Crystal sitting on her bed, crying.

"Auntie Sheryl," they called out when she entered the cabin, launching themselves at her.

She took the full brunt of two small but compact bodies catching her around the waist, almost causing her to stagger.

"What's wrong?" She disentangled herself from their arms, suddenly worried. "What happened, tell me quick."

"Daddy says you're going away tonight," Marla wailed, clutching Sheryl's hand, her tear-streaked face turned up to hers. "And that you're not coming on the pack trip with us."

"Why do you have to go?" Crystal complained, stamping her foot. "It doesn't make sense."

"Come and sit on the bed with me, before you push your foot through the floor like Rumplestiltskin," said Sheryl, trying to make this very angry bundle of girl laugh.

Crystal managed a faint smile, then frowned again and dropped onto Sheryl's bed so hard the springs sang.

Sheryl sat beside her and pulled Marla onto her lap.

"We asked Daddy to ask you to stay longer, but he said you had to leave," Marla sniffed.

"Mommy said you were leaving tonight," Crystal said, suddenly turning on Sheryl. "You can't go. We didn't even see much of you. Uncle Mark had you to himself all the time."

"I had to help with the baling. Your daddy had a broken leg, and Uncle Mark couldn't afford to hire anyone else."

"But now you have to go right away."

"Please," added Marla. "We didn't see you at all..."

Any further entreaty was broken off by the opening of the door.

''Here you are, you two urchins.'' Elise scolded, her hands on her hips. ''Sorry about this, Sheryl. I couldn't find them and finally clued in to where they went.'' She turned to the girls and stepped aside, pointing out the door. ''Now off to the house and the bathtub, on the double.''

Crystal glanced at Marla who sniffed again. Sheryl gave her a quick hug and then let her slide off her lap. They walked to the door, making each step seem like a monumental effort. At the door Crystal hesitated and turned back to Sheryl.

''If you stay one more day, we can get to know each other better.'' Crystal added. ''Maybe you can even come on the pack trip with us. Daddy says we can't go this year because he has a broken leg and Mommy has to cook.''

''Don't bother Auntie Sheryl with all of your troubles, Crystal. She has had a busy day and a long night ahead of her.'' Elise admonished.

''Don't you like us at all, Auntie Sheryl?''

A stab of pain pierced her heart at the innocent question. The only time she saw them was a brief glimpse of their heads each evening against the light of their bedroom window when Mark drove away.

''I suppose I could leave tomorrow instead.'' She hesitated. ''That is if it's not too much trouble.''

''Of course not,'' Elise said warmly. ''I'd love to have you around.''

Crystal and Marla looked at each other, mouths open, then whirled around and ran back to Sheryl. Again she was engulfed by arms and surrounded by cries, this time of happiness. She caught her balance and, reaching out, stroked their heads, missing Elise's smirk.

''I think you'd better go, girls. Your mom is waiting,'' she said, squatting down to look them in the eye.

Marla smiled at her and hugged her again.

''We can go riding tomorrow if you want,'' Crystal said. ''Or we can go for a walk.''

"Whatever you want," Sheryl replied with a smile.

Crystal nodded and turned.

"Let's go, Marla," she said with a grin.

"I'm sorry about that, Sheryl," Elise said as the girls ran down the walk, their whoops of delight drifting behind them on the night air. "They have been wanting to spend time with you all week, and when they found out you were going away tonight they were desolate."

"I just didn't want to impose on you."

Elise walked over to Sheryl's side and gave her a quick hug. "You're not imposing at all. Like the girls were complaining, we've hardly seen you at all. Mark had you to himself, and all he did was make you work. I'd like you to have at least some time to go riding. It's the least we can do after you helped us out."

"Well I suppose one more day wouldn't matter much."

"No, probably not." Elise smiled, then turning, left.

"The next bus doesn't leave until five Tuesday afternoon?" Sheryl frowned, winding the telephone cord around her finger. "Is there any other connection I can make before that?" She sighed, grimacing at Elise who lifted her eyebrows in sympathy. "Okay. Thanks a lot."

Sheryl hung up the phone and turned to Elise, wondering if she knew all of this when she'd convinced her to stay another day. "Well, unless I hitchhike, it looks like you're stuck with me until Tuesday." She bit her lip, planning. Her rent was paid until the end of next month. All she needed was a job, badly.

Elise shook her head. "Don't even think about hitchhiking. Mark would have a fit if he found out you were even considering it, and he'd end up driving you himself."

"So what must I do the next few days?"

"You can come on the pack trip with me and Crystal," Marla said, looking up from her coloring. "Daddy says we can't go if he isn't coming, because Mommy has too much work to do."

Sheryl looked at Marla's innocent blue eyes, then at Elise's gray ones, so like Mark's, and wondered if this hadn't been the plan all along.

''Catch Roany and F5 and get them ready to be rigged up.'' Mark handed two halters to Conrad. ''Tie them to the south hitching rail. I don't want F5 to get too close to Tia. She's ornery today.''

Conrad took the halters and headed off. Mark watched to make sure he shut the gate properly behind him and then shouldered himself between Two Bits and Tia. He began buckling up the rigging on Tia who pranced around. A warning thwack on her haunches made her settle down.

''Where should I put these?'' Elaine stood beside him holding a pannier. Mark glanced up from the latigo he was tightening and almost ground his teeth in frustration.

''Just set them against the tack shed for now,'' he answered shortly, ''and make sure you put them where they won't get kicked over.''

He turned back to Tia, giving her a shove, wondering for the thousandth time how he'd managed to let Allen and Elise talk him into moving the trip up a couple of days.

''Hey, Mark,'' Brad called from the other side of Two Bits. ''The buckles on this rigging are wrecked.''

''I thought you were farther along than that.'' Mark called over his shoulder, snugging up the latigo. Tia jerked back, and her rope flew loose. Mark grabbed for it, but she trod on the end, grinding it into the mud from the rain last night.

''Move over you ornery critter.'' Mark shouldered the horse aside, but she wouldn't budge. Two Bits sidestepped and almost crushed him between the two horses. Mark elbowed Two Bits in the ribs and, with one final heave, managed to move Tia and tied her snug to the rail.

''Just stay put you miserable creature,'' he warned, hoping he had used up his catastrophe quota.

He ducked under Two Bits' head, trying without success to quell his rising frustration.

"The breeching is too tight," he said shortly, running a practiced eye over the rigging. "You shouldn't snug it up till you're ready to pack the horse."

"Now you're going to be ticked," sighed Brad, resting a hand on Two Bits' haunches. "Which one is the breeching?"

"Breast collar goes across the chest of the horse, breeching across the rear end...like britches?" Mark loosened the buckles, wishing, almost praying for one person who knew what they were doing, instead of these weekend cowboys who made up his family.

"Well I'm glad enough I got it on the right way," Brad huffed, picking up on Mark's mood. "Anyhow, the buckles on the *breast collar*—" he put emphasis on the word "—are the ones that are broken."

Mark ignored him, praying as he felt the all-too-familiar tightening of his chest as he struggled with a mixture of impatience and frustration. He wished again he'd had four days instead of two to get everything ready.

"You have to ream out the hole on the strap," he told his brother. As he ducked under Two Bits' head, he knew that his underlying problem wasn't horses and inept wranglers, it was Sheryl.

She had dropped the news of her leaving on him without any preparation. They'd spent four days working together, talking in the evening each time he'd dropped her off, but never a hint of her departure until four hours before she left.

Mark tugged on a strap on Tia's rigging a bit too hard, netting him an antsy horse, and he took a deep breath, stifling the rising clutch of panic. He didn't know if he would ever see her again. She doubted she would expend a lot of energy on familial visits in the future. He paused a moment, looking past the horses, past his house to the hills beyond that so captured her fancy. He wished he could take her riding through them. He wished he could bring her to the very place where he instinctively knew she might drop her guard and show him the girl he had only caught tantalizing glimpses of. He knew there was a hungering within her for love, for God, for security, but she covered that need with a hard shell of independence because much as she yearned for these things, she feared them more.

"Yo, Mark." Rob's loud yell pulled him back to reality and the work at hand. Biting back a sigh, he vaulted over the hitching rail to handle yet another crisis.

"Oh, no," Brad yelled out. "Someone catch that horse!"

Mark looked up just as Tia thundered past, ropes trailing, loose rigging flopping around, kicking up great clods of mud. Three horses were right on her heels as Conrad let out a mighty yowl.

"I told you to watch that gate, Conrad," Mark cried out, running to the gate that Conrad was desperately trying to push shut.

Conrad eyed him warily, and Mark stifled his anger. He'd been owly the past couple of days. He knew it, and try as he might, he couldn't seem to keep from sniping at everyone. He dug in his pockets and tossed Conrad a set of keys.

"Take my truck and head them off before they hit Sweet Creek."

Conrad was over the fence and hit the ground running.

"And don't pump the gas," Mark called out after his retreating figure.

Everyone had stopped what they were doing, watching the latest drama unfold. Conrad got in, leaned over to turn the key, his head bobbing. It wouldn't start.

Mark groaned and dragged his hands over his face. Flooded. "What are you trying to teach me, Lord?" he sighed, drawing in a steadying breath and counting to ten.

"Hey, Mark," Brad called out.

Mark looked up in time to see a set of car keys arcing toward him. He caught them against his chest.

"Just remember it's a car, not a farm truck," Brad yelled as Mark ran toward the gleaming white vehicle.

Mark got in, pushed the key into the ignition and was about to turn it when he looked up and saw the three runaway horses galloping back down the drive toward the corrals.

''What in the world...'' he muttered, jumping out of the car. What miracle had occurred to make the horses turn around? He jumped out of the car and snapped out orders. ''Someone get in the corral and keep the other horses away from the gate. Brad, Allen, funnel the loose horses down. Don't let them get on the wrong side of the hitching posts. Elaine you open the gate.''

Conrad came at a dead run, vaulted over the corral fence and herded the horses into a corner. As the gate swung open the three free horses paused a moment, as if pondering their next move. Then a whinny sounded from behind them, and there was Tia being urged on by Sheryl riding Nate's gelding.

Mark stopped, shock and surprise coursing through him as Sheryl easily herded the horses through the gate. Tia stopped.

''Shut the gate,'' Sheryl called out as she swooped down and caught Tia's halter rope, preventing her from escaping one more time. Elaine pushed the gate closed, and all was under control.

Except Mark's heart. It lifted and ran at the sight of Sheryl's long blond hair, flushed cheeks and soft green eyes, unable to believe that she was actually here. Questions stumbled through his mind, all eager to be voiced.

Why hadn't she left on Thursday like she said she would? Why had she changed her mind?

Then she looked down at him. He sensed hesitation and indecision. Whatever her reasons were for coming he wouldn't find out directly.

It didn't matter. Her presence was an unexpected answer to a prayer he hadn't even dared to utter. It was nothing short of a miracle.

He held out his hand for Tia's rope. Wordlessly she gave it to him, and their gazes locked, neither able to look away. Mark rubbed Nate's horse, Spanky, with one hand, smiling up at her.

''Miss your bus?'' he asked, his voice quiet.

Sheryl nodded. ''Crystal and Marla managed to make me feel guilty for not spending any time with them, and since the next bus isn't leaving until Tuesday afternoon, they conned me into taking them on the pack trip."

"Good girls." Tia pranced away from him and Mark tugged on her halter rope. "And you returned my horses."

"I thought I'd ride Spanky here to get a feel of him, and when I saw the horses coming down the road, I figured they weren't supposed to be there."

Mark took refuge in humor. "Wow. Smart *and* good-looking."

A smile teased the corner of her mouth, but she seemed to ignore his comment. "Elise is bringing the girls and their horses right away. I hope it's okay they come. Nate thought they'd get in the way, but I promised to look out for them."

"I'm glad they're coming," he replied, leading her horse to the hitching rail. The entire congregation of Sweet Creek church could come along, if they had anything to do with her being here. "But I'm even happier that you're here."

Sheryl bit her lip and then dismounted, fiddling with Spanky's cinch. "So what can I do?"

Mark tied up Tia next to Spanky and leaned back against the rail, watching her. "Why don't you tell me?"

She looked him squarely in the eye as if challenging him. "Throw the diamond hitch."

"Now I'm really impressed," he said, a heaviness inexplicably falling off his shoulders. Ed was the only one who could throw a faultless diamond hitch that caught all the parts of the pack and held them with an even snugness on the pack horse. He hadn't managed to teach Nate, so packing up the horses invariably fell totally on Mark's shoulders.

"Well that's easy to do to some people," she joked, loosening the latigo on Spanky's saddle.

Mark pushed himself away from the rail and stopped directly in front of Sheryl, taking a chance and tipping her chin up.

"I'm really glad you came, Sheryl."

She only shrugged in answer, keeping her eyes down.

Mark let his glance idle over her hair as the sun danced off it. It was tied up again in her now-familiar braid. She was beautiful and she was here. For now that was enough.

The rest was in God's hands.

Chapter Nine

"Here, I'll help you with that."

Rick, Mark's older brother, stopped and helped Sheryl heave the tarp over the packed horse.

"I can't believe you know how to do this stuff," he said as he straightened it.

"I'm a little rusty, but it's coming back." Sheryl smiled at him. Mark's family accepted her sudden appearance with an equanimity that still surprised her.

"Are you hassling the help, Rick?" Mark poked his head over the horse's rump, handing Sheryl a rope.

"Don't be getting greedy, Mark. You've got at least thirty-five years of escapades to share."

Mark slanted him a warning glance, and with a laugh Rick sauntered off, whistling.

"Don't I just love my family," he sighed, handing Sheryl the lash cinch to which the forty-foot rope was tied. "Do you want me to help you?"

"It'll go faster." Sheryl answered.

They fell into the same easy rhythm they shared baling hay. Sheryl felt an accord that she didn't want to analyze.

She murmured softly to the horse as he danced around, and he settled down.

"Are you this good with cows?" Mark asked as she tied the final half hitches under the pack and they moved on to the next horse.

"Cows used to petrify me." Sheryl laughed. "Nate always got mad at me when a cow charged and I'd run the other way. Then he'd be stuck with a bawling calf and a protective mother." Sheryl laughed, setting the pack pad high up on the horse's withers and sliding it down.

"Nate tends to overreact," Mark responded. He bent over and handed her an extra pad. "Use this on F5. He's a bit high withered as well as high-strung."

They finished packing up the horses and together helped the others finish saddling, checking stirrups, adjusting cinches. Sheryl was amazed at Mark's patience, how easily he worked with the horses, not against them.

By early afternoon the horses were packed and everyone mounted up and ready to go. Mark walked down the line checking ropes, adjusting bridles.

Sheryl handed Brad the lead rope for one of the pack horses, Roany. "Don't tie this to the saddle horn," she warned as he took the rope. "If you meet up with a bear you'll have a rodeo you don't want to be in the middle of. Better to let Roany fend for himself rather than get tangled up in ropes and hooves."

"That makes sense." Brad mounted his horse. "Mark just hands me the rope, lowers his eyebrows and growls 'tie that rope to your saddle and you're wolf bait' so I don't ask why."

"I'm sorry," Sheryl apologized. "I didn't mean to preach."

"No problem. I'd sooner listen to you than Mark's yowling anyhow," Brad said loudly, as Mark drew nearer.

"Unlike yours, my yowling makes sense," Mark answered dryly, running a quick eye over Brad's saddle horse. "Check your cinch ten minutes after you've been riding."

Mark turned to Sheryl, the soft breeze lifting his long hair away from his face, a smile curving his well-shaped mouth.

"Ready to go, partner? I've got you leading F5. He seems quieter around you."

Mark's voice took on a teasing tone, then his rough finger

brushed a few wisps of hair out of her face, further confusing her.

Sheryl glanced at him, trying to gauge his mood. He smiled crookedly, his head tilted to one side. He let his fingers trail down her cheek, and his expression became serious.

A sixth sense warned her of his intention, and she silently pleaded with him not to. Then his head blotted out the sun and he brushed his lips lightly over hers. He straightened, winking at her, as if challenging her.

"Lets get the show on the road," he said quietly. He turned and ambled down the line of horses to Toby, his own mount, leaving Sheryl, her emotions in a turmoil.

Somehow Sheryl found her way back to Spanky, Nate's horse, ignoring Elise's approving smile. She untied F5's lead rope and mounted up, her cheeks burning.

She managed a quick wave at Lenore who had elected to stay behind with Benjamin.

"Have fun," Lenore called out as the line moved past her, out of the yard. "See you in a few days."

Sheryl drew in a steadying breath, wondering what she had gotten herself into, wondering what the next few days would bring.

The horses had been climbing for about twenty minutes, the trail winding through the dusky coolness of the towering fir trees. In the light-strewn openings in the foliage, Sheryl caught glimpses of the hay fields that lay below them, dotted with small stukes of hay.

Now and again she saw Mark at the head of the column. He rode easily, moving with his horse, the hand holding the pack horse's rope resting on his thigh. She let herself watch him, let herself wonder about him. She couldn't imagine that he hadn't been swamped by other girls. He was the kind of man her fellow waitresses would fantasize about during coffee breaks. If Tory could see her now, she would think her crazy for not taking advantage of the situation.

As if you had a chance, she chided herself.

He did kiss you, the other insidious voice reminded her.

"Hi, there." Elise fell back and drew abreast of Sheryl. "Isn't the weather great?"

Sheryl welcomed the intrusion into her thoughts and turned to Elise. "Have you done this trip in the rain?"

"Oh, yes. That's when we really depend on Mark's even temperament." Elise paused, as if waiting. "He's such a great guy," she added hopefully.

Sheryl recognized her underlying purpose and decided to humor Elise a little.

"So how long has Mark lived out here?"

Elise brightened at Sheryl's question, and Sheryl stifled a chuckle. They were good people, but they couldn't get away from their straightforward heritage, so different from her stepfather and brother's.

"Mark moved out here about seven years ago, the same year Nate and I got married, and bought out the Simpson place a year later." Elise sighed, looked ahead, as if making sure no one else was listening and drew her horse a little closer to Sheryl's. "He bought the place for Tanya but she wouldn't move from Vancouver. Guess she could get engaged to a manager of a successful real estate office, but couldn't marry a rancher."

Sheryl straightened as she absorbed this hitherto-unknown piece of information.

"Did she ever come out here?" Sheryl couldn't stop herself from asking. She had a sudden inexplicable need to fill in the spaces in Mark's own past.

"She tried to talk him out of it, but he wouldn't listen. He bought the ranch, and she came out once in a while, but we could see it was coming apart a little more each time she visited. When he had to make a choice, he chose the ranch."

"How did the girl take it?"

Elise sighed, biting her lip. "Badly. Mark was considered quite a catch. She finally offered to live here for half a year at a time, but Mark didn't want that. He is pretty even tempered but when it comes to the ranch, he is pretty definite."

Sheryl looked past the other riders to the trail that wound upward through the silent trees, remembering semitrailers, airplanes and the constant smell of exhaust. How could anyone choose that over this?

"So he's been unattached since then," Elise added hopefully. She settled back with a smile, moving easily with the rhythm of her horse. "There have been a number of girls who imagined themselves in love with Mark, but none of them have the temperament to live out here on their own, and Mark knows that."

Sheryl only nodded, which was all the encouragement Elise seemed to need.

"He seems to enjoy being with you, though."

"And what am I supposed to say about that, Elise?" Sheryl laughed, unable to feel uncomfortable around Elise's straightforward manners.

"You could get coy and accuse me of kidding you, meanwhile hoping that I'll reassure you, or you could freeze me out with a 'you're exaggerating' and since you did neither, I'm going to say it again." Elise tossed Sheryl a sideways glance, suddenly serious. "I haven't seen him this interested in anyone in a long time."

Sheryl decided to change the line of questioning. "Did you send the girls into my cabin or was it their own idea?"

Elise pursed her lips, tilting her head to one side, eyes glinting with amusement. "It was a group project."

Sheryl stifled a groan. The way the Andrews family operated everyone was in on the plan except her and Mark, of that she was sure. His surprise this morning was genuine.

"But that wasn't the only thing we had on our mind when we cooked up this scheme." Elise continued. "I guess we wanted you to spend some time with us as a family, to spend some time up in the mountains. Mark says you love them so much, and Nate has told me enough about how you used to spend hours riding up here."

Sheryl returned Elise's now-serious look with a smile. "You are really an interesting family," she said.

"I'm glad you feel that way," said Elise as if Sheryl had just bestowed the ultimate compliment.

They rode on in companionable silence, Sheryl enjoying the ease she shared with Elise and literally soaking in the smells and sounds of riding up the mountain trails. It had been years since she'd been on the back of a horse. The creak of the saddle, the jingle of reins, the soft sounds of hooves falling on packed ground as they worked their way up the hills brought back good memories.

The trail, guarded by fir and pine trees, angled upward now, and would continue until they crested the first range. From what Sheryl remembered they would be at the upper pastures and the first camp by late afternoon.

She shifted in the saddle, turning back occasionally to check her pack horse, who plodded along expending the minimum amount of energy required.

A sigh lifted her shoulders as she looked around, the sun warm on her neck and back, the occasional shade welcome.

Elise stayed close, and now and then Sheryl made a comment on the landscape, pointing out birds and some of the different plants.

"You love this country, don't you?" Elise asked finally.

Sheryl nodded. "I spent a lot of time up in these hills. My poor mom didn't get much help from me in the house. Nate always said he pitied the man who married me."

Elise was quiet, then turned to her. "You never really got along with Nate, did you?"

Sheryl felt as if it was her chance to spill out the injustice of what had happened. For eight years all her anger and frustration and guilt had been directed at Nate and Ed. It waited, stewing, and now she was given a chance to tell her side.

But Elise was married to Nate, and Sheryl didn't know if it was fair to push on the foundations of what Nate had built here, just to satisfy her own anger.

Sheryl shook her head. "Please don't ask me about that."

But Elise wouldn't quit. "Sheryl, he's my husband and I love him, but I also know he's not perfect." Elise bit her lip, nodding. "I guess it would help me understand him a little more if you could tell me your side of the story."

Sheryl tightened her hands on the reins, trying to balance her own memories with the changes that she had seen in Ed and even in Nate.

Sheryl looked ahead of them, at the long, drawn-out line of riders and pack horses as they meandered down the hill to a dried-out creek bed. It was almost symbolic of this family. A dependence, a caring, and Nate had a part in all of this.

"Please," Elise encouraged. "I think it's sad and wrong that you've been away from them so long without a word."

Sheryl cleared her throat and began. "It was difficult when we first moved to the farm." Her voice trailed off as she tried to catch the right memory. "But once I got over losing my dad, I realized that it could be a lot of fun. Nate and I had to work with each other a lot, and I didn't mind the first few years. But there was always work to do on the land, and my mom didn't help out much. She was busy enough running the house, but I think Nate resented that."

"Nate always said that Ed was a perfectionist...." Elise let the sentence hang as if encouraging Sheryl.

Sheryl felt tempted to leave it there, but somehow Elise's raised eyebrows and tilted head seemed to draw her out. She sighed, then said, "I don't think there were many things either Nate or I did that met with his approval. But Nate kept trying. I didn't. And that was when the trouble began."

"I guess Nate kept at it because he always knew he would get the ranch someday."

"And that's why I resented all the work after a while," Sheryl added quietly. "As a stepdaughter, I figured there was nothing in it for me."

Elise nodded in understanding, and Sheryl experienced the same feeling of relief she'd felt with Mark. And again she felt as if part of the burden she had been carrying had shifted a little, felt a little lighter.

"How did Jason come into the picture?"

"Through my own stubbornness."

''How did that happen?''

Sheryl shrugged. ''I was talking to him once, and Ed found out,'' she continued. ''He warned me away from this evil boy and I, of course, ran in the opposite direction.'' She fell silent, remembering how dangerously exciting it was at first to be with Jason, the thrill of defying Ed, but she also remembered her mother's anguished look each morning after she slipped in late.

''How old were you when you started going with him?''

''About sixteen. We went out for about two years, until I graduated from high school, then Jason and I eloped.''

''When did your mother die?''

The unexpected question was spoken in gentle tones, but the words cut and hurt. Sheryl thinned her lips, looked ahead and shut off her memories.

''I'm sorry, Elise, I don't want to talk anymore.''

''No,'' Elise said quietly, ''*I'm* sorry. I shouldn't pry and dig.'' She reached over, and squeezed Sheryl's hand. ''I'm glad you came and I'm glad you're here and I won't ask any more questions—'' she lifted her eyebrows as if she didn't quite believe the statement herself ''—if I can keep my mouth shut that long.''

In spite of the momentary tension, Sheryl smiled. Elise was uncomplicated and easy to be with. But the pain she felt at Elise's question showed her that she was better off to keep her thoughts to herself.

Mark dismounted, looking over his shoulder gauging the hours until sunset. Glancing around the site, he noted with approval the firm hitching rails and clear camping area. He hadn't had the time to supervise Rob, and he'd sent him up here right after the haying was done. He'd done a good job.

Mark tied up his mount and pack horse, easing the cinch on his saddle for now.

''I'll get you something to eat in a bit, Toby.'' He stroked his horse's nose, stepping back as the animal tried to rub the side of his head against him. ''Just settle down, now,'' he warned with a smile. He walked around to his pack horse, loosening the rope, keeping a lookout for Sheryl.

One by one riders pulled in, laughing, chattering. Horses shook and blew, riders dismounted, stretching, groaning.

"Watch that horse, Jennifer," Mark called out to his niece as she dismounted. "He's a little too interested in the ground for my liking."

Her father, Allen, looked up and jogged over. "Whoa, you mongrel." He caught him by the bridle. "Don't you go rolling over on my best riding saddle." He held the horse a moment while his daughter dismounted, then tied him up.

"The tents are on Brad's pack horse," Mark said to Allen, pulling the tarp off his own. "Get Diane and Lois to set them up while we unpack these horses. Those teenagers can help."

He carefully untied the boxes, making sure he took the same weight off each side to keep the pack frame from slipping. By the time Elise pulled up, all the boxes and containers were off the horse, lying in a neat pile.

"Working already, brother?" she asked, dismay tingeing her voice as she looked down.

"Don't wimp out on me now, sister. We're hungry, and since you're the chief cook, we have to wait for you."

Elise slipped off her horse with a groan. "Well, the least you can do is take care of this poor critter for me. I'll see what's on the menu for tonight."

Mark caught the reins, looking up just as Sheryl rode in, a curious half smile on her face.

He had spent most of the afternoon glancing past his family to the end of the train, catching only glimpses of her blond hair as it caught rays of the sun through the gentle dapple of the pine trees. Now that she was in front of him, he felt suddenly tongue-tied, an unfamiliar feeling for an Andrews.

"This really is God's country," she sighed as she slipped off her horse, running her pack horse's rope through her hands.

Mark felt a thrill at her words. That she could acknowledge

God as Creator was a beginning. He smiled at her as she brought her horses around to the hitching rail.

"So how does it feel to be back up in the mountains?" he asked, watching her slim hands working at the làtigo of her saddle, pulling it loose, her head bent. He half turned, still watching her, resisting the temptation to kiss her exposed neck.

She paused a moment, looking up again. "I've forgotten how much I missed this." Her voice caught on the last words, and she looked down again, busying herself with the saddle, the bridle and moving on to her pack horse.

Mark let her go, sensing her need for space, encouraged by the emotion in her voice. He returned to Elise's horse, thoughtful. If spending only one afternoon riding in the hills could open up even one tiny crack, he wondered what he might learn about her after two days.

Open her heart to You, Lord, he prayed, his mind imploring as his hands worked. *Let Your creation show her Your power and let us show her Your love. Help us to show her Your forgiveness and teach her to forgive.*

Mark paused, glancing over his shoulder once again. Brad and his wife, Lois, were helping Sheryl unpack, their voices carrying a murmur punctuated by an occasional laugh from Lois. Drew and Elaine were gathering the tack, and Allen and Diane helped Elise set up the kitchen. Their teenagers had found a frying pan lid and were already playing frisbee with the younger kids.

He felt the tension ease in his shoulders. He had been dreading this trip, and when Nate broke his leg, it put that much more on him. He had come so close to canceling, but now, as he saw his family so thoroughly enjoying themselves, he realized that all the trouble was worthwhile.

And when he heard Sheryl laugh softly, he knew that the patience he had unexpectedly received to finish the preparations for the trip was God-given, possibly for another reason.

Soon the clearing was full of tents, and Elise was ringing the gong for supper. Mark stretched, pushing a kink out of his back. The horses were hobbled, the more aggressive mares picketed to prevent them heading back home. Folded tarps hung over rails alongside saddles, blankets and bridles. He quickly scanned the sky. No clouds, but in the mountains you never knew. He would cover everything with the tarps before he went to sleep.

With a satisfied nod, he turned back to the camp, where his family had now gathered, waiting. They stood in a circle, a steady buzz of chatter flowing comfortably around them. He approached them and took his place beside Sheryl who stood off to one side, her hands clasped behind her back.

"Allen, can you say grace?" Elise asked as she held out her hands.

Mark saw Sheryl hesitate as a circle formed. Marla pulled Sheryl's one hand to herself and, with a wry grin, Mark reached over and caught her other.

She pulled away as Mark had known she would, but he only looked at her, his hand holding her smaller one firmly. When she looked up at him, a slight frown marred her forehead.

"Shall we pray?" Allen said, looking around the circle with a smile. Mark bent his head, still holding Sheryl's hand. She relaxed.

Allen's words were hushed, almost muffled by the largeness of the space they were in. His voice flowed, counterpointed by the whispering wind teasing the leaves of the trees above.

As Allen prayed, Mark added his own silent supplication, holding Sheryl's hand tighter, praying that she might be able to see God in nature around them, be able to see His love and His forgiveness.

When Allen said amen he felt Sheryl's fingers cling to his almost desperately. When he turned to her, her head was bent, eyes squeezed shut, lips clamped between her teeth. Mark resisted the urge to pull her close to him, to ease the tension that held her so stiff.

But then she pulled her hand away and looked up, not at

him or anyone else, but at the leaves above them as if in supplication.

''We'll eat the usual way.'' Elise's voice broke the moment. ''Parents help the little kids, and then the adults can eat once they're settled.''

Sheryl turned to Marla and away from Mark, as if shutting him off.

He waited, watching her as she ushered her stepniece to the line, helping her select a plate and cutlery and then get served by Elise. Sheryl found them a spot on a fallen log and sat down.

Mark waited until everyone was served, intending on sitting at the table. He had envisioned sitting with Sheryl, but sensed that she wanted to be left alone. Crystal suddenly appeared beside him.

''Come and sit with us, Uncle Mark?'' she asked, an overly bright smile wreathing her face.

''Why?'' he asked, looking past her to where Sheryl sat with Marla, her head bent over the little girl's.

Crystal leaned closer, her voice lowered to a theatrical whisper. ''Sheryl has tears in her eyes,'' she whispered.

Mark straightened, his fingers tightening on the plate he held. Ignoring his family's knowing looks, he affected a casual air, got up and sauntered across the clearing to where Sheryl sat.

He lowered himself slowly to the ground beside her, leaning against the log she sat on. ''Hope you don't mind that I sit here?'' he asked, glancing up at her.

''No, go ahead.'' Her voice was quiet, almost strained. Beside him he could see her legs stretched out, the toes of her scuffed running shoes tapping against each other in agitation.

Crystal joined them with a plate of food for Sheryl, and between the two little girls, they managed to fill up the silence that loomed between the two adults.

When Mark finished eating, he gave Crystal his plate, sent Marla on an errand and pushed himself up on the log beside

Sheryl. She sat, head bent over her plate, her fork pushing around the remnants of stew that he knew was now cold.

"You don't have to eat it if you don't want to," he told her, his hands dangling between his knees.

"But if I don't, the bears will," she said with an attempt at humor.

Mark took the plate from her and with two spoonfuls finished it off. Then he handed it back to her. "Now just wipe it with your bread and you're done."

She did as she was told. "Thanks," she said quietly.

Giving in to an impulse, Mark slipped an arm around her shoulders and squeezed her.

Her answering smile surprised and pleased him. She didn't resist. It was as if she was content to have him hold her beside him. She took a slow breath, and Mark saw the shimmer of tears on the corner of one eye. With a gentle forefinger he touched it and one slipped out.

Mark pulled her closer, wondering, praying, knowing that somehow she had been touched, but knowing, as well, that he would have to trust and wait.

Chapter Ten

The crackle and snap of the fire broke the stillness of the night. Sparks spiraled upward into the darkness then chased by others.

Sheryl watched the flames, her hands cupped around a coffee mug, her restlessness easing.

She had helped Elise put her girls to bed, told them a story about when she was young and then kissed them good-night. She had dawdled, hesitant to step out of the safety of the little girls' company and join the adults sitting outside, their words an indistinct murmur punctuated by the snapping fire. The single tear that had slipped out at suppertime was a mistake, she didn't know what to do about it.

Mark had wiped it away, and she knew he wouldn't leave her alone. So when she stepped out of the tent, safely out of the circle of the firelight, she scanned the bodies around it, checking for his distinctive hair, but she couldn't see him.

So why had she felt a twinge of disappointment as she stepped closer to the fire?

The circle had opened for her, and she had found a spot just within reach of the warmth of the flames, but slightly back from the group.

Sheryl took another sip of her tea, followed by a deep, cleansing sigh. She enjoyed watching Mark's family, enjoyed listening to their light banter. Unfinished jokes circulated, memories interrupted by laughter and other remembrances, the conversation a stream of consciousness that meandered over past and present.

"Where are you?" A gravelly voice murmured in her ear. Joy sluiced through her at the familiar sound. A large hand rested on her shoulder, long fingers curling around it. Sighing lightly she gave in to an impulse and laid her head back, enjoying the feeling of belonging that surged through her at his touch. He liked her, and she had to admit she was attracted to him. Why not just enjoy it?

"My mind's just wandering," she replied.

"Well, put this on and come and wander with me instead." Mark drew back and dropped her heavy jacket over her shoulders and turned her around to face him.

His eyes glowed with reflected firelight, his finely chiseled features accented by the shadows. "I have to check the horses and thought you might want to come with me," he said, pulling the collar of the coat up around her neck.

Sheryl hesitated.

"Please," he urged, his rough finger caressing her neck.

She felt her skin warm under his touch and, pushing aside the last of her own objections, slipped her arms into the overlarge sleeves, pulling the coat close to her and nodded. "Sure. If my expert opinion is any good." Keep it light and superficial and just savor, she reminded herself.

Mark smiled, dropped an arm over her shoulders and drew her away from the campfire and his family. "You can tell me if I have the hobbles on upside down."

"Well if you're worried about that, you probably tied the horses to the picket with the wrong end of the rope," Sheryl retorted, a teasing note entering her voice. It was time she proved that she could hold her own, play the game and not get involved.

The fire was behind them now, the noises of his family receding as they walked.

"Listen, I had a hard enough time finding a picket that had the point on the right end," Mark said, slipping his hands in his coat pockets, his eyes on her as they walked.

Sheryl laughed, the sound softened by the darkness. The sighing of the wind in the trees above them and the occasional nicker or snort from the horses beyond them were the only sounds accompanying their muted footfalls.

He reached out and took her hand in his, intertwining their fingers, and Sheryl let him, content to relish in his attention. When he stopped and leaned back against a tree and drew her close to him, she didn't stop him, either.

She laid her head against his chest, feeling more than hearing the steady thump of his heartbeat, the slow rise and fall of his breathing. He touched her hair and pulled her braid out from the jacket.

''Do you always tie it up?'' he asked, toying with it.

''Usually. It gets in the way otherwise.'' She was pleasantly surprised at how easy it was to just enjoy his company.

''Can I undo it?''

''Sure.''

''I've wanted to do this for days,'' he sighed, combing her hair with his fingers. ''It's so beautiful.''

Sheryl leaned back, her hands pressed against his chest, watching him as his eyes followed his own hands as they wrapped themselves in her hair. It felt good to be treated so gently, but she had to be careful to keep the situation under her control. ''What do you want, Mark?''

Mark looked bemused, his eyes still on his hands. ''I want a lot of things. A square-bale stacker, some more land...'' He paused, looking down into her eyes, his own glinting in the weak light of the moon. ''Lots of money,'' he whispered dramatically.

''Who doesn't?'' she replied softly, her tone bantering, her mouth curved up in a smile.

Mark tilted his head. As his smile faded away, his expression became serious, and against her will Sheryl felt her heart still. Don't let him do it, she thought grimly, remembering his unexpected kiss that morning.

But his gentle fingers rested lightly on her forehead, his other hand held her even closer.

"I want a lot of things," he whispered, his eyes intent. "But what I need is you."

He waited a moment as the words sank in, dropping so quickly past her guard, she couldn't stop them. They shot straight as an arrow to that deep, empty place in Sheryl's life that yearned for love and affection. No one had ever needed her before. Wanted, used, but needed?

She looked up into his soft gray eyes trying to discern what he really meant.

Stop this now, commanded the angry part of her.

But Sheryl was suddenly tired of anger, tired of fighting. This moment, this time up in the mountain was like a dream. Mark's family, the fellowship, the beauty of the surroundings, Mark's arms around her—all of this was so unreal it was easy to think that no matter what happened it wouldn't affect her, once she returned to the valley and reality.

He needed her.

His arm tightened about her, his hand slid over her cheek and suddenly his mouth was on hers creating an ache within her heart that almost hurt. His lips were warm, soft, and she drifted against him, clinging to him.

"Sheryl," he murmured against her mouth, his own moving to her cheeks, her eyes, his fingers following, touching, tasting.

She slipped her hands around his neck, tangling her fingers in his hair, her mouth seeking his hungrily.

Reluctantly he pulled away, tucking her head close to his chest, his mouth brushing her temple.

"Oh, Sheryl, I wish I could tell you how much I care about you," he whispered against her hair, his lips warm on her skin. "I think I'm falling in love with you."

That word, more than any, was sufficient to wake her, and she pulled back. "Don't talk like that," she warned.

Mark tilted his head to one side, brushing her hair out of her face. "But I have to," he said. "I feel like I found someone who belongs with me…you're the part of me that has been missing all this time."

''Please stop.''

''I can't,'' he murmured, tracing the line of her eyebrows. ''I want to tell you what you mean to me, how much I like just watching you. I like seeing you work with the horses, driving a tractor. You look beautiful with dust streaking your face and straw in your hair. And when you smile—'' he kissed the corner of her mouth, as if to encourage it ''—that's what I want to do.''

Sheryl felt confusion warring within her. Physical actions she could deal with, but not words. She had no defense against what he said. He wasn't supposed to be making her bones melt and her blood thin with words. This was just supposed to be an interlude, a brief moment, a light flirtation.

Her mind fought with the pleasure of what he said and the humility of feeling undeserving. Jason and, even earlier, Ed both had tried to pound the feeling into her without success, and now Mark, with only a few words, had succeeded where Jason and Ed had failed. She didn't want to feel unworthy, yet around Mark she knew she was.

Caught between her wavering emotions she looked up into Mark's glowing eyes and slowly shook her head. ''We don't fit at all, Mark,'' she whispered, desperately fighting his attraction, trying to keep her emotions under control. What he said was too beautiful, too wonderful, to be meant for her. It gently pried open cracks in her protective covering that let out the remembering. ''You're too different,'' Too good for me, she added silently to herself, too wonderful, too much God's child.

''Not so different, Sheryl,'' he admonished, running a callused finger down her cheek. ''We both love the same things...''

''No,'' she said, her voice suddenly thick with emotions that came so easily to the surface when she was with him, mocking her earlier intentions. ''I can't love.... I don't have it in me.''

Mark tilted his head to one side, his hand cupping her chin, slipping down her neck. "Yes you do. I've seen you with Crystal and Marla, with Benjamin..."

"Stop it," she said, her voice tightening. "You don't know what you're talking about..."

"You don't mind it when I kiss you," he continued undaunted, gently caressing her neck.

Sheryl stiffened as his hands drifted over her shoulder, reminding her. She stepped away, and Mark's hands dropped to his side. His chest lifted in a protracted sigh.

"You do that so well, Sheryl."

She ignored him, pulling her jacket around her.

"What does it take to crack that shell you have so firmly around yourself?" Mark's voice was soft, but his tone suggested he wasn't going to let her pull back this time. "I care about you, Sheryl, and I want to help."

"What can you do," she cried out. "You're just a man, just another lousy man, and what has any man ever done for me?"

Mark paused, reached out and touched her cheek, tracing the track of the lone tear that slid unheeded down her cheek.

"One man gave up his life for you, Sheryl."

She blinked, swiping the moisture from her eyes with the palm of her hand, watching him, suddenly still as she listened.

"Jesus took all that pain you're carrying around, all those burdens, all the mistakes, the punishment that we deserve..." He dropped his hand, his eyes watching her. "He took it all with him and then he died—just for you."

It was there again. That hovering feeling, that sense of great love waiting. But she knew too well what God wanted. Subjugation.

"Well I can't give him what he wants, Mark," she said suddenly, closing her eyes against his image, concentrating on who she was. "God wants too much from me. And so do you. I can't give you what you want, what you need. You need someone who can share that faith you have, someone you can pray with, not someone who is hauling around all this other garbage...."

''Then dump it,'' he replied softly.

She looked at him then, ''What?''

''Dump it. I've told you what Christ has done for you, what he's waiting to do for you...''

''It's not that easy,'' she faltered.

''It's a whole lot easier than packing it around yourself.'' Mark pushed himself away from the tree, but he didn't touch her.

Sheryl bit her lip, her arms clasped tightly across her stomach. She couldn't look at him, but she could hear him breathing, saw his hands hanging loosely at his sides, his feet slightly spraddled. It was as if he expected her to turn and run.

She couldn't.

There was no place left to go. God seemed determined to find her and He would use anyone who came in her path.

Sheryl looked up at Mark. The slight breeze that came with evening in the mountains lifted his hair and dropped it gently. As she watched him, he laid his hand on her shoulder again.

''I can only guess at what happened to you. I know it's more than what you've said,'' Mark sighed, tilting his head to one side, his eyes gleaming in the soft night. ''I just know that I care for you in a way I've never cared for anyone.'' He tightened his hold on her, lifting his other hand to her waist as if to pull her closer.

She resisted; she had to. If she let him hold her again she wouldn't be able to keep herself aloof, and her last barrier would be pulled down.

''Sheryl, please tell me about Jason.''

She stiffened, then forced herself to relax, to adopt a light tone. ''I told you already. He wasn't a good husband.'' She ran her finger down the front of his T-shirt, feeling the warmth of him through it. ''It doesn't matter anymore....''

''Yes, it does. It's a part of you that you keep hidden. I don't like that. I want to know—''

''All the details?'' she asked, her voice tight. She didn't pull away, but wouldn't meet his gaze. ''Is it important for you to know exactly how many times he humiliated me?'' She suddenly grabbed the front of Mark's jacket, the metal ridges of the button cutting into her hand. ''Why is it so important to hear how many times he hit me, how stupid I was, how helpless? Do you want to see the scars?''

Mark closed his eyes and drew in a deep breath. Sheryl felt his chest rise and stifled a clench of instinctive panic.

''No.'' He ground the single word out, his rough voice harsh. ''I want to share the burden you're carrying, to help you. I want you to see what God wants to do for you. But you have to tell me. You have to open up.''

Sheryl swallowed, feeling as if she hovered on the brink of a dark abyss, unsure of what emotions waited below—pain, sorrow, regret, fear…

''I can only guess at what happened to you. I just want to help you,'' Mark's rough voice softened as his words tugged on her barriers. ''Please let me help.''

Sheryl closed her eyes at his words. They were so tempting. Did she dare let go? Who could she trust to catch her?

I'll be there. The still, small voice slid into her mind out of another part of her life. A soft and gentle part that was always there, a part she never dared acknowledge in her battles to be strong. *I'll bear you up on eagle's wings,* the voice continued.

Sheryl felt a wave of pure love, pure devotion, pure tenderness wash over her as if erasing and removing all the stains and wearing down all the bars that she had held so tightly over her soul.

A sob shuddered through her. Then another. She tried to stop it, tried to pull it back, but it was as if she tried to hold back the sea.

A wave of sorrow washed over her.

''Just let go,'' Mark's voice whispered, somewhere above her, piercing the darkness of her soul. ''God will carry you through.''

Suddenly she went slack. Strong arms caught her, supported

her. Then the tightness that always constricted her throat, loosened its grip.

Sheryl clutched her chest, trying to stop the knot of pain unraveling in her chest. "Where were you?"

"It's okay," Mark whispered, pulling her close, wrapping his arms around her. "I'm here."

Strength. Warmth. She felt a melting.

Then the sound came. First a narrow keen, weak and meager. As Mark's arms held her the sound built in her throat, harder, heavier.

Then, with the swiftness of a summer storm, the sorrow poured out. A grief larger than she could articulate threw her around, sucking her in the maelstrom.

"Mama," was all she could say. "I want my mama." Huge, heaving sobs racked her body, sorrow held down too long engulfed her, trying to come out all at once.

She clutched her head as tears coursed down her heated cheeks. Mark pulled her tighter against him, drawing her head against his chest. She clung to him as her anguish grew, the sorrow threatening to rip her in two.

"Why, Lord?" she cried out clutching Mark's jacket, the metal ridges of his buttons digging in her hands. "Why did you take her away from me?"

She could say no more, her face pressed against his shirt as she wept away months of repressed grief and sorrow.

She cried for the loss of her mother, for the brokenness of her relationships, for the loss of her own innocence in the reality of living with Jason. Time drifted on, meaningless, as she unburdened herself, her mind empty of all but grief.

The sobs lessened, but still the tears flowed. She wanted to stop but knew she couldn't until the pain was lanced out…for now.

After what seemed like hours, the tears subsided and she felt strength surrounding her through her sorrow. Strong arms held her, hands pressed her close. Mark had become an anchor in the storm that had just washed over her. But even with her heated cheek pressed against his now-damp T-shirt, she knew that a greater strength had comforted and held her firm.

She had tried to run away, but God had found her.

Mark closed his eyes, his own emotions in a turmoil. He rocked Sheryl slowly, soothing her, praying for the right words, knowing he would never forget the sounds of her anguish or the feel of her now-pliant body resting against him, trusting him.

''Dear Lord, please grant her healing,'' he whispered, his hand holding her head close to him. ''Let her tears cleanse her.''

He felt a tremor drift through her as she drew in a shaky breath, her cries a soft mewling sound. He wanted to absorb her pain into himself, take it away from her. Their relationship had taken another turn, and now the bond between them could not so easily be ignored or brushed aside.

''Oh, Sheryl,'' he whispered against her hair, kissing her damp temple, tucking her head under his chin. ''I do love you.''

His leg was cramping. He tried to loosen Sheryl's grip on his waist but she clung harder.

''I just want to sit down, Sheryl,'' he whispered, stroking her hair away from her face.

Reassured she released her hold on him, and when he sat down he drew her onto his lap, wrapping his arms all the way around her as if she were a child, holding her as close to him as he could.

''Do you want to talk about it?'' he asked, his voice quiet as he stared off into the dark, surprised that his family had not heard the sound of her crying and come to investigate.

Sheryl took in a breath, shuddering. ''I'm afraid to.''

''Why?'' he prompted softly, laying his head against the rough bark of the tree he sat against.

''It's so hard,'' Sheryl said simply, her hands resting against his chest. ''I tried to push everything out of my mind, tried not to think.''

He hesitated, feeling as if he took advantage of her, but deeper than that was a need to know everything about her, everything that she tried to conceal. ''You said something about your mother and Jason...'' he said gently, stroking her head with his chin.

Sheryl drew a slow, deep breath. ''I missed her so much,'' she said softly. ''I wasn't the daughter I should have been. I made things so hard. Then Jason...'' she shuddered. ''The times he beat me...I felt I deserved it for what I did to my mom.''

Mark closed his eyes, feeling her pain, sharing her sorrow, swallowing down his own. She had lost so much, had endured so much, how could he comfort her?

''I wanted to be a good wife and I wanted a baby so badly,'' she continued, her voice quavering. ''He didn't. And now I have nobody.''

Mark held her, his own emotions a disarray of feelings, thoughts, questions. She had borne this sadness and grief on her own. Now her restraint and self-control took on another meaning, became pitiable instead of a source of frustration. Who did she have to help share her burden? She had pulled away from God, she had no family support, and he wondered what kind of friends she could have made living with Jason.

''Can I pray with you, Sheryl?'' he whispered, stroking her head, his fingers tangling in her hair.

''I don't know,'' she murmured. ''It's been so long since I prayed.'' She drew back, looking up at Mark, the darkness unable to conceal her puffy eyes, the tracks of her tears on her cheeks. ''I'd feel like an uninvited guest barging in....''

Mark palmed away the moisture from her cheeks, smiling down on her. ''He's waiting for you, Sheryl. He wants to be with you. His love is never ending, don't you remember?''

Sheryl shook her head slowly. ''I remember believing it when I was little, but somehow I haven't seen a whole lot of it lately.''

Mark almost cried, himself, at her honest declaration, and he struggled for the right words. He took a breath and pressed a quick kiss on her heated forehead. "God has never promised us an easy life, without problems," he said slowly, "but He does promise that whatever things come our way He will use for our own good."

Sheryl blinked up at him and lifted her hand to his face. Her cool fingers ran down his cheek and cupped his chin as she watched him, a sad smile trembling on her lips. "You make it sound so neat and tidy," she whispered. "But right about now the only good thing that has come out of this is meeting you."

Mark's heart skipped a beat. He was unable to tear his gaze away from her shimmering eyes. She blinked, and another tear coursed down her face. Bending over her, he kissed it away, and suddenly she clung to him, desperation in her movements.

"Please stop being so good to me, Mark," she whispered, her voice urgent. "I have nothing to give back to you."

He laid his chin on her hair, staring into the darkened forest, afraid to think that life had indeed sucked her empty. Was what he offered enough to fill it? All he could do now was pray her heart would open to what God could give her.

Without warning she suddenly straightened, drawing away from Mark.

"I must look a fright," she said with a curt laugh, pulling her hair away from her face. With one easy motion she stood up, finger combing her hair, looking anywhere but at Mark.

He stayed where he was, drawing one leg up, resting his wrist on his knee as he watched her hurried movements. How quickly she pulled back, drew her defenses around her. It would be admirable if it wasn't so heart-wrenchingly sad.

"Do you have my hair elastic band?" she asked suddenly, her fingers weaving her hair back into a braid.

He stretched his leg out as he dug in his pants pocket for it. He handed it to her, and wordlessly she took it, still looking everywhere but at him.

"So what happens now, Sheryl?" he asked, unable to keep silent.

She paused, her head bent, then resolutely twisted the elastic around the bottom of her braid, her movements erratic. Tucking it into her coat, she shoved her hands in the pockets pulling her coat closer around her. ''I don't know,'' she answered finally, sniffing lightly, wiping her nose with the back of her hand.

Mark pushed himself off the ground and came near to her, standing close enough, but not touching her.

''I can't say I do, either,'' he replied softly. ''We shared something tonight, God touched you tonight, and I don't think you will ever be the same.''

''Probably not.'' She looked up at him, her face confused. ''But old habits die hard. Maybe I just need some time.''

Mark kissed her lightly on the top of her head and drew her alongside him, walking back to the campfire. ''Then we'll wait,'' he said, comforted by her hesitant acknowledgment, praying, wondering, but also realizing that she was right.

They walked back in silence, the wind whispering above them, the cool darkness enveloping them. In the distance Mark could hear the snap of the fire, the murmur of his family's voices punctuated by occasional laughter. Unconsciously his arm tightened around Sheryl's shoulders as if to give her strength. She lifted her head to look at him.

''You look scared,'' he said, smiling down at her.

Her step faltered, and she looked away from him, her hands still buried in her pockets. ''I am.''

Mark stopped turning her to face him. ''Why?''

Sheryl shrugged, chewing on her bottom lip. ''What am I supposed to say, how do I act?''

Mark frowned, trying to find the meaning under the oblique words. ''Normal, I guess.''

''But that's the trouble, Mark,'' she looked back up at him, her face tight with suppressed emotion, ''I don't know what's normal. I don't know who I am anymore.''

As Mark watched her he remembered the cold, hardened girl he had met in the bar only a couple of weeks ago. Now she stood before him, her clothes and manner totally at odds with that same girl. He had gotten past her hard veneer to the soft and hurting core of her. But by doing this he had also taken away her own natural defenses, and she was lost.

"You're Sheryl—" he started.

"But which one?" she broke in. "Reilly, Krickson or Kyle?" She broke away from him. "Who do I belong to?"

"First and foremost you belong to God," he replied without hesitating.

Sheryl said nothing, but when she turned back to him, she was smiling lightly. "I guess that's where I'll have to start then." She looked over her shoulder at the soft glow of the fire through the trees. "We better go. Your family is going to wonder what happened to us."

As soon as they stepped into the clearing, Elise stood up and looked past Sheryl to Mark with a knowing smirk on her face.

Mark shook his head imperceptibly as he pushed a stump into the circle with his boot.

Elise frowned, but when she sat down Mark knew she got his silent message. He just hoped the rest of his family would leave Sheryl and give her the space and time that she needed.

He prayed that he would be able to, as well.

Chapter Eleven

The early-morning sun warmed the tent, and Sheryl rolled over, pain slashing through her head and right behind it, her memories.

Sheryl slung her arm over her eyes as if to keep both at bay. But images danced through her mind, painful, mournful. Her mother's sad face as Sheryl and Ed once again faced off over Jason. Jason's angry face when she hit him back for the first time. The screech of metal, the glass flying.

Sheryl rolled onto her side, pulling her arms close to her chest, wishing she could drift back to the painless void that was her life the past year. It had taken years of living with Ed and Nate to build a defense against emotions. When her mother died, she hadn't been able to cry. While being married to Jason, she hadn't allowed herself to.

Now Mark had peeled away the protective layers, had made a mockery of her strength.

She rubbed her temples, now damp with tears as she pulled herself into the present. Her pain still hung in her mind, and she knew that no matter what happened, by tomorrow she would be alone again.

The thought propelled her out of her lethargy. With a quick motion, she pushed back the sleeping bag and got up.

Elise stood by the table, yawning as she mixed up pancake batter, smoke wafting from the stoked-up fire. Sheryl pulled up her mouth in a semblance of a smile and walked resolutely over, her offer to help received with enthusiasm. As she kept busy, Sheryl felt the blessed return of equilibrium and control.

Until Mark appeared in the clearing. He said nothing, but as he walked past her he trailed his hand casually over her shoulder sending shivers down her spine and confusion through her mind, mocking what she thought she had just attained.

Breakfast was over quickly and devotions followed. Allen read from the Old Testament this time. "'For the Lord searches every heart and understands every motive behind the thoughts. If you seek him, he will be found by you.'" The words were unfamiliar but, much like Mark's words of last night, they found and filled an empty spot in Sheryl's life. And much like Mark's words they made her feel unworthy.

After devotions came the work. Sheryl quickly haltered Marla's and Crystal's horses, then tied them up.

As she snugged up cinches, adjusted stirrups and packed the horses she felt surrounded by Mark's family as they moved, asked her for advice and exchanged laughing comments with each other.

"How's it going?" The soft voice behind her startled her. Sheryl glanced over her shoulder at Elise who stood beside her horse, her hand resting on its rump, concern showing in her face.

"Fine," Sheryl replied, her tone noncommittal, determined not to answer the questions that she saw in Elise's eyes. "I just have to snug this up and F5 is all packed." She turned her attention back to the ropes, making sure the loops were taut, the pressure on them even.

"You look tired," Elise persisted, tilting her head so she could better see Sheryl's face.

Sheryl shook her head, pulling the last rope through and making it taut. "I'm okay, really."

Elise took a step closer and placed her hand on Sheryl's shoulder. "You don't sound okay."

Sheryl bit her lip, still holding the end of the rope. She swallowed and swallowed, willing the myriad of emotions that were roiling beneath her fragile self-control to settle down. ''Please don't ask, Elise,'' Sheryl whispered finally, still unable to face her friend.

''There you are, sis.'' Mark's voice broke into the silence. ''Rick told me you were pestering my chief wrangler.'' He ducked under the hitching rail, and Sheryl didn't know if having him around was any better. ''Is your horse all ready to go, sis?''

''Yes,'' returned Elise, sounding peeved. ''And so is Crystal, Marla and all the others.''

''Good; then we can head out.'' Mark untied F5, speaking to Sheryl as he did. ''I didn't think you minded if I got Allen to lead this critter.''

''Fine by me,'' she said, risking a glance up at him. Their eyes met, Mark's hands stilled, and she felt herself drifting toward him. She had to almost clench her fists to keep from laying them against his chest.

He blinked then cleared his throat. ''Good,'' he replied, his own voice unsteady. ''Elise, can you take up the rear. Sheryl is going to ride up front with me.''

''Sure...'' It wasn't hard to hear the smirk in Elise's voice, and Sheryl knew that the inquisition Elise tried to begin a moment ago was only forestalled. She took a breath and turned away from both of them, reminding herself that tomorrow she would be leaving.

''Do you remember that place?'' Mark drew his horse alongside Sheryl, pointing out a steep slide visible between the trees.

''Frying pan ridge,'' Sheryl replied. ''Nate and I were out riding when we found that old frying pan up there.''

The early-morning mountain air had had a gentle bite, which the sun had since warmed off. The hills spread away from the riders, their undulating stretches ridged with pine trees. Above them, the grassy slopes gave way to harsh, unyielding rock and benignly deceptive rock slides.

She glanced sidelong at Mark, disconcerted to see him

studying her with a bemused look on his face. Up till now his comments had been superficial and she had been grateful for his casual attitude.

"What?"

"You look beautiful this morning," he said softly, reaching out. But Sheryl's horse shied and his hand missed its target.

"My eyes are red, my hair is a mess..." Sheryl shook her head taking refuge in humor.

"You look softer, warmer, more approachable," he returned, refuting her deprecating remarks. "And you look great sitting on the back of a horse," he finished with a smile.

"Well, I guess the horse can take some credit for that."

"I said *you* look great, not the horse."

She only nodded.

"How are you feeling this morning?" he said his expression suddenly serious.

"I woke up with a headache."

Mark drew his horse closer, taking her hand in his, squeezing. "I was praying for you last night."

"What for?" Sheryl replied, trying to cover the jolt his words gave her. Not now, she thought, please don't talk about that now.

Mark winked at her, threading his callused fingers through hers. "That you would sleep well."

Sheryl knew she should take her hand out of his, but she couldn't break the connection. She enjoyed the feel of his large work-roughened fingers, as an undefinable peace flowed over her. She knew it couldn't last and was determined not to let the future intrude on this time out of time.

Mark looked ahead, his hand swinging Sheryl's, his hat pushed back on his head, eyes narrowed against the bright morning sun. Small wrinkles fanned out from the corners of his eyes, light lines in his tanned face, and a smile lifted one corner of his mouth. He moved easily with his horse, unconsciously attuned to its movements.

His jacket hung open, the ever-present mountain breeze ruffling his hair. Above him was the hard blue sky, behind him the rugged mountains.

The rightness of the scene gave Sheryl a stab of pleasure, almost painful in its intensity. As if he sensed her regard, he turned, his dark eyebrows frowning a moment, questioning.

''What's wrong?''

Sheryl shook her head, smiling as she squeezed his hand. ''Nothing at all,'' she returned, losing herself in eyes as gray as a soft summer rain.

They reached Mark's camp by lunchtime. Everyone dismounted, and pulled out the sandwiches and ate them standing, sitting or lounging against the wall of the cabin. Sheryl sat with Crystal and Marla, content to watch and listen. The girls found a ready ear for their excited jabber about their horses and near encounters with death on the trip up.

All too soon it was time to return to the main camp. A few moans and groans accompanied the mounting up. Brad, Allen and their wives said their goodbyes to Mark. It would be a while until they saw him again. Elise gave him a quick peck on the cheek, and he gave the girls a hug.

Sheryl helped Crystal and Marla into the saddles. Elise was already on her horse, and at a signal from her, they rode off, leaving Mark and Sheryl alone.

Sheryl toyed with the reins of her horse, unsure of what to say. How do you say goodbye to the first man you met that you felt at one with? How do you tell him that you can never be together?

Then his hand lifted up her chin, and she looked once again into soft gray eyes.

''I'm glad you came along, Sheryl,'' he said, his voice rough with unexpected emotion. He smiled carefully at her, his fingers caressing her cheek. ''If it wasn't so terribly improper, I'd ask you to stay with me out here and ride with me, help me gather the cows.''

Sheryl managed a shaky grin at his words, trying to grasp some kind of equilibrium in her own emotions, now so tender and vulnerable.

"Thanks for letting me come. It was good to be out here again." She bit her lip as she felt a sob rise in her chest, remembering last night, not wanting to think what lay ahead. She blinked carefully, but a tear coursed down her cheek.

"Oh, Sheryl," Mark sighed, drawing her suddenly against him in a fierce hug. "I'd say don't cry but you have so much sadness that has to come out."

She leaned against him, drawing from his strength, saying nothing.

"Whatever happens, Sheryl," he said, "please remember that Jesus's love is greater than mine."

Fresh tears flowed at his words, and Sheryl fought to regain control. She couldn't start crying now. She had to get on her horse and ride down to their camp and then down into the valley and then…

She straightened, palming her cheeks and wiping the moisture off on her pant legs. "I'm sorry," she murmured, "I don't know what's happening to me. I never used to be weepy."

"You never had the chance," Mark said softly, reaching into his pocket and pulling out a red polka-dotted hanky. Carefully, he lifted her chin with his fingers and dried the rest of her tears. He took his time, his gentleness almost setting her off again. When he was done, he folded the hanky in her hands.

"So, what happens now, Sheryl?" he asked.

Sheryl looked away, wrapping his handkerchief around her hands, clenching them tightly. "I still have an apartment in Edmonton. I'm enrolled in classes this fall, and I'll need to go job hunting."

"I still owe you for the one you lost." He shifted his weight, tugging on his ear. "And what about Nate and Ed?"

"I'll visit Ed just before I go and as for Nate…" She lifted her shoulders in a shrug. "Nothing much has changed. I don't imagine it will between now and when I leave."

"And forgiveness…?" His words were soft, but they cut.

"I don't know if I can do that, Mark."

"Not on your own, of course."

Sheryl bit her lip. "I don't think I have to forgive them. They have to live with what they've done, just as I have to live with the consequences of my own decisions."

"But you can't build a relationship until forgiveness has been granted," he urged, touching her cheek with one finger.

Sheryl looked up at him, shaking her head regretfully. "I don't know if I want a relationship...."

"You have all that you need," he finished for her.

Sheryl avoided the steady deepness of his gaze and said nothing.

"And now you have to leave?"

"Yes."

Mark sighed, shoving his hat back on his head. "Can you wait until I'm done up here?" he asked, then hurried on before she could reply. "I know I'm asking a lot of you, but can you stay at Nate and Elise's until I get back? I'll be finished here in a couple of days. It will only be four more days, tops. Could you wait that much longer?"

Sheryl's heart flipped over, stopped and then began to race. She couldn't think about what he asked, didn't dare let her thoughts venture further.

Mark caught her by the arms, as if sensing her withdrawal. "I'm not asking you to stay forever, at least not yet. But something's happening here and I don't know exactly where it's going." His voice became pleading. "Sheryl, you can't just go back without having settled what you know is building between us. Stay and let's give it a chance."

Sheryl closed her eyes, fighting the temptation to drift against him, to let him kiss her like she knew he wanted to.

"Please, Sheryl. Stop fighting, stop trying to be so independent."

"I don't know, Mark. I get confused by you." She looked up at him, pleading. "You want things from me, things I'm not ready to give."

"Give-and-take is all part of normal interaction."

"But that doesn't come easily for me." She almost cried

the words out. ''Do you think this trip has been easy? Do you think it's easy for me to jump from a life with Jason, Nate and Ed, into a trip like this with a family like yours?''

''What's wrong with my family?''

''Don't get all defensive.'' She pulled away, reaching out to settle her horse, jumpy from the rising sound of their voices. ''Your family is perfect. Too perfect,'' she added softly.

''No, we're not. We fight and bicker and get angry with each other. I have just as hard a time getting along with Nate as I'm sure you used to.''

Sheryl frowned up at him, surprised to hear that.

''But we keep on going because he's family and he's been placed in my life for a reason,'' he continued.

''And what about the things that happened to me? I still haven't found the reason I lost my father, my mother.'' Sheryl halted. ''Everyone who I ever loved…''

So many of her barriers had already been broken down by this darkly handsome man. So much she'd held so tightly had been pried open, leaving her vulnerable and scared. He talked easily of forgiving things that happened in the past, but it wasn't that easy. ''You talk about God having a reason for what happens. Was Jason placed in my life for a reason? And is there a reason you and I met?''

Mark laughed shortly. ''Yes, I know there is.''

''Well, God has a sense of humor, I guess.'' She turned away from him, wanting to get this parting out of the way, afraid to prolong it. But just before she could get her foot into the stirrup, Mark pulled her back, held her by the shoulders and looked down into her eyes, his brows meeting in a frown.

''There's a plan for us, Sheryl. I know it. You belong here as much as I do. Think about that when you're trying to find a job in Edmonton.'' And without any warning he pulled her against him and caught her mouth in a brief, hard kiss.

Sheryl turned away, stifling a sob, jumped on her horse and rode and rode and rode.

* * *

Sheryl slipped her jacket on and shook out the wrinkles of her skirt. She flipped her backpack over her shoulder, hefted her suitcase off the bed and took a last, lingering look around the cabin. Was it only ten days ago she had come here?

It seemed like weeks.

Nate waited in the driveway, she could hear the low thrum of the engine of their minivan. She wished Elise could have taken her to Sweet Creek. So many unresolved feelings hung between her and Nate. Their relationship was still wary, watching and unforgiving. It was easy for Mark to talk of forgiveness, but surely something had to come from Nate?

With a sigh Sheryl left, closing the door softly behind her. Moisture drizzled down through the trees, and Sheryl picked her way carefully through the puddles, heedless of the water that misted her hair.

She came around the corner of the cabin, and Marla and Crystal jumped off their perch on the verandah rail and came to her at a dead run, calling her name.

Dropping her suitcase, Sheryl bent over to catch them against her.

"Why do you have to go, Auntie Sheryl, why don't you stay with us?" Crystal cried, clinging to her waist.

Marla said nothing, only hung on to Sheryl her face pressed against her side.

Sheryl stroked their heads as a bleakness settled inside her. How much she wanted to stay, how much she needed to leave.

"I'm sorry sweethearts, but I have to go back to my own home. That's in Edmonton." And maybe there, she thought, away from the memories, she'd have the space to seek God.

"But you can have a new home here?" Crystal cried out, giving Sheryl a shake. "Uncle Mark wants you to stay, I know he does."

Funny that those innocent words could create anew the aching hunger that had gnawed at her yesterday with each fall of the horse's hooves, taking her farther and farther away from Mark.

''It's okay, Crystal. I might come back again,'' she promised quickly.

''When?'' Marla's head shot up, her eyes expectant.

Sheryl bit her lip and shrugged lightly. ''I don't know. I have to get a job and save up some more money.'' The explanation sounded lame in Sheryl's ears, but Marla seemed to accept it.

''You could work here,'' Marla offered.

Sheryl only smiled and stroked Marla's head, a rush of love flowing through her.

The door slapped against the frame, and Elise stepped onto the verandah, holding Benjamin. Sheryl released the girls and walked across the verandah toward them.

''So, you're going, then?'' Elise said quietly, her eyes sorrowful.

Sheryl didn't trust her voice and only nodded. She held out her hands for Benjamin who leaned toward her, the drool on his chin rolling down the soft fuzz of his blue sleeper, his bright eyes wide. She wrapped her arms around his soft warmth, holding him close, inhaling the sweet baby smell of him. She swallowed down a lump of pain, not wanting to cry again, not with a long trip beside Nate ahead of her.

Benjamin placed his chubby hands against her shoulders, pushing back, his blue eyes focused on her as if memorizing her. He gurgled and grabbed the braid that hung over one shoulder.

''You are such a sweetheart,'' she murmured, pressing a kiss on his warm cheek. Giving him another quick hug, she returned him to Elise's arms.

''Run upstairs, Crystal, and get that package on the bed,'' Elise said over her shoulder. She looked back at Sheryl with a sad smile, then hooked an arm around Sheryl's neck, drawing her close. ''I sure hope we can see you again,'' Elise murmured against her hair.

Sheryl returned Elise's hug, Benjamin hanging awkwardly between them, her backpack slipping down her arm. When she straightened she was surprised to see tears in Elise's eyes.

"Please don't start," she said, her voice breaking.

"Oh, Sheryl. I had so hoped you could stay."

Sheryl shook her head. "I don't belong here, Elise. There's too much history..." And pain, she added silently.

"I guess we've just asked too much of you, me and Mark," Elise replied softly, blinking back her tears. "But you have to keep in touch. Promise me you will?"

"Maybe," Sheryl said vaguely, avoiding the steady deepness of her eyes, too much like Mark's for comfort.

The screen door flew open, Crystal and Marla tumbling through the opening. "Here, this is for you, Auntie Sheryl." Crystal ran up to Sheryl, breathless, handing her a small, wrapped parcel.

"It's just a little something for the trip." Elise shrugged, pulling Benjamin close. "I hope you enjoy it."

"You have to open it on the bus," Marla piped up.

Sheryl looked down at the brightly wrapped package, trimmed with ribbons and a bow, swallowing down a knot of emotion. She couldn't remember the last time someone had bought her a gift, and she was afraid she was going to cry again.

"Thank you, very much," she replied softly, touching the springy curls of ribbon.

The blare of a horn broke the moment. She reached out and gave Elise another quick hug and, pressing a kiss on each of the girls' heads, she rearranged her backpack on her shoulder and picked up her suitcase. With a quick wave to the assembled group she ran down the steps of the verandah, through the drizzle to the waiting van.

She threw her knapsack and suitcase in the back seat, got in, and before the door closed behind her, Nate took off. She turned to look back. Elise's and the children's figures were indistinct blurs through the water than ran down the windows, but she waved anyhow.

The van topped the rise, turned the corner onto the road, and the ranch was hidden from view.

Chapter Twelve

Sheryl turned around, buckling up her seat belt, fussing with it, straightening her coat, trying to avoid Nate's gaze. The atmosphere in the van was heavy, weighted with memories and recriminations that neither had dared voice over the past week.

Finally she settled into the seat and stared resolutely at the windshield wipers slapping back and forth across the window, watching familiar landmarks slip by, now blurred with the haze of rain.

The silence bothered her. She and Nate had spent many years together, and now they couldn't even share more than a few mumbled questions and answers. It wasn't right. Especially after spending three days with the Andrews family and their constant chatter, the silence in the van felt unnatural.

''I'd like to thank you for letting me stay in the cabin, Nate,'' she said finally.

Nate only nodded in reply.

She bit her lip and tried again. ''Did you visit Ed while we were gone?''

At that Nate turned to her, his mouth curled up in derision. ''Spare me the false concern, Sheryl.''

His comment, all too familiar, wouldn't have hurt a week ago. She had grown soft in the past few days. ''It wasn't false concern,'' she said as her fingers tightened around the buckle.

''You were here ten days,'' he replied looking ahead again, his jaw clenched. ''You managed to see him three times.''

''You want it both ways, don't you, Nate.'' She drew in a deep breath. ''You've accused me of not finishing a job, and because I did, I couldn't see Ed as often as I might have.''

Nate bit his lip and changed tack. ''Why did you go on the pack trip?''

''I was invited.''

''The girls seemed to enjoy the trip. Although they said you didn't spend much time with them.'' He glanced at her, his eyes slightly narrowed. ''They said you had someone else you wanted to be with.''

''As in?'' As if she didn't know.

''Mark.''

''Well I guess now we're getting down to what you really wanted to talk about.''

He turned on her, his face angry. ''He's my friend, brother-in-law and partner and that makes his concerns mine.''

''I think Mark can take care of himself.''

''Mark is a different man from the kind of man you're used to....''

''How do you know what I'm used to? I've only ever had one boyfriend.'' She smiled derisively, ''And *one* husband.''

''The worst man in the county.''

Sheryl said nothing to that.

''Mark is a good man, Sheryl,'' Nate continued, his tone condescending. ''He's a sincere Christian.''

''Something I've never been, right?''

''And I've found out that marriage is difficult enough,'' he interrupted. ''And if one partner is a Christian and the other isn't, well that just makes it even more difficult.''

''He hasn't proposed to me, Nate.''

''Mark's a romantic,'' Nate continued, a white line edging his lips. ''I know he's fascinated with you.'' He spared her a brief glance. ''You're an attractive girl. I know where he's headed with you, even if you don't seem to care.''

Mark's words drifted over the anger that slipped so easily

into her mind at Nate's words. ''Anger drains you, Sheryl, it eats away at you until nothing is left.'' She didn't want to hear them. Didn't want to let go of her anger, because then what would she have left? Only sadness and an emptiness that yawned ahead of her, bleak and unwelcoming.

But Nate wasn't finished. ''When Mark bought the ranch he made plans to live on it with someone else…''

''Tanya,'' Sheryl said with quiet determination.

''So you know the story.''

Sheryl nodded, her hands clenched tightly together.

''Then you know what he is going through right now. You know how hard it must be for him to have met someone who seems to have the same interests as he does.''

Sheryl turned on him at that. ''What do you mean when you say *seems?*''

Nate plunged a hand through his hair with a quick sigh. ''You helped him with the haying, you went on the pack trip. Mark thinks you enjoy that kind of work.''

Sheryl shook her head in dismay. ''Your idea that I was a lazy girl who never lifted a finger is old, tired and untrue.''

''I didn't say that.''

''No, of course you didn't. You never come right out and say what you think, you skirt around it with vague words.'' Sheryl slowly unclenched her fists, almost afraid of her anger. ''Why don't you just come right out and admit to yourself that your feelings for me aren't the kind a Christian should have.''

Nate bit his lip; his eyes narrowed as he seemed to fight some internal battle. ''I've never known exactly what I've felt for you, Sheryl.''

More ambiguous words, more pieces to try to fit together.

Sheryl looked away, fixing her eyes on the hills that undulated away from them. This whole trip had been a waste of time. She would have been better off to have stayed in Edmonton.

And what about Mark?

Sheryl pressed her fingers against her lips. She couldn't

think about Mark. Because much as Nate's words cut and hurt, she knew he was right.

''He asked me to wait for him, Nate,'' she said softly, wanting to prick his self-righteous hauteur. ''Just before we rode away, he said that something was happening between us and that he wanted time to figure out what it really was.''

Nate turned suddenly at that, eyes wide. ''And what was your answer?''

''I'm in your van, heading out to Williams Lake,'' she replied, her voice tight. ''I don't know why you see it necessary to point out how unsuitable I am for him. But somehow, by showing me that he cares for me and by giving me what you and Ed never would, Mark has shown me, more clearly than you and Ed ever could, that I don't deserve him.'' She looked down, rubbing her hands over her skirt, forcing herself to relax. She wished she could appeal to their past, to the part of him that might remember rides up to a slide, finding a frying pan.

''I left because I know even better than you do that I can't give him what he needs.'' And as she spoke the words Nate had only hinted at, her anger seemed to dissipate, leaving only sorrow that even when they agreed on something, she ended up feeling vanquished.

Nate blinked, stupefied. He opened his mouth to speak, seemed to think better of it and looked ahead again.

As they drove, the silent swish of the wipers vied with the splashing of the tires through the puddles in the rocky road. The mountains, misted and gloomy, hung over Sheryl's shoulder, and as the river plateau broadened, she couldn't help turn for one last glimpse of them.

An hour later they pulled into the parking lot of the hospital. Sheryl swallowed, a heaviness weighing her down. Her first impulse was to tell Nate she wanted to wait in the van instead of seeing Ed. But deep within her she hungered for what he had offered on their first visit and much as she doubted his sincerity, she still yearned for it. Mark's love she couldn't give in to, but the love her stepfather belatedly offered her was her due.

She drew a deep breath, opened the door and stepped out into the rain.

"I've got to see the doctor," Nate said as he hobbled down the wet sidewalk to the front doors of the hospital. "I'll meet you at Dad's room." His tone was brusque and he didn't look at her.

She followed Nate until without a second glance he headed to the outpatient section of the hospital. Sheryl watched him go, wondering again what single event, if any, had created such antagonism.

With a sigh, she shook the moisture off her coat, shoved her hands in the pockets of her jeans and walked away, her measured tread squeaking lightly on the waxed floor. Each step brought her nearer to Ed, each footfall seemed to be a harbinger of an epiphany.

Sheryl knew her experiences in the mountain had buffeted her protective cover, had exposed her own weaknesses. And now what would her reaction be to her stepfather, given what happened?

He sat in the same place he had during her previous visit, the dull light softening the harsh angles of his now-thin face. Today he looked more alert, his eyes brighter, and when he saw her, his smile was a little broader.

"Sheryl..." He lifted his good hand and held it out to her.

She paused in the doorway, trying to let this actual image of Ed drift past her own memories.

All that was left was this old broken man, this old lonely man. She took a steadying breath and stepped into the room. He looked up at her entrance, and a tentative smile lifted one corner of his mouth.

"I've...been waiting." He spoke his words carefully, each sound an effort. "Please...sit...here."

Sheryl pulled her purse close to her and once again sat across from her stepfather, studying him with other eyes, other emotions. The sorrow that had engulfed her up in the mountains seemed to have smudged the clarity of her memories and feelings.

"Glad…you…came." Ed smiled his crooked smile at her, one side of his face staying resolutely in place. He tried to reach out to her, but Sheryl kept her hands stiffly folded in her lap.

But as she looked at his face, she saw sorrow and regret etched clearly in the lines. She remembered the tears he had shed the last visit she'd made, when she'd told him of Jason's death.

She remembered the words of love spoken each time and felt her own tense shoulders sag. It was so much work to keep up her anger against him. Each time she saw him he became more pathetic and less powerful.

He pushed himself up in his chair, his pillow falling off the chair. Sheryl got off her chair and picked it up, crouching down to tuck it between the metal arm of the chair and his frail body. As she did, she felt his good hand on her hair.

"I wanted…to love you," he said softly.

Sheryl looked up at him. "What do you mean by that?" she asked. "Why do you talk of love now?"

"Wrong…Sheryl…I've been so wrong."

Sheryl edged backward, lifting herself up onto her chair, her eyes never leaving his face. "How have you been wrong, Dad?" she whispered, wishing he could speak clearer, faster.

"When you were little…you were so strong…" Ed leaned back and sighed. "You loved your dad so much…I was jealous."

Sheryl lifted her eyebrows. Sad that she had never considered that aspect, she thought. Looking back, it made sense.

"Is that why I was never allowed to talk about him?"

Ed frowned. "I loved your mom…she was…everything… Nate's mom wasn't. Soft…warm…kind. I was…everything Bill Reilly…wasn't. I…know I never…treated her…like I should…." He paused, his brow furrowed in concentration.

Sheryl clasped her hands around her knees, mentally urging the words out of him.

"I was…jealous of your dad…I gave you…a home…a place…and you had…to move because of him. I don't…know if your…mom ever loved me…the same way."

"She wasn't in love with you?"

Ed shook his head sorrowfully. "She didn't love me…like I loved her." He looked up at Sheryl, his mouth curved up in a smile of memory. "She seemed to love you more. I was jealous of you. I thought you were spoiled…willful." His voice grew quiet. "I was so wrong. I'm so…sorry."

"I tried, Dad, I really did." She felt a need to tell him that, to make it clear that it wasn't all her fault.

"I know now." He reached out for her. "I've learned a lot…from Mark…from Elise…about love."

Sheryl closed her eyes. Mark again. Perfect, loving Mark. How much farther was he to be put beyond her reach?

"They showed me…loving is giving…it's letting yourself become weak." Ed sighed, a soft exhalation. "I didn't give…to your mother…to you…like I should have…like God did to me. I have been so…wrong."

Sheryl bent her head, still afraid to look at Ed and take what he so belatedly offered. It wasn't enough to fill the emptiness of her life, but it would take away the hollowness of it.

His hand touched hers and with her head still down, she wrapped her fingers around his. They squeezed hers with surprising strength. She looked at his hands, the raised veins, the heavy knuckles of a man who had worked hard. It had been difficult for him, as well. She knew he'd had a desire to get ahead. These ambitions were universal. It was just that Ed's were stronger than some, his motivation more powerful. How he had gone about it was questionable, but after working for a living, she understood so much better its daily struggle.

"Sheryl, I always loved you…just not the right way. I shouldn't…have driven you away. Can you please forgive me?"

Again Mark's words came back to her. "You can't build a relationship until forgiveness has been granted."

She looked up at him and saw such pain and regret in his face that it pulled at the bleak emptiness in her, opening it. She had no father, mother or husband. No one. And now a small part of her past was being given back to her.

She thought back to eight years ago, to the last days she'd spent with Ed and Nate before she'd left with Jason. She had always known that the decision to marry Jason was hers and hers alone. Suddenly she realized it was no longer right to put all the fault for the mess of her life on his shoulders.

"Jesus told us we had to forgive seventy times seven," she whispered suddenly. "I haven't filled my quota yet."

Ed smiled tremulously. He could say nothing, but the hand that clutched hers and the tears that drifted down his sunken cheeks said more than his halting words ever could.

"You always had…a big heart." He shook his head as his tears flowed more freely now.

Sheryl felt as if that same heart was being squeezed down to a small knot, and suddenly she leaned over and kissed Ed on the cheek. He reached up and held her neck, and it seemed only natural to put her arms around him.

Sheryl hugged him carefully, feeling the changes her eyes had noted. It suddenly struck her that he, too, had lost much.

"I didn't want…you to marry…Jason."

"I know, Daddy, I know," she said, her voice thick. She pulled away, reaching into her pocket for a handkerchief and came up with the same red polka-dotted one Mark had given her just the day before. She quickly blew her nose, wiped the spilled tears, a pain knifing through her as she caught the scent of Mark on the scrap of material. "I made a mistake leaving with Jason," she said, her voice hoarse with emotion. Sheryl stopped at that, afraid that if she spoke more she would be putting unnecessary burdens on his frail shoulders. "I guess you need to know that what happened was as much my fault. When my mother died…"

She shouldn't have ventured that far, she thought, swallowing down the tears. Ed could not help her; she needed to be strong on her own.

"It wasn't your...fault...Sheryl. She always loved you... always."

Sheryl wiped her face once more, sitting up. As she sucked in a deep breath, controlling her sorrow, she let Ed's words flow over her. She had received love, in different ways, she had just been too full of anger to see what had been happening. It wasn't all her fault, she knew that, but she also knew she wasn't innocent.

"Thank you for telling me that, Dad."

Ed smiled at her, reaching out for her hand. She took his again, tracing the blue veins. He still wore his wedding ring, and Sheryl rubbed it lightly.

"I have to also confess that you were always right about Jason. I should never have married him, and I admit that I did it all on my own." Sheryl paused, hoping he would understand her confession. "What happened was my own fault. I tried to explain that to you in the letter I sent."

Ed frowned, straightening. "Which...letter?"

Sheryl shook her head, not wanting to destroy the moment of harmony between them by bringing up something he had obviously forgotten.

"Did you send me a letter?" he continued.

"Hi, Dad."

Sheryl jumped as Nate's overly loud voice broke the moment. He hobbled into the room, the clump of his crutches the only sound.

Ed frowned as if wanting to ask more questions, but Sheryl turned to her stepbrother.

"So what did the doctor have to say?" Not that she cared, but she needed to change the subject. Nate's entrance couldn't have been better planned.

Nate glanced quickly at her, his expression wary as if he didn't quite trust her. "I have to be on this walking cast for another two weeks, and then it can come off."

"Good thing...haying is over," Ed put in.

Nate looked away and nodded.

Ed turned to Sheryl. "How long…are you staying yet?"

"I'm leaving tonight."

Ed frowned and looked back at Nate who merely shrugged. "So soon?" Ed asked of Sheryl.

"I have to, Dad. I'm taking some courses, and if I don't get them done, I can't be admitted to university this fall." Sheryl spoke hurriedly, hoping her explanation would satisfy him. His words sounded suddenly empty and mundane to her, sitting across from her dying stepfather.

"I thought you…were moving back home?"

Home. The word sounded so comfortable. She had no home in Edmonton, but she knew she could not live here.

"Sheryl only came up to see you, because she knew that it was only a matter of time for you." Nate said.

"And I haven't…conveniently died yet." Ed smiled, but Sheryl couldn't share the macabre joke.

"I'll try to come back again, Dad," she reassured him. If I can get a job, she added silently, wondering how she was going to work up the nerve to ask Nate to pay for her bus ticket to get her home. She didn't have enough cash to pay for it herself. "I'll keep in touch."

Ed nodded and turned back to Nate. "Did Mark…go to the upper…pastures?"

"A few days ago. He should be back by tomorrow or the day after if all goes well."

"How much…hay did you…get?"

"We did really well. Our banker will be pleased, anyhow. Looks like things are finally pulling ahead a little for us."

Sheryl smiled to herself. Bankers and crops and weather. The eternal tug-of-war that went on with ranching. Nate's and Ed's conversation hearkened back to many made over supper tables at the end of the day. When she'd lived at home, she'd been a part of it—how many bales today, how much do we need to put up, will we have to borrow money to buy more, will we have enough to sell, will the rain stay away, will cattle prices hold?

Ed lay back, his face pale. Sweat beaded his brow, his weariness obvious to Sheryl.

She let him and Nate talk for a while, and after a few minutes reminded Nate that the bus would be leaving soon.

''Okay,'' he replied, getting up, still avoiding any eye contact with her. ''I'll wait for you in the van.''

He left and Sheryl turned to Ed, surprised again at the change that had occurred from her first visit to now. A certain lightness and peace had entered a small part of her life, and she treasured it. One more time she leaned over to hug Ed, this time her motions easier, more spontaneous.

''I love…you, Sheryl.'' He drew back, cradling her cheek in his one good hand. ''But you have to know…God loves you more. Let Him love you…take His love…take it and live….''

Sheryl only nodded, afraid to speak, afraid to think too hard of the supreme irony of finding peace with him just before he was to die. ''I'll keep in touch with you, Dad,'' she whispered. She kissed him again. ''I love you.''

He smiled at that, nodding his thanks.

Sheryl straightened, turned and resolutely left the room. She walked down the hall, through the doors and stepped into the van that Nate had driven up to the door, her movements mechanical, her thoughts fully occupied.

Maybe the fact that she might never see him again gave his words so much weight. Maybe it was his closeness to death that made her mull over what he had said about God. But as they drove down the rain-soaked street, Ed's words resonated through her head.

They reached the bus depot, and much to Sheryl's surprise Nate paid for her bus ticket. She thanked him and, flinging her backpack over her shoulder, picked up her small suitcase and walked over to the empty chairs in the waiting area.

Her bus wouldn't leave for another hour.

Nate clumped behind her, and after hesitating a moment he sat down in the empty chair across from her, holding his crutches across his leg.

''Here,'' he said, handing her a few bills. ''Some cash for the trip. You'll need to eat I guess. Wages for the haying season,'' he told her gruffly.

Sheryl pocketed it, thankful for the small buffer the money would give her when she got home. ''I appreciate that,'' she said.

Nate nodded in acknowledgment, his fingers clenching and unclenching the crutches.

Nate sighed, fidgeted then blurted out, ''What did Dad say about the letter?''

Sheryl frowned. ''What letter?''

''You sent a letter to him asking to come back. I heard you asking about it. What did he say?''

''How did you know what my letter said? Dad didn't seem to.''

Nate turned red. ''I couldn't let him see it.''

Sheryl's mouth fell open. ''You read my letter? You kept it from Ed?'' She blinked, feeling the full extent of his repressed fury. ''Why?''

''After all you did to him, to me, you took what we were offering and threw it all back in our faces when you took up with Jason. You didn't want to be a part of our family, you never wanted to help.''

''I was ten years old when I came…''

''And at your age I was already pitching bales, stuking, riding fence.'' Nate stared at her, his blue eyes so much like his father's. But where Ed's had been softened by sorrow, Nate's were hardened with anger. ''I was fourteen when you came and in all the years I worked side by side with my father, he never cut me the slack he cut you. And how do you thank him? You take off with the one guy guaranteed to make him so angry that I had to suffer for it. And then you have the nerve to ask if you could come back.''

Nate spat the words at her so quickly Sheryl barely had a chance to absorb the shock of them before he threw more at her.

''I thought you knew how I felt, how I cared about you,

but all you could think of was ways to hurt us. I loved you, but I don't think you even knew."

Sheryl's breath left her, she stared at him, the busyness of the bus terminal receding in a rush of black, with Nate's face at its center.

What was he talking about?

"Nate, I don't understand." She grasped for coherency, trying desperately to make sense of what he had just spilled on her. "You said you loved me?"

"To my shame, yes." Nate's fingers on his crutches were almost white. "I loved you from the moment you were old enough. But you made it clear that you preferred Jason's company."

"I never knew, Nate." Sheryl stared at him in disbelief. "I really didn't know."

"Well neither does Elise or anyone else." He tapped his fingers against the wood of his crutches as he looked past her, not seeing. "I love Elise, and I'll do anything for her. I don't want her to know this. It's not something I'm proud of."

Sheryl pulled her hands over her face, as if trying to absorb what he had just said. Casting back over the past events, looks, comments thrown her way, it now made sense. Why didn't she see it before?

His words seemed to hover, buffeted by the emotions that swirled around both of them. But Sheryl wasn't finished.

"And what about my letter?"

Nate looked away, chewing his lip. Behind him a neon sign flashed red, then white, then red, each change synchronized with the pounding of Sheryl's heart.

"You knew what was in it..." she urged.

He turned to her then. "Yes I read it. I had to protect my dad from more hurt. I needed to know what you wanted after three years of silence."

"And you found out." Sheryl was surprised at how quiet her voice came out. "You found out what I had to live with. You read my pleas, my fear. You coldheartedly sent it back. I had to live with the consequences." She simply stared at him, her arms clasped tightly across her stomach, her fingers clenching the thin fabric of her coat. ''Do you know what I had to live with after that?''

Nate tried to shrug. Sorrow coiled like a snake through Sheryl, anger twisting her face. She drew back, and with quick, jerky motions pulled off her jacket and rolled up the sleeve of her shirt, exposing the two-inch scar on the inside of her upper arm. It was only a fine line now, a row of dots marching up either side of it from the sutures.

''Beer bottle, busted across the bedpost,'' she said, her voice flat as she struggled for control, remembering the pain, the humiliation. ''He discovered I had hidden my tips from him. It was my grocery money for that month. He blew it in an hour.'' She ignored his look of surprise as she drew up her skirt, exposing her thigh. ''This one is a souvenir of the one time he picked up the mail and found the letter that you decided to send back.'' She bent her head as she dropped her skirt. ''I'm sorry, but the broken arm doesn't show, or the bruises from the accident when—'' Her voice broke and she pressed her fingers against her mouth, wishing, praying, her silent pleas desperate.

Nate sat still as a statue while Sheryl battled her emotions. Around them life swirled on—people talking and laughing, saying hello and farewell. A baby cried and a father hushed it. Someone dropped a glass bottle, the brittle sound of smashing glass breaking in on Sheryl's pain.

''Last call for the five o'clock bus to Quesnel and Prince George.''

Sheryl glanced over at Nate, anger and bitterness vying with her sorrow and regret. ''That's what I had to live with. That was the consequence of your sending my letter back.'' As she watched him, she saw his face tighten, and he bit his lips, his gaze still downcast, his hands clutching his crutches.

Sheryl got up as the tinny voice over the intercom propelled her into movement. She bent over and picked up her knapsack.

''Sheryl.'' Nate's voice made her straighten. She looked

over at him, wondering what he would have to say. Their eyes met. Was that pain she saw in his eyes? Regret? Sorrow? Or only her deep desire that he show some kind of emotion? But he said nothing more, his face devoid of expression.

For a moment she stared at Nate as he sat, still holding on to his crutches as if they were his only defense.

Sheryl drew in a trembling breath, flipped her knapsack over her shoulder and walked away without a backward glance.

Chapter Thirteen

The steady thump of the wheels as they hit the frost heaves on the Yellowhead would have lulled Sheryl to sleep at any other time. But each time she closed her eyes thoughts, memories and events flipped and whirled around her mind like a kaleidoscope.

Almost two weeks had passed since she and Mark had driven down this road, and she felt as if she had lived a lifetime.

With a resigned sigh she turned her head and looked out the tinted windows watching the fields flow past. The grain had already turned a pale gold, and here and there swaths of hay lay, awaiting the baler.

In a month the harvest would begin, and back at Sweet Creek, Mark would have one more cut of hay. A month after that the cattle would be ready to be brought home, calves weaned and shipped. When she'd lived in Sweet Creek she had helped with each part of the operation.

In her mind she already saw Mark on his horse, herding the cattle down the trails from the far pastures, she could hear the din of the cows and calves bawling as they got separated for weaning, taste the dust of their milling feet as they were squeezed down to smaller and smaller pens until they were finally run through the chute one at a time for their shots and treatments.

And what would she be doing at that time?

Sheryl closed her eyes, trying to alleviate the momentary flash of panic. She was headed home to no job and an apartment she knew she had to move out of before it got condemned. All she had to show for eight years of living away from Sweet Creek was a pile of schoolbooks and mismatched furniture. She hoped she could find a job. Government and businesses all were downsizing, and the last time she had gone job hunting, there were thirty applicants for each of the jobs she had applied for.

I won't be scared, she thought, biting her lip. She looked down at her knapsack and pulled out the gift Elise and the girls had given her. She hadn't unwrapped it yet, preferring to savor the mystery of it and to just enjoy the notion that someone had thought enough about her to set something aside and wrap it up.

Now would be as good a time as any to unwrap it, she thought, carefully peeling off the ribbons and putting them in her knapsack. The tape was next, each piece meticulously pulled off, and then with a smile she folded back the paper.

A couple of bars of soap wrapped in a pretty handkerchief and a worn book. She sniffed the soap and turned over the book.

It was a Bible. Her old one.

Inside it was a short note from Elise. Sheryl unfolded it and read it. Elise and the girls had found the Bible when they'd cleaned up the cabin for her arrival. They thought she might like to have it back. On the bottom of the letter Crystal and Marla had scrawled their names, and Elise had signed the letter simply ''Elise'' and put their phone number and address on the bottom.

Sheryl folded up the letter and set it aside. She opened the Bible to the flyleaf, tracing the inscription there with trembling fingers. Ed's delicate handwriting, so at odds with his character, showed that the Bible had been presented to her on the day of her mother's marriage to him, sixteen years ago, and given to her with the hope that they might become a family that feared God.

They had feared God, at least Sheryl had learned to, she thought, flipping the delicate parchment pages of the Bible. And as for the family part…

Sheryl sighed lightly. It was no longer as easily decided who and what to blame. She had other experiences and other views to meld in with her own. She smoothed out a wrinkled page, her eyes falling on a childish scrawl in the margin. It simply said, "I love God and he loves me."

She remembered again the peace that had flowed over her whenever she'd prayed with the Andrews family and knew it wasn't just their presence that had created that.

How she longed for that peace now, she thought, turning the pages randomly, glancing at passages, remembering the cadences and the rhythms of words buried deep in her past.

She came to the New Testament. Partway through she found a paper wedged between the pages of 2 Corinthians. Curious to see what she had put there, she opened it up. It was an old church bulletin dated the same week she and Jason had left. She glanced over the familiar names, the announcements. Suddenly she noticed under the heading "Church Family," "Welcome to the Andrews family who will be moving from Vanderhoef and will be making their home here with their children, Brad, Elaine and Elise." Her heart thudded heavily in her chest as she read and reread it. She hadn't realized that their coming had been that close. Missed each other by days!

Her throat felt dry as she folded it up again, her fingers shaking.

God has a plan, Mark had said, a reason for things happening the way they did. What would have happened had she waited? Would she have met Mark? What would he have thought of her?

She knew the answer to that. Cocky, rebellious and angry. He would have had nothing to do with her then. So what had changed? She had spent eight years with Jason, she had been refused sanctuary from her father…correction her stepbrother…

Sheryl slipped the paper back into the Bible, trying to sort out her confused feelings. She should hate her stepbrother for what he did.

But somehow she couldn't. She had spent too much time hating, fighting down fears and trying to be strong. It only took from her and left her feeling empty.

Sheryl looked down at the Bible again, her eyes glancing over the familiar passage, and suddenly her eye caught it. A verse with a star inked beside it. God's words: "My grace is sufficient for you, for my power is made perfect in weakness." And then a little further on Paul speaking: "When I am weak then I am strong."

It didn't seem to make sense and yet it did. When she had broken down in Mark's arms, when she'd allowed someone to give to her, allowed herself to become weak, that was when she had felt renewal come into her.

When she'd allowed herself to forgive her stepfather, when she had confessed her part in what had happened, shown her weakness, then she'd felt peace and love overcome her.

Releasing her breath in a cleansing sigh, Sheryl laid her head back, her hand resting on the words she had just read. She didn't know what lay ahead, but she felt she would just have to trust that somehow maybe Mark and Ed were right. Maybe God did have a reason for things happening the way they did.

"Tory, this is Sheryl." She rubbed her forehead with her index finger, clutching the handset of the pay phone as she stared at the building across the street. If this was any indication of some great plan of God, she wondered if maybe the blueprint wasn't upside down.

The blackened hulk of her apartment block stared back at her, the acrid smell of smoke still lingering in the air. It had burned down last night, she was told. Had she come home when she'd originally planned she might have been able to salvage her books, the expensive correspondence courses that she had scrimped to buy.

"Hi, Sheryl." Tory's excited voice reassured her that she had done the right thing in calling. "How are you?"

Sheryl shook her head, grimacing. "Don't ask."

"Well, where are you?"

"Standing across from what's left of my apartment block..."

"Oh, no!" Tory's gasp came clearly across the line. "I wondered if that was your place when I heard it on the news this morning."

"Well, wonder no more. I've officially joined the ranks of the homeless...." Sheryl stopped herself, vowing she wasn't going to cry over a pile of rubble that had never been a home to her, only a dwelling.

"You stay right there. Don't move. I'll come and get you right away."

"No, Tory, that's okay. I just..." Just needed to connect with someone, needed to talk to you, she added to herself, and I didn't dare ask.

"Sheryl," Tory said her voice angry. "Don't you dare even protest or I'll get even angrier. Now promise me you won't move?"

Sheryl nodded. She couldn't speak.

"Sheryl?"

"I won't," she whispered. "Thanks." She hung up the phone, biting her lip. *I won't cry,* she thought, pressing her fist against her mouth as she sagged back against the telephone booth, staring at the mess across the road. *I hated living there, it was a horrible place.* But it had held all she'd had of eight years of her life. It had held her books and clothes and all her personal things.

Concentrate on something else, Sheryl thought. Count how many seconds it will take Tory to get here. But she didn't know where Tory lived. Had never asked her. Tory was a coworker, and any overture at friendship had come from her not Sheryl. Sheryl had never asked her about her husband, about her life.

What an empty life she had lived the past few months.

Come to think of it, the past few years. Jason had sucked everything out of her, had kept her from forming any kind of relationships.

The roar of a car engine made her look up. A small white vehicle screeched to a halt in front of her, and before it even rocked back, Tory was out and flying around the hood of the car.

"Sheryl, oh, you poor girl,"

Sheryl felt herself enfolded in arms that clung and hands that stroked. "You come and stay with us, girl. We have room. You come with me," Tory murmured over and over again.

And then Sheryl began to cry.

"Mr. Carlton's office, Sheryl speaking," Sheryl tucked the phone under one ear, typed the message on her computer screen and clicked Print, directing it to Dan's printer in his office. "Thank you, Mrs. Donalds. I'll see he gets the message right away."

She got approximately five characters typed when the phone rang again. A quick glance at the clock told her it was 5:10 and if she didn't watch it she would end up talking to another one of Dan's clients past suppertime.

It was Tory.

"How's it going, girl?" Tory asked, yelling into the phone.

In spite of Tory's raised voice, Sheryl could barely hear her over the background noise of the mechanic's shop. Compressors rumbled, pneumatic drills sang, and someone was clanging on a piece of metal.

Shortly after Sheryl had left for Sweet Creek, Tory's husband, Mike, purchased the shop where he worked, and Tory gladly had left her job at Dave's bar to help.

"Just fine," Sheryl said, raising her own voice. "I'm getting the hang of things."

"Great. I'm so glad Mike kept that lawyer's business card. I knew it would come in handy. Hey, before I left for the garage I got a call from someone named Elise. She just phoned to say hello and asked me to give you the message. Is this one of the Sweet Creek folk?''

Sheryl paused, her heart beginning an errant rhythm. ''Did she say what she wanted?'' Sheryl asked.

''No. Just phoned to chat.'' Tory spoke to someone, then she said, ''Hey, I got to run. I'll be working late, but I put a casserole in the oven. You'll be okay?''

''I'll be fine, Tory.''

''Good. See you later, eh?'' Tory clicked off, and Sheryl hung up the phone feeling slightly dazed.

She had phoned Elise the day after she'd moved in with Tory and Mike, to give her the number just in case something happened with Ed. Nate had answered the phone. The next day Sheryl went for a job interview and the day after started this job. Then she had called again to give them her work number. That time she got the answering machine.

''Sheryl, it's past quitting time.''

Sheryl looked up into the grinning face of one of the law students, Jordan Calder.

''I've just got this letter to finish, then I'll go.''

''Sheryl, has anyone ever told you that you work too hard?'' Jordan laid her arms across the smoked glass partition that separated Sheryl's desk from the hallway and rested her chin on them, her brown eyes narrowed. ''If you're not working late, it's evening courses at the university. You put in more hours than I do, and I'm supposed to be almost-a-lawyer. Is relaxation not in your vocabulary?''

Sheryl said nothing, only continued typing. ''I just want to do a good job,'' she murmured, frowning at Dan's scribbled note across a letter.

''Dan's been practically drooling since you came. You could ask for double what you earn now and he'd give it to you.'' Jordan finger combed her short hair, the dark strands falling perfectly into place.

''I'm making enough.'' Sheryl ignored her comment and turned the letter to Jordan. ''You've read enough of Dan's scribbles, what do you suppose that says?''

Jordan took the paper from her, squinting as she turned it first this way then that. ''It's getting clearer. It says, 'Go home.'''

''I doubt that.'' Sheryl laughed reaching for the paper.

''I'll hand it over tomorrow.'' Jordan held the paper out of reach and, bending around, switched Sheryl's monitor off, ignoring her polite protest. ''The way you type, you can have it done in a couple of minutes on Monday. Now put the cover on the computer. The weekend is calling.''

Accepting defeat, Sheryl stood, slipped on her sweater and closed the file on her desk.

''Someday you'll thank me for this,'' Jordan said, waiting as Sheryl walked past her. ''Believe me, work isn't everything.''

Sheryl smiled as they walked down the now-empty hall toward the reception area. Jordan Calder was not a typical student. She worked as much as she thought she should and didn't have the same hunger that usually typified student lawyers. And once she was off work, Jordan was fun and good for a few laughs.

Living with Jason had not given her much chance for social interaction. He had tended to discourage any relationship she might have had with anyone but himself. Since coming back from Sweet Creek she'd been given the time and space to rediscover relationships both with other people and with God. She was finding out who Sheryl really was.

''You're lucky Dan was out today, otherwise I'm sure I'd have to help you finagle your way out of yet another request for a date,'' Jordan said, punching the ground floor number as they stepped into the elevator. ''I've never seen him so stuck on anyone before.''

Sheryl let the comment pass. ''He's a good boss.''

''Of course he is, Sheryl,'' Jordan reassured her, tying the belt of her long, black trench coat. ''I'm not trying to cast aspersions on his sterling character. It's just that he can't keep his eyes off you.''

''I'm sure.''

Jordan rolled her eyes. "Goodness, girl, I've never met anyone so obviously unaware of her own good looks. If you dropped that cool and composed act you'd have guys hanging all over you."

"I'll keep it then. That's the last thing I need."

"Oh, don't tell me someone as gorgeous as you is a man hater?" Jordan wailed. "I hate it when that happens."

"I'm not a man hater."

"'I just don't want that complication.' As if guys are some kind of problem to figure out. I tell you, girl, this nineties garbage is really starting to get on my nerves." The elevator stopped, and the doors swished open. Jordan flung her purse over her shoulder and picked up her briefcase as they stepped out, their footsteps echoing on the marble floor of the foyer. "Now me, I've had to claw my way to the bottom of this little law firm. I'm allowed to be disillusioned and cynical. You're not."

"Men aren't a complication, Jordan. It's just that they want so much and give so little," Sheryl said as she paused to button up her coat.

Jordan narrowed her eyes at Sheryl. "You're basing your judgment on a narrow experience. There're lots of generous, good-hearted guys out there."

Jason wasn't, thought Sheryl, shoving her hands in her coat pockets. Ed wasn't, Nate wasn't...

Her thoughts quit as a gust of wind swirled through the foyer. The doors were shoved open and a tall figure strode into the entrance. Long brown hair hung on his shoulders, his jean jacket sat easily on broad shoulders, his long legs easily covered the distance between them.

Sheryl's heart leaped to her throat. Her purse slipped out of numb fingers spilling on the floor as she took a step toward him.

"Sheryl, what's wrong?" Jordan stopped, glanced at Sheryl's eager face, then at the man she stared at hungrily.

He paused, pulled a handkerchief from his pocket and as he wiped his nose he glanced around.

It wasn't Mark.

"Are you okay?"

"Yeah." Sheryl's shoulders sagged. Feeling slightly dazed she looked around, then, at her purse lying on the floor.

"You know that man?"

Sheryl bent over to pick up her purse, hiding her burning cheeks. "I thought he was an old friend."

Jordan slanted a skeptical look at Sheryl, retrieved a brush from the floor and handed it to her. "One of your 'give so little' friends?"

Sheryl drew in a deep breath as she straightened and shook her head at her lapse.

"I thought for a minute you were going to throw yourself at him..."

"Please stop, Jordan," Sheryl pleaded, feeling bereft and close to tears. She clutched her purse close to her, biting her lip.

Jordan laid her hand on Sheryl's shoulder. "I'm sorry. It's just that you're normally so cool and collected." She squeezed, then let go. "Anyhow, what are you doing this weekend? I've got tickets for a concert on Sunday."

"I don't think so." Sheryl flashed her an apologetic grin, pulling herself together. "I want to head to church on Sunday." She had been attending for a couple of weeks, finding peace and comfort there that she wouldn't at a concert.

"Probably a better idea," Jordan shrugged. "Well if you change your mind you know my number." She patted her shoulder once more, then turned and left.

Sheryl walked in the opposite direction to her bus stop, still feeling shaky. Mark was on her mind so much any little thing would bring back the memories—jeans on long legs, cowboy boots, a pickup truck on the city streets. One of the boys stocking shelves in the local grocery store was almost as tall as Mark and wore his hair just as long. Sheryl stopped going there because every time she saw him her heart stopped.

Living with Tory and Mike eased some of the emptiness that pervaded her life since she left Sweet Creek, but not totally eradicated it. Each time Tory said goodbye to Mike their leave-taking was reluctant, and Sheryl took painful pleasure in watching them, even though it was such an aching reminder of her own lack.

Loneliness was nothing new to her. But the angry loneliness of coming home to an empty apartment when she'd lived with Jason, or the sad loneliness that was her constant companion after the accident had never been as unmitigated, as heart-wrenching as the emptiness she felt when she'd arrived in Edmonton.

It frustrated her. Tory and Mike treated her almost like a daughter. She finally had a decent job that paid her enough so that she could attend evening courses at the University of Alberta.

But it wasn't enough. The courses left her feeling flat, the job was exciting but she felt stifled sitting inside day after day. The city was starting to get on her nerves with its busyness, its impersonal attitude.

The city bus sighed to a halt in front of her, and Sheryl climbed in, forcing herself past the people packed in the front of the bus to the back where there was usually a little more room.

She clung to a pole, staring out of the window as the buildings flashed past, her mind traveling with ease to a place surrounded by purple mountains, broken by creeks and rivers.

They would be baling again, she mused, thinking of Mark driving a tractor, a bandana around his head holding his long hair out of his face. It made her smile.

She wondered how he was doing. Now that Elise had called, maybe she would return the call. She could casually mention Mark's name, and she knew Elise would take off from there.

If she dared.

Two quick jabs of Mark's jackknife cut the last of the twine on the large, round hay bale suspended in front of him. With stiff fingers, he picked up all the ends, and in one jerk he pulled the twine loose. Backing up, he motioned to Nate, in the cab of the tractor, to drop the bale into the feeder.

The cows were milling about, bawling, trying to get past Mark to get at the hay. The crazy things were going to get run over with the tractor if they didn't watch it.

A bone-chilling gust of wind caught the strings and pulled a couple out of his hand, blowing them across the yard. Mark rolled up the remaining twine as he hunched his shoulders against the cold and chose to ignore the others. Later, later, later.

He and Nate had too much to do right now, and pieces of twine didn't concern him.

Another icy blast of wind pierced the cocoon of coveralls, sweaters and shirt, chilling him to the bone. The coldest day of the coldest October on record, and already that morning he'd fixed the well and taken their new bull in to the vet. Then he'd come home to a tractor that wouldn't start and a waterer that Nate had forgotten to put a heat tape down.

Mark's mood was as foul as the weather.

Nate picked up another bale, and it tipped precariously on the bale forks. Mark waved to him to stop but Nate was looking over his shoulder. The bale tipped past the center of gravity and fell off the forks to the ground.

Mark ground his teeth in frustration. Nate got out of the tractor to see how bad the damage was.

"Didn't you see that the bale wasn't on the forks?" Mark yelled.

"So I'll pick it up again." Nate yelled back.

"It didn't need to end up on the ground if you had done it right the first time."

The two of them faced off, glaring at each other as a plume of exhaust from the tractor swept between them. Nate turned, walked over to the offending bale, poked it with the toe of his boot and climbed back into the tractor without a second look at Mark.

Mark turned and got into the truck. He knew he was miserable, but he was also unable to stop himself. Nate could feed that last bale on his own. He had to get to the house to make a phone call anyhow.

With a sigh he put the truck into gear, hesitated a moment, then released the clutch and drove away. Elise had invited him to have lunch at their place, and he could apologize to Nate then. Maybe the drive from his place to Nate's would settle his temper.

Shivering, he turned the heat up full and stared at the gray clouds drifting over the mountains heading toward them. Snow for sure.

He'd been edgy the past couple of months, and no one knew it better than he did. He couldn't settle down, and lately he'd found any kind of excuse to go running around the country.

After finding out it would be cheaper to rent a truck and haul the hay himself, he had done so. Four trips to Langley had done little to improve his temper. If anything, driving a semi down the Coquihalla then the Trans-Canada had almost given him a nervous breakdown.

On his return, the third cut of hay had been ready to be baled. He'd run one tractor, Rob another and in a couple of days they'd had their feed for the winter rolled up in large round bales.

Then he'd saddled up his horse, packed up a second and ridden up into the mountains. He had spent a week longer in the hills than he'd needed to, rounding up strays and herding them back home.

It wasn't necessary that he personally take care of needling all the animals but with the help of a halogen lamp and a few all-nighters, he'd gotten it done.

Nate had helped with the baling, but after the second trip to Langley he'd told Mark he wasn't going to try to keep up. Mark had sensed Nate had his own problems to deal with, but wasn't going to drive himself into the ground doing it like Mark was.

Last week Mark had snapped at his mother when she'd

asked him if he was ever going to slow down and take some time out to be with his family.

The truck fishtailed, Mark pulled his foot off the accelerator, glanced at the speedometer and then at the hay trailer.

With a sigh he braked, slowing the truck down, pushing his hat further up his head, leaning back against the seat.

For a moment he let his thoughts drift where they did far too often, as he remembered long blond hair, green eyes lit up with laughter, delicate features.

Sheryl.

When he'd come back from the pack trip, two and a half months ago, to find out that she had left already, he'd felt lost, empty and even more alone than when Tanya had mailed his ring to him here at Sweet Creek.

Tanya was a good woman, prettier than Sheryl, more refined. Tanya was friendly, open and fun to be around. She had no major hang-ups and gladly accompanied him to church. But he had never felt the same feeling of absolute rightness with her that he felt with Sheryl.

Or that feeling of emptiness when she'd left.

He tried to see that it was all for the good. Each day he struggled with the same loneliness, the same sense of happiness, elusive, just out of his grasp. If he stopped to analyze his own actions, they didn't make much sense. Sheryl had only spent two weeks here. She had been gone nine.

In theory he should have forgotten her after the first two. So why had he spent the past couple of months wondering what she was doing? Why did he constantly remember exactly how the light caught her hair when it hung loose, flowing to her waist? Why could he still feel the slenderness of her in his arms?

Theories only worked on paper, not in life.

And the worst of it was his own fear. It had been difficult getting over Tanya. And she was pretty straightforward about her reasons for breaking up with him.

There was nothing straightforward about Sheryl. She confused him, puzzled him and scared him.

He knew Jason had abused her. She had said as much, and Nate had confirmed it only a month ago, telling him about her scars. Even now the thought made him clench his fists around the steering wheel, wishing it were Jason's neck. But knowing that had also created a distance. Did she hate men? Was she scared of him? He had bared his heart to her, given her as much as he could.

She had never called, never written. But then he wondered if he could expect her to. Given what she had lived with, would she make the first move to him? But also, given what she had lived with, could he expect to be welcomed?

He was torn between wanting to run to Edmonton and letting go and letting God take care of it all.

He sighed and slowed to make the turn into Nate's place. It had been a few days since he'd seen his sister and Ed. Initially he'd turned down the invitation to lunch, preferring to keep himself busy with nothing. But his loneliness became too much even for him and finally he accepted.

A few flakes of snow hit his cheeks as he stepped out of the truck, and he squinted up at the gray sky. It was going to be a full-blown storm by the time evening came. Feeling even more depressed, he pulled his coat closer around him and trudged around to the back of the house.

The porch was almost as cold as the outside, and Mark quickly shucked his coat, coveralls and boots. He stepped into the kitchen, and a wave of warmth, heavenly aromas and the sound of the coffeepot burbling on the stove wrapped around him. This was what a home should smell like, feel like, he thought, inhaling the smell, letting the warmth seep into his cold body.

''Hello, Mark,'' Ed greeted him, looking up from where he sat at the kitchen table. He slowly reached with his good hand and shoved a piece of paper across the table toward him. ''A message from...Calgary. Confirm...reservation for the Stockgrowers Convention.''

Mark picked up the paper and glanced at it before shoving it in his pocket.

''And Marla...is coloring...a picture...''

Marla was bent over her coloring book, her nose inches away from the paper, tongue between her teeth. ''It's a present,'' she said not looking up.

''Could you color one for me?'' Mark asked, hooking a chair with his stockinged foot and dropping on it across the table from his little niece. ''I'd like a picture to hang up in my kitchen.''

She pursed her lips at that, tilting her head to study the picture she worked on. ''When I'm finished this one,'' she replied, flashing him a mischievous grin.

''Got the...cows fed?'' Ed spoke up.

Mark nodded, picking up Marla's crayon box. ''Nate and I just finished doing the ones at the other corrals. He'll be by in twenty minutes or so.'' He turned back to Marla. ''Which color do you want now?''

''The gray one.'' She handed him the pink crayon, its paper peeled off.

''Shouldn't you make the sun yellow?'' he asked, leaning closer to Marla's picture.

''No. This is a sun in Edmonton. Auntie Sheryl told Grandpa that the days are gray where she lives.'' Marla finished coloring the sun a dull gray as Mark sat back, his heart hammering in his chest. The mere mention of her name, coming so close on the heels of his own thoughts, filled him with sudden longing. ''Grandpa talked to her on the phone,'' Marla continued, tilting her head to look at the picture. ''I talked to her, too. Mommy's talking to Auntie Sheryl now, and if you ask, maybe you can.'' She looked up at him and flashed him another grin.

Right then Elise stepped into the kitchen, the cordless phone tucked under her ear, a loaf of bread in her free hand. ''It's not been great weather here, either, like Ed told you,'' she was saying. ''Yes, Lainie had a baby girl and she's adorable. Nate's foot is just fine.... No, he's out feeding cows with Mark. I can give him the message.'' She looked up and just about dropped the phone when she saw Mark. ''Sorry, what were you saying?'' she asked, dropping the frozen bread on the counter.

Mark listened to the one-sided conversation, straining his ears for even the faintest sound coming out of the headset, almost hungry for even the slightest connection with her.

''Well...'' Elise leaned her elbows on the counter, staring down at it as if afraid to look at Mark. ''To tell you the truth, Mark's miserable.''

Mark felt his breath leave him as he realized what Sheryl was asking.

''He's been running around all over the country trying to keep busy. He looks exhausted half of the time. I don't think he's very happy, Sheryl.''

Mark glared at Elise, but she kept her eyes glued to the countertop.

''I think he's missing you.... Don't start that again, it's the truth.'' Elise bit her lip as she clutched the headset. ''I think he's still in love with—''

A few angry strides brought Mark around the table and across from his sister. He held out his hand, and without even looking up, Elise handed him the phone.

Mark held it a moment, his breath coming in short gasps as if he had just run ten miles instead walked ten feet. He blinked, swallowed and then, drawing a steadying breath, he put the phone to his ear.

''Elise are you still there?'' Sheryl's soft voice still held a hint of pain, he thought, his anger melting at the sound of it.

''Hi, Sheryl.'' It was all he could say. Nine cold empty weeks and he could barely say her name.

''Mark?'' Silence, then, ''Where's Elise?''

That hurt more than it should. ''If you want to find out how I am, why don't you ask me yourself?''

''Please don't do this, Mark,'' her voice pleaded. ''I can't take this.''

''Take? That doesn't seem to be something you do.'' Mark couldn't seem to keep the angry hurt out of his voice.

She said nothing.

Way to go, Mark, he thought, wishing he had held his tongue. You're tearing me apart, girl, he thought, wishing he could voice his inner feelings, wishing she would give him any kind of encouragement, any kind of reason. ''Sheryl—'' his voice became pleading ''—why did you leave?'' Mark leaned back against the counter, rubbing his forehead, eyes closed, silently pleading. ''Are you afraid of me?''

''Ye-es,'' she said, her voice breaking. Mark clutched the phone, her single word hitting him and hurting beyond understanding.

''Why? You know I would never hurt you....''

A sudden click in his ear told him that she had hung up. Mark lowered the phone, staring morosely at it. She hadn't even given him a chance to tell her that he loved her.

Chapter Fourteen

Sheryl lifted her hymn book, flipped it open to the page and, as the organ began playing, felt a lift of her heart. The songs, the music, all seemed to come together to fill empty spaces in her life.

Since leaving Sweet Creek she'd felt a deep desire to attend. Tory and Mike lived a few blocks from a small community church, and Sheryl saw this as a clear indication of what she should do.

Sheryl drifted back to the service she had attended in Sweet Creek. A light smile lifted one corner of her mouth as she remembered the emotions that had spun through her mind, tangling up her thoughts.

Much had happened since then. She had relaxed her guard, but not without a struggle. It had meant soul searching and required confession. Since her visit with Ed, they had written, and in each letter he repeatedly apologized, repeatedly offered her his love. It became easier and easier. She found the less she fought, the more she received.

Love was a peculiar emotion. Ed's love had been misguided, Nate's confused. She wondered if Jason had loved her or just needed someone to dominate.

And Mark…

Sheryl closed the book and dropped it in its holder with a "thunk." She didn't know what to do about Mark. It was easier to feel unworthy of God's love. He was perfect.

Mark was a man. A man she was attracted to with a depth that frightened her. If she were to give in to him and to find that once he really knew her he didn't want her…

It would break her, and she had no reserves to draw on. So she ran away from it.

Leaving Sweet Creek without seeing Mark had been a wise thing to do. It had been three months since she'd left and still she couldn't forget him. The power of her caring frightened her.

During that time he had never called her, and she knew she had saved herself from a heartbreak that would be deeper than any that Jason, Ed or Nate had inflicted on her.

The chords of the closing song broke into her thoughts, and with a sigh, she got up. She let the words of the song wash over her, soothing and comforting. God was faithful, his love perfect and sacrificial—that she was reassured of each Sunday. People were sinful and frail and disappointed, but each time she came to church she became more convinced of God's love.

She stopped a moment to chat with fellow churchgoers, turning down an offer for lunch. Tory was expecting her, and she hadn't seen much of her and Mike the past couple of weeks.

The walk home chilled her, and when she let herself into the apartment it was with a thankful sigh as the heat rolled over her.

"Is that you, Sheryl?" Tory called out as she hung up her coat. "Lunch is on the table."

"Be there as soon as I wash up," she replied with a smile. Every time she stepped in the door from church, lunch was on the table. She knew Tory kept an eye out, and as soon as she saw her coming down the sidewalk, went into action.

She spent an enjoyable hour with Tory and Mike. After three months of living together they had found a comfortable rhythm. They had been good for her, and they were part of the reason that Sheryl hadn't gone actively seeking an apartment on her own.

Mike excused himself for his usual Sunday afternoon nap, and the women lingered over the remnants.

"So I see you got another letter from Ed," Tory said, pushing her plate away. She took a slow sip of her coffee, savoring it.

"Yes. He's been writing quite a bit lately."

"I thought he had a stroke?"

"Elise writes his letters. She always adds a little on the end."

Tory nodded, pursing her lips. "And…does she say anything about Mark?"

Sheryl shrugged, hoping her disappointment wouldn't show. "Sometimes. He seems to be doing well."

"You don't sound happy about that."

"Of course I am. Mark, well, he's…"

"He's a good-looking guy. And I told you to hang on to him, remember? You didn't take my advice. You shouldn't complain that he's carrying on with his life."

"I'm not." Sheryl frowned, pulling Tory's plant toward her.

"Leave that poor thing alone," grumbled Tory, pulling it back. "You always leave the dead leaves lying around."

"They make the plant look ugly."

"It's all part of the life-and-death cycle." Tory grinned back. "Anyhow, the least you could do is throw them away or stuff them back into the dirt."

Sheryl plucked one off and with exaggerated motions, did as Tory suggested. "Anyhow," she mused, "I don't have time for anyone right now, and I'm not sure Mark is interested in me anymore."

"You don't have time because you don't make time. You mope around and pretend you want to be an independent woman and get a career, when I know you'd just as soon be living at home and having babies." Tory pulled a leaf off the plant, looking at it.

"I'm not moping around…"

"Oh, c'mon," Tory chided gently. "I knew you before you

went to Sweet Creek and I know you now. Something happened there, something that made you a little softer, a little less reserved, a little more lovable. Only you still like to pretend you're the same person.''

''It was because Ed and I had a chance to straighten out a few things.''

''That might be part of it. But making up with a stepfather doesn't put a dreamy look on a girl's face, doesn't make her stop what she's doing to stare off into space, like I've seen you, when you're supposed to be studying.'' Tory plucked off another leaf, inspecting it as if weighing her next words. ''And since you've come back, I've heard you crying. And not just once or twice.''

Sheryl swallowed. ''I've had a lot of pain that I've hidden, Tory, you know that.'' She stopped, then sighed. ''I hadn't had a chance to cry since I got married. Maybe it's like pulling out these dead leaves. Maybe I'm just getting rid of tears I held back all that time.''

Tory smiled a sad smile, reaching across the table to clasp Sheryl's hand. ''Interesting comparison. But I think some of those tears are new.''

Sheryl blinked, then looked away, out the window to the gray day outside. She knew that Tory was right, but she didn't know what to do about it. It had been three months since she'd left Sweet Creek. Mark had never contacted her.

''Have you tried calling him, writing him?'' Tory asked quietly.

''I can't do that, Tory. I can't go running after him. Not after all the humiliation that Jason dished out. I just can't.'' Sheryl bit back a sigh, her confusion mocking her resolve. ''Besides, I'm sure he's forgotten about me by now.''

''You're not that forgettable.'' Tory squeezed her hand. ''Do you love him?''

Sheryl laid her chin on her other hand, still looking out the window. ''I don't even know. I thought love was supposed to be so easy, just a straightforward emotion, but it isn't. I thought I hated Ed, but I don't. He said he loved me but didn't know how to show it. Nate said he loved me, and he hurt me so badly and yet, lately I find I can't dislike him as I should. I'm starting to feel sorry for him and bad for not paying more attention to him when I was younger.'' She laughed, a soft laugh, free from its usual bitter sound. ''I'm finding out that love is a complicated, frustrating business.'' She risked a glance at Tory, who smiled in understanding. Sheryl rubbed Tory's wedding ring with her finger, sighing deeply. ''I still miss Mark.''

''Well that's a good sign,'' Tory replied.

''Maybe. I'm afraid of him, too.''

Tory clucked. ''That's not.''

She was about to speak again when the phone rang, making both of them jump. Tory got up and Sheryl looked back outside.

December in the city was a dismal affair. The snow piled along the streets was streaked with gray and black, and everyone, including the cars, looked like they'd sooner be someplace else. The Christmas lights strung along buildings and houses provided the only cheerful note.

''Sheryl.'' Tory stood beside her, holding on to the handset. Sheryl looked up, surprised to see pain on her face.

''What's the matter?''

''It's for you. It's Elise.''

Sheryl's heart tripped, then raced. Ed. It had to be Ed. Sheryl grabbed the phone. ''Hello, Elise?''

''Hi.'' Elise paused, her voice strained. ''I'm phoning to tell you that Ed passed away.''

Sheryl sagged back against her chair, her hand covering her eyes. ''When?''

''Last night.''

''I guess it wasn't so unexpected, was it?''

''No.'' Sheryl could almost hear Elise swallow her tears. ''But it's still hard.''

Sheryl only nodded, a knot of sorrow building in her throat. ''When's the funeral?'' she managed to whisper.

''Thursday. Can you come?''

''Of course. I'll take the bus.'' Sheryl pressed her hand tight against her eyes. ''Tell Nate I'm sorry for him.''

''I'll do that. Are you going to be okay?''

In spite of her sorrow, Sheryl felt a rush of love for this considerate and caring person. ''I'll be okay. How about you?''

''My mom's here and Mark's coming later.'' Elise drew in a shaky breath, audible to Sheryl. ''I know I shouldn't be sad. He was waiting for the end. I should tell you that he told me, just before he died, that he was so glad you came and very thankful for your letters. He…he wanted me to tell you that he loved you.''

Sheryl bit her lip, wishing she could say goodbye and retreat to her bedroom. ''Thanks.''

Tory knelt beside her, her arm around her as she handed her a tissue. Sheryl smiled weakly at her and wiped a tear that drifted down her nose.

''I'll let you go, Sheryl. We'll see you on Thursday then?''

''I'll be there. Bye.'' Sheryl waited until Elise hung up, then pushed the button ending the connection. For a moment she stared at the phone, a heavy sorrow dropping down on her.

Without a word Tory gathered her in her arms. Sheryl dropped her head on her shoulder and wept.

Mark hooked his finger between his tie and his collar, stretching his neck. He disliked wearing the thing. And he disliked funerals. The music was always so dreary, so hushed.

We really should be rejoicing, he thought. Ed has gone to the place he's wanted to be for the past four months. Instead the church was hushed, the music sombre. No one spoke.

Quite a few people had come out on this cold December day, and Mark was glad for Nate's sake. Here and there he heard a sniffle, saw someone wipe away a surreptitious tear.

But Mark couldn't summon tears. He had spent enough time the past few weeks with Ed to know that he yearned to die. He had made his peace with Sheryl, and she had forgiven him fully.

Mark turned his head ever so slightly, looking for her. She was sitting behind Nate and Elise, beside a sister of Ed's Mark hadn't even known he had. Sheryl's head was bent, her hair loose, and Mark felt again the weight of longing press against his heart.

Three months had made no difference.

His only contact with her had been that intercepted phone call and the little bits of her life she wrote in her letters to Ed that he would read when he found one lying around Elise's place. As usual she gave him nothing. As usual he wondered why he still cared about her.

He shifted his weight, trying to catch a glimpse of her face, trying to make some kind of connection. They had shared so much. He knew what she had to live with, and he didn't know how to make a connection with her.

He didn't even know if she would want it.

He caught his mother's puzzled look, and he looked ahead again. He should feel guilty for thinking only of Sheryl when he should be contemplating Ed's life, but he couldn't dredge up the proper emotions.

The minister announced the final song, and as they stood, the funeral director motioned for the pallbearers to carry the casket out of the church.

Mark shook out the leg of his pants, straightened his suit jacket, borrowed from Nate, and turned. For a brief moment his gaze locked with Sheryl's. Awareness arced between them, tangible, real, powerful.

Mark almost stumbled, then drew in a shaky breath and, looking toward the doorway at the end of the church, walked out.

Because of the cold weather, the graveside ceremony was mercifully brief. When it was over, Nate, Elise and the children lingered a moment. Sheryl stood to one side, as if unsure of her place. Her lips were pressed together as she reached out and plucked a flower from the top of the casket. Holding it close to her she turned.

Mark watched her go. He wasn't going to run after her again. He wasn't going to go where he wasn't wanted.

Then she paused a moment at the headstone beside Ed's grave. It belonged to her mother, Blythe.

She stared at the inscription, her hand pressed to her mouth, tears coursing down her face. Mark remembered her crying in his arms, remembered her pain, and he couldn't stop himself.

A few steps was all it took and he was beside her, silent, waiting.

She glanced furtively at him, reaching into her pocket, and when she pulled out an old handkerchief of his, Mark felt as if he'd been hit.

He swallowed and, without stopping to think about his actions, took it from her, tipped her chin up and gently wiped the tears from her face.

He tried to be clinical about it, but his hands were shaking, and his insides were churning. When her soft green eyes, bright with tears connected with his, his restraint fell away. Slowly he drew her toward him. Fear flickered in her eyes, and she pressed her hands against him.

"Please don't, Mark."

Mark dropped his hands, heat rising in his face. The same words she had whispered over the phone just a couple of weeks ago. What was he? Some kind of ogre? What could he possibly have done to her that she felt she had to beg him to leave her alone.

He wanted to shake her, to give her a reason to be afraid of him. He wanted…to kiss her.

"Are you coming, Sheryl?" Nate had come up beside them. "We're going to have lunch at the house."

Sheryl nodded, avoiding Mark's eyes, her relief obvious.

Mark turned, staring at his brother-in-law, feeling betrayed. Three months ago he had rescued Sheryl from the uncomfortable situation of being with Nate and now, it seemed, the roles were reversed.

"Are you coming, Mark?" Nate asked.

He tried to affect a light tone, glancing back at Sheryl. "For a little while." He paused a moment, hoping for what, he didn't know. Some kind of sign, some kind of recognition.

When she looked down, he turned and stalked off, berating himself for being such a sucker.

All the way to Nate's place he wondered why he was so stuck on her.

Why he couldn't get her out of his mind. He had defended her to Nate, to Ed. Had argued for fair treatment for her. And now he had to live with the consequences.

The house was full. The scent of coffee permeated every corner, the subdued chatter of people drifted about. Mark and Nate set out chairs, talked to people. Elise sat in one corner beside Sheryl, while other ladies of the church served the coffee.

Mark made small talk, consoled some of the older folk, talked ranching with a few men, kept the kids from eating all the food and tried not to look at his watch. Ed hadn't planned his own death, but the funeral couldn't have come at a worse time. The Stockgrowers Convention in Calgary had been set up months ago. He had tried to find someone else to take his place as director, but no one could. The longest he could stay was another two hours.

One hundred and twenty minutes to find a chance to talk to Sheryl.

He picked up a few dirty coffee cups and with a quick glance to make sure Sheryl still sat in the corner, he walked into the kitchen to wash the cups.

Elise had a sinkfull of water running, and when he came close, she handed him a tea towel.

"You shouldn't be doing this, sis," he said, stroking her hair.

"I need to keep busy," she replied with a faint smile. "I'm

sure it will all hit me once everyone is gone, but for now I feel better pretending this is just another family get-together." She dropped a cup on the drainboard and glanced sidelong at Mark.

"Have you had a chance to talk to Sheryl?" she asked. "You don't have a lot of time before you have to leave."

He shook his head, picking up the cup and inspecting the soap suds that ran down the sides. "One hundred and eighteen minutes, to be precise." He wiped the bubbles with an angry swipe. "What am I going to say?"

"How about, 'I love you, I'm crazy about you,'" Elise replied softly.

"And how would that look with what Nate has to tell her?"

"Hey it was your idea to talk to Ed about his will."

"I know," he replied irritably. "I just didn't think it would jeopardize my own position with her. Besides she's scared of me."

"What do you mean by that?" Elise frowned at him.

The door to the porch opened and Lainie Jesperson came in, carrying a bundle of blankets, her husband right behind her, carrying a diaper bag and car seat. The baby, Mark guessed, putting down his towel to go and help her, ignoring Elise's question.

He took the bundle from Lainie as she took her coat off and dropped it on the pile on the table. Mark shifted the bundle around and the blankets slipped open. Tiny unfocused eyes stared up at him. Soft black hair stuck up from a head no larger than the palm of his hand. It wriggled, its mouth opening up in a miniature yawn.

He couldn't help the smile that curved his mouth.

"I didn't know if I should bring her along," whispered Lainie. "But I wanted to come, to see Sheryl." She turned to her husband. "Anthony can you take Deidre from Mark?"

"That's okay," said Mark to Lainie's husband. "I don't mind holding her for a while." Anthony shrugged, took a cup of coffee that Elise had poured for him. After offering her his condolences he went in search of Nate.

The baby lay lightly in the crook of his arm, and Mark couldn't keep his eyes away. Kids always brought out his mushy side, babies even more so.

"I'll finish up in here, Mark. Can you take these around?" Elise pushed a plate of squares across the counter at him. He settled the baby more securely, picked the plate and carried on with his duties.

He worked his way around the living room, avoiding the corner where Lainie now sat beside Sheryl.

Mark watched as Lainie stroked Sheryl's shoulders. She looked up at him as the baby squirmed in his arms and let out a gentle cry.

Their gazes locked, and all else fell away. Gray eyes held green for what seemed like forever till the baby in Mark's arms cried again. Sheryl broke the connection, looked at the bundle Mark held, her expression wistful.

"Here, I'll take her from you." Anthony came up beside him. Mark awkwardly shifted the red-faced baby into Anthony's arms, desperately afraid that he would drop it. But she settled against her father, and Mark couldn't resist touching the downy hair nestled against Anthony's shirt.

"She's beautiful," he said softly, a smile curving his mouth. He touched the creamy soft skin of her cheek, then turned.

Sheryl's mouth curved up in a smile directed to him. Just then Crystal tugged on Sheryl's arm. Sheryl reached down and hugged her. Benjamin toddled up to both of them, yanking on Sheryl's shirt. Sheryl grimaced and swung Benjamin up in her arms.

"You don't smell good, little man," Mark heard her say with a lilt in her voice. She dropped him on her hip, caught Crystal's hand in hers and worked her way through the crowd up the stairs.

Mark paused, tempted to follow up on the hesitant smile Sheryl had directed at him. It was the first acknowledgment she had made of his presence.

"Mark," an older lady stood beside him, tugging on his shirt. "My car won't start. I left the lights on."

Mark glanced at Sheryl's retreating back.

"Probably just needs a boost, Mrs. Newkiski," he said. "Just let me get my jacket and I'll be right out."

He still had time to catch Sheryl before he had to leave, he reassured himself.

Sheryl pressed Benjamin to her as she made her way up the stairs, and, undaunted by the smell of his dirty diaper, kissed him soundly on one sticky cheek.

"How can you kiss him, Auntie Sheryl, he smells so bad," Crystal complained, holding her nose primly with her thumb and finger.

"It's not bad, not for him." Sheryl gave him another squeeze at the top of the stairs and turned into his bedroom. She paused a moment in the doorway, looking at the changes made since she had slept here.

A wallpaper border decorated with rabbits ran around the room, halfway up. Elise had painted the room a pale green below the border and white above. Marla's bed had a pale pink quilt with rabbit appliqués and a green-and-white striped bedskirt. Benjamin's crib quilt matched Marla's except his was green. A rocking chair sat in one corner of the room. It looked cozy and inviting.

"What did this room look like when you slept in it?" Crystal asked, standing beside Sheryl as she looked it over.

"It was just plain white," Sheryl replied, walking to the far wall and plopping Benjamin on his change table. "I didn't spend a lot of time here. Mostly I was in the cabin."

Crystal handed her a clean diaper. "Are you sad about Grandpa?" she asked, leaning on the change table, her clear blue eyes gazing up at Sheryl.

"In a way," Sheryl replied, unsnapping Benjamin's pants, smiling at the difference between him and Lainie's baby. "I think he's happier now."

Crystal sighed, wiping away a stray tear with her thumb. "I wish I could be."

Sheryl paused, then bent over to press a kiss on Crystal's head. "You'll miss him a lot."

"Do you miss him?"

Sheryl smiled down at Crystal, her sweet face blurred by unexpected tears. "Yes," she said softly. "Yes I miss him."

A light tap on the door made them both jump. Nate stood, almost hesitantly, framed by the doorway. "Crystal, do you mind to go find Mommy. I would like to talk to Auntie Sheryl for a minute."

Crystal shrugged, then left. Nate watched her go, his expression melancholy. He closed the door quietly behind him, then walked over to his son.

Sheryl sensed a change in him. Anger and antagonism didn't surround him, as it had when she'd left. Since she'd come back, his overtures to her were of a tentative nature, as if unsure of how to proceed.

In his own gruff way he had been solicitous and caring. Sheryl had begun to see the side of Nate that Elise must have become attracted to.

"How are you feeling, Nate?" she asked, pinning up Benjamin's clean diaper. She didn't look at him as she pulled up the plastic pants and snapped his coveralls again.

"I'm okay." Nate bent over and kissed his son, letting Sheryl pick him up. He looked up at her, and Sheryl was surprised at his expression. Pain had pulled his features down, sadness tinged the deep blue of his eyes. "How about you?"

"It's hard. I'm just glad I could see him before—" Sheryl stopped, remembering. "I'm glad we could make some kind of amends before he died."

Nate blew out his breath in a sigh, tapping his fingers nervously against his leg. "Sheryl, I really need to talk to you. I know now isn't exactly the right time…" he let the sentence hang as if giving her an out.

Sheryl sat down on the rocking chair behind her, holding her nephew on her lap. Benjamin nuzzled into her, his thumb in his mouth. ''It doesn't matter, Nate.'' She tried not to feel afraid, wondering what seemed to weigh so heavily on his mind that he'd followed her up here while his community and family congregated below. Outside a car started. People were beginning to leave. He should be saying goodbye. Instead he'd come up here.

Nate lowered himself to Marla's bed, across from Sheryl. He plunged his hands through his hair, holding his head a moment, looking down at the floor.

''I don't know where to start, what to say.'' He rubbed his face, then shrugged. ''I've been thinking about you so much since you left. After what you showed me.'' He swallowed, loosening his tie. ''I feel terrible about this, but,'' he looked up at her, his eyes seeming to plead for understanding. ''About a month ago I went to your cabin. I knew you had a box of papers in it and—'' he hesitated ''—I read your diaries. I needed to know more about you.'' He pushed himself off the bed, walking over to the window, looking out of it, his voice softening. ''I found out a lot about you, your mother. I got to see me and Dad through the eyes of a little scared girl who was trying to become part of a family that didn't know what to do with a little girl. Some of what you thought was happening was wrong, but I couldn't discredit your reaction. My own feelings weren't exactly without prejudice.'' He turned to her. ''I guess I'm trying to say that Dad and I tried. We made mistakes and we pushed you too hard.''

''Please, Nate,'' Sheryl whispered, overcome with emotion.

''No, I really need to tell you.'' He rubbed the back of his neck, looking down. ''I wish I could go back. I wish I could take what I've learned from my wife, my children, and use it. I know better how a family works.'' He sighed and walked over to Sheryl, hunkering down beside her. He toyed with Benjamin's hand. Sheryl felt a wave of sorrow and regret, remembering happier times with Nate, allowing those recollections to brush away the last memory she had of him, sitting in the bus depot, telling her about the letter he sent back.

"Once I thought I loved you. I read in your books how that looked to you..."

"Nate," she whispered, "I'm sorry."

"Don't be sorry about the truth," he said bitterly.

He took her hand, and Sheryl had to stop herself from pulling back, like she always did.

Nate must have felt her reaction, because his lips twisted. "When you showed me your scars, Sheryl..." He paused, biting his lip. "It hurt me to see that. I had disliked—" he laughed bitterly at that "—no, almost hated you for so long. I heard that love and hate are two sides of the same coin, and when you showed me what Jason had done to you, it was like the coin flipped again," He stroked her hand lightly then dropped it. "I'm so sorry, Sheryl." His voice broke and he turned away.

Sheryl sat, stunned. She didn't know what words to use, what to say. The last time she had seen Nate his animosity was like a shield. Some sense of change had come through in Ed's letters, but this? This was a complete reversal of everything she had dreaded coming back to face.

"I'm asking you to forgive me, like you forgave Dad," he continued. "I don't deserve it..."

"Please don't say that, Nate." Sheryl hugged her now-sleeping nephew closer. "None of us *deserve* the forgiveness we've been given, either by people or by God. I have to forgive you."

Her stepbrother nodded. "Thanks," he whispered. "I wish I could take away everything that happened to you, I wish I could take it on myself..."

"Nate," Sheryl said, stopping him. "No one forced me to leave with Jason. No one pushed me out of the house. I left on my own."

Nate nodded, turning to her. "We could have made it easier for you." He smiled wanly. "I'd like to say we tried, but after reading your books, I can see that we failed, badly." He hesitated, as if he had more to say. "Mark read your books, too. In fact, he was the one who told me I should look them over."

Sheryl felt her heart skip at that, trying to picture Mark delving into her past. Why would he do that if he wasn't interested in her?

Nate pursed his lips, staring down at his shoes, unable to meet her eyes. "I don't know if I should be the one telling you this, but he was heartbroken after you left. He would spend hours in your cabin, sitting on the bed, reading your papers."

Sheryl closed her eyes, imagining his large form on her bed, delving into her past, creating yet another intimacy.

Nate was quiet a moment, as if giving her time to understand what he had said.

"There's more I need to tell you." He slipped his hands in his pockets, leaning back against the wall behind him. "I don't know if you're going to stick around for the reading of the will, but you'll find out one way or the other. Dad willed half of his share of the ranch to you."

Chapter Fifteen

"What?" Sheryl stared at Nate, trying to absorb what he said.

"I have to confess, it wasn't my idea."

"How did that happen?"

Nate sighed, lifting one shoulder up. "After you left, Mark came down from the mountains. He went straight to Dad and talked to him about you and the treatment you've received."

Sheryl frowned, trying to understand. "Why would he do that?"

Nate bit his lip, glancing over his shoulder as if making sure they were alone. "He wanted to make sure that you got what you deserved. But more than that, he did it because he loves you."

"I don't understand." Sheryl chose to ignore the last part of what Nate had said. It seemed too wonderful. "What am I supposed to do with a share in the ranch?"

"Well you would either get some income a month from us, or Mark was talking about giving you a lump sum."

Sheryl got up, agitated, afraid to probe too deeply the implications of what Mark had done. If she took a lump-sum payment she could get her degree in three years instead of six, the way she was doing it now.

But was that what she wanted? Tory's words came back to her. "You pretend you want to get a career when I know you'd just as soon be living at home and having babies."

Sheryl shook her head, holding the now-sleeping Benjamin closer. But babies required a husband and a husband required…everything.

"If I wanted a lump-sum payment," she asked, her voice muffled as she laid her head against Benjamin. "What would that mean for the ranch? I thought you guys were strapped."

Nate sighed behind her. "We are. I would be lying if I said different."

"So…"

"Mark was going to go back to work for a few years, at least until the river-bottom land was paid off."

Sheryl kissed Benjamin's warm head, staring off into the middle distance, trying to imagine Mark living in the city. Pictures of him flashed through her mind—Mark on the back of a horse, driving his pickup truck too fast, balancing on a stuker, pitching bales. She pulled herself to the present, glancing at Nate. "He doesn't want to, does he?"

Nate walked slowly around to the other side of the crib, his eyes on his son. "No, he doesn't. But he's willing to do it for you, because he loves you."

Sacrifice. Mark would sacrifice what he loved for her.

"Why didn't he call?" Sheryl asked, confused. "If he loves me like you say he did, like he says he does, why did he never call me?" She laid Benjamin carefully in his crib, arranging the quilt around him, her heart beginning an erratic rhythm.

"He was afraid to." Nate pulled the quilt around his son's face, stroking his cheek. He sighed and looked up at Sheryl. "I've had to work with him the past three months. He's been miserable, torn between wanting to chase you down and afraid that once you found out about the will you'd mistrust his motives. He knows you don't have a high trust level of our sex." Nate reached over and touched Sheryl's hand. "Mark's usually very even tempered but you've got him tied up in knots. Whenever we'd talk about Jason, he'd get furious. I told him about what Jason had done to you." Nate shook his head. "He grabbed me and asked me why we let you go. I thought he was going to deck me. I've never seen him like this. He knows what you went through with Jason. He thinks you're afraid of him.''

Sheryl clung to the top rail of the crib, the wood pressing into her hands, the implications of what Nate was telling her beginning to fall into place. ''But I'm not. Not the way he thinks...'' She looked up at Nate. ''What should I do?''

He straightened, tapping the crib lightly with his fingers. ''Like I said before, Mark loves you. I don't deserve your forgiveness, but I'm thankful for it. And as for the rest, I'm leaving it in your hands, Sheryl. I don't think you've had a lot of choices in the past.'' He bent over, gave his son a kiss, nodded to Sheryl and left the room.

Sheryl hugged herself, restless. She walked to the window, staring out at the snow-covered yard, now full of vehicles. She easily found Mark's silver pickup and she remembered sitting in it, sharing her life while he listened.

He loved her. She knew that now. His words, his actions, all made that very clear to her. So what should she do about it? Could she accept what he was giving her?

Sheryl touched the cold window, tracing her initials on it, just as she used to when she was younger. Sighing lightly, she let herself drift back, remembering her life with Ed and Nate, trying to fit everything in with what happened.

Somehow everything seemed to come back to Mark. Mark and Elise. They had influenced this family in so many ways, had shown them God's love in a different way. Mark had shown her a different kind of man, a different kind of love.

A tap sounded at the door. Sheryl jumped and without turning around, knew it was Mark. With an air of resignation, she turned to face him. He wore a jacket and hat as if dressed to go outside. His cheeks were red, and as he walked toward her, Sheryl could smell the clean outdoors on him. His eyes met hers as he came closer, and Sheryl felt her breath leave her in anticipation. Her heart sped up, her limbs felt weak, and when he stopped in front of her she had to clench her fist to keep herself from reaching out to him.

His unselfish act, which clearly showed her his love, also hindered her. How would he read her reaction to it?

''Sheryl...'' His voice faltered, and he cleared his throat. ''Sheryl, I've come to say goodbye.''

''No.'' The word flew out of her, protesting, afraid. ''No, don't say that.''

Slowly he lifted his hand and caressed the fine line of her jaw with his knuckles. Sheryl's eyes drifted shut as she swayed toward him, her hand grasping his hard wrist, keeping his fingers on her face. She turned her mouth toward his cold hand, touching her warm lips to his palm. She couldn't stop herself, couldn't keep herself from connecting to him.

With a sigh as light as a snowflake, he carefully drew her against him, his other hand sliding along her jawline to her neck, his fingers tangling in her hair.

''I'm leaving for Calgary.'' His deep voice was a soft rumble beneath her hands. ''I'll be back in a week.'' He said nothing more, as if waiting for her response.

She tilted her head, reaching up to cup his jaw, feeling its smoothness. ''What do you want me to do?'' she whispered, losing herself in the soft gray of his eyes. ''I don't know what to do.''

Mark looked at her, his expression sorrowful. Then be bent his head and found her lips with his own. Sheryl slid one hand around his neck, the other around his back, clinging to him as their mouths met, explored, tasted. He held her tighter, his fingers caressing her head, holding it, while his lips moved from hers, lingering on her cheek, touching her eyes then returning to her mouth.

She felt a hunger growing, even while his caresses created an emptiness within her, a need for more. She inhaled the scent of him, soap and cold air, reveled in the strength of his arms, the comfort and security she knew she would find there.

Mark straightened, his hand still entangled in her hair, his arm still around her.

''So, Sheryl,'' he lifted one corner of his mouth in a careful smile. ''Now what?''

"I don't know," she replied her voice subdued.

"Neither do I." He let his hand drop from her back. But his other slipped through her hair then lifted it to his mouth, brushing it softly. "I love you, I care for you, I want to marry you." He let her hair drop then stepped back. "But I can't make you feel the same."

Sheryl was surprised she could still stand. To hear him open himself up to her, to make himself so weak in front of her, showed her more clearly than anything, his strength. She couldn't speak, didn't trust herself to say anything.

A rustling in the crib made them both turn. Benjamin stood at the rail, rubbing his eyes, his mouth pulled down in a pout.

Mark was the closest and he picked him up, swinging him into his arms. He turned to face Sheryl, Benjamin sitting easily in his arms.

He would make a wonderful father, she thought. And an even more wonderful husband.

"I have to leave, Sheryl. I've got a long drive ahead of me." He kissed Benjamin on his forehead and handed him to Sheryl, bending over to pick up the briefcase she didn't even know he had brought into the room. He turned to leave, hesitated and looked back at her. "I won't forget you, and I pray you find what you've been looking for."

He left, closing the door quietly behind him, sending an ache spinning deep within her.

Holding Benjamin close, she walked to the window.

He loved her. He loved her so much he was willing to give up his own work on the ranch, work that he loved, to ensure that she would have enough money to make her independent.

She laid her hot forehead against the window, listening to the sound of the snow ticking against it. The wind, drifting down through the valley, was picking up. It was going to storm.

She felt as tossed about as the small flakes. Since her father died she had been seeking, trying to find home, trying to find a place she belonged.

And now Mark had offered her a chance to do something

on her own, with no outside influences. He had just given her power over him, she realized. By telling Ed to change his will, he had sabotaged his own life. If she decided she wanted her share of the will at once, he would have to go back to working in the city and away from the ranch she knew he loved. It would be her gain, but the sacrifice would be his.

She watched his tall figure, huddled in a bulky jacket, as he strode between the parked cars to his truck. As he opened the door he paused, looking up.

''Oh, Mark,'' she breathed, her heart winging toward him, her hand reaching out, stopping at the cold window.

He flipped her a wave as he stepped into his truck. He closed the door. A cloud of exhaust swirled around it, and in one motion he spun the truck in a turn and drove away.

Sheryl felt as if he had pulled part of her with him.

You belong with him, you love him. You need him more than he needs you. Still holding Benjamin, she ran out the door, down the stairs, past a group of startled people and out the front door.

But all she saw of his truck was a swirl of snow that disappeared over the hill and was gone. Weak with reaction, she hugged Benjamin closer and leaned against the verandah post, tears slipping unheeded down her cheeks. She had just discovered so much. She had just been shown unselfish, giving love.

The door opened behind her, and Elise came up, slipping an arm over her shoulders.

''I should have told him,'' she whispered. ''I couldn't talk, I couldn't think.'' She turned to Elise. ''What should I do now?''

''He loves you, Sheryl, that's all I can tell you.''

''He gave up his own happiness for me,'' Sheryl said, looking up. She had been so afraid to make herself vulnerable, and Mark did it so easily.

''Love is not selfish.'' The quote from the Bible wove through her confusion, melding her thoughts, weaving them

into a coherence. She knew she loved him. Loved him with a depth that frightened her.

"When is Mark supposed to come back?" she asked, shivering as another gust of wind blew across the verandah.

"A week from now."

Sheryl bit her lip, thinking, planning. She knew what she had to do.

"I'm sorry, Dan. I can't give you any more notice than this." Sheryl clasped her hands in front of her, keeping her eyes on the desk that sat between her and her boss.

Dan blew out his breath in a sigh, rubbing the bridge of his nose. "I guess there's not much I can do about it, is there?"

Sheryl shook her head slowly.

"Your mind is made up?" Dan stared over his hand at her.

She nodded. "Yes. I enjoyed working with you, but there's something I have to do that's more important."

"Are you going to finish your schooling?"

"No." Sheryl hesitated, then with a smile said, "I'm going to get married, live on a ranch and have babies." The words sounded so confident, and Sheryl didn't even want to examine her own doubts. She clung to what Mark had told her, and even more, what Mark had done. All for love of her.

"That's a waste," Dan snorted, getting up. "You have a lot going for you."

A discreet knock on the door intruded into what was becoming a hostile atmosphere. Jordan Calder opened it and walked in.

"Here's that brief you wanted on the Gerhard trial." She winked at Sheryl and laid it carefully on Dan's desk.

"Calder, I want you to help me out here." Dan gestured toward Sheryl as if she was some exhibit that he didn't know what to do with. "This girl here is going to quit this job, quit school and move out to some isolated part of British Columbia and…and—" he waved his hand as if what he was about to say was too preposterous to even voice "—get married."

Jordan pursed her lips, tilted her head to one side as if weighing evidence. ''Good idea,'' she replied succinctly.

''What?'' roared Dan. ''Are you out of your mind? You of all people?''

''No temporary insanity here, Dan.'' Jordan smiled. ''I think Sheryl made the right choice. No need for you to act like a jealous suitor.'' Dan glared at Jordan, who merely held her ground. ''I think marriage is a much-maligned institution,'' she continued.

''You should know, you've handled enough of my divorce cases,'' he growled.

Jordan ignored him and turned to Sheryl with a grin. ''So when's the big day?''

''I don't know. I have to ask him yet.'' Sheryl grinned, feeling suddenly free and confident.

''You're a real woman of the nineties, aren't you,'' Jordan said with a laugh, reaching over to give her a hug. ''I wish you a lot of happiness. Call me and let me know when I can start shopping for pasta makers.''

''How about diapers,'' grumped Dan from the corner of the office.

''That comes later, Dan.'' Jordan clucked disapprovingly at him, then turned back to Sheryl. ''I'll take you out for supper tonight, and you can tell me the details of the entire romance.''

''I'll do that.'' Sheryl smiled as Jordan gave her a thumbs-up.

The office was quiet a moment. Sheryl smoothed out a non-existent wrinkle from her wool skirt, waiting for Dan's next sardonic comment. Instead he only sighed and walked around the desk, parking himself across from her, his arms clasped over his chest.

''You're sure about this?'' he asked in his most stern lawyer voice.

Sheryl felt a momentary flare of panic. Then she remembered the notation on the copy of the will she had received. It was a verse from the Bible. The same verse she had read in her Bible on the way back from Sweet Creek: ''When I am weak then I am strong.''

''Yes, I'm sure,'' she replied quietly.

''Well then, I can only add my congratulations to Jordan's. I'll miss you, in more ways than one.'' Dan shook his head. ''Hope your future husband likes babies.''

Sheryl laughed. Then, surprising even herself, she reached over and gave Dan a quick hug. ''Thanks for everything, boss.''

In an elegant room of the Palliser Hotel in Calgary, Mark Andrews threw his briefcase on the bed and pulled the cupboard door open. With a complete disregard for the ironing Elise had done on his suit pants and shirts, he threw them on the bed, followed by his brand-new cowboy boots, bought especially for this conference.

By rights he was supposed to be sitting in on a banquet with a keynote speaker Dr. Something-or-other speaking on the potential of trade with Zambootyland, or some such place. He had forgotten. He stuffed the clothes in his suitcase, threw papers in his briefcase and snapped them both shut with a disdainful ''click.''

Come to think of it he had forgotten much of what he was supposed to be reporting back to his zone of the Stockgrowers' Association.

Three minutes ago he had called Elise to see how she and Nate were doing. Two minutes ago Elise had told him what Sheryl had done about the will. One minute ago he had hung up on her.

And for sixty seconds he had wondered if he was brave enough to risk running to Edmonton to find out for himself.

What if Sheryl had signed over her rights to him for Nate's sake? What if she felt she didn't deserve it, plain and simple.

What if she didn't want him?

But Elise's words rang in his mind, pushing him off the bed. ''She loves you, big brother. She told me, then she laughed and said it again. I've never heard her so happy.''

He glanced once more around the restrained elegance of the room, making sure he had everything, and left.

A quick punch on the elevator button, and Thank you, Lord, the doors glided open. He caught a glimpse of himself in the mirror on the side of the car on the slow descent. His hair hung in his eyes, and in the back it was tucked in the collar of his denim shirt. He quickly finger combed it into some semblance of order and pulled his shirt straight, tucking it better into his jeans. He could stop halfway to Edmonton to get prettied up.

He glanced at his watch. Five-thirty. It would take him three and a half hours to get to Edmonton, three if he could avoid any Mounties along the way. He would phone Sheryl's apartment when he stopped for gas.

The elevator stopped. Mark took a deep breath and stepped out. Leaving his suitcases parked by the elevator, he dug into his pocket for his room key and strode over to the desk, slapping it on the marble top with a clunk.

''I'm checking out,'' he said to the smiling clerk. ''There'll be a few long-distance calls on my bill, as well.'' He reached behind him for his wallet and pulled out his charge card.

''Name?'' Another hundred-watt smile.

''Mark Andrews.''

The girl nodded, then leaned back as if looking for someone. ''A lady has been asking for you,'' she said to Mark. ''She's waiting by the stairs to the mezzanine.''

Mark frowned as he dropped his card on the desk. He didn't know anyone in Calgary. He didn't feel like talking to anyone he didn't know. He was in a hurry.

''Thanks,'' he said, resisting the urge to drum his fingers on the marble top of the desk. He tapped his toes, shifted his weight and stifled a sigh.

''I'm sorry this is taking so long, Mr. Andrews. Are you in a hurry?''

''Yes, and I'm sorry to be so impatient.''

''Well, I don't blame you. She's very beautiful.'' The clerk flashed him a discreet smile and ripped the receipt out of the computer. ''Just sign here and you'll be on your way.''

Mark pulled a pen out of his pocket, scrawled his signature on the bottom and waited as she ripped his portion off and slipped it into the wine red envelope with the hotel's name scripted in gold on the front. All very elegant and tasteful, right down to taking your money, thought Mark, slipping the envelope into his pocket.

''She's right around the corner, Mr. Andrews.'' Another coy smile. ''And I hope you have a nice weekend.''

Mark heaved a sigh, shoved his wallet in his back pocket and walked around the corner to get this visit with this mysterious woman out of his way. He was a man with a mission.

He paused, scanning the length of the room. Only one person sat on a couch near the steps. Her blond head gave him a start, but when its owner raised her head, he frowned and took a step closer. Her hair was feathered in layers that framed her face and drifted to the shoulders of her bronze and gold sweater. She stood slowly, her hand on her chest, and when their eyes met, Mark's heart stopped, turned slowly over, then began to race.

It was Sheryl.

For a long moment neither said anything as they merely stared at each other, each fearful, each excited, each hurting.

Mark made the first move, his empty arms aching to hold her, his hands itching to touch her soft hair.

''Sheryl,'' was all he said as he bent over her, wrapping one arm around her slender waist, his other hand tangling in the soft silk of her hair, clutching her head.

''Oh, Sheryl, babe,'' he whispered brokenly, hardly daring to believe he had her in his arms so soon.

Mark buried his face in her hair, his warm breath flowing over her neck. Her arms clung to him, her face pressed against his chest as she murmured his name over and over again.

Reality pierced the haven they had created, and he straightened, ignoring the surprised looks of the other guests and hotel staff. His eyes traveled hungrily over her face, his fingers tracing her beloved features. She was here. She was real.

"You cut your hair," he whispered stupidly, brushing a wisp from her face.

"And you didn't," she replied, her voice breaking as she reached up to touch his hair, his cheek, his chin. "I was scared I would miss you."

"Well, I was on my way to Edmonton." He looked down at her, a fullness and richness welling up in him, Thank you, Lord, he prayed. This is too much to take in. "I called Elise. She told me you signed away your share of the ranch." He looked up, suddenly aware of an audience. With a wry grin he tucked a strand of hair behind her ear. "My bags are waiting by the elevator. Let's go to my truck. We need to talk."

Sheryl bent over to pick up her purse, but when she straightened, her cheeks were flushed, her eyes bright.

"Oh, sweetheart," he murmured, drawing her against him. "Please don't cry. You'll break my heart."

"Sorry." She sniffed, swiping a palm across her eyes. "It's been a long five days."

He gave her a reassuring hug and led her across the lobby. His bags lay exactly where he'd left them. An elevator waited, its doors open, and as they entered, Mark pushed the Down button and they slid shut.

Mark turned to Sheryl, his eyes drifted lovingly over her face, his mouth curved up in a wry grin. Not satisfied with merely looking, he reached out and pulled her toward him, lowering his head. She lifted hers, meeting him halfway. Their lips met, a hungry tasting, a sealing of what they both had been seeking.

When the elevator stopped, Mark pulled away, regret tingeing his smile. "This is our stop," he whispered.

"Okay," she whispered back, smiling carefully.

He laughed and, picking up his cases, strode down the carpeted hallway to the car park at the end.

His booted feet echoed in the cement parkade as he led her to the truck. Dropping his suitcase, he stretched up and fished his keys out of his front pants pocket. Mark opened the passenger door and gave her a hand in. He hung on the door, watching her buckle up, feeling like it was his right, his privilege.

He slammed the door, the noise echoing hollowly. Sheryl sat back, inhaling the familiar smell of his truck. He unlocked the door and in one easy step, got in. She drank in the familiar sight of him adjusting the mirror, settling in, shrugging forward to turn the key in the ignition. Then he sat up, draped his arm casually across the back of the seat as he looked almost disinterestedly over his shoulder and backed the truck up.

He flashed her a grin, pushed the truck into gear and they left the parkade with a roar. Soon downtown was behind them, then the suburbs and finally they were on the highway heading out of the city, the gleaming white fields stretching like a blanket toward the mountains.

The ride was made in silence, neither quite knowing what to say, how to say it.

After half an hour Mark slowed the truck and pulled over. He stretched his hands in front of him, almost popping the seams of his jacket. He laid his head against the back window, his eyes drifting shut. Sheryl half turned, watching him, indulging in the luxury of just looking. He looked vulnerable with his eyes closed, the long dark lashes lying like two small shadows. Lines etched around his finely shaped mouth, stubble shaded the sweep of his jaw. His hair hung in disarray over his coat collar. He needed it cut, she thought, reaching out to brush a lock out of his eyes. He scared her, made her feel unsettled and vulnerable. She loved him.

Mark turned his head to her and caught her hand, curling his fingers around hers, his thumb lightly stroking the side of her hand. Then her breath caught in her throat as he gently pressed it to his rough cheek. He turned his head ever so slightly, and warm lips grazed soft, cool skin.

"Sheryl," he whispered, his eyes still closed.

Trembling, her fingers spread out, touching his soft lips,

exploring the shape of them, moving over his jaw, fluttering up to his sculpted cheekbones, tracing his eyelashes.

He opened his eyes, catching her hands. "Tell me why you signed over your share of the ranch to me?"

"Nothing like getting to the point, is there?" She laughed, feeling as if they had come to an epiphany. She took his hand and gently traced the calluses on it. Even after four days of city life, grit still lined the cracks in his knuckles, the lines in the palm of his hand. The hand of a worker, a rancher. "I did it because I couldn't see you working in the city, couldn't see you giving up what you love just for me."

"And," he coaxed.

Sheryl looked up into his soft gray eyes. "I did it because I love you."

Mark relaxed, as if he had been holding his breath.

"I didn't think this could happen," he whispered, his expression bemused. "I thought you were afraid of me."

Sheryl smiled tremulously. "I was."

Mark shook his head, his eyes following his fingers as they drifted over her face, tangled in her hair. "I'm sorry," he whispered, leaning forward to kiss her forehead. "I'll never hurt you. You have to believe me."

"No—" she straightened, catching his hand, holding it close to her cheek "—you don't know what I mean. I was scared of how much you mean to me. I was afraid you would break my heart."

"I wouldn't do that, either. I love you too much."

Sheryl pressed her lips against his hand and brought it down to her lap. "You know, I thought I didn't know how to love, I thought I wouldn't be able to forgive." She ran her finger across his palm. "I learned a lot about letting go and looking in the right places, the past few months. Once I forgave Ed, many things became easier." She looked up at him. "You gave me so much, you helped me deal with something that was eating me from the inside out," she said softly, her voice breaking. "I thought I was going to crack. I think God knew I needed to be around family, so He sent me to Sweet Creek.

I've discovered how much love God has to give us, and once I let Him love me, it became easier to love others."

"I'm so glad, Sheryl," he squeezed her hand tightly. Then he sat up, brushing her hair from her face. "So is this where I can ask you to marry me?"

"Actually, I was going to ask you."

"Just what I thought. An independent woman." He smiled at her. Then, with a rueful shake of his head, he caught her and pressed her close to him, burying his face in her hair. "I promise you, with God's strength, I will love you and cherish you as long as I live."

Sheryl squeezed her eyes shut, her hands cradling his head, reveling in his strength, the safety he gave her.

"Are you crying?" he murmured against her neck, his breath warm.

"No," she said in a choked voice, trying not to. "Well, maybe a little."

"It's okay, you know," he said, pulling his head back, wiping her tears away with his thumb. He gently kissed the others away. "Crying is as important as laughing. I hope we can do a lot together."

He stifled a yawn.

"Are you tired?" Sheryl asked.

"Didn't get a whole lot of sleep the past few nights." He angled a mischievous glance at her. "Been thinking about you."

"Do you want me to drive?"

"That sounds great." He scooted over and lifted her past him, then helped her adjust the seat. "Just keep it around the speed limit, okay?" he said with a laugh.

He watched as she put the truck in gear, checked over her shoulder and pulled into the traffic. Sheryl tried not to feel nervous with him watching her and glanced over at him.

"I think I'm going to like this," he said.

Then, to her surprise, he stretched out and laid his head on her lap, staring up at her. "I think we'll do okay," he whispered, his eyes drifting shut, his head growing heavy and warm on her lap as he relaxed.

Sheryl glanced down at his beloved face, so close to her and let a full-bodied sigh drift out of her.

She stepped on the accelerator, looking down the highway to the hills as they graduated to the Rockies. They were the mountains of her youth, and beyond them was home.

She had come full circle. She and her mother had left Alberta seeking a home and now she had found it. She had found it not by becoming strong, but by becoming weak.

She glanced down at Mark's face, relaxed now as he drifted off to sleep. A wave of pure love washed over her, and she sent a belated prayer of thanks to Heaven.

In weakness is strength, she thought. I sought strength and found weakness. I sought independence and found a home.

Home. Next to *love,* the most beautiful word in the English language.

Epilogue

"The glasses are in the cupboard," Sheryl chided Mark as she dropped the bag of groceries and the mail on the counter of their kitchen.

Mark shrugged as he backhanded his mouth and shoved the milk carton back in the fridge. "Old habits, my dear wife," he drawled as he walked to her side. He leaned one hip against the counter and dropped a kiss on the top of her head. "How was the trip to town?"

"They didn't have the filters you wanted. They're still on order."

Mark grimaced and leaned back, crossing his arms across his chest. "So that means the tractor won't get an oil change until next week." He dismissed the problem with a shrug. He turned to her and slipped an arm around her waist. "And what did the doctor say? Everything okay?"

Sheryl leaned against him and nodded, relishing the feel of his solid body. She rubbed her cheek against his shirt and then leaned back. "There is one small complication though." She reached up and rubbed the frown off his forehead with a forefinger slanting him a mischievous grin. "It's not serious. Yet."

He gave her a gentle shake. "Don't do this to me, Sheryl. What do you mean?"

She smiled up at him, her love for him warming her to the

tips of her toes. ''Two,'' she said succinctly, holding up two fingers.

''Two?'' He stared, not comprehending and Sheryl laughed.

''Twins. Two little tiny babies,'' she said.

Mark blinked, looked away, then back at her, an incredulous expression on his face. ''Twins,'' he repeated. ''Two babies.''

''I think we've covered that.'' She leaned back, her arms still clasped around his waist as she watched with joy the play of expressions on his handsome face.

Suddenly he reached down, caught her by the waist and swung her around. ''Twins,'' he yelled. He stopped, realizing what he, in his exuberance, had done. ''Oh, no. I'm sorry. Are you okay, honey?''

Sheryl just grinned. ''I'm as healthy as a horse.'' She cupped his face in her hands and pulled him down for a kiss. ''And I love you.''

Mark wrapped his arms around her and held her tightly against him. ''Praise the Lord,'' he said softly. He buried his face in her neck, rocking her carefully. ''Thank you.''

Sheryl laid her head on his chest, silently echoing his prayers. Her own arms held her beloved husband close, his belt buckle pressed against her still-flat stomach. Hard to believe that two lives were growing and changing within her.

Outside the trees were tinged with the soft green of new growth. Life flowed from season to season, promises were made and kept.

She closed her eyes. God was good. He had taken her through trials and had brought her safely here. To a husband. A family.

A home.

* * * * *

Dear Reader,

Family is important to me. My husband and I have been blessed with brothers and sisters who share our faith and parents who have nurtured it from the very beginning. Through our family and relationships with siblings and nieces and nephews, our faith is strengthened. We are reminded of what God needs and requires of us.

What I wanted to do with *Homecoming* is to portray the consequences of ignoring the needs of family members. Sheryl had wanted to be a part of the Kyle family, but they didn't understand where she came from. By the time her stepfather realizes what he has done, Sheryl has become a person who mistrusts and wants to be strong on her own, thinking that leaning on God or family is a sign of weakness.

Mark, with his faith in God and his own loving family, shows her that, like an arch, leaning on each other creates strength. Through Mark, Sheryl learns to forgive and to lean on family and trust in God instead of trying to be strong on her own.

By writing this story, I found I had to reach back into our own families and search for the things that frustrate and yet strengthen. I like to think our families are a small reflection of the community of Christ. Not one of us is perfect, but we are united by one goal. We must always be forgiving and asking for forgiveness as we stumble along with our eyes on the One who is the epitome of love and forgiveness, Jesus Christ.

Carolyne Aarsen

Books by Cynthia Rutledge

Love Inspired

Unforgettable Faith #102
Undercover Angel #123
The Marrying Kind #135
Redeeming Claire #151
Judging Sara #157
Wedding Bell Blues #178
A Love To Keep #208
The Harvest "Loving Grace" #223

Silhouette Romance

Trish's Not-So-Little Secret #1581
Kiss Me, Kaitlyn #1651

CYNTHIA RUTLEDGE

grew up wanting to write books. She wrote her first book at fourteen, but when it received less than stellar reviews from those she let read it, she relegated it to the trash and didn't write again for years. She started writing again as an adult and sold her first book to Steeple Hill in 1999. That book, originally entitled *Faith on a Harley* and renamed *Unforgettable Faith,* will always be special to her beacuase it opened the door to her career at Steeple Hill. It remains the only book set in her home state of Nebraska.

THE MARRYING KIND

Cynthia Rutledge

To my husband, Kirt, for his love and support

Chapter One

Could her life get any worse?

Kaye ''Taylor'' Rollins outlined her lips in the ornate mirror gracing one wall of the executive washroom, amazed her trembling hand could still draw such a precise cinnamon line. Her hands shook as badly as an alcoholic in the throes of withdrawal, and ripples of panic were rapidly turning her skin to gooseflesh.

She tried to rein in her mounting fear. Surely, the man would listen to reason. To toss her out with no more thought than last night's garbage made no sense.

Her stomach flip-flopped, and Taylor lurched over the sink, fighting to keep down her breakfast. After several deep breaths the bile in the back of her throat retreated, leaving only the fear.

Dear God, what am I going to do?

The answer rose from deep within her. *God hath not given us the spirit of fear, but of power, and of love, and of sound mind.*

Taylor's fingers abandoned their death grip on the sink and suddenly she felt incredibly foolish. Why was it so easy for her to forget she wasn't in this alone? Even though she firmly believed the Lord helped those who helped themselves, she never would have made it through this last year without Him at her side. Today would be no different. He would be there with her when she walked into that large office on the twelfth floor.

Taylor straightened and wiped her mouth with a tissue, taking off most of the lipstick she'd so painstakingly applied. Even though she'd never met the company's young CEO, the man had a reputation for fairness. She had nothing to fear from Nicholas Lanagan III. And right now he was the one person with the power to make this wrong right.

Taylor scooped up the pink slip and headed out the door of the washroom to the elevator. Pushing the button with unnecessary vigor, Taylor stared at the piece of paper in her hand—"Effective immediately, your position has been eliminated...."

She crumpled the slip and lifted her chin. With the Lord on her side and Rollins blood coursing through her veins, this latest adversity was not the end of her world. It was just one more obstacle to overcome.

Nicholas Lanagan shifted impatiently and waited for the brass elevator doors to open. He glanced at his watch and scowled. It made good business sense to belong to the Chamber, but when these breakfast meetings ran an hour over and threw his tight schedule into disarray he had to wonder if doing his civic duty was worth it. He'd now play catch-up the rest of the day.

The doors parted smoothly, and Nick exited the elevator with long purposeful strides. He stopped in front of his secretary's large cherry-wood desk. "Good morning, Miss Dietrich."

The older woman calmly pushed the hold button on her phone and raised her steely-eyed gaze. The picture of a woman in control, Miss Dietrich's lined face showed no expression. She didn't waste her time, or his, returning the greeting.

"Mr. Lanagan, Mr. Waters is holding on your line. He says it's important." The woman's fingernail poised above the transfer button. "Do you want to take the call?"

Nick fought back a surge of irritation. Henry Waters had been a thorn in his side for months, and Nick was at the end of his rope. But the bottom line was he needed Henry's company to solidify Lanagan Associates's place in the increasingly competitive enterprise software market. To risk alienating the man would be reckless. Impulsive. It would be tantamount to business suicide.

"Put him through."

The door swung shut and Nick settled into his soft leather desk chair and took a deep breath. "Henry, what's up?"

The voice on the line radiated excitement. "I know we're meeting this afternoon, but I've got good news and it just couldn't wait."

Nick's grip relaxed around the receiver. "What is it?"

"Claire's coming home!" The restraint Henry normally used in his dealings with Nick had vanished. "I've been waiting for her to come to her senses. When she broke up with you and left town—"

"Henry." Nick spoke more sharply than he'd intended. "That was a long time ago."

The man didn't seem to notice his abruptness.

"Barely six months. There's no reason you can't pick up where you left off."

The cold chill that shot up Nick's spine had nothing to do with the room's temperature. This could be a major complication. But the ability to respond under pressure had always been Nick's strength. He ad-libbed, loosely covering the receiver with one hand and talking to the picture of his father on his desk as if the man had suddenly sprung to life.

"Can't it wait? I'm on the phone." Nick forced an irritated sigh. "Henry, I'm sorry to cut this short, but something's come up. We're still meeting at three?"

"I'll be there," Henry said, disappointment evident in his tone. "We can have a long talk then."

Henry's announcement was still ringing in Nick's ears when Miss Dietrich came in with a steaming cup of coffee. Two sugars already added, just as he liked it.

"It's very hot." She handed him the mug.

"Good." Nick ignored her warning and recklessly took a gulp, almost relishing the scalding sensation searing his throat; the pain took his mind off the implications of Henry's news.

"Anything else, sir?"

"Not now. I'll buzz if I need you."

Miss Dietrich nodded and pulled the door shut behind her. If only he could get rid of Claire with so little effort. Say a few select words and she'd be history. Out of his life for good this time. If only it could be that easy.

He plopped the cup down. The freshly ground Colombian coffee sloshed over the rim and spilled onto the hand-rubbed cherry-wood desktop.

He stifled a curse.

Claire! One word said it all. Raking back a strand of hair that dared fall across his forehead, he railed against the injustice. What had he done to deserve this?

Even as he asked, he knew the answer. He'd made the mistake of escorting the attractive brunette to a few social functions. All of a sudden they'd been labeled a couple. Dating the daughter of a potential business partner was risky under the best of circumstances, but when that woman was Henry Waters's little princess the potential for disaster increased tenfold.

When Claire had unexpectedly accepted a job at a prestigious public relations firm in Washington, D.C., no one had been more thrilled than he'd been.

An added plus was that Henry had been incredibly sympathetic when his daughter had taken off without a second thought. In retrospect, Nick couldn't help but wonder if that had given him an advantage in the bidding war for Henry's company.

Taking over Waters Inc.'s data warehousing niche in the enterprise software business had long been Nick's dream. Now, after endless negotiations and countless months of contract revisions, he stood on the verge of translating that dream into reality. The merger would be finalized in less than two months.

Unless Henry backed out.

Nick blew out a harsh breath. If the man took his business elsewhere, Lanagan Associates would be forced into major restructuring. Today's layoffs would be nothing compared to the massive cuts he'd be forced to make.

Why did she have to come back now? Like a dark storm cloud, thoughts of Claire Waters swirled in his head.

She could ruin it all.

If he let her.

Nick quenched his rising annoyance. He could stop her. She'd fare no better than any of the others who'd tried to come between him and what he wanted.

He'd come up with a solution.

He always did.

The office door flew open and slammed shut. Erik Nordstrom, his closest friend and chief legal counsel, splayed himself against it, looking more like a spy on the run than a corporate attorney in an Armani suit. "Quick, bolt the door. Your watchdog is ready to bite."

"Watchdog?"

"That drill sergeant you call a secretary." Erik heaved a theatrical sigh and pretended to wipe some sweat from his brow. "I wasn't on your appointment calendar. It's a crime, you know. Opening the door to your office if you're not on her schedule."

"She's just doing her job." Nick sighed and gestured to a nearby chair. "Since you're here, you might as well sit down. My morning's shot, anyway."

"I'm glad to see you, too." Erik slanted a glance at Nick and claimed his favorite leather wing chair. Up went his Italian loafers on a glass table. "What's got you so bummed?"

"Claire Waters. She's coming back."

"So?"

"So—" Nick tried to hide his irritation "—Henry thinks we should pick up where we left off."

Erik's hazel eyes flickered behind his thin wire-rimmed glasses. "But it's been months since the Catwoman left."

Nick's lips twitched at Erik's not so fond nickname for Claire. His friend had taken an instant dislike to the woman.

"If I remember right, you weren't sorry to see her go," Erik added.

"I know that. You know that. The only one who doesn't know that is Henry. And maybe Claire." Nick rubbed his neck. "Henry's thinking Claire and I are going to have some glorious reunion and live happily ever after."

Erik stifled a laugh. "He obviously doesn't know you're already committed."

"Committed? What are you talking about?" Nick frowned. "I'm not engaged."

"All right. Maybe the company is more like a mistress. It gets all your attention, your devotion." Erik placed one hand on his chest and topped it with the other. "Just tell Claire there's no room in your heart for anyone else."

"Cut it out, Erik. This is serious. There's no way I'm going to let Claire's return ruin everything."

"Maybe she doesn't want you, either. Have you thought about that?"

Nick shook his head, wishing that were true. "I didn't get that impression."

"Okay, then..." Erik paused for a moment. "What's the worst that could happen? She comes. She hits on you. You turn her down."

"And the merger negotiations fall apart." Nick pressed his fingertips to his temples. "You know what Henry's like. He'll take any rejection of his daughter as a personal slight."

"Okay, then string her along. Whisper a few sweet nothings in her ear. Just enough to keep her happy until those papers are signed."

"It's tempting." Nick knew it would be the easiest solution, one with the least amount of risk. Still, something held him back. "But I couldn't do that, even to Claire. Besides, I might get stuck with her forever."

Erick visibly shuddered. ''A life with that woman would be a fate worse than death.''

''I agree wholeheartedly.'' Nick laughed. ''Just don't let Henry know I said so.''

''So, what are you going to do?'' Erik glanced curiously Nick's way. ''If I know you, you've already got a plan.''

''Something did occur to me when you were talking about being married to the company.''

''I was just kidding about using that excuse.''

''Still, it did give me an idea.'' Nick leaned forward and rested his elbows on the desk. He lowered his voice, even though they were the only ones in the room. ''I could tell Henry I'm engaged.''

''Won't work.'' Erik shook his head. ''He'll insist on meeting her.''

''I'll say she doesn't live here.''

''Henry might buy it, but Claire? Not on your life.''

Nick thought for a moment. ''Then I'll find someone in Cedar Ridge to play the part.''

His friend collapsed against the smooth leather, his mouth twisting in a wry grin. ''It has potential. The only problem is you haven't even been seeing anyone lately.''

''Henry doesn't know that.''

''Fiancée's usually expect marriage as a follow-up.''

''This one won't. I'll make that very clear.''

''So—do you have anyone at all in mind?''

Nick shook his head. ''I haven't gotten that far.''

''How about that redhead you brought to the Christmas party?''

''Aimee?'' Nick shook his head. ''I don't think so.''

''Why not?'' Erik quirked an eyebrow, and a mischievous grin danced on his lips. ''She was really hot.''

''Keep in mind the reason we broke up.''

''Because you were more interested in work than her.''

The promptness of his friend's response brought back Nick's smile. ''Not that reason.''

''All right, so she was more interested in your money than

you.'' Erik's eyes gleamed. ''In this situation, she'd be perfect.''

''Probably. But she's out, anyway. I heard she's getting married next month. For real.''

''You really think you'll be able to come up with a fiancée on such short notice?''

Nick met Erik's questioning gaze with determination. ''I don't have much choice. I'll find someone if I have to take the next female that walks through that door.''

Their gaze shifted to the door and—as if on cue—it opened.

''Mr. Lanagan, I'm so sorry. I told her you were in conference.'' Miss Dietrich cast a disapproving glance at the young woman standing unannounced in the doorway's arch.

Obviously pretty.

Obviously furious.

Chestnut curls, highlighted with rich strands of deep red, tumbled past stiffened shoulders in loose waves. Delicately carved facial bones surrounded large almond-shaped eyes of glittering emerald-green.

The hand-tailored jacket's cut and rich sable color accentuated the woman's slim waist and gently flaring hips. Brushed with a hint of copper, her full lips tightened under his scrutiny.

''Mr. Lanagan, I apologize for interrupting, but I must speak with you.'' The woman's chin lifted a notch.

''Would you like me to call security, sir?'' The look in Miss Dietrich's eyes clearly said he'd be a fool if he didn't.

Nick glanced at Erik, and his lips twitched when he received a subtle thumbs-up. His gaze settled on the intruder, and her eyes darkened to a frosty jade.

''No, Miss Dietrich. I think I want to hear what Miss—''

''Rollins.'' She paused.

Nick shot a quick glance at Erik. Was the name supposed to mean something to him? His friend shrugged.

Nick checked his watch. ''I have a few minutes I can spare. Miss Dietrich, hold my calls.''

"Very well, sir." His secretary shot Taylor a narrowed glance. "I'll be right outside if you need me."

"Ms. Rollins, have a seat." Nick gestured to the chair in front of his desk.

The woman stepped forward, a belligerent look in her eye, and sat down. Undisguised interest glimmered behind Erik's gold spectacles.

Nick jerked his head toward the doorway. "Erik. We'll continue our discussion later."

Apparently not the least bit disturbed over his abrupt dismissal, Erik stood and walked toward the door, flashing Nick a knowing grin. He grasped the doorknob and turned, tipping his head toward the woman. "Ms. Rollins, a pleasure. And, Nick, good luck."

Nick ignored the comment and directed his attention to his visitor. "Normally I don't meet with anyone without an appointment."

A small muscle jumped at the corner of her jaw, but her voice was soft and controlled. "I realize that, however this is very important."

He smiled, hoping to put her at ease. "You have my undivided attention. What can I do for you?"

A pink slip sailed across his slick desktop. "You can explain what this is all about."

Nick reached out and picked up the computer-generated form. He suppressed a groan. This was just the reason he'd instructed Personnel not to deliver the termination notices until the end of the day.

He laid the slip on the desk and studied her. "Oh, so that's it."

"Yes. That's it."

He adjusted his cuffs and straightened the knot on his tie. "Well, Kay—"

Irritation flickered across her expression, then disappeared. "I prefer to be called Taylor. Assuming, of course, that you want to be on a first name basis, *Nick*."

"This form says *Kay*." He glanced at the sheet.

''Kaye is my given name. But I've always gone by Taylor.'' The slight tightening in her jaw indicated she probably wasn't as calm and serene as she appeared. ''And another thing, if you're firing someone, I'd suggest spelling their name correctly. My first name is *K-A-Y-E,* not *K-A-Y.*''

''Well, *Taylor.*'' Nick reclined slightly in his chair. ''We have a volatile marketplace out there. I'm sure you're aware that certain measures must be taken for a company to be competitive.''

Her emerald eyes raked him. ''Don't patronize me, *Nick.* I'm not a naive little girl. I know what the marketplace is like. That's why I checked this job out carefully before I even considered it.''

''If you'll—''

''I'm not finished. I gave up a good position to move back to Cedar Ridge. For what? For you to fire me after only three weeks? What's fair about that? I have bills to pay. Lots of bills.'' Her voice broke slightly then steadied. ''I never would have taken this job if I'd known a cutback was in the works.''

Bills. Any sympathy he'd started to muster vanished and he regarded her through narrowed eyes.

''You had to know this position was going to be eliminated. Why did you even fill it?'' Her voice cracked, and she pressed her lips together.

''We hired you only three weeks ago?''

She nodded.

''I apologize for the mix-up.'' He made a mental note to check with Personnel. They were only supposed to have been filling key positions, not ones scheduled for elimination. ''Unfortunately I don't have another job for you. After this downsizing is completed, we'll be in a hiring freeze until the end of the summer.''

Her face paled, and she took a ragged breath. Despite the fact he had no tolerance for those who lived beyond their means, Nick found himself feeling almost sorry for her. For all he knew, she could be the sole support of a couple of kids. ''Unless...''

"I'm willing to consider almost anything. I'm very versatile." Desperation made her voice husky.

He studied her intently for a moment, then slowly shook his head. "No, on second thought, I don't think it would be a good idea."

"Listen, I *really* need the money. I told you, I'll consider almost anything." Emotion whipped color into her cheeks in an appealing dusty-pink glow.

Nick leaned back and wondered if he'd taken leave of his senses. He was crazy to even think it might work.

"At least let me interview. Give me that chance." Her words stopped just short of begging, and her stricken eyes told him what it had cost her.

Nick tapped his pen on the desk, then without further thought plunged recklessly ahead. "Let's start with you telling me a little bit about yourself. That'll help me determine if you'd be right for this, ah, assignment."

She took a deep breath and flashed him a grateful smile. He found himself smiling back.

"I graduated from Swarthmore with a degree in computer engineering. I worked for ComTECH Industries in Denver for the past three years."

Nick raised one eyebrow. "I don't understand. With those credentials, I wouldn't think you'd have any problem finding suitable employment."

"Probably not," she agreed. "If I moved back to Denver. But right now I can't do that."

"I take it, then, your husband isn't willing to move?" He could almost hear his personnel director scream at the question.

"I'm not married."

He leaned back in his chair. "So, what's the problem?"

"I'm an only child. My mother died when I was fifteen. Last year, my father was killed in a car accident." She clasped her hands together and took a deep breath. "My grandparents are getting older, and I'm their only relative now. I want—I need—to be close to them."

Nick's eyes narrowed speculatively, ''What about evenings? Would you be free at night if the job demanded it? Or do you have to help care for them?''

She laughed, a full-throated laugh that brought a smile to his lips. ''Heavens, no. They're not dependent on me at all. But after my father's death, my grandfather suffered a mild heart attack. He recovered fully, but it was hard being two hours away.''

Nick stared thoughtfully. His gaze traveled over her face and searched her eyes. *It just might work.* ''Well, Taylor, I think I may have a job for you.''

Her face lit up, and a soft gasp escaped her. ''You mean, you've already decided? The job is mine?''

''It is. That's of course assuming you want it.'' Would she agree? Was she really that desperate? His pulse quickened.

Her whole face spread into a smile. ''Want it? Of course I do. Tell me about it. What position would I fill?''

''The position is—'' his gaze met her questioning eyes ''—my fiancée.''

Chapter Two

"What did you say?"

Nick repeated the words slowly, as if that would increase her comprehension. "I'm offering you a job. You'd be my fiancée. Just for the summer."

Taylor's heart quickened, and for the briefest of moments she allowed herself to wonder what it would be like to be this man's fiancée. With his classically handsome features, jet-black hair and piercing blue eyes, Nick Lanagan epitomized every woman's dream man.

"Shall we talk salary then?" A satisfied smile creased his lips, and he picked up his pen as if he planned to write out a check.

"No," she blurted, her voice stiff and unnatural even to her own ears. She realized her hesitation had given him the mistaken impression she was considering his outrageous offer. "Mr. Lanagan—"

Nick leaned back in his chair and chuckled. "First names, Taylor. No one will believe we're engaged if you're calling me Mr. Lanagan."

Irritation surged at the cool confidence reflected in his smile. "*Mr. Lanagan,* if this is some kind of sick joke, I'm not laughing."

"Wait a minute." His blue eyes flashed. "You're the one who said you needed money."

"Yes, but I believe I also said I wanted a job."

"That's what I'm offering." His gaze challenged her. "A job for the summer. Nothing more. Nothing less."

"As your paid honey."

"As my fiancée."

"Why me? You must have dozens of girls who'd like to play house with you."

His eyes glinted to steel-gray, and she smiled to herself. Good. She'd gotten under his skin.

"Absolutely. But they might expect more from me than a salary. And a paycheck is all I'm prepared to provide."

"A paycheck to pose as your fiancée?" She studied him thoughtfully like he was one of her data sheets she was having difficulty deciphering. What the man was proposing made absolutely no sense. She knew she should end the conversation now. But her insatiable curiosity wouldn't allow it. "Why would a man in your position need to hire a fiancée? And what kind of services would you expect this fiancée to provide?"

"Provide?"

"Don't give me that innocent look. You know very well what I'm asking. Is sex part of the deal?"

Nick threw back his head and laughed. His lips parted in a dazzling display of straight, white teeth. "No." He rose and leaned across the desk, "All I'd ask is the pleasure of your company. Maybe a few public kisses. A little hand holding. Nothing more."

"This is ridiculous. I came here asking for a job. A real job."

"At least consider my offer."

Her gaze lingered a moment before she shook her head and rose. "I know I told you I was desperate. And I am, but even desperate has its limits."

"Aren't you being a bit hasty? We haven't even discussed how much this arrangement would be worth to me."

"No amount of money—"

"Twenty thousand dollars a month."

Her breath caught in her throat, and she grasped the back

of the chair for support. That kind of money would make a serious dent in her bills.

A deep, rich fragrance enveloped her, and she looked up. Nick stood beside her, so close she could see the flecks of hazel in his blue eyes. A shiver rippled down her spine.

''This is very important to me,'' he said in a husky baritone. ''Just think about it.''

She opened her mouth to tell him that more time wouldn't matter, the answer would still be no. But his closeness drove the words from her lips.

''I don't—''

''I agree. Now is not the time to decide this.'' His hand rested firmly against her back, and he propelled her toward the door. ''I'll pick you up at six and we'll have dinner. I guarantee I'll be able to put all your fears to rest.''

Obviously he didn't realize there was nothing to discuss. Her mind was made up.

''What would dinner hurt?''

She could feel herself weakening, and as if sensing her weakness, he pressed on. ''We'll just talk. Then, if you still decide it's not for you…''

''It's not,'' she said with more conviction than she felt.

''Give me a chance to change your mind.'' He ushered her out of the office. ''That's not too much to ask, is it?''

She must have nodded, because he smiled that killer smile. He mentioned something about getting her address from Personnel before the door closed softly behind her. Taylor steadied herself against the doorjamb wondering if she'd just lost her mind.

The proposal didn't make any sense. But then neither did her reaction.

When his gaze had locked on hers and he stood so close she could scarcely catch her breath, for one brief moment, she'd been seriously tempted to throw caution to the wind and say yes.

Nick inhaled the rich aroma of Starbucks's finest blend, the dark brew steaming hot. Unlike many of the younger secretaries, Miss Dietrich considered keeping him well supplied with coffee part of her job. The woman was definitely an anachronism. A woman who insisted on being called Miss Dietrich instead of the more informal Margaret or the more modern Ms. A woman who steadfastly refused to call him by his first name. She was a top-notch secretary. And she made a terrific cup of coffee.

Nick grabbed the half-empty carafe and upended it over his mug. ''So, what do you think of Ms. Rollins?''

Erik Nordstrom took off his glasses, his normally boisterous demeanor strangely subdued. He flipped the frames from one hand to the other. ''She's pretty. Well-educated. Intelligent. I don't think you'll have any trouble convincing people she's your fiancée.''

''But...'' Nick's eyes narrowed, and he forced the rising irritation down. If Erik had reservations, Nick needed to hear them. The trouble was, he'd already made his decision.

Eyeglasses in place, Erik crossed his arms behind his head. ''One thing bothers me. She must be desperate for cash to even consider your offer. The question is why?''

Nick snorted. ''Probably overextended on her credit cards. That suit she had on certainly didn't come off the rack. My mother was the same way.''

Despite Taylor Rollins's reluctance, she'd end up agreeing to his offer. He'd seen the flash of raw hunger when he'd mentioned the twenty thousand dollars.

Erik regarded him with a speculative gaze, and Nick fought to keep his expression impassive. The man knew him all too well. They'd been friends since their freshman year in college.

''The reason doesn't matter, anyway. This is strictly a business proposition.'' Nick's gaze dared him to disagree.

''You seriously want me to believe you looked at those cat green eyes, those gorgeous legs and those—''

''That's right.'' Nick snapped.

If Erik heard the harshness in Nick's tone, he ignored it.

''Still, you didn't need to ask her to dinner. You could have worked out the details right in your office.''

Nick shook his head. ''She's a little hesitant. Dinner will provide the right atmosphere. I'll be charming and the money will do the rest. Remember—as of today—she's out of work.''

''Which brings up another concern.'' Erik's gaze grew thoughtful. ''If she's as desperate for cash as you say, it may have been a huge mistake offering her this, ah, opportunity. Especially since she'd just been fired.''

Nick rubbed his suddenly tense neck. ''What do you mean?''

''I'm talking sexual harassment. We may have left ourselves wide open for litigation.''

''Sexual harassment?''

''I know it sounds crazy, but it would be easy for a jury to misconstrue your actions.''

Nick sank into the thick leather of his desk chair and raked his fingers through his hair. Here he'd foolishly believed the day couldn't get any worse. ''A lawsuit? That's all I need.''

He cursed his own impulsiveness, knowing he had no one to blame but himself. Nick punched the intercom. ''Miss Dietrich, get me Harvey Rust in Personnel.''

Five minutes later, Taylor's file lay open on his desk. Her impressive résumé overflowed with the type of experience and credentials Lanagan Associates sorely needed.

What doesn't make sense is why we let her go.

Erik read the application and résumé over his shoulder. Nick looked up at his friend's sharp intake of air.

''Uh-oh. That's a problem.''

Nick frowned and glanced at the records. ''What's the matter?''

Erik's finger pointed to the name of Taylor's emergency contact. *William Rollins, grandfather.*

''Who is he?''

''I can't believe you don't recognize the name.'' Eric's expression reflected his surprise.

"I didn't grow up here, remember? Unlike you, I don't know everybody and his dog."

"But that name should be familiar, even to you. 'Don't mess around with Bill Rollins'?"

A fierce tightness gripped Nick's chest. "The judge that retired last year?"

Erik nodded. "Thirty years on the bench. He's still practicing law, but on a limited basis."

"I remember now. Didn't he have a heart attack or something?"

"That's right. It happened after his son was killed in that big accident on the freeway. His son was Senator Robert Rollins. Don't even try to tell me you don't remember *him.* His death made the wire services from coast to coast." Erik took off his glasses and massaged the bridge of his nose. "This couldn't get much worse."

"You don't think—"

Erik's nod confirmed his fears. "I do think we may have just delivered Judge Rollins a case he can't resist. And a case he can't lose."

Taylor took a deep breath and straightened her shoulders. Ever since she left the office, her mind had been as tangled and chaotic as her wind-whipped hair.

One moment she was headed home, the top of her convertible down, her favorite radio station blaring full blast. The next, she stood on her grandparents' steps, her knuckle poised against the six-panel door.

What had propelled her to her Nana and Grandpa Bill's clapboard colonial rather than her own modern town house? She hesitated, tempted to slip away while she still had time, when the door abruptly opened.

Her grandmother, half out the door before she saw Taylor, halted midstep and grabbed the door frame to steady her balance. "Honey, you startled me. I thought you were at work."

"I got off early." Her insides were like a mass of quivering

Jell-O, but Taylor was amazed at how calm she sounded. "If you're busy—"

"Nonsense, my dear. I'm delighted to see you."

She wrapped her arm firmly about Taylor's shoulders and gave the younger woman no choice but to be led into the foyer. "I'm just going to run out and get the mail. Your grandpa's expecting an important letter. Lunch will be on the table in a few minutes. Of course, you'll join us?"

Taylor couldn't help but smile. From the time she could walk, Nana had been consistent in her approach to life's problems. It didn't matter what the question or the concern, a little slice of one of her gourmet creations would make it better. It's a wonder they didn't all weigh three hundred pounds! Thankfully, her family seemed to be blessed with a high metabolism. She surveyed her grandmother's trim form out of the corner of her eye. At five feet six inches, Nana never weighed more than one hundred and twenty-five pounds. Despite her silver hair, her trim figure clad in the latest style made her look much younger than her seventy-plus years.

Taylor shifted her gaze to the den. Her grandfather sat hunched over the honey-colored oak desk that had come home with him after his retirement, totally immersed in a thick law book. Like a Norman Rockwell painting, the scene tugged at her heartstrings.

The click-clack of her heels on the hardwood floor must have alerted him. He looked up, and a fond smile lit his still-handsome features. "Taylor. This is a pleasant surprise. Come and give your grandpa a big hug."

His strong arms encircled her, and Taylor said a quiet prayer of thanks. Losing her parents had been almost more than she could bear. If she had lost him… She pushed the thought from her mind and hugged his lean frame extra hard.

"You're looking good." She pulled away and held him at arm's length. He reminded her so much of her father. The same nose, the same strong features. Only her father's hair had been dark brown, while Grandpa Bill's chestnut strands were peppered with silver.

"He needs to take it easy if he wants to stay looking that way." Nana said from the doorway, a bundle of letters in one hand.

"Oh, Kaye." Grandpa Bill rolled his eyes.

"You already had one heart attack. I don't want you to have another."

Taylor frowned. "Have you been having more chest pain?"

"No."

"Yes." Nana looked at her husband sternly. "Tell Taylor the truth, Bill."

"Okay, maybe a little now and again. But—" he pulled a small medicine container from his shirt pocket "—the nitro takes care of it right away."

"What does your cardiologist say?" Taylor tried unsuccessfully to keep the anxiety from her voice.

"The doctors say he needs to slow down and not let everything bother him so much." Nana's words were clearly as much for her husband's benefit as for Taylor's.

"Once this case is completed—"

Taylor looked at them questioningly.

"Bill's doing some legal work for a friend. It wasn't supposed to take much time, but—"

"It's almost over, Kaye. Then I'll have time to relax, maybe golf more." He turned to Taylor as if eager to get the focus off himself. "How about you, sweetheart? Been out playing lately?"

"I've been too busy. I think I've only played eighteen a couple times this year."

"I can't imagine what the two of you see in that game." Nana shook her head. "Bill, why don't you and Taylor relax in the living room? I'm going to put the mail away and then I'll make us all some iced tea."

"Sounds good to me," Taylor said.

"My dear." Grandpa Bill crooked his arm, and Taylor took it. They walked to the living room arm in arm. "I remember when we couldn't get you off the links. That new job must be taking up a lot of time. Or perhaps it's not the job. Maybe it's a young man?''

The image of Nick flashed in her mind, and Taylor's face warmed. She forced her attention to her grandfather, noticing the lines of fatigue around his eyes and mouth.

If only man troubles were all she had to worry about. She forced herself to breathe past the sudden tightness in her chest.

''Grandpa Bill—'' She stopped, not sure what to say.

''Taylor, is something wrong?'' A frown marred his worn face.

Did his complexion suddenly seem more ashen? Her breath caught in her throat. ''No, no, everything is going great.''

His brows drew together, and his eyes filled with concern. ''Princess, you can tell me.''

She met his gaze head-on and forced a bright smile. ''Everything's just great.''

''That's the second time you said that, and I don't believe it for a minute. Something's bothering my girl. I can tell.'' He pulled her to the couch and made her sit down. His large hand, so like her father's, gently cradled hers. ''You just remember, your grandmother and I are always here for you.''

She cuddled next to him like she used to when she'd been a little girl. Her head leaned against his shoulder, and his hand lightly stroked her hair. The familiar loving gesture brought tears to her eyes.

''Oh, Grandpa Bill. You're right. It is a man.'' Her frustrations centered on a man, all right. One man. Nicholas Lanagan III.

A twinkle returned to her grandfather's eyes, and a more reassuring color returned to his face. ''I thought as much. Who is he? How long have you been seeing him?''

''Whoa. Hold it a minute, counselor.'' Taylor jerked upright and realized he'd completely misunderstood.

''What's going on in here?'' Nana strode into the room, a silver tray with a pitcher of tea and three glasses balanced in her hands.

''Taylor's got a new boyfriend. And I've got a hunch it's serious.''

A flash of joy erased the worry on Nana's face. She hurried across the room, setting the tray on the credenza, the tea forgotten. ''Back up. I want to hear all about him. How you met. How long you've been dating. Don't leave out any details.''

Taylor groaned and stalled for time. ''What about the iced tea?''

''It can wait.'' Nana's eyes sparkled.

The love on their faces shone as bright as the afternoon sun, and at that moment Taylor knew she would do anything to spare these two people more hurt. Even if it meant telling a little white lie. Or two. She took a deep breath. ''We've been seeing each other casually for some time. It's getting kind of serious.''

''Enough of the mystery,'' Nana said. ''Who is he?''

''Do we know him? Does he golf?'' Bill added.

Taylor laughed and patted his hand. ''You're just looking for someone to round out your foursome.''

A brief flash of sorrow skittered across her grandfather's face, and guilt stabbed Taylor. Her father's death had left that slot vacant.

Grandpa Bill seemed to force a smile to his face. ''All I want—'' he grabbed his wife's hand ''—all *we* want is to see you happy. And if this man makes you happy—''

''I think he can, Grandpa Bill. I really think he can.'' The lies slipped off her tongue so naturally she could almost believe them herself. Taylor paused. She'd nearly passed the point of no return.

Could she do it? Accept an engagement to a man she didn't know? Even for a summer? Her belief in love, commitment and the sanctity of marriage hadn't changed. But love, commitment and the sanctity of marriage didn't enter into this arrangement. After all, she reminded herself, she wouldn't actually be getting married, and even real engagements often were broken. What harm would there be if she agreed to Lanagan's deal? What would happen if she didn't? For a long moment she studied her grandparents, then cast her eyes heavenward.

Dear God, is this really part of your plan?

Chapter Three

"Drat."

Taylor pulled the linen dress off and tossed it onto her bed with the other discarded outfits in a well-practiced move. If only she'd thought to ask where they were eating this evening.

Her hand reached into the closet, finally settling on a denim dress. With its scoop front bodice, shirred empire waist and long easy skirt, it definitely qualified as casual. The silver leaf buttons dressed it up, and she chose sandals of powder-blue to complete the outfit.

Hair up or down? Taylor grabbed a swath and twisted it upward, but released her hold, scattering the curls around her shoulders. Tonight she'd leave it down and pray the humidity left it alone.

She glanced in the mirror and frowned, rubbed off the pink lipstick and reached for her favorite cinnamon shade.

The doorbell chimed, and Taylor's head shot up. A trail of reddish-brown streaked across her chin. She grabbed a tissue and hurriedly scrubbed her face before heading down the stairs. She stopped in the foyer and cast a quick glance in the mirror. A flush stained her cheeks, and her eyes were brighter than normal.

The way her heart pounded in her chest, you'd think this was a date and not simply a business meeting. She took a deep, steadying breath, pasted a welcoming smile on her face and opened the door.

"Nick. Hello."

Like her, he'd dressed casually. With a blue chambray shirt deepening his eyes to the color of the ocean and his hair gleaming like the surface of her ebony piano, he was even more attractive than in his business suit.

"Come on in."

"I thought we'd start this out right." He held out an assortment of spring flowers interspersed with baby's breath.

"Oh. Thank you." Taylor smiled and took the bouquet. It'd been a long time since a man—other than her grandfather—had surprised her with flowers. She stepped aside to let him pass. "Have a seat and make yourself at home. I'll put these in water."

Taylor gestured to a chair in the living room and headed for the kitchen. Reaching into the upper cupboard for her mother's crystal vase, she caught a glimpse of him through the colonnade's arch surveying her living quarters. Most of the ornate furniture and limited-edition prints had been her parents'. She'd briefly considered selling them to help pay her father's gambling debts, but immediately discarded the notion. Her grandparents were well aware what these heirlooms meant to her, and no excuse for selling them would have been good enough.

Her hands shook as she quickly arranged the flowers. She adjusted one last sprig of baby's breath and carried the vase into the living room, the keen fresh scent of spring filling the room.

"I grew up with antiques." Nick reverently caressed the smooth finish of an early-nineteenth-century satinwood drum table. "This is beautiful workmanship."

Taylor smiled and set the vase on the mantel. The table had been her mother's favorite. "The inlaid purpleheart wood makes the piece."

"Obviously you like the good stuff. Is that why you need the money?" His arm swept out, encompassing the furnishings. "So you can live like this?"

Taylor took a deep breath and tried to keep the irritation

from showing in her face. "I like nice things. And from the looks of your car in my driveway, so do you."

He didn't tense up. Instead he carefully set down an ornate vase he'd picked up and studied her.

She shifted under his intense gaze. "The point is it's really none of your business what I need the money for—"

"You're right," he said. "So, you're still considering my offer?"

"Maybe. If you're still willing to pay me twenty thousand dollars a month."

He hesitated. "That's what I said."

"You don't sound so sure anymore."

"I'm sure. I need a fiancée, and you need money. We're the perfect couple."

"That's stretching it a little," Taylor said dryly, reaching past him for the sweater draped over the back of a chair. "By the way, I went to see my grandpa this afternoon. I told him about you."

"You spoke with your grandfather," he repeated softly, his eyes flat and expressionless. "The judge."

"Do you know him?" She'd never considered the possibility.

"I've heard of him. We've never met."

"Well, he wants to meet you. He had a lot of questions—"

"What did you tell him?"

The harshness in his tone took her by surprise. "What could I tell him?"

"Answer my question, Taylor."

His abruptness sent her temper soaring. No wonder the man didn't have a girlfriend. In a few minutes, he wouldn't have a fiancée, temporary or otherwise.

"Wait just one minute, buster. Don't you dare use that tone with me."

His eyes narrowed and his back stiffened ramrod straight. "There was nothing improper about my offer."

Shock tempered her anger. "I'm not saying there was."

"Then what are you saying?"

"We don't know if we even like each other, but you think we can convince our friends and family we're in love? I'm not so sure. I don't know if we can pull this off and I don't want my grandparents hurt."

"Are they suspicious?"

"Not yet." She shook her head, remembering their reaction. "Actually when I told them we were involved, maybe seriously, they were thrilled."

"You told your grandfather we were serious?" The tenseness in his jaw eased, and he expelled a deep breath. "Then his questions—"

Totally bewildered at his reaction, Taylor could only stare. "Were about you. Where you grew up, if you had any brothers or sisters, stuff that I didn't have a clue how to answer."

"We can take care of that," he said with a relieved grin. "Over dinner I'll bore you with my life story."

"That's a start, but..." Taylor paused, refusing to shove aside her concerns. "What makes you so sure you can convince everyone you're in love with me? You don't even know me."

"Well." A dimple in his cheek flashed. "I *was* in a few plays back in high school."

"Oh, I get it," she said. "You'll play Romeo. I'll be Juliet. Is that the plan?"

"I want this to work." His eyes blazed with determination. "And it will."

Taylor could only shake her head. Nick's confidence and self-assurance reminded her so much of her father. Robert Rollins believed there was no goal too high that it couldn't be reached and no obstacle too large that it couldn't be overcome. Until he'd gotten in way over his head.

Taylor pushed the disturbing thought away and answered Nick's confident smile hesitantly with one of her own. Lying had always been something she abhorred. Still, she needed the money. And who would it hurt? If only she could be as certain as Nick they could pull it off.

They walked in silence to the sleek silver-blue sports car

parked at the curb. Taylor waited while he opened the door. She'd barely settled into the plush leather seats of the Jaguar XK8 when an obvious thought struck her and she wondered why she hadn't thought of it before. "I've got an idea. Why don't we treat tonight as a sort of dress rehearsal? We could *act* the part of a couple in love and at the end of the evening critique our performance. Then we'll have a better idea whether or not we can pull this off."

"Sounds good to me." Nick reached over and brought her hand to his mouth, placing a kiss in the palm.

A surge of heat shot up her arm, and Taylor started to pull away, then noticed his impish grin. She chuckled and slipped her hand from his grasp.

Almost reluctantly he flipped the ignition, and the car sped away from the curb.

"Is the Lodge okay?" Nick turned the car off the highway onto a familiar dirt road.

"That's fine."

Built by a handful of wealthy businessmen, the exclusive private club was originally designed as a gathering place for sportsmen. Over the years, the tennis courts and golf course had been added, and the men-only rule had fallen by the wayside. The Lodge housed the Drake restaurant, famous in the region for its wild game cuisine.

He turned slowly onto the spacious grounds, and Taylor lowered the window. The soft fragrance of lilacs teased her nose, and she inhaled deeply. She reveled in the refreshing scent and ignored the breeze mussing her hair.

The headlights illuminated the award-winning golf course that lined both sides of the gently winding drive. She smiled as the eighth hole came and went. She'd had her first and only hole-in-one there. A sixteenth birthday present to herself.

"You look lovely tonight." Nick's voice broke into her thoughts.

Taylor had to give him points for trying. He'd clearly jumped into the role of adoring fiancée while she sat there blushing like some awestruck schoolgirl out for the first time.

She forced herself to envision what she would say—how she would react—if she loved this stranger sitting beside her. Taking a deep breath, she tentatively slid closer and leaned her head against his shoulder. It seemed unnatural to be so physically close to someone she'd just met, but she reminded herself it was no different than sitting in a crowded stadium at a Broncos game shoved up against some stranger.

But no stranger at a game had ever smelled so good or made her heart race so fast. Nick turned his head, and she could sense his gaze, but instead of looking up, she snuggled closer.

With a push of a button, Nick filled the Jag with strains of Beethoven's *Eroica* symphony, her favorite piece.

She raised her head and smiled. "Oh, you like classical music?"

"Actually I do. But I can switch—"

"No," she said before he could change the CD. "I like it, too. A lot."

His lips curved in a self-satisfied smile before he turned his attention to the road. Taylor returned her head to his shoulder and let the music transport her away from her worries, soothing the tightness in her limbs, allowing her to relax fully for the first time since she'd opened that envelope with the pink slip stuffed inside.

The car rounded the horseshoe shaped drive in front of the Lodge, and Taylor reluctantly straightened. Turning the car over to valet parking, Nick offered his arm to Taylor and they walked into the Great Room of the Lodge.

Nick stepped forward to give the maître d' their names. Taylor scanned the crowded room, hoping she wouldn't see anyone she knew. Breathing a sigh of relief, she glanced down at her denim dress and wished she'd chosen the more flattering turquoise-colored silk instead.

"The table will be ready in a minute," Nick said, his hand lightly resting on her shoulder. "Can I get you anything from the bar?"

"No, thanks. I don't—"

''Taylor, over here.''

Her heart caught in her throat. Even across the noisy room, she recognized Grandpa Bill's voice immediately.

''Nick.'' Another voice rang out from a far corner.

The arm around her shoulder tightened, and an expletive slipped past Nick's lips. A smile that didn't quite reach his eyes tipped the corners of his mouth, and he waved.

''Who's the guy headed this way?'' he asked softly, talking through a smile, his breath warm against her ear.

''My grandfather.'' She glanced at the balding man barreling his way through the crowd. ''Who's yours?''

''My soon-to-be business partner Henry Waters. His daughter, Claire, is the reason I need a fiancée.'' His fingers dug into her arm. ''Smile.''

''Just don't let on to my grandfather that I lost my job,'' she said under her breath.

What rotten luck! They hadn't even finished their first rehearsal and now they stood center stage. Apparently this was opening night, after all. She reached to push back a wayward strand of hair, and Nick grasped her hand, holding it tightly.

''Well, now, who do we have here?''

Nick turned in mock resignation to face the knowing smile lingering on the lips of the large, middle-aged man.

''Henry, I didn't expect to see you here tonight.''

''This must be your fiancée.'' The man chuckled. ''At least I hope she is.''

''Sweetheart, this is Henry Waters, the guy I've been telling you about. Henry, this is Taylor Rollins.''

Nick cast her a sideways glance, and Taylor knew the moment had arrived. A split second to decide whether or not to take on the role.

''His fiancée,'' she said. ''For now, anyway.''

Nick's blue eyes flashed a gentle but firm warning. ''Taylor and I can't wait for the wedding.'' He brought her hand to his mouth and caressed it with his lips. ''Isn't that right, sweetheart?''

''Absolutely.'' She swallowed hard and smiled brightly. ''Darling.''

Henry stared, his dark eyes sharp and assessing. ''Rollins, eh? Any relation to Bill?''

''I'm her grandfather.''

''Bill, old buddy. I didn't see you.'' Henry extended his hand and slapped Taylor's grandfather on the back. ''It's been a long time. How have you been?''

''Doing good.'' Bill cast a curious glance at Nick, who stood with his arm draped around Taylor's shoulders.

''I was just offering Nick and Taylor my congratulations,'' Henry said.

''Congratulations?''

''On their engagement. Don't tell me you didn't know.''

''Of course I knew. I just didn't know they'd made the announcement public,'' her grandfather said smoothly, shooting Taylor a glance that told her she had some explaining to do.

''Nick told me earlier he'd proposed but wasn't sure of the answer. I don't mind admitting it took me by surprise. I'd always hoped he'd be my son-in-law someday. But I can blame my daughter for that. She left him alone too long. It was only natural he'd find someone else.'' Henry Waters rambled on, and Taylor shot a glance at Nick. His expression didn't change but his hand tightened on hers. ''Anyway, that's water under the bridge. He certainly couldn't have done any better. Taylor seems like a lovely girl, and there's not a family in the state better thought of than yours, Bill.''

''Nice of you to say, Henry.''

Taylor swallowed hard against the lump in her throat. She'd made the right choice. No sacrifice would be too great if it preserved her father's reputation and her grandfather's health.

Her grandfather turned to Nick, and Taylor knew she should introduce the two, but Mr. Waters would wonder why Nick and Grandpa Bill had never met, and the whole deception would be over before it began.

"Son, it looks like congratulations are in order." For a moment Grandpa Bill studied Nick intently, and Taylor realized why he'd been so formidable in the courtroom. Nick returned the gaze steadily with a measuring one of his own until her grandfather smiled. "You'll have to come over to the house so we can formally welcome you to the family."

"Why don't you both join us for dinner?" Taylor said weakly, hoping they'd refuse.

Her grandfather shook his head. Regret laced his eyes. "I wish I could. But I'm here on business. In fact, we were just being seated when I caught a glimpse of you. And of course I had to come over."

"Of course." She smiled with relief, realizing again how much she loved this man. "I'll call you and Nana tomorrow."

"You do that." Her grandfather brushed a light kiss across her forehead, said his goodbyes and headed back to the dining room.

"Unfortunately I've got to get going, too." Henry clapped Nick on the back. "Jack Corrigan is over at the bar waiting."

Nick's face tightened. "I thought your negotiations with him ended when you accepted my offer."

"Jack and I are still old friends, Nick," Henry said with a hint of reproof, "although I don't think he's quite forgiven me yet for picking Lanagan Associates over his company."

Nick's biceps tightened beneath her arm, but the smile he flashed epitomized confidence. "Friendship or not, he has to know you made the best choice. Be sure and tell him hello for me."

"I'll do better than that. I'll tell him to expect a wedding invitation. Any idea when the happy day will be?"

"No," Taylor said at the exact same moment Nick answered yes.

Henry laughed.

Nick smiled and shrugged. "We've tossed around a few dates, nothing definite yet. But I guarantee you'll be one of the first to know."

Taylor leaned back against Nick and kept a smile firmly in place until Henry Waters was out of sight. How was she ever going to pull this off?

Taylor slipped the key into the lock and turned to Nick. "The evening wasn't as bad as—"

"Before you stroke my ego with more kind words—" Nick's fingers slid sensuously up her arm "—I think it would be a good idea to seal this engagement with a kiss."

"Why would you think that?" Her heart picked up speed.

"We need the practice." Nick's tone was half serious, half teasing. "And in case someone's watching."

Taylor laughed and glanced at a nearby tree. "Wave to Grandpa Bill."

Warm flesh closed over her hand, and the laughter died in her throat. Instinctively she tried to pull away, but his grip tightened.

"Okay, maybe he's not there tonight—" his lips brushed against her hair, as his other hand cupped her cheek "—but we still need the practice."

She shivered beneath his touch. Her heart pounded against the thin denim of her dress, but she didn't move.

His jaw relaxed, and he bent down, the warm smile more genuine now. His lips moved over hers, softly at first, as if testing the waters, then more firmly. Her arms unexpectedly wrapped around his neck.

Her heart pounded like a sledgehammer in her chest. More affected than she would ever admit, Taylor drew her head back and looked at this man she'd just kissed, this stranger, her temporary fiancé.

"Wow." He raised one dark brow. "That was some dress rehearsal."

He reached for her again, but Taylor shook her head and sidestepped his embrace. "I think we've practiced enough for one evening."

"Practice makes perfect." His heated gaze searched her eyes, and he smiled so enticingly she had to look away or give in. "Are you sure?"

Of course she wasn't sure. But she was sensible. Not to mention responsible. "Positive."

"Just one more for the road?"

She smiled, giving him a solid A for effort. "Not tonight. But since we're engaged, I'm sure they'll—"

"Engaged." He shoved one hand into his pants pocket. "I'm glad you reminded me."

He pulled out a tiny velvet box and pushed it into her hand. "Here. You'll need this."

Her heart twisted. She'd dreamed about receiving an engagement ring. But never had she thought it would be like this.

"Aren't you going to open it?"

"Sure. Why not?" She snapped the box open and gasped. The large emerald-cut diamond in an antique setting had to be at least five carats. "This is way too much. I can't accept this."

"Sure you can," he said, removing the ring from its velvet nest and slipping it on her finger. "It was my grandmother's. Just remember, I want it back when we break up."

She glanced at the stone. "Gee, thanks, Romeo."

He ignored her sarcasm and reached for her hand, holding it up to the porch light. "It looks good on you, Juliet. I guess it's official. We're engaged."

"Temporarily," she murmured.

The gem caught the light's rays, and a prism of colors shot from its depths. A beautiful prop. A precious gem to grace her finger for the next three months before being returned to storage. An outward symbol of deception, not of love and commitment. Was this really the road she was meant to travel?

"What are you thinking?"

Taylor pulled her gaze from the ring and shoved her doubts aside. "I'm thinking I can hardly wait to see what happens in Act Two."

Chapter Four

Nick leaned back in his leather desk chair and laced his fingers together behind his head. His gaze never left her face. "Mind telling me what's so important I had to leave a meeting that took me two weeks to arrange? The way you're acting, I can't imagine it's because you missed me."

It had been three days since she'd accepted his offer. Three days without so much as a phone call. Three days of offering excuse after excuse to her grandparents.

"The way I'm acting? How would you act if a man you've just introduced as your fiancé drops off the face of the earth, doesn't return—"

"I was out of town."

"I don't care if you were in China." Only death would have been a valid excuse for ignoring her fifteen voice messages. "You could have called."

"I was busy." A sudden thin chill hung on to the edge of his words.

"Busy?" she said sarcastically. "Too busy to pick up the phone?"

She stalked to his desk, picked up the receiver and shoved it into his hand. "How many seconds out of your *busy* schedule would that little gesture have taken? Five? Three?"

His lips quirked upward.

"Don't you dare smile at me, mister. Not after what you've put me through." She refused to be appeased. "What was I supposed to say when my grandparents asked why I wasn't bringing you over to meet them? I can't bring him because I don't know where he is? I can't set up a time because he won't return my calls? I wish I had a quarter for every time your secretary told me you were unavailable."

His smile vanished, and he set the receiver down with a slow, controlled gesture. "That's her standard response to callers."

"Even your fiancée?"

He had the grace to look slightly embarrassed. "I must have forgotten to mention—"

It was all she could do not to scream in frustration. "Nick Lanagan, if I had a rope you would be swinging from the chandelier in the lobby right now."

"What a romantic picture," a sultry voice purred.

Taylor's gaze jerked to the intruder in the doorway. The sleeveless white linen sheath emphasized the woman's deep rich tan, and the alligator belt around her waist accentuated her smallness. Her thick dark hair hung in long graceful waves over her shoulders.

"Although I must admit ropes don't do much for me. I've always been partial to satin sheets and champagne."

Shocked, Taylor could only stare at the unknown woman.

"Claire." Nick rose from his chair and circled the desk to stand at Taylor's side. "I'd like you to meet my fiancée, Taylor Rollins. Taylor—Claire Waters."

So this was the infamous Claire. Taylor narrowed her gaze, a tiny, superficial smile tipping her lips. The woman was a barracuda. In the political arena such women were well known. It didn't matter if the man was married or engaged, he was fair game. Consequently Taylor had developed a deep distrust of such creatures.

Claire smiled and crossed the thick gray carpet, her hips swinging seductively. Her dark eyes glittered, sharp and assessing. "Do I detect trouble in Paradise?"

Nick laughed and slid his arm around Taylor's shoulders.

''Just a little quarrel. In fact, if you hadn't interrupted we'd already be into the kissing and making-up stage.''

''Don't let me stop you.'' Claire waved one hand, her cherry-red nails cutting a bright swath in the air. She sat in the corner wing chair, crossing one perfect leg over the other.

For a long moment Nick stood silent, and a tiny muscle twitched in his jaw. Then he turned and curled his finger under Taylor's chin, tipping her face to his. ''I'm sorry I was so inconsiderate. Will you forgive me?''

Taylor nodded and shoved aside her irritation. Was this sincerity an act for his old girlfriend's benefit or was Nick truly sorry? With Claire watching their every move there was no way to be sure. Still, what could she do but lift her gaze and force a slight smile? ''Yes. I'll forgive you.''

As if on cue, Nick's mouth lowered to hers, leaving her no time to prepare.

She couldn't pull away.

She couldn't act repelled.

She couldn't do much of anything.

His lips covered hers, and for an instant all she *could* do was respond. Taylor jerked back, and a warmth crept up her neck. ''Nick, not here. We have an audience.''

Claire's brown eyes, so dark they were almost black, measured her with a cool, appraising look. Taylor lifted her chin and stared back, her fingers twisting the unfamiliar ring on her left hand. A plethora of blue sparks shot from the mounted gem, scattering the midday sun.

Claire's eyes widened, and an absurd sense of satisfaction swept through Taylor. She curved her fingers around Nick's arm, giving the other woman a clear view of the impressive jewel.

The slight smile that tipped Nick's lips told her the gesture hadn't gone unnoticed.

Claire's gaze moved slowly back and forth, studying Taylor's face for an extra beat before sending a brilliant smile in Nick's direction. ''Daddy and I have decided to throw you an engagement party. Assuming, of course, you and—''

Her hand fluttered in the air as if trying to recall some insignificant fact.

"Taylor," Nick told her, and Taylor smiled at the amusement in his voice.

"Oh, yes. Taylor. Assuming, of course, that you two will still be together then."

"Don't worry about that." Nick chuckled, and his arm tightened around Taylor's waist. "This is the woman for me."

For a fraction of a second, Claire's face stiffened then she shot him a sly smile. "If you're happy, I'm happy."

In a pig's eye, Taylor thought.

Claire reached into her bag and pulled out a notepad and pen. "I'll need your mother's current address so I can send her an invitation."

"Don't waste your stamp." Nick rounded the corner of the desk and hit his phone's do-not-disturb button.

"Now, Nick, I'm sure Sylvia loves your fiancée and would be crushed if she didn't have the opportunity to toast your engagement." Claire smiled brightly. "In fact, Daddy told me the cutest story yesterday and I said, 'Well, it sounds like Nick got himself a woman just like his mother!'"

Taylor shifted uneasily.

"You don't mind if I tell it, do you?" Claire's dark eyes flashed beguilingly at Taylor, her rosy lips turned up in a pouty smile.

"I'm not sure what story you're talking about," Taylor said.

"It's the one where you visited your grandparents for the summer and wouldn't wear the same outfit twice." Claire shot a slanted look to Nick as if to make sure he was listening. His smile remained, but his jaw was clenched. "Daddy said you maxed out your grandfather's credit card and then threw a fit at the mall when he told you no more clothes. It was the talk of Cedar Ridge for months. Sounds like your mother, doesn't it, Nick?"

His eyes narrowed, and Taylor shifted beneath his gaze. She remembered that time all too well. Her mother had died that spring, and her father had set off on the campaign trail. She'd been filled with resentment over being left behind. Grandpa Bill and Nana had borne the brunt of her teenage anger and angst that summer. "I'm surprised he remembered. That was so long ago. I was barely sixteen."

"But those are our formative years—aren't they?" Claire smiled sweetly.

Taylor opened her mouth to respond, but Claire cut her off. "I guess I always thought Nick was looking for a different kind of woman."

An inexplicable look of withdrawal came over Nick's face. He remained silent, forcing Taylor to answer.

"He was," Taylor said. "Me."

"Of course," Claire murmured. Her lashes swept down across her cheekbones, covering the satisfied gleam in her eyes. "Well, I need to scoot. Nick, I'll give you a call this week and we'll do lunch."

"I'm not sure I can make it. But maybe you and Taylor can get together."

"Sure." Irritation colored Claire's dark eyes but her smile never wavered. She grabbed her bag and rose. "Daddy and I are meeting at eleven, and he'll have my head if I keep him waiting."

The door couldn't close quickly enough behind her. Taylor breathed a sigh of relief.

"I don't think she bought it," Nick said, rubbing his chin, his gaze focused on the closed door.

"How could you tell?"

"She was way too nice."

"That was nice?" Taylor widened her eyes. "You're kidding, aren't you?"

"I wish I was," he said. "Seriously, she was being charming today."

"Charming? That wasn't quite the word I'd use. How could you ever have dated her?"

"We all make mistakes." Nick motioned for Taylor to sit.

He leaned against the desk, his expression thoughtful. "Claire was one of mine. And a big one."

"I think she's still interested, engagement or no engagement. Why, she practically threw herself at you."

"I expected as much." He paused and searched Taylor's face, for what she wasn't sure. "That's why you're here. To run interference so I can get some work done. But you're going to need to loosen up. Relax a little. Otherwise, she'll never believe this engagement is real."

"I'm doing the best I can, but—"

"I'm not saying you don't show promise. The kiss was pretty good." He shot her an irresistibly devastating grin, and despite herself, her heart raced. "With a little practice, I think we could really nail it. And since we don't have an audience now..."

His smile widened and brought out the dimples in his cheeks. She really liked those dimples.

In another instant she would have been in his arms. But it was the self-satisfied gleam in his blue eyes as he stepped forward that brought her back to reality. She pulled her gaze from his and took a deep steadying breath, forcing herself to remember the reason for today's visit.

"Since we don't have an audience, we need to talk about you meeting my grandparents."

He stopped. His smile disappeared.

"Tonight," she added.

He leaned across the desk and flipped open his planner. His gaze lowered briefly before he shook his head. "Tonight's not good for me. I've—"

"Tonight," Taylor said firmly. "I'm not putting them off any longer. Pick me up at seven."

His lips tightened, and his eyes darkened dangerously. For a long moment she thought he'd refuse.

He snapped the appointment book shut. "Seven it is."

She could tell he was angry, but she ignored his scowl. "Nick?"

He looked up from the pile of papers in front of him. ''Yes?''

''Don't forget to tell Miss Dietrich I'm your fiancée and she's to put me through when I call.'' Taylor's voice oozed with a syrupy sweetness at odds with the directness of her gaze.

''Consider her told.'' Nick's gaze never wavered, but for an instant, Taylor swore something that looked a lot like respect flickered in his eyes. ''See you at seven.''

Like actors with little in common except the performance, they headed their separate ways. Nick returned to his paperwork and Taylor pulled the door closed behind her.

With a little more effort on both their parts, this business arrangement could work. At the end of the summer she'd have her money and he'd have his merger. They'd go their separate ways and no one would be the wiser. No one would be hurt. It sounded reasonable. Then why did she have this sinking feeling that it wasn't going to be that simple?

Nick leaned back in the overstuffed sofa and took a sip of espresso. Taylor's grandmother—who'd insisted he call her Nana—sat a plate of tiny cookies on the table at his side.

His gaze slid over the festive platter, and he reached out and took a cookie. Nana's smile widened, and Taylor shot him an approving glance.

His temporary fiancée looked especially beautiful this evening, Nick thought taking a bite and reflecting on his impulsive choice. The warm glow from the lamplight brought out the red in her hair, and her green eyes glittered like a pair of emeralds. He reached over and covered her hand with his, giving it a little squeeze.

The large diamond was hard against his palm, but he'd expected that. It was the coldness of her skin that surprised him. Obviously she was not as relaxed as she appeared. Perhaps she wasn't as easy to read as he'd first thought.

Keeping his hand in place, Nick turned to Bill Rollins, who

thankfully hadn't insisted Nick call him anything but Bill. ''Have you known Henry Waters long?''

''Actually...'' Bill paused. ''I've known Henry for almost thirty years. He and I have served on a couple of committees together and we've golfed in the same league for years. How about you?''

''We met at a Rotary Golf Scramble a couple of years ago,'' Nick said, thinking back to his first impression of Henry. He'd dismissed the man as a loud-mouthed blowhard who drank too much. Since then he'd realized that although his first impression was correct, there was a little more to the man than met the eye. A shrewd businessman, Henry was intensely loyal to his friends and his family. Nick sighed. Hence the problem with Claire.

''I didn't know you golfed.'' Taylor's voice broke through his thoughts. It was a simple statement but Nick nearly groaned. Instead he smiled. ''Sure you did, sweetheart. Remember we talked about going out to the Lodge sometime?''

Understanding filled her eyes. She laughed. A pleasant musical sound. ''Of course...how could I have forgotten?''

Bill's eyes lit up, and he leaned forward in his chair. ''If you're free on Friday morning, some friends and I get together for eighteen. We tee off at nine.''

Nick could feel Taylor tense beside him. What was she so afraid of? That he'd bluntly turn the man down? If she knew him better, she'd realize he hadn't gotten where he was in the business world by alienating future contacts. He'd long ago learned the value of a tactful refusal.

Nick took a deep breath and mentally framed his answer.

''Grandpa, maybe Nick would like to know who else he'd be playing with.'' Taylor's voice was soft and low beside him.

''Of course, my dear.'' The smile Bill dispensed to his granddaughter was filled with love and indulgence. ''You might even know them, Nick. Jack Corrigan and Tom Watts?''

A band tightened around Nick's chest, but he kept his voice

offhand. ''Jack and I have met. He was one of the bidders for Henry's company.''

Bill's expression turned thoughtful. ''I think I do remember hearing something about that. Jack had really counted on getting that bid.''

Just as I thought.

No wonder old Corrigan was still cozying up to Henry. He was probably looking for an opening, any opportunity to get Henry to change his mind. Too bad he didn't realize he was wasting his time. There would be no opportunity. Nick would make sure of that. The refusal died on his lips. There might be some value in being a part of this foursome, after all.

''Fridays are usually good for me.'' The lie slipped easily from his lips.

Pleasure lit Bill's face, and Nick knew he'd scored some big points tonight. ''We meet in the clubhouse for coffee at eight, if you'd like to join us?''

''Works for me.'' Nick smiled and slipped his arm around Taylor's shoulders. There just might end up to be more benefits to this arrangement than he'd ever dreamed.

Utterly drained, Taylor leaned her head against the leather headrest and closed her eyes.

The smooth ride of the Jag acted as a soothing balm on her frayed nerves. From the time they'd set foot in her grandparents' house, every fiber in her body had been on alert; the enormity of the task that loomed before her was mind-boggling. What ever made her think she could convince these two people who knew her better than anyone in the world she was in love with Nick? And he was in love with her? She would have bet there wasn't an actor alive who could pull off such a feat.

But she'd underestimated Nicholas Lanagan.

Again.

With a warm smile and an engaging manner, he'd set about convincing her grandparents he was a man in love. He was so good she almost believed him herself. She could see why he'd been so successful in his business.

''Nick, did you feel—I don't know—uncomfortable at all this evening?''

He chuckled. ''Will you bite my head off if I say no?''

She heaved a heavy sigh. ''They loved you. Your champagne toast brought tears to Nana's eyes.''

''I'll take that as a compliment.''

''I'm just worried—''

''You worry too much.''

A year ago, worry and Taylor Rollins would never have been mentioned in the same breath. No one longed more for the carefree person she'd once been than she did. ''I just hope they won't be too upset when we break up. They've been hurt enough for one lifetime.''

''Losing their daughter-in-law and then their son, that would have been tough.''

A chill filled the car that had nothing to do with the air conditioner. Her mother had been dead over ten years, but discussing her father's death still brought tears to her eyes. ''It was horrible.''

''Did your father and his parents have a close relationship?''

''He was their only son. The light of their life.''

''You sound bitter.''

''Do I? I don't mean to. I mean I'm not. My father was a great guy.''

''Tell me about him.''

''Why?''

''Your grandfather mentioned him several times. He seemed to assume I knew all about him.''

''My grandpa obviously likes you. He doesn't talk about my father much anymore.''

''He did to me.''

''You played a convincing adoring fiancé.'' *Too convincing.* ''That toast—how did you put it again—to the woman—''

''—who made me realize that I could have all the riches in the world but be poor without her by my side. And then I added that part about you being my best friend.'' He shot her a crooked grin. ''Your grandparents seemed to find it very touching.''

''You're incorrigible.'' Her lips tipped up in spite of herself. No doubt about it, Nick had a certain romantic-hero type appeal.

Actresses always fall in love with their leading men.

Nonsense. She wasn't some naive Hollywood starlet. She was a responsible adult who knew the line between fiction and reality. She had a job to do. And as long as she remembered she was playing a role, she'd be just fine.

No matter how realistic the part.

No matter how handsome the leading man.

Chapter Five

Nick eased the Jag into one of the last remaining spots in the gravel lot and shut off the engine. He removed the key but remained seated, his gaze shifting to the blue skies overhead.

The often unpredictable northeastern Colorado weather had cooperated. The temperature was balmy, and there wasn't a cloud in sight.

"You couldn't have picked a more beautiful day for a company picnic." Taylor tried to forget her apprehensions and enjoy the day. As a politician's daughter she'd faced similar situations many times. The fact that this time it would be Nick's colleagues who would be watching her, assessing her, shouldn't change a thing.

"Actually the date is picked a year in advance," Nick said. "That way everyone can plan ahead."

"Now that you mention it, I seem to recall when I was first hired seeing some information regarding a picnic in my welcome packet." Taylor remembered being told to set the date aside. "What's the big deal, anyway?"

Nick opened his door, got out and rounded the front of the car to open her door. "Just wait. You'll see."

He took her hand loosely in his. A surge of electricity shot up her arm and it was all she could do not to pull away.

Why did his presence affect her so much? Every time she was close to him, it was like being in junior high again. Her heart picked up speed, excitement surged up her spine and she felt as awkward as a teenager on her first date.

She'd never reacted so strongly to a guy she knew well, let alone one she'd barely met. Even Tony, who'd been her friend forever, had never caused the slightest tingle to travel up her spine.

But at twenty-six she was no unsure teen, and over the years she'd become proficient in concealing her emotions, especially troublesome ones. She smiled and let Nick help her out of the low-slung sports car, ignoring the subtle musky scent of his cologne.

They strolled down a mulch-strewn path leading into the park, and Taylor concentrated on the beauty of the surrounding woods. A ground squirrel darted in front of them.

Delighted, Taylor turned to Nick, lifting her face to his, one hand lightly touching his shoulder. "Did you—"

His lips lowered to hers, and suddenly the question no longer mattered. The kiss ended quickly. With a warm hand Nick brushed a strand of her hair from her face. It was a tender gesture. Her heart lurched. "That's better."

"Better?" Confusion clouded her thoughts. "What do you mean better?"

"You have that 'I've just been kissed' look." His gaze searched her face. "Now you look like a woman in love."

In love? She wanted to laugh, but a tightness filled her throat and she couldn't pull her gaze from his.

"On second thought..." A dimple flashed in his cheek, and once again his mouth lowered.

The sounds of the woods faded and Taylor lost herself in the warmth and sweetness of Nick's kiss. She wrapped her arms around his neck, and he pulled her close, his fingers hot against her back.

"All right, you two. Break it up." Taylor jerked back at the amused masculine voice. Or as far back as Nick's unyielding arms would allow. Unlike her, his only reaction to the intruder was to raise his head and shift his gaze in the direction of the sound.

''Erik.'' A hint of annoyance crossed Nick's face. ''Shouldn't you be manning the grill or something?''

''I'd rather watch you.'' Erik leaned against the trunk of a tall tree, folded his arms across his chest and stared from Nick to Taylor with an innocent expression.

Taylor laughed. She couldn't help it. Although she'd only met Erik once or twice, her instincts told her that this behavior was classic Erik.

''Nick and I were just discussing the picnic,'' Taylor said, regretting the words the instant they left her mouth.

Nick raised a brow, his lips twitching.

This time it was Erik who laughed. ''Don't tell me. Let me guess. We're going to have a kissing booth and Nick was just checking to see if you'd be worth a dollar a pop?''

''Erik,'' Nick growled.

Erik ignored him, and his gaze slid up and down Taylor's form. For a second she wondered if her jeans were too tight or if the sleeveless cotton top clung too closely to her curves. They'd passed muster in the full-length mirror at home, but under Erik's intense scrutiny she wasn't so sure.

''I'd be glad to help out with the research.'' Erik reached for Taylor's arm. ''Give a second opinion.''

''Don't even try it.'' Nick's lips curved in a smile, but the warning in his blue eyes was clear.

Erik's hand dropped to his side, but instead of being upset at his friend, his amusement seemed to be even more pronounced. ''All right, have it your way.''

''Did we get a good crowd?'' Nick moved his arm so her hand slid down to his, and he gently locked his fingers with hers before starting down the path with Erik following behind.

''You bet.'' Erik's voice was filled with satisfaction. ''Miss Dietrich even showed up this year.''

Nick stopped suddenly and turned to his friend. ''She did?''

Taylor shot a questioning glance at Nick.

''She hasn't come since my father died,'' he said simply.

''Well, I for one wish she'd stayed away.'' Erik heaved an

exaggerated sigh. ''She's been hounding me for the last twenty minutes about when we're going to eat.''

''Hounding?'' Nick's expression was clearly skeptical.

''All right,'' Erik said. ''Maybe she just said something about making sure the meat didn't get too done, but I know what she meant.''

Guilt washed over Taylor. They'd been late because of her.

''Sweetheart.'' The word still felt awkward on her lips. ''If people are waiting we'd better get going.''

''You're right.'' Nick smiled but made no move to go. Instead he lowered his mouth to hers one last time.

Taylor resisted the urge to sidestep his kiss. She'd never been comfortable with public displays of affection, and Erik made no attempt to look away. But she had a role to play, and making the engagement seem real was part of it.

''Nick.'' Erik cleared his throat. ''Think about the meat.''

Nick's thoughtful gaze lingered for a moment longer, then he smiled. ''Now I'm ready.''

The picnic was unlike any Taylor had ever attended. She'd expected the long rows of tables covered with red and white cloths, overflowing with salads to satisfy any and all tastes. The chips were there, too, along with the roasted sweet corn and watermelon. It took three tables to handle all the pies, and Taylor's mouth watered at the sight of a pumpkin pie with pecan streusel topping.

But Nick pulled her past the beckoning tables, past the people standing in small groups staring with unabashed interest and past a stern-faced Miss Dietrich.

They stopped abruptly before a raised platform, and Nick gestured for Taylor to climb the two small steps to the stage.

She stood on the raw plywood, and Nick moved quickly to her side. Within seconds, the people who'd been milling around surrounded them. Everyone *had* been waiting for Nick to arrive. Her guilt intensified.

Nick turned on the charm the minute he began speaking, starting with a joke about why they were late and ending with the announcement they'd all anticipated.

"You all know how much this company means to me. I never thought I'd find anything that mattered as much to me. Well, I was wrong. When I met Taylor Rollins, it was no contest. And, although we'll be formally announcing our engagement in a few weeks, I wanted all of you to be the first to know." Nick pulled her to his side and grinned.

The crowd cheered, and Taylor pasted what she hoped was a properly adoring expression on her face.

The look of approval he shot her told her she'd hit the mark. He captured her hand with his, and from the broad smile on his face, he looked perfectly relaxed. But his hand gripped hers a little too tightly, and a barely perceptible muscle in his jaw jumped.

She'd grown up with a supremely confident male who never let on if he had worries or concerns. Knowing that this wasn't easy for Nick, either, made her feel closer to him. Impulsively, she turned and kissed him lightly on the mouth.

Surprise flickered in his eyes. He responded immediately. He tugged her toward him.

"Nick—"

He stopped her words by covering her mouth with his. It was an exquisite kiss and it made her forget for a brief moment in time that she stood center stage with hundreds of people watching.

The crowd roared their approval.

Nick released her, an odd tender look in his eyes. Taylor caught her breath and waved to the employees and their families.

Off to the side, Miss Dietrich stood, her arms folded across her chest, staring intently.

"Let's eat," Nick said.

As if on cue everyone scattered toward the food-laden tables.

Taylor's shoulders slumped in relief. The hard part was over.

Nick gave her hand a squeeze. "You did good."

"I don't think I'm cut out for this," she said with a sigh. "My stomach is churning."

"That's because—" he gently took her arm "—you're hungry. Come with me."

He pulled her toward the tantalizing scent of barbecue. A huge metal smoker loomed before them, and Taylor realized where Erik had disappeared to once they'd reached the picnic ground. Resplendent in a chef's hat and apron, the young attorney stood dishing out platters of ribs and barbecued beef.

Taylor's mouth started to water and she had to concede that maybe Nick was right. Maybe she was just hungry.

"Mr. Lanagan." A man Taylor remembered vaguely from her brief time at the company stopped them. "I hate to interrupt but could I speak with you a minute?"

Nick hesitated, and she knew he was remembering his promise to not desert her.

"Go ahead." She smiled. "I'll be fine."

Taylor took her place in line and filled her plate to the point of overflowing. She balanced it carefully in one hand, gripping a tall plastic cup of iced tea in the other.

The picnic tables were rapidly filling, and Taylor glanced around looking for a place to squeeze in.

"You're welcome to join me, if you like." The perfectly modulated voice sounded from her right.

Taylor turned and met the formidable gaze of Miss Dietrich. Her stomach clenched. They'd barely exchanged ten words since they'd met, but the woman still intimidated her. She was set to politely decline the offer, but something in the older woman's look and the fact that the secretary sat alone at the end of the bench while others seemed to be surrounded by family and co-workers changed her mind.

"Thanks." Taylor carefully lowered her plate and cup to the table's rough surface, then slid onto the bench opposite the woman.

She dropped a paper napkin onto her lap and lifted her gaze to find Miss Dietrich staring unabashedly.

Startled, Taylor shifted her gaze and popped a chip in her mouth.

Miss Dietrich hesitated for a second then grabbed a chip from her own plate and took a bite. "The sour cream and onion are my favorite."

The tenseness in Taylor's shoulders eased. Away from the domain of her office, the woman actually seemed pleasant. Maybe this wasn't going to be as bad as she'd thought.

Taylor picked up another chip, holding it loosely in her fingers. "You've known Nick for a long time, haven't you?"

"Since he was a little boy," Miss Dietrich said matter-of-factly. "I was his father's secretary for over twenty years."

"What was he like?" Though the barbecued beef on her plate beckoned, the desire to learn more about Nick overpowered her appetite.

"Nick? Or his father?"

"Nick," Taylor said immediately, then realized although she knew very little about her temporary fiancé, she knew next to nothing about his family. "Both."

Miss Dietrich dabbed the corners of her mouth with the edge of her napkin. "Nick was a sweet, serious little boy. He adored his father."

"It sounds like they were very close."

"As close as they could be." Miss Dietrich took a sip of her tea. "Nick's father faced a daunting task. When he started out, computers were in their infancy. There were constant changes in the field and Nick's father was determined to be at the forefront. Consequently he spent a lot of time at the office."

"But what about Nick and his mom? Where did they fit into his life?"

Miss Dietrich's gaze turned disapproving, as if Taylor had uttered an obscenity. "Mr. Lanagan was a good man. He did—"

"My two favorite ladies." Nick grinned and slid next to Taylor, his arm reaching up to rest loosely around her shoulder. "You both look so serious. What's up?"

An uncomfortable look flashed across the older woman's face, and she pursed her lips.

Taylor shifted her gaze and her breath caught in her throat. If she had to play this part, she couldn't have picked a more handsome leading man. She forced her thoughts to the conversation. "Miss Dietrich was just telling me about your father's accomplishments. It sounds like he was a remarkable man."

"He was." Nick nodded. "He was the reason Lanagan Associates flourished. It took a lot of time and effort, but to him, it was worth it. The company wasn't just his job, it was his life."

The question that Miss Dietrich hadn't answered still nagged at her. Taylor frowned. "But what about you and your mom?"

Nick shrugged and grabbed a potato chip from her plate. "We understood. Or at least I did. Dad always said for a business to be a success, it has to come before anything else in a man's life."

Taylor nodded as if what he'd said made perfect sense instead of being the antithesis of everything she believed. She wanted to ask him if he felt that way, too. But the thought of putting him on the spot before his employee kept the words from her lips.

And what did it matter anyway? She wasn't marrying the man. When she really did get married it would be to a man who shared her beliefs and values. A man who put God and family before his career. A man who loved her with his whole heart.

Taylor cast a sideways glance and sighed. And maybe if it wasn't too much to ask and she was really lucky, that man would be as handsome as Nick Lanagan.

Chapter Six

Taylor hung up the phone and heaved a sigh of relief. Since the picnic Nick had been extremely busy at work and he hadn't been able to fit any ''together'' time into his schedule. She'd wondered how he'd react to her invitation to attend church with her and her grandparents on Sunday. Would he refuse to go? Or see it for what it was? A way to convince her grandparents that this engagement was the real thing. Thankfully, he'd agreed to go.

Nana and Grandpa Bill hadn't wasted any time telling Pastor Schmidt about her engagement, and she'd been shocked to discover that the pastor had recently spoken to Nick. According to the minister, Nick was currently in the process of transferring his membership from a Denver congregation and was anxious to get involved with some of the standing committees. She'd had to smile and act as if she knew all about it.

Her grandfather had beamed at the news and made sure the pastor knew that the finance committee he chaired could use another member.

Taylor leaned back against the sofa, her mind a jumbled mass of confusing thoughts and feelings. As happy as she was to hear about Nick's interest in the church, something didn't ring true. If he was so interested in church, why had he insisted they attend the early service so ''only the morning would be wasted''?

She'd had to bite her tongue. Praising God wasn't ever a waste of time, but how Nick led his life wasn't her business. He was her employer. Maybe once she knew him better, she could subtly mention he might want to look at his priorities.

Once she knew him better?

She chuckled at the thought, a twinge of sadness underlying her amusement. Nick was a stranger. And she needed to remember that by the time she got to know him better, he'd be history.

Nick hung up the phone, unable to keep an irritated scowl from his lips.

He'd made his obligatory daily call to Taylor. As he'd told Erik, a phone call was a small price to pay to keep in touch and head off any unforeseen problems before they developed. And it didn't take a lot of time. After all, what was five minutes in the total scheme of things? If he called from the office, he could still be productive and review his e-mail or sign some checks while she talked.

Not that he didn't like Taylor or enjoy her company. And he especially liked kissing her. At the picnic there had been absolutely no reason for him to kiss her in front of Erik. Erik knew the score, knew the engagement was a sham. Nick didn't need to make a point. The simple truth was he did it for the pure enjoyment.

His gaze slid to the picture of her that now graced the top of his desk. She'd stopped by the day after the dinner with her grandparents and left it for him, along with a note. She'd been right on target, and he wondered why he hadn't thought of it. Surely, a man would have a picture of his fiancée somewhere in his office.

His lips tilted upward in a smile. The picture was a good one, but then, he reminded himself, Taylor was a beautiful woman.

Is that why he'd said yes to her request? Because she was beautiful? Or because deep down he'd really wanted to see her again?

All he knew was, when she'd mentioned church, his gaze had shifted momentarily from his computer screen with its endless e-mail messages to her picture, lingering on those full lips, and he'd found himself saying yes, he'd accompany her and her grandparents on Sunday.

Thankfully, he'd retained enough of his good sense to insist they attend the early morning service. Going to the late one almost guaranteed that not only his morning but the whole day would be wasted.

Eventually he would get to know the members of this congregation better and the time would be well spent. As his father used to say, church was a good way of making new contacts and of strengthening the old. His mother would always bristle, insisting that that was not the purpose of church. His father paid her no mind. He'd just laugh, slap Nick on the back and make some comment about women not having a head for business.

Sylvia may not have understood business but she certainly understood how to spend money. Nick's lips tightened. Lots of money. So much that the company had been on the verge of bankruptcy by the time Nick had taken over.

A familiar bitterness welled deep inside Nick. She should have spent more time tending to his father's needs when he was sick rather than dragging him to all those parties. And each time with a new designer dress or some ostentatious piece of jewelry bought specifically for the occasion.

According to the housekeeper, his parents had fought continuously about money that last year. Away at college, Nick heard all about it from the housekeeper, a woman intensely loyal to his father. She'd had nothing good to say about Sylvia Lanagan's behavior.

Nick's heart ached with sympathy for his father. He'd come home as often as he could, but he'd been a senior that year and it hadn't been near enough. If only he could have seen what was happening. If only…

Nick shoved aside the nonproductive thoughts. He had no time to waste on regrets. Only one thing was important—the merger with Waters Inc. Nothing else mattered. Nothing else was worth a second thought.

The door to Nick's office swung open. He spoke without looking up. "Just put the folders on the counter, Miss Dietrich."

"The old hag is down the hall at the copy machine."

The feminine voice was all too familiar. Nick could barely hide his groan. "Claire, I'm kind of busy here."

The overpowering scent of musk drew close. Nick kept his gaze on the troubling report from his new product chief.

Claire snatched the paper out of his hands. He jerked it back and glared at her.

She laughed, a pleased expression blanketing her carefully made-up face. "Still the same old Nick."

"Who else would I be?" This time he didn't even try to hide his irritation.

"I don't know." She pressed one finger to her lips and tilted her head as if pretending to think. "Maybe a love-struck fool?"

"Give it up, Claire."

She settled into the soft leather of the chair and looked at him innocently. "I'm just trying to make conversation. No need to bite my head off."

His fingers tightened around the edge of the desk. What was there about Claire Waters that pushed all his buttons?

"You're awfully cranky today. Are you and the girlfriend not getting along?" Her gaze turned sharp and assessing.

"Her name is Taylor," Nick said bluntly. "And for your information we're getting along just fine."

Claire twirled a strand of dark hair slowly around one finger. "If you say so."

He blew out a breath and gave in to the inevitable. Nick shoved the papers aside and leaned back in his chair. "Five minutes. You can have five minutes."

For the first time since she'd walked through his office door, Claire let some irritation show. Her dark eyes shot sparks, but her voice was well controlled. ''You're an arrogant jerk, Nick Lanagan. No wonder I find you so appealing.''

Nick raised a brow. ''The clock's ticking. You've got three minutes.''

''All right.'' Claire leaned forward in her chair. ''Daddy was going to call you but I said I'd stop by and ask you personally. He wants you to meet us for breakfast Sunday morning. Some guy that heads his operations area in New Jersey is going to be in town.''

A surge of excitement swept through Nick. After all these years, it was finally coming together. The Waters Inc. data warehousing operation would soon be his, and this meeting with Henry's operations chief only confirmed the reality. Sunday couldn't come soon enough.

Sunday.

His stomach twisted in a knot.

''Sunday morning's not good.'' He offered Claire his most engaging smile, wishing he'd been nicer to her earlier. ''How about in the afternoon?''

''He's leaving at noon.''

Nick raked his fingers through his hair. ''I can make it any other time.''

''That's the only time he's available.'' Claire rose effortlessly from the chair. ''What's the problem? If I know you, it can't be because you want to sleep late.''

Sleep late? There hadn't been a day in the last four years that he'd risen past seven.

If only his reason could be that simple. Bill Rollins might understand him skipping church, but he'd promised Taylor... Nick brought himself up short. Why was he so worried about her? She worked for him. He didn't owe her anything, least of all an explanation.

''On second thought, Sunday morning will work.'' Nick pushed back his chair, stood and rounded the desk. He gestured toward the door. ''Let Miss Dietrich know the time and place on your way out.''

Instead of heading toward the door, Claire moved closer.

So close the overpowering scent of her perfume surrounded him. So close it took only one simple movement for her to reach up and pull his face to hers. For her mouth to meet his. Her lips were warm with a hint of promise.

And left him cold.

''Mr. Lanagan.'' Miss Dietrich's disapproving voice sounded from the doorway.

''Yes, Miss Dietrich?'' Nick took a step back. He resisted the urge to brush away the taste of Claire from his lips with the back of his hand.

Claire smiled brightly at the secretary, her expression filled with satisfaction. At that moment Nick could see why Erik called her Catwoman. She looked like a cat that had just swallowed a canary.

Disapproval radiated from every inch of Miss Dietrich's ramrod stiff posture. The older woman's gaze slid dismissively over Claire before meeting Nick's head-on. ''Your fiancée called.''

Nick cleared his throat and forced an interested smile. ''Did she leave a message?''

''I told her you were in conference. She wanted you to call when you were free.''

''Miss Waters is just leaving.'' He'd done nothing wrong, so why did he feel like he had?

Claire ran a long red fingernail up his sleeve. ''But we were just getting started.''

Nick leveled her a warning glance. ''Goodbye, Claire.''

She hesitated then shrugged. ''I've got some business to take care of anyway.'' Claire's lofty gaze settled on the secretary. ''Mr. Lanagan is meeting me at nine a.m. on Sunday at the Heritage Hotel. Be sure and put it on his calendar.''

Her request was imperious and clearly designed to put Miss Dietrich in her place.

It didn't work.

Miss Dietrich drew herself up to full stature and turned with a disdainful sniff.

Shocked, Claire's eyes widened. Nick hid a grin behind his

hand. Claire would soon learn that no one got the best of Miss Dietrich. Not even Henry Waters's little princess.

Impatiently, Nick shifted in the high-backed wooden chair and wondered if it would be rude to leave. They'd started talking business the second he'd sat down, rather than wasting time in idle chitchat. He appreciated that fact since the purpose of the meeting was business, not social. But now the talk had turned personal, and bored stiff with the aimless chatter, Nick turned his attention to his surroundings.

The Pioneer Room of the historic Heritage Hotel had been recently remodeled and no expense had been spared. The rustic wagon-wheel motif had been replaced by more elegant appointments that few early settlers would have recognized. Stained glass depicting life in the old west topped each window, and original prints and artwork from the era were strategically placed along the walls.

Nick waved away another cup of coffee and glanced down the table, noting the linen tablecloth, the sterling silverware and the crystal glasses. Fine china replaced the rustic glazed mugs favored by the previous owners.

The waitress removed the last of the empty plates, and Nick couldn't have said what he'd eaten. Jack Corrigan's unexpected presence at the table when he'd arrived had effectively killed his appetite.

Clint Donovan, Henry's operations chief, sat with Jack on the other side of the table, while Claire sat between Nick and Henry. All through the meal Claire had rubbed her foot up the side of his pant leg. He'd done his best to ignore her.

"Nick, how's that beautiful fiancée of yours doing?" Jack added two spoonfuls of sugar to his coffee and took a sip.

"Great." Nick's smile was genuine. Taylor had surprised him and been a real trooper about the change in plans. Of course, he'd met her more than halfway by offering to call her grandparents and explain about the meeting.

"Fiancée?" Clint quirked a brow.

"Nick is engaged to Taylor Rollins." Jack explained before

Nick could answer. ''Her father was Robert Rollins, the senator who died in that car accident last year.''

Clint glanced from Claire to Nick, a puzzled frown on his face. ''But I thought you two...''

Nick's jaw clenched. ''Claire and I were dating at one time. She left town. I met Taylor. The rest is history.''

Clint shifted his openly curious gaze to Henry.

''I made no secret of the fact that I hoped my Claire and Nick would end up together.'' Henry heaved a sigh. ''But I can't blame him. She had to go take that job in D.C.''

Claire ignored her father's censuring glance and leaned across the table. She crooked a finger to Clint. He leaned forward. In a conspiratorial whisper, Claire spoke just loud enough for everyone at the table to hear. ''What Daddy is trying to say is Taylor got him on the rebound.''

Nick took a deep breath and counted to ten.

Claire smiled. Although she spoke to Clint, her gaze never left Nick's face. ''I've tried to tell him now that I'm back he doesn't have to settle for second best.''

''Claire!'' Henry exclaimed.

Jack Corrigan choked on his coffee.

Clint quirked a brow.

Nick's hands clenched into fists, and he forced a laugh. ''I don't think anyone who ever met Taylor would consider her a second-choice kind of woman, Claire.''

Claire shrugged and sipped her mimosa.

''It must have been hard to lose the contract.'' Clint turned to Jack in an obvious effort to change the subject and make up for his earlier gaffe. ''Those bids were so close.''

It was all Nick could do not to groan out loud. Of all the topics for the man to pick, why did he have to choose that one?

The uneasy tension that had settled over the table thickened.

''So I understand,'' Jack said with an easy smile. ''But that was Henry's call.''

Henry's call.

Nick could tell that even now Jack didn't understand why

he'd lost the bid. After all, Jack and Henry were friends from way back. What would have made him choose Nick?

Claire's hand on his thigh reminded him of the answer. Keeping a smile on his face, Nick reached under the white linen and captured her wrist, effectively stopping the upward migration of her fingers.

A twinkle of amusement flashed in Claire's eyes, and she blew him a kiss. Henry's gaze turned sharp and assessing. A glimmer of hope reflected in their dark beady depths.

Nick pretended not to notice. He lifted his coffee cup with his free hand and nonchalantly took a sip of the lukewarm brew.

He'd been right all along. Henry *had* chosen Lanagan Associates because he hoped Nick would one day be his son-in-law. Now Henry valued his reputation too much to back out of the deal without having a valid business reason. But if Nick should become involved again with Claire, all bets were off.

Nick downed the last of the cold coffee and settled back in his chair. As long as he kept this fake engagement on track and Claire at bay, at the end of the summer everything would be just as he planned. Waters Inc. would be his.

Chapter Seven

"I can't believe I let you talk me into this," Nick muttered and jammed his hands into his pockets.

"Will you relax?" Taylor snapped. "You look like you're headed to the gas chamber instead of a premarital counseling session."

"Same difference." Nick shook his head, and his dark hair glistened in the fluorescent light. "I can't believe I agreed to this."

"You already said that." Taylor took a deep breath and tried to slow her rapidly beating heart. Did he think this was easy on her? She'd known Pastor Schmidt since she was a child. And ever since her grandparents had surprised her by registering her and Nick for these classes, Taylor had been worried sick that the minister would see right through their sham engagement.

The door to the church office burst open. Taylor's and Nick's heads turned as one. A skinny blond woman with puffy bangs pulled a young man with glasses and a bad case of acne into the waiting room.

"C'mon, Tom." High and shrill, the young woman's voice grated on Taylor's already tightly strung nerves. "We're late."

"Mandy." Tom jerked his hand from hers. "Quit pullin' on me."

The irritation in his voice came through loud and clear. The blonde stopped suddenly and turned, her eyes wide with disbelief. Her lower lip, the pink lipstick half-chewed off, trembled.

"Oh, baby." The boy stepped toward her, his voice gentle and filled with concern. "Don't cry."

She sniffed loudly, and he hurriedly pulled a rumpled tissue from his pants pocket.

Taylor and Nick exchanged amused glances.

But Mandy wasn't through. Big tears welled in her blue eyes, and her bottom lip protruded further.

Taylor hid a smile. If she wasn't mistaken, Mandy had crying on demand down to an art form. She braced herself for a sob fest.

The door to Pastor Schmidt's office opened, effectively staving off the impending flood. Taylor offered up a prayer of thanks, and she and Nick rose to their feet as the minister entered the doorway.

"Welcome." The gray-haired minister smiled and stepped aside, motioning the four of them into his office. "We're a small group this evening, so we should all get to know each other really well."

Nick groaned under his breath. Taylor jabbed him in the ribs.

She ignored Nick's pained gasp and moved forward to greet the pastor. It was only with the help of God and Pastor Schmidt that she'd been able to survive the death of her father. Every time she'd thought she couldn't go on, he'd been there with words from the scripture to remind her that she wasn't alone.

"Pastor." Her smile was filled with genuine warmth. "I don't believe you've met Nick."

"Only over the phone," the minister said with a smile.

She introduced the two, and they shook hands.

"I've known Taylor since she was a little girl." Taylor squirmed under the approval in the pastor's eyes and wondered if he would smile with the same degree of fondness if he knew that her engagement was all a lie.

She squared her shoulders. She had a good reason for agreeing to this arrangement and she doubted that given the whole story even the good pastor could find fault with her motives. Plus, if she played this right, he'd never know.

As if he could sense her unease, Nick's arm slid up to rest briefly around her shoulders, and he offered her that heart-stopping grin she found increasingly hard to resist.

Taylor's tension melted away under the heat of his gaze and when his hand moved down to take hers she didn't resist.

They followed Tom and Mandy into the study with the minister bringing up the rear.

Once they were all inside, Pastor Schmidt shut the door and gestured toward a semicircle of chairs.

Nick waited for her to take her seat before sitting down next to her.

"Okay." The minister rubbed his hands together and paced the room. "Let's get started."

Taylor listened in horror as he described the agenda for the next six Together Forever premarital sessions. This was going to be harder than she thought. The minister seemed to be into everyone sharing their thoughts and feelings. She'd hoped for more of a lecture format.

"Nick, why don't you start by telling us what first attracted you to Taylor?" Pastor Schmidt leaned back in his chair, an expectant look on his face.

Nick paused, and his gaze shifted to study Taylor for a moment. She held her breath and smiled encouragingly.

"It was her spirit." Nick's gaze didn't waver. "She's one determined woman. I admire that."

Heat rose up her neck and into her cheeks. Though she and Nick had gone out many times during the past few weeks, their conversations had remained light and superficial.

"Taylor?" The pastor raised a brow.

What had first attracted her to Nick? She remembered how he'd looked when she first saw him. Like a *GQ* model in a hand-tailored suit.

"He was so handsome." The truth popped out before she could stop it.

Mandy laughed, a childish giggle of a laugh.

Taylor cheeks grew hotter.

"Okay." The minister's lips twitched, and he shifted his gaze. "Mandy?"

"What first attracted me to Nick?" Mandy giggled again. "Or to Tom?"

Nick's cough sounded more like a chuckle, and Taylor bit her lip to keep from laughing.

Pastor Schmidt didn't answer. He shot the young woman the same penetrating gaze he'd used when someone had gotten out of line in confirmation class.

Mandy straightened in her chair and cleared her throat. "What attracted me first to my Tommy boy?"

Nick rolled his eyes, and Taylor shifted her gaze to the ceiling and bit her lip again to keep from laughing out loud.

Once she started, the young woman wouldn't shut up. By the time Mandy finished her lengthy discourse on all of Tom's wonderful attributes, a hint of exasperation stole across Pastor Schmidt's normally jovial expression.

Thankfully, Mandy had taken so long that Tom had plenty of time to contemplate his answer, and he took only seconds to murmur something about Mandy's generous, fun-loving personality.

Mandy's face filled with pleasure, and Taylor found her irritation lessening.

"We've got a good group here," Pastor Schmidt said. "I think we're going to work well together."

Taylor smiled and nodded as if she understood, even though she didn't. Other than motormouth Mandy, the rest of them had barely said five words. How could he possibly know if they'd work well together or not? Still, if the minister wanted to be an optimist, who was she to be a naysayer?

Like a coach trying to rev up his players before a big game, the minister launched into a sermon on Christian love and commitment. Taylor leaned back in her chair and relaxed.

This was more like what she'd expected. He'd talk and they'd listen.

"At the end of each session, you'll be given a homework assignment."

Taylor straightened in her chair and shot Nick an incredulous look. "Homework?" she mouthed.

Nick shrugged.

"I want you to discuss what each partner expects from the other in a marriage."

"You mean like who should mow the yard? That kind of thing?" Mandy's brows furrowed.

"We could make a list," Tom added enthusiastically.

"No. I'm not talking about the day-to-day concerns, although those are important." The minister smiled. "I'm talking in terms of what role Christ and His church will play in your married life."

Mandy opened her mouth, but the minister waved her silent. "I'm not going to say any more. I want to leave it as open-ended as possible."

"Pastor." Mandy raised her hand like a child in school. "I have a question, but it's not about our homework."

"Yes, Mandy?"

"Why did you ask me what I liked about Tom?" Clearly puzzled, Mandy's thin features creased into a frown. "You asked all of us and then we didn't talk about it anymore."

That's because you talked about it enough for all of us, Taylor wanted to say. But a small part of her understood where Mandy was coming from. Taylor, too, had wondered what the minister had intended with that exercise.

"We were going to talk about it more when we meet in two weeks, but since you brought it up..." Pastor Schmidt paused. "Next time I'll ask you what made you first think you might be in love with your fiancé. The session after that there will be another relationship topic. Hopefully, by the end the reason for all the questions will be clear. I'd say more but I don't want to give the purpose away."

Forestalling any further discussion, the minister ushered

them out of his office. "Don't forget the homework. Mandy, what do you expect from Tom? Taylor, what do you expect from Nick? And, vice versa."

Taylor cast a sideways glance at Nick. What did she expect from him? Five thousand dollars a week and an uneventful engagement was all she asked. Hardly the stuff dreams are made of, but then she hadn't dreamed much in the last year.

Once her father's debts were paid off, her life would be her own again, and then maybe, one day, she could attend these classes again. This time with a man who loved her.

"Nick." Instead of immediately sliding into the convertible, Taylor paused at the open door. "Thanks again for coming tonight." Her lips quirked. "I know that when we discussed the terms of our engagement, premarital counseling wasn't mentioned."

"Neither was the company picnic," Nick said with an easy smile.

"Do you have time to stop for coffee?" For some reason, Taylor wasn't ready for the evening to end. "We could get our homework out of the way."

Nick paused as if seriously considering her invitation before he shook his head. "I can't. I have some proposals that I need to review before tomorrow. I'll be up half the night as it is."

"We'd better get going then." Taylor shoved aside her disappointment and reminded herself spending unnecessary time having coffee wasn't part of their business arrangement, either.

A loud curse echoed across the parking lot.

Taylor frowned and glanced over the concrete expanse.

Nick shifted his gaze to the only other car in the deserted lot. The vehicle was small and shaped like a tennis shoe with an oxidized yellow exterior highlighted by blotchy patches of rust.

"Isn't that Tom and Mandy?"

"Looks like they need some help." Despite his words about the work waiting at home, Nick didn't hesitate. He headed across the pavement with long purposeful strides, and Taylor had to run to keep up with him.

"Is the Gremlin dead?" Mandy's worried voice wafted on the breeze.

"It's not dead." Tom's muffled voice sounded from under the hood. "But the battery sure is."

"Can I help?" Nick stopped next to Tom. His gaze shifted to the grease-covered motor, and his head joined Tom's under the hood.

Taylor stood on her tiptoes and peered over Nick's shoulder. She glanced at his intense expression. Did Nick know anything about engines?

"It's the battery." In the waning light, Tom looked young and defeated. His glasses had slipped down his nose, and he pushed them back with a grease-covered finger. "Couldn't have come at a worse time."

"Do you have any cables? We could try to jump it."

Tom shook his head.

"There's an auto parts store a couple of blocks from here. You can pick up a battery there." Nick glanced at his watch. "They should still be open. I can give you a lift."

Tom shifted uncomfortably. "Fact is I don't have the money for a new one right now. But if you could maybe give us a ride?"

Taylor's heart went out to the boy. She wished she could offer him the money, but the twenty dollars she had on her had to last until her next fiancée payment.

"Don't worry about it." Nick clapped a hand on the young man's back. "I have some extra cash I can lend you. You can pay me later."

Pride warred with relief on Tom's face. Finally he nodded. "Thanks. I can pay you on the fifteenth, if that's okay?"

"That'd be fine," Nick said, and Taylor knew he didn't care if the young man paid him back or not.

Taylor shifted her gaze to the Jag. "Why don't Mandy and I just wait here? It's a little tight in that back seat."

"Is that your car?" Tom followed Taylor's gaze and gave a low whistle. "What is it?"

"Jaguar," Nick said. "An XK8."

Taylor and Mandy followed the guys over to the shiny silver-blue sports car.

"Twelve cylinders?" Tom ran his hands appreciatively over the sleek surface.

"V-eight," Nick said. "Thirty-two valves."

"Wow." Tom's eyes widened. "I bet it's fast."

"Zero to sixty in less than seven seconds."

"Unbelievable."

Taylor looked at Mandy, and they both smiled. Cars and sports seemed to be the universal language of men.

"Are you sure you don't want to ride with us?" Nick cast Taylor a questioning gaze.

"We'll be fine." She smiled reassuringly. "It's a beautiful night and this is a safe neighborhood. After all—" she gestured toward the church and the adjoining parsonage "—God is right next door."

Nick brushed a quick kiss across her lips and opened the car door. "Let's go."

He didn't have to ask twice. Tom couldn't get in the car fast enough. "I wish the guys at work could see me now."

The young man laced his fingers together behind his head and stretched back against the ivory-colored leather. "Man, is this livin' or what?"

Mandy giggled. Taylor smiled.

The engine roared to life and in a matter of seconds the car left the parking lot and sped off down the street.

Mandy waved until they were out of sight, then dug into her oversize purse and pulled out a tattered pack of chewing gum. "Want some?"

Taylor shook her head. "No, thanks."

"Let me know if you change your mind." Mandy shoved three pieces into her mouth and dropped the pack into her bag. "Want to go sit in the car?"

Taylor shrugged. "Okay."

Compared to the Jag, the Gremlin looked like a poor relative that was on its last leg. The passenger door stuck, and Mandy had to open it from the inside. She cleared some food wrappers from the seat and tossed them into the back of the car. "We drove through and got take-out on the way here."

Taylor smiled and brushed a French fry to the floor before she sat down. ''So when are you and Tom getting married?''

''October thirty-first.''

Taylor turned in her seat, not sure she'd heard the girl correctly. ''Halloween?''

''It's my birthday,'' Mandy said promptly.

Taylor paused. She'd sworn that she'd asked Mandy when she was getting married.

''You're getting married on your birthday?'' Taylor spoke slowly and distinctly. ''And your birthday's on Halloween?''

''That's right.'' A dreamy expression crossed Mandy's face. ''I told Tom if we got married on my birthday, then he could be my present.''

Taylor smiled weakly, unsure how to respond.

''Pastor Schmidt isn't too keen on it,'' Mandy continued. ''And he nixed my idea of having the reception be a masquerade party.''

''Did he?'' Taylor tried to keep her expression blank.

''When are you and Nick doing the deed?''

Taylor's eyes widened. She cleared her throat. ''Pardon me?''

''Doing the deed.'' Mandy repeated. ''You know, getting married?''

Taylor wondered what the young woman would say if she answered honestly and said never. ''Sometime this fall, I think.''

''You think?'' Mandy frowned. ''Don't you know?''

''We'll be firming up the date shortly,'' Taylor said smoothly. ''Now tell me all about this Halloween wedding of yours. It sounds like fun.''

''Tom was sure impressed by the car.'' Taylor cast Nick a sideways glance.

''I know.'' Nick shook his head. ''It's amazing how some guys are so into that stuff.''

''What are you saying, some guys?'' Taylor said with a smile. ''I heard that thirty-two valve, zero-to-sixty stuff coming out of your mouth.''

The corners of Nick's lips twitched. "I can talk the talk as well as anyone. But as far as spending seventy-five thousand for a sports car, that's not me."

"Why did you buy it then?"

"My father bought it." Nick's eyes darkened. "Shortly before he died."

He never talked about his father. Every time she'd tried to bring him up, Nick changed the subject. Even though it really wasn't any of her business, she was still curious. His father sounded like a fascinating man.

"Tom told me he and Mandy are getting married on Halloween," Nick said, changing the subject once again. "Said we're invited to the wedding."

Did you tell him we wouldn't be together by then? Taylor wanted to ask. Instead she forced a smile.

"Did he tell you that Mandy wanted to wear black and have her attendants attired in orange taffeta?"

Nick roared with laughter. "No way."

"It's true. But Pastor Schmidt *nixed* that idea," Taylor said, borrowing Mandy's word. "Now she's wearing white, and the groomsmen will wear black."

"She wanted a black wedding dress?" Nick shook his head in disbelief. "I can't believe she'd even consider it."

"Think who we're talking about here," Taylor said dryly. "Besides, it might have looked elegant."

"Would you ever wear black?"

The offhand question took her by surprise, even though it shouldn't have. After all, he didn't know her, didn't know what her plans for the future were, what type of wedding she wanted. Would they ever see each other after this summer? Would they be friends? Would he come to her wedding? Would she attend his?

"Maybe." Her heart twisted but her lips quirked up in a grin. "Who knows what the future holds? I certainly don't."

By the time Nick dropped Taylor off and got to his house it was after ten.

He quickly changed clothes and pulled out his laptop. Normally he'd be so lost in his work that the hours would go by and he'd scarcely notice. But tonight he couldn't seem to concentrate.

He'd never really thought much about his father's spending habits before. Seventy-five thousand dollars wasn't a large amount of cash, by any means, but the year his father was sick had been a critical time in terms of Lanagan Associates. The company had been in the middle of an expensive conversion project, and money had been tight.

Odd, he'd never considered his father might have had a role in the company's financial troubles.

He shoved the unsettling thought aside and returned his attention to the computer screen. If he didn't keep his mind focused on work, Lanagan Associates would be struggling again, and this time he'd have no one to blame but himself.

Chapter Eight

Taylor stood in the entryway, her gaze surveying the already crowded ballroom. The party she'd dreaded for weeks lay before her. The past four weeks had been a whirlwind of activity culminating in tonight's event. By evening's end her engagement to Nicholas Lanagan III would be official.

Engagement. The last step before marriage, Nana had proclaimed, unaware her happiness unknowingly added to Taylor's guilt.

"Would you relax?" Nick stood at her side, resplendent in his black tux, an easy smile etched on his handsome face. He lightly brushed back a strand of her hair. "It's a party, not an execution."

"Then why do I feel like my head's in a noose and I'm ready to swing?"

"Your body's telling you you need some—" he grabbed a glass of champagne from a passing waiter and shoved it into her hand "—of this. Give it a try."

"Wouldn't be trying to get me drunk, would you?"

"On one glass?" Nick grinned. "Not hardly."

Taylor glanced at the flute in her hand. Normally she didn't drink. She'd never much liked the taste of alcohol or the funny way it made her feel. Still, this tiny glass couldn't hold more than a half cup of liquid.

She raised the crystal and took a sip. Then another. The bubbles tickled her throat, and the sweet flavor was tasty.

Very tasty. Too bad the glass was so small. Upending the flute, she downed the rest in a single gulp. Before her lips were dry, a waiter appeared and replaced it with another.

This time Taylor took it without hesitation. She smiled her thanks and swirled the sparkling wine. "Maybe tonight won't be so bad after all."

Nick quirked one dark brow. "I think we'll make it." A faint light twinkled in the depths of his blue eyes. "One way or another."

She peered over the rim of the champagne glass and surveyed the crowd. *Small get-together, indeed.*

The casual event for twenty she'd envisioned had been replaced by black-tie formal for five hundred. Not quite the same intimate affair Claire and her father had proposed almost a month before. The party had become an event, the social event of the summer, and had taken on a life of its own.

The ball had started rolling when Henry Waters reserved the ballroom of the historic Heritage Hotel in downtown Cedar Ridge. It had picked up speed when he hired a designer out of Denver to do the decorations and an exclusive upscale caterer for the food. It had careened out of control when her grandparents insisted on doing their part by having tropical flowers flown in from Hawaii.

The results lay before her in all their breathtaking splendor. The sweet scent of the tropics invaded every inch of the massive ballroom. Reflections from hundreds of strategically placed candles flickered in the ornate beveled mirrors lining the walls. Tables, topped with linen and edged with lace, surrounded the mahogany dance floor. Sweet melodies reminiscent of a bygone era filled the air.

Waiters in black tie weaved confidently through the milling throng with silver trays balanced aloft, offering crystal glasses filled with golden bubbles. Three bars and double the number of bounteous buffets rimmed the room and offered everything from imported cheeses and breads to prime rib.

Taylor's stomach growled, and she realized she'd been so busy she'd not only skipped breakfast, she'd missed lunch.

She stole another glance at one of the buffet tables and promised herself she'd get something to eat soon. Thankfully—even without food—the tension in her neck had vanished with her second glass of the bubbly.

A conscientious waiter commandeered the glass she'd just drained and handed her another. Nick waved away one for himself, his eyes narrowing at the scene before him.

"This is really something."

Taylor turned, surprised at the edge in his voice.

"Henry and your grandparents certainly went all out to put on a nice party."

She forced an enthusiastic smile. "They sure did."

Privately, she could have done without the opulent extravagance. Especially when she knew this engagement would be over before her grandparents got the bill for the flowers. Goodness knows she'd done her best to stop them, but they'd insisted, telling her she needed to realize you only get engaged—and married—once.

Unless you're Taylor and Nick playing Romeo and Juliet.

"You look good." Nick's gaze met hers.

Her heart turned over in response, and she said a silent thank-you to her grandmother for insisting she wear something new.

The sleek ivory designer gown with threads of metallic copper fit like it had been created with her in mind. They'd discovered it in an exclusive showroom on Chicago's Michigan Avenue and, though the neckline showed a little too much cleavage, her grandmother had proclaimed it perfect and insisted on buying it. Nana hadn't batted an eye at the exorbitant price.

Last year I wouldn't have given a second thought to spending that kind of money.

This year, due to her financial situation, Taylor had planned to make use of one of the many beautiful gowns she already had hanging in her closet. Nana had been appalled, insisting a new dress would be her engagement gift and Chicago would be just the place to find it. Moments later her grandmother had the airline tickets on hold and a suite in Chicago's Palmer House Hotel reserved for the weekend.

Nick had raised an eyebrow when she told him about the shopping trip. Though he didn't say a word, she'd got the distinct impression he didn't approve. *Men.* Who could understand them? And here she thought he'd be happy to have a few days to himself.

His unexpected response confirmed she'd barely scratched the surface when it came to discovering what made her temporary fiancé tick. She'd grown acquainted with the public Nick Lanagan most people knew—the savvy businessman, the charismatic leader, the man who oozed charm when it suited his purposes.

She'd only caught glimpses of the private side of the man. The Nick who listened respectfully while her grandfather rambled on about his son's accomplishments. The Nick who'd surprised her and agreed to attend church services with the family. The Nick who swung by his secretary's apartment to check on her after she'd been involved in a minor fender bender.

"How *is* Miss Dietrich?"

"She'll be back on Monday. The cast came off yesterday." He studied her face with his enigmatic gaze for an extra beat. "Why?"

"Just wondering." Taylor gestured across the room, the large diamond heavy on her finger. "Isn't that Henry over by the potted palm?"

She pointed in the direction of a portly man looking very much like a penguin under a palm tree.

"That's him, all right." Nick tightened his arm around her. "Ready?"

She smiled and chugged the last of her champagne. Thankfully the butterflies in her stomach had flown along with her apprehension. "You bet."

Nick's lips parted in that charming smile she was coming to know so well, and they slowly made their way through the throng of well-wishers to the potted palm and their host.

Despite the earliness of the evening, Henry Waters's glassy-eyed stare told Taylor the man had definitely been enjoying the liquid refreshments. "You look lovely, my dear."

Her lips twitched. Up close, the man looked even more like a penguin. But she'd never been checked out so thoroughly by any bird. Henry's beady-eyed gaze swept her from head to toe.

"Doesn't Taylor look simply fabulous, my dear?"

Claire sauntered up to her father. She was dressed to kill—or shock—in a red sequined gown that fit like a second skin and left absolutely nothing of her ample curves to the imagination. She afforded Taylor only the briefest of glances.

"Very nice," Claire said. Taylor wondered if she could have been wearing a burlap sack and gotten the same response.

Claire moistened her lips and shifted her gaze to Nick. "Now you, darling, look positively hunky."

Taylor stifled a chuckle, and Nick shot her a warning look.

Henry glanced around and rubbed his hands together. "I'd say anybody who is anybody is right here at our party tonight."

"Speaking of anybody who's anybody—" Claire's voice dropped to a sultry whisper, and she looked like a tigress spotting fresh meat "—look who just walked in. I never thought he'd come. Not all the way from D.C."

Taylor automatically turned toward the front of the ballroom, but the broad shoulders of a tall man in a cowboy hat blocked her view.

Henry didn't bother to look, but his loud, boisterous chuckle attracted the stares of nearby guests. "Claire, darling, half the people here are from Washington. The room's crawling with politicians."

Taylor's grandparents, as well as her parents, had been well acquainted with the Washington social scene, and they'd sent invitations to many of their friends. From the size of the crowd, it appeared most had taken them up on their offer and had flown in for the festivities.

''No more for you.'' Claire drew an exasperated breath and took the champagne flute her father had just confiscated from a passing waiter and set it on a nearby table. ''Daddy, Tony Karelli is on his way over.''

A soft gasp escaped Taylor's lips. ''Tony? Here?''

Claire arched a brow, and her head swiveled slowly to stare at Taylor. ''You know him?''

''Yes. Maybe. I don't know. I guess there could be more than one.''

Yeah. Right.

Tony Karelli. They'd met as teenagers. Tony had been smart and incredibly sweet, but a bad case of acne, unfashionable thick-lensed glasses and a tendency toward chubby had made him a social outcast. Taylor had befriended him, and they'd been dubbed Beauty and the Beast by some of their crueler classmates. Over the years, they'd lost touch. Last she'd heard he was in Europe.

Claire's dark eyes glittered. ''His father used to be a senator from New York and now is the ambassador to Italy.''

''Then it *is* the Tony I knew—''

''I wondered if you'd remember me.''

Taylor's heart leaped at the sound of the familiar voice, and she turned toward it. ''I'd recognize that East Coast accent anywhere.''

''What accent?'' The tall broad-shouldered handsome man looked more like a stranger than the Tony she remembered. But the smile hadn't changed, and when he opened his arms for a hug, she wrapped her arms around his neck and let him twirl her around. She buried her face in his neck. Seeing him again brought a deluge of memories.

Almost as if he could read her mind, Tony whispered against her hair. ''I'm sorry about your father. I wished I could have been there for you.''

She blinked back the unexpected tears that pushed against her lower lids and hugged him tighter. ''I know you would have.''

''Why, it's little Tony Karelli.'' Grandpa Bill's amused

voice brought Taylor out of her old friend's arms. "See, Kaye, I told you that's who that was."

"Judge Rollins." Tony released her and turned to shake her grandfather's hand. "It's great to see you again, sir. But as you can see I'm not so little anymore."

"No, you're not. You're all grown-up. How's your father?"

"Busy as ever. He and Mother are still in Italy."

A warm glow filled Taylor, and she listened to her grandparents quiz Tony about the last few years, barely conscious of Nick's rigid form at her side and Claire's sideways glances. Her grandfather was right, Tony had indeed grown up. The dark hair, as black as Nick's but slightly longer, the brown eyes instead of blue, were just as she remembered, and confirmed this indeed was the Tony of her school days. But beyond that…

A tanned, smooth face gave no hint of the blemishes that had once caused such distress. He'd grown taller—a good six inches if she were guessing—leaving not an ounce of fat on his muscular frame.

"What happened to your glasses?" Taylor blurted when her grandfather paused for breath.

"Contacts." He grinned—something he hadn't done much of when he'd been younger—and she noticed the braces were gone, leaving behind a mouthful of straight white teeth.

Taylor returned his smile, happy that life had been good to her old friend.

"Isn't it funny? You two coming together after all these years at Taylor's engagement party," Nana said. "There was a time we thought it would be you and Taylor tying the knot."

Grandpa Bill shot his wife a disapproving glance, and Nana's face grew pink.

"A man would be lucky to have Taylor for a wife." Tony smiled and shook his head. "I can't believe you're getting married."

A warmth crept up the side of Taylor's neck and an awkward silence filled the air. Nick stepped forward and extended his hand.

"I don't believe we've met. I'm Nick Lanagan. Taylor's fiancé." His arm slid proprietarily around her shoulders. "I'm glad you could come and help us celebrate."

Tony shifted from one foot to the other, but his suave facade didn't waver. "Actually, I wasn't on the guest list. I—"

"He's here as my guest, Nick. We're—" Claire rubbed against Tony like a cat "—very good friends."

Taylor's jaw dropped. She shut it with a snap. "Tony?"

Nick's hand tightened around her arm. "Sweetheart, I feel like dancing."

He pressed one hand firmly against her back, and Taylor barely had time to smile her goodbyes before he whisked her onto the dance floor.

The tantalizing smell of his aftershave wrapped around her and she leaned lightly into him, tilting her face toward his. "Nick. Why did—"

Her last words were smothered by his lips. The kiss was sweet, tender, and it ended as quickly as it began.

"What was that for?" she said, slightly breathless.

"Can't a man kiss his fiancée without having a reason?" he teased. But his gaze slid around the room as if to see if anyone noticed.

Her heart plummeted. Of course it was all an act. For a fleeting moment, she'd forgotten.

Taylor shifted her gaze to the dance floor. Across the room Tony and Claire moved so slowly, they might as well have been standing still. Claire's voluptuous body molded tightly against Tony and they swayed back and forth, never moving beyond the same square foot. Tony's dark head bent over Claire's, and her fingers played with his hair.

"Look at them." She punched Nick in the back.

He turned and watched the two for a moment before shifting his gaze to Taylor. "Jealous?"

"No, of course not." Taylor frowned, and she stole another

glance at the non-dancing duo. "It's just that Tony's a good friend."

The faint glimmer of amusement that flickered in Nick's eyes infuriated her.

"Don't you care?"

"Why should I? I'm not interested in the woman. As far as I'm concerned, if he wants her more power to him."

A cold knot formed in Taylor's stomach at the thought of that barracuda with her friend. "Nick?"

"If it's about Tony," he said, "I wouldn't worry. He's a big boy. I'm sure he can take care of himself."

How could Nick be so insensitive? He, more than most, knew what Claire was like. She shifted her gaze away from Nick, preferring at that moment to look at anyone—or anything—else. Her gaze stopped abruptly at the sight of Claire kissing Tony.

"I get it now." His gaze followed hers. "This is all about him. You still have the hots for your old boyfriend and you're worried he may be taken by the time you're free again."

"You're crazy." Her and Tony? She'd never thought of him as anything but a good friend.

"Stay away from him, Taylor."

Taylor bristled. "Tony thinks we're engaged. He'd never—"

"Don't bet on it." Nick's mouth tightened into a thin hard line. "I saw the way he looked at you."

"You two having a good time?" Grandpa Bill and Nana danced to their side.

For a fraction of a second, Nick's face froze.

Taylor swallowed an angry retort and forced her lips to curve upward. "Just wonderful."

She gazed at Nick and hoped her smile looked genuine. "I was just telling Nick, engagements are fun but this one can't end too soon for me."

Grandpa Bill looked startled, then chuckled. "Can't wait for that honeymoon, eh?"

"Bill!" Nana said sharply.

The lively twinkle in her grandfather's eye incensed her grandmother, but Grandpa Bill glanced at Taylor and Nick and chuckled once again. ''Can't say that I blame you. Can't say I blame you one bit.''

Chapter Nine

Nick pulled out of the hotel's parking garage and activated the CD system. The *Eroica* symphony, the one Taylor always asked to hear, filled the quiet interior.

Nick glanced at his now official fiancée out of the corner of his eye. She'd rested her head against the seat and closed her eyes when she'd first got in, complaining of feeling light-headed, and hadn't looked up since. Thick waves of auburn hair spilled around her shoulders, and her normally rosy complexion seemed more like a soft pale ivory. Never had she looked more beautiful.

Other than their little argument on the dance floor, the evening had gone better than he'd expected. Taylor's performance had been flawless. Lovely and personable, she'd charmed his business associates and even—he swallowed hard—her leading man.

Unfortunately, her old boyfriend's presence had been an all too real reminder that this woman wasn't his. Had she really meant it when she said she couldn't wait for the engagement to end?

He pushed aside the image of her in Tony Karelli's arms and swallowed hard. ''I had a great time tonight. You were wonderful.''

Taylor's eyes fluttered open. She raised an eyebrow. ''Does that mean I get a bonus?''

''Hmm.'' He pretended to think. ''I might be able throw in an extra ten dollars in this week's check.''

''Scrooge.''

He grinned. ''Thanks for the compliment.''

''You're not welcome.'' Despite her words, a tiny smile played at the corners of her lips. ''Actually, it *was* a lovely engagement party.''

''The kind you've always dreamed of?''

A halfhearted laugh escaped her lips even as a wistful expression dimmed her smile. ''I couldn't help but wish my parents were there, though I realize if they were still alive, I wouldn't even be in this fake engagement.''

''Sometimes it doesn't feel fake to me.'' Nick's fingers tightened on the steering wheel.

She lowered her head and turned to the window. ''I know. Sometimes it doesn't to me, either.''

He leaned back. The tension in his shoulders left in a rush.

Taylor chuckled, a low husky sound. ''When Henry climbed on that table…''

Nick laughed. Henry had swayed precariously atop an antique side table, trying to make a toast for almost five minutes, a bottle outstretched in one hand, a glass of champagne in the other. ''He would have been okay if Claire hadn't got embarrassed and tried to pull him off.''

Taylor giggled. ''I thought for a moment, the way she was jerking his arm, she was going to split that dress right up the side.''

''Did you see the look she gave Tony when he pulled her away?''

''I don't think anyone could have missed that. Steam was practically pouring out her nose.''

''She should have been grateful. Another second or two and Henry would have ended up on the floor, on top of her.'' Nick pretended to shudder. ''That's one scary thought.''

''Claire's a beautiful woman,'' Taylor said matter-of-factly, casting Nick a sideways glance. ''Lots of men probably wouldn't mind rolling around on the floor with her.''

"They can have her. Now you and I—" he paused and his pulse quickened at the thought "—on that floor, that would be a different story."

"Does it seem a little stuffy in here to you?" Taylor fanned herself with one hand.

Stuffy wasn't a word he would have chosen. Warm? Hot? Intense? Those words better described his torture. He glanced over, hoping to see an answering flame smoldering in her eyes.

He narrowed his gaze. "Are you okay? You don't look so good."

"All of a sudden, I don't feel so good." She pushed a button and lowered the car's window, then rested her head against the door frame. The cool breeze fanned her pale face and lifted her hair like a dark cloud off her shoulders. In the dim light she looked positively green. "Could you pull over for a minute?"

His eyes glanced to the right and left. Concrete blanketed both sides of the well-lit thoroughfare. "Are you going to be sick?"

"No. I don't think so." Taylor shut her eyes. She took a deep breath, and the dark fullness of her lashes brushed against her cheek. "I just need some fresh air. I'll be okay."

Despite her assurance, Nick was not convinced. Cramping the steering wheel, he took a sharp right and headed for a residential area. He eased the car to the nearest curb, slammed it into park and turned off the motor. "Taylor?"

"I'm fine. Really." Her wan smile did little to reassure him. "It was the craziest thing. All of a sudden I got dizzy. And hot. If you're not in any big hurry, I might just walk for a few minutes. Clear my head."

She brushed the hair from her face with a trembling hand, confirming she wasn't quite as together as she wanted him to believe.

"A walk in the moonlight," he quipped, trying to put her at ease. "How romantic. Mind if I join you?"

Taylor shook her head, then winced at the sudden movement. ''I'd like that.''

By the time he'd gotten out of the car and moved to her door, she already stood outside, swaying slightly in the overgrown grass. But her skin had started to lose its pallor, and pink tinged her lips and cheeks.

''You're looking better.''

Her gaze shifted from the quiet neighborhood to him, and her eyes glittered. ''You're looking pretty good yourself.''

Nick moved a step closer. ''I had a wonderful time tonight.''

''Me, too.'' Her lips curved in a smile. ''Do you remember when I was dancing with Tony and you cut in?''

Nick stiffened, the memory dampening his desire. He remembered, all right. When one dance had turned into three, he'd had enough. Surprisingly, she'd gone into his arms willingly, almost eagerly. The air had been charged with the same electricity that surrounded them now. ''I remember.''

''When you put your arms around me—'' she smiled at him ''—I had the strangest thought.''

He quirked one eyebrow.

''What would happen, I said to myself, if I put my arms around your neck—'' she took a step forward, resting her hands on his shoulders ''—and kissed you. Right there on the dance floor.''

Nick cleared the catch in his throat. ''Now why would you have wanted to do that?''

Her hand stroked his cheek, and he felt the same nameless stirring deep inside as when he'd kissed her the night she'd agreed to be his fiancée.

''Because, even though I know we don't have a future together, I'm attracted to you.''

Her finger traced the firm line of his jaw, and he held his breath. ''You've got great-looking eyes, but I'm sure you already know that.''

Her hand slid up, her fingers parting his hair into short,

narrow rows, ''But did anyone tell you that you have really nice hair?''

He took a deep breath and grabbed her hand. ''I don't think this is such a good idea.''

She murmured in protest and leaned toward him, her eyes focused on his lips. ''Kiss me.''

''Taylor—''

''C'mon, Nicholas,'' she whispered, her long lashes fluttering provocatively against her flushed cheeks. ''One little kiss.''

She tilted her head just far enough for her lips to meet his. The electricity of the touch short-circuited his good sense. With a groan, he pulled her against him and kissed her. She wound her arms inside his jacket and around his back.

''Hey, what's going on out there?''

Nick stiffened, and his head jerked toward the voice. An elderly man peered from behind the screen door of a house ablaze with lights. A German shepherd barked sharply behind him, battering its body against the wooden frame of the door in an effort to get at them.

Great.

''Ignore them.'' Taylor's husky voice sent the blood coursing through his veins like wildfire.

His breath caught in his throat.

''You've got five seconds to get off my property or I'm calling the cops. This here's a decent neighborhood.''

The old man's words hit Nick like a splash of cold water. All of a sudden he saw them as the man had. Car doors open. Standing in the wet grass. He in a tuxedo. She in a formal gown. Wrapped in each other's arms.

Like two overage high-school kids on prom night with raging hormones and no common sense.

''We've got to go.'' Nick gently but firmly pushed aside Taylor's hands and her protests and settled her into the car, buckling her seat belt before shutting the door.

Back behind the wheel, Nick hit the gas, and the Jag responded, leaving the man and his decent neighborhood far behind.

"How are you doing?"

"I'm okay. Still a little dizzy." Her mouth twisted in a wry grin. "And a lot disappointed."

Nick silently agreed.

They rode the rest of the way to Taylor's house without speaking. The dark interior and smooth ride did little to ease his surging emotions. He assumed Taylor slept. But when he shut off the car, he turned to find a wide-awake gaze focused on him, the green eyes filled with an indefinable emotion.

"Want to come in for coffee?"

He shook his head regretfully. "I don't think that's a good idea."

He waited for her to argue, but she just sighed and released her seat belt.

"You're right." Disappointment clouded her features. "Don't you just hate it?"

"What?"

"Doing the right thing," she said with a heavy sigh. "Sometimes I wish just once I could do what I wanted instead of being so—so *responsible.*"

He knew exactly how she felt. When his mother had the business teetering on the edge of bankruptcy, he'd had to be the responsible one. He'd put his life on hold and cleaned up her mess. Yeah, he'd been resentful. And angry. Truth be known, he still was.

"Just once." She sighed again. "I wish I could be reckless instead of responsible."

"If you weren't so *responsible—*" he emphasized the word just as she had "—what would be the first thing you'd do?"

A flush tinged her cheeks. She hesitated, and he could almost see her wondering if she should speak freely. Her candid green eyes met his. "There's no need to discuss it, because it's not going to happen."

"So, what now?"

"I go to my bed. You go home to yours."

''What about Tony?'' He didn't know why he said it. All he knew was that he wanted an answer.

''What about him?''

''Are you going back to him once we break up?''

Taylor stared, a frown marring her forehead. ''Tony's my friend.''

''And Claire used to be my friend.''

She shook her head. ''I don't think we're defining friend in the same way.''

Nick's jaw clenched. He wanted to ask her more about her relationship with Tony but he kept his mouth shut. He had no right to question her. No right at all. In the eyes of the world he might be her fiancé, but her old friend probably knew her better than Nick did. The thought twisted inside him.

They walked to the front door in silence. Nick planned to brush a light kiss across her cheek and say a polite good-night. But she tilted her head at the last second, and the minute his lips met hers, he was lost.

Nick moved his mouth over hers, and in the end it was Taylor who called a halt, backing out of his embrace with a stumble. She stared at him, her breath coming in short puffs, her eyes large and dark with emotion. ''I'd better go.''

Without giving him a chance to speak, she was gone, the door closing with a thud behind her.

Nick strode to the Jag, and with one flick of the wrist the engine roared to life. He hit the accelerator, and the car jerked from the curb.

What was he thinking? Ever fiber in his body warned him against her. She was a woman with a house filled with priceless antiques, a closet overflowing with designer clothes and debts the size of Pike's Peak. Claire had hit it on the head when she'd said Taylor was just like his mother.

Getting emotionally involved with such a woman made absolutely no sense. But even knowing that, he still couldn't help wanting her.

And that made the least sense of all.

Chapter Ten

"This might take more time than I first thought." Claire sat forward in her living room chair and leveled at Tony a narrow, glinting gaze. "How long can you stay?"

Tony thought for a moment. The only thing waiting for him in D.C. was the gambling debt his father so unreasonably refused to pay. He had no job, and other than the money Claire had promised him, no source of income. He took a sip of coffee. "As long as you want, sweetheart."

"Good." Her lips curved upward. "We need to plan our strategy." She leaned back against the burgundy leather, and he could almost see her mind go to work.

His gaze lingered on the long expanse of leg visible beneath the pale yellow fabric. When Claire had greeted him at the door dressed in nothing more than a skimpy silk chemise and matching kimono he'd had high hopes. But those were quickly dashed. She'd informed him she'd just hopped out of bed even though it was past eleven. And unfortunately she'd made it clear business was the only thing on her mind.

"She responded to you," Claire said almost to herself.

"I told you she would." Tony spoke with more confidence than he felt. He knew Taylor had been glad to see him. Nonetheless he hadn't missed how her eyes had searched for Nick even while Tony held her firmly in his arms. "She and I have always been close."

''About that.'' Claire's gaze turned calculating. ''How close were you?

''You mean did I ever…?''

''Did you?''

Her hopeful expression said there might be some extra money in it for him if he said yes. Unfortunately if he lied and Claire found out, he'd be dog meat. He'd be better off facing a hundred hungry loan sharks than one angry Claire Waters.

He shook his head and heaved a heartfelt sigh. ''I'm afraid not.''

''Are you lying to me?'' Dark storm clouds formed in her eyes. ''Because if you are—''

''Now why would I do that?''

''Because you're old friends.'' She spit the words out as if they were poison. ''Maybe you're trying to protect her.''

''I'm telling you the truth, Claire.'' He took a long sip of coffee. ''But you're right, I do want to protect her. That's why I'm here.''

She raised a brow.

''Okay, I'm here because I need the money,'' Tony said. ''But I'm here because of her, too. If Nick is the jerk you claim I don't want her to be with him. If I can get her away from him and end up making a few bucks in the bargain, so much the better. Like killing two birds with one stone.''

He could see her weighing his words, and under her measuring gaze he felt sixteen again. Awkward. Unsure. The type of guy a woman like this would never look at twice. Tony straightened. He now ran with the beautiful people and got invited to the all the best parties. Any adolescent angst belonged in the past.

''I can't believe the two of you never fooled around.'' Like a dog with a bone, Claire wouldn't let the subject drop.

''Taylor's saving herself for marriage,'' Tony said with a shrug.

''You're kidding. She's twenty-six years old.''

''I don't know what to tell you.'' He shifted uncomfortably, once again feeling like he'd been judged and found wanting. "Nothing happened."

"Okay." She moved forward and rested her arms on her knees. "The first step is for the two of you to renew that old friendship. Then you find a way to break them up. It's as simple as that." Claire smiled slyly at him.

Simple? Tony groaned. Even he wasn't foolish enough to believe that.

Taylor stared at the phone, willing it to ring. Willing it to be him. It had been two days since the party, and the only time she'd heard from Nick was when he'd called early on Sunday to say he was skipping church.

Every time the phone rang she hoped she'd hear that rich baritone. But so far she'd fielded two calls from her grandmother and three from telemarketers.

Please let it ring.

As if on cue, the shrill ring split the air. She grabbed the phone. "Hello."

"Recovered from the party?"

Taylor recognized Tony's voice immediately. She pushed her disappointment aside. "I think I'm fully recovered," she said. "But then it's been a few days."

"I don't think I'd ever seen you drink so much champagne." A thread of amusement ran through his voice.

"And I can tell you, I won't be doing it again. Ever."

"Headache?" Tony teased.

"The worst. Yesterday, every time I moved, my head throbbed." She never drank. The evening had been so important to her grandparents and so critical to the success of her and Nick's arrangement that she'd tried to calm her fears with alcohol.

Dear Lord, I'm so sorry.

She offered up the silent apology. She'd never find the comfort and the strength she needed in a glass of champagne.

"Well, when you feel better, how about we go out? Catch up on old times?"

"I'd like that," Taylor said sincerely. She and Tony had been good friends and they knew a lot of the same people. "Why don't you give me a call in a day or two and we'll set up a time?"

"I'll call you tomorrow."

"I'll hold you to it." She hung up, grateful Tony hadn't asked to set a time now. Normally she would have been more than willing. But if her schedule was booked, she and Nick might not be able to find time to get together.

Her cheeks grew warm just remembering the way she'd acted when they'd last been together. Like a wanton woman. She'd practically thrown herself at him.

What must he be thinking? Was that why he hadn't called?

Taylor straightened and squared her shoulders. She couldn't change the past, she could only learn from her mistakes and move forward. Today she'd keep herself busy around the house. Tomorrow, if he still hadn't called, she'd find an excuse to call him.

"How was the party?" Erik Nordstrom put his feet up on the glass coffee table, ignoring Nick's censuring look.

Nick tapped his pen against the stack of computer reports piled high in front of him. It was only Tuesday, but Saturday night seemed a million light-years away. "Tell me why you weren't there."

"I already did. My mother was getting married. Again. And she insisted I attend."

Erik's answer barely registered on Nick's short-circuiting brain. Restless and agitated over the news he'd received that morning, Nick pushed back his chair and strode to the side bar. He grabbed his Denver Broncos mug and poured his third cup of the extra-strength coffee Miss Dietrich had brewed.

"I have it on good authority that stuff works just like drain cleaner in your stomach." Erik waved away a cup for himself.

"Forgive me for not listening to someone who relies on trash newspapers at the grocery store checkout lines for information."

"Hey, I'm an inquiring man."

Nick groaned and Erik grinned. His friend's fondness for the tabloids had been a source of dissension since their freshman year when Erik had convinced him it would be acceptable to list a popular tabloid article as one of their sources on a group research project. Thanks to that lapse in judgment, Nick had pulled the only B in his college career.

"How was the wedding?" Nick asked, more to change the direction of the conversation than out of any real interest. He'd attended the last two with Erik, and they hadn't varied much except for the groom.

"Typical. Same minister, same organist, same singer. If I didn't know better, I'd think she had them all on retainer." He chuckled. "The music was a little different. Remember how the last guy liked the Stones? Well, this one must have been into country because Mother dear walked down the aisle to a steel guitar rendition of 'Here Comes the Bride.'"

Nick choked back a laugh. "Sounds…nice."

"I might be able to get him to play at your wedding." Erik placed a finger to his lips and pretended to think. "If we play our cards right, he might give us a frequent-user discount. What do you think?"

"I think you've been drinking something with a little more kick than this caffeine." Nick gestured with his half-empty cup.

"Nicholas, I'm shocked. You know I never drink before noon," Erik said. "But seriously, doesn't all this wedding talk sort of get you in the mood?"

Nick smiled, remembering Grandpa Bill's words. "Let's just say you can keep the steel guitar and the ceremony. But the wedding night, now that's different."

"I knew you had the hots for her." A smile of pure satisfaction blanketed Erik's features. "I knew it the moment you told me you'd made her that crazy offer without even thinking it through. It was so impulsive. So unlike you."

Nick shifted uncomfortably. "Like you said, she's a beautiful woman. A man would have to be crazy not to find her attractive.''

The image of Tony Karelli's expression as he'd watched them dance flashed in Nick's mind. Karelli was definitely not crazy.

''So the pretend engagement's now official?''

''Announced before five hundred people on Saturday and made the society page in Sunday's edition. You don't get much more official than that.'' Nick took another sip of coffee.

''Seeing the way you two look at each other would have been enough to convince most people. If I didn't know better, I sure wouldn't have any doubts about whether it's the real thing.'' Erik shook his head, open admiration in his eyes. ''You two deserve Oscars for your performance.''

Nick smiled and accepted the compliment. Erik would be shocked if he knew how little acting was actually involved. Over the past few weeks the once clear line between real and pretend had blurred. Being invited to dinner parties as a couple, golfing with Bill Rollins and being treated as one of the family, even talking with Taylor every day had become part of his life. This morning that fact had been driven home when an employee stopped him in the hall to offer his congratulations and he'd found himself saying, ''I'm a lucky man,'' and meaning it. The closing curtain needed to fall on this charade, and fast. Or Nick Lanagan just might end up in love with his leading lady.

''I think now would be a good time for you to contact Henry's attorneys again. See if you can push things along. Get some of those last few contract issues resolved.''

''Merger means end of engagement.''

''It'll save me some cash.'' Nick dropped into his desk chair, picked up the pen and drummed it against the edge of the desk.

''You'll lose your fiancée.''

''She's never been mine to lose.'' He ignored the voice

deep inside that insisted Taylor was his girlfriend. His fiancée. *His.*

But she was so wrong for him. And if his heart didn't quite agree, he'd never let it direct his decisions in the past and he wasn't about to start now.

The ringing phone saved him from comment. He motioned for Erik to stay.

"Very well. Put her through." His fingers tightened around the receiver. "Taylor. What's up?"

"I just wanted to let you know that we're golfing Friday afternoon."

"We are?"

"My friend Tiffany called and they needed one more couple for this charity golf scramble. They were desperate and I thought we'd probably be going out anyway...."

"Friday's not good for me." Nick deliberately clipped the words.

"Why not?" she asked.

He steeled himself against the disappointment in her voice and reminded himself it was better this way. "I've got work to do."

"You can't spare one afternoon?"

"I gave you all last weekend," he said brusquely. "This engagement was supposed to give me more free time, not less. Just tell your friend we can't—"

"Don't worry about it. I'll find another partner." Taylor's voice lowered. "Nick, about the other night, I'm a little embarrassed. I never drink and I think the champagne must have affected me more than I thought. If I said or did anything to offend you, I'm really sorry."

"Don't give it a second thought. You didn't do or say anything I can hold against you." The lie slipped easily from Nick's lips, and he smiled when he heard her breathe a sigh of relief.

"Great. I was worried. And about Friday, if Tiffany and I weren't such good friends I would have said no, too. This consulting work is going to take more of my time than I thought.''

''I know they're glad to have your help.''

''It's sort of ironic. You fire me, offer me a job as your fiancée, then hire me as a consultant. What a deal.'' She laughed, and the lilt in her voice that had been there when she'd first called returned. ''Hey, Nick, my other line is beeping. I've got to go.''

Nick slowly lowered the receiver to its base and wondered if distancing himself from her really made the best business sense. She certainly hadn't seemed to mind. In fact it was almost as if she didn't care. Of course, he needed to keep in mind she got her five thousand a week whether they saw each other every day or once a month.

''Why aren't you going out with her Friday?'' Erik's voice broke into his thoughts.

''What were you doing? Listening to my conversation?''

''Of course. As much as I could hear, anyway. I should have suggested you put her on speakerphone.'' Erik's teasing expression turned solemn. ''Seriously, Nick, she's supposed to be your fiancée. Why wouldn't you want to be with her?''

Because I already like her too much.

''We been together way too much lately.'' Nick hoped the lie sounded convincing. ''Plus I'm not crazy about co-ed golf.''

''Still, you need to keep your woman happy.''

''That's what the money's for. Believe me, the ink was barely dry on that first check when she cashed it.'' Nick wondered why he resented paying her when it was all part of the deal.

''Hey, that reminds me of a rumor I heard this morning. Is Taylor going to be doing some consulting work on the Burkhalter project?''

Nick nodded. ''She was the team leader on that project before she got downsized. They were going nowhere quick without her.''

Erik shook his head. ‘‘It really makes no sense why she was let go. Did you ever check on that?’’

‘‘Harv from Personnel called me this morning.’’

‘‘And?’’

Nick sighed. ‘‘You’ve got to promise to keep this just between us.’’

‘‘I’m not sure I like the sound of this.’’ Erik’s eyes were serious behind his glasses.

‘‘Apparently there’d been a mistake. The pink slip Taylor received was supposed to go to a Kay, *K-A-Y,* Taylor in the audit department.’’ Nick recognized Erik’s shocked expression. He’d worn the same one when he’d heard the news. ‘‘Harv apologized all over himself then asked me what I thought we should do.’’

‘‘And what did you tell him?’’

‘‘What could I say? I told him not to mention this to anyone, especially Taylor. I said I’d take care of it. I made it sound like Taylor had a lot on her mind between the wedding and consulting and I didn’t want her to feel obligated to go back to work full-time.’’ Nick paused. ‘‘He bought it.’’

‘‘As if this whole fiancée-for-money thing wasn’t bad enough.’’ Erik slowly removed his glasses and rubbed the bridge of his nose. ‘‘When are you going to tell her?’’

‘‘I don’t know.’’ Nick set his cup down on the desk slowly and deliberately. ‘‘Keep in mind the only reason she’d even considered my offer was because she’d lost her job and needed the money. What’s going to happen if she finds out she still has the job?’’

‘‘Nick. Listen to me. You have to tell her.’’

‘‘I don’t have to do anything,’’ Nick said, a hard edge to his voice. ‘‘I’m paying her a bundle to be my fiancée. Not to mention the money she’s earning now as a contract employee. She’s not hurting under this arrangement.’’

The lines of concentration deepened along Erik’s brows. ‘‘Wake up and smell the lawsuit, Nick. I don’t have to remind you she was hesitant enough about agreeing to this engagement. If she finds out you've deceived her—there's no telling what she'll do."

"Once the merger is complete, I'll give her back her old job. With a raise," he added hastily.

Erik leaned back and fit his fingers together. "You can't believe she'd actually take it."

"Why not?"

"Because everyone thinks this engagement is real. It's bound to be awkward when it ends. You think for one minute she'll want to come back and work for you like nothing happened?" Erik shook his head. "No way."

"Then I'll give her a great recommendation."

An incredulous chuckle spurted from Erik's lips. "I can just see it. Last assignment—fiancée. Job duties—social companion, attractive escort, occasional golf partner."

Nick clenched his jaw. "Come off it, Erik. You know what I meant."

"I've said it before and I'll say it again. You'd better be thinking about keeping that woman happy." Erik stood and stretched. "Happy people are less likely to sue."

Nick pushed aside his unease and gave a dismissive wave. He'd had his fill of this subject. "You want to play racquetball Friday night?"

"I thought you were busy with work."

"We can just play a couple of sets. It helps me relax."

Erik shrugged. "Sure. But if you change your mind and want to do the golfing thing with Taylor..."

"I won't."

As soon as the door closed, Nick leaned back. He knew he should be going with Taylor on Friday. If he had his way, he'd see her every day. But he had to keep reminding himself no good would come out of getting too attached to a woman who was so wrong for him.

Chapter Eleven

Nick returned to his old habit of staying late and coming in early to catch up on the work he'd uncharacteristically let slide the previous week. Thankfully the pile on his desk was dwindling, and he knew he would have the time to golf with Taylor tomorrow. But then, he reminded himself, time had never been the issue.

The door swung open, and Nick groaned. "Miss Dietrich. I thought I told you—" He stopped midsentence and straightened in the chair. "Mother, what a surprise."

Sylvia Lanagan Childs smiled brightly and opened her arms. "What, no kiss?"

He rose, rounded the desk and brushed the obligatory kiss across her cheek. Her skin was soft and smooth, and the faint scent of lavender surrounded her.

"Have a seat." Nick gestured to the chair in front of the desk.

Even though they lived in the same town, it had been almost a year since he'd seen her. He took a minute to study her. Her auburn hair was longer than he remembered, pulled back low at her neck and secured with a tortoiseshell clasp. Although a few strands of gray were visible, her casual linen suit highlighted a still-youthful figure.

Her gaze shifted to meet his. Two lines of worry appeared between her eyes. "You look tired."

"Not tired. Just busy." Nick gestured to the stack of papers sitting before him.

"You're always busy," she said without rancor. "I won't keep you long."

She laid an envelope on the desk. "I'm sorry I missed your party. Charlie and I have been in Switzerland and the invitation must have come when we were gone."

Nick stared. Claire must have gone against his wishes and invited his mother.

"You look surprised." Sylvia's smile wavered. "Don't tell me I wasn't supposed to be invited?"

"Of course you were." He'd thought it would be hard on them both if she came to the party. But he'd failed to take into account how much it would hurt her not to be included. "I didn't know you were out of the country."

Her brow lifted, and he had the feeling she could see right through the lie.

She shoved the envelope across the desktop. "Please accept my congratulations. I hope you and Taylor will be very happy."

Nick stared. She'd given him money. An unreasonable anger rose within him.

"We don't need your money." He spoke more harshly than he'd intended. Didn't she realize everything couldn't be made right with money?

"There's no money in the envelope." Disappointment filled her blue eyes. "Only love and good wishes."

His heart sank lower, and shame filled him.

She rose, her face tight and controlled. "I'll leave you to your work."

"I promise I won't stay but a minute—" Like Erik and then his mother, Taylor burst into Nick's office unannounced. She stopped suddenly, and her eyes widened. "I'm sorry. No one was at the front desk. I didn't realize you had company."

"Miss Dietrich had some errands to run." Nick rose and rounded the desk, brushing a welcoming kiss against her cheek. ''Taylor, I'd like you to meet my mother, Sylvia Childs. Mother, my fiancée, Taylor Rollins.''

Sylvia stood, and Nick cursed himself for putting the wariness into her gaze.

Thankfully, delight swept Taylor's face and she moved forward immediately to clasp Sylvia's hand, ''Mrs. Childs, what a pleasure to finally meet you. I'd hoped to see you at the engagement party. Nick and I were so disappointed you couldn't make it.''

Thank you, God.

The strain in Sylvia's face eased, and Nick breathed a sigh of relief.

''That's why I stopped by. My husband and I were out of town and I didn't get the invitation until we returned.'' Sylvia gestured to the cream-colored envelope still unopened on the desktop. ''I dropped by with a card. I didn't have time to pick up any—''

''Don't you worry about that,'' Taylor said, giving his mother a hug. ''Your good wishes are all we need.''

For a second, Nick swore his mother was going to cry. But when the embrace ended, Sylvia's eyes were dry.

''You're a lucky man, Nick.'' Sylvia's gaze shifted from Taylor to her son. ''You take good care of her.''

He swallowed against the sudden lump in his throat. Why did her approval still mean so much? ''I will.''

''And, Taylor, you make him happy.''

Taylor met the older woman's gaze with a directness that surprised even Nick. She was really getting the hang of this acting. ''I'll do my best.''

''Good.'' Sylvia hurriedly gathered her purse and blinked rapidly. ''Congratulations. I wish you both only the best.''

In a matter of seconds she was gone. The door closed softly behind her, and Taylor sank into the chair Sylvia had just vacated. ''Your mother seems like a nice woman. I'm glad I got to meet her.''

Nick sat in his desk chair, strangely exhausted. His fingers toyed with the card.

"What does it say?"

"I haven't looked at it yet." He pushed it toward her across the slick desktop. "Open it if you want."

It was all the encouragement Taylor needed. "Do you want me to read it out loud?"

Nick shrugged.

"Wishing you love and happiness on your engagement." Taylor held up the card and showed him the outside.

"If you're going to take all day, I've changed my mind. Don't read it."

Taylor ignored him and shifted her attention to the card. "There's no verse inside, just a note from your mother. Maybe you should read it yourself."

He waved a dismissive hand. "Go ahead."

"Okay." Taylor took a breath. "'Dear Nick, Remember what I used to tell you when you were younger, If you always do what you've always done, you'll always get what you always got.'"

Nick groaned and raked his fingers through his hair. He'd heard that a million times when he was growing up. Even when he'd been in college, she'd spouted it to him. When he'd told her he wasn't any good at public speaking, she'd encouraged him to take some speech classes, join the debate team and practice before small groups. She'd said if what he'd been doing hadn't worked, he needed to do something different. She'd been right.

"Go on." Sensing Taylor's curious stare, he shifted his gaze to the ceiling.

She cleared her throat and resumed reading.

"'Make sure that the choices you make, the priorities you set as a couple are the ones that will give you both the true happiness you deserve. Love, Mother.' That's so sweet." Taylor smiled and lowered the paper. "I don't think I've ever heard that saying before."

"It was one of her favorites."

"Does she have any others?" Taylor lifted a brow.

You love that company more than you love me. More than you love Nick.

It wasn't a saying as much as a refrain heard over and over. Even now, five years after his father's death, he still railed against the thought.

After all, wasn't it Nick his father had asked to see while on his deathbed? Hadn't Nick been the one to hold his father's hand while his life slipped away? And hadn't Nick been the one he'd entrusted with his most valuable possession—the company?

Why did the thought suddenly make him sad?

"No," he said, shaking his head. "Anyway, none that I remember."

Her gaze narrowed, and she studied him thoughtfully but didn't comment. Instead she picked up her bag and rose. "And you're sure you can't golf tomorrow?"

He used an easy out and gestured to the papers littering his desk. Work had been his salvation after his father died. It would have to be again.

Chapter Twelve

"I hope Claire didn't mind you coming with me tonight." Taylor waited while Tony loaded her clubs into his 4x4 Cherokee.

Tony laughed. "You're incredible."

She smiled. "What's so funny?"

"If anyone's going to be upset about you and me being together, it'll be your fiancé."

His arched brow reminded her of Nick, and for a second her heart twisted. Try as she might, she still couldn't understand why he hadn't come with her today.

"You never told me why he bailed on you." Tony's eyes shone with a curious intensity.

"This golf match was last-minute." Taylor forced a shrug. "And Nick had work to do."

"So you're telling me he's not waiting in the wings? You're free for the whole evening?"

"Not free," Taylor pushed thoughts of Nick aside and smiled. "It'll cost you."

Playing along, Tony reached into his pocket and pulled out his wallet. "Okay, how much?"

"There's a Dairy Queen down on Main I've been meaning to check out. Do you have enough for a—"

"Vanilla dip cone with butterscotch?"

"How'd you remember?" She smiled with delight.

"How could I forget? Hanging out at DQ with you was a

big deal.'' Tony reached over and tugged her hair, a familiar gesture from the past. ''Tonight, we're going all out. Drinks are on me.''

Taylor giggled. The girlish sound made her laugh. ''Lime Mr. Mistys?''

''For you, darling, nothing but the best.''

She flung her arms around him. ''Tony Karelli, you're wonderful.''

He reciprocated and wound his arms around her, but instead of a brief squeeze the moment stretched. Was it her imagination or did he seem reluctant to let her go? She finally pulled back, breaking the contact, her gaze searching his face. For what, she wasn't sure. As if sensing her unease, Tony winked, and the warm friendliness in his grin reassured her.

Sitting next to Tony atop one of the weathered picnic tables in front of the Dairy Queen, she could have been eighteen again. Taylor tossed away the straw and sipped the slush straight from the cup. The bug zapper buzzed overhead and the ice cream turned to liquid faster than she could lick and talk.

Sparkling stars filled the dark sky, and the gentle breeze ruffled Tony's dark hair into little tufts.

Impulsively, Taylor reached over and touched his arm. ''I'm so glad we're still friends.''

''I've missed you, Taylor,'' he said quietly. ''You were the best part of my life for a long time. Actually, you were my only friend.''

Taylor murmured in protest, but Tony just smiled. ''It's true. Don't bother to deny it.''

''They just couldn't see what a special guy you were.'' She held up one hand and counted off each finger. ''You're loyal, kind, fun to be with—''

''Stop, stop.'' Tony held up one hand, a flush spreading up his neck. ''You're making me sound like a cross between a Boy Scout and Lassie.''

Taylor laughed. ''All I'm trying to say is you're a great guy. Don't settle for less than you deserve. Promise me that?''

"I promise." His gaze shifted to his drink. "Do you really think your father hoped we'd end up together?"

Taylor took another sip of her Mr. Misty and thought for a moment. She finally nodded. "Probably. He always liked you and your parents."

"He was a great guy. And your mother was the best. They were a perfect couple."

"Yes, they were." Taylor thought of the loving touches and the laughter that had flowed gently between the two. There had never been any doubt their affection ran deep and true. "I always promised myself that would be the kind of love I'd have."

"Do you think you'll have it with Nick?"

"That's an odd question." Taylor forced a laugh. "Of course."

Tony set her drink aside and took her hands in his. "I don't want you to take this wrong. I'm just worried you might have rushed into this engagement. Claire says you two haven't known each other very long. I can understand you being lonely, what with your parents gone and all, but please don't *you* settle for less than you deserve."

She couldn't be cross with him. Still, what if any of this got back to Claire?

"I appreciate your concern. I really do. But you don't need to worry. I love Nick. We're very happy together."

Skepticism shone on Tony's face.

"I'll admit the man's a workaholic, but I'm doing my best to change that."

He reached up and tipped her face to his, his dark eyes solemn. "I want you to promise me if you ever need—"

"If she ever needs anything or anyone, I'll be the one she turns to—right, sweetheart?" Nick dropped down next to her on the picnic table.

Her heart lodged in her throat, and hot guilt spread up her neck. She'd done nothing wrong, so why did she feel like she had?

"Nick. I didn't see you."

His gazed shifted between her and Tony. ''I don't doubt it. You two were so *involved.*''

''What brings you to this neighborhood?''

''I just dropped Erik off. We had some business to discuss this evening.''

''The scramble was really fun. When you couldn't make it, I called up Tony, and he was able to rearrange his plans. It's too bad you couldn't be there. I think you would have enjoyed it.'' Taylor stopped and took a deep, calming breath. She detested people who chattered mindlessly.

Nick glanced at Tony, then back at Taylor. His face creased into a sudden smile. ''Just being with you, sweetheart, would be enough to make it enjoyable.''

Even though she knew he'd slipped into his adoring fiancé role, a comforting warmth invaded her body and it seemed natural to lean her head against his shoulder. His arm wrapped around her. Maybe she'd caught the hang of this acting. Or maybe…

''I'll see her home from here, Karelli.''

A muscle twitched in Tony's jaw, but he smiled at Taylor and nodded to Nick. ''I need to get going, anyway. Thanks for inviting me, Taylor. If you ever need a partner—''

''Won't that be a little hard to do from D.C.?'' Nick raised a brow.

''Actually, I may be sticking around. At least for the summer. Henry wants me to help him with some project.''

''Tony, how wonderful,'' Taylor said, unable to believe she'd have her friend around for a while longer. ''Isn't that great, Nick?''

Nick smiled.

Tony stood and tugged Taylor's hair. ''Call me.''

''Thanks again for going with me. I had fun.'' She watched him walk away before turning to Nick. ''Maybe while Tony's in Cedar Ridge, you and he can get better acquainted.''

Nick stared for a moment then gave her a half smile. ''Maybe.''

Taylor picked up the slush and took a sip. ''I hope so. I think you two have a lot in common.''

''Right offhand, I can think of at least one thing,'' he muttered.

Taylor stared at him, baffled, until she remembered. *Claire.* They'd both been involved with that woman. Taylor frowned. ''Nick, about—''

He shook his head and stopped the words and her heart with a simple touch of his fingers against her lips. His solemn gaze swept her face. ''I've been doing a lot of thinking these past few days. I've decided as long as the whole world thinks we're engaged, I need to be your escort, your golf partner. After all, I'm supposed to be your fiancé. It's time I started acting like one.''

Acting like one? Dear God, how was she ever going to hold on to her sanity—not to mention her heart—if he really pulled out all the stops? He might be acting, but her response to his words and actions tended to be all too real.

His eyes twinkled, and for a moment she wondered if he knew what kind of thoughts ran through her mind.

Gazing into his deep blue eyes, it was all Taylor could do to resist the urge to venture from the firm solid bank where she'd always stood to a place where she could be over her head in minutes.

Like a shot of whiskey, she downed the last of her slush in a single gulp and jerked upright. Her sudden movement dislodged his hand, and it dropped from her shoulder. All at once she could breathe again.

Until he took the cup from her and set it on the picnic table. His eyes darkened. ''You know what I want.''

''A Mr. Misty of your own?'' she asked weakly.

His cupped hand slid up her arm. ''You're so beautiful you take my breath away.''

Her skin prickled, and a strange kind of electricity filled the air. Taylor forced a laugh and gestured at her shorts and top. ''In this? I don't think so.''

"It's not what you're wearing." Nick fingered the thin strap of her tank top.

Taylor froze, her heart fluttering wildly.

"Nick, don't."

"Shh, sweetheart." He leaned forward, his hands on her arms. His mouth lowered, and his lips moved over hers. Soft. Gentle. Incredible.

Her heart pounded an erratic rhythm and it took everything she had to make herself pull away. Trying to gain control of her rioting emotions, Taylor shifted her gaze and took a long, steadying breath.

She looked up a moment later to find his gaze on hers. Her mouth went dry. "I..."

"Taylor, I'd like for us to get better acquainted," Nick said softly, curling a loose strand of hair behind her ear. "Let me take you home,"

There was no doubt what he was asking. Taylor paused, thankful she had a ready excuse. "You can't."

"Can't?" His brows drew together.

"I'm spending the night with my grandparents," she said. "There was some kind of chemical spill in my neighborhood this afternoon. The fumes were terrible and the fire department suggested everyone find somewhere else to stay tonight."

She knew she was chattering again but somehow she couldn't stop. A tiny smile lifted the corners of Nick's lips, and he brushed his knuckles lightly across her cheek. "Call your grandparents and tell them you'll stay at my place."

She shook her head.

"Why not?" A small muscle twitched at the corner of Nick's jaw. "We *are* engaged."

"For the moment." She met his gaze without flinching. "And even if were really engaged, we're not married."

"You can't be serious."

Taylor knew the need that made him push the issue. It gnawed at her, too. But she also knew the difference between right and wrong.

"I'm sorry, Nick." She rested her hand lightly on his forearm. "It's just not going to happen."

"This is incredible." He raked his fingers through his hair.

"Nick, I—"

"It's okay." He jerked to his feet, frustration evident on his face, his fists jammed into his pockets. "It's probably better this way."

He blew out a short harsh breath. His gaze focused intently on the big flashing cone on the roof of the building.

"I know you won't believe this," she said in a soft voice, staring at his rigid features. "But this is hard for me, too."

"Good." Nick let his gaze drop, focusing for a moment on her lips. He forced a smile.

They walked to his car and talked around the tension draped over them like a shroud. The car ride to her grandparents' home was pure torture. Even though he worked hard to keep the conversation light and superficial, beneath the pleasant words an awareness of her fanned a fire that not even the knowledge that nothing was going to happen could douse.

Feeling all of sixteen again, he insisted on walking her to the door. Like a scene from an old movie, he half expected to see the porch light blazing and Gramps peering out the front window. But the night enveloped them in darkness, and the only light shone from the ornate pole at the end of the driveway.

Still, when they reached the steps Nick couldn't help but glance at the front window. The tension in his shoulders eased when he saw the curtains were drawn shut. He turned to Taylor.

Her lips curved in a smile, and she lifted her face expectantly. Nick slipped his fingers into her silky hair and pulled her close. If all he could have was a good-night kiss, he'd make it one she'd remember. One she'd dream about when she slept alone tonight.

He resisted her waiting lips and bent lower, smiling at her sharp intake of air, imparting light feathery kisses where her shirt collar ended and her skin began. She arched her neck, and he planted kisses along her jawline, moving upward, his lips still everywhere but on her mouth.

And then he covered her mouth with his, kissing her with an intensity that shook him to his very core. No one existed but the two of them.

Suddenly the raucous barking of a neighbor dog out for a midnight stroll interrupted them.

The porch light flicked on.

With one supreme effort, Nick pulled back from Taylor's arms. His breath ragged, he slumped against the railing and ran a shaky hand through his hair.

Taylor straightened herself and patted her disheveled hair with a hand as shaky as his. Her eyes glittered in the harsh glare.

It was all he could do not to pull her into his arms again.

''I'd better go in. How do I look?''

Like someone who's just been thoroughly kissed.

Nick's gaze lingered. How had this woman managed to get under his skin? ''Beautiful. You look beautiful.''

Her lips curved in a soft dreamy smile that made him want to kiss her all over again. She reached for the doorknob, then turned and brushed her lips across his. ''Sleep well, Nick.''

He smiled weakly. Was she kidding? It would be a miracle if he slept at all.

Chapter Thirteen

''What did you think of Pastor's sermon this morning, Nick?'' Nana added another dollop of jelly to her toast.

Stopping at the Pioneer Room after church for breakfast had somehow become a regular event, and despite his initial reluctance, Nick found himself looking forward to the Sunday tradition.

He paused and took a sip of coffee, contemplating his response. Technically, the minister was an excellent orator. He interspersed humor into his message, used vocal variation and gestures to full advantage and made good eye contact with his audience. But somehow Nick had the feeling that Nana referred to today's topic, the one that centered around the message of forgiveness. ''Excellent sermon.''

''What'd you think about it, Taylor?'' Nana shifted her attention to her granddaughter.

Taylor sat her glass of milk down. The morning light filtered through the stained glass window and fell softly on her hair, emphasizing the rich red highlights.

''Forgiveness is a hard one.'' Her brow furrowed in concentration. ''I still find myself not always wanting to forgive easily. I think it's because I feel forgiveness sometimes excuses bad behavior.''

''I know what you mean.'' Nana nodded thoughtfully. ''That's what I like about Pastor's sermons. They really make you think.''

They made you think too much, Nick thought. During the first few weeks he'd attended services with Taylor and her grandparents, he'd been able to tune the minister out. But lately the words had been getting through. It was the oddest thing. No matter how much he tried to concentrate on other things, his thoughts kept straying to the sermon.

And it wasn't enough that he was hit right between the eyes in church, they had to discuss it again over breakfast. It was enough to kill a guy's appetite.

"Nick?"

He glanced up guiltily to find the three of them staring at him expectantly.

Bill smiled knowingly. "I think Nick left us for a while."

"Nana wanted to know if you found it hard to forgive."

Back on the hot seat again, Nick shifted uncomfortably. Hard to forgive? He'd never been a person to hold a grudge. Except when it came to Sylvia.

"Not usually. No." He smiled at Taylor and took a bite of egg. "In fact I've even forgiven your grandfather for beating me at golf Friday."

"You should have seen the look on his face when we tallied up the scores." Bill chuckled. "Taylor, I don't think your fiancé is accustomed to losing to a senior citizen."

"Senior citizen?" Tony Karelli's voice sounded behind Nick. "No way."

"Tony!" Genuine pleasure filled Grandpa Bill's voice. He rose to his feet and clasped the younger man's hand. "And Miss Waters, what a pleasure to see you again."

The eggs Nick had just eaten turned to rocks in his stomach. He pushed back his chair and stood.

"Pull up a couple of chairs. We'd love to have you join us," Bill urged.

"You're so kind," Claire said, almost purring. "And please—" she batted her dark lashes at Bill "—call me Claire."

"Well, Claire." Bill held the chair for the woman. "What

brings you and Tony out today? I didn't think I saw you in church."

"Church?" Claire started to laugh, then stopped and waved a careless hand. "Tony wanted to go on some nature walk at sunrise. He caught me at a weak moment and I agreed."

"When we lived in D.C., Taylor and I used to walk almost every Saturday." Tony smiled at Taylor. "Remember?"

"Of course I remember." Taylor returned his smile. "Every week for almost a year is hard to forget."

Nick narrowed his gaze. He'd known the two had been friends, but he'd never guessed they'd been that close.

"Almost a year." Claire's eyes widened innocently. "Why, after all that talking, I bet you know more about Taylor than Nick does."

"I wouldn't say that." Tony appeared to discount the notion, but the smug look in his eyes told Nick differently.

"People change." Nick took another sip of coffee.

"Do they?" Claire gave a dainty shrug.

Nick glanced at his watch.

"We all change over time," Nana said and offered Nick a smile.

"I know, let's do a little test." Claire flashed a beguiling smile, and Nick's unease increased. He'd seen that smile in the past, and it always spelled trouble. "We'll see how much Tony remembers from those long intimate walks."

"They weren't intimate," Taylor said sharply.

"We were friends, Claire," Tony added.

"Okay, friends. But you knew Taylor pretty well, right?"

Tony nodded.

"Okay, question number one." Claire cast Nick a sideways glance to make sure he was listening. He forced a bored look. "Tony, how many children did Taylor want to have?"

One, Nick thought, maybe two.

"Now keep in mind she may have changed her mind." Tony paused. "But back then she wanted six."

"Six!" The word burst from Nick's lips like a bullet.

Grandpa Bill and Nana smiled. Taylor reddened. Claire laughed.

"I'm afraid he's right," Taylor said with a self-effacing smile. "Growing up as a 'lonely only,' I'd decided long ago that, God willing, I wanted a whole house full of children."

But six? Nick could only stare in amazement. Who would ever want that many children?

"So, Taylor, tell me." Claire raised a finger to her lips and studied the other woman. "Where do you think you're going to find a nanny for that many children?"

"I won't have a nanny." Taylor met Claire's disbelieving gaze head-on. "I plan to be a stay-at-home mom. My family will be my priority."

"What do you think of that, Nick?" One dark brow raised, Claire narrowed her eyes. "I seem to remember that at one time you weren't sure if you wanted *any* children."

All eyes shifted to Nick, and he resisted the urge to run a finger inside his suddenly tight collar. He settled for reaching across the table to take Taylor's hand and bring it to his lips. "You forget, Claire. That was before I met Taylor."

"When were you going to spring it on me that you wanted six kids?" Nick's hands clenched the steering wheel, and he kept his gaze focused straight ahead.

"How 'bout after the wedding that's never going to take place?" Taylor said sweetly.

Nick blew a harsh breath, knowing he was being unreasonable but somehow unable to stop. "Who in this day and age wants a half a dozen kids?"

She lifted her gaze, and her green eyes sparkled like emeralds. "I do."

"Well, I don't." He shoved aside an image of little boys with his dark hair and Taylor's green eyes.

"What does it matter?" Taylor said with a shrug. "Pretend you do."

"Pretend? How do you pretend to want six kids?"

"I don't know." Taylor's lips quirked upward, and she

leaned back in her seat as if she didn't care that she'd made him look like a child hater in front of her grandparents. "You're a smart guy. I'm sure you'll think of something."

Nick raked his hand through his hair. Clearly he was getting nowhere with this conversation. His foot hit the accelerator, and he pushed the troubling topic to the back of his mind, desperately hoping the subject wouldn't come up again.

The next day, after they'd played a round of golf, Bill Rollins stopped him on the way to the clubhouse and waved the others on. "Six children is a big family, and a big responsibility."

Nick stifled a groan. He ran an honest business. He didn't cheat at golf. Why couldn't he get a break?

"I know Taylor has always been willing to make that commitment, but you have to be willing to make it, too," Bill continued when Nick didn't answer. "Children need both a mother *and* a father around when they're growing up."

Nick knew this was Bill's tactful way of saying he'd noticed how much time Nick spent at the office. But that wouldn't change. Whether he had a wife and children at home or not.

"Are you sure that's what *you* want, Nick?" The older man's face was filled with concern.

Of course it wasn't what he wanted. But how would Bill react to the truth? Probably by worrying that his granddaughter had chosen the wrong man to marry.

Pretend you do.

Nick pulled on all those drama classes he'd taken and forced a chuckle. He slapped Bill on the back.

"Call me crazy," he said with what he hoped was a convincing grin, "but I really do."

Chapter Fourteen

"I had a wonderful time tonight." Taylor inserted the key in her front door and smiled at Nick over her shoulder. "I love to dance."

"It was fun," Nick agreed.

They'd gone to a club in Denver and spent the evening on the dance floor. It was the slow numbers that threatened Nick's resolve to keep things between them light and low-key. With her body pressed against him and her breath warm on his cheek he wanted nothing more than to kiss her senseless and go from there.

"Want to come in for a few minutes? I could make some coffee and…" Taylor paused and a twinkle lit her eyes. "I've got a pint of chocolate chip ice cream we could share."

Nick groaned. He loved ice cream, and she knew chocolate chip was his favorite. But to go in feeling the way he did right now would be reckless. Foolish.

"Sure. Why not?" He followed her into the dark house, pulling the door shut behind him.

In only minutes the coffee was perking and the small round container of ice cream sat on the counter in front of them.

Taylor reached into the silverware drawer. "One spoon? Or two?"

He knew she was remembering the time they'd stopped at Dairy Queen and shared a hot fudge sundae. And a spoon.

"One," he said.

''One it is.'' Taylor dropped the other piece of silver into the drawer and turned, dipping the lone spoon into the soft creamy treat. She took a bite, and her eyes half closed as she savored the taste. ''Oh, wow. This is so good.''

''I bet it is.'' He couldn't keep from smiling. Taylor was the first woman he'd known who liked ice cream as much as he did.

She held out the spoon and he hesitated, not wanting to end her pleasure.

''Sweetheart, I can get you another spoon,'' she said. ''It's no problem, really.''

He liked the way she said ''sweetheart.'' She'd started calling him that more frequently lately, even when they were alone.

''Now why wouldn't I want to share with you?''

''I don't know.'' She shrugged. ''I could be coming down with a cold. You could end up stuck in bed for a week.''

''I'm used to taking chances,'' he said finally. He moved closer and took the spoon from her hand, setting it on the counter.

''Don't you want some?'' Teasing filled her gaze. ''I can't eat it all.''

''I want something,'' Nick said, slipping his arm around Taylor and pulling her to him. ''But it's not ice cream.''

Soft and warm, she was next to him and all he could think was this was the way it was meant to be. He gently touched her face.

Her arms wrapped around his neck. Nick stopped talking and lost himself in their kiss. Not sure of what he'd planned to say, he was past the point of caring.

His resolve to keep his distance vanished in the moment. Suddenly he couldn't get close enough.

He wasn't even aware they were moving until Taylor's back hit the edge of the counter. Taylor seemed to have difficulty breathing and a rush of pink stained her cheeks.

''Let's go upstairs.'' His voice came out husky and shakier than he would have liked.

Taylor's gaze rose. ''Upstairs?''

''To the bedroom.'' All the reasons he should back off seemed inconsequential. He would make her his. Tonight he would make love to her until all doubts were swept away.

''Nick.''

Her sultry voice sent shivers of anticipation coursing through his veins.

''Yes, my love?'' Lightly he fingered a loose strand of hair on her cheek.

She drew a ragged breath and exhaled slowly. ''If I led you on, I'm sorry...''

He stared, disbelieving. She'd wanted this as much as he had, he was sure of it. ''What are you saying?''

She sidestepped his embrace and gestured to the door. ''I think it's time you leave.''

Too caught up in his feelings, he scarcely noticed the regret in her eyes or heard her words as she ushered him out the door. ''Before we both do something we'll regret.''

''I'll have a tall caramel macchiato, please.'' Taylor stood at the coffee shop counter. She'd have to settle for a dinner of only salad to offset the calories, but for once she didn't care.

''Whipped cream?'' The young woman behind the counter poised the can above the drink.

''Please.'' Taylor reached into her billfold and pulled out a five-dollar bill.

''Taylor.'' A feminine voice sounded from behind her, and she turned.

''Mrs. Childs.'' Taylor smiled warmly. ''I didn't expect to see you here.''

''I was out shopping and decided to take a break. The vanilla latte was calling my name.'' Nick's mother's smile wavered. ''I put my bags at the table over there. Would you care to join me?''

Taylor thought quickly. The few errands she had left could wait. ''I'd love to.''

They chatted while Sylvia got the latte that was calling her name, then they headed to the table by the window.

The shop looked out onto the town square. Several years before, the city planners had taken a good hard look at the blight and decay downtown and embarked on a massive revitalization project.

Most shoppers still frequented the mall at the edge of town, but the area known simply as Town Square had managed to achieve its own loyal following. The old brick buildings from the turn of the century had been renovated without losing the charm from that earlier era. Merchants had discovered that there were women and men willing to pay more for their high-end merchandise.

Taylor loved to browse in the exclusive shops, even though she could no longer afford the prices.

''Looks like you did some damage.'' Taylor gestured to the sacks Sylvia had propped up between them on the ledge lining the front windows.

''It's not as bad as it looks.'' Sylvia took a sip of her latte. ''Charlie desperately needed some new clothes, and McMurrays was having a big sale.''

''Really?'' Taylor raised a brow. Grandpa Bill's birthday was coming up, and he bought all his clothes at McMurrays. Although small, the shop always seemed to have a good selection of the finest menswear. And the service was superb. ''I might have to stop over and see what they have.''

''Georgine's is having a sale, too.'' Sylvia's gaze settled on Taylor's stretched silk boatneck sweater, obviously recognizing it as coming from the trendy boutique.

Taylor smiled. Little did Nick's mother know, the garment she'd coupled with a pair of linen slacks was three years old. ''I love that store.''

''I was just on my way over there. Would you care to join me?''

Taylor's purse was empty, and for the past year she'd used her credit card for emergencies only. Still, what would it hurt to browse?

''Sure, why not? It never hurts to look.''

''Or buy.'' Nick's mother laughed.

''I'll drink to that.'' Taylor held her caramel macchiato up in a toast.

If the two women weren't laughing so hard they might have noticed the attractive brunette standing on the sidewalk with a grin on her full red lips that would do a Cheshire cat proud.

''Daddy.'' Claire pushed open the door to her father's office, ignoring his secretary's frantic wave. She stopped in the doorway, her smile widening at the sight. This was going to work out perfectly.

The two looked up at the same time. Her father's lips curved in a welcoming smile, but after giving her a perfunctory nod, Nick returned his gaze almost immediately to the papers spread out on the worktable.

''Henry, about—''

''Nick, let's take a break. Helen.'' Henry bellowed to his secretary. ''Bring us some iced tea.''

Claire moved to her father's side and gave him a peck on the cheek. She slanted Nick a sideways glance.

The man was too handsome for his own good. And much too arrogant. He deserved to be taken down a peg or two.

''Daddy, I saw Jack Corrigan downtown this morning and he said to tell you hello.''

Nick's jaw tightened. Claire smiled with satisfaction.

''How's he doing?''

''Good.'' Claire pulled up a chair and sat down across from Nick. She wanted to be able to see his expression when she twisted the knife. ''He's considering an offer from some west coast firm.''

''An offer?'' Her father straightened. ''What kind of offer?''

''It's a merger thing.'' Claire shook her head and pasted a sad expression on her face. ''Poor Jack. I think it really hurt him when you didn't choose his firm. After all, you two have been friends for years.''

"Jack understood," Henry blustered, clearly uncomfortable. "It was business."

A muscle jumped in Nick's jaw. Claire's heart quickened.

"But I told him not to rush into anything." She widened her eyes innocently. "A deal's not done until the papers are signed."

She could almost see the anger bubble to the surface of Nick's carefully controlled features. Excitement raced up Claire's spine. Now came the real fun.

"By the way." She turned her gaze to Nick. "I saw your fiancée today."

Confusion clouded his gaze. Her adrenaline surged. She'd caught him off guard.

"You did? Where?"

"Downtown." Claire smiled brightly. "Shopping with your mother. Why between them they must have had a dozen sacks. Isn't it nice, Daddy?"

"Nice?" Henry frowned.

"Yes, nice." She shifted her gaze to Nick. Their eyes met. Her words may have been directed to her father, but they were strictly for the other man's benefit. "Nick really did get himself a woman just like his mother."

Just like his mother.

Nick's glove slammed into the punching bag.

If Taylor wanted to squander the whole five thousand dollars he'd paid her this week on clothes, he didn't care.

He narrowed his gaze and hit the bag again. Hard.

If Taylor didn't want him, he didn't care.

Like a bullet fired from a gun, his hand shot out, striking the leather. The force of the impact sent the bag swinging wildly.

He steadied the bag and took a deep breath, wiping the sweat from his forehead with the back of his gloved hand.

"Hey, Nick." A guy he vaguely recalled from a golf tournament last year yelled across the room. "Leave a little leather on that bag, will you?"

Nick acknowledged the greeting with a grunt and a nod then turned his attention back to the bag.

Right. Left. Right. Left.

Now he had the rhythm. After five minutes the tension in his shoulders began to ease. After ten, the unreasonable anger that had led him to cancel his afternoon appointments vanished. After twenty, he was exhausted, and the only emotion remaining was disappointment.

With all the women in the world, why did he have to go and fall in love with one just like his mother?

Fall in love? He sank down on a nearby bench, his mind reeling. He couldn't be in love with her. After all, this was all an act. Wasn't it?

Chapter Fifteen

"Nick, about the other night..." Taylor paused, then tried again. "I hope you don't think I'm making a mountain out of a—aargh!" Frustrated, Taylor whirled and plopped down on the bed. If it sounded stupid in the privacy of her grandparents' guest room, how would it sound when she tried to say it in person?

He'd wanted to spend the night with her. That had come through loud and clear. And she'd surprised him when she'd said no. She knew lots of women who would have jumped at the chance. Claire Waters, for one. She shoved the unpleasant thought aside.

Nick was a handsome man. She enjoyed his company. They laughed at the same jokes and shared a love of chocolate chip ice cream and golf. And she couldn't deny that underneath their friendship a current of desire surged like a raging river. She could control the lust. What made it harder to stay the course was the love.

The notion that she was falling in love with Nick had nagged at the edge of her thoughts for days. Taylor sighed, realizing she'd done just what she'd sworn she'd never do—she'd fallen in love with her leading man. That's why this role had become so easy to play. She didn't have to *act* like a woman in love because she *was* a woman in love.

But did he feel the same? That was the question that had

kept her up half the night. Somewhere around three she'd dozed into an uneasy slumber.

Taylor grabbed her robe and headed down the stairs. First she'd have a good breakfast. Then, on a full stomach, she'd think about what she was going to do about Nick.

"Taylor. What a surprise." A sinking feeling gripped Nick's gut, but he smiled past his unease. Her showing up unexpectedly at his office was not a good sign. He motioned for her to take a seat.

"Good morning." She flashed him a too-bright smile.

Although she was as beautiful as ever, with her hair shiny and soft and hanging in loose waves to her shoulders and her eyes that startling shade of green he liked so much, the lines of fatigue on her face were evident.

He could empathize. In the past few days his emotions had been on a roller coaster ride, and the trip had played havoc with his sleep.

He'd wanted her so badly he ached. But not just physically. Having Tony hanging around had sent a shiver of fear racing down his spine. In his haste he'd been reckless. He'd moved too fast. But he couldn't lose her. He couldn't lose what they had.

There was something about Taylor that made him feel warm inside, that made him think about sitting in front of a fire on a cold winter day with a dog at his feet and her at his side. Warm inside? Nick gave a strangled groan. He'd been burning with a different kind of fire last night.

"Did you say something?" She looked at him expectantly.

"Before you start…I want you to know I'm sorry about last night." Nick raked his fingers through his hair. Apologizing like this was awkward. He should have gone to her immediately this morning and cleared the air. Not made her come to him. After all, what would it have taken? A few minutes out of his day? Instead he'd done what he always did and had gone to the office and concentrated on his business.

If you always do what you've always done…

Nick shoved the disturbing thought aside and returned his attention to Taylor.

She shifted uncomfortably as if the soft leather of his office chair had suddenly turned hard. ''We need to talk.''

Were there four more dreaded words in the English language? He flashed her a grin. ''I thought that's what we were doing now.''

Her lips smiled but her eyes remained somber. ''Do you want to start or should I?''

There was that serious tone again. Did he really want to hear what she had to say? Unable to sit still for a moment longer, Nick got up and paced. ''Go ahead.''

''I'd feel better if you sat down.'' She gestured to the chair next to her, and he noticed her hand trembled slightly.

She looked so stressed Nick didn't have the heart to say no. He grabbed the chair and turned it toward her before he sat down.

A sudden chill hung in the air, and he wanted nothing more than to take her hand and tell her that together there was nothing they couldn't work out. Instead he flicked away an imaginary piece of lint and remained silent.

''Okay.'' The word came out on a long exhale. She clasped her hands in her lap and shut her eyes for the briefest time. For a second he thought she might be praying, but the moment passed too quickly for that.

Nick leaned back and rested his elbows on the arms of the chair, hoping he looked relaxed and unconcerned.

''My faith has been a part of me for as long as I can remember.'' Her gaze sought his, and he gave her an encouraging nod.

''I believe in God's word and I try to live a God-pleasing life.'' Taylor brushed a strand of hair behind her ear with a trembling finger.

Nick stifled a groan. He held up one hand. ''No need to say more. I get the point.''

''I don't think you do,'' Taylor said softly. ''I'm not just talking about you wanting more from me. I'm just as guilty of wanting more, too.''

''Then why...?''

''There's more to this issue than just the desire.'' Her voice was calm and matter-of-fact, but a telltale flush rose up her cheeks. ''I don't want to just sleep with or have sex with someone, I want to make love. And,'' she added, ''I want that person to be my husband. I want it to be something special, just between the two of us for the rest of our life. Not just with someone I'm hired out to for the summer.''

''Is that all I am to you?'' Pain made Nick speak more harshly than he'd intended. ''Your employer?''

A troubled look crossed her face, but her expression remained determined. She answered his question with one of her own. ''Tell me, Nick, what's the most important thing in your life?''

He didn't even stop to think. His response was automatic. ''This company. Making it stronger so it's the biggest and the best.''

''That's what I thought you'd say.'' A sad half smile creased her lips.

For one crazy instant he was tempted to take her in his arms and kiss that sadness away. Tempted to tell her that *she* was the most important thing in his life. But he held back as he always did when he got a wild impulse, and the urge passed. ''What does that have do with anything, anyway?''

''It shows how far apart we are on everything that matters.''

''We're not that far apart.'' Nick leaned forward and used his most persuasive tone. How could she act as if what had existed between the two of them these past months meant nothing? ''We get along great. You like to golf. I like to golf—''

''This isn't about golf. Or about chocolate chip ice cream. It's about who we are in here.'' Her hand rose in a fist over her heart.

''I guess I didn't think I was that bad of a guy,'' Nick said stiffly.

"You're not." Taylor drew a shaky breath. "I'm just saying that our priorities are worlds apart. What we want out of life is different and because of that there can never be anything more between us."

Her large emerald eyes glistened but he paid no attention. He clenched his jaw and drew a ragged breath.

"What's most important in my life is God and my family," Taylor said. "I don't put my job above everything else."

"That's easy for you to say," Nick said. "You don't have five hundred people depending on you for a paycheck every month."

"You're right, I don't," she said softly. "But I truly believe that all things work together for the good of those who love God and put *Him* first in their lives. And, as far as business is concerned, what does it all matter if we don't come home at night to someone who loves us?"

"I suppose this is where the pitter-patter of twelve little feet come in?" Nick said sarcastically.

"That's right." Her gaze met his. "When your father was dying, what mattered in that instant? Having his wife and son at his side? Knowing a loving Saviour was waiting for him with open arms? Or how many people he employed?"

His father's last breath? The memory was too vivid to ever be forgotten. "Take care of the company," his father had whispered to him. There were no loving last words for his wife sitting at the bedside. Or for his son.

"This is getting way too serious." Nick forced a light tone and an easy smile to his lips. "Why don't we just agree to disagree?"

"Agree to disagree?" Taylor's brow furrowed in a frown.

"Yeah," he said with a casual shrug that belied the pain in his heart. "Like you said, we're so far apart on what we believe, why even discuss it?"

"And what about us?"

"What us?" he said, proud he could sound so offhand while his heart was breaking. "You were the one that said there could never be anything between us."

"I was hoping I was wrong," she said softly. "That you wanted more from me than just a good time."

He steeled himself against the hurt in her eyes and shrugged. "You are a beautiful woman."

Taylor flinched as if he'd slapped her. She grabbed her bag and jerked to her feet, her eyes flashing emerald sparks. "I wish I'd never agreed to all this."

"Well, I wish I'd never asked." He felt like a recalcitrant child talking back, trying to one-up her, but he couldn't seem to stop. "I should have given you your old job back the second I realized it was all a mistake."

"My old job?" Taylor froze in the doorway. "What are you talking about?"

Nick's stomach clenched. He cursed his impulsiveness. This wasn't how he'd wanted to tell her. "I didn't find out until recently that there had been a mistake, that the pink slip had actually been meant for Kay Taylor in the audit department, not you. Funny, huh?"

Taylor's lips pressed together, and there was no amusement in her steely-eyed gaze. "Why didn't you tell me when you first found out?"

Because I was afraid to lose you.

"What would have been the point?" He kept all expression from his voice.

"I thought I knew you," she said slowly. "I guess I never did."

"I guess not."

Her gaze searched his face, and as she turned he could see her bottom lip start to tremble.

He could have stopped her. There was still time. But it had never been his style to beg.

You want me as much as I want you. He wanted to yell the words, to have the last say, but what would that have proved? Her response in his arms the other night told him she wanted him. Her words today told him she wouldn't have him. The door closed on his silence.

Hot anger surged, and suddenly Nick had to get away. From

the picture on his desk of his father holding up a trophy he'd been awarded for some business achievement. From Taylor's perfume lingering in the air making his chest constrict with each breath. From his own thoughts.

With no real purpose in mind, Nick drove downtown and parked. He walked the Town Square, glancing in the windows of stores with no real interest in going inside. Even on a good day he hated to shop. And although the sky was bright and sunny, today was definitely not turning out to be a good day.

The huge shade trees blanketing the center of the square beckoned to him, promising a welcome respite from the scorching midday sun.

He sent up a silent plea for some solitude as he headed down one of the concrete paths through the parklike area. His prayer wasn't answered. The place teemed with mothers and their children, older people resting on strategically placed benches and shoppers taking a shortcut across the square.

When the second stroller clipped his ankle Nick sought refuge on a nearby bench. He pulled out his electronic scheduler but quickly placed it back in his pocket. What did it matter what his next week's calendar held when the woman he loved wouldn't have him?

"Is there room for two on that bench?"

Nick lifted his gaze. Dressed in a yellow sundress that accentuated her deep rich tan, Claire stood with a shopping bag in one hand and her purse in the other. Under his scrutiny, she shifted from one foot to the other, an uncharacteristic blush stealing its way up her neck.

There should have been only one answer, a firm no. But it was that hint of uncertainty on her face that caused Nick to hesitate. That and the fact that, unlike Taylor, here was a woman who wanted him.

"Of course there's room." He shoved aside the little voice that said he was being disloyal to Taylor. After all, how could you cheat on someone who was only in it for the money?

Claire's wary look eased into a big smile. "It's a beautiful day, isn't it?"

Nick shrugged. ''I guess.''

''I'm surprised Taylor isn't here with you.''

''She has her life. I have mine.'' Disappointment made him speak more frankly than he'd intended.

''I've missed you, Nick,'' Claire said softly. ''We used to have a lot of fun together.''

If she'd said something negative about Taylor or his engagement, Nick would have been on guard, but her simple statement touched that part of his heart that had been wounded by Taylor's words.

''We did.'' Nick nodded, conveniently forgetting that those times were few and far between. ''But now you've got Tony to show you a good time.''

''He'd rather be with Taylor,'' Claire said.

The look in her eyes told him she was telling the truth. His heart clenched. Nick forced what he hoped was a disinterested smile. ''Is that so?''

''It doesn't matter.'' Claire shrugged. ''I don't want someone who doesn't want me.''

''Me, either.'' He thought of Taylor and the way she'd so callously dismissed him from her life.

''Anyway...'' Claire leaned toward him. ''I'd much rather be with you.''

With one hand Nick pushed Claire's hair from her face, caressing her cheek with a finger.

Claire put her arms around his neck and brushed his lips with hers.

''What's going on here!''

The angry voice sounded from the sidewalk. Nick immediately released his hold on Claire and slowly looked up, right into the horrified eyes of Bill Rollins.

''Bill!''

''What the...'' Taylor's grandfather took a deep breath and visibly reined in his temper. ''Will someone tell me what's going on here?''

The older man's words were sharp and curt, but it was the disappointment in his eyes that cut Nick like a knife.

''What does it look like?'' Claire smirked.

Nick resisted the urge to throttle her. How could he have let things get so out of hand? ''Claire, Bill and I need to talk. Alone.''

She opened her mouth, but he quelled her protest with a glance. ''Please.''

There was no softness in his tone and no question that he expected her to comply.

With all the drama of a born actress, Claire rose from the bench, making a great show of straightening her dress. ''Nick, sweetheart, I'll be home after six. Call me.''

Nick gritted his teeth and waited until she was out of sight before he spoke. ''I know what this must look like—''

''It looks like you're cheating on my granddaughter,'' Bill said with a level gaze. ''Is that what you're doing? Cheating on Taylor?''

Nick, who'd always prided himself on controlling his emotions no matter how stressful the situation, couldn't stop a hot guilty flush from creeping up his neck.

''Taylor and I have been having some problems,'' he said, forcing himself to meet the older man's gaze.

''And you think turning to another woman will solve them?'' Clearly incredulous, Bill could only stare.

Nick swallowed hard. He hadn't been fair to himself. Or to Taylor. Or to Claire. ''It was stupid.''

''You bet it was stupid,'' Bill said forcefully. The man's gaze turned sharp and assessing. ''I'm going to ask you a question and I want you to be honest with me. Do you love my granddaughter?''

Did he love Taylor? Nick thought for a long moment and searched his heart, pushing aside the angry words they'd exchanged this morning. ''I do. Very much.''

Bill heaved a relieved sigh. ''Then go to her. Work out whatever problems you're having *together*. Pray to the Almighty for guidance. He's helped Kaye and me through many a rough time. He can do the same for you. You just need to ask.''

Nick sighed. If only it could be that simple.

Chapter Sixteen

"Taylor, it *is* you." A thread of pleasure ran through Nana's voice. "I didn't expect to see you again so soon."

Taylor stiffened over the dresser drawer and didn't turn around. She hurriedly brushed the tears from her cheeks with the tips of her fingers. Certain no one would be home, she'd stopped at her grandparents' house to pick up some clothes she'd forgotten when she'd spent the night. "I thought you'd be at bridge."

"So did I." Her grandmother laughed. "I got all the way over to Betty's only to find that Margie and Eleanor have the flu. So we're skipping this week."

"That's too bad," Taylor mumbled.

A gentle hand settled on her shoulder. "Honey, is something wrong?"

Wrong? At this moment Taylor wondered if there was anything right with her life.

"What could be wrong?" Her attempt at a light laugh ended as a choked sob.

Nana turned her around, and although Taylor kept her gaze lowered she knew her grandmother would have to be blind not to see her swollen lids and blotchy face.

"Nick and I had a fight." Despite her best efforts, Taylor's voice quivered.

"Every couple has their disagreements," Nana said softly. "And it's not all bad."

"How can you say that?" Taylor lifted her gaze. "What's good about fighting with someone you love?"

The last word ended in a wail, and Taylor knew what she'd tried to deny for so long was true. Despite everything, she loved Nick.

"Let's sit down." Nana maneuvered her to the bed, and they sat next to each other on the edge. "Do you want to tell me what happened?"

Taylor shook her head. Tell her grandmother Nick didn't love her? That he didn't want to marry her but he'd sure wanted to spend the night with her? That he knew she'd been fired in error but for his own sake he'd withheld that information?

Nana remained silent, waiting for an explanation Taylor didn't want to give.

"We...we had words," Taylor finally managed to say. "I think it's over. He's not the man I thought he was."

"It hurts, doesn't it?"

That horrible ache returned, and all Taylor could do was nod. Whatever she'd expected, it wasn't this. Nana didn't even try to defend Nick or tell Taylor she could be wrong.

"I don't know who's right or who's wrong in this situation," Nana said, almost as if she could read Taylor's thoughts. "But I have lived long enough to know that at one time or another those we love will disappoint us."

"But the things he said to me—"

"Taylor." Her grandmother's voice was firm. "Stop and think about what I just said. *At one time or another those we love will disappoint us.*" Nana repeated the words slowly, emphasizing each one.

"So what am I supposed to do? Overlook it?" Strident and shaky, Taylor's voice rose. "Go on as if nothing happened?"

"No." Nana's troubled eyes met hers. "I'm saying you leave your pride at the door and search your heart. Turn it over to God. Ask Him for guidance. He knows better than you and I what is best."

"I don't know..." Taylor drew a ragged breath.

"Maybe you and Nick aren't meant to be together," Nana said slowly, her voice filled with regret and sadness.

Two months ago, if Taylor could have envisioned a perfect end to her temporary engagement, it would have been this, her grandmother agreeing with her that it was time for the relationship to end. But along the way, what Taylor saw as the perfect ending had changed.

"Do you believe that?" Taylor could hardly force the question past her lips.

"I don't know him as well as you do." Nana laid a hand over Taylor's. "But what I see I like."

"I thought I did, too," Taylor said. "After what he said this morning, I'm not so sure."

"Talk is cheap," Nana said. "Sometimes we say things because we're hurting or to cover up our true feelings. Or maybe he really is a mean person. But I can't believe you'd have agreed to marry someone like that."

"Nick's a good guy." The words slipped out automatically.

"Then don't make any quick decisions." Nana slipped her arm around Taylor's shoulders and gave a squeeze. "Mull it over, pray about it. Don't throw it all away unless you're sure."

Her grandmother's eyes were filled with love and caring. Taylor had no doubt both Nana and Grandpa Bill would support any decision she made. Her heart warmed, and she breathed a prayer of thanks. She'd been truly blessed to have been born into this family. "I love you, Nana."

"I love you, too, honey."

She leaned her head against her grandmother's, and Nana's arms closed around her.

"It's going to be okay, isn't it?" Her words were muffled against Nana's chest.

"It's going to be fine," Nana said firmly. "God will see to that."

* * *

Nick waited until Bill was out of sight before he finally rose from the bench and headed toward his car. His cell phone rang just as he slid behind the wheel. "Lanagan."

"Nick, it's Erik. I've got great news." Bubbling with excitement, his friend rattled on without waiting for Nick to speak. "We've come to a resolution on that final snag in the merger negotiations, and I think we're going to be ready to sign before you can say, 'How much money will we make on this deal?'"

It was what Nick had been hoping for, dreaming of, for the past four years. Why did it suddenly not seem so important?

If you always do what you've always done, you'll always get what you always got.

Well, he'd done what he'd always done and he'd gotten what he wanted.

But you lost Taylor. A band tightened around his chest.

"Nick? Are you there?"

"I'm here." Nick rubbed a weary hand across his forehead.

"Did you hear what I said?"

"I did." Nick forced some enthusiasm into his voice. After all, it wasn't Erik's fault he didn't feel like celebrating. "It's great news. Good work."

"I'll let you know when the papers are ready," Erik said. "We need to get these signed as soon as possible. Henry's too much of a powder keg. I won't feel good until his signature is on that contract."

An image of Claire striking a match to that powder keg flashed in his mind. "Call me when they're ready."

"Will do," Erik said. "I'll be in the office for another couple of hours if you want to run through these changes."

Nick thought for a moment. Even though he'd already approved the changes, he should review the final document. But he couldn't seem to summon up any enthusiasm. Not with so much else weighing on his mind.

"I'm not sure if I'll be back in today or not. Go ahead and have them typed up," Nick said. "Let me know when the final copy is ready."

"No problem," Erik said. "And, Nick..."

"Yeah?"

"Tell Taylor hello for me."

Nick clicked off the phone without answering and fired up the engine. He pulled away from the curb, despair seeping into every pore of his being.

Dear God, where do I go from here?

He drove automatically, not sure where he was headed. But no matter how far he drove, his thoughts kept returning to Taylor.

"Get the junker off the road!" a voice bellowed.

Nick's gaze jerked ahead. Traffic had slowed to a stop, but he'd barely noticed. Now he saw the reason. An all-too-familiar yellow vehicle with its hood up blocked the right lane. Standing to the car's side, looking young and forlorn, was Tom from their premarital counseling class.

The guy in the car in front of Nick laid on his horn. A woman in a small foreign car added her high-pitched beep to the fray.

Tom raked his fingers through his hair and stuck his head beneath the hood.

Without thinking, Nick put his car in park, opened the door and headed toward the Gremlin, weaving his way through the row of cars.

"Put the hood down," he said when he got close enough for Tom to hear him over the honking horns. "I'll help you push it off to the side."

Relief flooded the boy's face. He didn't argue. The hood slammed shut.

"Roll down the window and get in." Nick calculated the distance to a small shoulder area up ahead. "You steer and I'll push."

Tom slid behind the wheel, and Nick forcefully leaned against the vehicle. The car didn't budge. The boy still had it in gear! He stifled a curse.

"Put it in neutral," he ordered, and pushed again. Slowly the Gremlin crept forward. "Cramp the wheel to the right."

Nick put his shoulder against the car, and with one final

effort, the car rolled out of the traffic lane and onto the shoulder.

"Grab your keys and come with me." With his eyes focused on the Jag, Nick didn't even look back to make sure Tom followed.

The boy slid into the passenger seat just as Nick shifted into first gear and took off.

"What happened?" Nick slanted Tom a sideways glance. "Out of gas?"

"I wish," Tom said with a heavy sigh. "It just died."

"Do you want to call a tow truck?" Nick gestured to his cell phone. "Or I can drop you off somewhere?"

Tom thought for a moment. "Mandy's at the church for some meeting. She has a car. If it wouldn't be too far out of your way..."

"No problem," Nick said. Spending time with Tom might be just what he needed to help keep his mind off his own problems.

Unfortunately the trip to the church only took a few minutes.

"I think that's her mom's Buick." Tom pointed to a navy-blue Skylark in the lot.

"I don't want to leave you here without a ride. Better make sure it's hers." Nick pulled into the space next to the car. "I'll wait."

"Why don't you come in with me?" Tom said with an imploring look. "It's some ladies' circle meeting. The place will be crawling with women. I don't want to be the only guy."

Nick could have pointed out that Pastor Schmidt would probably be there, or that there was really nothing to fear from a group of women but he got out of the car and followed Tom into the church.

It didn't take them long to find Mandy. She was in the foyer talking animatedly to a whole gaggle of females. When Nick heard the word *Halloween,* he had to smile. He couldn't wait to tell Taylor.... His smile faded.

"Nick, man. Thanks so much." The boy reached into his back pocket and pulled out a well-worn wallet. "What do I owe you?"

Nick shook his head. "Not a thing."

"But—"

"What are friends for?" That Nick referred to the boy with that term surprised even him. But hadn't the pastor said, in one of those sermons that Nick couldn't seem to get out of his mind, that they were all friends in Christ?

"Thanks so much." Tom pumped his hand vigorously.

"Nick Lanagan." Pastor Schmidt's office door was open, and the minister stuck his head into the hall. "I thought I heard your voice. Do you have a minute?"

Nick forced a smile, hoping the minister didn't want to talk about the wedding that was never going to take place. Today had been hard enough. "Sure."

The minister opened the door wider and ushered Nick inside. "I just got through reviewing the questionnaire I had you and Taylor complete at the last premarital session."

Nick remembered that pop quiz all too well. They'd all thought the evening was almost over when the pastor had surprised them with the survey. Not only did each couple get no chance to discuss the questions, he'd also separated the men and women while they'd filled out the form. Nick had tried his best to anticipate Taylor's answers when he'd written his own. "Did I pass?"

Was it his imagination or did it seem like the minister was hesitating? "Don't tell me I failed?"

"Failed isn't the right word." Pastor Schmidt lifted a coffeepot.

The man was clearly stalling. Unease settled in the pit of Nick's stomach.

"Okay, give me the bad news," Nick said with a little laugh. "You've discovered Taylor and I aren't compatible."

"I wouldn't say that." The minister handed Nick a steaming mug. "At least not just on the basis of a questionnaire."

Even though a dozen words stood poised on the tip of his

tongue, Nick took a sip of the coffee and didn't respond. He'd learned the value in the business world of keeping silent until all the cards were on the table.

"There were some points that I did want to discuss with you."

Nick raised a brow.

"Children, for example."

Children? How could they have missed that one? Taylor had made it clear she'd wanted six children, so he'd made sure he'd put down six.

"Are you aware Taylor's not sure that she even wants children? And you put down six."

Nick choked on his coffee.

"I see it is a surprise." The pastor let out a long, audible breath. "The fact that you two haven't discussed it adds to my concern."

Taylor must have thought he'd answer honestly. The minister had stressed that in his instructions. "Above all, be honest," he'd said.

Nick cleared his throat. "We have discussed it, Pastor. What surprised me is that I thought Taylor had agreed to a…big family."

"She can't just agree." The minister leaned forward, his gaze intense. "Taylor needs to really *want* those children, not just do it for you."

At any other time this whole situation would be laughable, her taking his position and his needing to act like he embraced hers.

"I think Taylor has just been concerned that with work and everything else she might not have time for children."

"And what do you say to that?"

Nick resisted the urge to unbutton his suddenly tight collar. "I, uh, tell her that you have to look at what's really important. Your priorities should guide those decisions."

Now it was the minister's turn to raise a brow, and Nick realized he wasn't going to be let off the hook quite so easily. He remembered what Taylor had said, and he made her words his own. ''I believe if you put God and family first you can't go wrong. If that means scaling down your work hours, so be it.''

''Do you think Taylor would be willing to do that?''

''I do,'' Nick said. ''In fact we've talked about her staying home after we have children.''

''She'd be willing to do that?'' The minister was clearly skeptical. ''With her career being so important?''

''What is life about if you don't have someone to love?'' Nick realized with a start he wasn't just mouthing the words, he believed them. ''And this is the electronic age. There are ways to work at home. For both of us.''

''I'm glad to hear you say that.'' The minister flashed a relieved smile. ''Anyone can see how much in love the two of you are. I didn't want there to be any insurmountable problems.''

''Insurmountable problems?'' Nick shook his head and set his cup down. ''There's no problem that Taylor and I can't work out. That is, with God's help.''

''Nick!'' Surprise followed quickly by pleasure flashed through his mother's eyes.

''I probably should have called.'' He shifted uncomfortably from one foot to the other. In the two years since she'd remarried, he'd never been to her home. But after talking to the minister about the importance of family, he'd decided the time had come to clear the air and mend some fences. ''If I'm interrupting...''

''Nonsense.'' She grabbed his arm and practically yanked him across the threshold. ''I'm just puttering around. Charlie is out golfing. Can you believe it? In this heat? I don't know what that man was thinking.''

She chattered all the way into the living room. It was as if she thought he'd disappear if she stopped to take a breath. ''Can I get you some iced tea? Or I can brew some coffee?''

''Mother.'' His hand gripped her arm. ''Could we just talk?''

A stricken look crossed her face, and he cursed any and all of his past behavior that had put that look there.

"I need your help," he said softly.

"Is it the company?"

It was understandable she'd think it was work-related. The firm had been his life for the past four years. "No, it's not about work."

She gestured for him to take a seat, and instead of sitting on the sofa next to him, she took the overstuffed chair opposite him. Her face, which had been flushed with happiness and animated, was now pale and subdued. "What's the matter, Nick?"

"Were you and Dad happy together?" It wasn't the way he'd wanted to start the conversation, but the question had nagged at him for years.

"Happy?" Clearly caught off guard, she sat back against the plump cushion. "What a strange question."

"Are you and Charlie happy?"

"Yes, of course."

"Then why is it so odd for me to ask about you and Dad?"

His mother smoothed an imaginary wrinkle out of her crisp linen slacks. "Your father was a wonderful man with any number of fine qualities."

"Mother." Nick shot her a warning gaze.

She sighed heavily and offered Nick a beseeching look. "I always loved your father, Nick. But I have to admit toward the end, I didn't always like him that much."

"That couldn't have had something to do with the spending, could it?" Old habits died hard, and Nick couldn't stop his cynicism from showing.

Surprisingly, his mother didn't seem to take offense.

"To some extent it did," she said matter-of-factly, a shadow crossing her face. "When we were first married we were happy. But as the business began to grow, he began to spend more time at the office. We grew in different directions. We wanted different things in life. Especially that last year when he felt it was so important to keep up appearances."

Nick's breath caught in his throat. "Appearances?"

"You remember how he was." She shook her head. "Such a private man. When he started staying at home because he didn't have the energy to go to work, he worried about the rumors. To counter the speculation that the business was in trouble, he increased his spending rather than scaling back. He insisted we be seen at all the best parties."

"All that spending was his idea?" Nick stared in disbelief.

Sylvia stared back at him. "Well, of course. You know that. Take buying the Jag, for instance. He'd ordered it before he was diagnosed and he wouldn't hear of pulling the order. 'My dear,' he said, 'what would people think?' I mean, I'm glad that you've gotten your use out of it, but it was hardly a needed purchase. Much less a practical one." A trace of bitterness colored her voice. "He didn't seem to understand that his extravagant spending was putting the entire company at risk."

She was telling the truth. Nick could see it in her eyes. He cursed his foolishness. All these years he'd blamed her when it had been his father who'd pushed the company to the edge of bankruptcy.

He buried his face in his hands. If he was wrong about this, what else had he been wrong about?

"Nick." Soft and concerned, his mother's voice broke through his thoughts. She'd moved from the chair to sit beside him. Her hand rested lightly on his arm. "Tell me what's wrong."

He looked into her blue eyes, so like his own, and his heart twisted. What kind of man would have turned away from his own mother because of money? What kind of man would push away the woman he loved because of misplaced pride? What kind of man?

A fool. That's what kind of man.

"Mother." Nick reached over and took her hand. "I know I haven't been the kind of son you deserved." He silenced her protest with a raised hand. ''But I'm here to tell you that's going to change.''

And that's not the only thing, he thought. *That's not all that's going to change.*

''He's near the breaking point,'' Claire said with a satisfied smile. ''It's time to go in for the kill.''

''In for the kill?'' For a second Tony wondered if this was worth the money—until he remembered what Claire was paying him. Yes, the hassle was definitely worth it. Especially if Lanagan was the jerk Claire claimed. ''What do you have in mind?''

''Have him find you and Taylor in bed.'' She leaned forward, and her brown eyes sparkled.

''Not going to happen.'' He tried to keep the exasperation out of his voice. The woman had a one-track mind. ''I've told you what Taylor is like.''

Her gaze narrowed, and he wished he hadn't been quite so adamant. Obviously no wasn't a word Claire liked to hear.

''Maybe it's not her,'' Claire said with a decidedly malicious gleam in her eyes. ''Didn't you tell me you were a geek in high school? Maybe you didn't appeal to her.''

''Do I look like a geek to you?'' He ripped out the words impatiently.

''Exactly my point,'' she said. A smile of satisfaction crossed her face. Strange as it seemed, Tony got the impression his irritation pleased her. ''Ever hear the saying the past does not determine the future?''

Tony shrugged. ''I guess.''

''Keep it in mind when you're putting the moves on Taylor. Remember, just because you didn't score before, doesn't mean you're doomed to failure forever.'' Claire squeezed in next to him. Her breath was warm against his ear. ''You can do it. I know you can.''

He turned his face to hers, and she brushed her lips against his. ''That's for luck. Now remember, all you have to do is make Nick believe his sweet little Taylor has been unfaithful. If nothing happens just do the next best thing…say you did.''

''Then what?''

''He'll dump Taylor.''

A sense of unease coursed through Tony. He frowned. Something wasn't making sense here. ''If everything you say about him is true, why would you want him?''

''Because unlike Taylor, I like my guys bad.'' Claire laughed and ran a long red fingernail up Tony's cheek. ''In fact, the badder, the better.''

Chapter Seventeen

Taylor jerked on the mower cord for what seemed the hundredth time and wondered if it was worth it. She'd thought mowing the yard would help keep her mind off her troubles. But the mower refused to start, and her stress level was rising, along with the temperature outside. A trickle of moisture trailed down her neck.

"What do you think you're doing?" Tony's amused voice sounded from the driveway.

Startled, Taylor glanced up. Her friend stood leaning against his Jeep Cherokee looking cool and perfectly groomed. Feeling even more like a limp dishrag, Taylor blew at a piece of hair that straggled across her forehead. "What does it look like I'm doing? I'm trying to get this machine to start. I need to harvest this yard before the neighbors have me evicted."

She wiped the sweat from her eyes with the back of her hand and leaned over the mower. She pulled hard on the cord. Once again the engine sputtered. For a second she swore it laughed.

"I'd say it's time for a break." Tony's lips twitched. He crooked one finger and beckoned to her. "Before you kill it or it kills you."

Taylor shot a sideways kick at the mower and walked to the drive.

''I've missed you,'' he said softly. His gaze traveled over her face and searched her eyes. ''Is everything okay?''

''I'm afraid now is not the time to ask.'' Taylor couldn't help but laugh. ''I'm hot and extremely frustrated. Want to come inside for some tea?''

Tony smiled. A confident, lazy smile. ''I'd love to.''

He followed her into the kitchen, and she could feel his eyes watching her while she filled two crystal tumblers with iced tea and sat them on the table.

She took a seat across the table from him. ''Okay, what's up?''

Her directness seemed to take him by surprise. ''Does something have to be? Can't a friend just stop by?''

''C'mon, Tony.'' Taylor had known him too long to fall for that line. ''Something's on your mind. I can tell.''

Tony shifted as if his chair had suddenly turned from smooth cherry wood to a seat of nails. ''I wanted to talk to you about Nick.''

''What about us?'' Surely Nick wasn't already telling people they'd broken up? A pain pierced her heart.

''Be honest with me. Aren't you sorry you agreed to marry him?'' Tony's dark eyes never left hers for an instant.

Taylor hesitated. There were many things she was sorry for, but agreeing to marry Nick wasn't one of them. And as far as she knew, she was still his fiancée. She cleared her throat and forced a laugh. ''Not at all. Why would you even think that?''

Tony's eyes narrowed. ''Because from what I've heard, Lanagan seems to be a guy whose only real love is that company of his.''

Taylor stiffened. A chill traveled along her spine. ''That's ridiculous.''

A shadow of hurt flickered across his face. ''I'm sorry you think a friend's caring about what happens to you is ridiculous.''

He pushed his chair back and started to rise. She leaned

forward and grabbed his arm to stop him, her fingers curving in a firm grip.

"Tony, I didn't say you were ridiculous, and I certainly didn't mean to hurt you." She offered him an apologetic smile. "I just know Nick's not like that."

"He could—"

"Tony, no." Taylor pushed aside her doubts and kept her gaze firm and direct. She thought about Nick's kindness to Miss Dietrich, how he'd helped Tom with his car and the respect he'd always shown her grandparents. "Nick's a great guy. He sometimes comes across as self-absorbed but he'd do anything for those he cares about."

He nodded reluctantly. "If you're sure—"

"I am," she said firmly.

Tony's gaze traveled slowly across her face. "You love him."

"What?"

"You love him," he repeated, amazement blanketing his features.

"Of course I do." She twisted the diamond on her finger. "I'm engaged to the man. I told you from the first that I loved him."

"I know you did." He shook his head. "But I never saw it in your eyes. Until now."

He reached across the table and took her hand. "If he's the right one, then I'm happy for you, Taylor. I'm just not sure that he is."

Taylor stared at this man who had been her friend for so many years. Stared at his dark wavy hair and chiseled features. Stared at the face most women would describe as incredibly handsome. A man so many other women would find easy to love. A man who would forever only be her friend.

"You'll always be special to me."

"And you to me." Abruptly he shoved back his chair and rose to his feet, his smile forced. "I need to get going."

The phone on the counter rang, and Taylor jumped. Before

she could stop him Tony leaned over and picked up the receiver. ''Hello.''

His expression stilled and grew serious. He let out a long audible breath. ''She's right here.''

Taylor leaned forward, a sense of dread coursing through her veins. ''Is it Nick?''

''No.'' He held the phone out to her, and compassion darkened his eyes. ''It's about your grandfather.''

Chapter Eighteen

"Where is he?" Taylor's gaze swept the waiting room. There wasn't even a nurse in sight. Only Nick.

"Back there." Nick scrambled to his feet. He gestured to a closed set of double doors. "The doctor is with him now."

Taylor hated hospitals, all stark and white. The medicinal smell irritated her nose, and the overhead paging of every Code Blue sent fear racing up her spine.

"What room is he in?" Taylor headed for the doors without waiting for an answer. She would have been halfway down the hall if Nick hadn't grabbed her arm.

"Taylor, wait."

"Let me go," she said through gritted teeth.

"Listen to me—"

"Nick, not now." She tried to jerk away, but his grip was too strong. "We can talk later. Right now I want to see my grandfather."

"That's what I'm trying to tell you." His voice was firm. "Only one person can be with him right now, and your grandmother just went back."

Taylor stared, unblinking. All she'd wanted was to see her grandfather one more time and tell him how much she loved him. Just in case he... She shoved the unbearable thought aside and refused to let the tears pressing against her lids fall. He *was* going to make it. She wasn't going to let herself believe otherwise.

"Why don't we sit down?" Nick's voice was gentle and low.

Not trusting herself to speak, Taylor gave a jerky nod and let him lead her over to a smooth green vinyl couch that hugged the waiting room wall. Nick took a seat next to her.

It wasn't until she sat down that she realized how shaky her knees had become. It was a wonder she'd been able to stand at all. She took a deep breath and clenched her hands in her lap. "Tell me what happened."

"He started having chest pains," Nick said in a matter-of-fact, I-don't-want-to-alarm-you voice. "Your grandmother called nine-one-one. She said she tried to reach you at home but no one answered."

That stupid mower.

"She got me on my cellular, and I came right over. She thought you might be with me," he added.

Of course her grandmother would have thought that. Nana was the eternal optimist. Even now she probably believed everything would turn out okay.

"Your grandfather will be fine."

"You don't know that."

"No, but I've certainly bent God's ear since I've been here," Nick said. "I'm hoping that He'll make Bill well just to shut me up."

God would be shutting her up, too. Taylor hadn't stopped praying since she got the news. She'd hoped when she'd reached the hospital that her prayers would have been answered. A band tightened around her chest.

"He could be dying in there and I wouldn't even know." To her surprise Taylor spoke her fears aloud. She blinked back another round of tears and furiously dug deep in her purse. By the time her fingers closed around the tissue, a few tears streaked her cheeks.

"If they don't come out in five minutes, I'll go back and check," Nick said.

"If someone's not here in *two* minutes, *I'll* go check."

"You're one determined woman." A smile tugged at

Nick's lips. She could hear the admiration in his voice. ''Taylor?''

She glanced briefly at her watch and then at the closed doors. Ninety seconds left. ''Yes?''

His gaze locked with hers, and his blue eyes shimmered in the fluorescent glare. ''I'm sorry about this morning.''

''It doesn't matter.'' Again her gaze strayed to the end of the hall.

''I should have told you about the job the minute I found out,'' he said. ''I'm not going to lie to you anymore.''

The pain of his betrayal returned. She steeled herself against the ache in her heart. ''Nick, we can talk about this some other time?''

''Why not now?''

She drew a deep steadying breath. ''Because right now I'm worried about my grandfather and—''

The strident ring of his cell phone stopped her words. She glanced at her watch. Thirty seconds.

''Lanagan.'' The word was clipped, and she idly wondered if he was irritated with her or if there were problems at work. Either way she didn't care. He raked his fingers through his hair, and his gaze shifted momentarily to her. ''Now? Isn't there another time Henry— Erik, you'll have to reschedule. Of course I understand the risk. Anytime tomorrow would be fine.''

''You can go, Nick. I'm sure you must have a lot of work to do.'' Taylor rose to her feet. ''I'm going to check on Grandpa Bill.''

''I'm not going anywhere.'' He closed the cell phone with a firm snap and stood. ''And *we're* going to check on Bill.''

''But your phone—''

''Stop.'' His fingers against her lips stopped the words. ''Family is more important than work any day.''

In the back of her mind she noted the change in Nick's priorities, but she didn't have time to figure out what it meant. All she knew was having Nick share her burden of worry somehow made the load easier to bear.

"Thanks," she said simply.

"Ms. Rollins, I'm not sure if you remember me...."

Taylor's head jerked in the direction of the unexpected voice. She automatically extended her hand. "Dr. Pierce. Of course I remember you."

The middle-aged doctor looked much the same as he had a year ago, although a few strands of gray laced his black hair. With the white lab coat and a stethoscope looped casually around his neck, he was the picture of competence.

But she knew all too well how looks could deceive. The well-respected cardiologist had been on call the night of her father's accident. But he and the other physicians hadn't been able to save her father. Now Grandpa Bill's life was in his hands. A cold chill rippled through her body.

Nick's arm slipped around her waist and rested lightly against her side in a gesture of silent support.

"How is he?" She forced the words past her lips.

Dr. Pierce hesitated, much as he'd done when he'd given her news of her father's death. Her body went numb. Dear God, had she lost Grandpa Bill, too?

"He's stable. However, I don't want to minimize the potential seriousness of his condition."

Her heart pounded in her ears, and she took a deep breath, willing herself to stay calm.

The doctor's hazel eyes met Taylor's gaze. "His heart is in an irregular rhythm. We could wait and see if we could treat it with medication, but with the angina, it's best to treat it immediately. My associate is doing the procedure now."

"Procedure?" Taylor couldn't keep the tremor from her voice.

"Cardioversion," Dr. Pierce said. "Shock the heart back into normal sinus rhythm."

"It sounds dangerous."

"It can be, but—" a faint smile graced the doctor's face "—your grandfather's remarkably healthy otherwise. We've done a lot of these procedures with good success."

Nick squeezed her hand reassuringly.

"I'll keep you informed," Dr. Pierce said. "I want to assure you we're doing everything we can."

"Thanks, Dr. Pierce." Taylor swallowed hard against the lump in her throat. "He and my grandmother are all I have, and I love them both dearly."

"I understand." The doctor nodded before he left, but stopped short of giving her the reassurance she sought.

"What you told the doctor wasn't entirely accurate." Nick's voice sounded strained against her ear.

Taylor turned. He stood so close his breath was warm against her cheek. She lifted her gaze.

"You also have me," he said.

"For now," she said. *But for how long?*

Tony took a sip of coffee, keeping his gaze focused on the door to the restaurant.

Claire was late, as usual. He'd grown tired of waiting in the lobby so he'd taken a table by the window. Getting a seat in the normally busy eatery hadn't been a problem at this time of day. The large room was empty except for a group of businessmen at a large round table to the back.

Tony's gaze dropped to the airline ticket lying on the table. After leaving Taylor, he'd stopped at the local travel agency and booked his flight. Ten tomorrow he'd be on that big bird winging its way from Denver to D.C. He couldn't wait.

"I thought I said to wait in the lobby." Although Claire's words were censuring, she brushed her lips across his cheek before taking a seat opposite him.

"You also said we'd meet at three," he said, taking another sip of coffee.

"You're such a clock-watcher." She wrinkled her nose and picked up a menu. She didn't apologize for being a half-hour late, but then he never expected she would. That wasn't Claire Waters.

He gestured to the waiter.

"What can I get you?" The server couldn't have been more

than twenty, tanned with blond streaked hair, looking like he'd just stepped off a ski slope.

Claire preened under the man's openly admiring gaze. Tony had to admit she looked especially beautiful today. She'd pulled her dark hair from her face in one of the new trendy styles, and her makeup made her brown eyes appear even larger.

"I'll have a glass of strawberry apricot iced tea," she said.

The young man smiled, showing a mouthful of straight white teeth. "Will that be all?"

"For now," Claire said, looking up at him through thickly mascaraed lashes.

Tony resisted the overwhelming urge to gag.

Her gaze followed the waiter until he disappeared into the kitchen.

"You'd be robbing the cradle with that one," Tony pointed out.

"He's cute." Her smile was openly appreciative. "Did you notice?"

"I'll make sure to look when he comes back."

Her eyes narrowed, and he knew she'd finally picked up on the coolness in his tone. Her hand reached over and blanketed his. "Don't be jealous."

"Jealous?" Tony snorted. "As if."

A flash of hurt skittered across her face, and she jerked her hand back.

"Claire, I'm sorry."

"Let's get down to business." Her gaze hardened. "Did you succeed in your mission?"

Tony cleared his throat and shifted his gaze to the waiter.

Openly curious, the young man took his time lifting a tumbler filled with tea and chipped ice off a round tray before setting it on the linen tablecloth in front of Claire.

"That'll be all for now," Tony said, not giving the waiter—or Claire—a chance to speak.

Tony waited until the young man was out of sight before

he spoke. He didn't bother to hide his annoyance. "And what if I did succeed? Do you plan to broadcast it to the world?"

"You did it!" Joy flashed across Claire's face.

Tony relished the knowledge her happiness would be short-lived.

"Actually I didn't even try." He sat his cup down, lifted his gaze and waited for the explosion.

She glared at him. "What kind of game are you playing?"

Instead of a shriek, her voice was low and controlled. His estimation of her inched up a notch.

"No game." For the first time since he'd come to Cedar Ridge, Tony felt at peace with himself. "Taylor's my friend. She's in love with Nick. End of story."

Claire leaned across the table, her dark eyes spitting fire. "No, it's not the end. I've paid you a lot of money—"

"I'll pay you back." He'd made that decision after leaving Taylor's house.

"With what?" She sneered. "Your good looks?"

He deserved the jab. From the moment they'd met he'd shown her only his shallow, superficial side. He hadn't always been that way. Seeing Taylor again had brought back old memories, old dreams.

For the first time since he'd been a teen he found himself looking toward the future. Even considering again one particular dream he'd cast aside long ago.

It was almost as if he'd been given a second chance. He was back on track once again.

Thank you, God.

He smiled at Claire, praying she would one day find the sense of peace he'd rediscovered.

No, nothing was going to stop him now.

Unless, he mused, staring at Claire's thunderous expression, she killed him first.

Taylor let the hospital room door close silently behind her.

"He wants to talk to you." Utterly drained, she brushed a strand of hair from her face.

Thankfully, Grandpa Bill looked much better than she'd expected. But the day's strain had caught up with her.

Concern blanketed Nick's face. ''Are you okay?''

''I'm fine.'' Taylor forced a smile. She hadn't been sure he'd still be here when she came out. She'd asked him to come in with her, but he'd said he thought they needed some time alone as a family. ''Would you mind staying with my grandfather for a few minutes? He wants to see you,'' she added.

''I'm sure your grandmother—''

''Is going to go to the cafeteria,'' Taylor said, his hesitation taking her by surprise. If she didn't know better she'd think he didn't want to face the man. But that didn't make sense. Over the past months, Nick and her grandfather had become fast friends.

Nick shifted uneasily from one foot to the other.

''Please, Nick.'' She rested her hand lightly on his arm. ''Even if you won't do it for me, Nana needs to get some food in her stomach, but she won't leave him alone.''

He stared for a moment, then nodded. ''Sure. I'll stay with him.''

''Thank you.'' Her voice shook slightly. She clamped her lips together. The emotional upheaval of the past twenty-four hours threatened to derail her carefully held composure.

''Hey.'' Nick tipped up her chin with one finger. ''Don't go getting all weepy on me.''

''I'm not,'' she retorted, the moisture behind her lids evaporating in a spark of anger. She'd never been a woman who cried at the drop of a hat, and he'd been around her long enough to know that. ''I have...''

If the twinkle in his eyes wasn't enough, the twitch of his lips said it all.

She chuckled. ''What am I going to do with you?''

His voice dropped, and a strange look filled his eyes. ''I don't know. Maybe keep me around a while longer? Maybe—''

''Nana.'' Taylor cleared her throat and smiled at her grandmother over Nick's shoulder. ''Nick has agreed to stay with Grandpa while we grab a bite to eat.''

Her grandmother shook her head. ''I'm really not hungry.''

''Nana, you haven't eaten all day.'' Taylor slipped her arm around her grandmother's shoulders. ''And even if you're not hungry, I'm starved.''

''Kaye, go ahead and keep Taylor company. It'll give me a chance to talk to Bill. There's something I want to discuss with him.'' Nick sounded so sincere that even Taylor was impressed.

''If you're positive you can spare the time?'' Nana hesitated. ''I'm sure you've got lots of work to do.''

''Nothing that can't wait.'' Nick voice was firm and broached no argument.

Still Nana waffled. ''What if they need to reach me? Sometimes you can't hear or understand those overhead pages.''

Taylor glanced at Nick and lifted her shoulders in a silent plea for help. She could understand Nana's reluctance, but her grandmother had to eat.

Nick reached into the pocket of his suit jacket and pulled out his cellular phone. ''Take this with you.'' He waved aside Nana's protests. ''With all that monitoring equipment, I can't take it in the room anyway.''

Taylor took the phone from his hand. ''Thank you.''

He smiled. ''You ladies take your time. Bill and I will be just fine.''

''Thank you, Nick.'' To Taylor's surprise Nana reached up and brushed a kiss across his cheek.

But when Nick enveloped her grandmother in a hug and whispered, ''It will all be okay,'' Taylor could only stare.

''C'mon, honey.'' Nana stepped out of Nick's arms and headed for the elevator. ''A bowl of soup might be a good idea, after all.''

They'd barely made their way through the long cafeteria line and gotten settled in at a table when Nick's phone rang.

Her grandmother stopped cutting her grilled cheese sandwich into fourths. The color drained from her face. She and Taylor exchanged a wordless look of worry.

Taylor flipped open the phone. ''Hello.''

The cafeteria was in the lower level of the hospital. That fact, coupled with the noise from the supper crowd, made hearing difficult. She pressed one hand against her other ear. ''Hello?''

''Nick, it's Erik. We've got a bad connection. I can barely hear you.''

''It's for Nick.'' She mouthed the words to her grandmother, and Nana sighed with relief and turned her attention to her sandwich.

''Nick, can you hear me?'' Although filled with static, Erik's words were clearly audible.

''Yes, but—''

''Okay, you listen. I'll talk,'' Erik interrupted, and Taylor realized if he couldn't tell she wasn't Nick, he probably couldn't hear her well enough to understand her explanation.

''I was able to reschedule that meeting with Henry. You owe me big for this one, buddy. The old barracuda wanted to know what was so important that you wouldn't take time to sign the papers. Asked if you really wanted to merge. Of course, I improvised. Used an idea from a story I'd read in the tabloids and told him you'd been kidnapped by space aliens. I don't think he was fully convinced but at least he laughed. So, two p.m. tomorrow, no excuses. Ciao.''

Taylor ended the call in a daze. If she'd understood what Erik had said, Nick had given up a chance to finalize the merger to be here with her and her grandparents. She knew what that deal meant to him. This wasn't making any sense.

''Who was it?'' Nana took a bite of sandwich, her look openly curious.

''Nick's lawyer.'' Taylor frowned. ''Apparently Nick canceled an important meeting this afternoon. Why would he have done that?''

''Why, my dear, I should think that would be perfectly

obvious.'' Nana laughed for the first time today, a silver tinkle of a laugh. ''The man is in love.''

Nana handed Nick the phone and after thanking him profusely went immediately to her husband. Taylor and Nick slipped out of the room unnoticed.

''Thanks for staying with him.''

Nick shrugged. ''It was nothing.''

Taylor took a deep breath and clasped her hands together. ''We need to talk.''

He gazed into her eyes. Could he hear her heart beating?

''Yes, we do,'' he said softly. ''But not here.''

''The cafeteria's out. You can't hear yourself think down there,'' she said, half to herself. ''How about the park? It's just across the street.''

''Fine with me.'' He turned toward the elevator, but she stopped him with a hand on his arm.

''Wait a minute.'' Taylor stuck her head inside her grandfather's room. ''Nick and I are going to take a little walk. Maybe go over to the park and get some fresh air. Will you two be okay?''

Bill smiled at his wife and laid his hand over hers. ''We've managed for almost fifty years. I think we can handle a half hour or so.''

Taylor smiled and pulled the door shut.

Even though the day was bright and sunny, the park that bordered the hospital grounds was deserted. Taylor spotted a weathered picnic table under a huge elm and took a seat across from Nick.

''Erik called for you.'' It was an odd way to start a conversation, but Erik's words were foremost on her mind.

''He did?'' Nick raised a brow. ''What did he have to say?''

''We had a bad connection,'' Taylor said. ''He thought I was you.''

''Must have been a really bad connection.'' Nick smiled.

"Erik doesn't usually have any trouble distinguishing men from women."

The dimple in his cheek flashed, and her heart turned over.

"He wanted to let you know the meeting to sign the merger papers was rescheduled for two p.m. tomorrow."

"Good." Nick nodded in satisfaction.

"Why didn't you sign them today?"

"I was busy."

"Busy with us?" She knew more than most what this merger meant and how temperamental Henry could be. "You could have blown the deal by waiting."

"You needed me."

"You should have told me," Taylor persisted. "I would have been okay by myself."

Nick gave a deep, resigned sigh. "The point is I don't want you to have to be alone. I want to be there for you."

"That's very sweet." She'd misunderstood his intentions once. She wasn't going to make that mistake again. "But our contract is almost up. Once those papers are signed, we're done."

"This whole fake engagement thing was a stupid idea."

Her heart sank. "It was?"

"I don't like being engaged," he added.

"You don't?" Granted it had been awkward at first, but lately it hadn't been a chore, not at all.

"No, I don't." He reached across the table and took her hand.

Taylor tried to force a smile but couldn't quite manage it. "I'm sure you'll change your mind when you find a woman you really want to marry."

"I've already found her."

"You have?" For a second she could only stare, stunned. Then something snapped. How could she have ever thought there was a possibility he loved her? "Who is it? No, don't tell me. I don't want to know. What an idiot I've been." Taylor jerked to her feet, feeling like the worst kind of fool.

"No, wait." He scrambled up from the table and stepped in front of her, blocking her exit. "I'm saying this all wrong."

"You don't need to say more." Taylor blinked away the tears. "You've already said enough."

"I don't think I have," he said forcefully. "Have I said it's *you* I want to marry? Have I said it's *you* I love?"

She shook her head slowly, not trusting herself to speak.

"See, I didn't say it all." His hand gently brushed her hair over her shoulder. "I love you, Taylor. It's taken me longer than it should have, but I finally realize what's important in life."

"What about the company?"

"It matters to me. I can't say that it doesn't. But I was wrong to put it first in my life. You were right. God and family deserve top billing."

"Are you sure?"

"I'm positive." His hand cupped her face. "Will you marry me, Taylor? I'm asking for real this time."

She longed to shout her answer to the treetops, but one last piece of unfinished business held her back. "Nick, remember when you said no more lies?"

"I'm not lying—"

She closed his lips with her fingers. "You've been honest with me. Now I need to be honest with you."

Praying for strength, Taylor took a deep breath and told him what she'd kept to herself for so long. She told him the story of her father's gambling debts and her attempt to protect his reputation. Somewhere in the middle of the story, his hand slipped down her arm, and he laced his fingers through hers. When she finished, he wiped a few stray tears from her cheeks with his fingers.

"You must have felt so alone." His arms wrapped around her, and his voice was muffled against her hair. "I wish I'd known sooner."

Her heart warmed. Instead of focusing on what her father had done, his whole concern was on her feelings.

''I'm just glad you're here now.'' She lifted her head, and her eyes met his.

''Me, too.'' His gaze was warm against her face. ''You never did answer my question.''

''Maybe I need a little reminder.''

''Of the question?''

She laughed. ''No, of how much you love me.''

A thrill of anticipation shot through her as he lowered his head.

''Will this do?'' he murmured against her lips.

''For now,'' she said returning his kiss. Oh, yes, for now it would do just fine.

The nurse handed Bill the last of the paperwork.

Standing by the window, Nana barely noticed. Her gaze was riveted outdoors, on something more fascinating than any insurance forms.

''You're doing great. Your heart has stayed in normal sinus rhythm, and,'' the nurse added, ''once we get your meds up from the pharmacy, you'll be ready for discharge.''

''Hear that, Kaye?'' Bill rubbed his hands together. ''Sounds like everything's going to be just fine.''

Nana glanced briefly at her husband before her gaze returned to the window overlooking the park. A smile of satisfaction lifted her lips. Today had been filled with blessings.

Thank You, God.

''Kaye?''

She turned to her husband. ''What did you say, sweetheart?''

''I said everything has worked out just fine.''

''Yes,'' Nana said. ''Yes, it has.''

Chapter Nineteen

"I can't believe they knew all along about my father's debts." Taylor's gaze followed her grandparents on the dance floor.

"I'm sure your father would have eventually told you, too," Nick said. "But if you hadn't been so desperate for money, you wouldn't have agreed to be my fiancée, and we wouldn't be here now."

"I think God would have found a way to get us together," Taylor said, softly brushing her fingers against his cheek.

The sound of five hundred pieces of silver clinking against crystal goblets filled the ballroom of the Heritage Hotel.

Nick turned to his new bride and smiled. "Shall we?"

"It *is* tradition," Taylor said with mock resignation, even as her lips curved in a smile.

Nick lifted his napkin off his lap and dropped it to the linen-clad table. He pushed back his chair and stood, reaching for her hand.

Her fingers were warm against his skin, and a faint whiff of perfume stirred his senses. She turned and raised her arms so that her hands rested lightly on his shoulders. Her face tilted upward, waiting for his kiss.

Never had she looked more beautiful. He thanked God once again for the love and trust reflected in her gaze. Out of the corner of his eye he caught a glimpse of his mother and stepfather smiling proudly.

Yes, he had a lot to be thankful for.

"Are you going to kiss her or just stand there looking like a love-struck fool?" Henry's voice boomed from a nearby table.

Nick's smile widened, and he lowered his lips to his new bride, forcing himself to keep the kiss light and brief. There'd be time for more later. Much more.

The guests clapped. Nick chuckled. Taylor's cheeks turned pink. They sat down, and Nick rested his arm around the back of Taylor's chair, glad to be out of the spotlight. Unfortunately it didn't last long.

He stifled a groan as Erik pushed back his chair and stood, a mischievous glint in his eye.

"As the best man, I believe a toast is indicated." Erik lifted his glass of champagne, his gaze focused on Taylor and Nick. "I've known Nick for a long time, and he's made some smart moves in the past—hiring me as his attorney comes immediately to mind—but hanging on to Taylor wasn't just a smart move, it was a brilliant one. Seeing how happy they are almost makes me want to get married. Almost. But truly, Nick, Taylor, may you have a long and happy life together. Go forth and multiply."

Abruptly Erik sat down amidst laughter and a round of applause.

"Thank you, Erik." Nick rose, his smile widening. "That part about multiplying sounds especially intriguing."

Laughter erupted once again, but died down when Nick turned to the audience of friends and family, his face serious. "I'd like to take this opportunity to do a toast. I've said it before but never have I meant it more than I do at this minute." He raised his goblet, and his voice rang strong and firm in the silence. "To the woman who made me realize that I could have all the riches in the world but be poor without her by my side. To my lovely Taylor, my best friend, my love, and now, my wife. I am truly blessed."

By the time he finished, Taylor's eyes glistened with tears. Nana dabbed at her eyes with the tip of a napkin, and Grandpa

Bill cleared his throat. Even Nick had a lump in his throat, thinking how far they'd come.

He sat down and impulsively brushed a kiss across Taylor's lips. "I love you, Mrs. Lanagan."

Her fingers brushed his cheek. "I love you, too, Mr. Lanagan."

"Break it up, you two." Grandpa Bill leaned across the table. "There's plenty of time for that later."

"We're just getting warmed up," Nick said with a grin. "Erik did tell us to be fruitful and multiply."

"For once, a member of this family that listens to me." Erik laughed. "I threw that in because Bill over here was telling me you and Taylor want a big family. I couldn't believe it." His friend eyed him with a calculating expression. "You really want six kids?"

Nick's gaze slid across the crowded room. Past the little ring bearer in his tux dancing with the flower girl, past the children at the various tables nestled between their parents. He thought of what Taylor had taught him, about what is really important in life.

He leaned over and wrapped Taylor's hand in his before turning to Erik with a smile he didn't try to hide. "Hey, call me crazy. But I really do."

* * * * *

Dear Reader,

In *The Marrying Kind,* Nick Lanagan has a lesson to learn. Somewhere along the way he has lost touch with what's really important in life. He's put his career first, and although his professional life is flourishing, his personal life is floundering.

Taylor helps him to rethink his priorities and to realize that he's never going to be able to achieve true happiness until he embraces one simple truth: that God and family come first. It's a lesson we should all take to heart.

I hope you enjoy the book!

Warmly,

Cynthia Rutledge

Books by Valerie Hansen

Love Inspired

The Wedding Arbor #84
The Troublesome Angel #103
The Perfect Couple #119
Second Chances #139
Love One Another #154
Blessings of the Heart #206
Samantha's Gift #217

VALERIE HANSEN

was thirty when she awoke to the presence of the Lord in her life and turned to Jesus. In the years that followed she worked with young children, both in church and secular environments. She also raised a family of her own and played foster mother to a wide assortment of furred and feathered critters.

Married to her high school sweetheart since age seventeen, she now lives in an old farmhouse she and her husband renovated with their own hands. She loves to hike the wooded hills behind the house and reflect on the marvelous turn her life has taken. Not only is she privileged to reside among the loving, accepting folks in the breathtakingly beautiful Ozark Mountains of Arkansas, she also gets to share her personal faith by telling the stories of her heart for Steeple Hill's Love Inspired line.

Life doesn't get much better than that!

THE PERFECT COUPLE

Valerie Hansen

To Joe,
for being a great husband and father
and also being substitue "daddy" to Whiskers,
Harry (also known as Poopsie), Splash, Blackie,
Neek, Gypsy, Dumbo, Essence, Dinky, Duchess,
Beans, Shady, Big Molly and Little Molly.
Thankfully, not all at the same time!

Chapter One

Kara Shepherd loosed her ponytail and slipped the clip into the pocket of her jeans. Weary, she rubbed the back of her neck. It had been a long day. And it wasn't over. Sighing, she picked up the inventory list and went to work.

Intent on counting the supplies in exam room three, she didn't hear anyone approach. The first hint that she wasn't alone was a light tap on her shoulder.

She shrieked, whirled, her heart thudding. It took only an instant to realize who had innocently tapped her. "Oh, my!" Air whooshed out of her lungs all at once, leaving her breathless. "Susan, you startled me."

"Boy, no kidding. I thought for a minute there you were going to slug me!"

"Not a chance." Kara was still working to catch her breath. She managed a smile. "I'd never do anything like that to my favorite sister."

"I'm your *only* sister."

"Good point." Her grin grew. Mischief lit her brown eyes; the same lovely eyes her sibling had. "But don't push your luck by sneaking up on me like that again. I wanted a brother, you know."

"And I wanted a puppy. Maybe I should have been the veterinarian in the family instead of you."

Kara reached out and gave her sister a hug. "I'm glad we're

related. You're very special to me. I don't know what I'd have done without you, after—''

''Hey, no sweat. I like working here.'' Susan hugged her tight, then stepped away. ''Which reminds me. I finished all the billing. I figured I'd stop by the post office on my way home and mail everything. Want to come to dinner tonight?''

Kara wasn't fooled by her sister's overly casual manner. She knew Susan had purposely changed the subject for her benefit, to get her mind off her supposed loss. *If only she knew. If only someone did.*

Kara felt like a fraud every time she accepted an expression of sympathy. In truth, she was a lot less sorrowful than she should be about losing Alex, and her secret awareness of that fact left her feeling decidedly uncomfortable, especially at times like these.

''Well?''

Susan's voice drew Kara back to the present. ''Um, no, thanks. I still have a lot to do here.''

''Like what? Count pills? Roll bandages? Mop the floor?''

Kara chuckled. ''Mop? When I have a hired slave like you to do it for me?''

''Yeah, yeah. Rub it in. You always were a pain.''

''Isn't that what little sisters are for?''

''Maybe. If I ever manage to get pregnant and have a girl, I'll know if the problem was all little girls or just *you*.''

''If your baby's half as nice as you and Mark are, she'll be perfect. Now go on home and leave me in peace.'' Kara put her hands on Susan's shoulders, turned her and urged her out the exam room door.

Susan led the way down the hall. ''You really aren't coming to dinner?''

''Nope. If I keep you from having any time alone with that handsome husband of yours I'll never be an aunt. Besides, I've had dinner with you three times this week already.''

''You're avoiding the ranch, aren't you? You just don't want to run into Tyler Corbett.''

They had reached the deserted waiting room. Kara unlocked the heavy glass front door and held it open for her sister. ''He doesn't scare me.''

''Oh, no. You just hate each other's guts, that's all.''

Kara frowned. ''I don't hate anybody.'' She paused, sighed. ''Not anymore.''

Waving the bundle of outgoing bills, Susan said, ''I'm sending him another notice.''

''I told you not to do that. Mark's job as his foreman is more important than collecting on a bad debt.''

Susan shook her head. ''Look, Kara, if Corbett fires Mark because of a bill from you...which he owes, by the way...then he's a bigger fool than I thought. Trust me. I've gotten to know the man since we moved into the house on the ranch. I'm sure he's not vindictive.''

''Humph. I wish I could agree with you. The last time I saw him he avoided me like I was his worst enemy.''

''Hey, that sounds like an answer to a prayer to me,'' Susan said. ''You didn't want to get stuck making polite conversation with him, did you?''

As always, her sister was the voice of reason. Kara patted her on the shoulder. ''No, I guess not. Thanks for reminding me who's in charge of my life. I tend to get caught up in other things and forget.''

''You'll be back on track soon, now that you've started going to church again,'' Susan assured her. ''You'll see.''

''I suppose so.'' She brushed a goodbye kiss on her cheek. ''Now get going. I don't want Mark thinking I work you too hard.''

''Right. I'll stop by your place and feed your animals for you. See you in the morning.'' As she climbed into her car she called back, ''And don't forget to eat dinner!''

''I have a brownie in my desk drawer if I get desperate,'' Kara shouted, waving. ''I'll be fine.''

Watching her sister drive away, Kara locked the door and leaned against it for a few moments, thinking. Remembering. It *had* felt right to be back in the church in Hardy again after nearly two years' absence. The congregation had been wonderful. They'd welcomed her with open arms, accepting her as if she'd never been gone.

Kara made a derisive sound. Well, *most* of them had. The lone dissenter had been Tyler Corbett. They'd both been on their way out of the sanctuary one recent Sunday morning and their glances had met by accident. The brief, intense look he'd given her before turning away could have wilted the beautiful flower arrangement in front of the altar!

Working was Kara's favorite diversion. She often stayed long after the veterinary hospital closed, using her job as an excuse to escape the memories that still lingered in her house. The house she and Alex had shared. As his widow she didn't need all the room the old farm in Peace Valley provided but the place was paid for, so she'd stayed. Truth to tell, until she got her practice back on a more solid financial footing, she couldn't afford to move.

She had briefly considered hiring another large-animal vet to replace Alex, while she continued seeing the dogs, cats and assorted other smaller critters, as before. Then her flighty receptionist had quit and she'd had all she could handle to keep up with the office work, until Susan had arrived in Arkansas and volunteered to step into the job. After that, it had seemed to Kara that the practice was just as it should be and she'd abandoned the idea of adding anyone else to the staff.

She sighed. Looking back, it was easy to see that the Lord had been with her, even in the worst days of her marriage. And He was still looking after her.

"Thank you for everything, Father. Especially for sending Susan," she whispered.

Looking up at the darkening sky through the window opposite her desk, Kara noted gray clouds across the horizon. Evening storms were common in that part of the Ozarks, especially in the spring, but they could be frightening to some of her overnight patients. The dogs and cats were already anxious because they were separated from their owners. Thunder and lightning only made things worse.

"And thank you, Lord, that I'm still here tonight," she added, heading for the kennel area. A few kind words or even a mild tranquilizer would make the poor animals' night much easier.

She was petting a mongrel with a broken leg when she heard an echoing thud. Assuming it was the beginnings of thunder, she ignored the noise. Then it came again. Louder this time and accompanied by shouting. Male shouting.

Pausing, she listened. The dogs in the kennel runs had begun to bark but she could still make out a few words. Whoever the man was, he had a pretty colorful vocabulary.

Following the sound of the pounding, Kara stopped at the rear door. It was solid wood, not like the glassed-in front of the animal hospital, so she couldn't see who was making all the racket. Unwilling to unlock the door since she was there alone, she called out, "Who is it?"

"Open up," the man demanded. "It's an emergency."

"Go around to the front," Kara instructed. At least that way she could see who she was dealing with and make a sensible decision about whether or not it would be safe to let him in.

He mumbled something unintelligible, then said, "I was already there once."

"Well, go there again."

"I should have known I'd get this kind of treatment from you," he shouted through the heavy door. "Have a heart. It's raining."

Kara listened. The staccato sound of drops hitting the metal roof confirmed the man's statement. Since the porch where he now stood was dry, he did have a valid excuse for not wanting to circle the building. When she was in the kennel area she seldom heard anything over the uproar of barking and mewing, so it was highly likely he actually had knocked on the front door, just as he'd claimed. Which meant he was probably harmless.

Still cautious, Kara unlocked the door and opened it wide

enough to peek out. Her eyes widened. Tyler Corbett? It couldn't be!

She blinked as she combed a fall of hair back off her forehead with her free hand. It certainly was him. And he looked anything but cordial. His jacket was wet, water was dripping off the brim of his cowboy hat, and his scowl was even more pronounced than it had been the last time they'd met.

"What do you want?" she asked firmly.

"A pepperoni pizza." His tone was sarcastic. "With extra cheese."

Kara tried to slam the door. The toe of Tyler's boot stopped it from closing. "I don't like jokes," she told him. "Now go away."

"Not till you help this poor dog."

"What poor dog?" She let the door swing open and stuck her head out far enough to scan the whole porch. "I don't see any dog."

"He's in here." Tyler looked down.

Kara's gaze followed his. His arm was bent to support a slight bulge on one side of his jacket. When he lifted the fabric away from his chest, Kara could see the dark, soulful eyes of a floppy-eared, nondescript brown puppy.

"Why didn't you say so?" She quickly threw the door wide-open and ushered him inside. "Follow me. I'll have a look."

Tyler kicked the door closed behind him, took off his soggy hat and reluctantly trailed her down the hall. He hadn't intended to do more than drop off the pup and go home. If he hadn't thought the dog's condition was critical, he wouldn't have brought it to that particular animal hospital in the first place. And he certainly wouldn't be taking any orders from Kara Shepherd.

She moved lightly, with athletic grace, he noted, watching her precede him. Funny. He'd seen her before but he'd never noticed that. Nor had he seen how long and silky her hair was when it was unbound. He'd also never noticed what a take-charge person she could be. About the only times he'd talked to her was when she'd acted as her husband's assistant during veterinary visits to the cattle at his ranch in Ash Flat. She'd seemed more introverted then.

Kara led him to the closest exam room and gestured toward a stainless steel table. "Put him there."

"He's awful cold," Tyler said. He dropped his hat on a chair. "And I'm not sure how busted up he might be. I think it's pretty bad."

His concern brought her up short. So, there was a tender bone in Mr. Corbett's body after all. Well, well. What a surprise.

She reached into a cabinet beneath the supply rack and brought out a fluffy white towel, draping it over the exam table. "Okay. Lay him on this to begin with. If I need to do anything serious, we'll move him into surgery."

Tyler began to slowly part the front of his coat and lean toward the towel. The puppy whimpered. "I'm afraid to move him much."

"Here. I'll help." She circled the table without thought and reached for the jacket, folding it back carefully. There seemed to be more blood on the man's shirt and coat lining than there was on the dog.

Kara took a moment to caress the puppy's face and check his gums for color. Thankfully, they were pink and healthy. He hadn't lost too much blood.

"That's a good boy. I'm your friend, too," she cooed, sliding one hand along the length of his body and lifting gently. "Come on. That's it. You'll be just fine."

Tyler leaned toward her, bending over the exam table, and together they maneuvered the injured dog out of the crook of his arm.

Kara continued speaking softly to reassure the puppy as she eased him down onto the towel. "That's good. Almost there."

"Watch that front leg," Tyler warned. "I think it may be broken." He reached out to cradle the tiny bones. Kara did the same. Their hands accidentally touched.

She looked up, startled. Tyler was staring back at her as if he'd never seen her before. "You can let go, now," she finally managed to say. "I've got him."

"Right. I was just..." He frowned. "Never mind."

Well, at least he didn't look angry anymore, she thought, relieved. She quickly refocused on the job at hand. "He's in shock, like you thought. That's why he was acting so cold. You probably saved his life by keeping him warm the way you did."

"I didn't know what else to do. By the time I found him, he looked like he'd been there for some time. When I picked him up he started bleeding again."

Kara was swabbing the matted fur around the wounds with peroxide as she assessed her patient. "There's one deep laceration on his shoulder and a few other smaller ones. I suspect you were right about the broken leg. Can't tell yet about internal damage. How was he hurt?"

"I think a car hit him. I found him by the side of the road."

She nodded. "These injuries are consistent with that kind of an accident. How long have you had him?"

Tyler pushed up the sleeve of his jacket and looked at his watch. "About fifteen minutes, give or take."

"What?" She froze in midmotion.

"He's not my dog."

"I see. Do you know who he belongs to?"

"Not a clue. I suppose he was dumped. Lots of folks seem to think that the country is a wonderful place to abandon unwanted animals."

"I know what you mean. I got three of my own dogs that way. No telling how many others just wandered off and starved to death."

"Or became a coyote's dinner."

"Don't remind me." She shivered. So did the pup.

"Will you be able to save him?"

"I think his chances are good. He's young. That's definitely in his favor. We'll start by sewing up the gash in his shoulder, then X-ray the leg to see if it needs a splint or a cast."

Tyler raised one dark eyebrow. "We?"

''A figure of speech.''

''Oh.''

''However...'' She did need help. And he was handy. There was nothing wrong with having him assist her. Besides, he'd always been disgustingly overbearing. It might be fun to turn the tables for a change, to see how he behaved in a situation where he wasn't the one giving all the orders.

A slight smile lifted the corners of Kara's mouth. She bent over the puppy, letting her long, brown hair sweep across her cheeks to hide her amusement until she could get it under control. ''I could give him a general anesthetic instead of a local, but I'm afraid his already depressed nervous system might shut down if I do. That's why I'd rather not operate to pin the leg bones.''

''Sounds logical. So?''

''So, I'll need you to hold him still while I work.''

''I have a lot to do at the ranch,'' he alibied.

''Fine.'' She straightened, managed to face him soberly. ''I'll call Susan to come back in. Even if she's home, it could take her a while to get here, though. I'd rather do what's best for the dog.''

''Which is?''

''Start immediately. You don't have to help. I can always chase him around the hospital with a needle and sutures while he hops along on a broken leg.''

''Very funny.''

''Just making a point.'' Kara's smile crept back. Mischief lighted her eyes. ''Well?''

Muttering under his breath, Tyler shed his coat and began to roll up his sleeves. ''Okay. You win. What do I do first?''

Kara was amazed at how competent her drafted assistant turned out to be. All she had to do was tell him once and he did whatever she said. Correctly. His compassion for the injured little dog was even more impressive.

They had successfully tended to the puppy's wounds,

X-rayed his leg and started to set it. As soon as the bones were stabilized the pup had settled right down, exhausted.

Up to her wrists in the slippery solution that was part of the new, lightweight casting material, Kara realized she'd forgotten to pull back her hair and it was getting in the way. She blew it out of her eyes, tossed her head, rubbed her cheek against one shoulder.... Nothing worked.

Tyler was steadying the sleepy puppy, gently stroking its head and leaning close to speak softly to it as if Kara weren't there. "Your doctor's got a problem, kid. Yes, she does. I think she needs a haircut."

She tried her best to ignore the taunt. A wild hair stuck to the perspiration on her forehead and tickled her lashes. When she tried to wipe it away with her forearm, it whipped into her right eye. Squeezing that eye tightly shut, she wished mightily for a second pair of hands. Hands that didn't belong to smart aleck Tyler Corbett.

"I think she's winking at me," he told the pup. "Either that or she's making eyes at you." He glanced up at Kara, giving her a lopsided grin. "Want some help?"

That was the last straw. "Oh, no. I'll just sit here and go blind while my hands become a permanent part of this dog's cast."

"I take it that was a yes."

"Yes." She made a contrite face. "Please."

"That's better. I hate it when people aren't specific. What do you want me to do? Cut it off?"

"My hair? No!" she snapped back without thinking. His resultant chuckle aggravated her. Of course he hadn't intended to actually cut her hair! How dense could she be?

Kara pulled herself together, helped by the fact that her eye was really beginning to smart. "There's a big clip in the right-hand pocket of my jeans. Use that."

Hesitating, Tyler raised one dark eyebrow and eyed the slim hips encased in form-fitting denim. "I don't suppose you could hand it to me, could you?"

"Of course not." Kara suddenly understood exactly what

was stopping him and her cheeks warmed in a bright blush. ''Tell you what. Why don't you just come over here and hold the hair back for a few minutes. Get it out of my eyes. I'm almost done.''

Tyler wasn't in any hurry to accommodate her. He was still recovering from the bewilderment he'd felt when their hands had touched. Just because he was a widower and Kara Shepherd was a widow didn't mean he was interested in forming any kind of relationship with her. Or with any woman, for that matter. There would never be anyone like his Deanne. She'd been the perfect wife. Practically a saint.

Which meant he'd certainly be immune to any mild charm a prickly person like Kara might have, he reasoned logically. Pulling her hair back for her would be no more exciting than combing the tail of his favorite Quarter horse.

Reassured, he sauntered around the table. ''Okay. No sweat.''

''Thanks.'' She leaned her head to one side. ''It's this eye that hurts. See if you can clear that first, will you?''

Tyler lifted his hand. Hesitated. Discovered he actually wanted to see what it felt like to touch that beautiful, silky hair. Until now, that kind of act had been reserved for his late wife. Transferring those feelings to any other woman was totally unacceptable.

Kara peered over her shoulder as best she could without letting go of the puppy's cast. ''Well? This stuff is hardening. What are you waiting for?''

What, indeed? He didn't even like this woman. Surely, there was no reason to avoid touching her. He leaned closer so he could see the fine hairs against her cheek, reached out and carefully swept them back.

A tingle danced across Kara's face and skittered down her spine. His fingertips were rough, yet his touch was light, barely there. It was amazing that a man that big, that imposing, could be so gentle when he wanted to be. She shivered, aware of his closeness, of his breath on her cheek as he examined her eye.

"Did I get the hair out?" he asked quietly.

"I—I think so. Thanks."

Tyler straightened. Stepping behind her he carefully gathered the rest of her hair in both hands and held it back while she worked. "Okay. Just hurry up, will you? I've got other things to do besides hang around here." He knew his words sounded unduly harsh, especially since Kara was being a Good Samaritan, but he didn't like the feelings she'd awakened in him and he wanted to escape from her influence as soon as possible.

She continued to smooth the cast, glad the job was nearly done, because she could barely think straight with him standing so close. He made her miss the quiet companionship of a husband. Even one like Alex.

She blinked and sniffled, blaming the moisture pooling in her eyes on irritation from the stray hair.

Still holding her hair, Tyler leaned closer. "You all right?"

Kara felt his breath tickle her ear. She searched for words, *any* words, to answer and found none. His presence filled the room, overwhelmed her. All she'd have to do was turn her head and…

And what? Make a fool of herself? She was just overtired and stressed out. She must be. Only temporary insanity would make her think of Tyler Corbett as romantic.

She sniffled again, stalling for time to get her errant emotions under better control. *Please, Lord,* she prayed silently, simply, *help me.*

No bolt from the sky came to rescue her. No mountains crumbled. No seas parted. Tyler still bent over her, and her heart continued to hammer. The only change in the room was the sudden wafting odor of…*pizza?*

Kara's head jerked toward the door. Tyler hadn't been ready for such an abrupt move and inadvertently pulled her hair. She yowled.

He let go and jumped back. "What the—?" His gaze followed Kara's.

Standing in the doorway, with a broad grin on her face and a pizza box in her hands, was her sister, Susan.

Chapter Two

Susan giggled. "Well, well. What have we here?"

"Not what it looks like," Kara countered. "Mr. Corbett found an injured dog and we were…I was…just setting its broken leg."

"Okay. If you say so." Susan laid the pizza box on a chair and stepped up to the table so she could steady the puppy. It licked her hand and she smiled down at it.

"I *do* say so," Kara insisted, stripping off her latex gloves and dropping them in the trash. "If I'd known you were coming back tonight, I'd have waited till you were here to help."

"Looks like you did okay without me." Her eyebrows arched as she glanced over Kara's shoulder at the flustered man who was doing his best to appear unconcerned. He'd thrust his hands into the pockets of his jeans, hiding them as if they might be considered evidence against him.

Now that the atmosphere in the small room was no longer romantic, Kara was easily able to resume her professional bearing. "Give that a few more minutes to set," she told Susan, gesturing at the puppy, "then put him in one of the empty cages up here. I want him close so I can observe him tonight, just in case he has internal injuries, too."

Tyler spoke up. "You're going to stay here? All night?"

"She does that all the time," Susan explained. "That's why I brought the pizza. I figured she'd need something to eat besides the one brownie left over from lunch."

''I didn't mean for you to have to go to so much extra trouble,'' Tyler said, addressing Kara. ''I just didn't know what else to do with him. Once I spotted him, I couldn't drive off and let him die. I wouldn't have brought him here if there'd been any other vet hospital close by.''

''Of course you wouldn't,'' she said, trying to ignore the implication.

''I didn't mean it like that.''

''Don't apologize,'' she said flatly. ''And don't worry about me. I have a couch in my office where I sleep whenever I have to stay over. I'll be fine.'' She turned her attention to the drowsy pup. ''He looks good so far. I'll check on him every hour or so till I'm sure he's going to be all right.''

Susan was glancing around the room. ''Where's the paperwork?''

''Well...'' Kara's expression was apologetic. ''Would you believe we didn't get around to making any?''

''In a heartbeat,'' Susan said. She looked to Tyler. ''I'll need a name to put on the cage for identification. What do you call him?''

He drew the fingers of one hand down his cheeks to his chin, thinking. ''All I've called him so far is 'Road Kill.'''

''Okay,'' she said. ''Road Kill Corbett, it is.''

Kara interrupted. ''You can't give that poor little innocent thing a name like that.''

''Why not?'' Tyler was grinning broadly, obviously pleased with his witty selection.

The boastful look on his face did something strange to Kara's usually even disposition, making her decide to say exactly what she was thinking. ''Because it isn't fair. What's he ever done to deserve a terrible slur like that?''

''You mean besides get hit by a car and nearly die?'' Tyler's brows knit above deep-brown eyes that punctuated the question.

''Oh, that,'' she said sweetly, smugly. ''I didn't mean the Road Kill part. I meant Corbett.''

* * *

"I thought he was never going to close his mouth," Susan said, smiling at her sister as they got the puppy settled in his cage and went back to straighten up the exam room together. "Did you see the look on the poor man's face?"

"See it? I'll never forget it. It was all I could do to keep from busting up laughing. If he hadn't stormed out of here when he did, I might have exploded!"

"I couldn't believe you had the nerve to say something like that in the first place. What came over you?"

"I don't know. I guess he made me mad when he told us he only came here because he had no other choice. I wasn't very Christian, was I?"

"No. But the whole situation sure was funny."

"It was, wasn't it?" She grew thoughtful. "When, exactly, did you decide I needed a pizza?"

"On my way home. Why?"

"Oh, no reason."

"Come on, Kara. We've been sisters for too long. You can't hide stuff from me and you know it. Fess up. Why is the pizza important?"

She busied herself wiping down the stainless steel table as she answered, "I just thought it might have been the answer to a prayer. But the timing's wrong. I didn't even ask for anything until long after you decided to come back."

"It could still be an answer."

"I don't see how."

Susan put her arm around her sister's shoulders. "Because God knows what we need before we even ask Him." She stopped being serious and added, "Although, I must say, I've never asked Him to get me a pizza before."

"That wasn't what I prayed for."

"I figured as much. What was it you wanted? Me?"

"Sort of. I wasn't that specific."

"Then what?"

"You're not going to drop this subject till I tell you, are you?"

"Nope."

Kara made a face at her. ''Okay. I'd prayed for a little help. That's all.''

''With the puppy?'' Puzzled, Susan studied her.

''Something like that.'' A blush warmed Kara's cheeks. She turned away, hoping Susan hadn't noticed, but she had.

''What? Tell me. Maybe I *can* help?''

Kara was sorely tempted to make up a problem rather than have to let Susan in on the truth. Instead, she opted for honesty. ''I just wasn't comfortable with the situation, that's all.''

''Because of Tyler Corbett? You weren't afraid of him, were you? Oh, don't be. Mark says he was so goofy in love with his late wife that he won't even *look* at another woman. The man's branded for life.''

Kara understood completely. All her emotions blended together when she remembered Alex.

I won't ever let myself be hurt like that again, she vowed. Not ever again.

Susan had gone, leaving Kara to her thoughts and sole ownership of the now lukewarm pizza. Taking a piece of it with her, she strolled out to the waiting room to look over her practice and assess it while she ate.

Alex's death had left her with a lot of unpaid bills she hadn't expected. Most of those accounts had been settled but there was still the day-to-day running of the hospital to consider. Overhead like that wasn't cheap.

Susan had taken one look at the books and offered to work for no wages. Kara had insisted she be paid. As soon as they could afford to add another warm body, they planned to get a kennel boy—or girl—to keep the runs and cages clean. Until then, they shared the dirty work, too.

Sighing, she switched off the office light. Darkness had frightened Kara before she'd married Alex. After a few months with him, however, she'd welcomed the dark as a place to hide whenever he got so angry he lost control and began screaming at her. Living with him had been like sharing her life with a time bomb.

She was about to return to check on her latest patient when she saw headlights and the shadow of a truck bearing down on the glassed-in front of the animal hospital.

Startled, she stepped back just in case the driver misjudged the distance and didn't stop in time. Whoever it was, he sure was in a hurry. She wasn't up to tackling another emergency. Yet she knew she wouldn't—couldn't—turn anyone away.

The truck slid to a halt in a shower of mud reflected in the outside light. Someone jumped out and ran up the steps to the porch.

Kara dropped the slice of pizza into the trash, reached for her keys, and headed for the door. When she looked up she was face-to-face with Tyler Corbett. He was waving a white slip of paper.

She unlocked the door.

He burst through, his boots thudding on the tile floor. "I thought you didn't answer the door at night."

"I do when I can see who it is. What's wrong?" She followed him down the hall.

When he got to the place where light from her office illuminated the paper in his hand he stopped and whirled to face her. "This," he said, waving the paper.

Kara stood her ground. "Well, if you'll hold it still, I'll take a look."

"You don't have to look, *Doctor,*" he said, exaggerating her title. "You sent it to me."

"I what?" Suddenly, she realized what he had to be holding. Except he couldn't be. Not yet. Susan had only put the monthly statements in the mail that evening.

"Whoa," Kara said firmly. "That's impossible."

"Oh? Then what's this?"

"Well, it looks like one of our bills but it can't be. The postal service isn't that good."

"This didn't come in the mail," Tyler said. "It was hand delivered." He unfolded the bill and held it up in front of her face. "Look at the part on the bottom. If you wanted me to pay for the puppy's care up front, you should have said so when I was here, not fired off a new bill before I even had a chance to drive all the way home!"

Susan. Kara's shoulders sagged. Of course. Her sister knew how badly she needed to keep her accounts current and in a fit of efficiency, she'd changed Tyler Corbett's bill to reflect the latest charges and hand delivered it to him, rather than put it in the mail with the others.

"I'm really sorry," Kara said. "She…we…shouldn't have done that."

"Well, you're right about that." He reached into his pocket and pulled out a wad of crumpled money, thrusting it at her. "Here. Consider this a down payment. If there are more charges before the dog gets well, I'll pay whatever it costs. In spite of what you seem to think, I'm not a deadbeat."

"This isn't necessary." Cupping the bills in both hands so she wouldn't drop them, she realized she was trembling. "You can write me a check later. When everything's done."

"No way, lady. I came here to pay up and I intend to do just that. Your brother-in-law works for me, remember? The last thing I need is to have my foreman think I'm dishonest."

"I'm sorry. I'll see that Susan doesn't do anything like this again," Kara promised, chagrined. Her voice grew more faint. "It wasn't fair."

That sincerely apologetic attitude gave Tyler pause. The woman wasn't acting nearly as mercenary as he'd imagined she would. She hadn't even pocketed the money he'd shoved at her.

He had an attack of conscience. "I'm sorry, too. I didn't mean to scare you."

"You didn't," she said.

"Then why are you shaking?"

Kara stood taller, her chin jutting out, and alibied, "I'm probably just hungry."

"Didn't you eat that pizza?"

"I managed half a slice before you got here."

"Well, no wonder you're shaky. Come on." Without waiting for her consent, he ushered her into her office where the open pizza box rested in plain sight atop a file cabinet. He took the money from her hands, tossed it onto her desk and said, "You go wash up. I'll wait here."

"That's not necessary," Kara insisted. "I'm fine."

"No, you're not. And it's my fault. First I made you work overtime, then I kept you from enjoying your dinner." He scanned the office. "Got a microwave?"

"In the back. I use it to warm food for some of the animals." The wary look on his face made her smile in spite of her unsteadiness. "It's perfectly clean if that's what you're worried about. Anyway, I prefer my pizza cold."

"Good. Me, too. Go wash up while I find us some napkins."

"Us?"

Tyler shot her a lopsided smile. "If you don't mind, I'll join you. I was so busy blowing my stack I forgot to eat. I've just realized I'm famished."

Kara shrugged. "Sure. Why not?" Taking a deep, settling breath she left the room. There was no way she could tell anyone, especially not Tyler Corbett, why she'd been trembling. Hunger had nothing to do with it. When he'd burst in and shouted at her, her panicked response had been instinctive. Fresh fear had taken control. Alex's legacy of intimidation lived on.

After two years, she'd thought she was through being frightened. Tonight, when Tyler had confronted her, uncalled-for dread had returned as if it had never left.

Procrastinating, she splashed water on her face at the bathroom sink and stared into the mirror. "I'm going to be okay," she said to the image. "I'm smart and capable and I can make it on my own. It doesn't matter what Alex thought. He can't hurt me anymore."

And God loves you, she heard echoing in her head, in her heart. Kara nodded as she reached for a towel to dry her face. Remembering that she was a child of God was the most important part of her ongoing healing. It was His opinion that was important. No one else's counted.

* * *

"I looked in on Road Kill while you were gone," Tyler said. "He's asleep. I watched and he's breathing fine."

"I know. I checked him just before you charged in."

Tyler shrugged. "Yeah, well, I'm sorry about that. I'd had a pretty rough day. I had to throw away my favorite shirt and I'll probably have to give up my good jacket, too, thanks to the mess he made of it when I was trying to keep him warm."

"You don't need to throw the clothes away. A little household hydrogen peroxide will get rid of those stains. I use it all the time." She walked over to the file cabinet and picked up the flat, white pizza box, then returned to him and held it out. "Here. Help yourself. I could never eat all this anyway."

"Are you positive? Now that I think about it, I feel kind of bad about inviting myself."

"Nonsense. Somebody has to clean up the leftovers. If it hadn't been you, it would have been someone else."

Tyler took one slice and laid it on a paper towel. "You mean you have a steady stream of clients pounding on your door at all hours, begging for food?"

"Not as a rule. I was thinking of my dogs at home. They love leftovers." She placed the box on her desk and served herself.

"I'm taking food out of the mouths of your pets?"

"I won't tell if you don't. Besides, this has pepperoni on it. It doesn't agree with them."

"Oh, I get it." He started to smile. "Protect the dogs by feeding the spicy stuff to the testy client."

"Something like that." Circling the desk she plopped down in the leather chair and leaned back, pizza in hand. It was strange to be sharing an impromptu meal with a man again. The fact that they were alone in her office, the office that used to belong to Alex, made the encounter seem even more bizarre.

With that thought, Kara's appetite vanished. She laid the pizza aside on a paper towel and tried to suppress a shiver. Tyler Corbett wasn't acting at all intimidating. Yet she found herself nervous, as if an obscure threat lurked in the otherwise tranquil environment.

Thoughts of her late husband continued to intrude and refused to go away. Alex wouldn't have liked her eating at this desk. His desk. Alex wouldn't have approved of sharing a meal with a client, either, even if the person was also a friend. And he'd have been absolutely furious if she'd opened the door after hours and welcomed a man who'd once threatened a lawsuit. A man like the one casually perched on the edge of the desk across from her. Her mouth went dry in response to her mental rambling.

Tyler noticed Kara's psychological retreat. One minute she'd been fine. The next, she was looking at him as if he were an escaped criminal, ready to hold a knife at her throat. As far as he could tell he hadn't done anything to trigger that kind of reaction, except raise his voice when he'd arrived. Surely, that couldn't be what was bothering her now. She'd seemed normal enough, even friendly, once he'd apologized.

Tyler got to his feet and wiped his hands on a paper towel. "Well, I guess I should be going." He expected Kara to observe polite custom and disagree before finally giving in when he insisted on leaving.

Instead, she stood and headed for the office door. "That's probably a good idea."

Dumbfounded, he stared after her. "Who put the burr under your saddle?"

"No one." Starting down the hall she called back, "I'll unlock the front for you."

There was nothing more to say. Tyler grabbed his hat and coat and stomped out the glass door as soon as she'd jerked it open. He strode quickly to his truck. Kara Shepherd might be good with animals but she sure lacked the normal social graces where people were concerned. No wonder she'd stuck with that underhanded bum she'd married. They'd been perfect for each other.

Tyler jammed the truck in reverse and floored it. It didn't matter what that woman thought of him. After all, she was

Shepherd's widow. The widow of the swindler who had cost him the health of his herd and nearly ruined everything he and Deanne had worked for.

He swung onto the highway. It would be just fine with him if he never had to deal with Dr. Kara Shepherd again, personally or professionally. And as soon as he got Road Kill bailed out, that was exactly how it was going to be.

Kara maintained her composure until Tyler was gone. Then she collapsed against the wall, hugging herself. What was it about her that brought out the worst in men? First her father. Then Alex. And now…

She wanted to weep, to wail, to wallow in self-pity. Blinking, she waited for the flood of tears that usually accompanied such poignant retrospection.

Nothing happened! No hysteria, no devastating gloom, not even one solitary tear.

Kara was astounded. She took a deep, slow breath. She was healing! The nightmare was finally coming to an end.

Overcome with a sense of God's presence she closed her eyes, lifted her hands in praise and accepted the gift with a whispered, "Oh, thank you, Father."

The simple prayer didn't begin to express the soul-deep joy suddenly filling her heart. Peace flowed over her, enveloping her in the warmth of her Heavenly Father's abiding, miraculous love.

Chapter Three

Kara wasn't in her office when Susan arrived the following morning. She tracked her down in the kennels and held out the handful of crumpled currency she'd found on the desk.

"What's all this?" Susan asked. "You moonlighting as a bank robber?"

"Nope. It's payment of a bill."

"Really? Hey, that's great!"

"No, it isn't." Kara scowled. "It came from Tyler Corbett."

Susan looked around quickly. "He's here?"

"Not any more. But he was last night. And he was *not* particularly impressed by your efficiency."

"Oops." She made a penitent face. "I get the idea you're not crazy about it, either."

"That's an understatement. Now he thinks I don't trust him to pay his debts."

"Well, you don't, do you?"

Kara took a moment to mull over the question. If she judged by their past association she shouldn't trust the man at all. Yet for some crazy reason, she did.

"I believe he'll pay for the puppy's care," she finally said. "As for what happened before, well, that was between him and Alex."

"But, I thought..."

"Nothing is certain where Alex was concerned," Kara said.

"I know he did a lot of work for Corbett's ranch. But I don't know how accurate his record keeping was. That's why I dropped the idea to sue for the money after Alex died."

"You think he may have overcharged the ranch?"

Kara shrugged. "I hope not. Unfortunately, we'll never know for sure."

"But it is possible?" Susan was clearly disturbed by the thought.

"Oh, yes."

"I never dreamed Alex was like that."

Kara felt the urge to go on, to tell her sister everything. There was a great deal about Alex Shepherd that had remained hidden in the painful, private core of their supposedly perfect marriage. If she'd spoken out when Alex was living, maybe Susan could have offered some helpful advice. Now, however, the only benefit of confessing would be to know that someone else shared her suffering. Kara didn't want to lay that kind of burden on anyone.

She pressed her lips into a thin line. That wasn't completely true. She hadn't wanted advice or familial concern when Alex was alive. She still didn't. She'd purposely kept her misery to herself because she'd felt partly responsible for her bad marriage. Even now, that kind of thought kept nagging at the fringes of her consciousness, refusing to be banished.

Standing as tall as her five-foot-two-inch stature would allow, she said, "My husband is gone. I don't see any reason to discuss him, if you don't mind." The statement came out sounding so harsh she softened it with a tender smile and added, "Hey. Come on, Susan. It's a beautiful day and we should be praising the Lord that we have our whole lives ahead of us. Let's not dwell in the past, okay?"

To Kara's relief, her sister returned her smile and agreed. "Okay. It's a deal. So, let's talk about the patients. How's the infamous Road Kill Corbett doing this fine morning?"

"He's pretty chipper, considering. Last time I looked, he was happily shredding the newspapers we'd lined his cage with and tossing the soggy bits up in the air."

"Cute. Kind of like his owner, don't you think?"

Kara knew exactly what Susan was up to. Her loving but meddlesome older sister had been trying to play matchmaker for her ever since Susan had arrived in Arkansas. It was easier for Kara to pretend she'd misunderstood than it was to talk Susan out of continuing to do so.

"You'd know more about that than I do," Kara said sweetly. "You live on the Corbett ranch so you'd be far more likely to notice the condition of Mr. Corbett's newspapers after he's done reading them." She stifled a giggle.

"Very funny. You know I didn't mean Tyler tears up the paper with his teeth, like the puppy. What I meant was, don't you think he's kind of cute?"

"In what way?" Kara was determined to remain emotionally uninvolved. Anything to discourage her sister.

Susan threw up her hands. "I don't know. His eyes are gorgeous, so dark and brooding. And he has great hair. I wish Mark's was half as thick and nice."

"I can recommend a good coat conditioner," Kara teased. "It works wonderfully for all my dogs."

"You just aren't going to take me seriously, are you?"

"Why should I? You're not making any sense. First you tell me Mr. Corbett is still madly in love with his late wife, then you turn around and ask me if I find him attractive. That's ridiculous."

"Well—" Susan cast a sly smile her way "—nothing is carved in stone. Maybe he'll change his mind once he gets to know you better."

"No."

"Of course he will. You're smart, and pretty, and—"

Kara interrupted. "I mean, *no,* I don't intend to get to know the man any better than I already do. I've had enough of Tyler Corbett to last me a lifetime."

Susan was grinning. "I notice you didn't say you think he's ugly."

"He isn't ugly, he's—" Blushing, Kara broke off in midsentence.

"Aha! I thought so. You did notice how good-looking the guy is. Maybe there's hope for you yet."

"I am *not* interested in getting involved with another man, no matter how good he looks in a Stetson," Kara insisted. "Not ever. And certainly not a person as opinionated and short-tempered as Tyler Corbett."

"Don't be so sure. After all, just because a man isn't quiet and refined like Alex was doesn't mean he won't be every bit as easy to get along with, once you get to know him." Susan paused, studying her sister's pained expression. "What's the matter? What did I say? You look like you're about to cry."

Kara swallowed hard and steeled herself for the well-rehearsed denial she was ready to recite. Then it occurred to her that to do so would be to perpetuate a lie. What kind of practice of her faith would that be? Instead, she managed a smile and a diversion.

"I didn't get much sleep last night. I'm overstressed." That was certainly true. She eyed the crumpled money Susan was still holding. "I had company, remember?"

"Did he yell at you?" Susan asked, chagrined.

"A little. Don't worry about it, okay?" Turning, Kara looped an arm around her sister's shoulders and guided her toward the front desk. "It's almost time to open and you haven't put out the display of flea collars that came in yesterday. Think you'll have time to do it this morning?"

"Sure. No sweat." Susan smiled slightly. "I'm sorry if I seemed too pushy. I just hate to see you all alone like this. I feel kind of sorry for Tyler, too, so I thought—"

"What part of *no* don't you understand?"

She brightened, her eyes twinkling. "Hey. I've got an idea. How about the new manager at the feed store? Would you like to meet him? I hear he's single."

"Susan..."

"Okay, okay. But you can't enjoy being a recluse. I know you too well to believe that. There's a man for you somewhere. I'll just have to keep looking till I find him."

"Aaargh!" Wheeling, Kara gave up and headed for the

kennel. There was no reasoning with Susan when she was in one of her Ms.-Fix-It moods. As the younger of the two sisters, Kara had always looked up to Susan and admired her, even after they'd become adults. But this was one battle Susan was going to lose. No way was Kara going to allow herself to become romantically involved with another man. It was too scary an idea to even consider. She'd had her fill of men. And of marriage.

Shaking her head to punctuate her decision she made her way between the rows of smaller animal cages, her mind wandering. Yes, Tyler Corbett was good-looking. More than that, his tenderness toward helpless animals had spoken to her heart. But that was the end of her involvement. At this point, she didn't even care if she collected the full amount due for treatment of the injured pup he'd brought in. It would be worth it to write off the remainder of the bill if that meant she wouldn't have to face Tyler again.

Kara shivered. Truth to tell, she found she was actually starting to like him.

That inclination scared her far more than anything else had for a long, long time.

Kara was still insisting she wanted nothing to do with romance a week later, even though she was driving toward the Corbett ranch.

"This is all Susan's fault," she said to the drowsy puppy lying on the car seat beside her. "So help me, if she tries anything funny I'm going to disown her."

The pup thumped its thin tail and rested its chin on her lap, looking up at her with sad, brown eyes.

"If it wasn't for you," Kara told him, "I wouldn't be doing this." She laid her hand on his head and smoothed his fur. The cut by his ear was almost healed. His broken leg would take longer.

Recalling her recent conversation with her sister, Kara sighed in resignation.

"So, what are we going to do with Road Kill?" Susan had

asked that morning. ''We haven't had a single call on that lost-and-found ad you had me put in the paper.''

Kara remembered making a face. ''I don't know. I can't take him home with me. My neighbors are already complaining about the greyhound getting out and chasing game, and the rest of my dogs barking too much. Not to mention my cats hunting wild birds.''

''Well,'' Susan had drawled, ''I could always deliver him to Tyler.'' She paused and arched her eyebrows. ''Of course, since Mark works for him it might be better if I didn't make him mad. Again.''

''Meaning?'' Kara had a feeling she wasn't going to like the answer.

''I just thought, if *you* took the pup out to the ranch, I'd be off the hook and Mark wouldn't have to defend my actions to his boss, like before.'' She began to pout. ''I'm still in the doghouse over that bill I hand delivered.''

''No doubt.''

''Well?''

Kara's eyes narrowed as she studied her seemingly innocent sister. ''No tricks.''

''Cross my heart.'' Her index finger traced an invisible X on her chest. ''I just want to find a good home for the poor puppy, that's all. There's plenty of room on the ranch and nobody cares how much noise those dogs make.''

''Then you and Mark can take him,'' Kara said, certain she'd come up with the perfect solution.

''Sorry. Can't. It's not our house, remember? We're not supposed to have pets inside. And it would be too lonely for Road Kill, anyway.''

''Then leave him outside.''

''Where he can get into more trouble or get hurt, again? No way. Tyler has a big, fenced yard for his dog. It would be the perfect place for recuperation.''

''You're not going to drop this, are you?''

Susan had stood her ground and grinned with self-satisfaction. ''Nope. I'm right. Admit it.''

Which was why Kara was now driving toward the Corbett ranch in spite of her misgivings. She stroked the puppy's head slowly, gently, taking care to avoid his sore ear. The contact was soothing to both of them. Before she knew it, she'd arrived.

She turned into the gravel drive and drove beneath the ironwork arch marking the main ranch entrance. The only other times she'd been there was when she and Alex had come to treat Tyler's cattle. It seemed strange to be visiting in a quasi-unofficial capacity.

The Corbett ranch had always been impressive. The main house was a sprawling, brick residence that rivaled any in the area for both style and size. This time, though, Kara noticed that the flower beds needed care and the perennial plants were wildly overgrown. Tyler apparently wasn't interested in gardening.

Parking directly in front of the house, she carefully lifted the puppy and started for the porch. "Lord, be with me," she prayed in a whisper. "And help me find the right words to soften his heart."

Before she could ring the bell, the door was jerked open.

Kara gasped. "Oh! You startled me."

"I wish I could say the same," Tyler countered. "Susan told me you were coming. I called your office as soon as I got back to the house to try to stop you. I'm afraid you've made the trip for nothing. I'm not taking that dog."

His pigheaded attitude provoked her. "Then why did you bother saving his life?"

"You know I couldn't just leave him there."

"But you have no qualms about leaving him homeless?"

"That's different."

"Not the way I see it." She stood her ground, her chin jutting out stubbornly, her eyes issuing a clear challenge.

"I hate to tell you this, but your opinion doesn't cut it with me, lady."

"Do you think I'm surprised?" she snapped back. "I don't care what you think of me, or my practice. All I care about right now is finding a place for this poor little helpless puppy to recuperate.''

''So keep him at your place.''

Kara arched her eyebrows. ''I wish I could. Unfortunately, my neighbors are already upset about the menagerie I have out there.''

''That's not my problem. It's yours.''

''You're absolutely right.'' She extended her burden toward him and the pup began to wag its skinny tail excitedly. ''And this one is yours.''

''Now wait a minute....'' Tyler's instinctive reaction was to accept the friendly puppy when she thrust it into his arms. The minute he drew it to his chest it wriggled happily and stretched up to lick the bottom of his chin.

''See?'' Kara said, delighted. ''Road Kill likes you.''

''Yeah. I see that.''

She watched his telling reaction to the little dog. It warmed her heart. Tyler Corbett might act antisocial toward her but he clearly had a way with animals. He couldn't be all bad. As a matter of fact, he looked thoroughly appealing as he stood there holding the fractious pup. His eyes sparkled with amusement, his mouth was curved into a charming smile, and the weariness seemed to have gone from his face.

It suddenly occurred to Kara that Tyler needed the puppy as much as it needed him. He'd continued with his chores at the ranch and built a new way of life for himself after the loss of his wife, but apparently he didn't have anything in that life that needed his personal attention or his love the way Road Kill did.

Kara cleared the lump from her throat, then said, ''I tell you what. How about keeping him just until his leg heals? I'm sure we can find a home for him then.''

''I don't know....'' Tyler glanced over his shoulder. ''Buster doesn't usually like to share his turf.''

Leaning to one side, Kara peered into the living room. A big, yellow Labrador retriever was lounging on the sofa as if it belonged to him. His muzzle was greying and his eyelids drooped, indicating he was pretty old. "Is that Buster? He doesn't look like he'd even bother getting up to sniff a puppy this small," Kara said. "Why don't we see?"

Tyler scowled down at her. "You're a determined woman, aren't you?"

"Yup." With that, she sidestepped and slipped past him. Approaching the sofa, she spoke quietly and extended her hand. "Hello, old boy. Would you like a playmate? Huh? Would you? I'll bet you would."

Buster lifted his broad head and nosed it beneath her hand to be petted. In the background, she heard Tyler say, "Well, I'll be."

"What's the matter?"

"Oh, nothing." He approached slowly, still holding Road Kill up out of the way in case the older dog objected. "I just haven't seen my dog take to anybody that fast before."

"I love animals," Kara said.

"Obviously they know it." He stepped closer. "Okay. Now what? Do we put this one down for Buster to sniff or do you want to hold him to introduce them?"

Relieved, Kara smiled up at him. "I take it this means you've decided to give it a try."

"It'll be temporary," Tyler reminded her. "I have plenty to do on the ranch. I don't have a lot of extra time to spend taking care of a puppy."

Nodding, she said, "I understand."

There was a strange, faraway quality to her voice which made him wonder what she really meant. "You do?"

"Oh, yes. I threw myself into my work after Alex died, too. It helps. Until I go home and have time to think. I suppose that's why I've taken in so many homeless animals. They give me company and keep my mind occupied."

Tyler was ashamed of himself. It didn't matter what kind of man Alex Shepherd had been, he'd still been Kara's husband. And she'd suffered the same kind of personal loss he had. Whether he liked it or not, they had a lot in common. No wonder he'd sensed an unexplainable camaraderie when he was in her presence. He'd been unfairly judging her for her husband's sins. In reality she was as much a victim of a meaningless tragedy as he was.

He bent to place the puppy in Kara's lap. "Here. You do the honors while I get us some coffee."

"I can't stay for coffee."

"Why not?" he asked pointedly.

"I have to get home and feed my animals." She shifted Road Kill so his nose faced Buster's and carefully let the two dogs sniff each other. Neither seemed upset about the encounter.

"One cup of coffee won't take long." He flashed her an amiable smile. "Humor me, okay?"

Kara didn't know what to say. The last thing she wanted to admit was that she was actually enjoying his company, in spite of the way he'd welcomed her at first. There was something soothing about being with Tyler. It was as if she no longer had to worry about doing or saying the wrong thing. He seemed to accept her as she was, not as she thought she should be, and the resulting feeling was strangely peaceful.

"All right. One cup," Kara said. "Lots of sugar."

Tyler chuckled. "You've heard about my coffee?"

"No. Why?" She was continuing to monitor the dogs but chanced a quick peek at him. He looked thoroughly amused.

"Dee used to tell me it would dissolve a spoon. Nobody's ever proved it, though."

"Let's hope I'm not the first," Kara said with a smile. "Maybe you'd better put some cream in it, too. Just to be on the safe side."

"Gotcha. Back in a minute."

She held Road Kill in her lap and continued to rhythmically stroke Buster's head after Tyler left the room. What was wrong with her? Didn't she have any sense? She hadn't come to the ranch to pay a social call or to befriend Tyler Corbett. She'd come to foist an injured dog on him. That was all. So why was she looking forward to a leisurely cup of coffee as if they were old friends?

Because he understands, she answered. And I understand how lonely he feels, too, even though I didn't share the same kind of wonderful love he once had.

Kara gazed down at the puppy, smiled and nodded her head. It looked like the Lord was in the process of healing a lot more than the little dog's broken leg. He was mending Tyler's broken heart, too.

She was glad to be able to help.

Chapter Four

"Here you go." Tyler held out one of the two mugs he'd just filled. "Lots of cream and sugar."

Kara carefully lowered the puppy to the rug at her feet and made sure he was comfortable before she reached to accept the steaming coffee. Cradling the hot mug in both hands, she took a whiff. "Mmm, this smells wonderful."

"Thanks." He perched on the arm of the sofa, purposely locating Buster between them as a buffer. "I have a question. Why were you the one who brought Road Kill to me? Why didn't you send your sister, instead? She's usually right in the thick of things."

"No kidding." Kara blew on the coffee, then took a cautious sip. Her eyes widened. "Wow. You weren't kidding when you described this stuff. I'll bet it keeps you awake all night if you drink much of it."

"It's decaf," he countered. "Don't change the subject."

Eyes lowered, she sensed him studying her, waiting to see if she'd answer at all, let alone be truthful. She looked up as she said, "I came because Susan wanted me to do the honors, just in case."

"In case of what?" Tyler's brow furrowed.

"In case you got mad." Kara faced him squarely, surprised that she wasn't nearly as jumpy as usual, considering the gist of their conversation.

"What difference would that make to Susan?"

"Well..." Kara hesitated, taking time to chose her words carefully. "She didn't want to do anything that might adversely affect Mark's position with you, so she—"

Tyler got to his feet so quickly his coffee sloshed. He set the mug aside. "Whoa. Hold it a minute, lady. Do you mean to tell me that you and your sister think I'd be dumb enough to fire the best foreman I've ever had, just because his wife and sister-in-law happen to drive me nuts on a regular basis?"

"Well..."

He muttered under his breath. "You do have a pretty low opinion of me, don't you?"

"No. It's not like that at all," Kara insisted. Their pleasant conversation had deteriorated so rapidly she felt she'd better try to say or do something that would reverse the negative trend, if only for Susan's sake. Rising, she cautiously stepped over the resting pup.

Tyler folded his arms across his chest and remained resolute as she approached. "Oh? Then how is it?"

"It's a long story." Kara willed him to understand and hoped she wasn't making a mistake by confiding in him. "Susan and I come from a wonderful family, really we do. It's just that our father had a pretty short temper, sometimes. He yelled a lot. Especially when I was a teen. Susan used to intervene on my behalf all the time."

Tyler's frown deepened. "What's that got to do with me?"

"Nothing, directly. But we've discussed it more than once and decided that may be the reason she and I tend to avoid unpleasant confrontations whenever possible."

"I see."

Kara could tell by the leery look in his eyes and his standoffish posture that he didn't see a thing. That didn't surprise her. None of her friends had ever believed that her dad could be a monster when he lost his temper, either. His company-face was unblemished. Outsiders had never seen him behave irrationally or heard him shout at his family until he was hoarse, so why should they believe the wild tales of an uptight teenager?

And then, heaven help her, she'd married a man just like him. She'd been searching for someone who was kind and gentle, who loved animals as much as she did, and she'd been totally fooled into thinking Alex Shepherd was the perfect choice. She shivered. What irony.

Taking a deep, settling breath Kara managed a nonchalant smile as she turned her back on Tyler and started for the door. ''Well, thanks for the coffee. I have to be going.''

He opened his mouth to ask her to stay longer, then changed his mind. Having a normal chat with this woman was impossible. Every time he decided she was intrinsically anti-social, she came up with some revealing tidbit that tugged at his heart so strongly he was tempted to take her in his arms and offer comfort.

His breath caught. Now *that* would be a mistake to end all mistakes. Half the time, Kara was as prickly as a porcupine. Yet she could also be as gentle, as vulnerable, as a doe. With his luck, he'd give in and decide to hug her just about the time she stuck her quills up!

Following her to the door, he found he was smiling at the analogy.

Kara caught him grinning. ''What's so funny?''

''Nothing. I was just thinking.''

''About me?''

''Sort of.''

''I don't want to know more, do I?'' she asked wisely.

''Probably not.''

''I didn't think so.'' She extended her hand. ''Thanks for agreeing to take Roady. He really is a sweet-natured little guy. I'm sure he and Buster will get along fine.''

Instead of shaking her hand, Tyler opened the door and stood back. ''I'm only keeping the dog until he's healed up.''

''Of course.'' Kara felt like cheering! By the time she got around to removing the cast, Road Kill would be so much a part of Tyler Corbett's life he'd beg her to let the puppy stay. Naturally, she'd have to give in and allow it.

Stifling a triumphant smile, she hurried to her car, climbed in and drove away. Things were going to work out fine as long as Susan didn't interfere and try to "help." The Corbett ranch was the perfect place for a rambunctious pup, and having a canine companion might give old Buster a new lease on life, too.

Kara's smile turned wistful. What a lovely, tender scene she'd beheld when she'd first entered Tyler's living room. The elderly, yellow Lab was as much a permanent fixture in the casually furnished ranch house as the soft, leather sofa he'd claimed as his own. Clearly, he was a well-loved member of the family.

Tears began to cloud her vision. Disgusted, she blinked them back. What was the matter with her? The mercy mission had gone well. Roady had a good home with a loving man who'd watch over him and care about him. So why get emotional now? *Why, indeed?*

Suddenly, Kara realized what was bothering her. The concept wasn't rational, nor could she explain what had caused her to make such a ridiculous comparison. Only one thing was certain. In spite of her aversion to marriage and commitment, she envied the *dogs.* They'd found unconditional love. And someone they could always trust.

It didn't matter that their master was Tyler Corbett. The important thing was they truly belonged.

For the first time in months, Kara dreaded Sunday. She wasn't about to let anything keep her out of church, she just wasn't keen on running into Tyler there. To be on the safe side, she'd spent the two days since her visit to his ranch rehearsing a series of nonchalant comments to use in case they happened to come face-to-face.

Knowing that the Corbetts and their friends usually sat together in the third and fourth rows, Kara took a seat near the rear of the old stone church, greeting fellow worshipers with a demure smile.

This was the church she'd attended before her marriage. Afterward, Alex had insisted they didn't need to worship in a small, country church that didn't offer him much opportunity to further his practice by impressing wealthy, local ranchers with his intellect and supposed piety. Kara never had been able to make him understand how at home and peaceful she felt when she sat quietly in that little church and allowed the Lord to fill her heart with His love. She sighed. Words couldn't describe how good it felt to be back.

The day had promised to be warm so she'd wound her long hair into a twist and fastened it up with a large, tortoiseshell clip that matched the muted colors of her softly draped, rayon print dress. She was smoothing her skirt when all of a sudden her sense of peace vanished.

Wisps of hair on the back of her neck tickled, prickled and would have stood on end if they hadn't been so long. She tensed. It wasn't necessary to look over her shoulder to know what was wrong. Tyler Corbett had arrived. She could feel his presence.

The broad-shouldered man passed right by Kara as he made his way forward, down the center aisle. On his arm was a slim, blond-haired lady. Kara raised one eyebrow. *Well, well. And who might this be?* She wasn't surprised that she didn't recognize the woman. Since she'd only recently begun attending this church again, there were many people she didn't know, or faces she couldn't place.

What did bother Kara, however, was the unexpected twinge of jealousy when Tyler and his companion had walked by. What a silly response! Why should she care who he was with?

Susan slid into the pew next to her and nudged her gently. "Scoot over, will you? Mark's coming as soon as he parks the car. I was afraid we'd be late so I had him let me off at the door. One of the horses picked last night to foal and we were up half the night."

"Why didn't you call me?" Kara whispered. "You know I'd have come out to help."

Susan made a face. "I thought of that. Mark said no. It seems Tyler wasn't too pleased when you dropped by the other day."

''That's *your* fault.'' Kara wasn't about to back down. ''You talked me into doing it. I wanted you to take the puppy to him in the first place.''

''I know. My mistake.'' She shielded her mouth with one cupped hand and leaned closer. ''What did you say to the man, anyway? Mark says he's been a real pill ever since you were out there.''

Shrugging, Kara was at a loss. ''I don't know. We just talked. Made polite conversation. The usual.'' She remembered her confession about their father's bad temper but could see no connection between that and Tyler's mood. ''He seemed okay when I left.'' A sly smile lit her face. ''Of course, I did foist an injured dog on him. Maybe that's what's bothering him.''

''Maybe.'' Susan slid closer as her husband joined them. ''And maybe he's just naturally mean-spirited.''

''Oh, I don't think so,'' Kara said quickly. She noticed a look of smug satisfaction come over her sister and easily anticipated her thoughts. ''Don't start with me again about needing a husband,'' she warned. ''Don't even start.''

Susan almost managed to look innocent. ''Who? Me? I didn't say a word.''

''No, but I know what you were thinking. I told you, I have no interest in *any* man, least of all Tyler Corbett. Besides, he's got a special lady friend. Look. Third row. Second from the left.''

Leaning sideways, the elder sister peered between the heads of other worshipers until she spotted her quarry. ''Aha. I do see. How interesting that you noticed.''

''The man walked right by me. I couldn't help but see him. Now, will you please leave me alone?''

''Till the service is over,'' Susan said. ''Then you and I are going to find Mr. Corbett so I can properly introduce you to his lady friend.''

''It won't be necessary to go to…'' Kara began.

Susan pointed to the front of the sanctuary. ''Shush. They're starting. I can't hear a thing when you're talking.''

Disgusted, Kara closed her mouth. Her mind, however, refused to be quieted. No way was she going to permit her sister to drag her into another unnecessary discussion with Tyler Corbett. Especially since he'd brought a female companion to church!

Not that she cared one way or the other, Kara insisted. He was widowed. He was entitled to find somebody else to fill the void in his life.

On the other hand, the emptiness Alex had left in *her* life was a blessing. Yes, she sometimes felt guilty for thinking like that. There were even times when she missed the man she thought she'd married. But truth was truth. Alex had been a beguiling, blasphemous hypocrite with a volatile temper. It was only a matter of time before he'd have stepped over the line and done something truly horrendous—to her or to someone else. Maybe both.

She'd never wished him harm in a literal sense. She'd simply been frightened and unsure of what to do when he'd gotten drunk, flown into a rage and stormed out of the house for the last time. The decision to drive away had been his. Investigators had assured her that the fatal, single-car crash was no one else's fault. Alex had made many wrong choices. Ultimately, one of them had led to his death.

All she had to do was accept what had happened and get on with her life. Thank God she was finally healing; finally beginning to feel normal again.

Even if being normal meant she was beginning to notice a good-looking, appealing man when she saw one? Kara asked herself. She nodded. *Oh, yes.* She could handle her emotions. Thanks to Alex, she was no innocent, naive girl. Not anymore.

The Sunday morning church service was over far too soon to suit Kara. She gathered up her purse and bible, intending to make a quick exit as the rest of the congregation began to file out of the sanctuary.

Susan grabbed her arm. ''Hey! Not so fast. Come with me.

I'm going to introduce you to somebody special. Remember?''

''Sorry. I don't have the time. I have to stop at the grocery store on my way home, then drop by the hospital to check on the sheltie we took in on Friday.''

''And don't forget, you have to wash your hair, too.'' Susan grinned knowingly.

''What?'' Kara patted the twist at the back of her head to make sure it was still neatly in place. ''What are you talking about?''

''Just being a good sister and providing extra excuses, in case you run out.''

''Very funny.'' Kara tried to sidle past. The aisle was blocked. Short of being impolite and shoving somebody out of the way, she was temporarily trapped.

Taking advantage, Susan grabbed her by the hand and tugged her backward until they were once again standing between the two rows of padded pews where they'd been seated.

Only five feet two inches tall, Kara wasn't able to see over people's heads as well as her sister could. She strained on tiptoe, checking every glimpse of a dark-blue suit in the crowd, hoping that Tyler wasn't going to pass by before she could make a graceful exit.

It took her only a few seconds to realize she wasn't going to get her wish. She lifted her chin proudly and smiled as Tyler and his well-dressed companion inched past.

Behind her, Susan squealed so boisterously that dozens of people stopped to stare. ''Louise Tate! It is you! I'm so glad to see you decided to come today. Welcome!'' She leaned around Kara and extended her hand, grinning widely when the woman took it. ''This is my sister, Kara.''

Louise smiled pleasantly. ''How nice to finally get to meet you. Susan has told me a lot about you.''

Uh-oh. Kara couldn't help but smile in response to the woman's happy glow and the elfin look in her twinkling blue eyes. The only thing that amazed her was Louise's evident age. It looked as if Tyler preferred older women. *Much* older women. With ash-blond hair that hinted at grey.

"Louise is Deanne's mother. You know...Tyler's wife. I mean late wife." Susan blushed. "Oh, dear. I'm sorry. I shouldn't have put it that way."

Louise patted her on the arm. "Nonsense. We all want to remember Deanne. She was a lovely girl. I'm proud to have had her for a daughter. It bothers me when people avoid mentioning her because they think it will hurt me."

Worried about how Tyler might be affected by the candid conversation, Kara glanced up at him, expecting the worst. Instead, she found him staring at her as if he hadn't heard a word anyone had said. Their gazes met. Held for an instant too long. She blinked to break the silent bond and looked over at Susan, hoping she hadn't noticed. She obviously had.

"My sister's a widow, too," Susan volunteered, her voice brisk and enthusiastic, "but I guess I told you that already, didn't I?"

"Yes, you did," the older woman said. She smiled sweetly at Kara. "I hope I'm not speaking out of turn, dear. At my age it's a lot easier to get away with saying what I really think." She punctuated her statement with a soft chuckle. "I must tell you, now that I've met you, I'm surprised you're still single."

Kara opened her mouth to express her opposing point of view.

Susan cut her off before she got started. "She says she likes being on her own. I sure wouldn't. I don't know how I'd manage if I didn't have my Mark to come home to every night."

"I know exactly what you mean," Louise agreed. "I've outlived two wonderful husbands. If the right man came into my life right now, I'd marry again in a heartbeat."

Pointed comments were flying back and forth between Susan and Louise so rapidly, Kara felt like a spectator at a tennis match. She rolled her eyes in disbelief and looked up at Tyler for validation of her cynical attitude.

He nodded in agreement. Kara relaxed and smiled at him, secure in the knowledge that she could do so without giving him the wrong impression.

His eyebrows arched comically, one corner of his mouth lifting in a wry smile, as he took his mother-in-law's arm. ''Come on, Louise. I'll treat you to lunch and we'll brainstorm about finding you another husband. How's that?''

''Well, I—'' She was hustled away before she could finish the sentence.

When Tyler glanced back over his shoulder, Kara mouthed a silent, ''Thank you.''

He replied with an equally silent, ''You're welcome,'' and gifted her with a heartwarming smile.

Kara felt the effects of that stunning smile all the way from the top of her head to her toes. A shiver skittered up her spine. On its heels was a warm glow.

Taken aback, she waved her church bulletin like a fan to cool her suddenly flushed cheeks. ''Whew!''

A wide, satisfied grin split Susan's face. ''What's the matter? Too hot for you?''

''It is warm in here,'' Kara offered, still fanning.

Susan snickered. ''Hah! The air temperature has nothing to do with your being so hot under the collar, and you know it.''

''Don't be silly.''

''I'm not the one being silly.'' Susan bent to pick up her purse and bible. She was still grinning broadly as she waved goodbye to Kara with a blithe, ''See you tomorrow.''

Chapter Five

The veterinary office was finally empty, the last client on his way home. Exhausted, Kara sank into the chair behind the front counter, propped her feet up and sighed. ''Boy, I don't know what's the matter with me lately.''

Concerned, her sister leaned against the filing cabinet. ''Are you sick?''

''No. It's not that. I'm...well...distracted. Sort of befuddled. I have been all week. It's like I have spring fever or something, and it's wearing me to a frazzle.''

''I wasn't going to mention it, but you have been acting kind of *out to lunch,* lately. And I'm not talking about food.'' She laughed lightly. ''Course, I shouldn't talk. I'm the one who shaved Mrs. Pettibone's tomcat's tummy so you could spay him!''

''That was so funny,'' Kara agreed with a chuckle. ''You should have seen the look on your face when you realized what you'd done.''

''It wasn't entirely my fault, you know. His name's Miss Priss.''

''Not anymore. Mrs. Pettibone was so shocked to learn he was a boy that she decided to change his name. I think she finally settled on Rufus.'' Kara paused. ''Which reminds me, how's Road Kill?''

''A cat named Rufus reminds you of Road Kill? That's a stretch of the imagination.''

"He's been on my mind lately."

"Are we talking about the *dog,* here?"

"Of course we are." Kara made a silly face.

Susan's eyes glimmered with mischief. "And you have no interest in how Tyler is?"

"He's all right, isn't he?"

"Aha!" Susan was jubilant. "I knew you were thinking of him all along."

"What if I was? I'm still worried you and Mark will get into trouble with him because of me."

"Hey, don't worry about us. We're fine. Mark got a raise and he loves his job, so things couldn't be better." She studied her younger sister perceptively. "Except that I hate to see you sitting home all alone, night after night."

Kara's "Hah!" was loud, abrupt. "I live with four dogs, six cats, and keep a spoiled rotten, retired carriage horse in my side pasture. I'd hardly call that being alone."

"Okay. Besides the Kara Shepherd Home for Antique Animals, what do you have to look forward to?"

"Peace and quiet, for one."

"As opposed to an interesting human companion who cares about you? I'd hardly call that a fair trade."

"Well, I would," Kara insisted.

"Maybe." Susan gave her a friendly pat on the back. "But it's really none of my business so let's change the subject. What are you doing for dinner Saturday night?"

Kara scowled up at her. "I thought we were changing the subject."

"We are. I've got a really delicious-looking pork roast in the fridge. I thought I'd stick it on the rotisserie. Cook it real slow. Only it's way too big for just Mark and me to eat all by ourselves."

"You could serve it two days in a row."

Susan shook her head. "I could. Or I could ask my favorite sister to share it with us. That is, if she isn't too stubborn to admit she gets lonesome once in a while."

"Okay. Once in a while I suppose I do. But remember,

living by myself is my choice.'' She smiled to assure Susan she wasn't upset. ''So, what can I bring?''

''Yourself,'' Susan said enthusiastically. ''We'll have a great time. You'll see. I can hardly wait!''

Eyeing her suspiciously, Kara wondered why anyone would be so excited about having a sibling over for dinner. Especially since it wasn't that rare an occasion. She decided to ask. ''Why is it I'm getting the idea you're way too happy about all this?''

''I'm just a basically cheerful person. You used to be, too, before—'' Looking penitent, Susan said, ''Sorry.''

''Hey, don't be. I know I've changed since we were kids. Everybody has to grow up sometime.'' She smiled and pointed. ''Even you.''

''Not me,'' Susan countered. ''I plan to stay a big kid all my life. It's more fun that way.''

Kara's smile faded. *Fun* was a concept she'd put aside for self-preservation when she'd realized what kind of man her husband really was. He hadn't liked the sound of her normal laugh; said it was too shrill, too loud. So to keep the peace, she'd minimized it. During the course of her marriage she'd squelched her good humor so often she'd almost forgotten how to let go; how to have ordinary fun the way Susan did, especially when she and Mark were together.

That was one reason Kara didn't like to spend too much time in their company. It hurt to see what a good marriage could be like and to know how rare it was.

What a blessing it would have been to find that kind of husband, she thought wistfully. To have the kind of perfect partnership Susan and Mark shared. The same kind that Tyler Corbett had once had with his beloved Deanne.

''I don't know why she's so intent on putting on such a big spread,'' Mark said, dusting off his hands and facing his boss. ''All I know is, when my wife gets a bee in her bonnet, it's best to let her have her way.'' He flashed a wide grin. ''You don't mind, do you?''

Tyler shrugged. ‘‘No. I’m flattered. What time shall I come?’’

‘‘I don’t know. We usually eat around six. Just wander over an hour or so before that and you can help me light the barbecue. Susan’s been cooking a roast on the electric rotisserie all day but I still have corn on the cob and taters to do on the grill.’’

‘‘Sounds delicious. Can I bring anything?’’

‘‘Nope. As long as you show up and help me keep peace in my family, I’ll be satisfied. Susan left it up to me to invite you and I got the idea she wasn’t going to take it kindly if I didn’t succeed.’’

Tyler chuckled. He took his hat off and raked his fingers through his hair, combing it back. ‘‘She sure is something when she makes up her mind, that’s a fact. Has she always been so stubborn?’’

‘‘Far as I know. She’s been that way as long as I’ve known her. Ever since she was sixteen.’’

‘‘Is Kara older or younger?’’ Tyler asked.

‘‘Younger. Susan turned thirty in March—only don’t you dare let on I told you or I’ll be in the doghouse for sure. Kara’s twenty-six.’’

Tyler made a skeptical sound low in his throat. ‘‘You could have fooled me.’’

‘‘I know what you mean. Kara’s so serious all the time, it makes her seem older.’’

‘‘Was she always like that?’’

Mark shrugged. ‘‘I’m not sure. I was eighteen when I first met Kara. And so in love with Susan I couldn’t see straight. I’m afraid I didn’t pay much attention to her baby sister.’’ He grew thoughtful. ‘‘Seems to me she was always pretty studious, though. Had her nose buried in a book most of the time.’’

‘‘What about their parents?’’ Tyler asked, remembering Kara’s confession. ‘‘Were they strict?’’

‘‘Their father was,’’ Mark said without hesitation. ‘‘I used to hear him ranting and raving some nights when I was sitting out on the porch with Susie. She never seemed to take him seriously but I sure did. Believe me, I *always* got her home before her curfew."

Tyler had to know more. "Is he still living?"

"Nope. Flew into a rage one day and had a stroke. He didn't live long after that. Susan said his heart gave out." Mark snorted wryly. "If you ask me, he didn't have one."

"That must have been hard on the sisters."

"It was." He paused to recall. "They both flew back to Illinois for the funeral. So did I. Alex and Kara had been married about a year by then. He never bothered to show up. I thought that was kinda strange."

"Must have made it worse for her," Tyler ventured.

"You'd think so. But if I remember right, I never heard her mention his name the whole time we were at her mother's."

"Not even once?"

"Nope. Well, I'd better go get that corn."

Tyler didn't pay much attention. He was thinking about Kara and visualizing her as a sensitive child who'd buried herself in her studies to escape rancor in the home, while her sister had merely shrugged off the same situation and hadn't let it bother her. Too bad they couldn't have both been immune the way Susan was.

He quickly convinced himself it wasn't his problem. He didn't want to know what made Kara Shepherd tick. Or what experiences, good or bad, had formed her into the person she was today.

Except that she intrigued him, he admitted ruefully. There was something about her that drew him, caused his normally staid emotions to threaten to run amok when she looked at him with those soft, doe eyes of hers. It was almost as if he couldn't bring himself to look away, once their gazes met.

You're a fool to look at another woman in the first place, he told himself. You had the best. You had Deanne. She was one of a kind.

Tyler nodded slowly, pensively. His days had been blessed beyond imagination by his marriage. He firmly believed that a perfect love only came along once in a lifetime. In spite of what his former mother-in-law kept insisting about finding another husband for herself, he was certain his personal quota of miracles had been used up. That was enough to convince him he'd never court anyone else. Ever.

When Kara's winsome face popped into his consciousness unbidden and he muttered in disgust, "*Especially* not her," he was very thankful Mark wasn't there to hear him.

Kara arrived at Susan's just in time to help her set the dining room table.

"We were going to eat in the yard but the bugs have been terrible," Susan said. "Mark insists it's because last winter was too mild."

"Probably. We need a long, cold spell to kill off a lot of the worst pests. Of course, there is a plus side. We'll sell a lot more flea and tick killer."

"Good point." Susan grinned. "Hey, maybe we could breed the little critters and make even more money!"

Kara huffed in mock derision. "This is Arkansas, dear heart. Nobody has to try to breed insects here. They just appear in droves the minute the weather gets the tiniest bit warm. I don't know what I'd do without the Purple Martins that nest out at my place."

"Eating mosquitoes, you mean?"

"Those, and every other flying insect they can catch on the wing. I must have twenty pairs of martins in my birdhouses so far this year and they're singing like wild canaries to attract mates. It's wonderful. I wake up to a concert every morning."

Susan giggled. "I wake up to Mark's snoring."

"Well, to each his own. I prefer my birds," Kara teased. "They don't make funny noises. And they always clean up after themselves."

"But they don't keep your feet warm at night."

"I have an electric blanket." She made a face. "If it stops working, I can buy another one."

A pleasant voice coming from behind her made Kara jump. "Buy another one what?" Louise Tate asked.

Kara whirled. "Oh! Hello. You startled me." She smiled for Louise's benefit, then shot a questioning glance at Susan.

"I take it you didn't know I was coming," the older woman observed. "I hope you don't mind."

"No, of course not. It's nice to see you again."

Susan smiled broadly and reached past Kara for the bowl Louise was carrying. "Oooh, fruit salad. How delicious."

"I didn't want to come empty-handed," she said. "If you don't want to serve it tonight, you and Mark can always have it later, when we're all gone."

We? All? Kara was beginning to have serious misgivings about the forthcoming evening. She had a bad feeling that Louise might be only the first of the surprises her sister had in store.

Before she could ask, Mark burst in the back door, still dusty from work. "Sorry, ladies," he said in passing. "I got delayed. I'll go grab a quick shower and be right back." He stopped in the hallway and stuck his head back through the door to the kitchen where Susan, Louise and Kara stood. "If Ty gets here before I'm done cleaning up, ask him to go ahead and light the barbecue, will you?"

Kara's mouth dropped open. She wheeled to face her sister. "Susan..."

"Hey, it's a big roast," she countered. "No sense in letting it go to waste. Besides, there's nothing wrong with trying to make points with the boss." She smiled sweetly. "I kiss up to mine all the time."

Kara's, "Oh, save me!" practically rattled the windows. She quickly excused herself, spun on her heel and headed for the door. Of all the ridiculous tricks Susan had pulled, this one took the prize.

Jerking open the screen, Kara plunged outside, ran down the steps onto the lawn and nearly collided with Tyler Corbett.

He put out his arms to catch her. It wasn't necessary. She

managed to skid to a stop and regain her balance without stumbling, then step back out of reach.

Filled with annoyance, she put her fists on her hips, braced herself and stared up at him. It was easy to see he was as shocked to see her as she'd been to learn that he was also invited to dinner.

Kara nodded toward the house. ''I wouldn't go in there if I were you.''

''Why not?'' Scowling, Tyler stood his ground.

''Because there's apparently a plot brewing. I don't know why I'm surprised. My sister's done this kind of thing before.''

''Done what?''

''Gotten it into her head that I'm desperate for a husband and tried to hurry things along. I hate to tell you this, but I think she's picked you for the job.'' She grimaced. ''Louise is in the house, too. I suspect a conspiracy.''

His eyes widened. ''Dee's mother? Why would she be involved?''

''I don't have a clue. All I know is she seemed to know you were coming and didn't act a bit surprised to find me in the kitchen with Susan when she arrived a few minutes ago.''

Tyler was slowly, pensively shaking his head. ''I suppose you could be right. Louise has been repeating her marital history a lot lately. I figured she was getting senile. Now that I think about it, she may have been using those stories to try to get me to consider finding another wife.'' He looked directly into Kara's eyes as he added, ''That will never happen. Deanne was one of a kind.''

Kara began to relax. Taking a deep breath, she released it as a relieved sigh. ''I know what you mean. After Alex, I swear I'll never get married again.''

''Why can't they just leave us alone?'' Tyler sounded melancholy.

''I don't know. Probably because they care about us too much.'' She was starting to get an idea and didn't want to discuss it where they could be overheard. "Come on. Let's take a little walk."

He eyed her with suspicion as she urged him away from the house. "Why?"

"Because I know how we can get everybody to relax and leave us alone," she said brightly. "It's brilliant. And plausible. I've used similar tricks to get Susan to back off, before. It'll serve them right if they swallow the whole charade, hook, line and sinker."

"We're fishing?" Tyler teased. He was beginning to suspect where Kara's mind was going and couldn't help being amused by her enthusiasm.

"No, we're bamboozling. We're going to make them think we're a couple! We'll have to work out the beginning of our pretend relationship, of course. It has to look natural or we won't fool anybody. That'll be the hardest part."

"You're crazy. They'll never buy it."

"Sure they will. It'll be easy, especially if we throw in a suitable lovers' quarrel every once in a while." She grinned up at him. "How about it? Think you can argue with me convincingly?"

"I think we can manage that part all right," he said hesitantly. "The friendly stuff may be tougher."

"Not once we get used to it. Lots of couples have rotten home lives and still manage to present a loving image when they're out in public."

"That's not a very comforting picture."

Kara agreed. "No. But it does prove my plan is doable. What do you say? Shall we try it?"

"I'm not sure. Suppose Susan doesn't fall for the same trick again? And what about Louise?"

"If it doesn't fool them, then we're right back where we started. We won't have lost a thing." Kara's eyebrows arched. "But if the plan *works,* we can string them along for months, maybe even years, till we either get tired of acting the part or you meet somebody else and decide to move on."

Laying her hand on his arm she sobered. "I know what's

bothering you. It's deceitful. That part bothers me, too. If our friends were trying to manipulate us like this, we could just tell them off. But Louise and Susan are family. We can't disown them just because they're trying to do us a favor, even when they're wrong.''

Tyler looked down at where her warm hand rested on his forearm. If he wasn't so positive he'd never be able to replace Deanne, he'd never agree to such a bizarre plan. If it worked, however, there could be added benefits that Kara hadn't mentioned. ''Okay. I'll do it. But only because I think it will demonstrate to Louise and everybody else that I am *not* going to change my mind.''

''Ditto.'' Kara extended her hand. ''Shake on it?''

He complied, then quickly released her and stepped back, sliding his fingers into the back pockets of his jeans. ''Okay. You're the brains of this outfit. How do we get started?''

She smoothed the hem of her T-shirt over her hips while she gave her imagination free rein. ''Well, you could always kiss me and then I could slap your face.''

''Why would I *kiss* you?'' Flushing, he realized his initial astonishment at the suggestion had made him sound too hostile. ''I mean, doesn't that seem too quick?''

She subdued her bruised pride and managed a cynical smile. ''Hmmm. You're right. So why don't we just wing it? We've already decided we're going to have a few lovers' quarrels. I think you'll do just fine at that kind of scene without a script.''

Tyler didn't miss the extra dollop of cloying sweetness in her voice—or the smug look on her face. ''Cute. Sounds to me like you won't need one, either.''

''See? You're starting to appreciate my quick wit already. Come on.'' Kara started back to the house. ''I'll go in the kitchen door. You'd better wait a few minutes and use the front so we don't look like we're together.''

''I thought that was the idea.''

''Not yet. That's too easy. They'll never buy it if we give in too willingly.''

He slowed his pace. "Okay. I suppose you're right. You go on back. I'll follow in a few minutes."

"Right." Suddenly nervous, she paused and smoothed her pale-blue top again. "Do I look okay?"

He wanted to tell her she looked wonderful. The shirt fit her nicely, without being too tight the way some women wore them, and her jeans were so right for her they may as well have been tailored to her precise measurements.

"You'll do," he said dryly. "You're not auditioning for *Macbeth,* you know."

Kara giggled. "I feel like it."

"Scared?" Tyler stepped closer to speak in confidence. They were barely fifty feet from Mark and Susan's. The sun was low in the west, the ranch as quiet as it ever got, and he didn't want their conversation accidentally overheard.

"A little," she said softly. "I know it's crazy but it really bothers me to think of deceiving Susan. She's always there for me when I need her. I love her a lot."

"We don't have to go ahead with this, you know. It's not too late to change your mind." Stepping closer, Tyler waited for her final decision.

Kara's words were so soft he could barely hear them. He rested his hands lightly on her shoulders and leaned down, inclining his head to one side. "What did you say?"

She was about to repeat, "I know," when she saw a flash of movement past Tyler's shoulder. It was Mark. And he was staring right at them!

Before Kara could warn Tyler or step away from him, Mark let out a hoot of surprise, then bolted for the house.

Tyler spun around. "What was that?"

"I think it was the opening of act I, scene 1," she said, her heart racing, her cheeks turning crimson. "My brother-in-law just caught us out behind the barn."

Mark shot through the door and shouted, "Hey! You won't believe what I just saw!"

Susan and Louise froze where they stood. Susan finally found her voice enough to ask, "What?"

''Kara and Tyler.''

''So?''

''Together!'' he added, pointing. ''Out there.''

''Were they killing each other?'' Susan was rapidly drying her hands, preparing to go to Kara's rescue.

Mark snickered. ''That sure wasn't what it looked like to me. I didn't stand around and stare but I'd swear they were pretty friendly.''

Louise let out the breath she'd been holding. ''Whew. That's a relief.''

''I'll believe it when I see it.'' Susan was already headed for the door. She grabbed a handful of her husband's shirt in passing and tugged him along behind. ''Show me.''

Tyler was having trouble dealing with the unacceptable awareness he'd felt when he'd made the mistake of innocently touching Kara's shoulders. He told himself he should have already learned the folly of doing anything like that. It had happened for the first time when she'd asked him to hold back her hair while she'd doctored the pup's leg. This time was worse. This time, he'd had no reasonable excuse for his actions.

''What do we do now?'' Kara whispered.

''Don't ask me. I suppose we could claim we were quarreling, like we'd planned.''

''Even *I* wouldn't believe that one, and this story is my invention.''

''Well, what then?''

She pulled a face. ''I don't know. Maybe we can—''

Just then, Tyler saw everyone else rush out of the house. Mark was pointing.

''Go to Plan B.'' Tyler finished her sentence with a self-deprecating smirk, grabbed Kara and pulled her into a full embrace. As he bent to kiss her, he whispered a warning against her lips. ''Hang on. This won't hurt a bit.''

The moment he took her in his arms, Kara's brain curled

into a useless knot and ceased rational function. The touch of his lips only added to the turmoil. She wrapped her arms around Tyler's neck and held tight as he lifted her off the ground. If this was his idea of a make-believe kiss, she was glad he'd never give her a real one! It might be so wonderful she'd die from its sweetness.

Tyler released her almost immediately, although it seemed as if eons had passed while their lips were pressed together. Guilt assailed him. He'd pledged himself to Deanne for eternity, yet he'd savored the taste, the touch of Kara's kiss. That was wrong. It had to be.

He started to back off.

Kara blinked repeatedly, trying to focus her thoughts. She wasn't scared. She wasn't anything. Her brain was drawing a complete blank, leaving her feeling about as resourceful as a bowl of cold, week-old grits.

When Tyler looked down at her and gazed silently into her eyes, she could hardly breathe. "What—what did you do *that* for?"

"We have an audience. Plan B. Remember?"

Kara remembered all right. She also remembered exactly what she was supposed to do in return. "Well, you started it," she muttered. "I guess I can finish it."

Drawing back, she slapped his face so hard her palm stung, spun on her heel and stalked away.

Chapter Six

Kara stormed past her openmouthed sister and the others and reentered the kitchen, slamming the screen door behind her. If the idiotic plan to pretend she was interested in Tyler hadn't been her own, she'd have had someone else to blame. But there was no way to disclaim accountability. There was nothing left to do but try to carry out the entire plan.

Susan and Louise followed her inside a few minutes later. Kara's cheeks were still flaming, her eyes flashing, when she whirled to face the other women and peered past them. "Where's Mark?"

"Outside, attacking the grill so we can roast the corn," Susan said simply.

"And Mr. Corbett?"

"Outside." Susan half smiled. "Or were you asking if Mark was attacking him, too?"

"Very funny." Kara didn't have to act the part of a flustered woman. She was truly upset about what had just occurred between her and Tyler. The worst part was she could still feel the touch of his lips, still sense his nearness, still taste his kiss.

"Actually, I thought it *was* pretty funny," Susan replied. "You should have seen the look on your face afterward."

"I don't want to discuss it. And I don't appreciate what you tried to do tonight." She focused on her sister. "I'm never going to be able to trust you again."

Susan held up her hands in mock surrender. "Hey. I didn't tell him to kiss you. And I certainly didn't make you kiss him back." She chuckled quietly and smiled over at Louise. "It didn't look to me like Kara minded much. Did it to you?"

"No, I can't say it did," Louise drawled. "As a matter of fact, I'm not sure Tyler started it. It seemed to me that Kara was as much a party to what took place as he was."

"I was not!"

Susan cocked her head quizzically as she asked, "Do you mean to tell us the man knocked you out and dragged you off behind the barn so he could ravish you?"

"No. Of course not." Resolute, Kara faced her sister, hands on her hips, jaw clenched.

"So, you went with him all by yourself, right?"

"Yes, but..."

"Aha. I thought so. I couldn't see you letting any man take advantage of you, if you didn't want him to."

That's true, now that Alex is gone, Kara thought. I am much stronger willed than I used to be. She refused to be swayed. "We were just talking. That's all."

"About what?"

The knowing look in Susan's eyes told Kara her ruse was working, in spite of the plan getting off to a rocky start. She supposed that was better than failure, even though it had meant she'd learned something disturbing about herself. And about her vulnerability...or what was left of it.

Whether she liked it or not, she was attracted to Tyler Corbett, at least on a physical level. Of course, she'd never let him guess that was the case. Their scheme would still work. All she had to do was keep him from demonstrating any more of his romantic tendencies and all would be well.

Kara let herself smile as if she were hiding a delicious secret, then said, "Tyler and I were talking. That's all you need to know, nosy."

A triumphant expression bloomed on Susan's face. She glanced over at Louise, clearly pleased with herself.

Kara's troubled conscience did a back flip and landed as a

heavy lump of guilt in her chest. She averted her gaze. There were two ways to get her meddlesome yet devoted sister to leave her love life alone. One was the way she'd chosen; a sham romance with a man who could be trusted to keep a confidence and not misunderstand her motives. The second was to reveal the truth about her horrible marriage to Alex so Susan would understand why choosing another husband was not something Kara would ever consider.

In any fair contest the truth should prevail, she knew. And maybe someday she'd find the courage to confide in her sister. But not now. Not yet.

The urge to unburden herself faded. Forcing a smile, Kara reached for a paring knife. "Okay. Let's get back to work, here. Which do you want me to fix, the green salad or the potatoes?"

Without speaking, Tyler followed Mark to the patio and watched him light the barbecue grill. He felt like he ought to say something—anything—that would explain why he'd been kissing Kara. He snorted in self-derision. If *he* knew why he'd done it, he'd have a lot better chance of explaining the whole thing to someone else.

It had been a spur-of-the-moment decision. One he'd been regretting ever since he'd acted upon it. In retrospect, he realized he'd gathered her so close he'd even lifted her feet off the ground. Considering how short she was compared to Deanne, he supposed his reactions had been instinctive. *And stupid,* he added. What must poor Kara think of him?

His hand lifted to touch his still-tingling cheek. *Poor Kara, indeed.* For a little gal she sure packed a big wallop.

Mark was watching him and chuckling softly. "Sorry. If I'd known you were going to try to kiss my sister-in-law, I'd have warned you. She's not the most approachable woman in the world."

"No kidding." Tyler shook his head, remembering. "I don't think I'll try that again."

"Oh, I wouldn't give up on her too soon. She's one smart

lady. Once she sees you're not just stringing her along, she should come around." He paused, studying Tyler. "I'd hate to be the guy who messes up her life, though."

"Why? Do you think she'd deck him?"

"No," Mark said soberly. "But I'd have to."

It was crowded in the dining room when everyone gathered around the small, oak table for dinner.

Kara had judiciously avoided making eye contact with Tyler when he and Mark had come inside bearing their contributions to the meal, hot off the grill.

She'd already made up her mind she was *not* going to sit next to Tyler. Thankfully, he seemed bent on sidestepping any additional contact with her, too.

Planning ahead, Kara put her newly filled iced tea glass by the place setting between Louise's and Susan's. Then she waited for one or the other of them to try to maneuver her next to Tyler, instead. Neither did.

With a relieved sigh and prayerful thanks to her heavenly Father for the respite, she plopped into her chair, exhausted. It seemed to take a lot more energy to carry on a charade than it did to simply live one's life in a forthright manner. At least that was the way it worked for her. She wondered absently if Tyler'd felt the same weariness after he'd kissed her.

The thought of that kiss, *his* kiss, instantly made her heart rate speed up, her hands tremble. Kara held motionless for a moment, then chanced a look at the others. Did her embarrassing reaction to her errant thoughts show? Was she making a worse fool of herself than she already had?

Thankfully, no one was paying the least attention to her. Mark was carving the roast while he and Louise discussed the merits of rotisserie cooking. Susan was emerging from the kitchen with a bottle of barbecue sauce in answer to Mark's request for his favorite condiment. That left only Tyler.

Kara's glance rested on him for mere seconds but it was enough to make him aware of her scrutiny. He turned and stared back across the table without hesitation. His dark eyes searched hers, issued a clear challenge. Then, he slowly began to smile with satisfaction. ''Yes, Kara?''

Kara felt like her whole body had melted. She was a chocolate bar left on the dash of a car; a waxy crayon liquefied by the summer sun; a wildflower, wilted by a sizzling July without rain. As Tyler's grin spread, so did her sense of befuddlement.

She couldn't speak. Couldn't think. Could hardly draw an even breath. Dear Lord, what was the matter with her? Why did everything about Tyler Corbett suddenly seem to thrill her? Why did she keep thinking about running her fingers through his thick, dark hair? Why were his eyes so beguiling? What made the sound of his voice so captivating? And that killer smile! *Oh, dear.*

Kara swallowed the lump in her throat. ''I—I was just wondering...'' *What? Say something! Anything.* She finally managed to stammer, ''...how...Road Kill was doing.''

''Great. He gets around on three legs as well as Buster does on four. I was kind of surprised you didn't ask about him when you first got here.''

She made a pouting face. ''I had other things on my mind, thanks to my sneaky sister.''

''Yeah, well...'' Tyler continued to grin over at her as he rubbed his right cheek with a melodramatic flair. ''Whatever you say.''

She did a quick flashback to their scene behind the barn and realized he was purposely hassling her. That helped strengthen what little was left of her self-assurance. ''If you're going for the sympathy vote, Corbett, I suggest you get your facts straight. I slapped you on the other side.''

''Are you sure?''

''Positive.''

''Oh. Well, then...'' Switching hands, he concentrated on the left side of his face. ''Hey. You're right. This is the one that hurts.''

''So glad I could help,'' Kara said, her words mocking.

Susan interrupted. ''Okay, you two. Enough already. Let's

eat, shall we?'' She bowed her head and folded her hands in her lap. ''Mark, would you please say grace?''

As Mark began to pray, Kara chanced a peek at Tyler through her lowered lashes.

He was looking back at her the same way.

Kara didn't think the meal would ever end. She'd picked at her food and pushed it around on her plate until it was cold, eating very little. Tyler, on the other hand, seemed famished. She watched him surreptitiously, wondering how anyone could eat when there was such an undercurrent of tension in the room. When Susan got up to clear away the dishes from the main course, she jumped to help her, just as she always had. So did Louise.

''Mark and I can handle this,'' Susan said with a bright smile. ''The rest of you just sit there and relax. I made fruit compotes for dessert.'' She cocked her head at her husband. ''Come on, dear. You can help me carry everything.''

As Mark and Susan left the room, Louise settled back down in her chair and urged Kara to do the same. ''Let your sister play the hostess,'' she counseled. ''After all, she is entertaining her husband's boss.'' She cast a motherly look of affection across the table. ''Besides, I want you to tell me all about this dog you call Road Kill.''

''Tyler rescued him,'' Kara said. ''That's really all there is to tell.'' She thought back to the rainy night she'd answered the door to the animal hospital and found the handsome Good Samaritan standing there, cradling the injured puppy inside his coat. The vision brought a temporary lump to her throat. She swallowed hard. ''It was pretty terrific of him to stop to help a dog that wasn't even his.''

''He's always done things like that, even when he was little,'' Louise said.

That surprised Kara. ''You knew him then?''

''Oh, yes. Our families were neighbors. His mother and I were so close he sometimes forgot himself and called me mama, too.''

Touched, Kara decided not to comment.

"Tyler used to bring home all kinds of mangled creatures when he was a boy," Louise continued. "I remember one time he found a butterfly with a torn wing in my yard and wanted me to tape the wing to make it better. When I couldn't, he cried all the way home."

"Louise!" Tyler glowered at her.

"Well, you did."

"I don't doubt it," he said. "I just don't think we need to discuss what I was like as a kid."

Kara smiled warmly at Louise and ignored Tyler's outburst. "I think it's sweet. I haven't thought of this in years, but I had a butterfly collection when I was about seven or eight. It was beautiful. Then, one day, I felt sorry about killing the butterflies. I didn't know that most of them only live a few days, anyway. So I held a private funeral and buried the whole box in the backyard."

"And now you save animals' lives," the older woman added. "How wonderful."

"I try."

"I understand your husband was also a veterinarian."

Kara cringed internally. Obviously, Tyler hadn't told Louise about his feud with Alex. Silence hung in the room like morning mist over the Spring River. She fidgeted.

Louise reached out and touched her arm. "I'm sorry, dear. I didn't mean to upset you."

"You didn't. I'm fine. Really." She purposely changed the subject. "You should drop by Tyler's to see how cute Roady is before you leave the ranch."

"Oh, good," Louise said, beaming. "I'd love it. We can go together and you can give the puppy your professional attention while I fuss over him."

Kara withdrew. "Oh, I don't think..."

"Nonsense." Louise was patting her hand and smiling triumphantly. "I'm sure you'd like to look in on him. And if we're both there, you won't have to worry about my son-in-law getting out of line again, either."

Eyes wide with surprise, Kara glanced over at Tyler. The look of astonishment on his face was ludicrous enough to make her laugh aloud and turn back to Louise to say, "Thanks. I hadn't thought of it quite like that."

Tyler grumbled unintelligibly.

Kara could tell he was getting so aggravated he might bolt. She didn't want Susan's dinner party to be ruined, so she leaned closer to Louise and spoke aside, pretending to share a confidence but making sure her voice was loud enough to be heard across the table. "It was a surprise when he kissed me, but it wasn't all that bad, considering." She paused, then added, "I suppose I shouldn't have slapped him. It was just a reflex."

Tyler broke in. "Not all that bad? Hey, thanks."

"You're quite welcome." Kara barely managed to keep a straight face. "I do apologize for clobbering you."

Acting sullen, he rubbed his cheek again. "You should."

That melodramatic act was all Kara's overloaded emotions could take, given the fact that she'd been as edgy as a lone cat at a dog show ever since he'd arrived. She lost control and burst into laughter.

As soon as she could catch her breath enough to speak, she said, "How many times do I have to tell you, Tyler? It was the *other* side I slapped!"

By unanimous consent, everyone had retired to the patio to enjoy the evening breeze while they shared pleasant, after-dinner conversation.

Kara noticed that Tyler couldn't seem to sit still.

Finally, he got to his feet and excused himself. "Thanks again for the fine meal, Susan, Mark. I really have to be going. Morning comes early on a ranch, even on Sunday." He swatted at a mosquito that was homing in on his arm. "Besides, I'm about to be eaten alive."

"Me, too," Louise said. "Come on, Kara, dear. Let's walk him home and look in on that puppy of yours."

"Oh, he's not mine." She hung back.

Tyler shook his head and muttered with disdain. ''You might as well give in and do what Louise says. Believe me, she's not going to be satisfied until you do. I know. I used to be married to the younger version of her. Dee was a wonderful person but she did inherit a stubborn streak.''

That was the first time Kara had heard him say anything about his late wife that was even remotely critical. Usually, he praised her as if she'd been ideal. Perhaps she had been. Deanne Corbett had already been ill the few times Kara had seen her, so there was no telling what the woman had really been like.

Deciding it was prudent to use Louise as a neutral third party, as she'd suggested earlier, Kara looked to her sister. ''I'll go check the pup, then come back and help you straighten up.''

Susan's, ''Fine. Take your time,'' made Kara grimace. She fell into step beside Louise. More time with Tyler was *not* what she needed. Time *away* from him, however, sounded like a really good idea.

He'd started home without waiting for anyone. Watching his broad back, his athletic walk, Kara wished the night were darker so she couldn't see him; so she wouldn't have to struggle to keep from appreciating the way he looked, the way he moved.

Searching her heart, she sensed that there was more to her current perplexity than merely a superficial temptation. For some unknown reason she cared about Tyler; how he felt, how he thought, what he did. And how he hurt for his loss.

That was the crux of it. It had to be. Because they had both lost mates she was feeling unduly sympathetic toward him. Was he having the same kind of reaction to her? she wondered. Sometimes it seemed that way. At other times, well...Tyler Corbett was an enigma.

Kara huffed in self-derision. Tyler wasn't unique in that respect. *All* men were confusing to her. They always had been. If she'd known how to understand them in the first place, she'd never have been fooled into thinking she was in love and married Alex.

She slowed her pace to match the older woman's and watched Tyler turn the corner by the barn and disappear from their sight.

"I've been wanting to talk to you, alone," Louise said.

They stopped walking. In the moon's light Kara could see lines of worry shadowing the older woman's face. She reached out to her. "Are you okay?"

"I'm fine. It's Tyler I'm concerned about. He's practically been a recluse since my daughter's illness. When I saw him kissing you, it was like a miracle. My prayers were answered."

"Sometimes things are not what they seem," Kara cautioned. She thought about how hard she'd prayed that Alex would ask her to marry him. When he finally did propose, she'd been certain it was because of divine intervention. How wrong she'd been! That thought made her add, "And sometimes it's best if the Lord refuses to give us what we ask for."

Tears glistened in Louise's eyes. "I know. The hardest part for me is always letting go and leaving it up to God to decide what's best for those I love."

Kara took her hand. It was trembling. "I'm so sorry about your daughter."

"She did love Tyler," Louise whispered, "but she wouldn't have wanted him to brood. He needs to find love again. To know that God's looking out for him, guiding him to accept what's been and to look forward to what can be." She squeezed Kara's fingers. "Give him a chance to do that?"

Once again, Kara's conscience reared up to sit atop her heart. "I'd never purposely hurt anyone," she said sincerely. "But I can't promise you anything else."

"That's quite enough, dear. I'm sure God will handle the rest His way, when the time is right. He always does."

Kara knew she should stop rehashing the past and agree completely, yet she kept thinking of all the mistakes she'd made. Had the Lord actually sanctioned her marriage to Alex?

Or had He merely permitted it because she'd strayed from the path she should have followed? Probably the latter, she reasoned. If she'd gone against God's will, the problems that resulted were her own fault.

So what about now? What about Tyler? Was she merely dealing logically with a frustrating situation or was she playing with fire? The smartest course would be to call off the whole charade and eliminate the danger of…

Of what? Tyler Corbett posed no threat to anyone, least of all her. He might have a grumpy side but he could also be a funny, entertaining companion. The next prospective suitor Susan dredged up for her might be far harder to deal with. He also might have a different agenda with regard to romance. At least Tyler wasn't actually courting her.

She sighed. She'd wanted a perfect way to deter her sister's matchmaking efforts and that was *exactly* what she'd found. A man who wasn't interested in making a serious commitment was the answer to a prayer. The ideal solution.

So why did she feel so uneasy?

Chapter Seven

Road Kill hobbled to the door, barking, when Kara and Louise stepped onto the ranch house porch.

Kara spoke to him through the screen door. "Hello, boy. Remember me?" She was instantly rewarded when he stopped yapping at her and began wriggling all over with delight.

Louise laughed. "I'd say he remembers you. Look at that! I've never seen a dog wag his tail in a circle."

"He's just full of new tricks," Tyler called from inside. "Let yourselves in. I'm busy picking up the trash that idiot dog scattered all over the kitchen."

"Oh, dear." Louise pulled open the screen door. "I suppose we'd better go help him before he boots our little friend out on his fuzzy ear."

"Or worse." Lifting the pup gently, Kara looked him over as she followed the older woman through the house. "Except for some mustard on his cast, he seems to be fine. I hope he didn't eat anything bad for him."

Her eyes widened as she entered the kitchen behind Louise. There was shredded paper and assorted household trash spread from one end of the room to the other, beginning at an upended plastic receptacle that lay on its side by the end of the beige, tile-topped counter. Beneath the clutter, the floor was speckled with a delightful array of color. Unfortunately, it looked like the flooring was supposed to be plain off-white, or some similar hue.

Kara held tight to the little brown pup and stifled a giggle. Crouched in the middle of the floor, Tyler was stuffing handfuls of paper into a black plastic trash bag. Seeing that his master had joined the game, Road Kill squirmed and whined to be put down.

"Oh, no, you don't," Kara warned. "It wouldn't be a very good idea to try to play with your daddy right now."

Tyler mumbled a curse. At least Kara thought he did. She decided it was best not to ask for clarification. Instead, she said, "Uh, can I help?"

He looked up at her, scowling. The frown deepened when he saw the mischievous dog in her arms. "Yes. You can take that poor excuse for a pet with you and leave me in peace."

"I meant, can I help you clean up the mess?" She held the puppy to her and stroked the soft fur on his head. "It's not Roady's fault you didn't have sense enough to put the trash can where he couldn't get to it." She had a further thought. "Besides, how do you know Buster didn't do this?"

"He never has before," Tyler countered. "Why should he start now?"

"Maybe because he has a rival in the house." Kara glanced around the room, assessing the damage. Empty food cans lay in a loosely made group beneath the round dining table; the kind of group a retriever might instinctively make. "Where is Buster, anyway? I didn't see him on the couch when we came in." She leaned down to get a better look under the table. "Aha!"

Tyler pivoted. "Now what?"

"Oh, nothing. I just happened to notice a big yellow dog hiding over there." She pointed. "He looks pretty guilty to me. Of course, he can't be Buster because your wonderful dog would never get into any trouble."

"Well, I'll be." Tyler's jaw dropped. There lay his paragon of canine virtue with an empty dog food can trapped between his paws. Telltale bits of gravy painted a stripe across the top of his nose from where he'd tried to stick his whole muzzle into the can while he licked it clean.

Amused, Kara couldn't resist adding to her earlier comments. "I told you one little dog couldn't have made this big a mess. He's not tall enough to have dumped the trash bin over by himself, either…not to mention having one leg in a cast." She ruffled the puppy's pendulous ears and it licked at her hand. "Daddy didn't mean it, Roady. He's not mad, anymore. Honest, he's not."

"Daddy?" Louise said with a giggle. "Oh, my." She crossed to the enclosed back porch. "I'll go fetch a broom, two if I can find them, and a dustpan. Don't do anything rash while I'm gone."

Kara was surprised that no physical effort was necessary to coax Buster out from under the table. Tyler merely drawled, "Buster…" in an authoritarian voice and the old dog crept over to him, then rolled on his back in submission.

With a sigh, Tyler gave in and scratched the dog's tummy, speaking to him as if he could understand every word. "You, my old friend, are in serious trouble." He pointed to the nearest remaining refuse. "See this? You know better than to dig in the garbage. What's the matter with you, anyway? You getting senile?" He glanced up at Kara. "*Can* dogs get senile?"

"They can lose some of their sharpness," she said, smiling down at the touching scene taking place in the middle of the messy floor. "I don't see that as Buster's problem, though. I think the opposite may be true."

"Explain." Tyler straightened and brushed himself off.

"I think he may be feeling more like a pup, again, because of having Road Kill around. I'll bet they had a wonderful time ripping all this tasty stuff to shreds. I wish I could have been here to see it."

"You mean to stop it, don't you?"

"Well…no." Kara's grin widened. "I think I'd probably have let them have their fun for a little while, as long as I was sure they couldn't hurt themselves."

"That figures."

She didn't like the snide expression on his face and she said so. "Stop looking at me like that."

"Like what?"

"Like *that,*" she said, pointing at him.

Tyler knew he shouldn't encourage her, especially since he'd already been dumb enough to kiss her, but the natural comedy inherent in the situation got the better of him. Instead of remaining his usual aloof and dignified self, he said, "You mean like this?" then scrunched up his face, crossed his eyes, and purposely played the fool.

He heard a strangled gasp. Louise was standing in the doorway, broom in hand, staring at him as if he were demented. Then, she broke into gales of laughter. So did Kara.

Tyler's face reddened. What in the world had made him act like that? He certainly wasn't in the habit of making faces at pretty women. The thought deepened his color. Kara *was* pretty, in a natural sort of way. He just wasn't happy that he'd noticed.

He relieved Louise of the cleaning supplies. "If you two are through having fun, I suggest we get this mess cleaned up before it sets. I'll sweep and Kara can scoop." Raising an eyebrow he passed Kara the dustpan, fully expecting an argument. He didn't get one.

"Fine." She handed the wriggly puppy to Louise. "If you don't mind, I'd appreciate having his cast washed off so he doesn't start chewing on it. It's not like the old plaster ones. You can get it wet. Just try not to get any water inside, next to his skin."

Louise looked back and forth between the other two, like a spectator at a tennis match, then nodded. "Okay. We'll be in the bathroom if you need anything else. Come on, Buster. You could use a sponging off, too." Head hanging, the old dog followed at her heels.

Once they were alone, Kara faced Tyler and gave him a furtive smile. "Well, I think we did it."

"Did what?"

''Fooled everybody. Didn't you see the way Louise looked at us just now? She's sure we're hiding something.''

''We are,'' Tyler replied. His ingrained defenses sprang into play. ''We can't stand each other.''

''If you insist.''

She'd immediately looked away but he could tell he'd hurt her feelings. Her voice had lost its elation and there was a definite hint of dejection in her posture. Tyler flinched. Like it or not, he cared that he was the cause of her unhappiness.

''I didn't mean it that way,'' he alibied gruffly. ''It just slipped out. Force of habit, I guess.''

Kara was about to smile at him and offer forgiveness when he added, ''You're not so bad.''

She let her sarcastic tone convey far more than her words as she smiled sweetly and said, ''Wow. Thanks a bunch, Mr. Corbett. That's the nicest compliment anybody's given me for ages.''

''I can't win with you, can I?'' His brows knit.

''I didn't know we were having a contest,'' Kara snapped back. ''And stop glaring at me. You look like you'd love to use that broom to sweep me right out the door.''

''Don't tempt me.''

She faced him squarely, her hands on her hips, and scoffed, ''Take your best shot, mister. I was married to Alex Shepherd. After that, *nothing* fazes me.''

It was the surprised, shocked look on Tyler's face that made her realize how revealing her statement had been. She hadn't meant to disclose so much, especially not to him. It had slipped out. Denial or explanation, at this point, would only make things worse. The best choice was to try a distraction.

Kara thrust the dustpan at him. ''Here. You finish getting the worst of it off the floor and I'll mop up the sticky stuff.'' When he made no move to follow her orders, she added, ''The other option is for me to forget about helping and go on home. I would, except I figure I owe you. So, what'll it be?''

''The mop is in the tall cupboard over there. So's the bucket.'' He pointed. ''Soap is on the shelf above.''

She wasted no time. Jerking open the cupboard door she grabbed the mop and bucket, then looked up at the shelf. The soap was there, all right. It was also far too high for her to reach unless she stood on a stool. Having none, she dragged a chair from the dining table and climbed up on it.

Tyler'd had his back turned while he repacked the plastic trash receptacle. He turned in time to see Kara balanced precariously on the chair. ''What do you think you're doing?''

''Getting the soap. I'm too short to reach it.''

He started across the room. ''Why didn't you say so? I'll help you.''

''No need. I'm used to coping,'' she answered, straining to grab the large box of powdered detergent.

At that moment, Tyler reached the chair. In his haste he didn't notice a spot of grease on the slick floor. He slipped. One foot shot out behind him. Momentum slammed him into the backs of Kara's knees.

Her legs buckled. She flailed her arms. The soap powder went up in the air, then rained down on them like winter's first snow.

With a screech, she grabbed the edge of the shelf to stop her fall. Her heart was pounding, her breathing ragged. She was about to confront Tyler and lecture him about safety when the third member of their cleanup crew ran back into the room, accompanied by both dogs.

Louise's mouth dropped open when she saw what was going on. Tyler's arms were outstretched as if he were about to grab Kara around the middle and jerk her off the chair. Kara's eyes were wide with surprise. Louise found her voice enough to squeak, ''What in the world are you two doing?''

Kara realized how the situation must look. She giggled. ''Would you believe, getting the soap to mop the floor?''

''Not for a minute,'' the older woman retorted.

Kara had quickly finished mopping the floor, bid Tyler and Louise good-night, and stopped back at Susan's, as promised. The lights were still on so she knocked.

"Come on in," Susan called. She was drying her hands. "You waited just long enough. The dishes are all done and Mark's gone to bed."

"Hey, great." Kara gave her sister a hug. "I always was pretty good at timing my entrance."

"No kidding. Want a midnight snack?"

"It can't be that late!"

Susan chuckled amiably. "Not quite. Is there some rule that it has to actually be twelve o'clock before you can have a *midnight* snack?" Not waiting for a reply, she retrieved what was left of the roast and set the platter on the table.

"I don't think so." Kara got herself a cold soda, plunked down in the chair next to her sister, and picked a sliver of the tender meat to nibble. "This tastes good. Guess I am hungry."

"That makes sense. You didn't eat any dinner."

"I did so."

"Only if pushing it around on your plate counts. But I can understand your problem. It's hard to concentrate on eating and make eyes at Tyler at the same time."

"I did not make eyes at him!" Amazed, Kara stared at Susan. "What makes you think I did?"

"Personal observation," Susan said with a knowing smile. "And it's about time, too. You've been grieving for far too long." She reached to give Kara's hand a reassuring pat. "I know that different people handle loss at different speeds, but it hurts me to see you going on and on alone. I know you can find the same kind of happiness you had with Alex if you'll just open your eyes and look for it."

Kara's throat constricted. She began to cough.

Susan leaned closer and patted her on the back. "Are you okay? Did you choke on your soda?"

"No...I don't know," Kara managed between coughing spasms. Finally she settled down, breathless, and wiped tears from her eyes. Weariness loosened her tongue. She sighed. "I wish you were right about happiness."

"I know I am," Susan insisted. "You'll find somebody else some day. I pray for you all the time."

Kara cleared her throat, then made a sound of pure derision. ''Well, don't ask for another man like Alex when you pray, okay? That's the *last* thing I need.''

''What are you talking about?''

''My wonderful husband,'' Kara said flatly. ''He wasn't.''

''Wasn't what? Wonderful?''

''Bingo. Now you're getting the idea.''

''Nobody's perfect.'' Susan reached out to her again. ''All you have to do is look at the rest of us to know that.''

''Yeah, well…'' Suddenly needing Susan's moral support more than ever before, Kara decided to reveal a few extra details. ''Alex was a fraud.''

''What do you mean?'' Susan was frowning.

''He pretended to be kind and considerate when he was in public but he wasn't like that at all when we were alone.''

''He wasn't?'' The frown deepened. ''Is that why you stopped getting together with your old friends or going to church regularly after you got married?''

''That was part of it. I was naive enough to let Alex pick my friends. He also said he didn't want to associate with all the hypocrites in our church and he didn't want me to go, either. But that was just an excuse to change to a church with more people who could enrich his practice. He was the biggest hypocrite of them all.''

Susan sat back, awed. ''I don't believe this.'' She quickly corrected herself. ''I mean…I *do* believe it, I just don't know why you never said anything before.''

''What would have been the use? I married him for better or for worse. We just never got to the *better* part.''

''Oh, honey…'' Susan leaned forward, her unshed tears glistening. ''I'm so sorry.''

''Yeah. So am I,'' Kara said. She managed a smile. ''But that's all over now, so let's forget it. Okay?''

''If that's the way you want it.''

''It is. I just needed you to understand where I'm coming from.''

Instead of the continued somber outlook she'd expected,

Kara was surprised to hear her sister say, "Actually, it's not where you've been or who's hurt you in the past that concerns me. It's where you're *going* that's important."

There was no way Kara could refute such a basic truth. "You can understand why I'm in no hurry to remarry, though, can't you?"

"Sure. You don't trust the Lord, anymore."

Dumbfounded, Kara stared at her. "I do so."

"Really? Then why isolate yourself the way you have been? If you were trusting God to take care of you, there'd be no reason to hide from life."

"I'm not hiding from anything. I'm just being careful."

Susan was slowly shaking her head. "I don't buy that. I think you've decided that it isn't safe to care about another man so you've shut them all out." The corners of her mouth began to lift. "Well, all except one."

Tyler Corbett. Kara opened her mouth to explain, then decided against it. Telling Susan the truth about Alex had obviously been a mistake. The only way to salvage any privacy from the current situation was to continue with the romance charade, at least for a while. Once Susan settled down and quit trying to find her another husband, she'd be able to back away from the pseudo-relationship with Tyler without undue notice.

It was Kara's intention to sound secretive when she said, "I don't want to talk about Tyler." Instead, her words came out in a rush and she noticed she was breathing rapidly.

One look at Susan's smug expression told her she'd been successful in spite of herself. Clearly, Susan was assuming her baby sister was romantically interested in the enigmatic rancher, which was exactly what she'd wanted. The trouble was that interest was no longer a meaningless fabrication! Like it or not, she *was* interested in him.

Sighing inwardly, Kara shook her head slowly and tried to pull herself together as she searched for some positive element in the shocking self-revelation. It finally came to her. She'd hated the idea of lying to anyone for any reason, especially Susan. Now, she wouldn't be lying.

Disgusted with herself, Kara pulled a face. What kind of progress was *that?*

Chapter Eight

Kara had just about succeeded in putting the preceding weekend out of her mind when Louise unexpectedly showed up at her house.

Greeted by three levels of barking and a tan-and-white greyhound who raced around her car in wide circles, she waved to Kara, parked and got out. "Hi! I can see why your sister warned me to wear my jeans when she gave me driving directions. You have quite a menagerie."

"This is only part of it. The horse and most of the cats are back by the barn." She shouted, "Okay, boys. Go on," and the canine welcoming committee obediently fell back.

"Wow. I'm impressed," Louise said. "What's your secret?"

"They think I'm the Alpha dog," Kara explained. "They respect me so they try to do what I want."

"Oh, I get it. You're the leader of the pack!"

"In a manner of speaking. Come on inside and I'll show you my birds. I always clean house first thing Saturday morning, so the place is fairly neat." She refrained from adding that she'd been so uptight all week that she'd dusted and vacuumed every evening rather than sit still and give herself too much time to think.

Louise followed her up onto the covered wooden porch. "This is lovely. So peaceful and quiet." She glanced at the three dogs who had taken up places on the shady lawn and already looked sleepy. ''Well, most of the time, anyway.''

''It's a lot to take care of,'' Kara told her, ''but I can live here pretty cheaply and the neighbors are far enough away that they don't complain...much.'' She rested her hand on the head of the tall greyhound at her side without having to bend over. ''So, what brings you all the way out here?''

''An errand of mercy,'' Louise said.

Kara hesitated only a moment, then sighed. ''Uh-oh. Sounds serious. I just made a fresh pitcher of lemonade. Would you like some?''

''Yes, please.''

The greyhound waited at the open door for the signal to come in as Louise sidled past. Kara smiled down at him and stepped aside. ''Okay, Speedy. Come on.''

He shot past her and dashed up the hall, only to reappear seconds later, tongue lolling, eyes bright, to leap over the back of the rose-patterned, brocade sofa and circle the carpeted living room at a run.

Louise was clearly amused. ''I can see why you call him Speedy. Does he ever slow down?''

''That is slow, for him. He's a retired racing dog. You should see him go when he wants to. I could never catch him if he didn't want to be caught. Unfortunately, he's discovered there are real rabbits to chase around here so I've started letting him sleep inside to keep him out of mischief.''

Touching the dog's smooth coat as he trotted past, Louise was amazed. ''My, it feels so different. Almost like satin. The hair is so short you can hardly feel it. Doesn't he get cold in the winter?''

''And sunburned in the summer if I'm not careful. That's one more reason for letting him stay inside a lot.''

Kara led the way into the kitchen, then turned to face her guest. ''Okay. Are you going to stop trying to distract me and tell me why you're here, or am I going to have to drag it out of you?''

''Aren't we having lemonade? I'll get the ice.'' Louise

started opening likely cabinets, quickly found what she was looking for, and set two glasses on the counter beside the refrigerator. "It's the least I can do."

"The least you can do after what?" Kara cast a leery glance at the older woman. "You may as well tell me what you have in mind. Worst-case scenario, I say, no."

"Oh, you won't. It's just that I'm not sure how we're going to handle Tyler."

Aha! Now, she was getting to the ticklish part, Kara thought. No wonder she'd seemed so nervous. She waited until Louise had filled the large tumblers with ice and put them on the table before she said, "Well?"

"I just want you to know, Susan had *nothing* to do with what happened. It was all my fault."

Exasperated, Kara put the pitcher of lemonade down so hard it sloshed. "*What* was?"

"Well, I had this big ham bone left over and I thought I was doing a nice thing. I didn't know I shouldn't give it to Road Kill, and…"

"Is he okay? Did he choke on it?"

Louise quickly laid a reassuring hand on her shoulder. "No, nothing like that. He's fine. Well, almost fine, anyway. He loved chewing on the bone. But then Buster took it away from him."

Kara's patience was nearly gone. "Was there a fight? Did Roady get hurt?"

"Goodness no. He just rolled over on his back and surrendered. Only he'd been holding the bone between his front paws and I guess the flavor was still there, so when he didn't have the bone anymore, he started to chew his cast."

"Uh-oh. What did you do then?"

"I tried washing it off, like you'd told me, but that didn't seem to help, so I called Tyler. Boy, was he steamed."

Rather than dwell on thoughts of anger, Kara busied herself filling the glasses while Louise went on with her story. "First, he tried taping up the frayed parts but the whole thing was such a mess the tape didn't stick. Then he got the brilliant idea that if he put hot sauce on it, Road Kill would leave it alone.''

''Oh, no.'' Kara could picture all sorts of results, none of which were desirable. ''Did it work?''

''I suppose it might have if the dog hadn't loved the taste and licked at it so fast.'' She stifled a giggle. ''You should have seen it. One minute, Tyler was positive his plan would work, and the next minute we were both chasing that crazy puppy through the house. We wouldn't have caught him, either, if he hadn't stopped to rub his face on the carpet. What a mess!''

Kara sank into a chair, her fingers pressed to her lips to help stifle her amusement. ''Oh, how funny. Poor Roady. I can see it now!''

Relieved, Louise asked, ''You mean, the stuff won't make him sick?''

''Hot sauce? No. I'm sure he didn't like it, once he realized how spicy it was, but there shouldn't be any lasting harm.'' She did, however, have one other concern. ''What finally became of the cast on his leg?''

''Last I saw of the dog, Tyler had him tucked under his arm and was headed for the barn, talking to himself.''

Thinking of her life with Alex she reacted instinctively and jumped to her feet. ''Tyler wouldn't *hurt* Roady, would he? I mean, I never would have left him there if I'd dreamed anything *bad* would happen.''

''Tyler? Hurt an animal on purpose? Not in a million years. I know that boy as well as I know myself. There's not a mean bone in his body.''

''Oh, thank goodness.'' Kara sagged against the edge of the table. If the same misfortunes had happened to Alex, she'd have been certain someone or something would get hurt.

''I do think Road Kill may need a new cast, though. I don't know how long it was supposed to stay on, but it's only been a couple of weeks, right?'' Looking very apologetic, Louise added, ''I'm really sorry I made such a mess of things and upset you so.''

"You didn't upset me," Kara assured her. "As long as Roady's all right, there's nothing that can't be fixed. I'll go to the office and get things ready. You bring him to me and we'll either patch up the cast he has or fit a new one."

"Oh, dear." Louise's hands started to flutter like two pale butterflies caught in a whirlwind. "Didn't I mention? I just stopped by on my way to my first day on the job." She beamed. "I'm going to be one of those shopper greeters, like you see all the time at Wally-World."

"You're kidding."

"No. Not a bit. I decided I'd been retired too long and needed to get out more, so I applied and they hired me! Isn't that wonderful?"

"Peachy," Kara grumbled. Her mind was churning faster than Speedy had run when he was in his prime. "Okay. Use my phone. Call Tyler and tell him to bring the dog to the hospital. I'll get Susan to meet us there."

"Um…that may pose a problem."

"Why?" Kara was beginning to get a sinking feeling in her stomach, not to mention a doozy of a headache.

"Because I already suggested that," Louise explained. "And he absolutely refused to consider it. Kept saying something about money and honor and…oh, I don't know. It made absolutely no sense to me." She cast a hopeful look at Kara. "I don't suppose you make house calls, do you?"

"Not if I can help it."

"That's what I was afraid of." Louise shrugged. "Oh, well, thanks for the lemonade. I have to be going." She started for the door, then paused. "And don't worry, dear. Tyler's very resourceful. I'm sure he'll find a way to mend the cast and keep Road Kill from chewing off the rest of it."

Kara just stood there. Louise knew very well she couldn't abandon any animal that needed her, even if it meant another trip back to the Corbett ranch and another head-to-head dispute with its owner. There must be another way. By the time she heard Louise's car start and back out the driveway, she was already dialing Susan's number in the hopes she could persuade her to bring the puppy to town instead. No one answered.

Talking to herself, Kara slammed down the receiver. It wasn't Roady's fault he was in trouble. If she didn't give in and go to the ranch to repair the damage Louise's folly had caused, he might lose enough support to rebreak his leg where the bones were starting to knit. She was stuck. Trapped. If only Louise hadn't had to report to work…

Kara's eyes widened. Her lips pressed together into a thin line. Every other time she'd seen Louise Tate, the woman had been dressed impeccably. This morning, however, she'd been wearing blue jeans and a plain blouse. Would she have worn that kind of outfit her first day on a new job? Not likely.

"I've been had," Kara muttered as she began to throw medical supplies into a duffel bag. "If that puppy doesn't really need my help, there are going to be a couple of people who hear exactly what I think about their interference. And that's a fact."

Kara found Tyler alone in the main barn. He still held the puppy in his arms. She burst out, "Oh, thank goodness!" without stopping to consider anything but her own relief.

Scowling, he faced her. Sunlight was streaming through the unshuttered windows and the main door. The brim of his cowboy hat shaded his eyes, making him appear even more gruff than usual. Kara didn't care. She was too elated to give his disposition more than a brief notice.

Tyler raised one dark eyebrow. "I see nothing in this situation to be thankful about, unless you count the fact that you've finally come to collect your useless dog." He tried to pass Road Kill to her.

"Oh, no, you don't." She held up her hands, palms out, to ward him off. "I'm only here because Louise told me the cast needs repair." Peering at it, she leaned a little closer. The dog's whole leg was swathed in so much excess elastic bandage it looked three times its normal size. "What have you done to it?"

"Kept it together with whatever I could find," Tyler said dryly. "I don't dare put him down because the minute I do, he starts ripping it off."

"That figures. He's a smart pup. It only took one experience to teach him he didn't have to put up with bandages if he didn't want to." She smiled proudly. "I knew he was special the first time I saw him."

"I'm so glad you're pleased," Tyler said cynically. "What do you suggest we do about it?"

"We?" Kara's smile widened.

"Yes, we. This is as much your problem as it is mine."

"Oh, I don't know about that. It seems to me that you have possession."

"Only because you forced it on me."

"Well," she drawled, "the way I see it, you can either ask me nicely to repair the cast, or you can hold on to him like that for another four to six weeks, until his leg heals." The astonished expression on Tyler's face made her snicker. "Hey, don't worry. It's a plus. You two will form a much closer emotional bond that way."

"I don't want to bond with this troublemaker. I want to get rid of him just as soon as he's well. Understand?"

"Oh, sure. No problem. So, what'll it be?"

"What will *what* be?" Tyler knew the kind of response Kara was waiting for but he didn't intend to give in unless she forced the issue.

Her smile never faltered. "Okay. I'll spell it out. Do I go home and forget about helping you, or are you going to ask me for my expert assistance?"

Tyler's jaw muscles clenched. "Okay. I'm asking."

"No, no, no. Politely. The way you'd treat anybody else, if you wanted them to do you a favor."

One corner of his mouth twitched, lifted slightly, before he got it back under control. Kara Shepherd was obviously enjoying aggravating him and he couldn't help admiring her spunk. It was an aspect of her personality that seemed to strengthen every time they met, which meant the present situation was unlikely to improve on its own.

He decided to capitulate and get it over with. Tucking Road Kill under one arm, he doffed his hat with a flourish, bowed from the waist, and said with an overly sophisticated air, "My dear madam, would you kindly do me the honor of repairing this flea-bitten excuse for a dog before I toss him out on his ear?" He straightened and put his hat back on, resuming his normal tone of voice. "There. How was that? Polite enough for you?"

Kara laughed gaily. "I guess so. I brought some supplies so we could take care of everything on the spot. Would you like me to work on his leg out here, or shall we go into the house to do it?"

He was about to answer when he noticed a familiar-looking shadow inching across the bare ground in front of the barn door. Louise was trying to sneak up on them to eavesdrop! That gave Tyler an idea. If she hadn't heard all of his prior conversation with Kara, she wouldn't have any idea they were discussing veterinary care instead of something a lot more personal.

Raising one finger to his lips, he whispered, "Shush," and softer, "Louise."

Kara's gaze followed his. Sure enough, they had company. "What now?"

"Watch and learn." He was grinning. Raising his voice and enhancing it with alluring sweetness, he said, "I'd like to do it in the *house,* darlin', if you don't mind."

Blushing, Kara understood the ruse perfectly. Trying not to snicker she made her voice a sultry purr and played along. "No, not at all. I never did like doing it in the barn...even when I was with my husband."

Behind her, Kara heard a sharp intake of breath that ended in a high-pitched squeak. If she hadn't quickly clamped her hand over her mouth she'd have burst into laughter in spite of her temporary embarrassment.

Still in character, Tyler shifted Road Kill to one side,

slipped his other arm around Kara's waist, pulled her close, and ushered her out the barn door toward the house. As they passed the place where his nosy, former mother-in-law hid, he leaned down to place a believable kiss on the top of Kara's head.

The kiss was meant as a prank. A farce. It wasn't until after he'd acted that Tyler realized it didn't feel nearly as much like a joke as he'd thought it would.

Kara cleared the kitchen table, laid a plastic sheet over it, and told Tyler to spread a layer of newspaper on top of that. Placing Road Kill in the center, she began to unwrap his leg while Tyler held him still.

Thoughts of Louise's clumsy attempt at matchmaking wouldn't stop running through Kara's head. After the illusion of flirtation she and Tyler had created she felt like a misbehaving teenager. A fresh blush warmed her cheeks. "I hope we didn't shock poor Louise too much."

"I hope we *did*," Tyler countered. "Her curiosity is getting out of hand. Next thing we know, she and Susan will actually join forces. Then we'll really be in trouble."

Kara finished unwinding the elastic bandage and laid it aside while she concentrated on the tattered cast. "They do seem to think they have to coerce us into seeing each other."

"They sure do." He wished he could let go of the little brown pup and finish this conversation from a safe distance…like maybe Mars! Going across the room or across town definitely wouldn't be far enough. He couldn't believe he'd been so simpleminded, so preoccupied with fooling Louise, that he'd actually kissed the top of Kara's head. What a mistake. Not only had he liked the feel of her silky hair on his lips, it was the first time he'd noticed the clean, floral scent of her shampoo. Worse, he was still close enough to enjoy its lingering fragrance.

Kara looked up at him, studying his expression. "They only feel they have to push us at each other because we haven't done a good enough job of convincing them otherwise."

"I suppose you're going to tell me you have another wonderful plan," Tyler grumbled. "I didn't think much of the last one."

"Oh? And I suppose it was my idea for you to manhandle me and waltz me past Louise just now?"

"That was a spur-of-the-moment decision."

Nodding, Kara agreed. "That's been our problem. We've ad-libbed too often. What we need is a definite script and mutually acceptable rules of conduct."

"You mean make a *list?*" He was incredulous.

"If need be." She turned her attention back to the job at hand and cut away what was left of the cast as she continued to explain. "I think it would be best if we talked it all out and made notes. Then we'll each keep a copy of what we've decided, so we know ahead of time what to do."

"Or what *not* to do."

"Exactly."

Tyler leaned down to look her in the eye. "You're serious, aren't you?"

"Completely. If you have a better idea, I'll be glad to listen to it."

He snorted in self-derision. "I'd rather just tell everybody off and forget it."

"Get serious. Susan's too stubborn to take no for an answer. And Louise is overly sensitive because of losing her daughter." Kara paused. "Sorry."

"It's okay." His voice was purposely empathetic. Maybe she did have a valid point. If they made an agenda and worked out specific guidelines, there'd be no chance of error…like the unforgettable one he'd made when he'd forgotten himself and kissed her. Twice.

Remembering made him decidedly uneasy. "Let's start with a No-kissing rule."

"Fine with me." She refused to look up at him as she spoke. "We'll probably have to hold hands once in a while, though, or nobody will believe we like each other." Waiting, she expected Tyler to respond with, "We don't like each other.'' Instead, he remained quiet, stroking the puppy evenly to keep it calm while she resplinted its leg.

Finally, he said, ''I suppose you're right. Do you mind going that far? Holding hands, I mean.''

Kara was glad he had no clue as to how attractive and appealing she thought he was, especially when he was ministering to the injured puppy. She watched the steady rhythm of Tyler's touch on its short fur and marveled at the gentleness in the man's large, capable hands. Would she mind holding one of those hands? Not hardly. Instead of saying so, however, she alibied. ''I'll muddle through if you will.''

''Good.'' He sighed in quiet resignation. ''Okay. That's settled. What else?''

''I think we should go out to dinner. Somewhere we can talk without being overheard.''

Tyler seemed taken aback. ''Dinner?''

''Dinner. Tonight works for me,'' she said flatly. ''I'll pick you up. If we're going to get the most out of this, we'll need to be seen leaving together. I can't think of a better place for that than right here.''

''I can. Why don't I come to get you at work someday next week? We can make a big deal about it, then.''

''Okay. That'll do.'' Finished with the puppy, Kara washed her hands, dried them on a paper towel, and smiled. ''Tomorrow's Sunday, so we're bound to run into each other anyway.''

Beginning to see what she was getting at, he studied her upturned face. ''You mean…?''

''Of course.'' The complaisant smile widened. ''I'll meet you in church. Save me a seat and we can impress Louise, too.'' She lifted the puppy and held him close, ruffling his droopy ears. ''In the meantime, I'll take our little friend with me and fit him for an Elizabethan collar so he won't be able to reach his leg to chew on it.''

''What about our list?'' Tyler was backing away.

''You make one, I'll make one, and then we'll combine them,'' she said brightly. She eyed the table. ''I put all my instruments back in my bag. You can just roll up that plastic and throw it away. Want me to stay and help you clean up?''

''No.'' He waved her off as if she were a pesky insect. ''No, just go. Go. Leave me in peace. *Please.*''

Giggling, she tossed a mock warning back over her shoulder and headed for the door with the puppy. ''Watch it, Corbett. If I didn't know better, I'd get the idea you didn't like me.''

Chapter Nine

When Kara had finally given up and gone to bed that night, her list of no-nos had begun with, ''No kissing.'' It had ended with, ''No hugging.'' There was nothing else in between.

The more she'd thought about Tyler on a personal level, the worse her dilemma had become. Naturally, she wasn't going to embarrass them both by listing the most obvious things she wouldn't do. He knew what kind of woman she was. And she was certain he was the kind of man who wouldn't press her for unacceptable intimacy. That was one of the main reasons she'd agreed to their mutual deception in the first place. She trusted him. It was that simple.

The rest of her feelings, however, were much more complicated. By dawn Sunday morning she'd developed a sizable tension headache. What she'd wanted to do was pull the covers up over her head and pretend it wasn't time to get ready for church. What she'd done instead was choose the most attractive dress in her closet, put on light makeup, and head for town to keep her promise.

The old stone church sat atop a rise, giving it a heavenly quality when viewed from the base of the hill. Folks parked all the way around it. Kara pulled into her usual spot. She'd often heard it said that the pickup truck was the official vehicle of Arkansas. Church parking lots helped confirm that idea. There were at least as many trucks as there were cars, and a lot of the people who drove cars on Sunday had a truck at home, as well.

Kara gathered her bible and purse and hurried into church before she could change her mind. Pausing in the rear of the sanctuary she scanned the backs of the parishioners who were already seated. It was easy to spot Tyler. Dark-haired and taller than half the men present, he was sitting in almost the same spot he'd occupied the week before.

Kara smoothed her softly draped, sea-foam-green dress, gathered her courage, and was just about to start down the aisle to join him when she felt a tap on her shoulder. As usual, she jumped. As usual, it was her sister.

"Morning, kiddo," Susan said brightly. Her husband, Mark, came up behind her. She gifted him with a loving smile and took his hand. "We swung by your place on our way, to offer you a ride, but you'd already left."

Kara could feel her pulse pounding in her temples. She pressed her fingertips to the sides of her throbbing head and took a deep breath. "Thanks, anyway."

"Hey, are you all right?" Susan leaned closer to study her sibling's expression. "You look kind of spaced out."

"I have a terrible headache."

"I wondered why you wore your hair down, today. Too much weekend?" Susan probed.

Kara could hardly tell her the whole truth. "Too much everything. I've thought so hard lately, my brain hurts."

"I'll bet you have. I noticed your truck parked out at the ranch yesterday."

Kara's head snapped up. She looked quickly from Susan to Mark and back again. "You did?"

"I did. And I'm a little miffed that you didn't stop by my house to say hi while you were out there."

"I didn't think you were home," Kara alibied. In truth, once she'd clashed with Tyler and they'd outwitted Louise, she'd been so befuddled she'd forgotten her sister even lived there. "I did try to phone you earlier. Nobody answered."

"I went to have my hair done in the afternoon." Susan

patted the smooth curve of the cut at the nape of her neck. ''What was it you wanted?''

''I thought you could bring Roady to the office so I could fix his broken leg.''

Instantly concerned, Susan forgot all about her new hairdo. ''The same leg? What happened? Where is he now?''

Kara sighed again. ''Resting in an inside run at the hospital. It's a long story. I'll fill you in, later.''

''Good,'' Susan said. ''Right now, we'd better go grab some seats or we won't find three together.''

This was it. The first well-planned step. Suddenly as nervous as if she were about to act the lead role in a Broadway play, Kara managed to smile sweetly. Starting to walk away, she said, ''You don't have to worry about me. Someone else is already saving me a place.''

''Oh, yeah? Who?''

Susan's question was nearly drowned out by the thudding of Kara's heart. The rapid beat echoed in her ears, drummed in her temples, and ricocheted off her rib cage like a pair of rubber-soled sneakers trapped in a whirling clothes dryer.

By the time she reached the pew where Tyler sat she was getting pretty woozy. That was when she realized she'd been holding her breath!

He stood and stepped into the aisle, politely taking her elbow to guide her. ''Are you all right?''

''You're the second person who's asked me that this morning. I'm beginning to get the idea I look bad.''

''No, no. You look...'' He wanted to say, *absolutely beautiful,* but thought better of it. ''Fine. You look just fine.''

She cast him a disbelieving glance. ''Would you be willing to swear to that?''

''I never swear,'' he countered with a wry smile. ''Especially not in church.''

Kara nodded a greeting to the woman on her left as she sat down, then turned back to Tyler with a questioning scowl. ''Where's Louise?''

''Visiting her sister. The one in Batesville, I think.'' He

lowered his voice. ''Don't look at me like that. How was I supposed to know she was going to take off?''

''Does she do that kind of thing often?''

''Not often enough,'' he said. ''When Deanne got so sick, Louise started acting like my shadow—and she's never stopped. I've been trying to get her to lighten up, for her own sake, but she keeps insisting I need companionship.''

In that light, Kara attributed a deeper significance to Louise's absence. ''Then it's a good sign.'' Feeling contrite, she looked up at him. ''I apologize.''

''For what?''

''For misjudging your motives. When Louise wasn't with you, I jumped to the wrong conclusions.''

''Why?''

''Because you're a man.'' Unwilling to witness the judgment she knew must be in his gaze, she lowered her eyes.

''Oh, I see.'' And he did see. Clearly, Kara's late husband had left behind a powerful negative influence. How sad, when she was otherwise such an amiable person. He noticed that her trembling hands were clasped atop the bible in her lap. The urge to comfort and reassure her was strong. He reached out.

As his warm, strong hand covered hers, Kara's vision got misty. When he said, ''It's okay. I forgive you,'' she was so touched she felt like weeping.

If she'd looked at Tyler at that moment, she knew she would have burst into tears.

All through the service, Kara was acutely aware of who sat beside her. If anyone had asked her to list even one of the important points of the sermon she'd just heard, she couldn't have done it.

The congregation stood to leave. Tyler pivoted and scanned the crowd behind them before turning to Kara. ''Okay. What now?''

''Don't ask me. You're the tall one. I can't see a thing from down here.''

He nodded. ''Sorry. I forgot you were so little.''

Kara stood straight, her chin jutting out proudly. ''I'll have you know that both my feet reach the ground just fine, Mr. Corbett. Therefore…''

''Therefore,'' he said with a chuckle, ''your legs must be the perfect length. I've heard that joke before. What I meant was, I can see Susan and Mark headed this way. What have we decided to tell them?''

''Oh, dear.'' She grasped the problem. ''We haven't decided yet, have we?''

''Not as far as I know.'' Tyler flashed a self-assured grin. ''Sitting together this morning was your idea, remember?''

''Don't remind me.'' Kara pulled a face. ''I know, I know. You just did.''

Tyler reached out, then paused to see what her reaction would be when he took her hand. He saw her eyes widen like a frightened deer, so he raised their joined hands between them and said quietly, ''This was on our okay list. Remember?''

When she nodded, he stepped into the aisle and started making his way to the front of the church, tugging her along behind, while most of the other worshipers went the opposite direction.

She gave only token resistance. ''I feel like a salmon swimming upstream. Where are we going?''

''Out the side door. It's that or wait till your sister catches up. Last time I looked, she was gaining on us.''

''Well, why didn't you say so sooner? Come on!'' Still holding his hand, Kara sprinted ahead and ducked through an archway, two steps in front of him.

Tyler was laughing softly. ''I would have if I'd known it would light such a fire under you. I thought for a minute there I was going to have to pick you up and sling you over my shoulder like a sack of grain to get you moving.''

''*That's* going on my no-no list, for sure,'' Kara shot back. ''No tossing me over anybody's shoulder, least of all yours.''

''Oh? Why not? I promise not to drop you.''

They had reached the outer door. Kara flung it open and shot out into the bright sunlight. She shaded her eyes and squinted up at Tyler. ''Because I'm afraid of heights. Besides, I could get a nosebleed from the altitude up there.''

''Spoken like a true munchkin,'' he replied with a chuckle. ''Now where to?''

That was the first time Kara had thought that far ahead. If they stayed in the parking lot, Susan was sure to catch up to them before they had a chance to discuss strategy. ''I'll make a run for my car.''

''Okay. Where are you parked?''

''Over there. By the—'' Kara broke off as she peeked around the corner of the church. Mark's truck sat directly in front of hers, blocking her exit. The chances of a simple, quick getaway were slim and none. ''Look. I have a problem.''

''I see what you mean.'' He made a snap decision. ''Come on. My pickup's parked on the side street. We'll take that.''

''To where?''

''Does it matter? All we have to do is give Susan the slip, wait till she's gone home, then come back for your truck.''

A marvelous thought popped into Kara's frazzled brain. ''I know! We'll go to my office and get Roady. It's a perfect excuse to leave together. That way, when Susan finds out, she won't be mad at me for ditching her!''

Tyler wasn't totally sold on her rationale but he went along with it as a temporary measure. Following her around the side of the building to his truck, he opened the passenger door and helped her in while he mulled over what she'd said.

It might be only his imagination, but it seemed to Tyler that Kara was unduly worried about making other people angry. Yes, she was intrinsically kind and therefore wouldn't want to upset anyone, yet there was more to it than that. She visibly tensed whenever she thought someone was cross with her. When she'd had that reaction to him, he'd assumed it was because of their prior conflicts. Now, he wasn't so sure.

Climbing behind the wheel, he started the engine and pulled away from the curb. ''Why would Susan be mad at you?''

Kara opened her mouth to tell him, then realized she had no valid answer. She shook her head, bewildered. "I don't know."

"You'll do anything to avoid conflict, won't you?"

"Any sensible person would."

Tyler didn't argue. He merely said, "Would they?"

Road Kill was so glad to have company he wriggled all over. When Kara opened the gate to the small dog run he paused only long enough for a brief pat from her, then headed directly for the man he considered to be his master. Kara beamed. "See? He loves you."

Casting her a cynical look, Tyler snorted. "Hah! He sees me as a meal ticket—nothing more." But he began to smile as the puppy awkwardly circled his legs. "What is that plastic thing around his neck? He looks like he got his head caught backward in a funnel."

"That's the Elizabethan collar I told you about. It keeps him from reaching his leg to chew on it."

"Oh." When he bent down, the pup collapsed in a heap at his feet and rolled on its back, tongue lolling and tail still thumping wildly.

Tyler scratched its pale pink-and-beige-spotted tummy as he softly said, "You are a no-good, worthless mutt, you know that? You trashed my kitchen and turned my innocent old dog into a delinquent. What am I going to do with you? Huh?" He examined the repairs to the cast as he went on. "Well, don't just lay there. Speak up. What have you got to say for yourself?"

Road Kill raised his head and looked at the man quizzically. An instant later, he lunged.

Caught off guard, Tyler rocked back on his heels, lost his balance, and wound up sitting on the floor. That was all the advantage the puppy needed. He jumped into Tyler's lap, cast and all, and planted a wet kiss right in the middle of his cheek!

Kara would have loved to comment but she was laughing so hard she couldn't talk.

* * *

Tyler stayed on the floor long enough to gain the upper hand. Gently but firmly, he insisted that Road Kill sit when he was told, even though the puppy quivered with the effort.

"Good boy. That's it," Tyler said. He looked up at Kara. "Maybe you were right. Maybe he is smarter than I gave him credit for."

She was still trying to recover from seeing him sprawled on the cement floor with Roady's cast poking him in the stomach. "Whoa. Do you mean to say *you* were *wrong?*"

"It does happen once every ten years or so," he countered wryly. "But I could be wrong about that, too."

"Then that's twice in one day. By your reckoning, you should be safe from error for the next twenty years."

Muttering, "Don't I wish," Tyler got to his feet and dusted himself off. The puppy immediately began to frolic at his feet again. He looked at it and shook his head. "I suppose you expect me to take him with me."

"It would be best. I only left him here overnight because I was afraid he'd get hurt if my dogs got to roughhousing with him too much. Your house is better because Buster is more laid-back."

Tyler stuffed his hands into his pockets and watched the pup investigate a corner of the room by hopping on three legs and swinging the longer cast out to the side. "Buster *used* to be laid-back—and well-behaved—until a certain bad influence polluted his mind."

"Dogs are scavengers. It's natural for them to rob the trash. Smart owners eliminate the temptation by keeping their refuse out of reach."

"Are you trying to tell me I made a *third* mistake, Doctor? That's preposterous."

She watched his countenance darken, his eyes narrow. Then the corners of his mouth began to twitch upward. He was making fun of her! And she'd almost taken his criticism seriously. Talk about mistakes.

Intent on distracting her companion and herself, Kara opened the door to the corridor leading to the outside runs.

Raucous barking was the instant result. She had to shout to be heard. "As long as I'm here, I may as well get my chores done. I usually go home and change after church, but all I have to do is feed and water, so it shouldn't be a problem to do it in a dress."

Joining her, he closed the door so Road Kill wouldn't follow. "I'll give you a hand. Show me what to do and we can be finished in half the time."

That surprised Kara. "I didn't bring you here to put you to work."

"I know. You brought me here to con me into taking that useless mutt home again."

Kara smiled up at him sweetly as she handed him the scoop for the dry dog food and lined up six clean dishes on the counter. "Did it work?"

"For the present," Tyler said with a sigh. He waved the empty scoop in the direction of the dishes. "What do you want me to put in these, and how much?"

"One full scoop of kibble and half a can of the gravy-covered stuff in those cases over there." She reached under the table, added one more dish to the group, then said, "Except for this one. It gets three scoops and two whole cans."

Tyler eyed the dish. "That looks like a turkey roaster. Even Buster doesn't eat that much." Pausing, he glanced down the row of dog runs. "What in the world *does?*"

"Big Bertha," Kara said, pointing. "You'll find her in the end run. Go have a look if you want. She's enormous but she's also the sweetest one of the bunch." As he started down the passageway, Kara added, "She drools when she's about to be fed, though. I wouldn't stand too close to the fence if I were you."

Overcome by curiosity, he had to see for himself. The dog he found in the last run looked like a cross between a Saint Bernard and a black Labrador retriever. There was benevolence in her sad, brown eyes and a lethargy to her movements that was somehow restful. She got to her feet and met him at the chain-link gate. Her nose was jet-black, her muzzle droopy, and her tongue wider than Road Kill's whole head. All four legs and her tail were sopping wet, as if she'd been swimming.

Amazed, Tyler called back to Kara. "I see it, but I still don't know what it is."

"I'm not surprised. Bertha's a full-grown Newfoundland. They're fairly rare, especially in the south, partly because they suffer so much in the summer heat."

"Is that why you've got a plastic wading pool in there with her? Or does she need that much water to drink?"

Laughing, Kara brought the Newfoundland's dinner and handed the heavy dish to Tyler to hold while she unlocked the gate to the run. "They like to lie in the water to cool off so I got her a pool of her own. She's actually an easy keeper, considering her size. Newfs are a pretty quiet breed, so they don't expend a lot of energy, especially when they get as old as Bertha."

"What is she, fifteen or sixteen?"

"Oh, no. She's barely seven," Kara said sadly. "The giant breeds have a notoriously short life span." Opening the gate slightly, she ordered, "Sit," then, "Stay" and the dog did exactly as it was told while Tyler placed the food inside the fence.

The dog's gentle disposition and kind expression touched him deeply. What a shame it had grown old before its time. Buster was already fifteen and he was just beginning to show his age. Tyler straightened and backed away while Kara latched the gate.

"I have to lock this one because Bertha's so smart," Kara explained. "She taught herself to unfasten the simple catches that I use to keep all the other dogs in."

"It must be sad to love a magnificent animal like that, only to lose it so young."

"I suppose you could look at it that way. I think the people who choose to own one of the giants feel that a little time with a dog like this is worth whatever heartache comes afterward. Most of them get another dog just like the one they lost, in spite of knowing the same thing will probably happen again.'' Kara suddenly realized the bittersweet turn their innocent conversation had taken. Holding her breath, she hoped and prayed that Tyler would not make the same connection.

''It's because they're looking for the same perfect love they found before,'' he said pensively. ''I wish the rest of life was that easy.''

What could she say? That he'd find another wife as wonderful as the one he'd lost? Platitudes were not only useless, they would cause him more pain. According to everyone who knew Tyler, he'd elevated his late wife to the level of a saint. It didn't matter that no normal mortal could ever be that perfect. As long as he thought Deanne had been a saint, he'd be content to cherish her memory. Kara was not about to argue with a dream like that.

All she could think of to say was, ''I'm so sorry.''

When he responded with, ''So am I,'' Kara wanted to wrap her arms around him, hold him tight, and rock away his sorrow the way a loving mother comforts an injured child.

Big Bertha chose that moment to shake, flinging swimming pool water all over everything and shattering the poignant mood.

Tyler shouted and fled. Kara was right behind him. Neither stopped until they were safely back at the other end of the aisle. He was muttering to himself.

''I *told* you to be careful,'' Kara prompted.

''You didn't tell me she was going to be all wet to start with.'' He was brushing at his slacks.

''A little water won't kill you.'' It was Tyler's quiet reaction, the solemn look in his eyes, that made her realize exactly what she'd said.

The temptation to curse was strong. Instead, she waved her hands in the air and closed her eyes. ''I'm sorry. I did it again, didn't I? I don't mean to. It's just that our language is filled with expressions like that and I wasn't thinking. I...''

Shaking his head, Tyler stepped closer and stilled her hands by taking them in his and drawing them to his chest. ''It's not you. The problem is mine.'' His fingers caressed hers while he searched for the right words. ''Sometimes I let myself dwell on the things that have gone wrong and forget to thank God for my blessings. Like you.''

Kara was speechless. Did he mean that she, also, forgot to give God the glory? Or was he saying he considered her one of his blessings? Before she could ask, he answered the unspoken question.

''When I'm with you, I feel...I don't know...kind of liberated. Like it's okay for me to be sad when we're together, because you'll understand and not try to talk me out of it. And it's okay to laugh, too, because you aren't judging me for being too happy when I should still be mourning.'' He paused, looking into her eyes and searching for the empathy he knew he'd find there. ''Does that make sense to you?''

''Perfect sense,'' Kara whispered. She rested her forehead against their joined hands and closed her eyes. ''I feel exactly the same way.''

Chapter Ten

It took Kara only a few moments to realize how unacceptably intimate she and Tyler were behaving. It took a little longer, however, for her to convince herself to break the comforting contact.

She finally stepped back. He let her slide her hands out of his grasp without argument. She knew she should offer some kind of excuse for her behavior. The trouble was she couldn't seem to come up with any reasonable rationalization.

Nevertheless, she made an attempt to explain. "I...we...I mean..."

Tyler's expression was cynical. He nodded. "Yeah. Me, too."

They parted awkwardly. Kara immediately busied herself filling all the outside water dishes with a hose, then went inside to take care of the animals recuperating in smaller cages. She didn't want to even look at Tyler again, let alone engage in any more in-depth conversation with him. What had happened already was bad enough.

He followed her inside. "Where's Road Kill?"

"I saw him headed for the office." Her words were clipped, her tone contentious.

"Oh." Tyler casually strolled closer. "Is there anything else I can do to help?" When she kept on rinsing feeding bowls in the utility sink, pointedly ignoring him, he tried a more direct approach. ''Hey, don't be mad at *me.* Holding hands was on the 'okay' list, wasn't it?''

It was his virtuous attitude that irritated her the most. To listen to him, a person would think they hadn't just looked through a mutual window into both their souls. Anger was her best—her only—defense against that kind of unwelcome closeness.

She sent a brief, icy stare his way. ''I meant in public. When we want to be convincing.''

''Oh. Sorry.'' Tyler stuffed his hands into his pockets as if hiding them would negate the social error. He stood back and watched her for long moments. ''Speaking of lists, I had some trouble making mine. How about you? Did you come up with many rules?''

''No.'' She tossed her head to sweep her long hair back over her shoulders without touching it while she dried her hands on a clean, white towel. ''I had a terrible time deciding.''

''So how many did you write down?''

Kara made a face. ''Two. But I've since thought of a couple more. Like, 'let's not be nice to each other when we don't have to be.'''

''You don't mean that.''

''Oh, yes, I do,'' she insisted. ''Look at us, Tyler. All we have in common is our grief. What kind of basis is that for anything?''

He sensed the enormous protective wall she'd built around her broken heart. How sad to have nothing more than that to represent her years of marriage. And how truly blessed he was to have had the opposite kind of life with Deanne.

Rather than express thoughts that would only intensify Kara's hurt and resentment, he kept silent and gave in. ''Okay. If that's the way you want it, that's how we'll do it. But I won't guarantee I'll remember I'm supposed to act unfriendly when we're alone. It's not my nature.''

''I know.'' Kara's voice was barely audible. Then she raised her chin proudly and stood ramrod straight. ''Leave the hostile stuff to me. I'm very used to handling it.'' She saw a new tenderness start to shine through his eyes; a sentiment she wanted no part of. ''And stop looking at me like that.''

''Seems to me we went over this subject once before, back in my kitchen. So how do you want me to look at you?''

''Not at *all* would be fine with me,'' she snapped. ''I felt like an animal in the zoo when we were in church this morning. Everybody was staring at us and whispering.''

''Well, not everybody,'' Tyler said with a half smile. ''There was that old bald guy in the back pew, second from the left. But I think he was asleep.''

He ducked just in time to miss being hit in the head by the wadded-up towel she chucked at him. Grinning, he caught it as it tumbled past and hefted it in his hand as if testing its weight.

Kara noticed his eyes narrowing while his sly smile spread. She warned, ''Whatever you're thinking, Tyler Corbett, don't you dare do it.''

One eyebrow arched. ''I didn't start this.''

''Yes, you did. I was trying to be serious and you made fun of me.''

''Of *us,* Kara. Not of you. I know exactly what you mean about feeling like you're always on display. People mean well, but their morbid curiosity gets in the way.''

''Well, maybe.'' Noting that he was still holding the balled-up towel in his hand, she edged to her left until her hip bumped against the rim of the sink. She'd been rinsing the kennel dishes with warm water from the spray nozzle and the main water supply was still turned on. If Tyler did what she thought he was planning to do, she'd be ready to retaliate immediately.

Looking at her askance, he drawled, ''Kara…I see a funny look in your eyes. What are you thinking?''

''Why, nothing, Tyler.'' The words were coated with far too much cloying sweetness to be believable.

He fisted the towel. ''Get away from the sink.''

''Uh-uh. Not till you put that down and back off.''

''This could get nasty,'' he cautioned.

''I'll take my chances.''

He charged.

She lunged for the sprayer. Grasping it, she swung it toward him without taking aim. As close as he was, she couldn't miss.

Tyler bellowed but kept coming. He grasped her wrist to divert the spray. It shot straight up in the air and rained down on them both like a private cloudburst.

''Let go of me!'' she screeched.

''Not till you turn off the water!''

''I can't,'' Kara shouted. ''You're holding my hand shut.''

''Why didn't you say so?'' Releasing her, Tyler started to laugh. ''You're a mess, Doc. So's your hospital.''

''Well, so are you.'' She was sorely tempted to shoot one last spritz at him. If he hadn't been drenched already, she might have given in to the whim.

''I'm not as bad off as you are,'' he countered, wiping his face with his hands. ''I hope your dress isn't ruined.''

''It's washable.'' Kara looked down at the limp, soggy fabric. ''I don't remember if the directions say I'm supposed to take it off first, but I suppose I am.''

''Undoubtedly. They probably figured it wasn't necessary to explain that part.'' Still chuckling softly, he eyed the disorder they'd created. Water dripped from the overhead beams and puddles had formed on the concrete floor, especially where they'd stood. ''I think it's my turn to mop,'' he said.

''It's only water. It'll dry.'' She handed him a fresh towel. ''Here. Your hair's all wet. Just toss the towel into the hamper under the sink when you've finished with it. I have a laundry service.''

''Maybe you should jump in the hamper yourself,'' he quipped.

''Naw. I'll dry, too. Eventually.'' She glanced at her reflection in the window over the sink. One side of her hair still looked fairly good. The other hung limp and soggy. ''I do think it might be best if I didn't go back to get my truck until later, though. No telling what rumors will get started if folks see me like this.''

''People mean well,'' Tyler offered. ''They don't know they're doing anything wrong when they pay so much attention to us. I think we scare them.''

That gave her pause. ''Scare them? How? Why?''

''Because they can identify with us on a basic level. Whether they admit it or not, they know that what happened to us could just as easily happen to them.''

Kara sighed. ''I'd never thought of it quite that way. You may be right.'' A slight smile lifted the corners of her mouth. ''Of course, if you tell anybody I agreed with you about anything, I'll deny it.''

''You mean you'd lie? Tsk-tsk-tsk. Weren't you listening to the sermon this morning?''

''Since you insist on the absolute truth,'' she said stubbornly, ''the answer is, no. I didn't hear a word of it.''

''Why not?''

Kara shook her head slowly as she studied the handsome rancher. His dark hair was tousled from towel drying, his eyes sparkled with wit, his smile made her toes curl every time he flashed it, and his openness made her feel totally unequipped to cope on an equal level.

Starting for the door leading to the rest of the animal hospital, she looked back over her shoulder. ''Only one embarrassing question per customer. You've already used yours. Sorry.''

''Where are you going?''

''To look for Roady and see what kind of trouble he's gotten himself into this time.''

Pensive, Tyler watched her leave the room. *Trouble? Hah!* That scrawny brown pup's antics were nothing compared to what was happening between him and Kara. He was starting to like her. Really like her. They could become friends, perhaps even confidants, if she ever got over being so blasted standoffish.

He sighed deeply. It was easy to believe Kara's claim that

she was an expert at handling hostility. She should be, given her past. But there was more to her than that. Much more. Tyler just wasn't convinced that he wanted to get close enough to her to find out what else there was to know.

Kara's dress was still speckled with damp spots by the time Tyler drove her back to the church to get her truck. Road Kill napped on the seat between them, providing the barrier both of them wanted.

When she opened the door to get out, the puppy acted like he expected to go with her. Kara put out her hand to stop him from trying to jump down and hurting himself. "No, Roady. You go home with Daddy."

"I wish you wouldn't keep calling me that." Tyler pulled the pup to him so she could safely close the truck door. "It's embarrassing."

"Don't be silly. There's nobody else here to hear me say it," she countered, waving her arm in a wide arc.

Road Kill cuddled up to Tyler as Kara peered in the half-open window. "Besides, I do see a family resemblance. For instance, you both have brown eyes."

"Sweet of you to notice," Tyler grumbled. "So, how much longer am I going to have to baby-sit this monster?"

"I'll probably need to work on his leg a couple more times, depending on how fast he's growing. On an adult dog, we could just cast the break and leave it alone, but on a growing pup the dressings can get too tight if we're not careful." She noticed that Tyler had laid his arm across the puppy's back, like an armrest, and was absentmindedly scratching his fur under the Elizabethan collar. Road Kill's eyes glazed over, then drifted half-shut with utter bliss.

Tyler nodded. "Okay. How about this funnel-shaped thing you put on him? When can I take it off?"

"Whenever you want. I'd probably give him a few days, then remove it and watch to see what he does. If he leaves his leg alone, it should be safe to stop using the collar."

"Do you think he will?" Tyler asked.

Kara chuckled. ''Not in a million years. He has your stubborn streak, too. Must run in the family.''

Susan was lying in wait for her when Kara got home. ''Aha! I knew you'd show up here, eventually. You might abandon your only sister and run off after church without a word, but you'd never leave your helpless animals to fend for themselves.''

''Did I forget to put out bowls of kibble and water for you, sis? Sorry.''

Susan giggled. ''You should be.'' She trailed Kara into the house, continuing to badger her. ''Well? Give? What happened with you and Tyler? Where have you been all this time? Do you know it's after three o'clock? I've been going nuts, waiting and wondering.''

It suddenly occurred to Kara that she wouldn't have to tell a single fib. Not one! Susan's wild imagination would supply enough lurid details all by itself. ''There's absolutely nothing between me and Tyler Corbett,'' Kara declared, relieved.

''Oh, sure. I saw the way you two looked at each other in church. And then when he hustled you out the side door the way he did, I thought I'd faint. What a hunk!''

''I'm afraid I don't know what you're talking about. We just left that way to avoid the crowd at the other door. There was nothing romantic about it.'' She almost laughed at the disbelief in her sister's expression.

''Sure, sure.''

''It's the truth. Actually, I'd expected to sit by Louise this morning, but she's out of town. I understand she went to visit her sister.''

''Oh, yeah, I see. Be nice to the former mother-in-law. Good plan, kiddo. If Louise Tate is on your side, you've won half the battle.''

''I'm not being pleasant to Louise because she was Deanne's mother. I happen to like the woman. I probably would have liked Dee, too, if I'd had a chance to get to know her.'' Pausing, Kara decided to go on. She stared directly at her sister to reinforce the point she was making. ''The only thing I *don't* like about Louise is her nosy attitude.''

''Oh, really?''

Kara couldn't believe Susan's blameless demeanor. ''Yes. Really. There seems to be a lot of that kind of interference going on around here. Have you noticed?''

''Nope.'' Susan giggled again. ''Must be your imagination.''

''I doubt it. And if you don't want me to disown you, you'd better not set up any more surprise dinner parties with me as the patsy. Got that?''

''Sure. You don't need my help. At least not anymore. I can't believe how fast you and Ty took to each other. Has he forgiven Alex, too?''

Sobering, Kara shook her head. ''I don't know. I haven't asked. Don't you bring it up to him, either. The less said about Alex, the better.''

''Was it really so bad...living with him, I mean?'' Susan laid a comforting hand on Kara's arm.

Now that Kara had spent a little time with Tyler Corbett, she could see how much she'd missed—would continue to miss—in life, simply because she'd chosen to wed the wrong man. That knowledge intensified the depth of her remorse. ''It was what it was,'' she said softly. ''I have no one to blame but myself.''

''Why? Because Alex was a skunk? That wasn't your fault, it was his.''

''I married him,'' Kara said flatly. She pressed her lips into a thin line. ''I made the choice. That makes it my fault for the way my life turned out.''

Susan raised her voice, nearly shouting, ''Phooey! You're as bad as Tyler.''

''What do you mean?''

Shaking her head, Susan huffed in disgust. ''As close as you two have been, lately, I thought you'd know already. He blames himself for Deanne's death. Talk about dumb.''

''What?'' Kara's knees felt suddenly rubbery. ''Why?''

"I don't know all the details. Just what Mark's told me. I guess there was a problem getting the treatment Dee needed, because of the cost involved. Ty finally worked it out by mortgaging everything, but in the meantime, her condition got a lot worse. More than one doctor told him the short delay didn't affect the inevitable outcome, only he refused to believe it."

"Oh, how awful for him." Unshed tears filled Kara's eyes, threatened to spill over. She blinked rapidly to hold them back.

Susan was nodding with comprehension. "The poor guy went through hell. So tell me again how you don't care a thing about him."

What could Kara say? Of course she cared. But that didn't automatically mean there was anything else brewing between her and Tyler. On the contrary. Susan's story further underscored his phenomenal love for his wife. A perfect devotion like that was a once-in-a-lifetime gift from God, not something that could ever be replaced.

Sniffling, Kara turned away to hide the consequences of her overwrought state. Naturally, Susan wouldn't be fooled, it just helped to avoid seeing the sympathy mirrored in her eyes.

"I do care about Tyler," Kara said. "Not for personal reasons, but because I understand what he's going through."

"Is that why you're crying?" Susan asked tenderly.

Within the jumble of Kara's emotions, one unwelcome fact continued to surface until she could no longer deny its existence. All her tears were not for Tyler. Or for his loss. Some were for herself. She'd wasted her chance for the kind of happiness he'd found, and, like it or not, she was envious of a woman she'd hardly known, simply because he'd once loved her.

Oh, Father, forgive me, Kara prayed silently. *I don't mean to be covetous. I just wish...*

Breaking off, she tossed her head stubbornly and started for the kitchen. "Forget it. I'm acting silly. I'll be fine as soon as I can find a tissue and blow my nose." She managed a smile as she glanced back at Susan. ''I've been shutting Speedy in the laundry room while I'm gone. Let him out for me, will you?''

''Sure. Why's he in the doghouse?'' Susan was still a bit subdued.

''Because he's tried twice to chase a rabbit by jumping through the screen on the front window. I don't want him to try it sometime when the glass is closed. He'd probably be cut to ribbons.''

''Ugh! No kidding.'' She finally started to smile. ''You and your menagerie. I swear, I don't know why you keep taking in so many strays.''

''They don't have anybody else. They need me,'' Kara said. To herself, she added, And I need them for the same reason.

Chapter Eleven

Kara was surprised when Tyler showed up at the animal hospital just after closing the following Wednesday.

Susan unlocked the door to let him in, gave Kara a broad wink, and promptly headed for the kennel area. ''Well, there's work to be done. You two take all the time you need. I'll clean up and feed by myself tonight.'' She giggled as she looked back at her sister. ''And, no, I did not invite him to stop by, so you can't blame me this time.''

Puzzled, Kara frowned up at Tyler. ''What are you doing here?''

He politely removed his cowboy hat and held it casually in one hand. ''You forgot we had a date? Shame on you.''

''We didn't have a date.''

''Yes, we did. You wanted to get together and go over our lists. Remember?''

''Well, yes, but we both said we weren't able to think of much to add, so I figured—''

''You figured I wasn't serious in the first place,'' he concluded. ''I thought you knew me better than that.''

''I don't know you at all.''

''That's not what you said right before we had the water fight last Sunday.''

Kara waved her hands wildly at him. ''Hush! Susan will hear you.''

''So? We didn't do anything wrong. Unless your dress was ruined after all. Was it?''

''No. At least I don't think so. I just tossed it in the washer and dryer. It looked okay when I took it out and hung it up.''

''Good. I like it on you.''

''What's that supposed to mean?''

''It means I like the dress. Nothing more. Nothing less,'' he said, starting to get annoyed. ''Now, are we having dinner together, or shall I take the hint and just go away?''

''I didn't mean...'' Kara felt about two inches tall. ''I'm sorry. It's been a rough day.''

''I can see that from here.'' Looking her up and down, Tyler stopped at her stained white coat and pants. He raised one eyebrow. ''I hope the other guy fared better than you did.''

''The other guy's fine, thanks.'' She realized how she must look. ''But I can't go anywhere looking like this. And I didn't bring a change of clothes. Maybe another time.''

''Nope. You're not going to brush me off that easy. If I can have my hair cut and take the time to shave—twice in the same day—you're going to go out to dinner with me. Tonight.''

She couldn't tell if he was teasing or serious. His hair did look marvelous—dark, shiny and neatly trimmed. As for his lack of beard stubble, all she could see was the compelling cut of his jaw and the way the fine lines on his face accentuated his smile and made his eyes twinkle. ''You're pretty sure of yourself, aren't you?''

''I'll be even better once I've seen your list and made sure you haven't added anything scandalous.''

Kara gasped. ''Me? Don't you dare—'' Her sentence was cut off abruptly when he picked her up, swung her feet off the floor, and started to carry her toward the door. ''Put me down!''

''Susan!'' Tyler shouted over the uproar. ''Hey, Susan. Come unlock this door and let me out before your sister gives me a black eye.''

''That's a good idea,'' Kara sputtered. Instead, she pushed against his chest, hoping to break free. It didn't help a bit.

Tyler was laughing. ''My second good idea of the day. The first one was when I decided to treat you to a nice dinner. I just didn't dream it would be so hard to get you to go with me.'' He looked beyond Kara. ''Ah, Susan, there you are. I seem to have a problem. The door's locked and I need to abscond with my date. As you can see, she's being difficult tonight.''

''She's *always* difficult,'' Susan said with a wide grin. Hesitating, key poised, she looked at Kara and added, ''I suppose I should ask you if you want me to let him out or call the police instead.''

''Look at me! I am *not* going out in public looking like I've just been dragged through the mud,'' Kara shouted. ''I tried to tell him that, but he's not listening.''

''Well, why didn't you say so? Wait right there.''

In a few seconds, Susan was back with a pile of neatly folded clothes. ''Here we go. My favorite denim blouse and jeans to match.'' She ignored the face Kara was making and spoke directly to Tyler. ''Put her down so she can go take a shower and change. I'll make sure she doesn't duck out the back door.''

''Well…I don't know. She's pretty sneaky.''

''You're telling me. That was quite a disappearing act you two pulled after church last Sunday.''

''It *was* good, wasn't it?'' He lowered Kara's feet to the floor and carefully released her as he said to Susan, ''Let's you and me sit down and have a little talk while Kara's changing. I'll bet you can tell me all kinds of interesting things about her. For instance, was she this stubborn when she was a little girl?''

Kara's loud, ''Aargh!'' filled the room. She snatched the clean clothes out of Susan's hands and headed for the bathroom next to her private office. The last thing she heard her sister say, was, ''You wouldn't believe it. I remember one time, when she was about six and I was ten…''

Picking up her pace, Kara ran down the hallway and flew into the bathroom, shedding her lab coat as she went. The sooner she got back to Tyler, the less time Susan would have to regale him with inventive tales of her childhood.

She jumped into the shower, washing automatically while her memory zipped from one event to another. What had she done when she was only a six-year-old? The butterfly collection? No, that came later. Maybe Susan was referring to the time she'd been caught sneaking food to a dozen stray cats behind her uncle's garage. Nope. Couldn't be that, either. She'd been at least eight, then.

Maybe it was— Oh, no! Not that! Susan wouldn't… Kara gritted her teeth. Yes, Susan would. Especially if she thought it would soften Tyler's heart.

Jumping out of the shower she grabbed a towel, quickly dried herself, and dove into the borrowed clothes. There was no time to waste.

Tyler was lounging in the office chair behind the counter, his boots propped up, when Kara returned. Susan had perched on the edge of the computer desk. They both looked terribly pleased with themselves.

"Okay, break it up," Kara ordered. "I'm ready to go."

"I knew she'd hurry," Susan said aside. "She didn't dare leave us alone too long."

"I have nothing to hide," Kara said flatly. "And I also have all night to get even by telling my version of our family secrets." The pseudoscandalized look on Susan's face led her to qualify her statement. "I didn't mean literally *all* night, and you know it, so don't look at me like that."

Tyler chuckled. "She's been warning me to stop looking at her funny for weeks, and I still don't know what she's talking about."

"Maybe her conscience is bothering her," Susan offered. "She always did have an extra strong dose of scruples. Wouldn't let me get away with a thing. I remember one time, when I was about fourteen—"

"Stop!" Kara ordered. She tugged on Tyler's arm. "Come on. We're leaving."

He feigned reluctance. "Aw, do we have to go? I was just getting interested."

"I'll bet you were." She unlocked the front door, pushed it open before he could do it for her, and pointed stiffly. "Out. Now. Go."

Tyler went without comment. After the fact, Kara realized she'd sounded like an irate parent lecturing a naughty child! That was very wrong. She ought to know. If she'd so much as raised her voice to Alex she'd have been in for a vicious tongue-lashing. The recollection made her stomach churn, her temples begin to throb.

Tyler put his hat back on and sauntered around to the passenger side of his truck. Kara hesitated, waiting for him to turn so she could see his expression and decide if she'd inadvertently made him angry.

He opened the truck door. "Well?"

"Sorry. I'm coming."

Puzzled, Tyler noticed how reluctant she seemed. How she averted her gaze. When she was close enough, he reached out and gently touched her shoulder. Startled, she flinched.

"I didn't mean to scare you," he said quietly.

"You didn't."

"Then what is it? What's wrong?"

His tone was kindhearted. It matched the look on his face, putting her more at ease. She sighed. "Nothing. Nothing's wrong. I just thought..."

"What?"

"It doesn't matter. I was mistaken." She angled past him, climbed into the fancy vehicle, and promptly changed the subject. "This is a really nice truck. Is it new?"

"Compared to the others on the ranch, yes." He got behind the wheel. "I'd wanted one for years but I couldn't convince myself it was okay to buy it. About six months ago, I finally gave in."

"Oh." She couldn't believe how tongue-tied she suddenly

felt, alone in the truck with him as they drove away. They'd been together like that before, so what was making her so apprehensive this time?

"Aren't you going to ask me why I waited?"

Kara blinked to clear her head. "Okay. Why did you wait?" Turning to look at him, she noticed his powerful hands clamped hard on the steering wheel and imagined the muscles of his arms tightening beneath the long sleeves of his Western shirt. Quickly, she added, "You don't have to tell me if you don't want to."

Tyler shook his head. "I do want to. I think it may help you if we talk about it."

"Help me? I don't understand."

"You will. I hope." He continued to watch the road. They'd left Hardy and were headed toward Ash Flat. "At first, I didn't know why I wasn't willing to buy the truck. I found lots of excuses to put it off. Then, one day, I realized what was holding me back." Tyler paused to give his declaration more emphasis. "I didn't think I deserved it."

"Why not?"

"Because Deanne wasn't going to be here to enjoy it with me."

A heaviness bore down on Kara's chest. She wanted to reassure him, to tell him he had no reason to continue to feel obligated, yet she couldn't force the words out. When Tyler pulled to the side of the road, stopped the truck and reached for her hand, she didn't resist.

"Do you see what I'm trying to tell you, Kara? It was a real awakening for me. I had to accept the fact that my life is not over, in spite of my thinking for a long time that it was…that it should be. If I make myself go on, regardless of how I feel at the moment, things will get better. Easier. I'll never forget Dee. I don't want to. But if I deny my individuality, if I withdraw from life, I'm wasting the time and talents the Lord has given me."

"That's pretty profound," Kara whispered.

"I know. I just thought you needed to hear it."

What had it cost him to expose his private emotions like that? she wondered. It couldn't have been an easy thing to do, yet he'd done it. For her. Because he had a kind heart. Her fingers threaded between his and tightened. "Thank you."

Tyler's resulting smile was both benevolent and triumphant. He lifted her hand to his lips and brushed a light, friendly kiss across the backs of her knuckles before letting go. "You're quite welcome, Doc. It was my pleasure. Now, where would you like to go for dinner?"

Kara didn't want to travel far in the intimate confines of the truck so she suggested a small restaurant close by. "How about Bea's?"

"Over on Highway 62? I thought you wanted some privacy so we could talk?"

She wasn't about to tell him she'd had enough time alone with him to last her the rest of her life. Maybe longer. "It's so noisy at Bea's nobody will be able to overhear a thing we say," she countered. "Besides, tonight their special is catfish. And hushpuppies to *die* for." A few seconds later, Kara squeezed her eyes shut and said, "Oh, no! I did it again."

Tyler was amused. "Hey, don't sweat it. I might not agree to give up my life for a hushpuppy but if that's what makes you happy, fine."

"You know what I meant." She pulled a face. "Every time we talk I seem to put my foot in my mouth."

"Well, spit it out," he said with a laugh. "It'll spoil your dinner."

Bea's Family Café was famous for its country cooking. A restaurant of one kind or another had occupied the same space for over a generation, which was why Kara could still see the faded remnants of other names painted on the side of the building beneath the current sign. As usual, the parking lot contained as many pickup trucks as it did passenger cars.

Seven people greeted Kara and Tyler with a nod, an amiable wave, or a brief Hello when they entered the cramped dining room. The waitress did, too. ''Hi, there, folks. Have a seat if you can find one. I'll be right with you.''

Kara led the way to an available table in the farthest corner. She'd expected Tyler to sit down across from her. Instead, he took the chair next to hers, trapping her between the wall and his broad shoulders.

She nudged him with her elbow. ''Aren't you crowded?''

''Nope. You?''

''Yes, now that you mention it. How about moving over there?'' She pointed to the chair she'd wanted him to choose in the first place.

''Too far,'' he whispered. ''We can't talk about personal stuff if I'm way over there.'' He scooted his padded, metal-framed chair six inches to the left. ''How's that?''

''Oh, *much* better,'' Kara gibed. ''I can actually move one arm, now. That should make eating a lot easier.''

''I aim to please.'' He flashed a smile at the approaching waitress. ''I don't think we need menus. Kara's been raving about eating your catfish special all the way over here, so we'll have that. And iced tea, please.'' He looked back at his companion, surprised to see a return of the stress he thought he'd banished. ''Did you change your mind about what you wanted?''

Kara lowered her eyes, her hands clasped together tightly and lying in her lap. ''No. Catfish is fine. So is iced tea.''

As soon as the waitress left, Tyler asked, ''What's wrong?''

''Nothing.''

''Bull,'' he mouthed. ''Something's bothering you. Either I upset you or she did. Common sense tells me it had to be me. Now, give. What did I do?''

''Well, if you really want to know, I can order my own dinner. I don't like to be bullied.''

Confounded, he rocked back in the chair until his shoulders bumped the wall behind them. ''Bullied?''

''Well, what would you call it?''

''How about courtesy? Or polite consideration? Maybe I was trying to be nice and take good care of you?'' Judging by the confused look in Kara's eyes, he was making headway so he pressed on. "It's only bullying if I refuse to listen to your opinion, to consider your feelings. It doesn't matter whether we're discussing what to have for dinner or how to save the world. The principles are the same. You talk. I listen. Then I talk and you do the same for me. We don't have to agree. All we have to do is give each other a chance to speak honestly."

Fighting to keep the outer corners of her mouth from turning up, she asked, "May I speak honestly, right now?"

"Of course."

"Do you have any idea how *pompous* you just sounded?"

"No. Is it my turn?" Tyler waited for her nod of agreement, then continued, "Do *you* have any idea how hard it is to read your moods? They change faster than the weather in Arkansas, and that's infamous for its instability."

"Thanks."

"I didn't mean to be derogatory. I want some help, here. Talk to me, Kara. I won't bite your head off."

"Oh, yeah? Promise?" She didn't give him a chance to reply. "I suppose that's part of the problem. Every once in a while you do or say something that reminds me of Alex and I have a strong reaction to that. To you. I can't help myself. He used to pretty much manage my life—and my work—for me. I didn't like it any better then than I do now. The difference was, he *did* bite my head off if I even acted like I might object to his decisions."

Kara let herself smile and shook her head, remembering. "Face it, Tyler. I'm warped."

"Then the problem isn't me."

Rather than reveal more, she answered, "In this case, I think we can safely say no. However, you're far from perfect, in spite of what Louise and Susan keep telling me."

He placed his hand over his heart and sighed with a melodramatic air. "I'm *not* perfect? Oh, no!"

"Stop that." She elbowed him hard in the ribs. "People are staring."

"Only because we're such an imperfect pair." He purposely rubbed the side opposite to the one she'd hit, to tease her. "Ouch. That hurt when you poked me."

There was no way Kara could miss getting the joke. "I poked your *other* side, Tyler. If you don't learn your right from your left pretty soon, I don't know what I'm going to do with you." The instant the shortsighted words were out of her mouth, she wished she hadn't uttered them. They made her think of the future and Tyler Corbett at the same time; a dangerous concept if she'd ever heard one.

"I think I'm teachable," he said lightly. "For instance, I know that this shirt pocket is on the left side." Patting it for emphasis, he felt the paper inside. "Which reminds me..." Drawing it out, he unfolded it on the table between them and leaned closer with one arm casually draped across the back of Kara's chair. "I managed to add a few more things to my list and made a copy for you. See how it grabs you."

The lined yellow paper was there, all right. She was sure of that. And there was writing on it. Beyond that, she was at a loss. Everything was a blur. Her senses were so inundated, so overwhelmed by Tyler's nearness, the room might as well have been pitch-black. She felt the warmth of his breath on her cheek as he spoke.

"I tried to be fair and to put myself in your place, too. Most of these ideas came to me at night, while I was trying to fall asleep." His breath became a silent sigh. "I have a lot of trouble with insomnia."

"Me, too," she managed to say.

"Since you've been alone?"

"Not entirely." Tyler's presence offered enough sense of sanctuary to allow Kara to explain further. "Most of my worst nights were when I was married." She felt him tense, perceived the faint tightening of his arm around her shoulders, offering protection from a threat that no longer existed.

It didn't matter to Kara that Tyler's concern for her welfare came too late. It still warmed her heart.

Chapter Twelve

"You should have married the first guy you proposed to," Tyler said, later.

"What are you talking about?" Kara paused with a crispy, round hushpuppy halfway to her mouth and peered up at him. "I never proposed to anybody."

"Sure, you did. Remember the zoo expert on television? Susan said you were six years old when you wrote and offered to marry him. You volunteered to take care of all his animals for him, too."

Kara's cheeks flushed pink. "So *that's* the secret Susan blabbed! Well, it's true. I didn't know how to spell some of the words in my letter, though, so I asked my big sister for help. Naturally, she couldn't keep a secret. Not about something as crazy as that. She told Mom what I was doing and I got in trouble." Kara bit into the hot hushpuppy. "Mmm. Delicious. I love the onion flavor with the cornmeal."

"Me, too." Tyler ate one off his own plate, then asked, "What made you decide you wanted to marry some old, gray-haired geezer?"

"That's easy. I thought all those exotic animals he showed on his TV program were his personal pets and I wanted desperately to live in a wonderful household like that. I could picture dozens of wild creatures running free in every room." She laughed at herself, remembering her childish zeal. "It never occurred to me that they'd probably eat each other the first chance they got!''

Tyler concentrated on his meal for several minutes before he made up his mind to ask, ''Is that why you married somebody like Alex Shepherd? Was it his connection with veterinary medicine that appealed to you?''

Kara finished the bite of deep-fried catfish she was eating, then blotted her lips with her napkin to delay answering. Finally, she spoke. ''In retrospect, I suppose that was part of it. Alex and I met in vet school. At that time he seemed like a very compassionate man.'' And I really didn't want to go back to my parents' home and listen to more of my mother's unfair assertions about my father's death, she added to herself, pushing her plate away.

''Hey, don't let my stupid questions spoil your dinner,'' Tyler said solemnly.

''I wasn't as hungry as I thought, that's all.''

''What have you eaten so far, today?''

''I don't know. A little of this, a little of that.''

''Uh-huh. The brownie in your desk drawer?''

She was surprised he remembered. ''Nope. That's long gone. I suspect Susan grabbed it when I wasn't looking. Either that, or the mice are getting big enough to open and close drawers. If that's the case, we're *all* in trouble.''

''Right.'' Tyler returned to his dinner, eating automatically. He didn't know why, but he'd begun to worry about every aspect of Kara's daily life. Was she eating right? Had she gotten enough sleep? Was she capable of handling her largest patients without getting hurt? Was she coping okay financially?

In the back of his mind lurked additional questions he knew he'd never ask. For instance, had she known how Alex ran their joint practice, yet kept quiet, condoning his unscrupulous methods by her silence? Had she been so intimidated by the man that she'd abandoned the strong code of ethics which now seemed to govern her work; her life?

He didn't want to believe any of that about Kara.

He didn't want to...but he did.

Tyler got home to find Mark sitting on his front porch, waiting for him.

Weary, he raised both hands in surrender. "Don't worry. You can tell your wife I never laid a hand on her sister."

"Did Kara lay anything on you?"

"Yeah. A guilt trip," Tyler said. "Just about the time I think we understand each other, she starts acting moody all over again. I can't figure her out."

"Do you have to? Figure her out, I mean."

Poking the brim of his Western hat with one finger to tilt it back on his head, Tyler propped his booted foot on the step beside Mark and leaned against a porch post, mulling over the question. "I'm not sure. It's like Kara needs me. I don't mean in the usual sense, man to woman, I mean something deeper."

Mark shrugged and shook his head. "I won't pretend to know what you're talking about. But then, I've never lost anybody who was close to me the way you two have. Maybe that's it. Maybe Kara senses that you know how she feels."

"Except half the time I don't," Tyler admitted ruefully. "It's as if she's two different people. She can be so moody she drives me crazy, or so playful we wind up having fun together. To tell you the truth, it scares me."

Chuckling low, Mark got to his feet. "Sounds to me like everything is normal. That alone is a miracle. Susan says Kara hardly ever used to cut loose and have a good time when they were kids. She kept to herself a lot, studying or reading or doctoring some stray animal and trying to keep it hidden in her room so their father wouldn't see it and blow his stack."

"That reminds me. What else can you tell me about his death?" Pausing for a moment, Tyler guessed, "It had something to do with Kara, didn't it?"

Mark nodded. "Maybe. In a roundabout way. She'd brought home an abused horse, of all things, and stashed it in the garage. Her father heard a noise, opened the garage door, and came face-to-face with the poor old nag. He yelled at Kara till his blood pressure was probably going through the roof. A couple hours later he had his first stroke.''

''First stroke? He didn't die then?''

''No. But he wound up paralyzed on one side. Susan tried to smooth things over with their mother. It didn't work. Kara got all the blame for him being stuck in a wheelchair.''

Tyler's heart went out to the altruistic young woman. ''How old was she then?''

''Let's see...'' Mark thought for a few seconds. ''It was after Susan and I got married. Kara must have been almost eighteen. She won a scholarship and went away to college that summer.''

''And married Alex Shepherd.''

''Not right away. Vets have to have as much training as MDs. She met Alex when she finished college and started in the veterinary program at Purdue.''

Tyler took off his hat and raked his fingers through his hair, combing it back while he pondered what he'd just learned and tried to put it into logical perspective. Except for Susan and Mark, it looked like Kara had no family to rely on, no one else to support her emotionally and help her heal. No wonder she was still suffering so.

The more he thought about it, the more Tyler began to see the Lord's hand in what was currently taking place. Kara just needed someone to lean on for a little while. Someone who understood what she'd been through. Someone to show her that no one could change the past, no matter how hard they prayed or how much they wished things had turned out differently.

Someone who had cursed and shouted at God for what had happened to Dee—and still been forgiven.

Someone like him.

Kara had tucked Tyler's list in her purse. As soon as she got home, she kicked off her shoes, brewed a cup of hot chocolate, curled up in the corner of her sofa with Speedy at her feet, and unfolded the paper.

It started out predictably with, ''no kissing,'' then progressed to, ''no unnecessary hugging.'' So far, so good.

Below that, he'd made two columns. The one on the left was headed with a big, Yes. Kara scanned that, first. It listed teasing, winking, squirting with a hose, sneaking out of church, sharing a busted-up dog, eating cold pizza, acting silly and kissing behind the barn. He'd crossed out the part about kissing but left enough of it showing that she could tell what had been written there.

Chuckling to herself, Kara took a small sip of her hot chocolate and started to read the No column. She nearly strangled. Gasping, she blew chocolate all over her lap, peppering the yellow paper. The first items dealt with neck and ear nibbling! After that, the list got even more ridiculous, including rolling in the hay and eloping! Why couldn't the man ever be serious?

As soon as she got her coughing under control, she grabbed the telephone directory and dialed his number, not caring how late it was.

Tyler answered on the third ring. ''If you're selling something, go away. I'm beat.''

''I'm not selling, and I'm not *giving* anything away, either. I'm not that kind of woman, in spite of what you seem to think.''

''Ah.'' He was laughing. ''Who is this? Could it be the cute little vet who dumped a mutt on my doorstep?''

''You know very well who it is,'' Kara said. His comment about her being cute was pleasing but she wasn't too thrilled with the *little* reference.

''I take it you finally got around to actually reading my list. I wondered why you took it so calmly when I showed it to you when we were at Bea's.''

''This is not funny, Tyler.''

''Sure, it is. Give yourself time. You'll eventually see the humor.''

Unfortunately, she already did. Stifling a giggle, she pantomimed an exaggerated look of disdain at the telephone in place of scowling at him in person. "Did you really think it was necessary to tell me *not* to do all those things?"

"I don't know. Was it?" He heard her muffled, predictable grumbling and broke into loud laughter. Getting control of himself he finally said, "Okay, okay. I'm sorry. I know you'd never elope with me. Not even if I promised to take you all the way to Tahiti."

"That's right, mister. Go find yourself another pretend girlfriend. I quit."

"Uh-oh. I think we're having our first lovers' quarrel."

Kara was really having trouble sounding mad. She couldn't think of the right words to express her supposed anger. "Tyler Corbett, you are the most…"

"Yes? Go on. I'm all ears."

"You're all *something,* all right, but it isn't ears," she retorted. There was no way to hide the smile in her voice or her delight with the absurd conversation they were having. "I'll fix the list and have it ready the next time I see you."

"Well, okay, but leave the part about no neck nibbling in public. I have a reputation to protect, you know."

That did it. Kara managed to hang up the receiver moments before bursting into giggles. Reacting to her upbeat mood, Speedy jumped halfway into her lap, eager to share in the fun.

She hugged him, speaking as if he could understand every word. "Oh, that Tyler Corbett. He's a…a…" Describing the situation rationally, even when talking to a dog, was impossible. The things about Tyler that kept coming to mind were so complimentary they were embarrassing. Visualizing his kind face gave her a peace she'd never known. His sparkling gaze blessed her all the way to her soul, even when he wasn't smiling. And that smile! It warmed her all the way to her toes. Half the time it made her feel like she was floating.

"Know what the best part about him is, Speedy?" Kara cupped the dog's narrow face in her hands and held him still so she could look into his eyes as she spoke. "The man makes me laugh. Really, truly laugh. I don't remember ever feeling this way before.''

The greyhound's tongue shot out, aiming for her face, but Kara was too quick for him. ''Oh, no, you don't. No face licking.'' She giggled. ''Would you believe it? That's on his goofy list, too!''

Kara's bedside phone rang just before dawn. Groggy, she answered with a slurred, ''Hello?''

''Kara. It's me. Tyler.''

''Mmm. If you think it's funny to wake me up like this, just because I called you so late last night, you're wrong. I'm not laughing. Bye, Tyler.'' She started to replace the receiver, heard him shout, and brought it back to her ear. ''What is it? Is Susan okay?''

There was profound sadness in his voice. ''Susan's fine. It's Buster. I went to let him outside this morning, just like I always do, and when he tried to get up, he couldn't walk.''

Kara was suddenly wide-awake. She sat up in bed. ''No other symptoms?''

''Not that I can tell. He's been eating well and hasn't seemed run down or sick. I thought maybe he had a muscle cramp or something like that, so I lifted him into a standing position. He collapsed the minute I let go.''

''How about his pupils? Are they equal and reactive?'' She rephrased. ''I mean, do they both dilate at the same speed and look the same size?''

''I don't know. Hang on. I'll check.''

While Tyler was away from the phone, Kara quickly began to dress. She had the receiver tucked between her ear and shoulder and was fastening her jeans when he returned.

''It's hard to tell for sure. I think both his eyes look the same,'' Tyler said, breathless. ''What should I do?''

Kara hesitated for a moment, praying the problem wasn't serious. ''If you can carry him to your truck without hurting him, it would be best if I saw him at the office so I have all my equipment handy in case I need it.''

''I'll get him there. Just say when.''

''I live out on Peace Valley Road. It'll be driving time from here to Hardy. I'm leaving right away.''

''Okay. We'll meet you there.''

Kara headed for the door, hopping on one foot while she tried to slip her other foot into a sandal. The fact that Tyler had called her for help was pretty profound, considering his former negative opinion of her practice. She didn't even want to think about how he'd feel—how she'd feel—if poor old Buster didn't pull through.

Tyler was waiting when Kara arrived. She skidded her truck to a stop next to his and leaped out. ''Where is he?''

''Here. On the front seat,'' Tyler said, opening the door wider. ''He seemed happy to be taken for a ride, even if I did have to lift him into the truck.''

''Oh, good.'' Kara let the dog sniff her hand, then began to systematically touch his whole body, beginning at his head. When she got to his hips, he winced.

Tyler crowded in behind her to watch. ''What is it?''

''Probably an injury. Maybe hip dysplasia. I can't tell without an X ray. He wasn't showing signs of breaking down when I saw him in your kitchen with Roady, so I suspect he just hurt himself.''

''Will he be okay?''

The poignant note in Tyler's voice touched Kara all the way to her soul. If there was ever a time she needed to pull off a miracle, it was now. Keeping one hand on Buster so he wouldn't try to move and make things worse, she looked up into the man's eyes and spoke honestly. ''I think he'll be fine. But no one can give you a positive guarantee about something like this. All I can say is that I've had a lot of experience with big dogs and I'll do my best to help him.''

''That's all I ask,'' Tyler said soberly. ''Is there anything I can do?''

''Yes. You can carry him inside for me as soon as I unlock the door and get an exam room ready.''

"Of course. Anything else?"

She thought about how she'd been asking the Lord for help ever since Tyler's call had awakened her. "Well, I don't think it's against any rules to pray for a pet."

"If it is, it shouldn't be."

Kara saw the beginnings of a smile lift the corners of his mouth and her heart warmed. This was why she'd gone into veterinary medicine in the first place; to help animals and to soothe the people who loved them. Expressions of her personal faith didn't always fit the situation but she didn't hide her beliefs, either. In a case like Tyler's, where she knew how he felt, she saw no reason not to include God in the equation.

"I'm glad to see you're feeling better," Kara said kindly. "If you're upset, Buster will pick up on your mood and he'll worry, too."

"I hate to imagine what he was thinking when I found him, then. He sure scared me."

Kara laid her hand lightly on his arm. "I understand. I know how special he is to you." With a little smile, she added, "And I'm flattered that you brought him to me. Just wait here a minute. I'll come back and get you when I have everything ready."

Tyler's jaw went slack as he watched Kara unlock the door and disappear inside. When she'd said she was flattered to be chosen, he'd realized that he hadn't even considered looking for a different vet. He'd found Buster ailing, panicked, and immediately called Kara, as if she were the only one qualified to help.

And she'd responded exactly as he'd known she would. Promptly and without reservation.

Buster was panting. Tyler stroked his side and spoke softly to help keep him calm. "I don't know whether you look better because you liked the ride over here, or if you just wanted to come see Kara again. Either way, you scared me silly, you know that?"

The golden Labrador thumped his tail and looked at his master as if he understood every word.

"Yeah, I know what you mean. I feel better now that we're here, too. There is something special about Kara, isn't there? You wouldn't happen to know what that special something is, would you old pal?"

Buster cocked his head, looking supremely intelligent but remaining silent.

"No, I didn't think you would. You're every bit as bumfuzzled by her as I am, aren't you? There are times when she really gets to me."

Tyler broke off. He didn't even want to contemplate the possible significance of what he'd just admitted. "Thank goodness you can't talk the way those dogs in the TV commercials do," he told Buster. "I could be in real trouble if you told anybody what I just said."

Chapter Thirteen

Tyler was an emotional wreck by the time Kara had finished X-raying and treating Buster.

"He'll be groggy for a while," she said as she and Tyler slid the dog into a small holding cage to keep him from moving around too much. "He needs to be kept inactive until the anesthetic wears off. I don't want him trying to get up and falling."

"You're sure it's not serious?"

"Like I said, his hip snapped back into its socket when we stretched him out for the X-ray. There's very little sign of wear on the joint, so it should stay in place. I'll give him some muscle relaxants and painkillers when he's fully conscious. You should be able to take him home late this afternoon."

Tyler exhaled in a noisy whoosh. "Okay. Thanks."

"You're both quite welcome." Pleased, she checked the wall clock. "Uh-oh. I need to get going."

"Why? You're already at work."

"True. But I didn't let Speedy out or feed any of my other animals before I left home."

"I could go feed them for you. That is, if I knew where in Peace Valley you lived."

"You could," she said, starting for the door, "but it might cost you an arm or a leg. I'm not sure how Harry and Peewee would react to a stranger on their turf, especially when I'm not there. And I'm sure Whiskers would go after you, even though he isn't big enough to do much damage, which would probably inspire the other dogs to follow his lead."

"Then at least let me drive you home."

Kara grinned up at him. "My, my. You are a brave man, aren't you?"

"I'm wearing my cowboy boots," he countered, holding out one foot. "Anything that tries to bite my ankles will hit leather."

"How high, exactly, do those boots go?" she asked, giggling. "Whiskers is a little terrier-mix, but Harry's part German shepherd."

"What's Peewee? Or shouldn't I ask?"

"Well..." She was getting a kick out of the guarded look on his handsome face. "Tell you what. Why don't I take you up on your offer of a ride and let you see for yourself?"

"That big, huh?"

"Don't say I didn't warn you."

Peewee was first to bound up to greet Tyler's truck. The other dogs followed. Several gray-striped cats watched cautiously from the sidelines.

Tyler slowed to avoid the boisterous lead dog. "What is *that?* Wait. Let me guess. That's Peewee?"

"You've got it. As near as I can tell, he's part Rottweiler, part brindle Great Dane, and part fence jumper."

"He looks more like a man-eater. Reminds me of how I always used to picture the hound of the Baskervilles when I was a kid."

"My favorite books were the ones about Irish Setters and sled dogs," Kara said. "And Lassie, of course. For years, I begged my parents to get me a collie."

"Do you have one of those, too?"

"No." Talking to her dogs to calm them, she climbed down from Tyler's truck and was instantly surrounded by the affectionate pack. She spoke to each dog and gave it a pat before she looked back at Tyler. "Purebreds are wonderful, of course. There are just too many strays in need of a home for me to go looking for another dog. As you can see, I have plenty already."

"No kidding. Think they'll let me get out, now? I know they haven't had any breakfast yet. I'd hate to be their first course."

Chuckling softly, Kara took hold of Peewee's collar and told him to sit. The other dogs did, as well, although the brown-and-white terrier was so excited he had trouble staying in one place. They all looked to their mistress for further instruction.

"I'd like you to meet Mr. Corbett, guys," she said to them. "He's okay. Well, sort of okay. He likes animals so he can't be all bad."

"Oh, that was a wonderful introduction. Now they *will* eat me," Tyler said with a mock scowl.

"It's my tone of voice more than my words that they pick up on, and you know it. I could tell them you were the dog-catcher and they'd still welcome you if I said it with love."

"Is that where they all came from? Animal control, I mean." He slowly opened the truck door and put one foot on the ground.

"Mostly. Each one has its own sad story. Speedy used to be a racing dog. The others were basically throwaways."

Tyler joined her, letting the dogs sniff his jeans and boots before chancing to offer a hand. "Which one is Speedy?"

"He's still in the house," Kara said. "Come on." Satisfied that Tyler had been accepted, she released her hold on the largest dog and started to walk away. The whole group tagged along at her heels, Tyler included.

"I feel like I'm in a parade," he joked. "Is it always like this around here or are they just hungry?"

"They're my friends. When you make the rounds at your ranch, don't you take Buster with you?"

"Not much anymore," Tyler said pensively. "I used to. Then I started leaving him in the house because Dee didn't want to be alone. I just never started taking him with me again, after...''

''You don't have to explain. I think he'd benefit from daily exercise, though, once he's back on his feet. You might consider it.''

''I will.'' Watching her open the front door without unlocking it, he asked, ''Do you always go away and leave the place wide-open?''

Kara laughed again and pointed to her pack of furry escorts. ''If you were a burglar, would you come here?''

''Not on your life!'' The thought made him grin. ''One look would be enough to end my criminal career for good.'' Following her into the living room, he was greeted by a flash of tan and white that leaped at him like a specter, landed with its front paws on his shoulders long enough to give him a kiss, then got down and spun in circles at his feet. Tyler stifled a yell of surprise and stood his ground.

''That's Speedy, in case you haven't guessed,'' Kara said. ''He's very friendly. He's also very fast in comparison to my other dogs. For a greyhound, he wasn't all that speedy, though. That's why his owners stopped racing him.''

''Judging by the look on your face, Speedy was one of the lucky ones. What usually happens to them when their racing days are over?''

''You don't want to know,'' Kara said. ''If I had all the money in the world, I'd probably spend it taking care of the unwanted pets that had been shoved out on the street to fend for themselves.'' Thinking about how close she'd come to losing everything after Alex had died and left her saddled with a pile of debts she didn't know about, she shivered. As long as her veterinary practice continued to grow, she'd be okay. But one hiccup in the normal operations and she could still lose everything she'd worked so hard for.

Tyler noticed the negative shift in her mood and tried to change it for the better. ''I can see it now,'' he teased. ''The Kara Shepherd Home for Elderly Animals. Our motto is, 'You shove 'em, we love 'em.' How does that sound?''

"About as ridiculous as you meant it to." She sent a smile his way. "Thanks. Once I get on my soapbox there's no telling what I'll say."

He reached for her hand, relieved when Speedy didn't object. "There's no reason to be ashamed of caring about injustices or for trying to put some of them right. Just because you can't cure all the world's ills, doesn't mean you shouldn't want to. The way I see it, when you're led to the special ones you can help, you just do what you can. That's all anyone can ask."

Kara looked into his eyes and saw an empathy equal to hers that took her breath away. This man did understand what she was trying to do. And why she'd never stop. His touch was warm and strong, but more important, it was compassionate. Without that remarkable quality, holding his hand would mean little. With it, his touch was momentous.

Sighing, she laid her free hand on top of his as he continued to gently clasp her fingers. She had no doubt she was supposed to help the lost, lonely animals that crossed her path. But what about the lonely people? What about this man in particular? Had she been led to him? Or, worse, had they been led to each other?

Oh, Father, Kara prayed silently. *Not me. Not yet. I'm not ready for this. Besides, I'm a veterinarian, not a social worker.*

Tell me you're not lonely, a voice inside her said.

She tightened her grip on Tyler's hand. Mere seconds had passed since he'd reached for her, yet it seemed as if they'd been standing there for an eternity.

I'd rather be lonely, she insisted. *I tried marriage. Anything is better than that.*

Kara felt, rather than heard, echos of rich, wholesome laughter. Her eyes widened.

"What's wrong?" Tyler dropped her hand and scanned the room in the direction of her anxious gaze.

"I thought I heard something." She humphed in disgust. "Never mind. It was probably just God, laughing at me."

Before Tyler could comment, she added, ''I always did think the Lord had a sense of humor. He'd have to, dealing with us.''

''Us, as in mankind? Or, us, as in you and me?''

''Take your pick,'' Kara said. Starting for the kitchen, she added, ''Come on. You can open cans for me.''

Tyler considered her house as he followed. The living room was neat but sparsely decorated. Larger pieces of furniture, such as a sofa and chairs were present. What was missing were the smaller objects, like lamps, knickknacks, end tables and anything that might be breakable. Considering the way Speedy raced around the house leaping over anything in his path, that was understandable. Whatever Kara hadn't removed to start with had probably been broken the minute the dog had arrived.

Her old-fashioned kitchen was a pleasant surprise. Tyler paused and began to grin. ''Wow. This looks just like my grandma's kitchen when I was a boy. She even had a Hoosier cabinet like that.'' Reminiscing, he ran his hand over the well-used, white-painted finish of the upright, freestanding cupboard. ''If I remember right, this enamel countertop slides out.''

''I was lucky to find one that still works,'' Kara said. ''Most of them have been altered to fit into modern kitchens where nobody cares about function the way folks used to. That one even has the flour bin still in it. Go ahead. Take a look.'' She was pleased to see he felt enough at home to open the upper compartments as she'd suggested. Truth to tell, he seemed more relaxed in her kitchen than he had in his own house.

Tyler turned to her. ''Do you bake?''

''Occasionally. When I get the urge. I'm afraid the cabinet doesn't get the regular workout it did in the old days, though. It's hard to imagine having to bake enough bread and pastries to feed a whole family.''

Watching her line up the dog's dishes, he chuckled. ''In

your case, it shouldn't be too hard. Everybody in your family eats off the floor!"

"True." Kara wasn't at all put off by his candid remark. "And they're not fussy." She set two large cans on the counter beside her.

Tyler took them. "I'll open these. What else?"

"That's it for the morning meal. I sure wish I could leave dry food out all the time but the dogs are so lazy they let the raccoons and possums steal it if I do." She was going to mention the added cost of feeding wild creatures as well as her own animals, then thought better of it. Considering the way he'd acted the last time Susan had billed him, the less she and Tyler discussed the specifics of their personal finances, the better off they'd be.

Mulling over their past conflicts, Kara led the way into the backyard. Now that she was getting to know Tyler better she had serious doubts he'd have withheld payment of a bona fide debt. Yet that was what he'd apparently done, judging by the information she'd been able to glean from Alex's records.

Doing her chores automatically while her imagination churned out one unbelievable idea after another, Kara fed the dogs, put cat food up on a high, secure ledge so the cats could eat in peace, then threw a fresh flake of hay to the old carriage horse and made sure all the water troughs and buckets were filled.

By the time she was through she'd decided what to do. Somehow, she was going to find out what had actually gone wrong after Alex had vaccinated the Corbett herd, even if it meant she had to personally go through every scrap of paper and every supplier's bill in the boxes and boxes of disorganized files she'd put into storage after Alex's death. The answer must be there somewhere.

All she had to do was find it.

Buster was sitting in his cage looking fairly alert by the time Tyler returned Kara to the animal hospital. Susan was already at work. She started to greet Kara, saw Tyler with her, and froze, speechless.

"Good morning to you, too," Kara teased. "What's the matter? Cat got your tongue?"

"You could say that." Susan grabbed her arm and pulled her aside. "Where did *he* come from?"

"Texas, originally, I think. Why?"

"Stop that. I'm not kidding. When I got here, saw your truck out front and couldn't locate you, I was worried sick."

"I left you a note. At least I think I did. I know I meant to."

"But you had other things on your mind, right?" She nodded toward Tyler. "Him, for instance."

"Buster was sick. Tyler called and I came in early. That's all there was to it."

"Uh-huh. If I hadn't recognized Tyler's dog in the recovery area, I'd have probably called the police and reported you missing."

Tyler stepped up and joined the conversation. "It was my fault, Susan. Buster couldn't walk. I panicked. I only drove your sister home so I could help her with her morning chores. I figured that was fair, since I was the reason she hadn't stopped to do them before she left."

Susan was not about to be placated. "I don't care if you two decide to elope to Las Vegas," she declared, hands on her hips, "I would like to be told what's going on if Kara decides to disappear, again."

In unison, Kara and Tyler both said, "Tahiti," then shared a chuckle at the private joke.

Finally, Kara looped an arm around her sister's shoulders and started to lead her away. "Come on. I'll tell you all about my adventure while we get ready to open."

"You'd better," Susan warned, scowling.

Kara glanced back over her shoulder and called, "Thanks for your help. You can come back for Buster this afternoon."

"Okay. See you then." Tyler tipped his hat and left.

As soon as the door closed behind him Kara let her exhaustion show. ''Whew.''

Susan immediately softened. ''Are you sick?'' She put her hand on her sister's brow. ''You don't have a fever.''

''No, I'm not sick. At least not the way you mean. I just can't seem to shake off an absurd compulsion to find out what actually happened to Tyler's cattle, back when Alex was treating them. Maybe the vaccine was bad. Or maybe the lab made a mistake on the tests we ran. I don't know. Something.''

''Why bother? That was years ago. What difference will it make at this late date?''

''It makes a difference to me.''

Susan was slowly shaking her head. ''You may be sorry if you go digging into the past. What you find out could change the way Tyler feels about you.''

Kara opened her mouth to say she didn't care, then realized the opposite was true. She did care. But only because they'd become such good friends. She trusted him and she knew he trusted her. That element of their relationship meant she owed him the absolute truth, no matter what it was. And if her search proved her business blameless in his misfortune, as she believed it would, they'd no longer have an outdated suspicion standing between them.

''I have to know,'' Kara finally said, starting for her office. ''For my sake as much as for Tyler's.''

Susan followed. ''And if the whole thing was Alex's fault? What then?''

''It can't have been. Alex wasn't perfect but he was a good vet. Smart and capable.''

''And honest?''

Kara froze. Her head snapped around. ''Is there some problem with the books you haven't told me about?''

''Nothing I can't fix,'' Susan said. ''You may have to go back and file an amended tax return for the last couple of years you were married, though. Alex was pretty creative when he made out the original forms he had you sign.''

"Oh, wonderful. I suppose that means I'll owe the government more money."

"Probably. But maybe we can average your income and break even. I'll give it a try. In the meantime, I don't suppose you'd like me to try to collect on any more bills that are years past due, would you?"

"Who's on that list besides Tyler Corbett?" Kara asked, anticipating the answer.

Susan merely shrugged and smiled sweetly. "Never mind. Bad idea." She quickly spun around and headed for the reception area. "Guess I'd better get back to work."

Watching her go, Kara thanked God for her sister's loving presence and willingness to share her skills. Without Susan's proficient management there would have been no way Kara could have kept the animal hospital going. Alex had left the books so jumbled it had taken a professional like Susan to make any sense of them.

A shiver of foreboding skittered up Kara's spine like the delicate scamper of tiny, invisible mouse paws. "Alex was just disorganized," she countered aloud. "That's all. As soon as I find the original records I'll be able to prove he had nothing to do with Tyler's terrible losses."

In her subconscious, however, lingering disquiet refused to be banished. Kara knew she'd have no real peace until she sought out the truth.

Chapter Fourteen

Buster was more than ready to go home by closing time. Kara delayed leaving work, expecting Tyler to come for his dog, as he'd promised.

She walked into the front office just as Susan was hanging up the telephone. "I just called the ranch. Mark says they had an emergency with one of the horses and lost track of time. I'm supposed to give Buster a ride home."

"That'll be fine. You told him you would, didn't you?"

"Actually, no." Susan displayed a self-satisfied smile. "I'm planning to buy a lot of groceries after work. My car will be way too full. Guess you'll have to do the honors."

"Susan…"

"Hey, don't look at me. I'm just the messenger."

"Then we'll trade vehicles. You take my truck. Put Buster in the front with you and load all your groceries in the back."

"What if it rains?"

Kara was getting frustrated. "It's *not* going to rain." She marched through the reception area to the glassed-in front. "There's not a cloud in the…" The instant she peered out, she realized her flawless rationale was no longer valid. "Okay, so there are a few clouds. That doesn't mean a thing in Arkansas. It might not rain for a month."

"Or it might rain right away and ruin my groceries before I can drive home. Sorry. The way I see it, you have two choices. You can either take Buster to the ranch yourself, or leave him here, alone in that cramped, little cage, all night long.''

Kara pulled a face. ''You know I'd never subject an animal to unnecessary confinement.''

The older sister shrugged. ''Whatever. Like I said, it's up to you. I'm sure Tyler will understand why Mark couldn't manage to arrange to have Buster brought home.'' She retrieved her purse from the lowest drawer of her desk and slung the slim strap over one shoulder. ''Well, gotta go. See you tomorrow.''

Kara's plea of, ''Hey, wait!'' was fruitless. Susan had already ducked out the door. ''I'll get you for this,'' she muttered, stomping off toward the kennel area. ''You knew just how to get to me, didn't you?'' Her voice mimicked her sister's, ''*Poor dog, alone all night.* And when that didn't work, you brought up Mark's obligations to his boss. Talk about great strategy!''

Buster wagged his tail happily when Kara leaned down to unlatch his cage. Speaking softly, she petted and reassured him as she snapped a leash to the ring on his collar and started to lead him carefully across the concrete floor. ''That's it, old boy. Take it easy. You'll be fine.'' Her tone never changed as she continued, ''Of course, *I* may wind up a basket case if I hang around your owner much more, but nobody seems to care about that. No, sir. They sure don't. They just throw Tyler and me together and watch the fur fly.''

She locked the door and walked to her truck, the yellow Lab ambling along beside her. Rather than encourage him to jump in when she opened the truck door, she placed his front feet on the floor of the cab, then eased his rear end in by lifting it herself so he wouldn't further injure himself. If he'd been much heavier—or much lazier—she couldn't have accomplished the task without help.

By the time she'd circled the truck to climb behind the wheel, Buster was lounging on the seat, looking terribly pleased with himself. He was panting, his wide, pink tongue lolling out the side of his mouth.

Kara laughed and ruffled his velvety ears. ''You old faker. You aren't having a bit of trouble getting around, are you? I'll bet your daddy will really be relieved.''

The thought of Tyler's reaction to her use of that silly nickname made her smile. Come to think of it, so did everything else about the man, from the color of his hair, to the mischievous sparkle in his eyes, to the warm, reassuring feel of his hand when it touched hers.

Sighing, she realized she was beginning to feel a lot like a teenager experiencing love for the first time. At least she thought she was. Her younger years hadn't been particularly enlightening where romantic relationships were concerned. There was a good chance she was merely imagining what falling in love would be like.

That conclusion brought her up short. Surely, she'd loved Alex once. She must have. After all, she'd married the man! But she'd never noticed thinking about him all the time. Or worrying if he was okay. Or constantly reliving their time together.

With Tyler, she'd done all those things. She hadn't wanted him to become such an integral part of her life; she simply couldn't stop her subconscious from dwelling on the joy and peace that blessed her whenever he was near. Lately, all she had to do was remember being with him and a similar awareness flowed through her, soothing away her hidden fears and calming her jumbled emotions.

''Oh, Buster,'' Kara crooned, laying her hand on the dog's broad head for mutual comfort. ''I think I'm in big trouble. Your daddy is starting to look far too good to me. And I have absolutely no idea what I should do about it.''

Kara saw Mark standing by the barn when she arrived at the ranch, so she drove straight to him.

''I brought Buster,'' she said, leaning out the truck window. ''Will you lift him down for me? I don't want him to jump yet.''

''Sure.'' As soon as the dog was firmly on the ground,

Mark straightened, dusted his hands on his jeans, and cocked his head toward the open barn door. "Ty's in the foaling stall down at the far end. We had a colt coming breach and had to pull it."

"Are the mare and the foal both all right?" Kara asked.

"Just fine. I was about to head for the house for dinner. You staying?"

Her brow knit. "I beg your pardon? I thought Susan was going grocery shopping after work."

Mark shrugged. "First I've heard of it. I saw her drive in a few minutes ago." He looked down at the dog. "Hey, why didn't you have her bring Buster home? Would have saved you a trip."

"I know." Kara's voice oozed pseudosweetness. "I guess I got confused." She handed the looped end of the leash to her brother-in-law. "Here. You do the honors. Just warn Tyler to keep him fairly quiet for a few more days and he should be fine."

"Okay, but…"

"Thanks. And don't hurry home. Okay? I want time to have a nice, private, sisterly talk with your wife."

Kara got back in her truck and took off, wheels spinning, leaving Mark behind in a cloud of dust. By the time she reached Susan's she'd managed to think of more than one choice comment to express her displeasure. When she barged into the kitchen, however, her sister grabbed her hands and greeted her with such delight it floored her.

"So, how did it go? Was he impressed that you went to all the trouble of bringing his dog home? He sure should have been. For a minute there I was afraid you weren't going to take advantage of the opportunity."

"Opportunity?" Kara said, confused.

"Sure! You've been playing too hard to get. I mean, the man did bring you his favorite dog when he could have taken it to another vet. How much more does he have to do to convince you he likes you?"

"Of course he likes me. We're friends…well, sort of. I like him, too."

Susan cheered. "Yeah! About time. I was beginning to think you'd never stop brooding."

"I don't brood," Kara argued. "I just don't dance around the room when something pleases me."

"Not anymore, maybe, but you used to. Don't you remember when we put on that talent show in the backyard? I was a clown. You were a ballerina. And we'd organized the other kids in the neighborhood into our stage crew." Her smile grew wistful. "Mom and Dad laughed and applauded so hard I thought they were going to fall off their seats."

Kara spoke softly, sadly. "I don't remember it happening that way."

"That's because you always take things too seriously. We all had a wonderful time."

"Till our father lost his temper, started yelling, and the other kids all went home."

Leading her to the kitchen table, Susan pushed her gently into a chair, then pulled another one close. "You don't know why? You really don't?" She shook her head when Kara didn't answer. "It was because one of the little boys knocked you down and made you cry, then wouldn't apologize."

"That can't be right." Tears began to sting Kara's eyes and blur her vision. "Dad was always getting mad and shouting for no reason."

"I know, honey, but you were the only one who ever took him seriously. Even Mom didn't listen when he acted like that. I suppose that's why she paid no attention to his hollering and he laid there in the driveway for so long."

"When?"

"When he had his first stroke."

Kara's eyes widened, spilling rivulets of tears down her cheeks. No one had ever told her that part of the story. "It doesn't matter. He'd have been fine if I hadn't brought that old horse home and hidden it in the garage."

"No way. Dad might have done better if he'd gotten medical attention faster, or if he'd cooperated with his physical therapist, or if he'd kept his blood pressure down and dieted like he was supposed to. But he had a volatile temper he couldn't, or wouldn't, control. That was his problem, not ours. Even Mom has finally realized she wasn't to blame for what happened."

Kara was adamant. "She never blamed herself, she blamed *me.* So did he. They told me so."

"Oh, honey..." Susan reached out and pulled her sister into a warm, forgiving hug. "They blamed everybody at first—you, me, the doctors. Even God. But later, when they'd had a chance to accept Dad's illness, they both changed for the better. Toward the end of his life they seemed very happy. I think they even fell in love with each other again."

Weeping, Kara clung to her sister. "But—but they never said. They never told me. I always thought..."

"You'd moved away and finished college by the time I realized our father had finally grown up. You had a life of your own. A husband. Your career. I never dreamed you were still hurting over that stupid misunderstanding or I'd have said something sooner. I'm sure Mom would have, too."

She reached for a box of tissues, took one for herself, then offered the rest to her sister. They blew their noses in unison. Their eyes met. Compassion and acceptance flowed between them.

Susan was the first to break into a smile. "You look awful, kid."

"Hah!" Sniffling, Kara made a silly face and blotted her tears. "You don't look so good yourself. Besides, you're older. You're supposed to look worse than I do."

"Oh, thanks a heap."

"You're welcome." She glanced toward the door as Mark entered. When he saw what was going on, the bewildered look on his face was priceless.

Coming to an abrupt halt, he held up both hands in surrender. "Oops. Sorry to intrude. Do you want me to go outside and wait until you're through?"

"Through with what?" Susan asked, sniffling. "There's no problem here, is there, Kara?"

"Nope." She felt as if an enormous burden had been lifted from her soul. All along she'd been praying that she'd be able to accept her guilt for her father's affliction and be forgiven. Instead, she'd been presented with a much better answer. There was no guilt to forgive!

Mark lingered by the door, acting as if he didn't believe their assurance that nothing momentous was taking place. "Um. Okay, I guess. If you say so."

Gazing at him fondly, his wife walked up, took his hand, and tugged him through the kitchen. When they reached the hallway she slipped into his embrace and kissed him. "Stop worrying. We were just having a little woman-to-woman talk. Those are like watching old, romantic movies. They almost always require three or four tissues."

Observing Susan's and Mark's loving rapport as they kissed again made Kara painfully aware of how truly alone she was. She slipped out the open back door without saying goodbye so they could have some well-deserved privacy.

As she made her way to her truck, Kara realized her heart was finally at peace with regard to her parents. At least they'd found happiness before it was too late. How wonderful it would be to live in the kind of family Susan had built with Mark. All a person had to do was look at them to see they were deeply in love. Surely it wasn't covetousness to wish the same for herself.

The problem was, she kept making stupid mistakes about men. The first time, she'd been fooled by Alex's shrewd deception. This time, however, she'd walked into trouble with her eyes wide-open and fallen in love with a man who'd once enjoyed an ideal marriage, had an ideal wife. No one could ever live up to those kinds of standards. Especially not her.

Kara was so numbed by her heartbreaking conclusion she literally bumped into Tyler before she noticed him.

He caught her arm to steady her. "Hey, Doc. Glad you're

still here. I saw your truck was here so I came on over. Thanks again for what you did for Buster.''

''It's my job,'' she said soberly.

''Fixing his leg was your job. Giving him a ride home wasn't. Mark told you why I didn't make it back to Hardy?''

''Yes.'' She tried to edge past him but he was blocking the way. ''I'm glad the mare and foal came through all right.''

''Me, too. Which gives us a great reason to celebrate. How about letting me take you out to dinner again?''

''Not tonight.''

Tyler tilted up her chin with one finger, forcing her to look at him. ''Are you mad at me for some reason?''

''No.'' She twisted free. ''I'm just tired. It's been a long day. All I want to do is go home and crash.''

He knew a lame excuse when he heard one, especially since Kara was such an atrocious liar. What he didn't know was why she was putting him off. ''No problem. We'll get takeout and eat it at your place. That should prove pretty challenging, considering the animals you have under foot.''

''Really, Tyler, I don't feel much like celebrating.''

''Okay. Have it your way.'' Stepping aside, he opened the truck door for her, slamming it as soon as she was settled behind the wheel. ''I'll share my special dinner with Buster and Road Kill. They'll love it.''

Kara purposely avoided looking at him again. She'd been fighting additional tears ever since she'd admitted she was in love with him. All she wanted to do now was escape before she made a worse fool of herself—not that that would be easy, given the scope of her primary idiotic mistake.

Spending time with Tyler Corbett was supposed to have been a safe alternative to serious involvement for both of them. Instead, she was hopelessly in love. And he was just as hopelessly ignorant of it.

''Good thing,'' she muttered to herself, driving off with a brief wave instead of bidding him a normal goodbye. ''If he had a clue how I felt he'd probably run so fast to get away from me he'd put Speedy to shame.''

* * *

The doldrums would have been a step up for Kara that evening. She did her chores mechanically, then showered and changed into shorts and an over-size T-shirt to take full advantage of the cool night air. Lying on the sofa, she'd almost drifted off to sleep when the barking of her dogs roused her. By the time she got to the porch, the bedlam had ceased. It was easy to see why.

Tyler had backed his new pickup into her driveway. He was seated on a lawn chair in the truck bed, pitching tidbits over the side to pacify the milling pack below. He waved. "Hi, Doc. Want to join us for dinner? We're having country fried chicken."

"Stop that! You can't give dogs chicken bones," Kara shouted. "The splinters can kill them."

"I know. I bought a bucket of nuggets for them. You and I get the parts with the bones in them."

She could see how proud he was to have come up with such a unique approach. The sight of him was so endearing she couldn't bring herself to refuse his offer. "What am I going to do with you?"

"Well, you could start by helping me control Peewee. I'm running low on nuggets and he looks like he's about to jump in here with me and make me prove it."

Kara padded barefoot to the truck. "You're crazy, Tyler. These dogs have only met you once. How did you know they wouldn't bite?"

He waved the paper take-out carton. "Bribes. Works every time."

"Oh, sure. As long as you don't run out of food." It amazed Kara how rested, how invigorated, how radiantly alive she suddenly felt. "Did you bring sodas? Napkins?"

"Yup," he answered, holding out his hand to her. "Come on in. The food's getting cold."

Kara climbed into the back of the truck by stepping on the bumper and letting him help her over the tailgate. She had to speak firmly to her dogs to make them stop trying to follow.

Smiling so widely her cheeks hurt, she gazed at the party

Tyler had prepared, complete with two folding chairs and a tray-table. "I see you thought of everything."

"I tried to. All that's missing is a fancy tablecloth, candlelight and violins. I was afraid that would be overdoing it."

"Not if you were trying to court me," she said lightly, hoping for a positive response to the blatant cue.

"Which I promised not to do, remember?" he countered. "Here. Sit down. I'll get you a plate and a fork. Nothing but the finest paper and plastic for my guests."

Kara resigned herself to making the most of the precious gift of his presence, however temporary. No matter what eventually came of their friendship, Tyler had made her feel alive again, as if the future was something to look forward to instead of dread. He'd blessed her spirit more than he'd ever know. She'd always be grateful to him for that. Her fondest wish was to know that she'd made a favorable difference in his life, too. Judging by his upbeat mood, she had. All she needed to do now was keep her own feelings at bay and everything would be fine.

By the time Kara and Tyler finished eating, the sun had set and the luminescent green flashes of courting fireflies were starting to appear above the lawn and low shrubs. In the distance, a whippoorwill called.

"Is that one of your Purple Martins I hear?" he asked.

Kara shook her head. "No. They're strictly daytime hunters. Mosquitoes are their favorite food, which is why we can sit out here at night without being bitten."

"Hey, you're right!" Tyler leaned back in his chair, laced his fingers behind his head, and used the edge of the tailgate as a footstool. "Think Martin houses would work if I put them up at my place?"

"Sure. It's probably too late to attract any nesting birds this year but you could always get ready for next spring. Martins migrate to South America to spend the winter. They'll all be gone soon."

"You're kidding."

"No. I mean it." He looked dubious so she added, "I can lend you a book about their habits, if you like. They never nest alone, which is why we put up houses with lots of compartments. Each colony is one big, happy family."

Tyler didn't particularly want to read about big, happy families, even if they were only a bunch of birds. He also didn't like the feelings of affection for Kara that kept popping into his head. Birds had it easy. They just grabbed a mate, made a nest, and that was that. He'd tried to build a family with Deanne and failed. Once was enough.

"I don't need to read a book," Tyler said flatly. "Just tell me what kind of stuff I need and I'll buy it."

"You mean make you a *list?*" Kara saw his color deepen. Even with only moonlight to illuminate the scene, it was evident he was embarrassed.

"Yeah, well...writing all that stuff down was a mistake. I think we should forget about it." The silly list he'd made as a joke had ceased being funny as his personal awareness of Kara had grown. She was a desirable, witty, intelligent, attractive woman. *Too* attractive, considering their pledge to be no more than friends.

Tyler could see he'd made a big mistake by insisting he and Kara spend more time together. The only way to control his impulsive thoughts was to leave, as soon as possible. He got to his feet. "Looks like it's time I went home."

"Awww. The party's over?" The hours had passed swiftly. Kara had no idea how late it was. Nor did she care.

"We both have to get up early tomorrow." Tyler busied himself gathering the residue of their feast and stuffing it into a trash bag. "I'll take this with me so your dogs don't get into it and hurt themselves."

"Okay." Puzzled, Kara handed him an empty carton. For a guy who'd been so insistent that she dine with him, he was sure acting put off all of a sudden. She tried to recall exactly what she'd said or done that had triggered such an adverse reaction. Nothing came to mind. Still, *something* had definitely destroyed their earlier tranquility.

Deciding she should ask what was bothering him, Kara silently rehearsed speech after speech, trying to make up her mind what to say. No approach seemed suitable. Soon, her uncalled-for nervousness had built to such heights she could hardly form a coherent thought.

Her heart fluttered. That unique frame of mind was all too familiar. And decidedly unwelcome. Her body was reacting to Tyler's mood change in *precisely* the same way it had whenever Alex or her father had gotten upset!

That honest analysis absolutely floored her.

Kara was still dealing with the possible ramifications of her disturbing conclusion long after Tyler had driven away.

Chapter Fifteen

Sunday after Sunday, Kara continued to sit with Tyler in church and try to act as if nothing had changed in their so-called relationship. But it had. She'd analyzed her innermost thoughts and decided that, although she did love him, she obviously wasn't trusting him completely. As Susan had pointed out, she wasn't even trusting God the way she should, and she had no idea how to change that, either.

Now that Road Kill's broken leg was healed and the pup no longer needed her care, it was getting easier to avoid Tyler during the week. Sundays, however, were a different story. She'd begun to dread going to church. She knew she could ask Tyler to worship somewhere else, only then he'd wonder why she'd suggested it. Which would mean either lying or admitting her emotions had gotten out-of-control. Neither would do. She was stuck in a no-win situation.

Still, Kara knew she must stop seeing Tyler…anywhere. Period. The more they were together, the harder it was to pretend she didn't care; to behave as if they were just casual friends. Given enough opportunity she was bound to say or do something that revealed how crazy she was about him. Once that happened she'd never be able to face him again. Because he was Mark's boss, that attitude could hurt Susan's family, too.

Thinking about the mess she'd gotten into by agreeing to a supposedly harmless little fib, Kara decided there was no such thing as a harmless lie. She felt like kicking herself. Instead, she simply stuffed her raw emotions into the farthest corners of her mind and refused to show anyone how much she was suffering.

Catching her between patients, Susan was the first to mention the symptoms of her withdrawal. ''Hey, Kara.'' She snapped her fingers. ''Wake up. What's the matter with you lately?''

''Nothing. Sorry. What were you saying?'' There was no enthusiasm in her tone.

''So,'' Susan drawled, ''you'll give me a big raise?''

Kara's mind jerked back to reality. ''What?''

''I figured that would get your attention. I was actually talking about Ty's hayride idea for the fall festival at church. Do you like it?''

''Sure. The kids will love riding in a wagon.''

''So will the adults, if they're anything like Mark and me.'' She giggled. ''Are you working a booth, again?''

''No. I'm not up to it this year.'' Placing one hand on the small of her back, Kara stretched to ease the strained muscles. ''I carted all those boxes of old receipts home so I could rummage through them in the evenings. It's amazing how much trivia we accumulated when Alex was keeping the books. He sure didn't have his act together the way you do.''

''Thanks.'' Susan smiled, then sobered. ''I wouldn't be so sure all that confusion was due to his lack of skill, though. I've been going over your personal records, the way you wanted me to, and I suspect the man was a lot smarter than we've given him credit for.''

Kara couldn't honestly refute her sister's theory. She had never caught Alex doing anything deliberately unlawful but she had corrected a few mistakes in his accounts once. Soon after, he'd started updating the bills on the computer terminal in his private office.

''Nothing was correctly filed, that's for sure,'' Kara said. ''Trying to put everything in order is a nightmare.''

''Are you close to being done?''

''Close enough.'' She rubbed her back again. ''I think I'll have the job finished this weekend, at the latest.''

''Then what?''

Kara arched her eyebrows and shrugged. ''I don't know. Depends on what I find when I start matching our suppliers to the actual usage. I still can't bring myself to believe Alex purposely endangered the Corbett herd—or anyone else's animals—the way Tyler claimed he did.''

''I don't suppose you've asked Tyler for his version of the story, have you?''

''Of course not! Why would I bring that up? You're the one who told me he blames himself for his wife's death.''

''So?''

''So, it all ties together. If his herd hadn't gotten sick he could have sold it off, or used it as instant collateral, instead of borrowing against the ranch property to pay his wife's extra medical expenses. That would have been much faster and easier. Only nobody wanted anything to do with unhealthy cattle.''

''That's not your fault,'' Susan argued.

Nodding, Kara sighed. ''I just hope I can prove to myself that it wasn't my husband's fault, either.''

By late Friday night, Kara knew the worst. Alex had bought enough vaccine to cover the Corbett ranch's needs, all right. But he'd also treated a large herd out near Ravenden. That meant he'd either diluted all the vaccine or skipped half the inoculations he'd claimed to have given. Either way, she didn't think she could ever face Tyler again. Truth to tell, she was having enough trouble facing herself. How could she have been so stupid? So naive? So trusting?

She bit her lip as her actual weakness became clear. She'd been cowardly, not stupid. It had been easier to overlook Alex's faults than to face him, incur his wrath and insist on a clear accounting. Which meant she shared the blame for everything.

But what could she do to make amends? *Nothing.* She

didn't have the monetary resources to pay anyone back for their losses, no matter how much she wanted to. Nor could she do anything about Tyler's personal hardships. The worst part was knowing he blamed himself for the tragedy Alex's dishonesty had sparked.

In need of comfort, Kara picked up the phone and dialed her sister. The minute Susan answered she blurted out the whole sordid story. When she was through, all her nervous energy had been spent and she plopped into the nearest chair, exhausted.

Susan offered reassurance. "Don't blame yourself, Kara. You didn't know what was going on."

"I do now."

"True, but so what? It's all in the past."

Slowly, pensively shaking her head, Kara voiced the truth she'd been avoiding. "No, it's not. I have to tell Tyler. He deserves to know everything, so he can stop blaming himself."

"Are you sure?"

"Yes." She pictured the ruggedly handsome face she'd come to love and imagined the loathing she'd see in his eyes once he heard the truth. "You and I both know it's the right thing to do," Kara said with a shudder. In her heart she knew that facing Tyler and revealing the wrongdoing her search had turned up was absolutely essential.

It would also be the hardest thing she'd ever done.

On the morning of the bazaar, Susan drove her car to church so she could safely transport the cakes she'd baked. Mark rode with Tyler in the rubber-tired ranch wagon. They'd hitched a team of sorrel mules to it and lined it with bales of clean straw to use for benches. Tyler was driving.

"Susie called her sister, just like you wanted," Mark said. "But Kara wouldn't budge. Says she's too busy to come today." He plucked a shaft of loose straw, twirled it between his fingers, then stuck one end of it in his mouth. "I don't know what's gotten into her lately. I haven't seen her act so gloomy in years. Not since—''

''Since her husband was alive?'' Tyler offered.

''Yeah. How'd you know?''

He shrugged. ''I knew her then, too. Not as well as you, of course, but well enough. In those days I never would have guessed she was so smart and funny, and—'' He stopped talking when Mark began to laugh.

''You forgot *beautiful,*'' Mark said. ''And *lovable.*''

Tyler started to glare at him, then softened. ''Yeah. And you forgot *tenderhearted.* I don't know why she insists on taking in all those stray animals.''

''I think it's partly because it's her nature to rescue things. Always has been. I suppose that's why she became a veterinarian in the first place.''

''What do you know about Alex Shepherd?''

''Not much. I never liked the guy. Don't have a clue why, though. He was always pleasant to me when we ran into each other at family gatherings.'' Concentrating, Mark squinted and stared off into the distance, then added, ''There was just something about him that put up the hackles on the back of my neck the minute he walked into a room. And that was back before I knew he was abusing Kara, so I can't blame my reaction on that.''

Tyler stiffened and brought the team to a halt with an abrupt, ''Whoa!'' When he turned to Mark there was fire in his eyes. ''What do you mean he abused Kara? When? How?''

''Hey, don't look at me like that,'' Mark said, flinching under his angry stare. ''I just found out about it a couple of weeks ago, right after she finally told Susie.''

''Told her what?''

''That she'd been afraid of Alex. Apparently, he had the same kind of volatile temper their father used to have. Only Alex was better at hiding it. He saved his tantrums for his wife, when they were alone. One night he went nuts and broke every dish in a fancy set they'd gotten for a wedding present.

It was a gift Kara had really loved, so I guess he figured he was punishing her.''

''And Kara put up with behavior like that? I can't believe it.''

''I know what you mean. I had the same problem when Susan first told me. But you have to remember how much Kara has changed since she's been on her own.'' Starting to smile, Mark added, ''She's gotten even more independent since she started seeing you. Obviously, being in love is real good for her morale.''

Tyler's gut knotted. Kara wasn't in love. She'd made it perfectly clear on more than one occasion that she wasn't interested in romance. And no wonder. Thinking about her appalling life with Alex Shepherd made Tyler want to lash out. Since Mark was the only target available, he squelched that urge and replaced it with a more acceptable one. He *had* to see Kara. Immediately. Eyeing the church in the distance, he told Mark, ''Get out.''

''What?''

''You're walking from here. It's not far. A little exercise will do you good. Tell them I'll have the wagon back in plenty of time for the hayride.''

Mark did as he was told. ''Okay. You're the boss. Where will you be?''

''I'm going to Kara's.''

Grinning knowingly, Mark stepped away to give Tyler room to turn the team. All he said was, ''Well, well. What a surprise.''

Kara heard the jingle of the mules' harnesses before she actually saw the low-sided wagon turning into her driveway. She quickly called her dogs so they wouldn't spook the team.

Shading her eyes with one hand she recognized her visitor. Apprehension washed over her. ''Oh, please, Lord, not yet. I know I asked for the opportunity to tell him the truth, and I will. I promise. But you can't expect me to do it now. I haven't even *begun* to decide what I should say or how I should say it.''

Heart beating wildly, Kara watched Tyler's approach. Normally, she would have admired the matched pair of mules. This time, however, she had eyes only for their driver. Tyler's hat was set low, shading his luminous, dark eyes. Strong hands held perfect command of the reins. One boot was propped on the footboard, the other on the brake. The sight of him was so dear, so heart wrenching, it caused her actual physical pain. So did her guilty conscience. She didn't have a clue how she was going to cope with both problems at the same time.

During the drive, Tyler's contemplation about how Alex had treated Kara had left him so upset he was barely able to curb his temper. He brought the team to a halt a few feet from her. Instead of his usual pleasant greeting, he ordered, ''Get in.''

His overbearing attitude restored a measure of Kara's lost self-control. By focusing on being miffed she was able to reply with suitable sarcasm. ''Good morning to you, too, Mr. Corbett. What brings you here like this?'' She gestured at the wagon. ''Did your truck break down?''

''I came to get you for the fall doings at church. Mark had some crazy idea you weren't planning to come.''

''I'm not.'' Kara stood her ground.

''And why is that?''

''Because, I...'' Hands on her hips, she scowled up at him. ''Hey. Hold it, mister. I don't have to explain a thing to you.''

Tyler knew she was right. He hadn't meant to come on so strong. Or to start ordering her around, either. He was just so furious and so frustrated by what he'd recently learned from Mark, he hadn't been thinking straight. And now he'd made a bad situation worse.

Wrapping the reins around the wagon brake he climbed down, intent on looking directly into Kara's eyes when he apologized. He had to be sure she didn't fear him the same way she'd feared her late husband. A slightly built woman like Kara would have been crazy to stand up to Alex Shepherd when she'd already seen proof of his violent tendencies. Leave him, yes. Challenge him, no.

All Tyler wanted to do at that moment was take her in his arms, hold her tight and promise to protect her forever. Instead, he stepped closer and solemnly removed his hat. ''I'm sorry, Kara. There's no excuse for my lack of manners. Will you do me the honor of letting me drive you to church in my wagon? Please?''

She didn't know what to say or do. In all the times they'd been together she'd never seen him act so earnest. When he added a second, ''Please?'' it was hard to refuse.

''I have a lot of chores to do,'' she alibied. ''I really can't spare the time.''

Placing his hand gently on her shoulder he felt her flinch. The unconscious reaction to being touched tore him up inside. Speaking softly, comfortingly, he reassured her. ''You don't have to be afraid of me, Kara. I'd never, ever hurt you. I swear it. As God is my witness.'' There was a quick flash of doubt in her upturned gaze. It was replaced by a subtle yet perceptive smile that reached into Tyler's soul and calmed his uneasiness.

''I know.'' Kara slipped her arms around his waist and stepped into his waiting embrace. Laying her cheek on his chest she listened to the heavy, reassuring beat of his heart. If she could have stayed there like that for the rest of her days, she'd have gladly done so. Unfortunately, that was impossible.

Acting lighthearted to keep Tyler from seeing how deeply his vow had touched her, she leaned back and smiled up at him. ''I suppose this means you'll expect me to give in and go with you now?''

''Only if you want to.'' He brushed a conciliatory kiss on her forehead. ''I've been praying hard that you'd change your mind, though.''

She rolled her eyes dramatically. ''Oh, great! So, if I refuse you, you'll blame me for undermining your faith?''

''It could happen.''

Kara watched his grin spread, crinkling the corners of his eyes. This was the kind of cheerful give-and-take she'd missed so much when she'd stopped spending extra time with him. She knew it was foolish to resume the sham relationship that had already caused her to lose her heart, yet the urge to allow herself a few more hours with him was very strong. Besides, she reasoned, if they spent the day at the church get-together, maybe she'd have a chance to explain what Alex had done.

Kara sighed. Who was she kidding? All she wanted was the opportunity to enjoy a few more special moments with the man she loved. To make memories that no one could ever take away. Once Tyler learned who had been responsible for his loss, there was no way he'd ever be able to look at her again and not remember, not think the worst.

''All right. I'll go,'' Kara said, feigning a casual attitude. ''Give me a few minutes to change.''

''Why? You look fine to me.''

The compliment made her feel like she'd just been handed first place in a beauty contest. ''Thanks. You're not so bad yourself, cowboy.''

''It's the hat,'' Tyler quipped, squaring it on his head. ''Gets 'em every time.'' He held out his hand. ''Come on. Let's go before you change your mind.''

''I won't change my mind,'' Kara promised. ''But I do intend to change to newer jeans. If I go to the church in these, my friends are liable to take up a collection to clothe me!''

''If you ask me, you'd even look good in a feed sack,'' he insisted, ''but I won't argue. Just hurry. A lot of kids are waiting for hayrides. I don't want to disappoint them.''

''Right. Be back in a flash.''

Kara was still reeling from his compliments as she ran toward the house. Could he have meant them, or was he just being polite to add emphasis to his apology for being so grumpy? It had to be the latter. After all, he'd been married to Deanne, a tall, beautiful blond who looked like an angel and was so perfect she was practically a saint.

"And I'm neither," Kara grumbled to herself. "I could lighten my hair but I'd still be short. And seriously imperfect."

She grimaced. It was a good thing God loved her, no matter what, because even after surrendering to His will and becoming a Christian, she still had plenty of flaws left.

Halfway to the church, Kara was so convicted she had to speak out or explode. "Tyler?"

"Mm-hm."

"There's something I have to tell you." When he glanced over at her and opened his mouth to speak, she shushed him. "No. Be quiet and just listen. I don't know if I can get through this if you talk to me."

"You don't have to explain anything. I already know all about Alex," he said softly.

Kara was awestruck. "You do?"

"Yes. Mark told me this morning. He said Susan confided in him. I suppose most married couples would do the same." After a soul-wrenching sigh he went on. "Dee and I never managed to reach that point. She had the idiotic notion she was supposed to hide the bad stuff from me, for my own good. That's why I didn't find out how sick she really was until it was already too late."

"Oh, Tyler, I'm so sorry. For everything." Kara reached out to him and laid her hand over his as he gripped the reins. He didn't look at her but she could see his eyes glistening with tears.

"I guess that's why I was so upset this morning. Why didn't you tell me what your marriage was like?"

"What good would that have done? I didn't want to be pitied. Besides, I had to admit my weaknesses, and Alex's, before I could hope to overcome anything." Her fingers gently stroked the back of Tyler's hand as she rested her head on his shoulder. "I thought I'd never..."

Kara wanted to say she'd thought she'd never fall in love again, but now that she fully comprehended the significance of Tyler's promise that he'd never hurt her, she realized there was far more to her change of heart than mere romantic love.

"Go on," he urged.

Kara was so relieved, so joyful, she didn't know where to begin. "Oh, Tyler. I can't believe how blessed I am. I didn't think I'd ever meet a man I could trust the way I trust you. After what Alex did, I was sure you wouldn't want to have anything more to do with me. But here we are. Still together. It's a miracle. I can't wait to get to church and tell Susan!"

He chuckled. "Then I suppose you don't want me to stop this wagon and give you a kiss, huh?"

"Nope," Kara said, laughing with him. "I want at least *two* kisses. And that's just for starters."

As soon as Tyler released the reins she fell into his arms, gave up the last of her reservations against loving him, and lifted her face to his.

Tyler's kiss was gentle at first, then grew more and more demanding. Kara's head spun. Her heart raced. Her soul rejoiced. This was not the kind of intimate awareness she'd expected when she'd released the last of her misgivings and admitted how much she loved him. This was truer, deeper, absolutely flawless. It was unexplainable. Unfathomable.

Kara closed her eyes and returned his kiss with every ounce of her being. Surely, no woman in the entire universe had ever been as happy as she was at that moment.

Chapter Sixteen

The churchyard was decorated with bundles of dried cornstalks, gourds, squash and pumpkins. Streamers of crepe paper in rich autumn colors hung from the trees and fluttered in the breeze amid the falling leaves.

As soon as Tyler brought the wagon to a halt, he was mobbed by giggling, tussling, shouting children.

Kara reluctantly left him and went looking for her sister. She found her in the church kitchen with three other women, slicing cakes and pies into individual servings.

Everyone was startled when Kara burst through the door and screeched, "Susan! Guess what just happened."

"From the look on your face, it must be something pretty good." She laid down her knife, licked icing from her fingers, then rinsed her hands in the sink.

"Not good...wonderful!" Kara rushed to join her. "I just left Tyler. You won't believe this. He's not mad. Not at all."

"About what?"

"About Alex, of course." She lowered her voice. "I didn't expect you to tell Mark right away but now I'm glad you did. He blabbed the whole thing to Tyler this morning. I didn't have to explain a thing. Isn't that terrific?"

"Whoa." Susan took her by the arm and led her to a distant corner of the room where they could talk more privately. "Slow down and start from the beginning. What makes you think Tyler knows what Alex did?"

"He said so."

"In so many words?"

Kara's brow knit. "Well, no. I guess not. But I'm sure he knows. He said you'd told Mark all about it." She didn't like the additional sympathy that had begun to color her sister's already concerned expression.

"Mark was in bed, snoring, when you and I talked on the phone last night," Susan said. "The guy sleeps like a rock. I couldn't have tattled on Alex if I'd wanted to."

"Surely this morning..."

She shook her head. "No. Mark grabbed his breakfast on the run and headed for the barn so he could get his chores done early and ride into town with Tyler."

"That's not right. It can't be. Tyler was alone in the wagon when he came to pick me up."

"I know. They were almost to the church when he made Mark get out and walk the rest of the way. That's really all I know, except that my poor husband was grumbling about his sore feet by the time he finally got here."

Dizzy, Kara leaned against the wall for support. If only she could recall exactly what she'd said to Tyler. Or what he'd said to her. Her thoughts were a hopeless jumble being stirred by a growing sense of foreboding. What a fool she'd made of herself, babbling on and on about how wonderful Tyler was! When he *did* find out the truth, he'd probably imagine she'd only kissed him to keep him from demanding restitution for his losses. Not that she'd blame him. If she were in his shoes, that's *exactly* what she'd think.

Susan slid a comforting arm around her shoulders. "I'm sorry, Kara. Don't you see? It couldn't have been Alex's dishonesty that you and Tyler were talking about this morning. Mark doesn't know about it, yet."

See? Oh, yes, she saw plenty. In the shattered mirror of her mind everything was becoming agonizingly clear. "I guess it must have been Alex's awful temper that Tyler meant. It all makes perfect sense now that I think about it. That's what made him say he'd never hurt me." Her lower lip quivered with repressed emotion. "Too bad he isn't going to be able to keep that promise."

"Maybe..." Susan began.

Kara interrupted her. "No. It's over. You know it and I know it, so don't try to kid me."

"What are you going to do?"

"What should I do? Go home? Forget him? Forget about dreaming of having his children?" Tears crested her lower lashes and trickled down her cheeks. Sniffling and fighting the urge to sob out loud, she added, "If I live to be a hundred, I know I'll never be able to forget him. Never stop loving him."

When Susan opened her arms to offer a motherly hug, Kara lost her battle with her raw emotions and collapsed on her sister's shoulder, weeping as if she'd just lost her best friend. As far as she was concerned, that was exactly what had happened.

Time with the children was so hectic it was after twelve before Tyler realized how long it had been since Kara had left him. He passed the reins to Mark and went looking for her. Instead, he ran into Susan.

"Hi. Have you seen Kara? She was supposed to come back and ride the hay wagon with me after she talked to you." Grinning, he pushed his hat off his forehead and wiped his brow. "I need her help. Those kids are tough to handle."

"I haven't seen her for hours," Susan said flatly. "But don't worry about Kara. She can take care of herself."

"Not according to Mark."

Her eyebrows arched. "So he did tell you something. That explains a lot." She pointed to some chairs in the shade next to the old stone building. "I think you'd better sit down. Apparently, you only know half the story."

"Okay. Sure." Concerned, Tyler offered Susan a chair, then spun another one around backward and straddled it like a horse, facing her. "What else is there? Mark already told me Alex used to lose his temper and scare the fire out of Kara." He stiffened, scowling. "He didn't hit her, did he?"

"No, but he might as well have. If that man were alive

right now and I caught him in a dark alley, he'd be real sorry.'' She folded her arms across her chest, made a dour face and snorted in disgust. ''I guess I might as well get this over with. Remember this morning, when you and Kara were talking? She thought you meant you weren't angry that Alex had shorted you when he vaccinated your herd.''

Tyler was on his feet in a heartbeat, sending the chair flying. ''What? Is that true?''

''I'm afraid so. Somehow, Kara got the idea Mark had already told you all about it. Only he couldn't have. She didn't phone me with the bad news until late last night, long after Mark had gone to bed. There was no way to change history, so I didn't wake him.''

Tyler couldn't believe what he was hearing. Indignation hardened his heart. ''And what about *before?* How long has Kara known about this? Months? Years? Since it happened?''

Susan stood rigid and returned his anger in kind. ''If you really think that, then I'm glad you and Kara are through. She was married to one stinker. She doesn't need another husband like that, now or ever.''

''Who said anything about us getting married?'' he shouted. ''Kara and I were just pretending to like each other in the first place!''

Their raised voices had attracted a crowd but Susan didn't back down. ''Look. Kara already knows she was a fool to fall for you. She always was too naive, too loving, too empathetic. That's her biggest problem. She never did have enough sense to turn away lonely, helpless critters when she thought they needed her.''

''Meaning *me,* I suppose? Well, I'm not lonely. And I'm not helpless, either,'' Tyler snapped.

''Oh, yeah? If you're so sure of yourself, then why are you yelling?''

Like it or not, he had no ready answer.

Susan nodded and stared at him knowingly. ''That's what I thought. How long have you been in love with my sister?''

''I'm not...''

''Careful, Tyler,'' she drawled, ''you're standing in a

churchyard. I don't think it's a very good idea to tell a fib here...or anywhere else, for that matter." The moment she detected a softening in his expression, she stepped closer and laid a hand on his arm. "Kara didn't know what Alex had done until she'd finished sorting out some old statements he'd left behind. It was only late yesterday that she had enough information to put it all together."

Tyler realized he'd been holding his breath as Susan spoke. He exhaled with a whoosh. "Why didn't she *tell* me?"

"She thought that's what you two were discussing on the ride down here. I was the one who had to break her heart and explain she was mistaken."

He glanced into the crowd of onlookers, searching in vain. "I have to talk to her. Where is she?"

"I don't know. I suppose she went home to lick her wounds. Personally, I'd have run as far away as I could get, but Kara's not like that. I hope you realize how easy it would have been for her to destroy the old bills and hide the real truth from all of us."

"I'm beginning to see a lot of things I missed before," Tyler said soberly. "Can I borrow your car?"

"Why?"

"Because I'm temporarily afoot. Unless you expect me to chase after Kara in the hay wagon. If she's not at home, it could take me forever to catch up to her that way."

Susan began to smile. "Oh, I don't know. The cowboy heroes in the movies always manage to arrive in time to rescue the damsels in distress." The consternation in his expression made her giggle. "Of course, they usually ride beautiful white horses. The scene might lose some of its romance if you trotted up to her driving two other jackasses...besides yourself, that is."

"That's another reason I'd rather take your car," Tyler countered wryly, "so Kara doesn't get me mixed up with the mules. We're all stubborn and hardheaded. Considering the ridiculous mistakes I've made recently, I don't want to take the chance she might get the three of us confused."

* * *

Kara was so engrossed in cleaning the barn she didn't hear Susan's car approach. Her first clue that she was no longer alone was a tall shadow falling across her path.

Startled, she spun around and gasped. That was enough to bring Peewee to her side, growling a warning until he recognized their visitor.

Tyler paused and calmly held out his hands. "It's just me, Kara. I didn't mean to scare you. I knocked on your front door. Nobody answered." He chanced a slight smile. "I figured I'd find you wherever all the animals were gathered. And sure enough, here you are."

Realizing she'd pushed herself to exhaustion as a temporary means of taking her mind off her troubles, she leaned wearily on the handle of the pitchfork. "I know why *I'm* here. The question is, why are *you* here?"

"To finish what we started this morning."

Kara drew one wrist across her forehead to push back wisps of damp hair, then shook her head sadly. "Look, Tyler, I've been giving this whole mess a lot of thought. I made a big mistake this morning. I guess I wanted to believe I could get away with not telling you something important because I didn't want to be the one to hurt you. So I interpreted our conversation to my advantage. Only it wasn't. To my advantage, I mean."

His smile widened. "Are you through?"

"No. I have to explain. It's just very hard to do."

"I can see that."

"I'll bet you can," she countered. "Will you please take me seriously and stop that silly grinning?"

"Honey, I'll take you any way I can get you," Tyler said with clear affection. Approaching, he held out his hand. "But first, I want you to put down the pitchfork." He eased it from her hand and laid it aside before continuing. "Susan told me everything. And I mean, *everything*."

When Kara tried to speak he silenced her by placing one finger lightly across her lips. "Hush. I admit I was pretty mad, at first. Who wouldn't be? But I thought it all through on my way over here. It wasn't your fault. I don't want us to ever talk about what Alex did or didn't do again, in private or in his veterinary practice. None of that matters."

"Yes, it does." Kara's voice quavered, her eyes filling with unshed tears.

"Only if we let it," he insisted. "Neither one of us had a perfect marriage, in spite of what we led people to believe." Seeing the doubt in her eyes he added, "No. Not even me. If my wife had trusted me, loved me the way you do, she'd have known it was unfair to withhold a portion of her life, simply because the details weren't pretty. Keeping me in the dark like that wasn't a kindness. It was cruel and unfair."

Kara placed her palms on Tyler's broad chest. His arms encircled her. Pleading for understanding with her gaze, she said, "Alex and I ran the animal hospital together. I should have kept closer track of the details. Maybe I could have stopped him."

"You know that kind of a man wouldn't have paid any attention to your moral objections, even if you had figured out the hoax he was pulling. I thank God you didn't realize what was going on. Alex could have hurt you—or worse—if he saw you as a threat to his schemes."

Tyler's arms tightened, pulling Kara closer, protecting her from unseen danger simply because he loved her so deeply, so completely, he could do no less.

She wrapped her arms around his waist and laid her cheek on his chest. Their heartbeats merged, became one rhythm, as if the Lord were joining them to each other, body and soul. Maybe Tyler was right. Maybe God had kept her blinded to the truth for her own sake. This was the first time she'd considered the possibility of being in her heavenly Father's safekeeping all along.

And now? Kara wondered. She started to rehearse what she should say to Tyler, then realized it was unnecessary. No longer worried, she tilted her head back and looked up at him without reservation. The sight of his dear face thrilled her beyond belief. It was a good thing he was holding her so close because she doubted her wobbly legs would support her if he let go.

Happiness and perfect peace flowed over, around and through her. She grinned at him through a mist of joy. "Hey, cowboy?"

"Yes, ma'am?"

"Are you just going to stand there, or are you going to kiss me?"

"I could do that," Tyler drawled. "But first I want to ask you something."

"Talk, talk, talk. That's all we seem to do." To Kara's delight he silenced her with a long, firm kiss that stole her breath away. She was still struggling to regain her equilibrium when he began to whisper against her cheek.

"I was going to ask you to marry me, but if you don't want to talk..."

Wide-eyed, Kara leaned back and stared at him. "I—I might be willing to make an exception."

"That's mighty gracious of you," Tyler teased. "Well?"

"You're really serious about this? I mean, you're not going to let me answer, then laugh hysterically and tell me it was all a joke, are you?"

She saw his countenance start to darken and began waving her hands in front of her as if she could shoo her words away like pesky gnats. "Never mind. Forget I said that. I'm a little nervous, that's all. I never thought I'd even *consider* getting married again, and now, here I am with—"

Tyler interrupted. "Was that a *yes?* I couldn't tell."

"Yes!" she squealed, throwing her arms around his neck. "Yes, yes, yes."

Tyler caught her up and spun them both in circles. Sharing the excitement, Kara's dogs began barking and running back and forth. The little terrier dashed up and nipped at Tyler's ankle, giving the leg of his pants a good thrashing. Thanks to his boots, he wasn't hurt.

He set Kara on her feet and pointed down. "Um, would you mind explaining to your furry friends that I'm one of the good guys? They seem to be confused."

"Whiskers!" Kara scooped the terrier up and spoke to him like a naughty child. "Shame on you. That's your new daddy.

You can't bite him anymore.'' Elated and giddy, she knew she was grinning comically but she didn't care. She set the dog down and turned to Tyler. ''There. How was that?''

''Wonderful.'' He gently cupped her cheek, then slid his fingers into her silky hair and drew her closer. ''Is there any way I can break you of making me surrogate daddy to all of your pets?''

Kara immediately thought of the very personal dream she'd confessed to Susan back at the church. In the past, she'd have kept the idea of having children to herself and hoped Tyler would eventually guess what she was thinking, what she wanted.

Now, however, she blurted out her reply before she had a chance to modify it. Or to change her mind. ''Well, I suppose...if you were a *real* daddy, it wouldn't seem quite so appropriate.'' The passion lighting Tyler's eyes told her she'd done the right thing by speaking her mind.

''I'd love that. I've always wanted kids,'' he said softly, tenderly. ''I guess there are a lot of other important things you and I need to settle, too, before we get married. I don't want to rush you into anything.''

Kara's smile was so expansive her cheek muscles were beginning to ache. ''Oh, really? Shucks. Then I suppose next week would be too soon for the wedding, huh?'' The look of astonishment on his face made her giggle. ''Okay, okay. I'll give you a little more time if you insist. How about two weeks? I don't know if I can stand waiting three. I've been really, *really* lonesome. Especially lately.''

''Oh? Why is that?''

She playfully punched him in the shoulder. ''Stop grinning at me like that. You know perfectly well what I mean. I'm tired of cooking dinner for one. And coming home to a dark house. And not having anybody but the animals to talk to at night. And...'' Blushing, she broke off.

Tyler finished the sentence for her. ''And sleeping alone? Me, too. Come on.'' Tyler slid his arm around her shoulders and guided her out of the barn.

Kara was afraid he'd gotten the wrong idea until he stopped

at Susan's car and opened the passenger door. She got in. ''Where are we going?''

''To round up a best man and matron of honor, reserve the church and tell the preacher what we have in mind,'' he said, joining her. ''How long is it going to take you to find a wedding dress?''

''I'd get married in denim if I had to, as long as you were the groom.'' She scooted over close to him and laid her hand on his thigh as if it were the most natural gesture in the world. Somehow, it felt like they'd always been together. Always been a couple.

Tyler put his hand over hers. ''Did I mention how much I love you?''

''How should I know? I hardly remember my own name when I'm around you.''

His laugh was rich and deep. ''I know what you mean. After your sister told me why you'd left the festival, I decided to chase after you before I realized I didn't have a car! That's why I borrowed this one.''

''I suppose we could drive back separately so you could return Susan's car and I'd have a way home,'' Kara suggested logically.

''No way, lady. We don't need any other transportation when we have a perfectly good wagon and team waiting for us back at the church. You and I are taking a nice, slow hayride in the moonlight tonight. I might even stop once in a while and give you a few more kisses, if that's okay with you.''

''It's *very* okay.'' Kara snuggled closer to him and sighed. This was turning out to be a wonderful day, and he'd promised her an equally wonderful evening.

With a start like that, and a man like Tyler to love her, the rest of her life was bound to be blessed.

No one could ask for more.

* * * * *

Dear Reader,

There are many decisions in life that can help make the difference between success or failure, health or illness, joy or sadness. But in the final analysis, no mater how hard we struggle or how much we scheme, we're still not in charge of the final outcome. We never were.

Do we always understand why things happen the way they do? Of course not. Maybe that's why it's so easy to get caught up in worrying about our personal problems and forget that we don't have to face *any* of them alone. Not only does Jesus promise to send the Holy Spirit to comfort us, God also uses perceptive, empathetic people to help us bear our daily burdens. There is not adversity that others have not already successfully overcome, thanks to their faith in Christ.

Sad or happy, our past is a part of us. It never goes away. There's not a thing we can do to change it. But our future is another story. There, we have a choice. We can spend the rest of our days struggling through life alone, or we can reach out to the Lord, turn our lives over to Him and be assured He will never forsake us.

Jesus is waiting to wrap us in His loving arms and heal our broken hearts. All we have to do is let Him.

Valerie Hansen

Valerie Hansen
P.O. Box 13
Glencoe, AR 72539-0013